ARKHAM HORROR

It is the height of the Roaring Twenties – a fresh enthusiasm for the arts, science, and exploration of the past have opened doors to a wider world, and beyond…

And yet, a dark shadow grows over the town of Arkham. Alien entities known as Ancient Ones lurk in the emptiness beyond space and time, writhing at the thresholds between worlds.

Occult rituals must be stopped and alien creatures destroyed before the Ancient Ones make our world their ruined dominion.

Only a handful of brave souls with inquisitive minds and the will to act stand against the horrors threatening to tear this world apart.

Will they prevail?

ARKHAM HORROR™

VISIONS & NIGHTMARES

An ARKHAM HORROR *Omnibus*

First published by Aconyte Books in 2025
ISBN 978 1 83908 324 2
Ebook ISBN 978 1 83908 325 9
Mask of Silver first published by Aconyte Books in 2021
The Deadly Grimoire first published by Aconyte Books in 2022
The Bootlegger's Dance first published by Aconyte Books in 2023

Cover art by Daniel Strange.

Printed in the United States of America and elsewhere.

9 8 7 6 5 4 3 2 1

ACONYTE BOOKS
An imprint of Asmodee North America
Mercury House, Shipstones Business Centre
North Gate, Nottingham NG7 7FN, UK
aconytebooks.com

ARKHAM HORROR™

VISIONS & NIGHTMARES

An ARKHAM HORROR *Omnibus*

MASK *of* SILVER

The DEADLY GRIMOIRE

The BOOTLEGGER'S DANCE

INCLUDING THE SHORT STORIES:

OLD TERRORS

GATHERING SHADOWS

ROSEMARY JONES

ARKHAM HORROR™

MASK *of* SILVER

An ARKHAM HORROR *Novel*

Smoke filled the air and confused the senses. He was raging somewhere in the rooms above her head, waving his silly sword about and shouting words that she didn't understand.

"Never mind," she whispered to the children clutching her skirts. "Never mind."

The corridor seemed to go on forever. It was the mirrors. She hated those mirrors, having to dust them daily and clean them with soap and water every two weeks. Useless things, mirrors, just showing reflections of a plain New England house and her own plain face. Except when they didn't. Sometimes, she saw things in the mirrors. Shadows of things that weren't there. But she never told anyone that. The women in her family had learned to hold their tongues a long time ago. Speaking of shadows brought them closer.

The children were coughing and crying, wanting their mother. "Never mind," she said to them. "Never mind. Just follow me."

He had brought the long narrow mirrors and all the other fancy furniture to Arkham, wagonloads of the most silly stuff, chairs gilded and sitting on lion's feet, little useless tables topped with even more useless vases. Just things to dust and no more practical than those endless rows of mirrors.

The mistress was a sweet gentle lady, soft spoken and shy, often overshadowed by her big shouting husband. But she adored her children. She tried to keep them safe.

Not like him. Typical of the master of the house to thrust his enormous portrait in her arms and tell her to save it, along with the chest of papers that he shoved into the grasp of the bewildered little boy now clutching her skirts with one hand and his father's papers under his other arm. His sister toddled beside her, weeping openly now, frightened by all her blustering father's curses, the smell of fire, the smoke, and, if one dared to admit, the shadowed figure watching them from every mirror as they passed.

"Never mind," she said, as much to herself as to the children, "never mind."

They ran, burdened by fear as much as the items they carried, to the back of the house, to the kitchen where she had blessedly left the door propped open for a little breeze on a warm midsummer day.

Out the door they went, the strange trio of weeping children and grim maid, down the steps and into the vegetable garden. With a sigh or perhaps a sob of relief, she dropped the wicked portrait in the radish patch and pulled both the children close to her. The boy still carried his father's wooden chest of papers. The girl clutched a mirror, almost as large as herself, that her father had foisted on her. How the child had held onto it and still clutched her skirts, Rebecca Baker would never know.

She turned back to look at the house. The flames were sprouting through the roof now. Smoke poured from every window. Such heat, such fury. She listened for the shattering of glass, the destruction of the other mirrors, but heard nothing. Later when they shifted the ashes and found those six mirrors still intact, she would suggest burying the wicked things. But nobody listened to her. She was, after all, only the maid.

But she had gotten the children out. As she sat, suddenly exhausted, on the ruins of her radish plants, she gathered both children into her arms and gave them the same awkward comfort that her own mother gave for bruises and scrapes.

"Never mind," she said. "Never mind."

In the upstairs window, a silver cloaked coldness was outlined by the flames. The shape of a hooded man, a faceless man, who watched her nevertheless without eyes. She pretended that she did not see it. She was good at that. All Baker women were good at ignoring such shadows. It was looking straight at such silvery, shadowy figures that entrapped the soul.

The crows in the wood were cawing with dissatisfaction. Crows liked dead spirits. They knew that their job was to guide them. The dead that escaped to other starless places glimpsed in the depths of mirrors. Such an unnatural occurrence would confuse and alarm the crows. She knew that, but there wasn't a single thing that she could do about it. She had no bell, no book, no candle powerful enough to ward off such evil. Still, strange incidents were not uncommon in Arkham. There were others to come that could deal with such events. That much she knew from her dreams.

"Never mind," she said to the crows as much to the children. "Never mind."

The day was done, the sun was setting, red behind the flames flickering now in every window. Shouts and cries drowned out the fussing of the crows as the neighbors finally roused themselves to come up the long drive and begin the battle to save the house. They would fail. The place would be ash by dawn. Rebecca Baker knew that too from her dreams.

She waited there, both children now leaning against her, too stunned and exhausted to cry any more, as the flames ate the house and all left within it, all except that which could not burn. Rebecca Baker mourned the mistress, small and kind, who had thrust the children into her arms and told her to run.

As for the master, she cursed him a little, but under her breath so as not to disturb the children.

The house collapsed completely by midnight. Smoke and sparks swirled up in the air, obscuring the stars and the rare blue-tailed comet that streaked across the solstice night sky.

The neighbors carried away the children along with the bits and pieces that had been saved from the house. She tried to keep them from taking the mirrors, but failed. They even carried off the master's fire-blackened sword, after they detached the remains of his hand from the hilt. Why anyone would want that nasty blade, she could not imagine.

Rebecca Baker sat and waited for the ones who took charge to leave, one hand trailing in the cool green leaves of her garden, threading them back and forth through her fingers. Then the others came up the long drive. The widowed women of the town, the servant girls, the cooks, the laundry ladies, and all the others who worked behind the scenes to keep things orderly. All towns had them, all towns needed them, even a town like Arkham.

Someone thrust a cup of cool water into her hands. Another draped a shawl around her shoulders. The murmuring of women rose around her as they watched the final sparks of fire to fade and waited for the house to die.

When the dawn finally came, cool but with the promise of summer heat, she rose very stiffly and walked down to Arkham town proper with that huddle of women. She didn't look back. She had done what she could.

"Never mind," she told herself. "Never mind." But Rebecca Baker felt a deep sorrow for those who would come to Arkham later. She wished there was a warning that she could leave them.

CHAPTER ONE

The dreams still come at night. Not as many. Not as fierce. But the shadows are there, tinged with silver and fire. Dreams of a mask that I wish I had never made. I wake far too early in the morning, throw open the windows, and breath the salt air from the Pacific. But in my dreams I smell smoke and something else, something not altogether of this world. The scent of a shadow, a perfume of death, that clings to me even awake. Sometimes, out of the corner of my eye, I even see a shadow on the wall or glimpse a hooded face. But then I turn and face it directly, and there is nothing there.

Eleanor said that writing our story would make the dreams fade. But in her last letter she spoke of waking still to the visions of Lulu in the coffin. So I am not sure if writing this down will make it better. But I will try. I will always try, for the sake of those who could not escape the mask that I made.

It started at a party. Most of Sydney's worst ideas did. Perhaps because we were tired, and I must admit, a little drunk, it sounded like a good idea. Sydney's proposals often seemed like good ideas until they weren't. Until people got hurt. Until, in Arkham, people died.

But, in the beginning, that late May night in California, we were enjoying a "reviews are in" party, the type of party we always held in Renee's pretty garden apartment. The French doors stood wide open to the courtyard so couples could wander in and out. The open windows also kept the worst of the cigar smoke and whiskey fumes from overpowering the fresh flowers that filled the McCoy vases lining the mantle. For this particular Saturday night, we mingled late orange blossoms with jasmine. People always expected red roses, but Renee hated them. She said red roses were a cliché if you were a dark-haired beauty. She allowed white roses in the winter when we couldn't get anything else. Later, after Arkham, hothouse flowers smelled too much like funerals and the vases sat empty.

As usual, Sydney made us wait days before giving the party. He wanted all the reviews to read out loud, even those sent express from New York, Boston, and Chicago. Which meant Max, Sydney's assistant, had driven down to the train station and bribed a porter or two to turn over the studio's mail to him. Once Max had collected every possible clipping, and Sydney had read them in secret in his apartment, then the party was allowed to properly begin at Renee's.

As I recall, it was well past midnight when Sydney began talking about the next film. Max leaned against the oak bookcase behind me. Renee concealed his beloved imported whiskey there. She kept his bottles stashed inside the hollowed-out works of Walter Scott. I was in my leather chair in that corner, neatly tucked in with a sketchpad and an idea for dress that would resemble a shooting star.

Renee and Sydney had their usual place in the center of the room. Renee reclined across her chaise lounge, the one that we called Marie Antoinette's fainting couch. We'd found the frame in a sweet little secondhand shop in Pasadena. I'd covered it all in material left over from some French Revolution costumes. Renee hadn't played the queen, of course, but she received great reviews as the Parisian fortuneteller who cursed Marie and all her court after a royal carriage ran down her only child. Sydney adored Renee in that role. It led to her starring in his first nightmare picture. Renee liked to say that the Queen died for her career. We certainly sacrificed a dress or two for the upholstery.

While Renee reclined with one shoulder slipping out of the simple little silk dress that I made for her flapper girl appearance in an earlier comedy, Sydney sat straight upright on the other end of the chaise lounge. He had his usual unlit cigarette in an ivory holder clenched in the corner of his mouth. His hair was perfectly pomaded and the shine made the lamplight seem to shimmer around his head. There was always a sense that all lights shone directly on Sydney, even when he was outside of the spotlight and yelling at all of us to "get that scene right."

The rest of the actors were busy drinking everything we had, and a few stray bottles that somebody had brought from another party, while the crew wandered in and out of the dining room in search of something substantial to eat. But everyone kept an ear tilted toward Sydney to catch his every remark.

"Listen to this," he roared, pulling the cigarette holder out of his mouth and gesturing at the page spread flat on Renee's coffee table. "'The Showman's latest nightmare picture is simply wonderful and probably unfit for public exhibition.'"

"Is that the *Times*?" asked Max.

"No, *Variety*." Sydney was obviously pleased. He adored his nickname, "The Showman to Know", and added to the legend by always wearing his top hat, tails, and crimson-lined cape to openings. Renee often teased him that it made him look like a ringmaster from a seedy circus. To which Sydney retorted, "I wore a red coat in the circus, never black, so they'd follow my every move."

Sydney grabbed another newspaper and spread it open. "This is even better," he said. "Quite the most terrifying thing to be seen on screen so far in 1923."

                    Arkham Horror – Visions & Nightmares

"Isn't that the one when they mention Chaney's new picture?" said Max, which earned him a terrible frown from Sydney.

"There might be something at the end. Nobody reads to the end," Sydney said.

Max bent over to me and said softly, "It says that Chaney will deliver his most spectacular film yet. Universal is spending nearly a million dollars on the sets, costumes, and hundreds of extras."

Sydney, who had the hearing of a bat when someone was talking about the movies, chimed in: "Anyone can make a movie for a million dollars. It's making quality with far less that shows talent. Why, give me a thousand dollars and I can outshine Wallace Worsley any day."

Max smiled a bit and asked: "Should I tell the studio that you're cutting your fees?"

"Never!" cried Sydney with an exaggerated shudder. "After all, I need to pay all of you." He waved his hand at the actors and crew laughing at the exchange. Sydney's spending on sets, costumes, and extras could be, and often was, far more extravagant than the studio liked. Max was sent to us by the studio a couple of years ago "to keep an eye on Sydney." He did his best to hold the expenses in check, but in the end Sydney nearly always won. The studio paid because, whether they liked his terror pictures or not, his films certainly sold tickets. By 1923, Max was clearly one of us, rather than a studio flunky, and had even taken to dressing and talking a bit like Sydney. He certainly shared his more expensive tastes for good whiskey, among other things.

Fred wandered in from the garden, smelling faintly of pipe smoke and engine oil. He dropped onto the floor, leaning back against the arm of my chair to peer at my sketch. "Nice dress," he said. "Which role?"

"Sydney is talking about casting Renee as a mesmerist who lures men to their doom. The dream maker, he calls it," I said. I rolled my knees out of the way so Fred could get a better look. For comfort, I wore my black pajama pants, made out of silk, and an embroidered tunic top to all of Renee's parties. I hated fussing with garters and stockings. And rolling your stockings down and rouging your knees was even worse. Besides everyone knew I was half Chinese and figured that the outfit was inherited. It wasn't. I got the tunic from Anna Wong, who had it from some director or other who was trying to impress her. She wasn't impressed. Rather like being told that you had to like chop suey just because you had black hair and dark eyes. I never did like chop suey. Mostly because it tasted all wrong, a mix of American ingredients trying to look like Chinese food. But I loved the tunic. Not for where the tunic came from or what it represented. But for the gorgeous flower embroidery that started at the shoulder and spiraled down my back. When I wore it, I felt glamorous but not Hollywood. Someone both inside and outside the crowd of flappers in their beaded dresses and the men in their suits. Fred teased me about wearing the same outfit to every party to avoid having to think about clothes. Except I thought about clothes all the time.

Anna traded the tunic in return for my making her a tailored velvet coat with a fur collar. She wanted to impress a director and prove that she could look like a flapper, and didn't have to play a girl named Lotus Blossom. Didn't work. They cast her as Lotus Flower in her next film. That's the trouble with being Chinese-American in Hollywood. They only see you as one type of character if you're in front of the camera. It's a bit better behind the camera, even if you do have to work twice as hard to prove yourself. So I worked hard, sketching ideas constantly for movies that we made and movies that we might make.

"What material will you use?" said Fred as he looked at my sketchbook that night. As our cameraman, he always wanted to know ahead how something might translate to black-and-white film.

"I've got a few bolts of a silver lamé. It will shine in the lights."

"As long as it doesn't reflect Sydney waving his arms."

"No more mirrors. I promise you."

Our last picture dealt with a cursed circus, which Sydney knew something about, having once been a ringmaster. He read out his own quotes from the newspapers with glee. "'My time in the circus taught me how spellbinding and terrifying these acts could be. And how an audience can be trained to look where you need them to look. It is a combination of wicked magic and temple ritual, all triggered by the smell of greasepaint and the whistle of the calliope!'" he said. "You know that's what we should have done for the opening. Had someone blow in the smells of a circus ring. Sawdust, peanuts…"

"Horse manure," muttered Fred. "To say nothing of elephants." He filmed several small circuses as additional footage for the picture. I often went with him for costume and makeup ideas. We'd both been horrified by the poor battered creatures in cages and tiny traveling stalls.

In our circus picture, which had only one lovely horse on set, Renee played the charming, mysterious performer who rode that white horse round and round the ring, mesmerizing the hapless males in the audience. Mesmerizing was a label that Renee began to despise that year, but it was the way that Sydney wrote her characters, mystery women who lured men to their doom. And, as she often said to me, that was better than being the screaming ingénue victim.

The doomed circus performer role turned out to be more difficult than usual. Renee hated horses and was furious with me when we found that the mirrors on her costume reflected Sydney directing off camera. That ruined nearly a day's filming and meant she needed to mount the beautiful but bouncy horse for a second day's shooting. I smeared all the mirrors with grease before we reshot the entire scene. And then we all suffered through another day of Sydney yelling about Renee's posture on a horse as the silly creature trotted instead of cantered in all of its scenes, despite being able to do a lovely canter the day before. Which meant even more bouncing about by Renee. And more yelling by Sydney. Perhaps even a little weeping by the trainer who swore that Rex was a wonder horse and should be in pictures. Fred, as always, stayed calm and kept the camera rolling. He even salvaged some of the earlier footage. But afterward, I swore to Renee to never ever let Sydney put her on a horse again.

The whole crew was glad to be done with horses and circuses. I hoped our next picture would be full of sophisticated party scenes. We'd been talking about another hypnotist picture, with elaborately staged sets.

Fred rested his head against my chair and traced the lines of the dress in my sketchbook with one stubby scarred finger. The man fiddled with engines and anything else that whizzed or whirred, and his hands bore the traces of his work in a network of tiny scars and freshly healed cuts. If I turned my hands over, I could see every callus, every prick, every mark that costuming left there. People always said that we didn't work, that we just played, when we were making movies. Our hands told a different story.

"If I adjust the lights, she'll look like a silver ghost emerging from the shadows. And that head dress!" Fred said, tapping the page. I had drawn a close-fitting cap set with long silver spikes that formed a star-shaped frame for Renee's head. "That's finer than a 5th Avenue getup. Good work, China girl."

I slapped his hand away before he smudged my drawing. "Not China girl, just plain Oakland, that's me."

Fred grinned up at me. "Hello, Oakland. I'm Brooklyn. Want to dance?"

"You just like me because I'm the only woman in the room shorter than you."

"Nah," said Fred. "Adore you for that. And your mean game of croquet. The way you'll play gin rummy when we get a rainy day. Oh, and your costumes. That one is something. Sydney will love it."

"I'll love what?" said Sydney from across the room. Mention his name and he always heard you.

"Jeany's new costume for the mesmerist."

"Oh, that tired old idea, I'm not making that. It's too close to *Caligari*. Even with Renee as the hypnotist."

"Well I'm delighted not to play a hypnotist, but I do love Jeany's idea for the silver dress. Can we use it in the *Mask*?" Renee said.

"Oh course. I'm sure it's exactly what Camilla should wear on the night that she calls for the stranger. Along with a silver mask," Sydney put his cigarette holder back in his mouth and waited for everyone to catch up with him. The crowd grew quieter and moved a little closer. This was the boss talking about the next job, the one that we all hoped to be part of. "This is my best idea ever."

"You want a mask with this dress?" I said. I liked making masks and had built a couple for past pictures. I thought about how the material could be applied to the form. "How much of the face should it hide?"

Sydney thought for a moment and then slid into his storytelling voice. "I see a woman emerging from the shadows. Her face is covered in a silver mask, so highly polished that she appears to be wearing a mirror or liquid mercury, a mask that reflects our world and distorts it. She pauses on the threshold of light and shadow. The audience grows uncertain. Is she a beauty or a grotesque hiding behind the mask? The audience will be both attracted and repelled. Slowly the mask of silver reflections becomes transparent, revealing the face of a lovely woman, our gorgeous Renee, but then her face in turn changes. She becomes a creature of glamorous horror, a siren both alien and familiar. And the audience will know that is the face of truth."

I was scribbling as fast as I could on the corners of my sketchbook page. A full mask, with the barest slits for eyes, to give Sydney the blank form that he wanted? Polished silver to make it reflective? But that would create the same problem that any mirrors on a set created. Perhaps a metallic paint that mimicked metal but would not create reflections? With the right lighting, it would give off a luminous shimmer like the dress itself. Fred could film that, stop the filming, Renee would remove the mask, and then Fred could resume filming. We had done a similar dissolve two pictures back, when Sydney turned Renee from a withered ancient corpse to an enchantress who lured the hero to his final doom.

Fred, like me, was obviously working through the sequence in his head. "So will the siren be a second mask or something else? Makeup like Chaney is doing for his hunchback?"

"Oh something else entirely," smirked Sydney. "Something that hasn't been seen before."

Fred and I both sighed. That line normally meant that Sydney hadn't decided what he wanted and we'd be doing trial after trial of possible combinations of costume and makeup. When we had to make the witch woman turn into a werewolf to avenge her dead husband, Sydney had ranted for days on the combination of furs, wigs, and makeup because everything made Renee look too hideous. We ended up creating the shadow of a wolf on the wall with one of the crew manipulating a puppet head that I built. Then Fred filmed Renee stepping out of the doorway and wiping the blood from her lips with the white cravat of her husband's supposed killer.

"So we're not filming the hypnotist story? But, Sydney, the studio has started on the sets," said Max. Three lines appeared on his forehead. You can take the guy out of accounting, but you can never quite erase the bookkeeper from the guy. Fred called him "Brooks Brothers down to his second pair of pants." I told Fred he was just jealous that Max owned a suit that fit him. Also, the girls liked the Harold Lloyd tall and skinny type. Fred tended toward tweed jackets and canvas pants, stuff that was constantly being pulled out of shape by the gadgets stuffed in his pockets. Fred was a Brooklyn tough, who powdered out of Brooklyn as soon as he could talk the army into taking him. He drifted to California after he was invalided home for losing a toe in France. At least, that was Fred's story. We all had stories that were a little bit true and much more what we wanted people to believe.

"Call them in the morning. Tell the studio that I don't want their tacky interpretation of a historic haunted house. I'm taking you all to Arkham, Massachusetts. We'll film where Puritans mixed with witches and Colonial ghosts still ride the lanes."

That set up a storm of comments and questions. Sydney sat grinning like the Cheshire Cat in the middle of it all until we stopped. Then, having gained everyone's attention, he started to tell us his latest, greatest idea. He would make a movie, a wonderful, terrible, frightening movie set in an ordinary little New England town that none of us had ever heard of.

"But what's the story?" said Max.

"Later, Max, just arrange all the necessary bits and bobs for travel," said Sydney, who could be maddeningly Continental when he felt it made him sound important. "Jeany can start by designing the mask now. That's key. The rest we can do when we get to Arkham."

I nodded, not really listening, because I had an idea. I drew a nearly perfect oval over the face I sketched. Shading it lightly with the pencil, I then extended the shadow behind the woman on the page so another, stranger being stood behind her. The spikes on the crowned headdress took on a more fluid, twisted shape in this shadow image. The points of the shadow's sleeves also flowed down, like the strangely delicate tentacles of jellyfish, dwindling away. Then, further behind both figures, I drew the hooded man. The last was Sydney's signature creature, a man dressed in a hooded cape. The character never appeared more than once in a film and never in the same type of scene twice, played by whoever wasn't already in the scene. Also, oddly, the hooded man never did anything. Never spoke or interacted with any character. He was just there. Watching. Often it was so subtle that many people missed it, but the critics had taken to looking for those appearances and speculating what Sydney meant by it. None of us knew. Sydney liked to say to the reporters that it would all be revealed later. But that movie had not been made yet, despite the topic being raised frequently by Max since he joined our company. Apparently the studio felt a hooded man picture would be the biggest seller yet. Sydney tended to go sly during those discussions, telling Max to mollify the studio for a little while longer. Poor Max, he was stuck between two difficult and very different bosses: the unseen and, for the rest of us, unknown studio heads and Sydney, the driving force in our daily lives.

"That's clever," said Fred as I sketched out the two figures behind the woman in the mask. "We could create the second shape behind her by backlighting a screen. Does it need to move?"

I looked at my drawing. "I think so," I said slowly, the idea sparked by Sydney's words growing inside of me. A terrible, wonderful idea, quite unlike anything we'd done before. "Can we make the shadow reach out from the wall and engulf her? Like ink, or blood, running dark over the mask and revealing the woman beneath for just a second or two. Then they both disappear."

Fred nodded. "Good idea, Oakland. I predict half the audience faints and the other half leaps out of their seats with a yell."

This was why we worked with Sydney. Because with just a few words, he could set a mood that inspired all of us. I knew Fred was right, that we would weave the shadows and reflections into something just as terrifying as anything Chaney could create with a hump and a limp. But Chaney's specialty was grotesque makeup. Our terrible monster was beautiful, always chillingly beautiful, that glamorous horror that Sydney talked about.

I added a few more lines to my sketch and then stopped. Too much and it would disappear into a mess of charcoal on the page. Restraint was the most important lesson that I'd learned from Sydney, the most flamboyant showman. The suggestion of a shadow cast by a man in a hood, the merest glimpse of the monster in the mirror, a pallid mask of silvery shadows, those were the things that would terrify the audience. Why we should we want to evoke terror, that was the question that I failed to ask myself that night as Fred and I sat up long after the rest had left.

Finally Renee came over to our corner. "Go home," she said to Fred. He rented a tiny house all the way out in Santa Monica and had borrowed a friend's car to avoid being stranded by the Los Angeles streetcars shutting down in the early hours. With a friendly grumble, he unfolded himself from the floor and wandered out the garden doors into the predawn pallid gloom. I wondered if he'd sleep in the car or drive himself home. Either was possible with Fred.

"Are you done?" Renee asked me. "Can you get home all right?"

"I only have an elevator ride of one floor," I said, as if my only sister didn't know that. Of course she did, but everyone else only knew that I lived in the building. Our relationship was a closely guarded secret, from the press, from our friends, and, most especially, from the studio where we had been working for the last five years. Because while everyone knew that I was a Chinese-American from Oakland, nobody knew Renee's true heritage. If the studio knew, she would not be a leading lady. And if Renee was not a star, the rest of us might not work. So while we knew exactly what lies we were telling, the rest didn't have much reason to ask uncomfortable questions. Everyone understood Renee and I had always worked together in Hollywood, and left it at that.

I eyed Sydney stretched out on Renee's chaise, still leafing through the magazines and newspapers that Max had brought. At this point in the night, he was past the reviews and reading about others' triumphs and failures. He knew how to turn such knowledge to his advantage. He could, and often did, stay up for hours after the rest of us had collapsed. One disgruntled extra conjectured that

Sydney didn't sleep, just rested lightly in a coffin like some creature from one of his films. It wasn't true. Sydney slept very soundly when he did sleep and not, as some speculated, at Renee's apartment. He had his own a floor above. She always threw him out before she went to bed herself. Sometimes she used as an excuse the need to put up someone at the party who had too long a journey or had too much to drink. Then that unfortunate soul, quite often me if she had no other sacrifice to avoid Sydney's snores, slept on her wildly uncomfortable chaise lounge.

"I'd rather sleep in my own bed tonight," I said, uncurling from the leather seat that I had claimed earlier.

"Come to lunch," Renee answered. "I'd like to talk about this costume." She pointed to my sketch, set aside on the table as Fred and I had gone over possible ways to trick the audience's eyes into seeing what did not, could not, exist. She glanced at Sydney. "He'll be gone in a few hours and I want some sleep too. But we'll order something splendid for lunch, just the two of us."

I nodded. When a picture was done, Renee tended to withdraw into luxurious comfort. She tipped generously and had a dozen restaurants nearby ready to deliver whatever she felt like eating. Renee adored her slender candlestick phone and welded it like a fairy godmother's magic wand to deliver the bounties of the Los Angeles shops and restaurants to us. She called it her "cocoon before the butterfly time."

Sydney called it "hiding," but he was the exact opposite. After a picture was done, he would drive all over town, even up the coast to San Francisco, to talk to people about everything and anything that interested him. With Sydney that could mean visiting the latest airplane demonstration or a strange occult shop hidden down a back alley. The occult was a particular obsession that we all knew about. We even joked that his forays were Sydney researching terrors for his next picture. Séances weren't quite as popular as they had been a few years before but there were still plenty held around Hollywood. Sydney knew all the tricks and liked to reveal frauds to his friends. Sydney was never fooled by slate writing, spirit pictures, table tipping, or rapping. But he collected odd "safekeeps," as he called the items that he picked up from people who did not like to tell where their treasures came from. Renee called these artworks ghastly and refused to have any in her apartment.

"Thank you very much," Renee said when she clapped the lid on some box or other that Sydney had handed her as a gift. "But it still looks like a bunch of bird bones and feathers to me. Put it in your apartment, please."

"But, dearest muse," Sydney would reply. "What if the spirits take you from me too soon?" For Sydney, spirits were less ghosts of dead ancestors than emissaries from a world that we could not see except out of the corner of our eyes or in the reflections of a mirror. In his best scripts, the ones that he wrote for Renee's villainesses, Sydney turned hauntings into an "invasion from beyond," where spirits or supernatural creatures lured humans, usually males, out of the world as we know it and into a twisted landscape besides and beyond our world. The "safekeeps" acted as locks, according to Sydney, to keep shut doors that should not be open. Anything could be a door, even a mirror upon the wall or the reflection in a silver mask.

"It's casting the right reflection, at the right moment," Sydney said that night as he discussed the script with Renee and me, while we struggled to stay awake. "The right reflection allows us to control the door and the spirits beyond. The right reflection, at the right time, in the right place. While the mask protects the priestess or the Muse."

"But it has to be a silver mask, a reflective mask," I said, thinking once again about the problems with the mirrors in the last picture.

"Oh, yes," said Sydney, "a mask to cast its own reflection back into the mirror." I shuddered considering all the issues that would cause for Fred in filming such a scene.

Renee yawned and punched Sydney's shoulder lightly. "Go work on your script and let us sleep. If we're going to someplace on the East Coast, we'll have days of travel to work this all out."

That night, when I reached my bedroom, Sydney's idea of the silver mask consumed me. Even after I climbed into my bed, I continued to sketch variations on my first idea, often surrounded by a circle of mirrors casting reflections back and forth until endless repetitions appeared. In the glow of the electric lamp, the images on the page turned into a chorus of featureless faces, watching me with the empty eye sockets of a drama mask. These fanciful thoughts slid into nightmares, and I woke with an aching head atop the crumpled pages of my notebook.

At lunch, as I consumed cup after cup of black coffee, Renee described her own nightmares to me.

"It began after Sydney left," she said. "I must have been asleep for less than half an hour, but the nightmare felt like it lasted forever."

"We all ate and drank too much last night," I said. "And then Sydney started telling us about his latest horrid idea."

"I'm quite sure that you're right," said Renee with a sip of her own black coffee. Both of us usually preferred our coffee sweet, with plenty of sugar stirred in, but this morning nothing would do but the bitterest of brews. "I dreamt that the film went in reverse. Rather than the mask dissolving to reveal my face, I was watching my face become the mask, just a silver mask that reflected everything but me. It was as if I was being erased."

My nightmares of a lost Renee reflected in a mirror showed me a tangle of hallways, all leading into shadows. Behind the shadows, someone watched us. Sydney? It felt like something older, something more terrible. But I shook off my memory of the dream, and convinced Renee of the source of her fears. "Sydney's ideas for the mask. I'm sure that prompted your dream."

"Sydney called me this morning, just to talk more about Arkham," Renee said.

I felt relief that he had just telephoned and not come downstairs to share our breakfast. An excited Sydney, planning a new picture, was the worst companion for a headachy morning. "He kept talking about how long it had been since he had been in Arkham but how he was sure that it hadn't changed. How much he was looking forward to going home."

"It's hard to imagine," I said. "Sydney as a boy in an idyllic little New England town."

Renee smiled. "Yes. I never think of him as anything other than the Sydney Fitzmaurice striding through the world in his silk cravats and stylish hats. Do you suppose he wore short pants and had skinned knees from falling off his bicycle?"

For some reason that thought doubled us up with laughter. Wiping those cheerful tears from her eyes with some choice words about the impact on her mascara, Renee swore that this would be her last nasty nightmare picture for a while.

"Sydney's brilliant," she said. "But I need to find a lighter script, a romance or a comedy, or I'll end up playing nothing but murderous women in impossible hats. Remember what Sennett said to me? That I had a flair for comedy."

"That's just because he wanted to stick you in one of his silly bathing suits," I said. "And those caps are far less fetching than any hat that I designed for you."

She shrugged. "Better that than another terror role with a costume that weighs two tons."

"My costumes never weigh more than one ton," I countered and we both giggled again.

I left Renee's apartment feeling much more cheerful. She was right. Sydney's nightmare stories were starting to turn into real nightmares. What we needed was a picture that wouldn't stay with us in our dreams.

One trip to Arkham, and a summer trip at that. By the time we returned in July, at worst August, if filming went long, we could look around for the perfect project for the fall. Renee's contract was with the studio, not Sydney, and they always wanted her to work with other directors. Fairbanks had approached her about an *Arabian Nights* fantasy that summer, but she disliked the script and especially the character of the girl who betrayed the hero to his enemies. "Not another scheming spy," she said. "I don't want to be known only as the beautiful but murderous woman." But I loved the idea of working on such a picture, with palace scenes and fairytale characters. I discussed it with Fred, who had heard about the flying carpet being built, and he suggested that I go to United Artists with my costume designs and see what was available. It would be easier for me to work outside our studio too. Our studio was less possessive of costumers than they were of their few proven stars like Renee and Sydney.

Chatting with Renee that morning, I asked, "Would you mind if I talked to other studios? Just when you're not working on a picture."

Renee looked a little startled. We'd been together our entire careers in Hollywood, but now it seemed like we might have reached a time to grow more apart.

"Jeany," she said, reaching across the table to squeeze my hand, "you should do what you want. As long as you promise to design all my hats when they cast me as the romantic lead!"

"All your hats and your party dresses," I promised.

So I packed for Arkham with far too light a heart. While my sketches of shadows and masks, still scattered across my unmade bed, made my hand tremble a little as I gathered them up, I stuffed the pages with great determination into my portfolio and knotted the ribbon around it twice. Thus I thought that I could contain the nightmares spawned by Sydney's description of the silver mask.

CHAPTER TWO

The first problem with Arkham was that it was in Massachusetts. "Could have been worse," said Fred. "Could have been Maine."

I looked at the map spread across the table in the train's dining car. Then I checked my timetable. "I think we have to go through Maine to get there," I said. "Isn't Boston in Maine? Don't we change trains there?"

"Well, ma'am," said Joseph, the porter, coming to fill our water glasses, "you'll transfer in Boston but that's in Massachusetts. And your company paid for all your cars to be switched. So you folks don't have to do more than sit tight and wait for a little bump."

I found the right spot on the map. It still seemed a terrible long distance from California, the only state that I'd ever known. Unlike Joseph, who had worked as a Pullman porter all across the country, I'd never been farther north than Oakland or farther south than Los Angeles.

"How did Max talk the studio into paying for our own cars all the way to Arkham?" said Fred.

"Because it was cheaper than the private train that Sydney wanted them to commission. As is, we have four cars, including baggage, on this one," said Max, shifting a cup so Joseph could see that there was no coffee in it. The porter smiled and took the water carafe away to exchange it for a silver coffee pot. Four private cars, including baggage, meant the studio had bought out first class. The first class dining car was ours throughout the day and night, although we probably didn't tip as well as the regulars would. The porters were nice about it, and nice about me riding up front with the rest. We were taking a northern route, and Joseph didn't anticipate any objections, although he warned me to stay away from compartments further down the train. "There's some folks with no manners at all sitting in second class," he said. I looked into his warm brown face and wondered what he'd heard over the years.

"Just tell them that we're in pictures," said Fred on the first day, when some conductor or other fussed about the sleeping arrangements and, possibly, a Chinese-American woman riding with the others. Even after nearly five years at the studio, I ran into stupid prejudices despite others like me in Hollywood. There were successful actresses like Anna May Wong, cameramen like James Wong Howe, who started with DeMille in 1917, and more. I wanted to make my own career, my own way, but it was a battle. I owed my early assignments to Renee and later Sydney insisting on my designs. It probably helped that I worked behind the camera and not in front of it. Still, I appreciated that Sydney kept the executives and other busybodies off his sets, insisting on working with his favorite artists in picture after picture. In return, he made the studio a lot of money and they gave him funding for his next picture. And, for the last couple of years, that studio funding came with a Max tied to it. Luckily we liked him.

And, for this trip, Max had persuaded the studio to pay the extra expense of leaving California in style.

Renee and Sydney each had a private compartment and a sitting room in between in their car. The rest of us, the men and women, were bunking in two open-section sleepers but it was only us, no other passengers allowed. All the bunks had privacy curtains and converted to seats during the day. A furiously contested poker game raged there when people were not sleeping, which is why Fred, Max, and I preferred to work in the dining car.

Joseph, with his knowledge of train gossip and ready hand with the coffee pot, was another reason to stay there.

"Oh, everyone working on the train knows you work in the movies, sir," said Joseph. "Couldn't miss you all getting aboard at La Grande." Our parade of luggage and chattering actors had been followed to the steps of the train by an equally large crowd of reporters and fans. Also, Fred made the biggest fuss as we boarded the train in Los Angeles, because they wouldn't let him sleep with his nearly new Bell and Howell camera. They insisted on stowing all the gear in the baggage car. Fred wanted to move his bed to the baggage car, just to keep close to his equipment. A couple of porters and the stationmaster finally convinced him that the camera was safe enough where it was.

Now we were east of Chicago, passing by cornfields, and trying to get as much work done as possible in the nearly four-day trip. The dining car turned into our workshop. Joseph kept us well supplied in coffee and ignored the times that Max or Fred tipped a little extra into their cups from their hip flasks. He even brought me a pot of tea on the first morning, but I told him that I preferred coffee with sugar.

"I still don't see what Sydney wants in our opening scene," said Fred. He looked at some notes scrawled in Sydney's atrocious handwriting. "They enter a house, it is not clearly their house," he read. "How do we show that?"

"They carry luggage but nothing too large," I suggested. "As if they were gone for just a few days. Or it could be that they are new to the house and moving in. The audience decides."

Max scribbled something in his notebook. Because this was the start of production, his tiny pocket notebook had neat crisp corners and a blank cover. By the end of the shoot, it would be dog-eared, dripping with receipts, and numbers would be scribbled on every corner of the cover. The notebooks were legendary. Rumor stated that each one was specially done for him in a stationer's shop. Max did have his name stamped in gold inside the front cover of every notebook that I saw, which argued for the truth of the custom-made rumor.

Max never lost a notebook, no matter how many times he pulled it out and was interrupted by some request by Sydney. His ability to hang onto it, and to turn all the many jotted notes into coherent reports to the studio, was truly magical. What happened to the notebooks after a film was done and the final report filed, I never learned. Fred was of the opinion that they deserved a ceremonial burning, like a Viking funeral, and more than once offered to build a little ship so Max could launch them flaming on the Pacific. As far as I knew, Max never agreed to that.

"Do you need to buy bags or can you just use ours?" Max said with a pencil poised to jot down that potential expense. "It would make the studio happy if we could keep away from too many purchases on this trip." Max liked to keep the studio bosses happy, and apparently endless reports on expenses made them very happy indeed. We all suspected that the studio paid Max a bonus whenever he whittled down Sydney's budget. Which was good, because Max liked buying costly clothes and accessories for himself.

"Renee can carry her hat box," I said. "The one with black crocodile trim. She has that white ensemble with the small round hat that would look good with it." I flipped open my sketchbook, quickly turning past page after page of masks sketched with shadows dripping across them. The nightmares continued on the train. I often found myself awake and drawing to relieve my terror. Joseph had become used to me arriving in the dining car well ahead of everyone else and juggling my breakfast around my propped-open sketchbook.

"That settles Renee's costume. What about the other girl?" Max asked.

"Is she supposed to be the maid or the best friend?" We hadn't seen a full script from Sydney. Not unusual. He often hid details until he was filming, just to shock the actors and create a stronger reaction from them. At least that's what Sydney said. Often we felt it was because he didn't know the end of the story until he was halfway through it. "Is Betsy playing her?" Our usual ingénue, Betsy Baxter, was back in a sleeping car, betting next month's salary on poker. Betsy most often portrayed girlish servants, the kind who flirted madly in the corner and caught the audience's eye with her smile and dimples. Betsy always cleaned up in card games, as she looked so sweet and spoke with a bubbly squeak that made the men go mushy and miss that she was counting the cards. Fred refused to play with her after she took twenty dollars off him in one night of gin rummy.

Max checked his cast notes. "Betsy is the maid. Renee is the older sister and Lulu plays the younger."

"Renee has a sister?" I drew a belt to add to Renee's traveling coat so it wouldn't look so much like what she wore in the last picture. I could borrow a belt from another dress that we probably wouldn't use. I wondered how we could dress the other actress to make her relationship clear with Renee. It would be a new challenge. Renee usually played the lone temptress. The hero often had family, a kid brother or kid sister, that helped him out. Or mourned him after he died. Sydney could go either way with his stories. "Who is playing her? Maggie stayed behind for that role with Chaplin." Maggie often played the hero's kid sister or an innocent friend of the heroine.

"Maggie is never going to get cast with Chaplin," said Fred, fiddling with a bit of wire. He had spent the morning checking his hand-cranked Bell and Howell model 2709 (serial number 242, as Fred would tell anyone foolish to ask about the camera) and the rest of the gear still stored in the baggage car. Though he visited his beloved camera regularly to make sure nothing was joggled loose, there wasn't much else that he could do until we arrived in Arkham. Except drive the engineers crazy by pestering them to let him ride up front and see how all the engine's levers and switches worked. Actually the engineers liked Fred. He disappeared for several hours each day to return coal-dusted and grinning, his ragged old checked cap further scarred by smuts and stray sparks.

"Sydney isn't planning to bring Maggie later, is he? We don't need two faint-ers," asked Max.

"No, Sydney hated that Maggie stayed behind for that *Hollywood* film," I told Max. "Where everyone in the cast is a star playing themselves except the girl who comes to town to become a star. There's a bit with Chaplin. Maggie wants the role of the flapper who goes off with the tramp." The film itself was a stunt, a gimmick more than a script with famous actors in dozens of parts. Sydney sneered when he heard about it, and frowned even more when nobody from our company was invited to take part. His nightmare movies might sell well at the box office but we definitely weren't as famous as some. Even if Maggie got a bit in *Hollywood*, she wouldn't be playing herself like Chaplin and the rest. She'd just be a "Flapper" in the credits.

"Maggie never hits her mark and has two left feet," said Fred. "Can't see her making the final cut with Chaplin. So, Max, who is our fainter for this picture?"

Once Maggie got into place – and Fred was right, she never remembered where she was supposed to walk – she was a champion fainter. Sydney often had her hit the floor just as a shadow crept up the wall or a hand reached around the door. It never failed to make the audience jump. It was hard to imagine a terror picture without a fainter.

"Yes," I said, "who is going to be terrified by Sydney's tricks so the audience knows when to gasp? Is he planning to use Renee? She hasn't played the innocent for a while, but it worked in *The Vampire's Doom.*"

"Lulu McIntyre," said Max. He flipped a page in his notebook and looked over some information there with the suggestion of a sigh. "She's driving from New York and meeting us in Arkham. She asked for quite a lot to do this picture."

The name sounded familiar but not too familiar. "She's not in the movies," I said, and it wasn't a question.

Max nodded. "She's been on Broadway the last few years in those plays by Eleanor Nash. That's part of the contract. She's coming with Nash, who will be working on the script with Sydney."

"Sydney hates sharing a writing credit," I said. He generally got first billing as "Written and Directed by Sydney Fitzmaurice," in letters that filled the screen. Renee had been arguing for the last few pictures that her contributions to the scripts be acknowledged, but so far Sydney had slithered out of that.

"Oh, he wanted the writer as much as the actress," said Max. "But it was the headlines about Lulu's performances that caught his eye."

"The Screamer?" said Fred and then I remembered. There was an actress famous for her "haunting wail" starred in something very like *The Bat.* Except it wasn't *The Bat.* Sydney had been obsessed with the reviews for that show, especially about the technical tricks played on the stage to terrify the audience. He kept reading Lulu's reviews out loud almost as often as his own. Something about her voice driving men mad.

"What does it matter if she can scream?" I asked. "Nobody will hear her except us."

"She can open her mouth," said Fred, "and the organist can let out the train whistle or something like that. Will there be a score for these films?"

"There will be a score. You know Sydney. But he doesn't want the organ tricks," Max said. "Sydney wants you to try recording her. Something about sending a cylinder with each film for playing."

Fred shook his head. "Won't work. Better to just mark the score and have the organist or piano player make a shrieking noise."

Max objected to that. Fred started a long explanation on why recording sound to sync with film was a fascinating idea but not practical for large distribution. Something about microphones, and speakers, and why nobody would bother to convert a movie theater because it would just be too much money. Also everybody was making more money with silents than live theater, so why bother going backwards and adding spoken dialogue to a story. Then he talked about the work being done by DeForest that had been inspired by a Finnish scientist. For a kid from Brooklyn who never quite finished high school, Fred liked to read, only he read the type of articles in magazines that sent the rest of us to sleep. He also went to demonstrations, as many as he could find. Inventors flocked to Hollywood, all convinced that they could make a fortune in pictures. Fred loved to listen to them and discuss their new ideas. He'd been terrifically excited with some radio magazine that had reported a director using a radio to signal directions to large groups of extras in an outdoor scene. He thought it would be much more efficient than Sydney's megaphone.

"But can we record her scream?" Max finally said. "That's important according to Sydney's notes."

Fred shrugged. "I can rig up a microphone. If that's what he wants. Waste of time. Waste of money. We would have to record the scream and then film her screaming."

"He wants everyone to hear her scream in the movie."

"They'll hear the clatter of the camera if I record while we are filming," Fred explained. "Old 242 is the darling of my heart, but noisy as hell. We'll have to match the sound and picture later. It's an effect that any big organ can do better."

"But can you make it work?" said Max.

"One theater, one time, might be able to do that." Fred looked a little more intrigued and asked to borrow some paper from my sketchbook. He started doodling notes with a stub of a pencil that he pulled out of a pocket along with a couple of screws, a toffee wrapped in wax paper, and a ball of string.

Max looked satisfied with Fred's promise. Myself, I didn't like the sound of how this was developing. As if Lulu's scream was more important than anything else. As if she was taking top billing over Renee. I needed to talk to Renee about this, find out if she knew. We watched each other's backs, that's what we always did, because everyone knew that success only lasted until the next picture, the next darling embraced by an increasingly fickle public. If Sydney thought someone else could sell tickets better than Renee, then the studio might think that. And if the studio thought that, so much for roles that needed fantastic hats and fabulous dresses. I excused myself and went forward through the smoky sleeping cars. Betsy waved from her seat where she was holding court with a deck of cards, a pile of matchsticks standing in for chips. Paul and Jim, two other actors who worked in almost all of Sydney's movies, were about to be parted from their money.

"Want me to deal you in?" Betsy giggled. "The boys need someone easier to bluff."

I shook my head. Walking through the cars, I could still hear Betsy's usual chatter about the next stop, and whether there would be time to get off and pick up something from the station. An older actress, Pola, was catching a catnap wrapped in her coat, head bobbing a bit with the swaying of the train. Watching cornfields made everyone sleepy after a while. Hal, one of my favorites, was reading a magazine that he'd picked up during an earlier stop.

"Hey, Jeany," said Hal, whose rotund shape and balding head made him the perfect judge or doctor in Sydney's films. "Seen the script yet?"

"Not yet," I said, steadying myself against the back of his seat as the train creaked and rattled round a curve. "Just some notes on characters and how they are supposed to look."

Hal chuckled. "That's Sydney. Has to be the most mysterious man in Hollywood. Don't know why we bother working with him."

"The reviews?" I said. It was an old joke, shared among the crew and cast.

"Nope, the cash. Max always makes sure we are paid on time," said Hal. "Got my eye on a chicken farm in Salinas. That's the life for me."

"What do you know about chickens?"

"Absolutely nothing! That's the allure. I know too much about other things to try them." He waved his farming magazine at me. "There's always a need for chicken farmers. I'll just buy some eggs, wait for them to hatch, and then have lots of more eggs."

"I am not sure that it works that way," I said.

"Everybody needs eggs. Chickens produce eggs. Seems like a sure bet."

I wished Hal well with his dream, knowing that by the next picture he would be talking about buying an orange grove in Anaheim. It changed with every picture, but one thing stayed constant. Hal loved acting, and dreaming about not acting, more than anything else.

After the chatter of our cars, the private salon shared by Sydney and Renee seemed deathly quiet. Neither were in the parlor area but that wasn't unusual. Sydney had barricaded himself in his room with loud orders that nobody but Max was to disturb him while he wrote.

I went to Renee's door and knocked quietly. She called out and I entered. The bed had been converted into a long seat with a small table unfolded beneath the window. Another seat was opposite that. I slid into it.

Renee was playing solitaire, the red and black cards in a fan pattern taking up the small table.

"How much longer?" she asked me. She asked the same question every time I visited her, but she rarely came forward to the dining room or mixed with the others in the sleeper car. It was, she once said, part of her mystique. It was easier to maintain in Hollywood, where she could go straight from the apartment to the studio and home again. Nobody ever wondered there why she was always in full makeup or hidden under a hat and veil during daylight trips. On the train it was harder to stay out of the direct light and away from too many close looks. Still I never felt she had to hide. With this crowd, she had established her persona. Sydney's beautiful muse. But Renee was firm. She kept her distance from everyone except Sydney and me, the two people that she trusted not to betray her secrets. But I was the only one who knew all her secrets. As far as I know, she never told Sydney her real name or where she came from. And, to be fair, he never seemed to care about that. As long as she was willing to be his inspiration, he was happy to accept whatever story she told to the press as her true biography.

"Less than two days until we are in Arkham," I said. "We switch trains in Boston, and it is just a few hours beyond that."

She sighed and flipped another card into a growing pile on the side. "Why did I agree to this? Mile after mile of boredom."

"For the reviews?" I said again.

One eyebrow flew up. I always envied Renee's ability to do that. She achieved that perfect lift from practicing with her reflection. She used to do it over and over when night turned the windows over the kitchen sink into murky mirrors. We spent a lot of time staring into those windows while washing dishes in the orphanage. From the time she was fifteen, Renee knew exactly what she wanted. She wanted to be famous. She wanted to be rich. She wanted to arch her eyebrow at anyone and everyone who ever called us a dirty name. She wanted to make them feel small. My sister wanted us to be safe from them all.

I was jealous of her certainty then. Her ambition and her single-minded pursuit of her goals. At twenty-one, I still wasn't sure exactly what I wanted. Not the way that Renee knew.

"Has Sydney given you the script yet?" If anyone had seen it, it would be Renee. He generally turned to her first, to sound out his ideas. She said it was because he loved her. I knew it was because she had a flair for adding the details that gave strength to a scene. Renee remembered small gestures that people made, the ways that they picked up and fidgeted with objects when they were angry or sad. Playing a lovely poisoner, she once rearranged a set of combs and brushes on a dressing table in a way that gave her "a chilling authority," according to one review.

"I haven't seen a scenario yet. Why?"

I picked up the discarded cards, running them through my hands, flipping them over to finish off Renee's fan.

"Jeany, what is it?"

"You have a sister."

Renee stopped dealing her own hand of cards. "Are we having this discussion again? You know I cannot tell anyone…"

"No," I said. "Not that. In the script. A sister. It's in Max's notes about costumes needed."

Renee cocked her head, a little intrigued. Sydney never gave her any family in his recent stories. She was always alone. "Is it Betsy?"

"No, he's bringing someone from New York. The actress who can scream. Lulu something."

Renee placed the ace of spades over the king of hearts. She looked up at me. "Lulu McIntyre. Sydney keeps talking about her. Some review or other caught his eye. And then there's the divorce stories in the newspapers."

"Whose divorce?"

"Hers. She married a banker and he decided that he didn't want an actress wife. And he named Eleanor Nash as co-respondent."

"A woman?" Such affairs were known around town but rarely mentioned in the press. The studios knew that it didn't sound good in Peoria and worked hard to keep that type of story out of the newspapers. I wondered at Sydney daring to cast Lulu if she was that big of a scandal. With Taylor's murder last year and Reid's drug-related death in January all the Hollywood and New York studios and theater chains felt strongly about the morality of their players. At least the public perception of their morality.

"Sydney thinks the scandal will attract attention. He said that the first director to cast her after the divorce would see even more people flocking into the theaters."

That sounded like Sydney. If there was any person more single-minded about becoming famous than Renee, it was Sydney. I thought it was the thing that they truly had in common. Perhaps terror pictures could be a bit more scandalous than love stories or domestic dramas. Certainly our studio wanted to sell tickets more than anything else, if Max's account of meetings was accurate.

I finished up the tail of the fan; three of clubs and then two of hearts and then ace of clubs. Six, it added up to six, and that was a lucky number. Maybe this would all work out.

Renee also counted and sighed. "I was hoping for seven. That's lucky."

"Not for us. Mama always said people got that backwards. That six was luckier."

"Maybe for you, little sister," said Renee, naming the private relationship that we never shared in public. "Maybe six is your lucky number. But I'm not Mama's daughter any more. Seven is my number now. And this is my seventh movie with Sydney. This is the one that will be lucky for me."

"Perhaps. But I feel better with six," I said. Something about Sydney's secrecy bothered me. Renee was certain of his loyalty to her, but I had never felt so sure about him. Maybe this was the movie where he would replace Renee with another actress. That was our greatest fear, that someone would find out about Renee and me, that we were sisters, the daughters of a Chinese mother who could never marry our big Swedish immigrant father under the laws of California. All of which would make Renee a less desirable star with the studio's new drive for toeing the line and conforming to how they thought the world should look.

"So I have six and you have seven. Maybe Arkham will be lucky for both of us," I said, trying to quiet my own fears.

"Or at least not as bad as that circus pony," Renee said. "I made Sydney swear that the only thing I will ride in this movie will be a motor car. Driven by someone else."

"Oh, I'd like to learn to drive," I said.

"Wasn't Fred teaching you?" Renee asked.

"I only drove about ten feet before he decided to do something to the engine. After an hour of waiting for him to come out from under the hood, I left. But it was fun. Next time, he promises to have it tuned up before the lesson."

"After we get back, I could buy you a car," Renee said. "And some driving lessons."

"Renee, you can't. You know you can't. People would ask questions if you gave me a gift like that."

Renee shrugged. Pretending that we were just friends and occasionally admitting that we grew up in the same orphanage when pressed about how we became friends – that had all been Renee's idea. I looked too obviously like our mother's daughter for anyone to believe that I was white. But Renee was taller, thinner in the face, and her eyes were almost hazel in certain lights. With wigs, makeup, and later a good hairdresser to bob her hair and give her auburn highlights, she passed. Especially after we made up stories for the press about her descending from the family of a Hungarian princess. After all, Hollywood was all about the make-believe. Nobody really wanted to know that Theda Bara was the daughter of a Jewish tailor named Goodman. They preferred to believe that Bara was the half-French daughter of an Arab sheik or an Italian sculptor. Backgrounds and family histories were fluid in Hollywood, shifting with an actor's current roles and needs.

"I may not tell people about who we were," said Renee. "But I will never forget my responsibilities. I'll always take care of you, Jeany. You know that."

"I know," I started to shrug too and then stopped. We tried very hard not to have the same gestures. She did take care of me. From her very first picture, she found work for me. Work that I loved, making her costumes and now the costumes for the entire cast. People came to me to tailor clothes or design outfits even when they weren't connected to one of Renee's movies. Whatever she had, Renee shared with me. Everything except her name. And why that would bother me now, after so many years in Hollywood, I didn't know. It wasn't smart, wanting to tell people, tell someone, anyone, that we were sisters.

"So, according to Max, what type of person am I? Sydney is being more mysterious than usual about this script." Renee continued shuffling cards, trying a little too hard to sound calm. Sydney rarely kept secrets from her these days. But he had secrets, we all knew that, and sometimes Max was a more reliable source of information.

"Max doesn't seem to know much as usual since Sydney abandoned the mesmerist idea," I said.

"I'm glad he dropped that. There's too many films about hypnotists. I don't think we could make that truly frightening," Renee said. "This picture sounds different."

"So did Sydney say anything about your role?"

"Only that I am the catalyst of all terror."

"He said that about your last two roles. What about the plot?" I asked.

"That it was terrible in its simplicity and irresistible in its truth."

"What does that mean?"

"Absolutely nothing. At least to me. He probably stole the line. The man is a magpie when it comes to stories. He collects them from everywhere and never remembers where they came from."

"Well, as long he remembers that you are the star of the picture."

"Oh, I won't let him forget that. I'm sure Lulu is just a casting stunt and a small part," said Renee. "After all, what good is a screamer when you can't hear a thing she says?"

We both laughed at that. Then, after a long chat about how Renee could show up Lulu in the first scene by carrying her white travel bag with the crocodile trim, we both felt better about what was to come in Arkham.

We were both wrong.

CHAPTER THREE

For those who wonder, our deception began when we ran away from the orphanage in Oakland. Well, I ran away. Renee was eighteen and old enough to leave. I was barely fifteen and the nuns wanted me to stay in school. Since Renee wouldn't leave without me and they wouldn't let her take me with her, I climbed over the wall. We walked nearly a mile to the train station with Renee's cardboard suitcase banging the backs of our legs as we switched off carrying it. The War was just starting for our boys in 1917. Soldiers and sailors filled the train to Los Angeles. Some were on leave, heading home and chatty about what they would do when they got there. Some were heading back to their camp and quick to tell tales of what they'd seen in San Francisco. Only the brand-new recruits were silent, too nervous in shiny crisp uniforms to talk much. We stood up part of the way until two older ladies got off. Then one soldier shoved another soldier in the aisle so Renee and I could sit together.

Several flirted with Renee. She flirted right back as if she'd been flirting with boys all her life. Watching her, I bet none of the sailors guessed that she spent the last five years of her life in a Catholic girls' orphanage. Our landlady in Oakland, Mrs Ryan, sent us there after our mother died during an influenza outbreak. Our father had been dead for three years by then. "Better you have an education with the nuns than try to support yourselves," the apologetic but firm Mrs Ryan said. "When you're older, you'll thank me."

I'd been sick, same as Mama, and remained frail for weeks afterward. If I hadn't been so ill, I think Renee would have run off then and there. But she agreed to the orphanage in 1912 and there we were for five bitter years. Bitter for Renee, at least. I never minded the nuns, but Renee disliked all their rules. She hated missing high school and high school dances, and snuck out whenever she could to visit dance halls and practice all the latest steps. That was how we knew about the window that didn't latch properly and the best tree to climb to get over the wall when it came time for me to run away with her.

We never wrote to Mrs Ryan. Even after Renee did become famous in the pictures. We probably should have thanked her. Because we learned a lot from the nuns. At least I did. I used my education, especially art with Sister Theodora and sewing with Sister Dorothy Anne. I think Renee actually learned something too. After all, Renee developed her patience, her persistence, and her ability to raise one eyebrow. Without those years of doing dishes after being caught climbing back in the orphanage windows, she would never have gone so far, so fast, in Hollywood.

Of course, Renee's tenacity started long before the orphanage. Mama always said that mountains should bend out of the way when Renee came marching toward them. If she couldn't go over, she'd go straight through. But the orphanage sharpened her skills, especially when it came to winning fights with the other girls who tried to bully me.

I was, from the first, the odd one out. The only one obviously Chinese-American amid a group of girls abandoned by fate to the care of the nuns. Because I was frail due to a bout of influenza, small for my age, and, later proved to be good at school, the nuns made something of a pet of me. Which didn't help in the dormitory where daughters of Italian, Mexican, and Irish immigrants, tired of being called dirty names outside the convent walls, decided to knock down someone even more obviously *other*. Many didn't realize that Renee was my sister until she punched them on the nose or knocked their legs out from under them. Then Renee was disciplined for fighting. I would stay beside her in the kitchen, drying the dishes that she washed, and talking about what we could do when we finally left Oakland.

"For we are not staying here," she said. "There's nothing here for us."

"Where will we go? San Francisco?"

"There's nothing there either," said Renee with decision.

"Tye Leung," I said, very bravely disagreeing for once with my big sister. "She lives in San Francisco." My heroine was the first Chinese-American woman to cast a vote in 1912. I carefully cut out all the newspaper stories and pictures of her and pasted them in a scrapbook for us both.

"New York or Los Angeles, that's where we should go," said Renee, whose interest in politics was then and forever minimal compared to her interest in the movies. "Some city where we can be in pictures. That's what we will do. Become famous. Look at the Gish sisters."

"There's sisters in the movies?" I said.

"Of course. Dorothy Gish and her sister Lillian. They are renowned beauties of the cinema." That last sentence I recognized as a quote from one of Renee's magazines. She had a fearsome memory and could repeat a line days after she read it or remember a dance step after only one try.

Renee snuck out to the nickelodeon once and loved Dorothy Gish in *Little Meena's Romance*. After that she'd bartered and begged for newspapers and magazines about movie stars. She slipped scraps and smiles to the garbageman's son. He saved things up for her. She never minded if a story was weeks old, as long as she could read it out loud to me and the other girls in the kitchen or in the back of the choir loft. Anywhere that the nuns didn't hear us. There was as much debate then as now on whether the pictures destroyed a young girl's morals or improved her knowledge of the world. The nuns, except for Sister Theodora, fell firmly into the camp that cinema was a fearful source of sin. Sister Theodora was known to catch a picture at one of the many nickelodeons in the neighborhood.

"I rather think it does no harm," she once said to us, quietly after hours when we had finished putting all the dishes away and she was inspecting our handiwork. She ignored the stained movie magazines spread on the clean kitchen table. "To have some place where a body can go, and see something that makes them laugh or makes them cry, and know that everyone around them, no matter where they came from, is feeling just the same. That might be a powerful force for good. For not since the Tower of Babel fell have we all been able to understand each other. It may be that the pictures will be our common language given back to us."

Many years later, Sydney expressed the same view but from a quite different motivation than Sister Theodora.

As soon as she turned eighteen, Renee decided that Hollywood was closer than New York, and easier to reach on the small sum that the nuns had given her upon graduation to purchase clothing for an office job, also arranged by the diocese. Renee spent her money on the two cheapest train tickets possible to carry us out of Oakland. Then she packed what clothes we both had into the cardboard suitcase, walked down the stairs, and said a very cheerful goodbye to the nuns. Many regarded her docility with suspicion. Sister Theodora just shook her hand and winked at me.

That night I dutifully followed Renee's directions, climbed the correct tree, and ran off to the train station with everything I cared about, namely my sketchbook and pens, stuffed in a satchel that I had won for good deportment. Years later, when I told Fred some but not all about running away from the orphanage, he asked "But weren't you scared?" Of course I wasn't scared. I was with my big sister, who had protected me all my life, even though I just called her my friend when discussing this with Fred. Being without Renee would have frightened me, would have broken my heart, for she was all the family that I had. As for our destination, the whole world was moving to California in pursuit of a fortune in pictures. Hadn't Fred done just the same once his war was over and the army let him go?

"But it is different for men," said Fred, who joined the army the same year that we boarded our train for Hollywood.

I swatted him with a fabric swatch for that comment. "It wasn't different for me," I said. "Hollywood was the place where I could do what I wanted to do. Isn't that why we all ended up in Sydney's little troupe? Because he let us be us."

Fred had to agree.

In 1917, while being jostled by soldiers of all types in a slow-moving train down the center of California, we made the discovery that made all the rest even easier. Outside the orphanage, much as inside, people did not take us for sisters. "Who's your shy little friend?" one sailor asked Renee. "Where did she come from? Shanghai or Singapore?"

I started to say "Oakland", but Renee pressed down on my foot. I resented the "shy" comment, something so many assumed just because I wore an orphan-age dress and walked behind the nuns to church. I was about to tell the sailor that I was as bold as brass, brave as Tye Leung, because I climbed a tree to freedom that very night. I wasn't shy, but it was hard to get a word out before Renee started talking. Over the years, I developed the habit of letting her speak first. Otherwise she'd kick my ankle in that way that didn't bruise but definitely smarted. As much as I loved my sister, I knew from age three that it was best to let her do most of the talking.

"Where do you think that I'm from?" Renee asked, opening her hazel eyes wide and staring straight at the sailor.

"San Francisco," chorused several returning soldiers. "All the beauties are from there!"

"New York," said another.

"St Paul," said a third. "You've got cheekbones like a Swede. And you're tall like the girls I knew there."

Renee smiled and then picked a city straight out of our geography lessons. "Providence, Rhode Island," she said. Then she added the plot of *Little Meena*, mixed with stories that we had read in the *Saturday Evening Post*. "But my family was Dutch. I was educated in Paris and all over the world. That is how I met my friend, Miss Jeany Lin. She kindly agreed to accompany me to Hollywood."

The soldiers may have hollered and hooted a little at that, but nobody out and out called her a liar. As Renee said later, nobody ever says they come from Providence, Rhode Island, and it did sound pretty grand.

"But's what your name, lovely?" asked the first sailor who had forgotten all about me when Renee started talking. That was something else that I was used to having happen and one of the things I noticed first about Fred, when we met him. Fred was friendly with everyone, but he never lost track of me when Renee was in the room. Now he did tend to lose track of everyone when he had a new invention going, but that's just Fred being Fred. I'm the same when I'm drawing or sewing, said Renee, more than once.

With a gleam in her eye, my not shy older sister told the entire train car, "Why, I am Renee Love."

So my sister acquired her new name. Later that night I swore to her that I would never tell what her name was before Renee Love. And I never have.

It was during that train ride that I took on the role that Renee had cast me in: best friend. After we arrived in Los Angeles and started making the rounds of the studios looking for work, she never told anyone that we were sisters. We shared a room in a boarding house, one run by a Japanese landlord who wasn't going to make trouble for me but wasn't too sure about Renee living in the neighborhood.

Renee started by playing the same parts that every newcomer was cast in: the partygoer, the maid, the hatcheck girl, and so on. But she quickly caught the attention of directors at the studio with her penchant for adding just a little extra to a role. A turn of the head, a way of walking, that wasn't quite like the other girls. Because she was an extra, she had to supply her own costumes, and that's where I came in. After her first picture, the other girls started asking me to help fit their dresses or add some trim to make them as noticeable. I did help, but I saved my best ideas for Renee's characters. Then Renee played the fortune teller who cursed a queen, and Sydney snapped her up to star in his movies. By their third picture in 1919, the movie magazines dubbed them the king and queen of terror. Eventually the studio bowed to both Sydney's and Renee's demands for a piece of the box office profits. One night, pooling our money on the worn little table in our shared room, Renee announced, "I'm moving into Alhambra Luxury Apartments and so are you."

"Together?" I said. We rarely admitted we lived in the same building, let alone the same apartment. We took different streetcars at different times from the studio to get home and practiced other small deceptions.

"You'll have an apartment upstairs. I'll have a garden apartment downstairs. It's all arranged."

"And what about Sydney?" By then they were tangled in a romance. How deeply, I did not know, and tried hard not to think about it. She was my older sister. I didn't want to know, mostly because of the one fact that I was certain of. She could not marry Sydney. Not without lies or leaving the state. He was white. She had a Chinese mother. The state of California had laws against such marriages.

"Sydney's divorce is final and he's deeding the house to his wife. He's taking an apartment at the Alhambra as well," Renee said. Sydney married an heiress from Pittsburgh at the end of 1918, just before he arrived in Hollywood and met Renee. The heiress financed his first films and built a mansion with a great sea-shell-shaped saltwater swimming pool. Sydney held exactly one party there for all the cast and crew, but we never met her. As we were leaving, stumbling a little in the early morning light after hours of dancing, swimming, and an impromptu tennis match in the empty ballroom, I'd looked back at the mansion and seen the silhouette of a woman in a lighted room on the second floor. I wondered at the time if that was Sydney's wife and what she thought of us. What she thought of Sydney became the stuff of legend in the newspaper articles that came out after Arkham. It all added to his reputation. But at the time of the divorce, she remained quiet and faded from view. At least, from our view. I don't think we ever knew her full name.

"Well, she paid for the house," I said, a little spitefully. "It is only right that Sydney gives it to her."

"He says that no man needs two mansions, and he'd rather keep the one that his family built," Renee said, ignoring my tone and answering in a way that told me that she understood my unvoiced objections to Sydney all too well. I had my own romances, mostly sweet boy-and-girl stuff like drinking a soda or going to the movies. But after Renee started working with Sydney, and insisted on me making all the costumes for her pictures, I found myself wanting to do even more. I worked with Sydney's chauffeur turned cameraman, Fred, on how to create ghosts or werewolves for Sydney's terror pictures. Designing props as well as costumes consumed more of my time, and romances with silly actors seemed a waste of it.

"Sydney has a family mansion?" I asked that night as we discussed moving out of our boarding house and into separate apartments.

"Yes, he comes from some town called Arkham."

"Well, why doesn't he live there?" I said, and was instantly a little ashamed of how petty that sounded. I tried hard not to be jealous of Renee's relationship with Sydney. But I didn't like the deceit that had to go with it, with Sydney's marriage and Renee's heritage. And, of course, I never quite trusted Sydney's charm. He switched it on so easily, and there was always something rather cold about the way that he'd watch people in a movie theater. Of course, all directors did that. Went to their own pictures to watch not what was on the screen but how the audience reacted. But with Sydney, it seemed more calculating, more considering, as if he was waiting for something other than a scream or a sigh from the collected people in the theater.

"Sydney is in Hollywood because he needs to make movies starring me," said Renee with her wicked grin that undercut all the conceit in her statement. That's why everyone loved her on set. She never acted like a leading lady, even when she had top billing. And that's why, even after Arkham, people asked after her and wondered how great a star she could have been, if only the shadow had not consumed her.

CHAPTER FOUR

Sydney's family home was not what we expected. Although in Arkham proper, it gave off an air of isolation, hidden behind a high hedge and iron gates. But once past those gates, a short drive led to a pleasant country house, weather grayed to a dull silver on the outside. The back of the house revealed an altogether different aspect, with a steep lawn leading down to a tangle of woods.

The other houses of French Hill were hidden behind the trees or the high hedges that bordered the back lawn as well. There was something about the entire neighborhood that made me feel strangers were not welcome in this part of Arkham. Once we drove up the drive, the high hedges around the Fitzmaurice house effectively cut off all views of the neighbors. It was as if we were alone on an empty island. Empty except for a flock of crows that cawed and wheeled overhead, streaming like a black cloud past the crooked chimneys and sagging roofline of the Fitzmaurice house to destinations unknown.

"There's a gate to the woods, and a path leading to a pond," said Sydney as we climbed out of the cars that brought us and the luggage from the train station. Max paid the drivers, who seemed eager to be away after they dumped our trunks in the drive and on the porch. Sydney ignored this activity, describing instead his ancestral grounds. "We will need to investigate the woods. I have an idea for a scene out there."

"But, Sydney, we are not staying here, are we?" asked Renee, looking a bit forlorn surrounded by all her luggage on the front veranda. "Isn't there a hotel?"

"We have twenty-two rooms and five baths here," said Sydney. "And my idea is to film at all hours of the day and night. It will be much easier if we are together in the house."

"But what about meals?" said Fred, who would have slept in the barn as long as he knew he would be fed.

"I telegraphed my old housekeeper, Mrs Mayhew. She's already arranged all the rooms as well as a cook for the days. There's Humbert, too, he lives down the road, to handle the outdoor work."

Inside, the house continued to reveal its divided nature between Colonial antique and country summer house. Obviously some attempts had been made to update it, probably when it was electrified, so the lower floor rooms had been joined together with arches and columns, each room flowing into the next. The electric lights snapped on without any fuss. Fred expressed his satisfaction with the fuse box positioned in the kitchen and even wandered down to the basement to check on the furnace arrangements. With summer heat already making its sticky impact, we were unlikely to need the furnace. Fred just wanted to see what was there and how it worked.

But the house was odd. A row of long, thin mirrors hung in the downstairs hallway. Although all the same size, each mirror's narrow frame bore distinctly different hieroglyphics around the edge. With the opening of King Tut-ankhamen's tomb the year before and the popularity of Bara's Cleopatra movie last decade, Egyptian motifs were common in Hollywood. But these mirrors appeared much older than even Bara's 1917 smash hit. Standing in the center of the hallway, I realized that the mirrors captured the reflections in strange and crooked ways. Walking into the dining room, I had the clearest view of the front door, and the shadows of people moving around on the veranda, even though I had turned a corner from the entry to get to where I was. It felt like I was spying on everyone. Or something else was spying on all of us.

Beyond that, I felt warned off as I wandered through each downstairs room. Although warm enough inside, shivers coursed through me as I looked at the interiors where we were supposed to film. I sensed that strangers were never welcomed here.

"Ghost catchers," said Betsy, looking down the hall lined with mirrors.

"What?" I said.

"My mother used to talk about it. How ghosts can be caught in a mirror. How you should cover a mirror during a funeral to keep the ghosts out."

"I never heard that."

Betsy laughed. "I used to have a Halloween card, one that proclaimed that I could see my fate in a mirror. How did it go? *On Halloween look into the glass and your future husband's face will pass.*"

We both glanced at the mirror. Max's reflection could be seen as he moved across the veranda to talk to Sydney. For a moment he paused. In the narrow mirror, it appeared as if he stood shoulder to shoulder with Betsy.

Betsy winked at me. "Do you think it counts if it isn't Halloween?"

I laughed, shaking off my depressed reaction to the strange mirrors. My uneasy feelings stemmed from the difficulties of filming in such a location and nothing more, I told myself. Discussing Betsy's interest in mirrors and marriages was a far more cheerful subject. "Who knows. Maybe your rhyme counts double. We are here for a month or more. Isn't June the month for weddings? You could honeymoon on the trip back to California."

Betsy's pursuit of Max waxed and waned. Sometimes she seemed set on attracting his attention. Other times she talked solely of her career and plans. Betsy was smart and she had an amazing confidence, something that Max, who was often overset by Sydney, didn't seem to share. "I don't think he sees himself quite as wonderful as I do," she told me once. "And some days, I'm not sure if I should wait for him to find out how truly magnificent I am."

Upstairs revealed a much more old-fashioned and cheerful warren of tiny bedrooms spread across two floors as well as the five promised bathrooms. Renee immediately claimed a room with double windows that looked out over the front veranda. A four-poster bed, not old enough to be Colonial but trying very hard to look important, dominated the center of the room. It had been made up with a satin quilt and several pillows. All the pillowcases were lushly trimmed with lace.

My sister eyed with disfavor the oil lamp sitting on the table closest to the bed. "Why is that there?" she said to Sydney, who poked his head into the room to see how she was settling.

"What where?" he said.

"That oil lamp. Don't you have electric lights upstairs?" Renee said.

"Oh, they turn off the electricity at midnight unless someone has paid to keep it on longer. I'll have Fred or Max call the plant manager. We'll want power on the nights that we are filming."

"Every night," said Renee. "I don't want to be stumbling about in the dark after sunset. Neither do you. You're usually up until midnight or later working on your papers."

"Yes, yes. But for tonight, you might need to use the candles or the lantern. Mrs Mayhew always puts a fresh box of matches in the nightstand," said Sydney. "It is so wonderful to be back. I can feel my family history inspiring so many ideas, so much that's never been seen before."

Renee sighed and muttered something about a modern hotel, never mind family history.

I continued to explore, looking for a room to sleep in. Toward the back, I found a place where somebody had added more rooms, building out over the kitchen and the old back porch. The hallway had an odd half-step as I went past the bedrooms to a tiny screened-in sleeping porch. The cot there was made up, just like the four-poster bed in the room that Renee claimed, with a bright crazy quilt and well-worn sheets. Under one window, an old bookcase was filled with battered favorites. I pulled out *The Emerald City of Oz, The Window at the White Cat,* and *The Lightning Conductor* to pile on the bed. I'd read all three several times at the orphanage. It felt like discovering old friends at Sydney's house.

Renee stepped down onto the sleeping porch while I was re-reading the endings of all three books and trying to decide which one to start from the beginning again. "You always choose the funniest corners," she said. "It's like that apartment of yours."

I loved my efficiency unit on the second floor of Renee's building, with my east corner windows at the end of the kitchenette. The building super cleared out the table that was there and moved my drafting table into that corner. Since I usually ate downstairs with Renee or at the studio, I kept the kitchen drawers and cupboards filled with my sewing and art supplies. With a Murphy bed that folded up into the wall when I needed more room for pinning costumes together on fidgeting actresses, the apartment suited me. But Renee felt it lacked dignity and, over the last year, kept trying to talk me into a larger apartment on the ground floor near her. She pointed out more than once that she could afford it on the salary that she negotiated with the studio. I reminded her that there was no reason for her to be paying my rent. My apartment looked right for my position at the studio.

"I like it," I said to Renee about the screened-in room, stating the obvious as I slid my suitcase beneath the cot. I set my handbag and sketchbook on the table next to the bed. "It will be airy, and I can hear the birds singing in the woods." At the moment, all we heard was the cawing of crows, but I refused to give up my ideal image of a country house stay, with birds singing at dawn.

Renee gave an exaggerated shudder. "Birds. Just another reason to regret this idea. Do you remember those seagulls when we filmed *The Siren's Net*?"

One of Sydney's earliest nightmare films cast Renee as a strange creature who either was the daughter of a mad lighthouse keeper or came from another world beneath the waves. I made Renee a long wig, one that cascaded nearly to her knees. I knotted shells and large fake pearls into her braids. Sydney wanted to suggest that her hair was the net that dragged men under. The press raved about the "blonde siren" who lured men to their watery deaths. One reviewer said, "At first it appeared that the only persons who looked likely to escape drowning by the end of the picture were the director and his cameraman." And my favorite part of the review: "Miss Love wears such remarkable gowns as she walks along the seaside that all the women patrons in the audience may wish to shop wherever the siren does."

What the reviewer didn't record was that the seagulls, perhaps attracted by the shells in Renee's wig, or perhaps by Fred's famously greasy bacon sandwiches, harried us for one memorable afternoon at the beach until even Sydney lost his glossy look and fled wild-eyed back to the cars.

We didn't make another picture outdoors for nearly a year. Renee also turned down Mack Sennett's proposition to be a bathing beauty on the grounds it meant filming near the shore and those malevolent gulls. That didn't discourage Sennett. He kept sending her flowers and reminding her that he always had room for another beauty in his casts.

Betsy popped her head in the door. "Are you taking this room? It's darling."

I nodded. "Where are you?"

"One floor up. I'm sharing with Pola. We decided those were the best mattresses. And it's right next to a bathroom. You know I never mind sharing with her. She's always so calm and never takes any time at the mirror." Pola Vasily had worked for years in vaudeville before films. She took every "matron" role that Sydney dreamed up, usually the mother or the housekeeper of the hero. Her favorite parts required her to be murdered early in the plot, so she could spend the rest of her time on the set knitting stockings. She also made endless scarves. We all had a few pieces given to us from Pola's generous work bag.

"Max is on this floor, in the room next to Sydney. Jim, Paul, and Hal took a bedroom with an attached sitting room next to us and are going to rotate who sleeps alone on the couch by the strength of who snores the loudest. Fred's down the hall from them, converting what looks like a broom closet into a workshop with a cot. He liked the shelves," Betsy crooked a finger at both of us. "I was sent to tell you that Sydney is having a talk downstairs. Before the New Yorkers arrive."

Sounded like everyone was settled, although I wondered if there would really be enough bathrooms. We weren't a large crew but we'd filled the house quickly. Luckily everyone could double up on roles in front or behind the camera. Our films often seemed like we had large casts but we weren't DeMille or even Sennett. Sydney liked to work with a small hand-picked company and fill in with locals when available. In Los Angeles, with an extra on every corner, it wasn't so big a deal if we needed additional players. But in Arkham, we might have to do everything ourselves.

Pola and Betsy, of course, could transform themselves into a range of ladies, from the matron to the flapper. Hal played the wise father or the malevolent uncle, and loved being a butler too. Jim could be made up into young crooks, servants, and men about town. Paul played the older versions of those roles. He helped Fred with the lights and could even double as a cameraman. Paul had been an electrician before the War, according to Fred. I never knew much about Paul. He was one of those men who tended to grunt when you asked him a question.

"So are you ready to meet the New Yorkers?" Betsy asked us as we made our way down the hall

"Ah, the New Yorkers," said Renee. "The screaming Lulu and her partner. I suppose Sydney wants to tell us about them."

Betsy giggled. "I think we're about to be lectured on being professional and all that. Or maybe Sydney just wants to boast some more about this house. Oh, Fred said that he found sandwiches in the kitchen and might be persuaded to share."

"For sandwiches," said Renee, "I'll come down."

I hurried after the pair, realizing that I was also hungry. My morning cup of coffee and bread roll on the train seemed such a long time ago. As I followed Renee, I noticed a small alcove that I'd missed on my earlier exploration. Hidden behind a half-drawn chintz curtain was the landing for a small staircase. It twisted up to the second floor and also went down. I took the downward twist only to find myself in a sizable pantry, well stocked, with one door leading to a side terrace and another, upon opening, into the kitchen. In the kitchen was Fred, balancing a large tray of sandwiches and trying to hook a coffee pot under his arm.

A sour-faced woman, who introduced herself as Mrs Mayhew, and another tiny little lady, who said "Call me Ethel," were clustered by the stove.

"It's a beast, Mrs Mayhew, that stove. Should have been pulled out years ago," said Ethel.

"It is indeed, Mrs Roxbury, a beast of a stove," said Mrs Mayhew. "But I trust you'll be able to keep it under control. Three meals a day for five dollars a week, I think we agreed. I will be bringing the supplies each morning from the farm and twice a week will come with my girls Maggie and Hilda to sweep out the place."

I wondered what Max would make of the cost of the cook, to say nothing of Mrs Mayhew's supplies and girls, but decided that was the studio's problem.

"I'll take that," I said to Fred, grabbing the coffee pot

"Thanks," replied Fred. "Max took the cups in already."

I followed Fred and the sandwiches into the spacious main room. A deep fireplace occupied one whole end. Sydney arranged himself in front of the fireplace, one arm along the mantel in a pose that I recognized from a past photo essay entitled "The Great Showman at Home." Over the mantel hung an oil painting, very dark, showing a man with Sydney's features but in a fine uniform tunic with a fur-edged jacket slung over his shoulder like a cape. Both tunic and jacket were adorned with silver braiding and several rows of buttons. Below the portrait hung a curved sword, oddly blackened and burned about the tip.

"My friends," said Sydney. "My fellow artists. My most brave adventurers into the wilderness of Arkham."

I settled into a cozy chintz chair and took a large bite of chicken sandwich. From the introduction, I expected Sydney to tell us the plot of the movie and exhort us to reach new heights of creativity. The coffee was black and bitter, and strong enough that I guessed Fred had made it or that Ethel had Fred's attitude towards the liberal use of coffee beans.

"It is fitting that we gather here, under the gaze of my most revered ancestor, that daring French hussar who brought his little family to Arkham following his own grand adventures with the Emperor Napoleon in Egypt."

"I was in a film about Napoleon," Betsy whispered to me as she settled in the chair next to mine. "Maid to Josephine."

Sydney glared at her. Betsy mimed "sorry" to him and the great man continued his speech.

"It was Saturnin Fitzmaurice who battled in the shadow of the mighty pyramids, and later served as part of his emperor's envoy to the young American Congress. It is his stories that my grandfather so lovingly preserved within our library. It was Saturnin's discoveries and the descriptions in his journal that inflamed my youthful imagination. From his writings, translated from the tablets unearthed by this very sword," he flung up a hand to point at the fire-blackened blade, "we will draw our latest script and create a story in silver and shadows to enthrall and terrify audiences around the world."

Sydney paused. From long habit, nobody said anything. The pauses were for dramatic effect only. We knew he disliked being interrupted in full flow. Besides, we all wanted to know the plot.

Gravel crunched beneath tire wheels. A long melodious horn blast sounded outside the windows. The New Yorkers had arrived. Sydney swung around with a wide smile to stride from the room and greet them on the veranda.

Fred swallowed the last quarter of his sandwich in one enormous bite. "So," he said to me, "how do you unearth something with a sword?"

"It looks like somebody used it as a poker," I said, eyeing the soot stains along the blade. It was thoroughly blackened, and I wondered if the chimney smoked. But I liked the look of the uniform still vaguely visible in the painting over the fireplace. I considered taking such braid and trim, and adding it to the hero's coat for a continental dash. "Fred," I said, "who is playing the hero?"

Fred shook his head. "Max never said."

I thought about the actors who had accompanied us. Sydney liked to switch the actors playing his heroes from film to film. Sometimes, instead of a romantic hero, he wrote in a charming but hidden male villain manipulating events until caught.

Hal wouldn't do for such roles. He was too short, too round, too bald, and too old to fit the studio's idea of a romantic lead, good or bad, which was a pity because he had more charm than most.

Skinny Jim Janson played everything from jewel thieves to rustlers, but again looked too juvenile for a lead. If a villain, Jim was the second villain, the one that was easy to spot in Sydney's scripts.

Same for Paul Kopp, who either played an obvious heavy or a detective. He often showed up just for the denouncement in the final act, which was good as he worked best as Fred's back up for the camera and lights. Fred, after one unbelievably bad scene in *Siren*, never acted in any picture. He was a genius at capturing emotion on film and a complete bomb at portraying it on film. Besides, he hated having anyone crank the Bell and Howell except himself. Said it took days to get 242 feeling right if Paul or someone else turned the handle. He had an older Pathé that he preferred to give to Paul.

I never even tried to act. That was Renee's talent. Mine was to make everyone look good in their clothes and makeup.

My theory, never expressed to Renee, was that Sydney's constant rotation of leading men was to prevent her from becoming part of a couple for one of the studio's publicity pitches to the press. She was Sydney's muse and his alone. Although his marriage and her own reasons for concealment kept them from being an obvious couple around town, much to the distress of more than one publicity agent.

The men who consistently worked from film to film with Sydney never posed a romantic threat, at least in Sydney's eyes. As for the women, I suspected he kept with the same ones because they understood his tricks. It wasn't unusual. All directors had their "regulars" for supporting characters. Working with Betsy, Maggie, and Pola was comfortable for Sydney. He never liked change and insisted on loyalty and even some secrecy on set, to better surprise the public when our terror pictures opened. Maggie leaving us for the *Hollywood* picture had been a blow to Sydney. I heard him tell Max earlier in the trip that he wouldn't work with her again. Sydney could, and did, carry grudges.

Still Renee was his only leading lady once he started directing his own pictures. He always wrote her into the leading role as either *femme fatale* or ingénue. Although, by 1923, Sydney liked her best as a mystical and deadly otherworldly creature. The press and the public loved her in those roles too. When she played the wolf woman, the studio staged a photo with Renee standing over the bones of her devoured victims. It was a clear copy of a Theda Bara publicity photo. Later we heard that Bara's studio wasn't happy that our studio was pushing Renee as a new breed of vamp. Although Bara's career was nearly over by then.

Bringing in an outside actress, and a New York stage actress, like Lulu McIntyre, marked something new. I wondered if Sydney was assigning her the hero or villain role that normally went to a male actor. Or, as I feared, Lulu might be meant as a replacement for Renee in the supernatural category. A hidden villainess, perhaps.

"Maybe our male hero would be another New Yorker?" I said to Fred. "Or would Sydney cast a local as the hero?"

"Could be." He turned in his chair and yelled at Max. "Didn't you say something about a theater in Arkham? Any actors coming from there?"

Max wandered over, distracted by trying to watch Sydney and the New York ladies through the window. "Yes. Sydney directed something locally, several years ago, before he came to California. But we may not need more actors. Sydney says this script is very focused on just a few characters, the sisters in particular."

"Will we need more costumes?" I asked, thinking about what we had shipped from Los Angeles. Most were general items that we used on our regular troupe and fitted for them. Hal's butler outfit and his dining out suit, Pola's matron dress and another longer dress for being the wife of a distinguished gentleman, usually Hal, at a party. Various ensembles for Betsy, from the parlor maid to the flapper on the sidewalk. Same for Paul and Jim, outfits that turned them into anything from servants to menacing toughs. And, of course the cape.

"Will we be using the man in the hood?" I said.

"Can't have a Sydney Fitzmaurice film without him," said Fred, and he wasn't joking.

The hooded man scene was our signature scene and made a horror film a Fitzmaurice terror picture.

Sydney loved that cape, which could cover a large man from foot to head, and had a deep hood that hid the wearer's face. I made it for the very first picture that we ever filmed with him. It was yellow material, lined with gray, and we could turn it inside out, depending on how Fred wanted it to film. Over the years, I draped that one costume over multiple actors to make them look far more mysterious and menacing than they were. Luckily the camera didn't show how many times I'd hemmed it up or down, depending on who had to wear it. That cowled and caped figure always stood somewhat out of focus in each of Sydney's pictures. Also the hooded man just watched the scene for a moment or two, and then disappeared. A few enterprising reporters asked Sydney when he was going to reveal all about this recurring character, but he just laughed and told them to come to the next picture.

My speculations with Fred on leading men and plots were interrupted by the return of Sydney with a lovely blonde clinging to his arm. Her other arm was clutching a pug of particularly unpleasant expression. Ropes of glistening glass beads were entangled with embroidered scarves that floated all around her. Sliding off her bare shoulders was a gorgeous coat trimmed with feathers and fur. The effect was, as intended, quite startling. An elegant brunette followed them into the room. She wore the most beautifully tailored checked suit and dangling earrings that emphasized her long neck and narrow features.

"My dears," said Sydney, "my company. Here's the famed Lulu McIntyre and her writer friend Eleanor Nash." The blonde Lulu waved at all of us with a great fluttering of scarves and a slight growl from the pug.

The brunette Eleanor bared her teeth in a smile that radiated even less good humor than Lulu's dog. "Sydney, it's been in the headlines for weeks. For goodness sake, call us lovers. That's what we are. And if any of you gossip to the press about us, just know that I am descended from Salem witches and will curse you from here to California."

"Oh, Nell," said Lulu, "you don't mean it. We're just so very, very excited to be in pictures."

Renee rose out of her chair and crossed the room to shake hands with Lulu and Eleanor. "We are delighted that you could join us. I hear that you are quite the screamer."

Lulu blinked at her. "Oh yes, you're the one who plays my sister. So fun to have a film actress to work with. I've only worked with real actors before. In a legitimate theater."

At that fatal statement, silence filled the room. Renee ignored it. With a smile just as broad as Eleanor's and just as deadly, she said, "Yes, Sydney cast you as the younger, sillier sister. So lucky that the camera doesn't reveal true ages. Mary Pickford is able to carry off young girls even though she's past thirty now. I'm sure as a real actress that your age won't set you back at all."

Eleanor gave a snort that might have been a laugh. Lulu let out a howl for Sydney, still standing close at her side, that argued for the veracity of the claim that she was the greatest screamer in showbusiness. Renee continued to smile.

And thus that particular battle began. Later it would seem trivial.

CHAPTER FIVE

By Friday, Fred and I decided to leave the house, and the warfare within, to find a diner. While the meals served up by Ethel were large, filling, and often even delicious, the ongoing battle between Renee and Lulu over the importance of Camilla, Renee's role, versus Cassilda, Lulu's character, continued to engulf the whole company.

Lulu's inexperience with movies didn't help. Her first attempt at makeup proved to be a disaster and delayed filming for a couple of days. She was used to preparing for the stage but almost everything she did was wrong for film. Fred explained, patiently, that red would photograph black, so she couldn't use her normal lip rouge. She didn't believe him until he carefully photographed her with a still camera he used for such tests and processed the pictures in the darkroom that he'd created in the basement.

"We sometimes rouge the cheeks," I explained as Lulu moaned about how hideous she looked in the photos. "That creates dark shadows and makes your face look hollow. You can put it on your eyelids for the same effect. But light carmen looks best on the lips."

Betsy chimed in. "Yes, don't worry. We all looked terrible at first. Once you've got the grease paint and powder on, it's just finding the right shade for your eyes. Jeany and Fred are a whiz at it."

Many older actresses and actors still preferred to do their own makeup, figuring that they knew best how to make themselves look right for their parts. After all, many made their own costumes until just recently. Chaney famously insisted on creating all his creature makeup himself. But as I started to design costumes and props for each of Sydney's pictures, I'd also taken over the initial design of the makeup for the characters. The greatest emphasis, of course, was on how Renee would appear as the mysterious temptress, but Pola and Betsy were used to my laying out their basic makeup, even though both were quite capable of doing themselves up without my help. Fred added a few more tricks that he learned from cameramen around town, like Howe's technique of placing black velvet in a large frame around the camera to make somebody's eyes appear larger and darker.

Of course, the studio, and their proxy Max, loved that I could double up as both costumer and makeup person. Probably if I hadn't done it, they would have insisted on all the actors continuing to do their own. They definitely didn't like it when I started buying Factor's shades, deeming them more expensive than other brands, but his blends were meant for movie work. I had nearly thirty colors by then in my kit and kept them locked up when we weren't filming. Not that Pola or Renee would ever steal my makeup. But Betsy and Maggie both "borrowed" some when going out on dates. Hence the locked case by the time we went to Arkham.

"Listen to Jeany," advised Pola. "The stage is not the same as film. We all must learn this."

"I am known for my beauty on stage," said Lulu. "That's why all my husbands married me." Turned out that Lulu's divorce was her third and, according to Lulu, the only one that gave her any trouble. The others, again according to Lulu, were sweethearts who had been most generous and understanding when she decided that the time had come to part. As she probably was still in her early thirties, it was an impressive history. Later, Eleanor would tell me not to be deceived by the feathers and beads. Like Betsy, Lulu was far sharper than she pretended to be. Although married at a very early age, in part to escape a managing stage mama, she had left her first husband before she turned eighteen. She quickly went from being in the chorus in Chicago to headlining Broadway shows in New York.

"The important thing was," said Eleanor, "Lulu really married men for love and the fun of it. The first two were creative but very poor. One was a painter and one was a trumpet player. She still sends them gifts every now and then to help them out. She always sends money to her mother and even lets her visit. Lulu's biggest mistake, and probably her only one, was marrying a rich man the third time. He was used to owning things. Lulu will never be owned."

"And her affair with you?" I said in those days after Arkham when I tried to understand all the motives of the people who Sydney gathered under his roof for his horrific film. "How did that come about?"

"She rather swept me off my feet," said Eleanor with an uncharacteristic blush. "I just was looking for the perfect woman to place in peril in my horrid little plays. And there she was, all feathers and pug dog, and as perfect for me as she was for my plays. You saw her at her worst, at the start. She was terrified about going into moving pictures and didn't want to show it."

Finally during that first week of filming, to mollify Lulu's anguish about how different it all was, Eleanor intervened. With her help, we got Lulu to listen to our advice as we changed her look into something that would work in the movies.

"We can shadow the corners of your eyes with brown," I told Lulu. "And then outline them. You will look lovely." Lulu had very light blue eyes. Renee and I had learned various tricks to make Renee's eyes look rounder and lighter. Looking at the photographs rather than Lulu herself, I could see a different style was called for. Perhaps even a little red near the ears to make Lulu's face longer and less full.

"Lulu's character is supposed to be the frailer of the two sisters," said Eleanor, looking at notes that Sydney had given her. "Perhaps recovering from an illness. So her older sister has brought her to this house for her convalescence. Can you convey that and not make her look like a walking corpse?"

I nodded as I showed Lulu how to powder her face properly, a tricky technique until an actor got used to layering the grease paint and film powder for the right effect of flawless skin. "You'll look very lovely and frail," I promised her.

And she did. After a few more experiments, and photographs quickly processed by Fred, we settled on a look for Lulu that made her appear very young and innocent. So much so that Eleanor laughed and asked if she could send a few copies of the photographs to the press that had bothered them so much in New York. "Not that those hounds would care," she said. "But given all the stories that her husband spread about us, it might make a few of the readers doubt his claims of Sodom and Gomorrah on West 57th Street."

Lulu professed herself equally charmed and ready to start her film work. Which led to the next disaster, a simple scene in which Sydney wanted Renee and Lulu to enter the house with "bewilderment and trepidation."

Lulu had taken one look at Renee's ensemble, which I had created by retrimming her traveling coat and hat, and insisted on an entire new costume for herself. Which had to be sent from her apartment in New York, another delay but one that gave us a couple of days to settle the question of her makeup

After Lulu's desired coat and hat arrived, and were approved by Sydney, with Max muttering about telegrams and express charges, Lulu then upstaged Renee's entrance twice. The first time she dropped her bag as they descended from the car. The second time she stepped in front of Renee in an awkward cross that left them both teetering slightly on the stairs.

Fred sighed and stopped the camera. With the clatter stilled, we all stood in awkward silence.

"Twelve cents a foot for film," muttered Max beside me. "And this is only the first scene." He took the slate in his hand and changed the chalked take number to a three. Max excelled at numbers, was a disaster at acting like Fred, and never could be trusted with anything too mechanical. But from the beginning, when we all wondered what to do with the upright accountant that the studio had sent to keep an eye on Sydney, Max had fallen in love with the slate. Keeping track of the take numbers was an important task. We all knew of productions where somebody forgot to do it, which led to disasters in editing. Max never made a mistake. He always had the right numbers written on the slate and waved it with quiet dignity before the camera lens at the start of every take.

The second time that Lulu ruined Renee's entrance, Sydney removed his cigarette holder from his mouth and used it to gesture Lulu up the stairs. Renee, recognizing what he was about to do, stood with great tranquility by the open car door. Jim, costumed as their chauffeur and disguised with a large pepper-and-salt mustache so he could play other roles later in the picture, leaned against the hood and napped in an upright position.

"Lulu, my dear, I fear you may have misunderstood my directions," Sydney said with the purr that indicated that his voice could grow much louder. "You are not to rush into the house in girlish glee, knocking over your sister on the way."

Lulu laughed. The rest of the cast, knowing Sydney, kept quiet. I watched Paul and Hal, neither of whom had any part in this scene, head around a corner of the house with their pipes. We'd put a couple of decrepit willow cane chairs on the back lawn. The gentlemen had turned those seats into their favorite smoking spot.

"While some directors prefer to film the scenarios willy-nilly, I follow the course of a script as closely as possible," Sydney continued. "The emotions seen on the face of my actors must remain as true to nature as can be contrived. This is your first encounter with the house, your first trip to Arkham. In this scene we should see a vague fear, the trepidation that some great shadow is about to descend upon you. That is what must show in this scene. Not your petty desire to be first through the door!"

The latter came out as a roar. Lulu, neither foolish or reticent, stood her ground and stared Sydney straight in the eye. "I have been acting since I was three and my mother placed me in a lion's cage," she said. "If there is one thing I know is how to walk into a room so the entire audience notices and cares about my character."

Renee now added her bit. "Sydney, be patient. Circuses and vaudeville shows call for exaggerated motions. You can't expect Lulu to know about your technique of absolute realism. That movie actors must act as naturally as possible. What did you tell me? That our expressions must be no more pronounced than they would be in real life. That the slightest deviation leads to mortifying results on the screen. Petty physical tricks cannot be a crutch for the performance. Unless we are thinking about what we are trying to portray on the screen, the audience will become instantly aware that the emotion is false."

Sydney thrust the cigarette holder between his teeth and rushed down the stairs to grasp Renee's hands. "You are always my bright muse," he said. "My wise Camilla. That is it exactly. Now, Lulu," he turned and faced her. "Do you think that you can contain your natural enthusiasm and portray a delicate young lady beset by illness and fear?"

With a huff, Lulu turned on her heel and marched back to the car. "Of course," she said. "Shall we begin again? Lead, dear Renee, and I will follow, properly fearful of shadows."

After that, Lulu behaved, but Sydney struggled to find the angle that he wanted, making Fred circle about and film them from various positions, through a half-open door, looking up the steps, and once halfway down the drive looking back at the house. All of that took time as Fred shifted the black metal camera and its solid wood tripod from place to place. Then he would begin to crank again, smooth and even, and the clatter of 242 would drown out the crows cawing from the trees.

"Twelve cents a foot," Max groaned with every change of Fred's position as he jotted notes in the notebook he carried in his breast pocket. The take number on his slate was erased and rewritten and rewritten again.

Betsy discovered a croquet set stashed under the veranda and dragged it out. Half the balls were missing. But the iron wickets still bore white chipped paint and very little rust. We set it up on the lawn and played round after round while the filming dragged on. Pola proved particularly wicked at knocking away her opponents' balls. Even Hal and Paul abandoned their pipes to join the game.

When the sun finally dipped below the hills and real shadows swamped the veranda, Sydney called a halt for the day. Renee and Lulu trod up the stairs a final time. Both disappeared into the house with strained smiles. Eleanor had pleaded a need to work on the film scenario for the next day's shooting and had left much earlier.

Fred stowed his camera and then collapsed on the lawn next to Betsy. He watched me ricochet a ball through two wickets and smack the final stake. "How about dinner in town tonight?" he asked.

I glanced at the house. If they came to dinner, there was sure to be tension between Lulu and Renee. And Eleanor dropping her own barbed comments to Sydney about the scenario that they were supposed to be scripting together. Although Sydney had hired her to script out the entire film, and seemed to want her talent for creating terrifying scenes as much as he wanted Lulu's scream, he had decided that he wanted her to write only "the next twenty-four hours of filming" rather than a complete scenario for the movie. It was an unusual choice. His vagueness about what was to happen next had reached new highs with this film and was not to Eleanor's liking. The rest of the cast and crew tended to tuck their heads down and swallow their dinner without comment. Even voluble Betsy grew uncommonly quiet at the table these days. None of us wanted to be drawn into the warfare raging between Renee and Lulu, and, in a slightly different but equally poisonous manner, Eleanor and Sydney. I would, of course, support my sister, but I found that I quite liked Eleanor and even the vainer Lulu. I think the rest of our small company felt the same. Eleanor and Lulu made us all laugh, when we weren't wincing at the barbs flying around the table.

"I think a dinner in town would be splendid," I said. I hadn't been past the hedges since we arrived. Max had taken various trips down to the train station and into town to fetch items for Sydney. Fred had gone with him as he waited for filming to begin. I'd been spending most of my time sketching out ideas for Sydney's silver mask as well as various possible designs for costumes and props. Like Eleanor, I was frustrated by Sydney's vagueness. I felt more than ready for a night away from the house. "Where do you want to go?"

"Max and I found a diner not far from here. They aren't fussy. The food's good and cheap," said Fred. "We can take the big car."

Max had hired an ancient but stately touring car for the arrival of the sisters in the first scene. Sydney loved the double row of leather seats and yellow painted wheels. As soon as he saw it, he told Max to keep the car for future excursions. Max had sighed, made another note in his notebook, and arranged that we would have the car for the rest of our stay in Arkham. "Do you want to ask Max and Betsy to come along?" I said.

"Still trying to promote that romance?" said Fred with a chuckle.

"I have no idea what you mean," I said. "But she's sweet and better at math than he is. He'd be lucky to have her."

"I'm sure you're right," Fred said. He turned his cap right way round. It had been pushed backwards so he could peer into the lens without interference. "Let's grab them and go."

I was still wearing my working slacks. "Do I need to change?"

"It's just a diner. They'll think you're an amazing Oakland doll when they see you."

"So none of the other women in this town wear pants?"

Fred shrugged. "Not that I've seen. But they have a university. There's women students and professors. Bound to have been a few pants wearers among them."

In the three years since women got the vote nationally, hemlines had crept up. But pants were still considered fairly scandalous outside of certain cities. I glanced down at my working pants, a pair that I'd styled for myself off the linen trousers favored by many men for the summer. Side-fastened, wide-legged, and with deep pockets, I had more than one actress approach me after a shoot and ask where they could purchase a pair. I'd run up several for the more daring women of Hollywood. But I wasn't sure that New England was ready for ladies in trousers.

I said. "I'll change. Meet you by the car."

Fred nodded and ambled over to Betsy to explain our plans. She squealed a little and lit out for the house. No question that Betsy would change into a prettier dress for a dinner with Max. So it appeared her interest in him was on the rise again.

Neither of us took much time. We both beat Max to the car. Fred finally had to go back to the house to pull him away from changing into a new silk tie for a dinner out. Max and Betsy took the back seat. I rode up front next to Fred so I could get a better look at the gears and pedals. I reminded him that he still owed me a driving lesson.

"The steering's stiff," he commented. "But I knew gals who handled worse, driving ambulances in France. Tell you what, let's take this car and a picnic basket down some farm lane when we get our next break. You can practice then."

"You mean when Lulu decides to halt filming for another dress order from New York?" I said with a laugh.

Max groaned in the back and Betsy giggled.

Fred just clashed through the change of gears and grinned. "You can drive back and forth while I eat all the sandwiches."

As we rolled into the Easttown neighborhood, the houses started to look friendlier and more ordinary. The high hedges, walls, and locked gates that separated the mansions of French Hill were left behind. We all started to laugh and talk about Lulu's mishaps. It felt like an ordinary day again, with Max complaining about the waste of money to pamper a New York theater actress, Betsy wondering if Sydney would give her a scene dressing Renee and Lulu for a party, and Fred complaining that they didn't even know if there would be a party scene.

"Oh, there's sure to be a party," said Betsy. "Sydney knows the audience wants to see a crowd all dressed up and looking lovely. Especially for a story set in a big fancy house."

"We'll need to get more extras from town if we do that," I said. "I wonder what the society types would wear in a town like this."

"Perhaps some girls and boys that we can recruit from the university?" said Betsy. "They'd be thrilled to be in a film."

Max brightened at that thought. "You're right. I suspect we could cast students for little or no wages."

"Max!" we all cried.

"Well, we'll pay something," he grudgingly said.

We parked the car right in front of Velma's Diner and tumbled through the doors a very merry crew, debating the ethics of making extras work for experience and little else. We'd all had that happen to us. It was a common trick.

"When I think of all the dollars that I've spent on my munitions," said Betsy, "I used to think that it would be cheaper for me to pay the studio to work. I always hated how the studio kept saying we should invest in our look." Her moan about the money that any actor had to put out for good makeup or clothes was common. Sydney and many bigger directors were starting to want more control over the look of a film. Some were starting to costume their entire casts and outfit makeup artists. But, as Renee also complained, our studio often operated like it was 1913, not 1923, and we were making serials for the nickelodeon crowd.

We plopped down into the seats nearest the window. A young woman was adding up her tips behind the till. She headed toward us with menus and stopped when she got a clear look at me. Then she said, "We don't serve chop suey."

Max and Betsy looked puzzled. Fred, who had been out with me before, started to scowl but switched to his biggest grin. "Well, then, that's too bad. I love chop suey. But can you cook a steak? Or should we try La Bella Luna instead?" said Fred.

The girl stood there with her mouth hanging open. It was a common reaction to Fred. A second waitress came up behind her and smacked her shoulder. "Suzie, go on back to the kitchen and help Ted with the dishes."

"But I don't wash dishes, Florie," said Suzie with an edge of whine in her voice.

"Now you do," said the older woman. "I'll finish up your tables and maybe split the tips with you if you don't break anything. Go on. Scoot. Or do you want me to tell Velma that you tried to chase away the famous stars of the only movie ever filmed in Arkham."

Suzie gulped a little and fled to the kitchen.

"Not the brightest thing," said the waitress. "But she's Velma's niece. We have to keep her or Velma's sister raises a ruckus. Now coffee's on the house, here's some menus. I recommend the fried chicken myself, but Joe does a nice steak too."

I buried my head in the menu. Once Suzie was gone, I thought of several things to say in response to such a cheap and common insult. And a couple more things to say to Fred about how he did not have to play knight errant. I could fight my own battles. But everyone was looking at me and it was easier to read through the whole menu twice. I agreed with Florie that the fried chicken sounded like the best choice.

"Joe makes the best fluffy mashed potatoes to go with the chicken," she said. "Now, do tell me that you are from the Fitzmaurice place and are making a movie in Arkham."

"Yes, ma'am," said Fred with a twinkle. "But we are not the stars. Just working stiffs."

"Oh, call me Florie, Florie Wilson is my name," she said. "You're something new and that makes you newsworthy in this town. The *Arkham Advertiser* has been writing up stories about Sydney Fitzmaurice coming back to town and making a movie here for months."

"Months?" I said. "But Sydney only made this decision weeks ago. Max, didn't you say that the studio was furious that he changed plans after they'd agreed to the budget for his mesmerist idea."

"The studio is always upset," said Betsy. "That's why Max is going gray around the edges." She looked at him expectantly, waiting for Max to respond about how the studio always knew best.

Max, funnily enough, didn't trot out his favorite phrase. Instead he just shrugged and asked about the steak, the most expensive item listed. Betsy and Fred picked the chicken.

"Well," said Florie, tucking her notepad into her apron pocket after getting all our orders. "Mrs Mayhew got a telegram more than three months ago asking her to open up the house and get it ready. Can't keep a secret in Arkham, that's for sure. Now, you leave room for pie. We've got both apple and cherry tonight."

"Sydney might have said something about Arkham earlier," Max told us after Florie walked away. "He wanted to do a different approach. The studio said that if he filmed here, he had to deliver on all his promises."

"His promises?" I said, wondering what that meant.

Max pursed his lips. "The hooded man."

Fred looked up at that. "What about that gimmick?"

Max fiddled with his napkin and silverware. Betsy glanced at me, but I shrugged. The hooded man got people talking about Sydney's pictures, but the appearances never seemed to mean much.

"You know how the fans have been," Max said. "A big reveal. The power of the hooded man. Sydney said that the mesmerist picture would do that. But then he said that he had to film here. All the right occult signs and so on. It's been hard to pin Sydney down. You know what he's like."

Betsy patted his hand. "I'm sure that nobody blames you, Max. Everyone knows how hard you work to stop Sydney spending money."

Max shook his head. "It's not the expenses. It's the other promises Sydney made to the studio. That this picture will be the one. He had better be right this time. The studio knows that I can keep the money under control."

Fred and I both laughed at that. Nobody could ever stop Sydney from spending, certainly not gentle Max with his perpetual lines of worry carving his forehead. Most people thought Max had been with us forever, but he was actually the third attempt by the studio to organize Sydney. The first one lasted through two pictures but fainted nearly as much as Maggie at the sight of blood. Real faints too, unlike Maggie, even though the blood had been fake. The second kept trying to get Sydney to sign invoices, usually right when Sydney was in the middle of reading reviews out loud or doing other activities he enjoyed more. Sydney banned him from all sets for all time. Max had been a relief. He never argued with Sydney, and he was even mildly useful during filming with the managing of the slate and his perpetual note taking.

"Enjoy your dinner," Fred said to all of us, "and don't worry about Sydney's plans. He'll tell us when he feels like telling us."

"Excuse me," said a woman seated at the next table, "but did you say that you are staying at the Fitzmaurice house?" Dark-haired and closer to Florie's age than mine, she had a careworn face, with noticeable circles under the eyes, and the slight squint of a woman who spent a lot of time with her nose in a book. But there was something compelling about her gaze as well.

Since I was sitting closest to her, I answered, "Yes, we're staying there. We're making a movie with Sydney Fitzmaurice."

"Oh, yes," she said. "I knew Sydney. I was teaching a course at Miskatonic University when he directed a play with an amateur theater troupe. A very odd play. It killed one of my students."

I blinked, certain that I had misheard her. The woman swiveled away from me to pour cream in her coffee. She stared into the cup and refused to meet my eyes. I had the distinct feeling that she deliberately ignored me. I turned to Fred to ask if he had overheard what she said, but was interrupted by Florie's return. She thumped down the plates, distracting me from my contemplation of the stranger at the next table. The fried chicken smelled wonderful. Then she turned to the woman who had spoken to me. "Need anything else, professor? How about a little dessert?"

"No, nothing," said the woman, standing up. She collected her handbag and moved toward the cash register. As she passed my chair, she looked straight at me again and said, "Be careful."

The others didn't notice, being busy with a debate about how much they could eat and still have room for pie. Betsy declared that she was willing to leave half her chicken on her plate if it meant she could have cherry pie. Fred, of course, said that he'd eat her dinner and his, and manage two pieces of pie. For a small man, he was perpetually hollow. He claimed it came from too many years of trying to eat inedible army food.

Their laughter and chatter shook me out of the anxiety caused by the stranger's remarks. I decided that she surely couldn't have meant that Sydney actually killed someone. She must have mixed up the man with one of his movie plots. People did that, thinking what they saw on the screen was real.

"Are you going to eat that?" Fred said, pointing his fork at my pile of mashed potatoes.

"Every bite," I declared. And I did.

When Florie came back to clear our plates and take orders for dessert, I asked her who the woman was.

"That's Professor Krosnowski," said Florie. "She teaches at Miskatonic. Knows all sorts of interesting stories."

"What kind of stories?"

Florie shifted the plates around so they rested on her hip. "All types. Quite a bit about the town and the families who built it. People like my grandmother's great-something granny. She was supposed to have been a Salem witch."

"There's more than a few of those around," said Fred, recalling Eleanor's claim when she first arrived.

"Reckon it's true," said Florie. "Women in my family have some peculiar talents, that's for sure."

"So were the Fitzmaurices one of these founders?" I asked.

"The Fitzmaurice family? No, latecomers they are. Arrived well after the Revolutionary War. Didn't even send the British packing in 1812," said Florie.

I thought about my parents, who hadn't arrived in Oakland until 1897, and wondered what Florie would call them. "So your family has been in Arkham longer than the Fitzmaurices?"

"Oh, yes," she said. "Earliest was Remember Wilson. She arrived in Arkham by the 1770s. Now there's Wilsons all over New England. Probably isn't a town within a hundred miles where I couldn't find some kin, even if it is only names carved on a tombstone."

"Really?" said Betsy. "Imagine knowing your history that far back. All I know is that my grandmother worked in a shirt factory and my mother decided that sewing wasn't for her. So she married a tailor. Said he could do the hemming at work and at home."

"Smart woman," said Florie. "Yeah, there's many in Arkham that know their family history. Sometimes a little too well, I think. Old grudges have a habit of lingering, if you know what I mean."

None of us had a good answer to that, since we all lived in a city where new people arrived daily, so we gave Florie our orders for pie. Three apples and one cherry for Betsy. The pie came out just as a number of people entered the diner. Suzie was released from her exile amid the greasy dishes. Both women bustled around the tables for several minutes.

Keeping her promise for coffee on the house, Florie returned to refill the cups and, as she put it, take a breath. She plopped the pot on an uncleared table and swung a chair around. "This is my break and if any of you have a cigarette, I'll thank you kindly for it," she said. "I'm fresh out."

Max handed over his case. Florie "la di dahed" when she saw the gold-plate engraved with Max's initials. Like his suits, Max's cigarette case was the best quality. He kept it stocked with Chesterfields. "Very pretty," she said, knocking out a cigarette with an expert twist. Fred provided the match. "My mother never did approve of ladies smoking," said Florie, "but then I never claimed to be a lady. I figured with you being theater type folk, you wouldn't mind."

We all assured her that we didn't. I never liked to smoke but it was common enough around a set. "Now tell me," said Florie. "What is Sydney doing back in Arkham?"

"How long has he been gone?" I said.

"Oh, it's been a long time," Florie answered. "He left in 1912, no, it was later than that. Summer of 1913. I remember that because my mother always claimed thirteen was an unlucky number and an unlucky year it was. Also it was right on a hundred years since the Fitzmaurice family built the first house."

"The house was built in 1813?" asked Max. "It doesn't feel that old."

"It's not," said Florie. "They cleared the land and started building in 1813. The woods and a little house burned down in 1818. Then the big house went in the 1823 fire. It was the second fire that killed the first Fitzmaurice, the one with the funny name who had been a soldier in Napoleon's army. They were lucky to save his portrait and papers. One of the maids got the children out with a handful of treasures that Fitzmaurice handed her. He went back for his wife and neither made it out. At least that's how my family remembered it. Took his son right out of the maid's arms and filled her hands with things, made his children carry his treasures too, so the story goes. Later the son rebuilt the house. Been Fitzmaurices on French Hill ever since."

"But Fitzmaurice died in the fire?" asked Max, clearly fascinated with all this gossip.

"Oh yes, he never came out. According to the maid, he went running up the stairs with his sword held high to find his wife."

"His sword?" I asked, remembering the blackened blade hanging beneath the portrait.

"Oh yes. They say that's all they ever found of him and his wife. Just the sword with his hand clinging to it."

"Just the hand?" squealed Betsy.

Florie nodded. "Everything else was burnt clean away."

Fred looked at me. "Didn't Sydney do that in *Winter's Rags*?"

"He did," I said. Max looked puzzled. I remembered that the studio sent him to us after that film. Sydney had just banished his second assistant and went a little wild over how he was going to tell a story in a new way. We'd filmed most of it on a stage, but Sydney wanted real snow and insisted on a day long drive into the mountains. Where we found mostly rain and rocks.

Betsy nodded. "That's the one where poor Selby broke his leg."

"He slipped," I said to Max, "and fell down a ravine. Fred and Jim pulled him out."

"And Jeany held him flat in the truck bed all the way down the mountain," Fred added.

That had been a true nightmare, with Selby moaning at every bump and me sure that we'd crippled him for life. He did have a nasty limp after that but found work in cowboy movies doing character parts.

"Well, my heavens," said Florie. "I never knew that filming was so dangerous."

"It can be," said Fred. "We try to keep it safe. But Selby was a fool, always just following Sydney's directions and not thinking about what he was being asked to do. I told him that the rocks were too slippery."

Fred worked harder than anyone to keep us safe. Besides being a wizard at figuring out the optical illusions that Sydney wanted, he wasn't afraid to point out when Sydney's ideas might cause problems. He nearly quit one time when Sydney wanted to send his hero up in a hot air balloon with no ropes anchoring it to the ground. Given that the actor didn't have any experience with flying, Fred refused to crank the camera unless a rope was attached or an experienced balloonist added to the scene.

"It's odd," said Betsy, "that Sydney would use something from his own family history, something like a dead hand."

"Sounds like Sydney to me," I said. "Renee always calls him a magpie for stories. He picks up pieces everywhere and adds them into his films. It's part of his extreme realism. Don't you listen to his lectures?" Of course, *Winter's Rags* had been the most extreme of Sydney's attempts at realism and also one of the few flops that we'd made in the last five years. Renee's part as the mysterious wife of the lost soldier never made much sense. The audience was confused about the ending too, with the soldier vanishing into a fire while staring at the reflection of a hooded man.

"By the time Sydney starts talking about the scenario, I'm usually too busy writing down figures to listen to his lectures," said Max.

Betsy giggled. "Nobody can listen to Sydney all the way through. Remember the time that he started to lecture us about the daily torture of mediocrity and the lure of mutability. Nobody understood him."

"He got that from his grandpa," said Florie. "I remember him, toward the end. Old Mister Fitzmaurice used to rent a lecture hall and talk about his days in the theater. About how he knew the Booth brothers when he was young and how they were going to change the world. He'd go on and on about some play even greater than *Julius Caesar*, about something in Egypt."

I asked: "*Antony and Cleopatra*?"

Florie stood up and shook her head. "That doesn't sound right. It was two women's names. You'll have to ask Professor Krosnowski sometime. She'd remember. It's the same play that Sydney directed, his last year at the University."

"The one that caused a fire," I said, remembering the woman's strange comments to me earlier that evening.

"That's it," said Florie, grinding out the last of her cigarette in an abandoned saucer. "Back to work!" She collected all our dishes in a teetering pile. The bell over the door rang, and a young man walked in. Florie shrugged a shoulder at him, her hands being full of dirty plates. "Darrell, it's been awhile," she said. "These folks are working on that movie that you were talking about."

Darrell came up to us. "Are you with the Fitzmaurice production? Do you know Renee Love?"

I blinked at his enthusiasm as he pumped the hands of Max and Fred.

"Darrell Simmons, *Arkham Advertiser*," he said. "I'd be thrilled to take a few pictures for our paper. Especially Miss Love. She's a favorite." He blushed a little. "Um, I mean she's a favorite with our readers. Everyone knows that Sydney Fitzmaurice is from Arkham. They always show his movies at the theater. And, of course, Miss Love is a great star. I saw *The Net of the Siren* seven times. I hear that *Nightmare at the Circus* is even better."

Betsy smiled and pumped his hand right back. "It's a doozy," she said. "I played Miss Love's dresser. There's this scene where she rides a white horse round and round. Then the hero dreams that his death is riding for him. Everyone comments on that."

Fred and I exchanged glances. Besides the mishap of the mirrored costume, the actor playing the hero had been terrified of horses. Sydney kept making Renee ride straight at him until the poor man, shaking and sweating in his seat, finally yelled and ran away. None of us had been happy with how Sydney treated poor Rodolfo.

Once Darrell learned that Betsy was an actress, he ignored the rest of us and peppered her with questions. It was a relief. I never knew quite how to talk about Renee to a stranger like that, and always was afraid that I'd say too much. Or not enough. Betsy loved to "play the baloney card" as she called bantering with reporters. She spun fantastic tales of highly unlikely adventures. Betsy might have been just a bit player in 1923, but she had ambition and she could turn on a glowing smile when it was her turn to shine.

Betsy agreed to being photographed at the diner so Darrell could have a picture of the movie stars stepping out in Arkham. She beamed and twirled on one of the counter stools while Max, Fred, and I stayed in the background. Darrell even put her behind the counter with Florie, pretending to pour cups of coffee for a bewildered pair of old men trying to eat their dinner. Florie was very pleased with all the attention and reminded Darrell twice to send over copies for her and Velma.

As we walked out into the cooling night air, Florie had one last snap at Suzie. "See, told you that they'd be good for business," she said. "Next time, be polite when strangers come through the door. You'll get better tips, too."

Darrell held the car doors for Betsy and me, hanging through the open window to ask if he could take pictures at the Fitzmaurice house. Max told him to come by in a day or so, and he'd see what could be done.

"Oh, that would be swell," said Darrell. "My editor is going to love this. She's always after me for more society pages stuff."

"What do you usually do?" I said.

He paused, an odd look crossing his face that made him suddenly seem much older. "Well, there's stories in Arkham that not everyone likes to hear." He lifted his camera up. "Or see. I try to be honest. I think that helps anyone who runs into something that they don't understand. But my editor keeps saying folks want happy stories too."

Betsy reached through the car window. "Well Sydney's films aren't always happy, but they do have glamour. Wait until you see us in Jeany's costumes. We look swell."

Darrell blinked at Betsy's informality and then nodded. "Photos of Miss Love in her new costumes. That will be something."

"He better take a few of Lulu too," said Betsy as we pulled away. "Or we'll hear shrieking."

"I'll make sure that both of them are wearing something wonderful," I said. "And, Max, you better let Sydney know. He'll want his picture to be in the paper too."

We arrived back at the house to find it plunged into darkness. Going through the door, only a single candle lit the downstairs hallway. The multiple narrow mirrors lining the hall reflected the faint light and made our shadows overlap into a bulbous shape with elongated tentacles.

A shout from Sydney roused us from where we had paused in the doorway. "Fred!" he bellowed. "Is that you? Did you call the power plant?"

Fred led the way into the living room where the crew was gathered around a number of oil lamps. In the grate, a smoking fire, lit more for light than warmth, added to the flickering shadows around the wall.

"What happened?" I asked Renee.

"Sydney was talking about the script and all the lights went out," she answered. "We staggered about and found some candles. Paul tried to fix the fuse but failed. Then Hal went upstairs and fetched the oil lamps out of the bedrooms. After that, he, Paul, and Jim went out for a walk. I think they took a flask with them and some cigarettes."

"Sounds like those guys," I said. When things got chaotic, the actors were good at sliding out the door for a long smoke and quick nip. They'd return when things calmed down.

"Yes," said Eleanor, from her chair. "All very effective drama, that blackout. But we still haven't finished the scenario for tomorrow's filming."

"Are we moving past the entrance to the house?" I said.

"Oh, yes," Renee answered. "That's done."

I refrained from saying anything more, like, "Thank heavens." In the kitchen, I could hear Sydney, Fred, and Max mumbling something about fuses. Drawers clashed open and shut. Sydney yelled, "When am I going to have light again? I need light. Eleanor and I need to write. We cannot write in the darkness."

"I thought he liked the candles," I whispered to Renee, who rolled her eyes.

"Not after he stubbed a toe trying to walk across the room," she whispered back.

Lulu looked immensely bored. She teased her pug with the end of her scarf. "Filming seems so slow to me," she said. "Imagine taking a whole day to walk up a set of stairs."

"And there weren't even very many stairs," Renee murmured. I pinched her shoulder. Last thing we needed was to start a row again. She shrugged me off.

Eleanor spread out some notes on the table, shifting the lamp so she could see the pages more clearly. "Now that the doomed sisters Camilla and Cassilda have returned to their ancestral home…" she began.

"Are they doomed?" said Lulu. "Isn't one going to escape? The audience does like a happy ending."

"According to Sydney's notes, they are fated to disrupt the cosmos with their doom. That does not sound like a happy ending to me, dear." Eleanor squinted a bit more at Sydney's scrawl. "Although it's not clear that anyone dies."

Renee offered "Sydney doesn't necessarily spell out what happens after. He loved *The Turn of the Screw*. He thinks all endings should fire the imagination the way that James did."

"Oh, yes," Eleanor said. "I saw a copy of *Two Magics* in the library room. I always thought the governess was the most dreary of creatures. If it had been me, I would have locked both the brats in their room and left the house immediately."

"Perhaps she had nowhere else to go," I said.

"Any woman of intelligence can find some place else to go," said Eleanor. "By the time I was seventeen, I had learned enough to pack my bags and take the train to New York. Which must have been a great relief to Leiper's Fork. My family never knew what to do with me. Of course, they didn't approve of me reading Henry James or the Brontës. Indecent reading according to my mother. But then I'm sure that there were parts of the Bible that would have widened her eyes if she had ever read them."

"You didn't like *Jane Eyre* either, darling," said Lulu. "And you were positively vituperative about Heathcliff. How can anyone not adore Heathcliff?"

I tried not to show my surprise that Lulu knew English literature or could use "vituperative" in a sentence. With her wavy blonde curls and feathery scarves, I assumed that the *Argos* was as heavy reading as she ever did. Then I decided that I was no Sherlock Holmes, able to judge people correctly at a glance. I'd need to know more about Lulu to guess at her tastes in literature.

"I prefer Brontë to James," said Eleanor to her lover, "but you are right. Give me Louisa May Alcott any day, even though those March girls were damn Yankees."

"*Little Women*," I said with a smile. "But not as good as *Anne of Green Gables*."

"Interesting choice," said Eleanor looking at me. "Did you want to be Anne, red hair and all?"

"No," I said. "I like my hair. And my eyes." More than once in the orphanage, I'd been asked if I wanted to look different. Truth is, I never did. I knew who I was when I looked into the mirror, my mother's daughter.

Eleanor nodded. "Good for you. Too many women try to batter themselves into a shape that they can never have."

More crashing came from the kitchen and then a shout of triumph from Sydney. Someone must have found the fuses.

"So," said Eleanor, "Sydney wants a shocking scene that suggests the mansion hides many secrets."

"They could be forced to sit in darkness, waiting for the lights to come on," suggested Renee.

"That lacks a certain amount of suspense," said Eleanor. "How about family portraits coming to life? A suggestion of ancient history haunting them?"

I looked up to the shadowy portrait of the first Fitzmaurice. His face was mostly bare. Jim sported luxuriant mustaches as the chauffeur. With his false whiskers removed and some shadowing on his cheekbones and around his eyes, we could make him into a fair match for the picture. An old coat could be dressed up with some braid and buttons to appear like the uniform jacket.

"I wonder if there's an attic," I said. "And trunks of old family clothes. We could use that to mimic the portraits. There's a couple of women in the other room."

"Sydney's mother and grandmother, I think," said Eleanor. "I noticed them too. We could move this gentleman into that room. Easier to have all three together."

"Betsy can be the younger woman and Pola the older," I agreed.

"Now how do we make them ghosts?" Eleanor mused, jotting notes on a blank page.

"Makeup. Cheesecloth. We stop the film and restart it. Fred can splice it together afterward. We sell the audience on the impression that they've seen more than we have shown. Sydney will have Fred concentrate on the reactions of Renee and Lulu," I said. Nothing new in these techniques but all of it reliable for building a mood of unease in the opening scenes.

"Yes," said Renee. "Lulu can scream."

"I can faint too," said Lulu, perking up and looking interested. "That slow crumple that I did for *His Bloody Hands*. Do you remember, Eleanor?"

"It made the audience gasp," said Eleanor. Seeing our skepticism, she added. "It did. Lulu can faint."

"Oh, good," said Betsy. "Our regular fainter Maggie stayed behind."

Suddenly it seemed like we could all work together. Even Pola, carefully counting her stitches by the fire, looked interested and cheerful.

Then the side brackets snapped on and we saw the dead bird.

CHAPTER SIX

A crow lay on the windowsill. When the lights were out, the black feathers blended into shadows. Pola stowed away her knitting. She walked over to it and looked down. "The neck is broken," she said. "It must have flown into the window."

"From the inside?" said Renee. She didn't get up. She never liked dead animals or birds. It was one of the reasons that we never kept any pets. We had a kitten once. Finding it dead on the back porch of Mrs Ryan's boarding house made Renee weep for a week.

"It probably flew in and then became confused. I'm surprised it didn't brain itself on one of the mirrors," said Eleanor.

Sydney, Fred, and Max returned from the kitchen carrying a triumphal bottle of wine and several glasses. The wine bottles had come up out of the cellar when we'd first arrived. Despite Sydney's assurances that his grandfather's stash was drinkable, the average was two bottles of vinegar to one bottle of mediocre red or slightly bitter white. At the rate we were progressing through it, we needed to find the local bootlegger soon.

"Problems solved," Sydney said. "Fred found the fuses. Max found the corkscrew."

"And we found a dead crow," said Renee, pointing at the cold mound of feathers on the windowsill.

Sydney went over to take a closer look. Unlike Renee, he adored dead things. His apartment was full of bits of taxidermy, some of it game that he claimed to have shot, as well as creatures turned into occult objects. Sydney even showed us a lion's head once, claiming he bagged it on a safari, but on closer questioning admitted that it was an old circus beast that he had stuffed and mounted

I had expected similar objects in the Fitzmaurice house. But other than a wistful grouping of poker-playing frogs under glass that had belonged to Sydney's grandmother, the place was remarkably free of dead things and occult relics. Perhaps Sydney's obsession with such objects had been picked up during his travels.

"Ah, a winged harbinger of death," said Sydney.

"A dead crow," repeated Renee. "You take it out."

He left the glasses on the table. Cradling the crow in his hands, Sydney seemed fascinated by the dead bird.

"Sydney," said Renee. "Eleanor suggested ghosts for the next scene."

"Excellent," said Sydney, still staring at the crow. "It is a good time to start haunting, with ways opening into the house. Max, I told you this picture would work better in Arkham."

We all looked at Max, who frowned at Sydney. "You said you could do this anywhere."

Sydney looked up from the crow. "Of course, I'm Sydney Fitzmaurice, I can make pictures wherever I am. But this will work, Max."

"We need more costumes," said Renee.

"Something for Pola, Betsy, and Jim to turn them into ghosts," I said.

"Oh there's piles of old clothes in the attic," said Sydney. "Use whatever you find. Grandfather was an actor and never could throw away a costume. I stored a few things up there from my theater days at the University too."

"Wonderful," said Renee. "Now let's discuss how to make the library properly haunted. I like Eleanor's portrait idea."

Sydney opened a window and dropped the crow outside. "Humbert will clean it up in the morning," he said.

We poured the wine and found it drinkable, and spent the rest of the evening talking about how to haunt the Fitzmaurice house.

CHAPTER SEVEN

The next morning I sorted through the extra set of keys kept hanging by the
back door and found some room keys. Two or three looked promising and I
eased them off the ring. Then I climbed to the top of the house. The locked
door at the end of the corridor, near where Pola and Betsy slept, did not lead
to another room. Instead, opening when I tried the second key, it revealed a
narrow little staircase leading upwards. "Attics," I said to myself with satisfaction.
While playing croquet the previous day, I had spotted a small round window at
the top of one roof peak. I had been certain that it marked an attic window.

Indeed it did. The attic stretched the length of the house, but only the one
window gave it any light. The splintery boards of the floor were almost completely hidden beneath piles of boxes and broken furniture.

Remembering what Sydney said about old clothes and costumes, I looked
for trunks. Shoving aside a crate of mismatched teapots, pitchers, and cracked
saucers, I found a large old-fashioned steamer trunk. Although it was locked,
someone had thoughtfully tied the key to a handle with a bit of string. I pulled it
free and released a cloud of dust when I dragged the heavy lid open. Inside were
a number of dresses and hats, all neatly sheathed in muslin. I set the cloth to
one side, as it might be used in any number of ways, and pulled out the dresses.
These were a near match to the style worn by Sydney's mother in her portrait. I
picked one or two that could be easily altered to fit Betsy.

Worming my way through the boxes and broken chairs, I found a bulbous
trunk, strapped closed rather than locked. It provided the skirts and blouses
necessary for making the grandmother's ghost. The full petticoats that would
have held the skirts wide were missing. But I could rig up something for Pola
that would suffice for a short scene. Considering the grey and purple mourning
colors of these skirts, I thought about draping the muslin over them to achieve a
lighter, more ghostly effect.

A third trunk looked more promising for gentlemen's clothes, but it was
locked and had no key. I poked through a few more boxes but nothing caught

my eye. Eventually I grabbed a large wicker hamper with broken leather handles. Bundling my finds into it, I dragged the lot to the top of the stairs. With a little pushing and pulling, I thumped my way to the lower floor.

Fred came trotting up the back stairs as I maneuvered my basket toward my room.

"I thought you were rolling a body or two down the stairs," he said. "Or did you stuff it in that hamper?"

"Ghosts," I said with satisfaction. "We can dress Betsy and Pola with these pieces."

"What about Jim?"

"There's a man's trunk up in the attic. I didn't see a key but maybe you can get it open."

Fred patted his pockets and came up with a pocket knife, a screwdriver, and last night's corkscrew. "Probably can," he said. "Lead on, Macduff."

"It is 'Lay on, Macduff'," I said. We had held this discussion many times before.

"How should I know?" said Fred, as he always did. "My education ended at age twelve when I became a shoeshine boy."

"I thought you ran away to join the army," I said.

"I was so good at polishing shoes, the army drafted me later," said Fred. "To keep the generals all shiny."

Whatever his past, or because of it, Fred did know how to break a lock. After a few minutes of tinkering, he popped open the trunk. Inside were a stack of old leather-bound journals and an odd assortment of men's clothes. By age and style, it looked like the coats and pants of two different men bundled together. Unlike the women's clothes that I had found, these had been carelessly packed and were heavily creased. I spread them across the boxes, trying to find something that could be made into a uniform jacket for Jim. Nothing looked quite right, although one cutaway coat might work for Hal if we needed him to play a doctor.

Fred kept burrowing through the boxes behind the trunk. I could track him across the attic by his sneezes and the occasional swear word as he knocked into something hard or sharp. "Hey, Jeany, this might work," he said, squirming back into the small cleared space where I stood. In his hands was a uniform coat that looked to be of Civil War vintage. It was dark blue and the buttons were all missing. Stray threads hung from the sleeves and shoulders. Still, with braid stolen from a few curtains downstairs and some buttons from the other coats, it might do. I could cut into a woman's fur tippet that was in one of the other trunks and drape it across the shoulders to match the cape effect of the portrait.

"We'll need to hide Jim behind the women," I said. "It's a crude match."

"If we just show his head and shoulders, it will be fine," said Fred.

I looked around the attic. A broken picture frame about the same size as those downstairs leaned against an equally shattered chair. The outside edges of the frame were scorched but still visible were the same type of hieroglyphics as encircled the mirrors in the main hallway. The portrait in the center was hacked away but the oval hole gave me an idea.

"We could paint this up," I said, hefting the frame out of the stack of broken furniture where it rested. "And put Jim behind it."

"Shoot him through the frame?" said Fred. "Yeah, I like that. The frame is a close match to those downstairs."

"In the long shots, show the real painting," I said.

"And in close-ups Jim's head and shoulders," Fred nodded. "We could even have him move slightly."

"Then all the ghosts step off the wall into the room," I said.

"I think we film all of them through this," said Fred, holding the picture frame up and peering through it at my head and shoulders. "Film the paintings in the same spot. And then film them again outside the empty frame. It's a stop trick, simple enough."

Although the stop trick was an old technique, almost nobody could do it as well as Fred. In an earlier film he'd turned Renee into a tree and back again, when Sydney wanted a murderous dryad. By lining up the shot carefully and paying absolute close attention to the light angles and shadows, Fred could make anyone appear, disappear, or transform by altering just one or two elements in the scene.

"It will give Eleanor the look that she wants," I said. "But we need another stop trick later, when we film the scene with the mask. To make Renee's face appear and disappear. Too much of the same thing in one film?"

One of the things that kept the audiences guessing was never to repeat ourselves. It's why Sydney never did the same type of plot twice in a row, even in his sequels. If we had ghosts in one film, then it was sure to be mythological monsters in the next. Similarly, we tried not to use too many of the same scares. Shadows, stop tricks, a bloody hand, they were all good. But show them too often and the audience grew to expect it and even laugh at the effect. Fred and I joked one time that we should deliberately do some grotesque trick repeatedly, just to make the audience laugh. "I'm not sure that the world is ready for horror comedy," said Renee. But she would have been brilliant at it, with her ability to evoke laughter as well as gasps. It was something that Sydney never quite understood, as he believed that his terror pictures should be serious and evoke a breathless reaction in his audience.

Fred hitched the picture frame over his shoulder. "I'll take this out to the barn to paint," he said. "And think about the mask. Have you made it yet?"

"No," I said. "I have so many sketches, but nothing looks right."

"Something simple," Fred said. "That always works best." He was right. The more elaborate the prop, the more it could and often did look poorly made. Simple objects often photographed better.

I knelt before the trunk that Fred had forced open, rooting under the clothes and journals to see if there was anything else I could use. Something cold and metallic shifted under my hand. I reached in and pulled out a dull black mask. "Fred, look at this. It looks like an old tragedy mask. It must have belonged to Sydney's actor grandfather." It was so heavy that I couldn't imagine anyone wearing it, but it could have hung on a wall as a decoration.

Fred squinted at the mask in my hand. "It's not silver."

"Paint," I said. "Light colors. If the title card says it is a silver mask, that's what the audience will believe."

Fred nodded.

"We can make this look like silver," I insisted. "And make a second one out of silver paper that's transparent enough that a shadow of Renee's face can be seen through it. Especially with the right backlighting." With the light behind Renee but pointing towards the camera, the material should appear to glow around the edges. Twist the light a little to the side and a suggestion of Renee's face should be visible.

"Two masks," said Fred. "That's a good idea."

I stashed the basket full of old clothes in my room, intending to work on them later, and followed Fred out of the house to the small barn that currently stored our touring automobile and an old-fashioned lawn mowing machine. I'd seen the hired man, Humbert Welles, leading a mule up the drive two days ago to pull the creaky contraption and reduce the grass to a neatly trimmed length, suitable for playing croquet.

After mowing, Humbert led the mule away, back to the farm that housed it, but came by each day to see if "Mr Sydney" had any more work for him.

Humbert made the unlikely claim that his mother had named him for a prince. If she had hoped for something charming, she'd failed. He was, as Eleanor put it, "the most dolorous sort, who looked as if he spent his life sucking lemons and eating prunes." Tall too, topping both Fred and me by nearly two feet, and so skinny that Pola declared that he disappeared when he turned sideways. He had exceptionally knobby wrists and ankles, clearly visible with his too-short sleeves and trousers. Fred kept telling me that we could use him for a rendition of Frankenstein's monster if Sydney ever decided to film that story.

We found Humbert in the barn. He reluctantly agreed that there might be some white paint stored in the back that could be used for what we wanted. But why we wanted to paint up that fire-blackened frame and old mask baffled him. "Nothing but rubbish," Humbert rumbled above our heads.

"Props," I explained.

Humbert took the frame from Fred. Squinting at it, he shook his head slowly. "That went around the portrait of Mrs Fitzmaurice, the one that died in the fire."

"Sydney's mother?" I said. I hadn't heard that, but I was beginning to realize for all that Sydney talked about himself, he never said much about his family's long history in Arkham.

"Nah," said Humbert. "The first one. The one that died when the house burned down."

"We heard about that," I said. "The 1823 fire?"

"Yup. Nearly one hundred years ago exactly. The solstice fire."

"The solstice fire?" I hadn't heard that before.

"Yup. June 22, 1823. That's the fire where they found the first Mr Fitzmaurice's hand. And this picture frame, with the picture all burned up. She was supposed to have been a pretty little lady, all dark hair and wide eyes, like your Miss Renee."

"Ah," said Fred. "So they found this after the fire along with the old man's hand."

"And the sword," said Humbert. "That's still up at the house. And his picture too. That Mr Fitzmaurice made the maid take that out. But her picture was lost."

It was the story that Florie told. Apparently everyone in Arkham knew about the maid rescuing the Fitzmaurice portrait.

"Odd the frame survived the fire," I said, turning it over again to see why the wood hadn't burned. The feel of it, hard and cold, gave me a clue. "I don't think this is wood," I said to Fred.

"It was heavy," he agreed, taking it back from me and scraping a little at the charred edges. With an application of his pocketknife, he was able to lift enough paint off it to show the dull green metal beneath.

"Copper?"

Fred shook his head. "Maybe. Or an old bronze. It's strange, not like any metal I've seen before."

Humbert also took a closer look. "One of the first Mr Fitzmaurice's finds. Unlucky things he dug out of that grave in Egypt. Mr Sydney's granddaddy made quite a fuss about them. Went round and round the house collecting them up when I was a boy. Made me polish a few, too."

Fred took his knife to the mask, chipping off what appeared to be more soot than paint to reveal the same type of greenish brown metal.

"Humbert, how long have you been here?" I said.

"Well, now," he said, rubbing the back of his neck, "I've been working round the house since I could toddle. My auntie cleaned for Mr Sydney's mother and so did my other auntie. And my sister for a time, until she married that Innsmouth fellow. My cousin Florie never liked cleaning. She went to high school and got an education. Now she waits tables at Velma's."

"So there's artifacts from Egypt in that old house," I said.

"Yeah, quite a few. Couple times some professors came out with their students from Miskatonic University to take a look. Mr Fitzmaurice, the one that was Mr Sydney's grandfather, liked that. Sitting and talking to them about what an important man that first Mr Fitzmaurice had been and how he'd brought those treasures to Essex County."

"I wonder if this mask was part of the Egyptian find?" I said to Fred. "It doesn't look like anything I've seen called Egyptian."

Humbert shook his head at it. "Mr Fitzmaurice used to keep that in a drawer in his study. Said he had to hide it from the crows."

It sounded like Sydney's grandfather was stranger than his grandson. Neither Fred nor I could think of any response to that comment.

I said finally, "Do you think Sydney would be all right with us painting family heirlooms?"

Fred shrugged. "I doubt these are valuable or even from Egypt. The mask is probably an old stage prop. And even if the picture frame is old, it was pretty badly burned. Just junk. Sydney said to use what was in the attic. Besides, we can always clean the paint off later."

"Unlucky things in that house," said Humbert with one of his big sighs, looking at the objects that we had handed him. "Bad luck that rubs off on everyone, my aunties used to say. One of the students who came the most often went out to sea and never came back. During the War that was."

"Lots of men lost at sea during the War," said Fred.

"Anyone else?" I asked, beginning to feel very uneasy about the mask that I had just handed Humbert.

"Nothing's happened to other students, at least nothing too bad," admitted Humbert. "They all came back from the War. Couple even went to Boston to set up a medical practice. Hear others are trying to raise funds to explore Antarctica. They had a talk about that down at the library. Exploring the South Pole or some such thing."

"That's a long way from Egypt and New England," said Fred.

"Yup," said Humbert. "Can't see the appeal myself. Wouldn't mind going to Boston. But the rest is all too far away for me."

After leaving Humbert with the picture frame and the mask that he promised to paint before the end of the day, we walked back up to the house.

"They're a strange lot," I said.

"Who?" said Fred.

"The Fitzmaurices and the rest of this town."

"Isn't that what they think of us?" said Fred.

I stopped, looking at the lawn mowed so neatly by a machine that was twice my age, and down to the hedges that surrounded the property. Over the hedge top, I could see the occasional peak or gable of a fine mansion, houses that had been sitting on French Hill for one hundred years or more. But I couldn't see more than that. And certainly nobody could see us. It was as if we were all alone on an island, far away from other people, even though we were in Arkham. "It's all so old," I said.

"In Paris they'd laugh to hear you call this little town old," said Fred. "I went out for a walk one night, just a ramble because I figured this boy from Brooklyn ought to see what made everyone claim that we wouldn't want to go home again after we saw Paris."

"And what did you find?"

"It's old. Real old. True old. What Sydney would call ancient. And for once, he would be right. There's parts of New York that I thought were there forever. But you walk through Paris and you realize that everything we've built since George Washington crossed the Delaware is brand spanking new compared to the streets of Paris."

"So what?" I said. "That's Europe. It's supposed to be old. It's like my mother's stories of China, where you could visit your village's graveyard and find a hundred generations."

"Now wouldn't that be something?" said Fred.

"Maybe. Maybe not. My mother didn't want to stay there. And her family were happy to sell her to a bride merchant who was smuggling girls to Chinese men who couldn't get married here." They did not call it selling to my mother, but she saw her parents receive money from the man. When she talked to the other girls on the ship, she realized that they'd all been promised the same thing: a young, rich, handsome man from their village who would marry them and let them live like an empress. Being of a skeptical turn of mind, my mother doubted that many rich young Chinese men lived in America and wondered who they'd really have for her to marry. Instead she decided to run off with the tall Swedish sailor who made her laugh when he helped her practice her English on the voyage. She'd been happy to slip away from the bride merchant and make her way to Oakland. But she never dared write to her parents back in China or even visit San Francisco across the bay where there was a proper Chinese groom waiting for her. As far as I know, my father never wrote to his family in Filipstad either, to tell them that he'd settled in California with a Chinese bride and made his living working on the small ships that carried goods up and down the coast.

"That's it," I said to Fred as if he could hear me thinking through all my family history, the very small bit that I knew well. Being Fred, he waited for me to explain and maybe did understand, a little. "That's what's so odd about Arkham. Where we come from, Brooklyn or Oakland, nobody knows a hundred years of family history. Oh, they might know a parent's or a grandparent's tales coming from somewhere else. But they don't know their history back to when Benjamin Franklin tied a key to a kite and flew it through a thunderstorm. They don't have the kite sitting in a box in their attic, just waiting for somebody to talk about how crazy old Ben was."

"I don't remember seeing a kite in the attic," said Fred, trying to kid me out of my mood.

"Doesn't mean that it isn't there," I replied, remembering all the boxes and bags that we'd left behind. "But it gives me the shivers, how they all talk about these people long dead. Humbert, and Florie, and even Sydney. Talking about things that happened almost a hundred years ago as if it just happened. As if the first Fitzmaurice sat down with them and told them about losing his hand in that solstice day fire."

"Bit like being haunted," said Fred.

I looked around again at the garden enclosed by high hedges, and the tops of mansions like old-fashioned tombs looming in the distance. "More like living in the graveyard all the time," I said. "And the Fitzmaurices and other Arkham families never leave. They never want to go anywhere else." It really was like being trapped on an island, one where the past never let a person go.

"Sydney's grandfather left. Acted in New York, according to Florie," Fred protested.

"For a few years, she said. Then he came back and spent his time in that house looking at unlucky objects dug out of a tomb."

"According to Humbert. Who takes a pretty dim view of everything. And Sydney left too. For ten years. Now he's back," said Fred. "But he's only back to make this film. Then he's off to the next one. You know Sydney. As soon as it's in the can, he'll be dreaming up vampire ladies or ungodly doings in a crypt."

Fred did not see Arkham quite the same as me.

The hedges leaned in, I realized. Not a great deal. Just enough to make it clear that their purpose was as much to keep people inside the grounds as to protect the house from strangers. Or to hide the house from prying eyes. To keep the Fitzmaurice family and their doings invisible from the rest of Arkham. Except Arkham had a very long memory.

"I don't know Sydney," I said, and realized it was true. "I know the man that he's pretending to be. The one that the press wants him to be, the one that the studio wants him to be." The one that my sister said loved her. "I don't know the Sydney that Arkham remembers."

"And do you need to know Arkham's version of Sydney?"

"Yes," I said. "I think we do." Because a woman in a diner talked about Sydney killing someone. Because there was something wrong, very wrong, with the crooked shadows creeping across the lawn toward me. With the crows wheeling overhead and then streaming towards the woods pressed up against the back gate. We'd barely started filming but I felt like we were caught on the wrong side of the camera. That we'd all become characters in one of Sydney's horrible stories.

But I couldn't explain it properly to Fred.

"It's just the jitters," he said. "Get a few more days filming in and everyone will settle down, even Sydney. We'll know how it all turns out. Let's go move some paintings and set up the next scene. Time to put a few of Sydney's ancestors to work in the movies."

The shadows crept across the lawn. The house waited for us to return to it and start playing at hauntings within its walls. It was beyond foolish what we had done already and would do in the days to come, but it was all because we did not know enough about the Fitzmaurice family and Arkham then.

CHAPTER EIGHT

The ghost scene took a couple of days to stage but looked good by the time we were done. The paintings seemed ominous clustered together at one end of the long library room. Fred and Humbert did a little carpentry that created a false wall at one end of this grouping to hold the empty frame. Surrounded by other paintings, it deceived the eye at first glance, especially when somebody stood behind the wall and pretended to be a portrait. Paul and Jim shifted furniture around and moved in a few mirrors from the hall to reflect light from the windows. It set up much like we would at the studio, with the actors at one end and plenty of room for the camera and the rest of us behind it.

We stationed Pola, Betsy, and Jim behind the fake wall, peering through the empty frame, one after the other. Fred cranked the camera slow and steady, muttering at them if they twitched. The idea was to keep them as still as possible for this bit of fakery. Later Fred would cut the film between the long shots of the oil paintings hanging in what appeared to be the same spot and the close-ups of the trio so the audience would be convinced that the paintings turned into ghosts.

Betsy had the hardest time being still, as she was distracted by two Arkham visitors that morning.

One was Darrell, who shadowed Renee around the room, taking various photographs every time Renee paused. She wasn't happy about it. Renee wanted to concentrate on Sydney's directions as he went over his ideas for how the sisters would enter the library and be surrounded by their ghostly relations.

The other distraction was the violinist that Sydney hired to play during the scene. He'd read somewhere that United Artists were starting to use musicians to create a mood on their sets. She was a pleasant, round little lady who taught violin but also played the piano at the local movie theater, which was how Max had found her. She arrived at the house still in her Sunday best, complete with a new cloche hat, and clutching a well-used violin case.

The violinist, Virginia Murphy, listened patiently while Sydney insisted that he wanted a dreaming mood for the sequence. "It is not a nightmare," he said.

"Not yet. The sisters are enthralled to see the ghosts of their ancestors. They teeter on the edge of terror, as will the audience, unable to deny the melancholy attraction of the tomb. Your music will convey that to the actresses, and they shall in turn create a living embodiment of the grief-stricken melody."

Like everyone encountering Sydney for the first time, Virginia seemed a bit overwhelmed. "Chopin?" she finally said. "His Nocturne in C Minor?"

Sydney shrugged. "If that is what you think is appropriate for ghosts."

She pulled out her violin and played a few bars.

Sydney turned to Renee.

"Does that evoke a haunting mood?" he said.

Renee crossed the room away from Darrell. "It's fine, but you know I don't need music to act," she said. Then turning to the violinist, she added, "Not that I have anything against your playing. You're very good. It was kind of you to come."

Virginia smiled. "I was so excited to be asked to work on a movie set. Everyone in town is talking about it since the *Arkham Advertiser* published that story yesterday. Florie told me about meeting you." The photos of Betsy pouring coffee in the local diner had dominated the front page of the little newspaper. "And, of course, Mr Fitzmaurice being back in town."

"Did you know Sydney when he lived here?" I asked.

Virginia continued to adjust her violin, trying out a trilling run of melodies. "Not really. I heard talk about the Fitzmaurices. Every time one of the pictures opened in the movie house, somebody would mention that Sydney Fitzmaurice came from an old Arkham family. And that his grandfather had been a very famous actor as well."

"Yes," I said. "Everyone seems to know about Sydney's grandfather. I've never heard anything about his parents." It was odd. Nobody ever mentioned anyone but the actor grandfather who was obsessed with family history and artifacts as well as the more distant ancestor who brought those objects to Arkham. It was as if the rest of the Fitzmaurice clan were bit players in their own story. Except for Sydney. He would always insist on being center stage.

"No, I don't know much about the family," said Virginia. "I haven't lived in Arkham that long. You should ask Darrell. He writes the most curious articles, weaving the town's history into the news. Some of his stories read just like a Fitzmaurice picture."

I watched my sister dodge the eager photographer. "He's quite a fan of Renee Love."

"Oh, yes. I'd see him every time one of her movies played the theater. For the siren picture, I swear that Darrell sat in the front row the entire run," Virginia said. "I do enjoy a long run. Doing the same picture several times gives me a chance to adjust to the film. It's always much better the second or third time, when I know what's coming next."

She was right, of course. I'd seen movies done in small houses and in larger theaters where they were beginning to bring in full bands. Even with cue sheets, the music could vary wildly and the mood created didn't always match the action on the screen. Good accompanists, the best really, reacted to the film as it progressed. The worst were like that poor chap who played "Waltz Me Around Again, Willie" and "Love Me and the World is Mine" no matter what was happening on the screen.

Sydney had argued several times that the studio should pay for musicians to go out and accompany his movies from town to town, just to ensure that the mood was correct in every showing. They wouldn't do it, of course, but they did let him hire a composer and then printed sheet music to be sent around with the reels of film. The stunt had earned a certain press, especially since the composer famously jumped off a bridge and drowned after writing the music for *The Return of the Siren*.

None of which I discussed with Virginia. Instead we talked about the practicalities of living the artistic life. For as much as she adored playing the great composers, she was not above rehashing a ragtime melody or other popular song if it meant a payment at the end of the evening. "I teach and play for parties," she said. "Mostly University events. There's a few of us in town, enough for a quartet or a trio, if they want to add some dancing. Those professors, going round and round the room in a stately box waltz, it's something to see. There's one old dear, a very tall and thin Scot, with a darling plump German wife. They've been married almost fifty years. They always ask for a proper waltz to end the evening. And pay promptly, too."

"It must be nice," I said, "to live in a town where you know everyone. It's a bit like that in the studio, where we work with the same people all the time. Sydney's crew, they call us. But in Los Angeles, it seems like there's hundreds getting off at the train station every day. It's changing so quickly."

"Oh, you should see New York," said Eleanor, who left Sydney fussing over some business with Lulu. "When I got back from Europe, I couldn't believe the crowds and how they all seemed to have arrived yesterday." She turned to Virginia and held out a hand. "Eleanor Nash, writer. So here I am, having proposed that they see ghosts. Now we are all waiting for the ghosts to appear."

At her words, Virginia shivered a little. "How odd," she said. "I felt as if something cold brushed my back."

I felt it too. A chill, not like a draft, but more like some cold creature had settled on my head and then writhed slowly down my neck. Once, in the orphanage, another girl dropped a small frog down the back of my dress. The feeling was the same damp, cold touch. I tried not to shriek but whirled around, craning to glimpse my back in one of the omnipresent mirrors. Everything looked normal.

Across the room, the others made hesitant steps and glances at each other.

Max, who had been moodily watching from an open door, probably calculating the expense of having a violinist on set, began slapping his back like a man suddenly overwhelmed by small creatures crawling across his skin.

Lulu screamed. Eleanor, who had been uneasily glancing over her own shoulder, twisted around. She strode over to her lover. "What is it, dear?" she said, catching Lulu's hands.

"Ugh," said Lulu. "It must have been a mouse. It ran right over my foot. I could feel its horrible little cold paws on my skin." At the edge of the room, Lulu's pug, Pumpkin, growled at something that wasn't there.

Sydney shouted for everyone's attention. "Right," he said. "Let's get started. The sisters enter the room. They hesitate in the doorway. Something chills them. A feeling of foreboding."

I shuddered as Sydney's words seemed to intensify the feeling of frogs and other creepy things crawling across my skin. The rest looked just as tormented. Only Sydney seemed immune.

"Where's that violinist? I need the music playing!" Sydney shouted.

Virginia lifted her violin and bow. Settling her instrument under her chin, she drew the bow across the strings in the same quick motions as before. But no melody emerged. Rather, it gave out an unearthly wailing noise.

Sydney blinked. "Not Chopin. But that works. Fred, begin. Renee. Lulu. To your places."

Virginia dropped her bow and said to me, "That's not what I meant to play."

"Try again," I said with as much confidence as I could. Just like the day that we arrived, I felt something, something unwelcoming, gathering in the shadows of the house. Something watching and judging, most unsatisfied with our actions and malicious in its reaction. Then I glanced across the room and saw Fred bending to the viewpiece, taking in the scene as the camera would see it. Beyond him, Betsy and Pola took their places. Jim, ordinary Jim, stepped behind the picture frame to play the ghost of an ancestor. It was all the very normal fakery of a movie set, a tale to cause the audience to shriek a little but no great threat to any of the actors I told myself, and hoped that I was not lying.

"Play. This should be fun," I said with greater confidence than I felt to the woman standing beside me.

Virginia nodded and with trembling hands began to play. This time the melody stayed true. The nocturne sounded throughout the room. Fred began cranking the camera, and its resounding clack nearly drowned out the violin. Renee entered first, heading to the end where the portraits hung. As the elder sister, Sydney informed her as she walked across the room, she must take the lead. "You are drawn to the picture!" he yelled. "You know that it reveals a terrible secret. A secret you long to know."

Lulu stepped across behind her. "You are frightened!" Sydney yelled at her. "You tremble in anticipation of what your sister will find. You fear the reveal of the stranger." Lulu stumbled a little and glanced at Sydney. "No, no," he yelled, "eyes on your sister. React, react, you stupid girl!"

"Well, that's the end of that," said Eleanor as Lulu froze in place.

"What did you say to me?" Lulu asked Sydney.

"Fred!" Sydney screamed. "Cut."

Fred stopped cranking. Renee walked back to her starting point with exaggerated care. Virginia wobbled through a few more bars of the nocturne, looked confused by the sudden lack of action and silence, and then stopped as well. We all waited for what would come next.

Lulu and Sydney lit into each other.

"Don't scream at me when I'm acting," said Lulu. "I'm trying to concentrate on my character. How can I do that when you're calling me names?"

"I am the director," Sydney reminded her. "You do what I tell you to do."

"I'm open to notes," she said. "You can give me notes when the scene is over. But during the scene, I'm working. Don't distract me."

Renee shook her head. "We do our notes while the camera is rolling. This isn't the theater where you need to stay silent for an audience."

Lulu stamped one foot. "This is ridiculous. That violin. Sydney screaming. You walking off your line."

"I am never off my line," said Renee with chilly finality.

"Of course you are," Lulu returned. "You are supposed to be going to the first portrait of our ancestor, not the frame that Jim is hiding behind. The picture with the soldier in the stupid uniform."

"That is my great-grandfather Saturnin Fitzmaurice," Sydney said. I could hear his teeth grinding against his cigarette holder from across the room. "A descendent of French nobility."

"Well, Renee is supposed to be walking to his portrait. And why is she always entering first? And if she's supposed to be walking to it, why is the portrait over there?" Lulu pointed across the room to where the painting hung upon the wall, considerably to the left of where it should be.

"That's not right," said Fred, looking up from his camera. "I hung him with his ladies." By which he meant the old woman portrait of another Fitzmaurice, the one that Pola was playing in her broad skirts, and the empty frame that Betsy filled playing the young Madame Saturnin.

Sydney changed the story for the film, making out that his young and handsome nobleman successfully saved his child and wife, sacrificing his own life for love. At least that was how he told it to Darrell during the young reporter's interview. The part about Saturnin handing off his real children to a maid, insisting his portrait be saved, the wife burning to death, and Saturnin himself being reduced to a single charred hand, none of that came up in the tale that Sydney spun to Darrell. But he convinced Darrell that this movie was based on actual Arkham history. Darrell was nearly breathless with excitement about this "exclusive" for his newspaper.

"It's all a bit complicated, isn't it?" Virginia said to me as I whispered explanations of what was supposed to have happened next while Sydney and Lulu continued their argument.

"Sometimes Sydney changes things around. He probably moved that portrait" I said, although I couldn't remember seeing him near it at all. "Just to shake up the actors. He says it makes the reactions more real." But Sydney usually told Fred, so he knew where to point the camera. And I'd been by Fred for most of the morning and never heard any new instructions. It was all very strange.

Because now Monsieur Saturnin's real portrait was clearly exiled from the group, hanging some distance away from where we put it earlier.

"Who moved that picture?" Sydney roared.

Nobody answered. Looking around the room, everyone appeared confused. It made no sense for somebody to have moved that prop. It would have been physically difficult, too. The frame of Saturnin's portrait was made of the same metal painted over to look like gilded wood as the empty frame that we found earlier in the attic. The portrait made for a heavy burden, as Fred and I learned when we had shifted it about.

Darrell turned his camera on the portrait and snapped a few pictures. "Ghostly picture moves across the room, does it warn of doom to actors?" he intoned. Then he laughed. "That's quite a trick, Mr Fitzmaurice. You shook them up good."

Sydney looked confused for a moment, then a little shifty around the eyes. "Yes," he said, drawing it out as he considered both Dennis and Virginia, two outsiders who might tell tales around Arkham. "Never reveal all your secrets to your actors. That's the signature of a Fitzmaurice nightmare picture."

Darrell nodded eagerly, slinging his camera to one side and drawing out his notebook. "I thought so," he said with satisfaction. "Can you tell me more about what's planned for this picture? Is it a haunted house story? Is this the picture where you reveal the meaning of the hooded man?"

"Yes, darling Sydney," said Eleanor with a snap. "Do tell us what all this spookery is leading to."

"Isn't that your job, my dear Eleanor?" said Sydney. "Didn't your scenario call for the sisters to feel as if their eyes are playing tricks on them? That the ghosts of their ancestors are drawing them into a waking nightmare from which they can only be freed by a masked stranger."

Renee gave a little theatrical yawn. "Are we going to film the scene or discuss it? Sydney, if you want me to walk in a different direction, just say so. Don't make me hunt for that portrait of your ancestor."

Sydney shook his head and waved his arms in a way that he probably thought looked theatrical or authoritative. It always reminded me of a duck flapping its wings. He quacked a bit, too.

"Places, places, again. Fred," he shouted, "get ready."

Max grabbed the slate and chalk, scribbling the scene number and that it was the second take, and then held it in front of the camera.

"Action," yelled Sydney. Max whipped the slate away. Fred kept rolling, his hands as steady as clockwork on the handle of 242. No matter how flustered everyone else got, Fred always made the cranking of the camera look easy. I never once saw him miss a beat.

Renee altered her course, heading toward the portrait of the hussar, with Lulu trailing along behind her, and Sydney running parallel across the room, careful to stay out of camera range. "That's it. Go toward the portrait. Stretch out your hand. You feel as if he is about to speak, to impart great secrets if only you have the wisdom to hear his painted words."

Virginia, still looking a bit bewildered, whispered to me, "Do I start playing again?"

"You might as well," I said, although it was obvious that Sydney had forgotten all about the music teacher trying to accompany our film.

"Twelve cents a foot," muttered Max as he walked behind us. "How many takes today?"

"As many as it takes?" I said. Max winced at the almost pun.

Renee reached the portrait. She stretched up her hand. Darrell had packed away his notebook and was just watching her. It appeared that he was holding his breath. Renee's fingers lightly brushed the frame. She gave a quick little cry of pain, as if shocked by the touch.

At her cry, I started forward, almost committing the sin of getting into frame and ruining the shot. I felt a brief burst of fury, convinced Sydney was indeed playing tricks on us for a reaction. I don't know how he did the frogs and mouse feet, but he could have hidden a pin or something sharp on the frame to prick a reaction out of Renee. Directors did things like that. One even shot off a real gun on his set just to see the actors react. "How could he," I muttered, even though I'd never known Sydney to play such tricks on Renee before.

Unaware of the camera, Darrell yelled and lunged toward Renee, knocking my sister to the floor. After a brief, startled moment, we all started shouting as the portrait flew away from the wall. This time I ran toward Renee, no longer caring about the shot. The portrait of Saturnin Fitzmaurice crashed to the ground, crushing Darrell's leg under its heavy metal frame.

Lulu began to scream in earnest.

CHAPTER NINE

The doctor pronounced Darrell fit enough to go home. The leg was bruised but not broken, but she advised staying off it for a day or so.

"You've twisted that knee pretty badly," said Doctor Wills. A blunt-faced woman with a mop of frizzy hair twisted back into a bun secured by a pencil, she snapped her bag closed authoritatively. "However, you'll do."

"As long as my camera isn't broken," said Darrell, who had been more concerned about that than his leg.

We'd called the operator and she'd called Doctor Wills to the house for us. By the time the doctor arrived, Fred had Darrell settled on a couch in the parlor. A closer examination of the portrait showed no damage to the wire or the nail from which it hung. Nobody could explain how it fell on the young reporter. And no one admitted to moving it from one end of the room to the other. As for that moment when it appeared to fly through the air, well, none of us mentioned that either to the doctor or discussed it among ourselves. Darrell only said that he'd seen the picture move toward Renee when he'd jumped to intercept it.

I dragged Fred to the other room while the doctor examined Darrell and quizzed him about Sydney's instructions. He claimed, and I believed him, that Sydney never said anything about changing the scene. Which left me stumped. Why would Sydney play an elaborate hoax, especially one that might have endangered Renee, if it wasn't for a filmed reaction? For the first time, I considered if someone else had sabotaged the scene, perhaps to remove Renee altogether. I didn't want to believe that of Lulu or Eleanor. But nobody else would gain from Renee breaking an arm or leg, or even her head, when that portrait fell.

When Doctor Wills asked about the accident, Sydney came forward. He told her that a prop had fallen off the wall and struck a blow to Darrell's leg.

"I'm glad to see that you are still in practice," said Sydney, shaking her hand as she collected her things.

"Not many towns tolerate a woman doctor," she said with a shrug. "Of course, Arkham couldn't afford to be choosy after the typhoid epidemic of '05. They had trouble enough staffing the hospital. It's a decent practice now we've added that youngster McPherson to help out Simmons and me."

"Dr Simmons is making rounds too?" said Sydney. "I remember him calling on my grandfather."

"The old goat's over eighty," said Doctor Wills, "and he keeps trying to retire. But you know Arkham, never enough doctors. It's steady work. I'll send you my bill in the morning."

Max told her to address her bill to him in care of the Fitzmaurice house. "The studio will pay for any medical costs," he told Darrell.

"Won't be much," said Doctor Wills. "He'll heal quick enough. Come along, Darrell, and I'll give you a lift home. I've another patient out your way."

"I will be fine," Darrell said, waving away Renee's expressions of concern as he tried to slide off the couch. "It's been a real honor to meet you, Miss Love. And you, too, Mister Fitzmaurice. Your pictures are terrific. The way that your films show things that… that, well, I didn't know other people saw."

Fred and Max helped the limping Darrell into the doctor's battered Model T. The car belched a bit of smoke out of its exhaust pipe as it rounded the gate and took to the main road.

"Well, that's been exciting," said Sydney with a bit of a sarcastic laugh. "Now, shall we begin again? I'd like to get this scene done before it gets dark."

"Sydney," protested Lulu. "You can't ask us to go back into that room."

Sydney turned and gave her a patient look. "Of course I mean to finish this scene. The sisters must encounter their ancestors prior to discovering the mask."

At the mention of the mask, I heaved a sigh of relief that I'd found something suitable in the attic. All I had to do was make the lighter paper version to mimic it for Fred's trick shots.

"Yes, about this mask," said Eleanor. "What exactly is it meant to signify? Why do the sisters even want it?"

"Without the mask, the transformation cannot be complete," said Sydney. "It's all there in the script."

"And about that manuscript," said Eleanor, "it would be helpful if you simply gave it to me. I could write all the scenarios."

Sydney waved her off. "First, let us finish this scene. Fred, where's Fred?"

"Here," said Fred, who had been hanging the portrait of Sydney's ancestor in the correct location for filming. "Are we starting from the top?"

"I think we must," said Sydney. "So many interruptions. Where is that violinist?"

Virginia stepped away from Sydney as he swung toward her. "I am sorry, Mr Fitzmaurice, but I must be going. I have a music lesson across town. Yes, that's it. A music lesson. One of my best pupils. I cannot be late." Despite her interest earlier, she now looked slightly desperate to be away. She kept edging toward the door as she talked.

"What's this? You are leaving? Surely we'd agreed that you'd stay until the scene was done." Sydney motioned to Max. "Max, Max, pay this woman something extra so she can skip her music lesson."

Max tried not to look horrified at Sydney's suggestion.

"No," said Virginia, waving off Max. "I must be going. I probably shouldn't have come. I was just so curious to see how a movie was made. And that's all been very interesting. But this house! Darrell's accident! When I was playing, it felt terrible. I really cannot stay." She continued backing toward the door as she spoke. "Oh dear, I thought all those things in your movies were just imagination. I didn't think a Fitzmaurice picture was truly scary."

Sydney looked a bit bemused by her statements. "Thank you," he started to say, but she didn't stop. Virginia hurried out the door, clutching her violin case under her arm as if one of us would snatch it away from her. I almost wished that I could have gone with her. I too had no real desire to reenter the room or watch the "ghosts" come to life.

Renee tapped Sydney on the shoulder. "I didn't like having music. It's a distraction. Let's finish this scene. We can always use the Victrola if you want more music later."

With a huge sigh, Sydney walked back into the other room. "No one understands me. No one appreciates me. Except you, my wonderful muse. You understand what must be done."

"Yes, yes," said Renee. "Let's just get through this scene. I don't like this room."

The room felt clammy and cold, as if it was the middle of winter instead of a pleasant June day. Outside, the crows set up their insistent cawing. Inside, our crew twittered at each other as we took our places. I helped powder Betsy and Pola, improving their ghostly pallor. Betsy stepped back behind the empty frame so Fred could film her full face and then, after a long pause, in profile. She kept the turning of her head smooth. Although I knew it was Betsy simply standing behind an empty frame with the center filled with gauze, the effect was uncanny. As if a ghost had peered through the frame and watched with deadly gaze as the two sisters walked across the room.

This time Renee walked right up to the portrait of Saturnin Fitzmaurice. She held herself still for one beat, two beats, and then stretched a trembling hand up to the canvas. Then, at Sydney's yelled instruction, she dropped her hand sharply and stepped back into the arms of Lulu. The pair stood still, leaning a little against each other as sisters will at the end of a long day of sorrow, when the only thing that keeps them upright is each other.

Sydney yelled "Cut!" Renee stepped out of the pose.

Lulu turned to Sydney and said, "Now what?"

"We begin preparation for our next scene," said Sydney. "The discovery of the tramp in the woods. Then the nightmare of death. And finally the discovery of the mask." Eleanor looked intrigued by this recital and grabbed a piece of paper off one of the tables to jot down notes.

"Can't," said Fred, carefully packing up the camera, as I wondered how to tell Sydney that the mask was not ready yet. That I hadn't started the paper mask. "No more filming today."

"Why can't we film in the woods this afternoon?" said Sydney.

"Because we're short on film and the light's going," said Fred. "I need to go down to the station and pick up some new reels. Studio's last telegram said it would be arriving on the next train from New York."

"Twelve cents a foot," muttered Max.

"Then I shall go wash off this makeup," said Lulu, "and take a gloriously hot bath. Eleanor, can you take Pumpkin out for a short run? Poor darling has been waiting for me all day."

Eleanor glanced at the pug snoring in the corner of the room. "I doubt that dog knows the meaning of the word run, but I'll boot it onto the grass for a bit."

"Eleanor," fussed Lulu. "You're always so mean to poor Pumpkin."

"I'm a saint around that dog," said Eleanor. "Especially after it ate my best pair of gloves."

"That was not Pumpkin's fault."

"Oh, God, must I listen to the sins of a dog," moaned Sydney. "I am trying to make art."

"Such a lot of bother about a flicker," said Lulu.

At that fateful word, we all turned to look at Sydney. "Films are not just…" began Fred under his breath.

Sydney went for it with his full director's voice. "Films are not just cheap flickers, meant for a moment of quick entertainment! Movies have the power to rebuild the Tower of Babel and create a universal language. With the right picture, I can unite all the people of the world. They will see our work and understand the power that links us all. There will be no war, because we will speak the same language. We will all understand each other's deepest dreams and greatest aspirations. We will be united in our efforts to build the perfect civilization."

Lulu started to open her mouth, but Betsy, who was closest to her, trod heavily on Lulu's foot. At her squeak of annoyance, or possibly pain, Betsy whispered: "Hush. It's one of his best speeches."

It was, too. Sydney presented a dream of a world. A dream that began in a quiet movie house, with an audience waiting breathlessly for the first note of the organ and the first moment of light as the film began.

"I felt it once," said Sydney, "in the crudest of nickelodeons. I was broke, despairing, ruined in all the ways that a man could be ruined. I paid my nickel and wandered in to escape the rain. And there they were. All manner of people. Dock workers still stinking of their labor, washerwomen with hands so chapped and scalded that they bled onto their aprons, and the street's children who spoke no English. Waiting together for a film to begin. The piano was out of tune, the player atrocious. It didn't matter. We all came together in the darkness. Those who could read recited the cards to their neighbors; those who spoke English translated the lines to the friends that surrounded them. But that was not necessary. Speech itself was silenced into a more universal connection. The film itself, the images that glowed upon the wall in shadows of silver and black, that we all understood. We all laughed together. We all cried out with the same terror. We all wept as one. And when we stumbled out onto the street, we fell apart, each going back to their own sorrows and joys. But still we were connected. For we still held within ourselves that precious moment when we experienced each emotion as one entity, one soul. That is what a movie can do that no other art can. That is what we are creating here."

There was a moment of silence, then Betsy began to clap, and the others picked it up. For we did believe, we always believed that what we were making was a little different from all the other films being churned out by the score. Sydney was right. There were moments in his films that were unforgettable. Once experienced, a scene or a gesture would stay with you forever. Years later, people would talk about movies, about the thrills or the scares, and they would always conclude, "But it wasn't like a Fitzmaurice terror picture. That stuck with you."

We all knew that. And we all stayed with Sydney because what he made was beautiful. And lasting. And we all, at that moment, wanted to be a part of what came next.

"The key," Sydney insisted to Lulu, who now looked as entranced as the rest of us, "is the right piece. I've been searching for that perfect movie, the one that will never be forgotten. The one that will be shown around the globe and open doors to worlds that we have never imagined. That piece is this picture. And the key to this picture will be the final sequence, when a beauty is transformed."

"I'm still uncertain how you expect that scene to go," said Eleanor.

"You will see," said Sydney. "We will create a perfect construction of terror. We will cause the audience to search their hearts. To pray for relief. And then, then they will be swept up into the shadow. The masked beauty will become them, and, like her, they will be transformed. Transfigured. Transported elsewhere and then brought back to earth again. United as minds have never been united before."

"Yes, but–" Eleanor said.

Sydney kept talking without pause. "The mask ripped aside to reveal the cosmos. The perfect mask for the moment," he said, swinging around to point at me. "Jeany's creation will set the final scene. It will be magic!"

I felt a moment of terrible doubt. Would an old stage prop repainted by

Humbert really work? But it was only needed for a moment or so. Of course it would work, I reassured myself.

The others chattered with excitement about Sydney's vision.

"It's better than being on stage," Betsy said to Lulu, who looked skeptical. "No, really, how many people see you in a play?"

"Our theater seats nearly five hundred," said Lulu. "And Eleanor's plays run for months."

"Yes," said Betsy, "but even if a play ran for an entire year, the most people who could see you would be under two hundred thousand." That was Betsy, ever calculating numbers in her head faster than the rest of us could write two down and carry one. I liked that about her, the way she used numbers to explain bigger ideas. That, and how she believed the best of everyone, that they could be better than they were, even after they betrayed her. Very few in Hollywood, or anywhere, had Betsy's courage when it came to forgiveness. Certainly I could never forgive Sydney's later betrayals of our company.

"One picture can play in thousands of theaters," Betsy told Lulu. "There are more than twenty thousand movie houses operating in America right now. And every day they are building them bigger and bigger. Thousands of people in one theater to see you in a movie. That's millions of people who might see you in the same week."

Lulu's eyes began to gleam. She understood fame. And she'd forgotten about the frights of a few hours before. I could see that. I'd seen the same expression on Renee's face when Sydney began talking about acclaim and riches and all the other things that came with being a star in the pictures. It kept her coming back, even when Sydney was his most impossible. And I'll admit, I felt the same. Sitting in the audience and listening to them scream during a Fitzmaurice picture and knowing it was our work that united them in terror was an unbelievably exciting feeling.

Max, this time, slid in the last word to Sydney's little speech, something he didn't normally do. "The studio is keeping a very close eye on how this goes," he said to Sydney.

"Do they doubt my talent?" said Sydney.

"No, of course not, your last two pictures were smashes," said Max.

"Of course," Sydney said. "There's never been anything like a Fitzmaurice picture in the history of the human race. I make movies that are the very height of diversion. The audience cannot escape the emotions, the very thoughts, forged in my world of silver shadows."

"Nobody's disputing your artistry, Sydney. But things are changing. The studio wants more control. Being so far away, in Arkham, it's making them nervous," Max said.

"Tell them to take a tonic," said Sydney. "I was wrong to think I could do this any place but Arkham. This is the place. This is the script. This time it will work."

"It's the expense," said Max.

"Dreams cannot be bought cheaply," retorted Sydney.

"Actually, Sydney," said Max, "that is what you promised them."

The dry finality of Max's tone made me wonder again exactly what Sydney was planning this time.

CHAPTER TEN

My mother talked about ghosts. But not as something that inhabited the house that you lived in. Rather ghosts were something far off, and part of the history that she had left behind. But if a light went out suddenly and left us in darkness, she would laugh and say, "the spirits have come to eat." When we questioned her about that, she said that her grandmother used that phrase whenever a candle blew out.

The spirits must have been very fat indeed at the Fitzmaurice house, for the lights constantly went on and off. Fred muttered at the fuse box on a daily basis, calling it a deceitful thing of beauty. Max had several long calls with the power company, who denied all malicious intent and inquired when last the wiring had been checked. The rest of the company, myself included, made sure to have candles or lanterns close to our beds with a matchbox conveniently nearby. The days were long, and the nights warm, so the inconvenience of finding a bathroom at midnight by candlelight was more a minor annoyance than anything else.

Still I found restful sleep increasingly hard to achieve. Every night, I dreamed of masks made of shadows, masks made of snakes, masks made of smoke, and masks made of silk that shredded into the webs of spiders. But when I woke and stared at the painted mask propped on my desk, the empty eyeholes stared back. Next to it was set its fragile paper twin, an equally unsatisfying prop. No matter how close these were to what Sydney described, I felt as if something vital was missing. Some otherworldly force, Sydney would say, except there was no such thing. "Props, just props," I muttered and pulled out my sketchbook to distract myself.

I tried to take my mind off the movie, sketching out costume ideas for future projects. Ideas I could present to United Artists and other studios. Ideas that would get me away from Sydney's horrid stories. Yet every night, I could draw nothing except a cloaked man with no face who nevertheless stared out from behind a masked woman. I threw my pencil across the room more than once, only to feel compelled to pick it up and start sketching the horrid creature all over again.

Eleanor seemed to have the same problem with her script. She typed page after page on a typewriter that she'd brought from New York. The clatter from her Underwood threatened to drown out Fred's darling 242 at times. Yet most of Eleanor's ideas were crumpled up and discarded as Sydney proclaimed that it was not quite what he was looking for or Eleanor herself would re-read what she wrote and sigh, "Not that shadowy masked woman and her cloaked friend again. That's such a useless idea."

By the following Saturday, we had barely filmed another page of the scenario, a slight scene where Pola played a visiting neighbor who gossiped about a magic mask hidden in the house. All the company was a little on edge and complaining about being cooped up indoors. Sydney proposed that we drive to the country. "A Sunday picnic in June," he said. "Just like my childhood."

Renee declined. She'd been suffering from headaches throughout the week and wanted to stay indoors and rest. On Sunday, I went to her room and asked if she wanted me to sit with her.

"No," she said, shaking her head with a wince. "It is just a headache. A day of quiet. That's all I want."

She did look pale. Her restless energy seemed diminished. She often wore herself out during filming, putting so much of herself into the performance that she could barely move by the end of the day. It was one of the reasons that she rarely attended or gave parties. The other, of course, is that we could never be sure when somebody outside our group would spot that she wasn't quite what she appeared to be. So Renee needing rest, and wanting to stay out of strong sunlight even with a group of friends, was not unusual. But it was rare for her to be this fragile when we'd completed so little.

"Do you want me to call the doctor?" I said. "I liked her. Doctor Wills seemed a sensible woman."

"I'm sure she is," said Renee, "but I don't need her. Go to the picnic. Enjoy yourself. I just need a few hours of uninterrupted sleep."

She lay back down on the bed with its fussy canopy and piles of lace-edged pillows. Curled up in the center, she looked so small. I'd never thought of my big sister as anything less than ten feet tall, a warrior woman who protected me all my life. This picture did seem to be draining her energy at an alarming rate.

"Perhaps we should go home," I said.

Renee just waved one hand at me without opening her eyes. "We will. When this is done. It will be worth it. You'll see."

I wanted to argue that nothing was worth night after night of frustration, but then took pity on my big sister. I left quietly, shutting the door as gently as possible behind me.

After collecting a hat and stuffing my sketchbook into a large straw bag, I descended the stairs with some relief. Perhaps out in the country, away from the house, I would finally discover the proper design for the mask.

The touring car was filled with Sydney, Pola, Betsy, Paul, and Max. Lulu, Eleanor, and the pug named Pumpkin went in Eleanor's sporty two-seater. Fred had borrowed an old truck from Humbert for the rest of our gear, including two picnic baskets, several blankets, some old bolsters, and a ratty collection of golf clubs in a mildewed canvas bag. The latter had been unearthed from the back of the barn. Sydney thought they belonged to his university days. I squeezed into the front seat of the truck between Fred and Jim. Hal, like Renee, declined to picnic and waved us goodbye from a chair on the veranda.

Driving through the town, I remarked how pleasant, how ordinary, even quite pretty it was in spots.

"Yeah," said Fred. "Pretty as a picture postcard."

"Don't you like it?" I said.

Fred, the lover of science and all things mechanical, grimaced. "You're right about the shadows."

"The shadows?" I said, not sure what he meant. I didn't like the shadows at the house, the cold crooked patches of dark, but what did that have to do with driving through this pretty New England town?

"Noticed it when I was fetching stuff for Max," said Fred. "Some days, there's more shadows than there should be."

"It's probably because we are used to California sunshine," I said, because there was no sensible, rational reason to be worried by shadows. Even though I was.

"Yeah," said Fred. "That makes sense."

I wished again that this picture was over and we were heading home to Los Angeles.

Once we passed Arkham's boundaries, the road meandered pleasantly up and down the rounded hills. Everything was the new green of early summer. It was hard to imagine that redcoats and Colonial soldiers had once marched across these fields and peppered each other with shots. Fred had been reading up on the American Revolution, there being a lack of scientific literature in the Fitzmaurice library, and speculated now on how far we might be from the protests, riots, and other acts of rebellion.

"Wasn't that all closer to Boston?" I said. My knowledge of that time period was sketchy at best although I could remember Sister Martha reciting such names as Paul Revere and John Adams, with nearly as much fervor as she named the saints.

"Maybe," said Fred, shouting over the rattling of the truck. "Arkham seems to have missed a lot of history. No pilgrims to speak of, no revolutionary shots heard round the world. Nothing much ever seems to have happened here."

Jim snored on my right side. The man could, and did, sleep through anything. His ability to lean himself up against a piece of set and snooze until called upon to act was something of a legend.

"Perhaps that is why the Fitzmaurices settled here," I said. "Because it was quiet and safe." Except as I said it, I realized that the town never felt safe to me.

We climbed a hill, slowly. Fred ground the gears and shifted down. The touring car, although loaded with more people, made better time in front of us. Fred shouted over the engine noise about valves and engine power.

The road smoothed out and we started to talk about the next week's filming.

"Humbert is good with tools. As good as Paul," said Fred. "He's helping us build that box for Sydney's next big scene."

"Oh, the one that Eleanor was talking about at dinner?" I said. "The bed that becomes a coffin in the sisters' dreams. Did Sydney decide to do that next?"

"Yes."

"That's grim." I hadn't liked the sound of it when we had discussed it a couple of nights ago. It reminded me too much of my recent nightmares. There'd been a lot of talk about who would be trapped in the coffin and, after much discussion, it was decided that this would be Lulu's first big solo scene. Renee as the older sister had been the focus so far with the haunted pictures and even the major character for the minor scene of gossiping with the neighbor.

Eleanor proposed the bed sequence, because it was similar to something that they'd done on stage in New York and had gotten a lot of press at the time. Sydney liked the idea as it established that this was *the* Lulu, the screamer and scandalous darling of the New York stage. Renee expressed herself delighted to give the scene to Lulu and not have to sleep in a coffin.

"It will be a good trick when we're done. I'm taking a real bed and fixing up the coffin sides and a lid to slide up around Lulu. We should be ready by Monday. It will be a great scene."

"Well, let's make Lulu look amazing," and as I said it, I suddenly realized how to fix Lulu's hair and makeup so she appeared to be halfway between a sleeping beauty and a beautifully preserved corpse. I knew it would be gorgeous but terrifying, and Sydney would love it.

"You'll make it amazing," said Fred. "You always do, Jeany."

Fred's confidence cheered me considerably. Ahead of us, Eleanor tooted the horn of her car and turned onto a narrow lane after Sydney's group. We followed them to a meadow where the long grasses were intertwined with wildflowers. Butterflies and small birds darted about. Far off in the distance, the Miskatonic River glittered silver in the sun as it ran east toward the ocean.

Fred pulled the truck behind the cars. With a snort, Jim woke up and amiably lugged picnic baskets, blankets, and bolsters into place. Most of us collapsed around the largest basket, unearthing various sandwiches, cakes, cookies, cheese, crackers, cold chicken, and three jars of pickles packed earlier by Mrs Mayhew. Pola, as usual, drew out a bag of knitting as soon as she settled herself on a bolster.

After eating everything but one jar of pickles, we all sprawled in splendid post-feast repose. Fred grabbed Jim, Paul, and the bag of golf clubs. They wandered a little ways away and used the rejected pickles in place of the missing golf balls. Soon small bits of green were streaking across the meadow with a wet thwack.

I pulled out my sketchbook and began to doodle. Flowers and butterflies intertwined in geometric and angular shapes. I thought about how they could be printed as a border of a gown or beaded onto a scarf and sketched some more. As I turned the page to shade in a long stem of grass, I saw how other shapes formed between an outstretched wing and curling petals. Shapes that looked like angular skulls and rounded creatures of a vaguely aquatic nature. The shadows growing behind them turned into the shape of a woman, oddly blurred and masked, with a shadow that stretched in all the wrong directions. Behind her stood a cloaked man. I slammed the sketchbook shut and stuffed it into my bag, determined not to work any more that day. I truly hated the hooded man in that moment and never wanted to draw him or his mysterious companion again.

With a giggle, Betsy pulled Max off his blanket and persuaded him to walk with her down the hill to find a better view of the river. Pola shook her head at them and then took a finer wool out of her bag. She cast it on her needles and began to knit a pattern of interlocking circles.

"That's beautiful," I said.

"A shawl fine enough to pull through a ring," answered Pola. "In my hometown, every bride had one in her trousseau."

The others were asking how Sydney knew about this idyllic spot.

The meadow was part of the Mayhew farm, according to Sydney.

"We always came here for picnics," he continued, waving one hand in a lazy circle much as a king might describe his kingdom with a wave of a scepter. "I used to chase butterflies with a net."

"And stick them in a killing jar," guessed Eleanor. She lay back on a blanket, her face tipped up to the sun. Lulu nestled at her side, a large hat shading her face.

Sydney laughed. "Well you can't catch and release them. The net breaks their wings. I wonder what happened to my old butterfly collection. I used to have a hundred or so, all pinned on cards with the Latin names written underneath. *Papilio polyxenes* or the black swallowtail. The painted lady or *Vanessa cardui*. How very long ago that was."

"How very ordinary. To chase butterflies with a net," said Eleanor.

"I found them endlessly fascinating," admitted Sydney. "As a boy I believed all manner of stories about butterflies. That they were the souls aflutter from a cooling body, the psyche that emerges from the dead man's mouth."

"So this obsession with death began at an early age?" Eleanor gave him a doubtful look. "Or is that a story that you made up to impress the press?"

Sydney shook his head. "I was a precocious child and quite my grandfather's shining hope. The Fitzmaurices have always had a fascination with ancient mythology. Particularly Egyptian. My grandfather collected an extensive number of books on the subject. I devoured every tale that I could find in his library. Especially the ones about psychopomps."

"Pumps? Lunatic pumps?" murmured Lulu, but something about her smile said that she knew very well what Sydney was talking about.

"Lulu, don't tease," said Eleanor. "We had discussions with the most darling little professor from Bryn Mawr about the creatures that escort newly deceased souls from Earth and where exactly they escort those spirits to."

"The horrors of research for one of Eleanor's plays," said Lulu. "You thought the professor was darling. I thought she drank too much of our gin."

Sydney looked a little put out to be upstaged and plunged back into his explanation of how ancient civilizations had lists full of creatures that led souls, both dead and living, to a place somewhere outside the cosmos that we knew.

"A liminal space," said Sydney, staring hard at Lulu.

"Oh, one of those places," said Lulu, "where we are in space between one point in time and the next. A doorway, just on the verge of being open or closed or that moment in a dream when you take a step and haven't started falling yet."

"Well, yes," said Sydney, a little disconcerted.

"I don't know how she does it," Eleanor said to me, not without some pride. "As far as I know, she had no formal education, grew up in the back of vaudeville theaters, and her mother actually did put her in a lion's cage in a melodrama at the age of three."

"She most certainly did," said Lulu. "I remember it clearly."

"And you never read anything but the most dreadful romances and the stage papers," Eleanor said to Lulu.

"Now, that is not true," said Lulu. "I often read your dull reference books when I want to go to sleep quickly. How about that New England history tome with the impossibly convoluted sentences right beside my pillow back at the house? Pumpkin has chewed the cover twice and declared it virtually inedible."

Sydney tipped his hat further over his face to shade himself from the sun. "I gave my best occult histories to Eleanor for her work. Not for the pug's supper."

"Very tiny nibble," said Lulu. "Barely a scratch." Eleanor swatted her with her hat and mouthed "Behave" .

To Sydney, Eleanor said, "Your grandfather was an actor. Quite famous, I hear."

"In his younger days," said Sydney. "It was all glories of the past by the time I was old enough to be interested. It was hard to imagine. That he actually knew the Booth brothers and saw them all play together at the Winter Garden. About how they had power, but didn't understand it. How John was a fool who thought he could change history with a gun when he could have done so much more."

"I would argue shooting Lincoln did change history," said Eleanor. "The death of the great man will do."

"So crude," said Sydney. "And, I don't believe a single shot, no matter where it happens or to who, really changes the world. It may bend history for a decade or a generation, but things do slide back. Same old problems crop up again."

"How very cynical of you," said Eleanor.

"How very noble of me," said Sydney with a flash of a smile. "After all, I'm the first to say that violence is useless. Shoot a man, and another takes his place. Win a war and another war is just waiting around the corner to begin. A war to end all wars will never happen. Change, true change, must come from outside. A radical change driven by a new consciousness. Or the return of a very old one."

Eleanor shook her head. "There's no new consciousness. Our perception is formed by our experience. To create something that nobody has ever experienced is impossible, because we all draw from the same conscious or unconscious well of experiences."

"Isn't that what we have been doing with our films? Creating something never experienced before?" said Sydney. "My grandfather thought you could bring it forth with theater, with ritual, but that all goes back to an idea that has been around for uncounted generations. I cannot tell you the number of times that it has been tried. And failed. There's some very interesting stories about that, especially around Arkham."

"But what we are doing is a form of theater," said Eleanor, who was obviously becoming more intrigued with Sydney's proposition. I recognized it, of course. It was Sydney's idea of a universal language, much as Sister Theodora once argued at the orphanage. A way to end the division caused by the fall of Babylon.

"Film is something completely new and growing stronger every day," said Sydney. "A collective communication, understood wherever you go, made of electricity, light, and shadows, a visual medium that progresses straight into the mind, without any common language needed at all. I too tried the theater, based on my grandfather's recommendations, and found it sadly lacking. But luckily I made that discovery while still in college. Next I thought it would be the circus, that art known round the world. That failed too. But I am convinced now that it is the movies."

Lulu teased her pug with a bit of ham taken from a sandwich. "It must have been a happy childhood. Living here in Arkham."

Eleanor sighed, "Oh Lulu. That wasn't what we were talking about."

Lulu winked at me. I understood immediately that she knew exactly what she was doing. Not arguing with two intellectuals sparring over vague concepts. Just pulling them back to earth a bit. It was one of the reasons that I couldn't dislike Lulu. Sydney's speeches on controlling the common consciousness made as much sense as Fred's speeches about using radio waves to convey sound and pictures. However, Fred's ideas had some practical merit. Sydney, especially when he started on the occult and metaphysical, made my skin crawl. Somehow, with him, it sounded more like universal hypnosis than communication. I never liked the character of Svengali and a Svengali who controlled populations through film was an idea that I hoped Sydney never wrote into one of his films. It would appeal too much to the wrong type of people.

"What?" Lulu said to Eleanor. "I meant it. Sydney seems to have been blessed. To grow up in a large house. To come on picnics to a pretty meadow full of butterflies. It sounds much happier than my childhood. Don't forget my mother put me in a lion cage at the age of three."

"As you never fail to remind me," said Eleanor. "It was one melodrama that ran less than three weeks. And the lioness was toothless, according to your mother."

"I didn't know that," said Lulu. "But still, Sydney, you sound as if you had the perfect happy childhood."

"Happiness was never a particular goal of my family," said Sydney. "We were far more set on other things."

"That's an interesting question," said Eleanor. "What's more desirable? Happiness? Wealth? Fame? Power?"

"Doesn't wealth, fame, and power bring happiness?" said Lulu.

Eleanor sat up. "I used to think that. But now, I find myself less sure. I chased through Europe for stories, certain that being a war correspondent would be the path to fame. And all the rest that you listed."

"Eleanor, your stories were printed in the *Saturday Evening Post*," said Lulu.

"And that did pay well," said Eleanor. "Although our horrid plays, all full of blood and screaming, paid even better. Then we fell in love and that certainly made both of us famous."

"I'm not sure that was what Sydney meant," said Lulu. "But it hasn't been that bad."

"No, dear," said Eleanor, giving Lulu a quick kiss and hug, "there's been a lot of good in the last year. But it proves my point. Or rather makes one think. I've been rich, well, as rich as a writer can be, and famous, or at least infamous. And has it made me happy? At least as happy as a simple picnic, sitting in the sun, arguing about what brings happiness."

"But you haven't been powerful," said Sydney with a sly look sideways. The sun slid under the down-tipped brim of his boater and made his eyes gleam. "Not the type of power that true fame and fortune brings. Where you can ask for anything and be given it."

"That's making three wishes off a magic fish," said Eleanor. "Nobody should ever be able to ask for anything and be assured of having it. Makes them spoiled. Makes what you are asking for worthless."

Fred wandered back to the blankets, swinging his golf club at daisies in the grass. "Is there any ginger ale left?" he said.

I pushed the picnic basket closer to him with my foot, relieved to be distracted. "Look in there."

"What's the argument this time?" he said, nodding toward Sydney and Eleanor.

"Fame versus happiness, I think. Or perhaps power."

"I'll take happiness," said Fred. "If we can order it off some menu."

"Don't think that is quite what they mean." But I thought he had it right. I loved my work, but I never cared, as Renee did, who knew about it. I never wanted to be famous. At least, I didn't think I did. Renee occasionally accused me of lacking ambition. But it wasn't that. I wanted to design for the movies. I wanted to have people clamor for my clothes or put my drawings on the cover of *Harper's*. I just didn't want to have my picture taken by reporters or have people speculating about my love life in the gossip columns. I watched Renee manage that, and manage it well, but it meant hiding part of herself. That I never wanted to do. If happiness meant forgoing fame, I'd take that.

Eleanor was keeping up the argument with Sydney, despite Lulu's best attempts at interjecting a little levity. "Changing the world through your creation. That's every artist's dream. But no art has that power. To bend the world to the image that you want."

Max and Betsy wandered back to the blankets. Max, as always, looked pressed and tidy. Even on a picnic, he wore immaculately tailored trousers, jacket, shirt, and tie. Even his boater sported a broader ribbon than Sydney's. "What are you talking about?" he said.

"Which is the most desirable: happiness, fame, wealth, or power," said Eleanor.

"Wealth," answered Max without hesitation. "The rest all follow the money."

"You have a mercenary soul, Max," said Sydney. "Art is the power to change men's minds."

"What about the women? Oh, we're already in our right minds and so don't need to change," retorted Eleanor.

Max just smiled. "If you can pay the bills and still have money left over for luxuries, wouldn't you be happy? There's nothing more miserable than being poor."

"Quite true," said Sydney. "I was miserably poor once. Down to nothing more than a nickel, and I spent that to go to the movies. Wisest decision that I ever made."

Max shook his head. "Sydney, you have never been poor. You may have been out of money once or twice, but you have always known that you could come back to this." He pointed at the picnic baskets. "A house full of treasures, servants, the luxury of a lazy Sunday afternoon spent discussing what is the most important thing in the world."

Betsy looked startled at this outburst. We all were. Max never spoke out or spoke up around Sydney. That's why Sydney liked him better than the studio's last two assistants. Max just totaled the numbers and moaned a little about Sydney's extravaganzas before figuring how to make it all work out.

"Why, Max," said Sydney, his mouth half crooked in a condescending smile, "you sound like a socialist."

"Oh, not me," said Max. "What do I care about the masses? My grandfather might have subscribed to the *Workers Times,* but it was a waste of his money. It did him no good at all."

"Not a fan of Emma Goldman either?" asked Eleanor, citing the outspoken radical who had finally been shipped back to Russia. "I heard her speak once or twice before she was deported."

"I have no time for anarchists, socialists, or communists," declared Max. "Or any other radical. And as for the government thinking they can solve problems by simply shipping people out of the country, that's as foolish."

"Careful, Max," said Sydney. "Next you'll be saying that you disagree with Prohibition."

"You can't legislate people into being prudent, sober, or good, however you define good," said Max with some bitterness. "None of that works. All decisions in the end come down to the irrational and the emotional."

"In that," said Sydney, "we are in some agreement. Fear speaks directly to the irrational mind. Terror is the key."

Max sat up even straighter. Like Sydney, his face was shaded by his boater. Weirdly shadowed, like a black hood fell across it. Suddenly Max – sweet, note-taking, cost-obsessed, creased-pants Max – seemed like the figure of my dreams. It was the most ridiculous idea that I had ever had.

"Terror is the key," repeated Max.

Eleanor continued to watch the two men with a considering look. "Keys can be dangerous," she finally said. "Look at Pandora and what she found when she unlocked her box."

Lulu broke up this sobering discussion, rising with a shaking of her skirts and tumbling her dog into the grass. "Come along, Pumpkin," she said. "Let's take a walk and enjoy the sun." She gestured to Eleanor. "Want to join us or continue arguing politics?"

"Darling Lulu," said Eleanor, getting to her feet. "You are always far more fascinating than men arguing about power versus wealth." She wound her arm around Lulu's waist. The pair wandered down the same path that Max and Betsy had taken earlier.

"Want to join our game of pickle golf?" Fred asked me.

"Oh yes," I said jumping up, wanting more than anything in that moment to leave behind my new and disturbing vision of Max. "How do you score a hole in one?"

"Smash the pickle completely?" Fred wondered as he handed me a golf club. "Or maybe turn it into relish?"

Betsy grabbed another club and followed us. "Who wants to talk about boring politics," she said. "Everyone has tough times. Why not enjoy what we have now?"

So we left Max and Sydney behind to discuss terror and keys, when we should have stayed and asked more questions about Sydney's ideas. That night the electricity went out again. The nightmares began in earnest.

CHAPTER ELEVEN

We were hot and tired, and just a little sticky with pickle juice, by the time that we got back to the Fitzmaurice house. Lines formed outside the bathrooms. The hot water had definitely cooled by the time I could fill a tub. Still, it felt lovely to wash my hair and pull on my silk pajamas. I dropped into bed convinced I would sleep forever.

Instead I dreamed of coffins, masks, and endless rooms filled with smoke. And I was alone, terribly alone. I knew in my dream if I could find Renee or Fred, it would be all right. But they were gone. Everyone was gone. Mirrors reflected flames behind me and muddled the way. I came to doors that were locked or doors that opened into infinite darkness. Nowhere could I see a clear path out of the smoke.

Smoke smothered my screams. Muffled, blinded, lost, I wandered the endless and hostile corridors of the Fitzmaurice house. No matter which way I turned, mirrors blocked my way and taunted me with the reflection of a door, a door that I could not reach but that promised freedom and clean air.

I choked on smoke and despair. I never knew such sorrow, more bitter than when Renee held my hand and told me that our mother died. I never knew such terror, not even as a child, when the influenza pinned me helpless to my bed with fever and I was convinced that I would never be well again.

In the depths of each mirror swam the shadow of a woman, a strange and amorphous creature of coiling smoke, and a hooded man standing further away. I could barely see him. He was more of an impression, but I would catch greater glimpses of her the closer that I went to the mirror. Her hair spilled down her back, writhing like snakes. She was constantly walking away from me. When I would turn and hurry in the opposite direction, trying to catch a glimpse of her amid the fumes, I would confront another mirror and a vision of her retreating back.

The man never moved. Instead he watched us engage in this lunatic race, looking for the right way out of the smoke and fire.

Weeping with fear and frustration, I banged my hands against the mirror, almost as if the woman was on the other side of a window and could hear me. The creature slowed and then turned, presenting to me a perfectly blank face, an oval of polished silver that reflected flickering flames and my own frightened face.

I woke gasping and almost screaming, convinced that I could smell a fire. But there was nothing but darkness, a warm smothering darkness. As I groped for the matches and the candle beside my bed, I heard small cries and startled exclamations coming from the hallway. Finally a lantern shone outside the door of my bedroom.

"Jeany? Jeany, are you awake?" Renee stood there with her bedside lamp casting wild shadows up and down the wall. Her hands were shaking too badly to hold it steady.

"I'm here," I said, tumbling out of the bed and making my way to the door. I heard the crackle of paper underfoot as I trod upon my sketchbook. "What's wrong?"

"Nothing," she said. And then, almost in a whisper. "Old nightmares. Would you mind sleeping in my room tonight?"

I nearly made some sarcastic remark about how that would look, but then I saw her face. She was biting her lips to keep them from trembling. I had not seen such sorrow and worry in her face since the day we went to the orphanage. But the moment I came close enough to touch her, Renee straightened her shoulders and assumed that look that only big sisters can give to little sisters.

"I'm all right," she said. "But I dreamed that something was in my room tonight. A bird trapped in the house? I kept hearing wings. I swear I felt it fly past me. Please stay with me."

"Of course. Don't worry. I'm sure it's nothing." Dreams, I told myself. It was only dreams and dreams could not hurt us.

As we went down the hall, we found a number of the bedroom doors were open. Eleanor and Lulu were in the hallway, arguing about whether or not to go downstairs and find something to drink. "I just can't sleep," said Lulu. "But it's so dark on the stairs."

"That's why we have lanterns," said Eleanor, hoisting hers above her head. "Please remember that our mothers managed stairs quite handily in long skirts and with no electric lights."

"We never lived in any place big enough for stairs," muttered Lulu.

"There's a smaller stair here," I said, pulling back the chintz curtain that hid the back stairs. "You go right into the kitchen on this."

"There," said Eleanor, shepherding Lulu onward. "Let's go down and see what we can find. I might even manage to light the stove to make a cup of Ovaltine."

When we reached the kitchen, we found the stove already lit. Fred pulled a boiling kettle from the top. "Hello," he said. "Anyone for a hot toddy?"

"Dear man," said Eleanor, "do you actually have whiskey for that?"

"Hot water, honey, and Max's favorite bottle of scotch," said Fred. "I remembered where he hid it in the library."

Betsy and Pola came tumbling down the stairs next. "Oh Fred," said Betsy. "That smells wonderful."

Fred filled up cups with generous dollops of Max's imported scotch and hot water. Eleanor stirred in the honey and handed us each a toddy.

"It would be better with schnapps," said Pola, sipping her cup, "but a good thought all the same."

Hal and Paul joined us next, claiming that Jim's snoring had woken them up but looking equally glad to have a toddy pressed into their hands. Max was the last to arrive.

"Is that my scotch?" he said, eyeing the empty bottle.

"Here," said Fred, handing him a cup. "You'll find it medicinal."

Only Jim, who could sleep through earthquakes and thunderstorms, and Sydney failed to join the party.

"But what did wake us all up?" Eleanor asked after her cup was empty.

"I thought there was a rat in the room," said Lulu. "It was climbing on the bed."

"Not likely," Eleanor answered. "Pumpkin was still wuffling away on his pillow when we left. Even that dog would wake up if he smelled a rat."

"I smelled smoke," I said. "Or I dreamed I did."

"I thought I heard a bird beating against the window," said Renee. "Maybe that was what started my dream."

Renee spoke of mirrors that cracked while she tried to fix her makeup and reflected a scarred face. "It was a bird, a crow," she said. "A crow flew into the mirror and cracked it. Cracked me too. Like a porcelain doll face, shattering on the floor."

Pola admitted that she dreamed of knitting shrouds for all her family. Betsy bit her lip and said "I couldn't make the numbers work in my favor. No matter how I added it up, I couldn't save him." But she refused to say who she was trying to help.

Eleanor sighed and said, "I dreamed that I was surrounded by paper and none of the ideas in my head would come out as coherent words. Every time I started to write, it turned into blobs of ink that meant nothing at all. And all the time I knew I was dreaming and was afraid to wake. It seemed as if awakening would release even more terrible dreams lurking inside of my dreams. Those were my terrors of the small hours."

Lulu hugged her and Eleanor hugged her back. "All ridiculous," said Eleanor. "I've seen far worse awake and survived quite sane. No matter what the New York critics say about my scripts."

Paul wouldn't say what woke him, but Hal told of a nightmare where he was being chased by chickens.

Max reached for the scotch bottle and tipped the remaining drops into his toddy cup. "I dreamed that I was poor again," he said. "I dreamed of the steps leading down to my childhood apartment and how they always smelled of garbage and damp. And I knew if I went into that basement apartment again that I could never leave. That's frightening enough."

"Oh, Max," said Betsy and tried to pat his hand. But he turned half away from her and took a long drink.

Tidying up the kitchen, Fred said, very quietly, "I was back in the trenches. And a mortar blew my hands off."

I watched Fred's clever hands stack the cups neatly into the sink. I could not think of a worse nightmare. All of them had already lived their worst nightmare. More than ever, I hated the Fitzmaurice house and wished we were anywhere else.

But what could I say? That the house was haunting us? The script that Eleanor and Sydney hadn't even finished writing? The mask staring with sightless eyes at me whenever I looked up from my bed? We made up stories like this all the time. We knew that such tales were just tricks of light captured on film. No wonder Sydney slept peacefully above. He was the storyteller who directed these scenarios. Why would he be frightened? Why would any of us suffer from nightmares when we were the creators of terror?

CHAPTER TWELVE

I went into the pantry to fetch the bread and cheese as well as some leftover bacon. Fred found the skillet and between the two of us we made a hearty middle of the night meal for everyone.

We sat up the rest of the night, talking of the next scenes to be done, what we thought Sydney wanted, and where we intended to go when this film was over. Lulu and Eleanor wanted to return to New York. Hal still spoke of a chicken farm so eloquently that Paul offered to go halves with him. Turned out Paul had raised chickens as a boy on an Iowa farm, so that Hal's plans made more sense than usual. Fred, of course, had ideas for improving 242, this time centered on the sidefinder that he had built for the camera. He even talked of applying for a patent.

"I'd need help drawing it up, and filing the paperwork," he said. "But there's guys I knew in the army who do such things. Engineers."

"I can help you with any drawings," I said.

Conversations ended when we heard the rattling of the dairy truck delivering the day's eggs and milk. Ethel arrived not long after with Mrs Mayhew and a couple of girls who did the Monday laundry and heavy housework. They chased us out of the kitchen with only a few words about the dirty dishes in the sink.

A second round of baths and naps followed, despite Sydney coming downstairs for breakfast and to chide us all for being unprepared for the day's filming. "If you slept normal hours…" he started but Renee stopped him.

"We don't all take powders before we go to bed," she said. "It was an uncomfortable night."

"Storm's coming," said Mrs Mayhew, passing through the dining room to direct some business around the polishing of mirrors. "You could feel it last night. That sticky heat."

"Yes, yes," said Sydney. "I'm sure that was all it was. A long day outdoors and a warm night. If we get some rain, everything will cool down."

"Solstice in a few days," said Mrs Mayhew. "Always brings bad weather. And trouble."

Sydney waved her off. "Nonsense. It's the best day of the year. The most light, the least dark," he said.

"That's why," said Mrs Mayhew. "Dark gets jealous. Tries to grab more than it deserves. It's a bad time to be opening doors. Worse time to be standing in doorways."

Sydney frowned at her and started to say something. But then he turned to Max and began talking about the scene to come, the coffin to trap Lulu.

Mrs Mayhew watched him leave the room with a dissatisfied expression on her face. She looked over the rest of us. Only the women were still lingering at the table.

"Some of you appear to have more sense than others," she said, looking directly at me. I glanced at the others, but they were occupied with letters, newspapers, or just peering with tired eyes into the bottom of their coffee cups.

"Thank you," I said to Mrs Mayhew, when nobody else responded.

"It's not my place to interfere," she said while gathering up the dishes left behind. Like Florie in the diner, she balanced a tray skillfully on one arm with all the plates neatly stacked on it. "It's not my place to gossip."

"Of course not?" I said, still unsure on why she was looking so hard at me and ignoring the others.

"Watch the mirrors," she said. "Count how many doors you see in them."

I glanced through the dining room archway into the long hall. We had moved the long narrow mirrors back into their original places after finishing the ghost portrait scene. One of the mirrors reflected the edge of the table, and Mrs Mayhew looming beside it. Except she wasn't a large woman. Taller than me, as most women were, but not by much. No, there was a larger shadow behind her, someone almost as tall as a man. I turned my head to look down the table, but nobody had moved from their seats and the angle was all wrong for that.

Mrs Mayhew didn't move herself, other than to watch me look over her shoulder, but she gave a little nod. "Sensible. You turn and count noses when you see people in a mirror. Keep noticing. It will help," she said. Then to the room at large, "More coffee?"

A murmur of denials ,but Eleanor asked where she could find more paper for the typewriter. "I've finished almost all that I brought," she said.

"There's probably some in the library," said Mrs Mayhew, "or you can go into town. The stationers would have what you want. If it's just plain and not fancy, the five-and-dime would have it too."

"Let's go to the five-and-dime, darling," said Lulu. "I love a good small-town five-and-dime. There's sure to be something that I need and a half a dozen things that I don't."

Eleanor groaned a little but agreed to a trip. Betsy looked intrigued. I asked if they could fetch some notions for me. "Bits of trim and other things that I could use," I said.

"There's a five-and-dime?" said Fred, wandering back into the room to grab another slice of toast. "I need some wire. Maybe some nails."

"Don't take Fred," I advised the others. "He takes hours in those stores."

While we made plans for shopping, Mrs Mayhew slipped from the room.

After lunch we gathered in the long parlor where we'd filmed the scene with the ghosts. Paul, Hal, and Jim were all rigged out like undertakers with top hats, long black coats, and black gloves. All the outfits were taken from the attic and there was a strong smell of moth powder lingering around them.

Taking advantage of the long windows, Fred and Humbert placed the rigged bed in the center of the room and moved sun reflectors, made out of silvered canvas screens, around it. Lulu arrived in a long pale champagne silk negligee straight from her trunks. She'd brought several. Sydney earlier rejected those with ruffles, fox fur, ostrich feathers, silk fringe, or ribbon flowers. This particular robe was the simplest of her collection, with only a few wide panels of lace for decoration.

"Mind you," said Lulu as we powdered her for the scene, "that lace came from Belgium before the war. They said it was made by nuns."

"I'm sure the sisters will be delighted that their work is in the movies," said Eleanor. "Are you sure about her eyes?"

"Yes," I said, painting a little extra arch onto Lulu's eyebrows. "Sydney wanted them emphasized." As I'd imagined the day before, Lulu looked even frailer, as if she was made out of porcelain, a doll or a corpse. But an exquisite corpse.

Betsy, who loved fiddling with makeup as much as me, took a long look at Lulu. "It's perfect," she pronounced. "She looks unearthly."

"Not too dead," said Lulu.

"No, no," said Betsy. "Just right. You'll match the ghosts from the earlier scene."

We lowered Lulu into her bed and arranged her hair so it became a blonde halo surrounding her. She looked lovely against the linen and lace draped pillows from upstairs. Betsy whispered to me: "What will Mrs Mayhew say?"

"Something unpleasant about making powder stains on the best linen," I responded, "but she's working for Sydney. He can talk to her."

Sydney leaned over Lulu to give her his instructions. "Wake up slowly. You have dreamed of strangers. Of gods in distant cosmos, vast beyond your comprehension, stirring in shadows. And, and… oh damn, what did you write, Eleanor?"

Sydney waved his hand at Eleanor, who handed him a scenario page. Sydney skimmed down it. "Oh yes, here we go. You wake in your comfortable, ordinary bed. You realize that your night terrors are simply dreams. Relieved, you stretch up your hands to pull down the sheet. But you cannot. You are trapped. You are tied to the bed by these simple luxuries that have so comforted you… Max, are those my monogrammed silk sheets?"

Max, who had been conferring with Fred about something, swung around. He glanced at the bed where Lulu was still lying, waiting for us to start. "Yes, Sydney, those are your sheets. You said she's trapped in a bed by the silk sheets. You have the only silk sheets in the house."

"Damn it, Max, what am I to sleep on tonight?" said Sydney. "You'll have to go out and buy more."

"Sydney, we will have to send to New York. Or you can sleep on cotton or linen like the rest of us until these are laundered," said Max. "And do not tell me to hang the expense. The whole point of filming in Arkham was that you could have the atmosphere that you wanted for half the cost of creating it in California. Remember?"

Sydney, who had been halfway through saying "hang the expense," just sighed. "What one sacrifices for art," he said and started to read from the scenario again. "You are trapped. You are tied to the bed by these simple luxuries that have so comforted you. You and the audience slowly realize that the silk sheets and lace pillows do not decorate a simple virginal repose."

Lulu giggled at the last. "Really, Eleanor, simple virginal repose?"

"It was late, my dear," said Eleanor. "And I was longing to get done. One puts in some words to fill the space and hopes to change them later."

"I like it," said Sydney. "Now will you all stop interrupting?"

I heard a muffled laugh from Renee but when I looked over my shoulder, she was innocently sitting in her chair, apparently helping Pola with her knitting. They would have a scene after this one and were partially costumed with towels around their necks to keep their makeup from staining their dress collars.

"Do you think it will take as long as the stair scene?" said Betsy.

"I hope not," I said. "We'll be here all summer at this rate."

Sydney growled and continued on, reading over the whispered conversations floating around the room. I was thankful that there was no Arkham reporter or violinist today to create even more distractions.

"Your silk sheets and lace pillows," bellowed Sydney above all the noise, "are the decorations of a coffin. You realize that you are trapped and about to be buried alive!"

Lulu pursed her mouth. "How can I be buried alive if there's no top to the coffin? Can't they just see me struggling? Oh, and you're not throwing dirt on me. Not this negligee! It's Belgium lace."

Sydney clenched his teeth against his cigarette holder. "You wake up. You look happy. You look distressed. You look terrified. Then the sides and top of the coffin come up and close around you! Can you do that?"

"Of course," said Lulu, snuggling down into the silk sheets. "Just yell when you want me to open my eyes."

"Fred!" said Sydney. "Max. Places. Now, begin!"

Max waved the slate in front of the camera to mark the scene and the take.

Fred cranked steadily. Lulu remained absolutely still, looking beautifully asleep or perhaps even dead. The audience would not know at the beginning of the scene, according to Sydney and Eleanor.

"Now," said Sydney.

Lulu's eyes fluttered open. She allowed herself the faintest of relieved smiles, portraying the sister who had awakened from a disturbing dream to find it *was* only a dream. Then she shrugged one shoulder. Her negligee slipped, revealing a silken strap and bare skin.

"Show off," muttered Betsy as she mimed the same movement with her own shoulder. I was sure I'd see it in one of her future movies. Eleanor shifted to stand beside us to get a clearer view of the action.

Then Paul and Jim shoved on mechanisms that cranked up the coffin sides and lid built by Fred and Humbert. The coffin banged into place around Lulu.

"Thank God that nobody in the audience will hear that," said Eleanor to me. "About as scary as a trunk lid being snapped shut."

"Depends on whether or not you are in the trunk," I said. "What did you do in the theater?"

"Oiled the hinges and had the orchestra play extra loud," said Eleanor.

Fred straightened up from the camera. "Good enough. Take it apart, boys."

Jim and Paul pulled on the lid. Nothing moved.

"Oh hell," said Fred. "It just snaps loose from the side. Twist it."

"It's stuck," said Paul. "Stuck fast."

Muffled banging sounded through the room. Eleanor swore. "She's terrified of small spaces," she said. "We never left her in our box past the curtain banging down."

The banging from the coffin increased in its fury. Appalled for poor Lulu, I joined Fred pulling on the lid.

"Get her out," Eleanor cried. "Oh, please get her out."

I knew how Lulu felt. I once got locked in a closet by another girl at the orphanage. It seemed to last forever, even though Renee tore open the door only minutes later. I glanced up and those horrid mirrors reflected us all banging on what looked like a real coffin.

"Pull!" yelled Fred.

We all pulled. Even with all of us shoving and pushing, the lid of the damn fake coffin stayed firmly shut. The banging inside became more frenzied.

"Lulu, Lulu," yelled Eleanor, "keep still. We'll get you out."

Sydney broke off a discussion with Max about the next shot to wander over. "What's wrong?" he said.

"The coffin won't open," Eleanor panted as she twisted the lid.

Fred left the room running. The frenzied knocking inside the box continued and a wailing shriek rose from within. At least we knew Lulu wasn't suffocating. Fred raced back with a crowbar. He shoved Eleanor to one side and applied it to the coffin lid. Made of cheap wood, it splintered apart. Lulu rose out of the shreds of wood and tangle of silk sheets.

"I am never, ever doing that scene again!" she cried. Tears coursed down her face. Her makeup streaked her cheeks. No movie corpse ever looked more appalling.

And the mirrors reflected it all. Except, as I turned fully to the door, the mirrors were back in the hallway and there was no earthly reason I should see the room so clearly in them.

"Watch my sheets," retorted Sydney. "Don't snag them."

"Damn your sheets. Damn your movie!" Lulu clambered out of the wreck of the coffin and stalked across the room. There were bits of wood in her blonde hair and she'd ripped out at least one seam on the negligee. Eleanor hurried after her.

Sydney eyed the wreck of the coffin bed. "I don't know," he mused. "That has a certain Gothic charm. She wakes in the ruins of a coffin."

"I don't think we can get Lulu back," I said. I looked out the door. I could barely see the edge of the mirror or Lulu's passing as she stalked toward the stairs. The disorientation made me feel strange, as if I had taken a step and missed my footing. That odd fall that happens somewhere between waking and dreaming.

"Renee, darling, come here." Sydney motioned to my sister. "What do you think?"

Renee looked over the ruins of the bed as she would have looked at any set up in any movie. Props did fail, all the time. Walls fell down. Glasses shattered. Actors tripped over footstools. All of this was simply the stuff of an ordinary day of filming. I looked down at my shaking hands. Why was I suddenly convinced of some supernatural malice? It was ridiculous.

Renee discussed possible solutions with Sydney. She shone at this, the ability to quickly adapt a scene and get an extra thrill out of it. "Show one sister going to bed in the coffin and then show another rising from it?" she said.

Sydney nodded. "That's the ticket. Fred, can you cast a shadow across Renee's face to make the suggestion of the mask that is to come?"

Fred nodded and started to shift the curtains and reflecting walls about. Using one lamp, he was able cast a dark shadow across the pillows left disarrayed by Lulu's escape. "Like this?" he asked.

"Very good," said Sydney.

"I need to change," Renee said. "I have a robe that is similar to Lulu's upstairs."

"I'll help," I said and ran up the stairs ahead of Renee to fetch her white robe out of the closet. Once she joined me, I helped her take off her dress and placed the robe over the simple peach slip that she wore.

"No need to change completely into a gown and robe," Renee said. "Especially if Sydney's concentrating on my head and shoulders."

"Do you want to redo your makeup so it's closer to how we did Lulu?" I sorted through the brushes and pots on her traveling case. It opened out in three tiers, with trays stored above and below that were filled with makeup that Renee favored.

As she sat on the stool next to the dressing table, I widened her eyes and drew shadows along her cheekbones. Over Renee's shoulder, I watched us both in the mirror. The reflections looked murky despite the clear summer sunshine streaming through the lace-curtained windows.

"Are you sure about this scene?" I said. My lingering unease bothered me. It was just a failed prop. Horrid for Lulu, but nothing supernatural.

"Of course," Renee said. "More screen time is always good. Sydney and I were talking last night about the relationship of the two sisters, how the audience should see them as two halves of one personality."

"Why?"

"We make it unclear who the monster is until the end. It's all part of this grander plot."

"Have you seen this manuscript? Eleanor keeps complaining that Sydney won't show her the end."

"He hasn't told me everything yet," Renee admitted as I drew the line of her eyebrows to match the arch we gave Lulu. "But it's all about how a very human woman can be transformed into a goddess of shadows, a divine and terrifying creature, that opens the door into another world."

"And what happens to the sister that isn't transformed?"

"She's destroyed," said Renee, turning around on the stool to examine her face and plucking the brush from my hand to add a little more shadow along the line of her left brow.

"But would a sister do that?" I said. "Allow the other to be destroyed." Because sisters protected each other. That was what they do, I wanted to say to her.

"It's just a story." Renee smiled into the mirror. The curtain stirred in the breeze, and the shadows in the mirror moved with it. For a moment, it looked as if someone was peering over her shoulder, looking back at me. But just the two of us were in the room and it was too warm.

"Let's go," I said. "I want to finish this scene today." I wanted done with the horrid scene and all the rest to come.

Lace shadows draped across Renee's face as she turned away from the mirror. I considered a lace mask, a pattern rather than the pale smooth oval that Sydney described. Black lace, like a widow's hat veil, that dissolved to something more eerie. And I would lock the masks in my room back in a trunk in the attic. For some reason, I was starting to hate them, even though the pair, metal and paper, matched Sydney's vision so exactly.

As we descended the stairs, I discussed the possibilities with Renee. If she liked the idea, she could easily sway Sydney into changing his plan for the masked woman. He knew that she had a better eye for the small detail and what suited her characters best.

"Black lace," she mused. "That might work. But, Jeany, it seems so clichéd for one of Sydney's films. A dangerous woman in black lace. I'm sure we can find something more unusual."

"But isn't it all about the glamor?" I said. "Look how Lulu fusses over her lace trimmings. I thought that it should be a half mask, something that leaves your mouth free and visible. Something human that the audience can focus on. That's more intriguing."

"I don't know. Sydney has been so sure that it needs to be a full-face mask. Something about that was what a priestess would wear."

"Are you a priestess? I didn't know that about your character."

Renee half turned on the stairs to look back at me. "Perhaps. You know Sydney. Vague, always so vague. But he said something last night about Camilla being descended from an ancient line of priestesses. Something about the real Saturnin's wife coming from Egypt and bringing that legacy to Arkham."

"That seems unusual," I said and wondered if Florie or Humbert knew about that. They seemed full of gossip about the early history of the Fitzmaurice family. If the wife had been Egyptian rather than French, surely someone would have mentioned it.

"Yes, something about Saturnin finding her in a temple along with a bunch of treasures. That's why he left France for America. As a French Hussar, descendent of nobility, he didn't have a choice. Nobody would have let him come home with such a wife."

"I cannot think he would have been that welcome in New England, either."

Renee descended the staircase with a laugh. "Oh, he probably just told everyone that she was French like him when he got here. Isn't that what America is for? Making up new stories about yourself? It's been going on a lot longer than Hollywood. However, I doubt Sydney got it right. You know him. Probably half the tale is from some Haggard novel that he read and forgot he had."

Perhaps she was right, my clever sister who never forgot anything that she read. Perhaps Sydney had fooled himself into thinking some Haggard story was his family history. As for changing your history to suit your vision of yourself, well, nobody knew more about that than Renee.

Downstairs, we arranged Renee on the bed surrounded by the wreckage of the fake coffin. She was an even more beautiful corpse than Lulu. Suddenly struck by an unreasonable feeling of horror, I wanted to pull her out of the coffin. It was too deathlike. Once again, I nearly made the unpardonable mistake of walking into the shot and ruining the take.

Fred adjusted his beloved camera and peered through the sidefinder. "That shadow is falling all wrong," he complained to Sydney. "I can't see her face at all. It looks like a mess of black snakes."

Sydney also bent to the camera and then straightened up. "No, it's perfect," he said. "She looks as if she is covered in a mask of shadows. Just what I want."

Fred grumbled as he cranked, and every click sounded like a gunshot to me. "Jeany," he said, and I nearly jumped to the ceiling, so concentrated was I on the strange attitude revealed by Renee's pose. "Jeany, would you move that pillow just a little to the left. I still don't think that her face is visible. Sydney, are you sure about this shadow?"

"Yes, yes, of course," said Sydney.

I readjusted the pillow under Renee's head as she smiled up at me. There was something about that smile, with her makeup so heavy upon her cheeks and brow, that made her look even stranger. I tried not to shudder as I fluffed her hair across the pillow in the same manner as Lulu.

Sydney caught a glimpse of her smile and told Renee to hold her face just so.

"That's my Camilla," he cried. "My lady of the shadows and doorways, my key."

The sun sank lower, and longer shadows crept into the room. For June, it felt ice cold. Even Renee began to shiver a bit between takes, despite being nearly buried under silk sheets and lacy pillows.

But Sydney was right. There was something mysterious and enthralling about her pale face surrounded by the ruins of the fake coffin. The black wood, white lace, and Renee's own elegant features blended in the shadows cast by Fred's cleverly placed lights. She appeared as much a ghost, or more, than Betsy and Pola from the first scene. While there was not a suggestion of blood, the entire scene reeked of violent death and resurrection. The fact that it was unclear whether it was a bed or coffin just added to the aura of sin.

This scene alone would earn Sydney his usual title of "king of terror."

Max certainly noted it. After the fifth take, he pulled Sydney aside to ask how long he intended to film Renee in bed and how much time that would take up on the screen in the finished film. "The ladies in Peoria won't like it," said Max.

"But everyone else will," said Sydney. "They don't pay for pictures that are sweet and safe. They pay to be enthralled. To have their emotions twisted about. A lovely lady, dressed for bed and surrounded by death, that sells. You know that, Max. The studio will tell Hays that everyone is clothed and we're really teaching morality to the kiddies by equating sex with destruction."

For the last three years, various church groups protested any theater that allowed young children to watch movies, especially those that were immoral – and what suggested immorality to those critics seemed to be everything that occurred in films, especially films like we made. There'd been testimony in Washington, DC, before Congress when one preacher had professed to watching hundreds of hours of films, documenting carefully each time a suggestive look or flash of skin occurred. The result had been a stunning stack of paper, thumped on the legislative desks. Now William Hays was out in Hollywood, promising to help the studios keep their pictures clean, but nobody quite knew what that meant. And everyone in the business knew that the movie producers and theater owners, not Congress or some church group, paid Hays a handsome salary.

Max muttered that if we kept on filming a girl on a bed, wearing nothing but her negligee, we'd get banned by at least one bishop.

"Banned by the bishop," Sydney chortled. "That's money in the bank, guaranteed."

Renee spoke up from the bed, "If you don't want me to really fall asleep, let's finish this scene. I've done horror, delight, desire, and panic. What next, Sydney?"

Sydney looked down at her. The shadows created by Fred's rearrangement of the curtains and lamps fell in stripes across her face. Some window left slightly ajar created a draft, and shadows stirred like snakes crawling across the bed.

"Utter stillness," said Sydney. "Eyes wide open but staring into the nothing that comes from the end of dreams. That moment when the dreamer begins to fall forward into the abyss."

Fred cranked the camera. The ordinary, simple sound of the whirring click of the film advancing echoed through the room like the beat of a funeral drum.

Suddenly I hated this scene more than anything that we had done. It reminded me of those horrible days after our mother died, when people came and went in our rooms, discussing how to organize our lives without giving us any voice in the matter. I clasped my hands around my arms and shook in my corner. I shivered so violently from the sudden invasion of memories that it was all I could do to keep from running forward and pulling my sister from that horrid bed. With each turn of the camera's crank, the cold increased, and my dread roared through my body like a fever.

I almost moaned with relief when Sydney finally called a halt for the day.

"Now for the woods," Sydney declared with satisfaction.

"What happens in the woods?" I asked Eleanor later that night.

She was scribbling on the scenario, sitting at the small table at the back of the parlor, while the others played cards and argued about their bets. As usual, Betsy was intent on winning all their spare cash.

"Dog bites man," said Eleanor.

"What?" I was distracted by watching Betsy flirt with Max and take the pot from Paul.

"I was reading one of Sydney's occult books, Anubis and all that. I had the clearest vision of a dog-headed creature carrying off a man at the command of a priestess. Only we will make it more vague, more horrifying than that."

I turned back to Eleanor. "We haven't made any costumes for a dog man. Would Jim play that role?" We had made a wolf's head once. Sydney hadn't liked it.

"No, it will be more subtle than that. The dog man will be a creature of shadow, never fully seen." Eleanor wrote this down as she said it. "Besides, I cannot wait to be out of this house."

"It can be harder, filming outdoors," I said, thinking of the problems that we had with seagulls during the *Siren* picture.

"Better than in this house," said Eleanor. "It's always so cold. I know many people don't like New York in the summer, but I love the heat. Even the smell. It just feels like life. This place is cold as…"

"As a tomb," I said. Eleanor stared at me and then nodded.

I looked through the door of the parlor. It shouldn't have been possible, but I saw Eleanor and myself reflected in a mirror. We both looked pale, with exaggerated eyes and mouth, like ghouls or ghosts.

I turned away, arguing with myself that this was just a trick of reflections, the flickering electric light.

When I looked again, there was nothing there. No mirrors were visible from this angle. None at all.

Two days later, we lugged all the equipment across the lawn and into the woods. Finally Paul Kopp had a part to play, a hobo who surprised the sisters as they walked on a wooded path. As Eleanor explained it, this character would at first be menacing as he begs for work upon the sisters' estate and then menaced by an unseen threat. Later the sisters would chance upon the hobo's bloodied and shredded coat blocking the garden gate.

Of course, that scenario meant we needed two coats. One for Paul to wear and one that was probably destroyed. The night before I asked Eleanor how the destroyed coat should look.

"Oh, like a wild animal attack," she said as she scribbled more details on the scenario for Sydney. "Something large and vicious with claws that snatch and teeth that bite. It's my jabberwock of a scene."

A search through one of the downstairs closets had turned up a number of dark men's coats of an age to have belonged to Sydney's grandfather. Men's coats being men's coats, there were two black coats of a similar cut. One I roughed up with an old metal file that I found amid Humbert's tools in the barn. That made it look like our tramp had been sleeping rough. As for the other, I stared at it for a long time, thinking about how an animal might attack a man. Would it come from behind, catching at his back and shoulders? Would it attack him from the front, ripping down a lapel and biting through the coat to his heart? How would the blood seep through the coat? Could I even make the blood show on the dark cloth?

When Fred wandered into the barn in search of a screwdriver or a wrench from some adjustment to the camera's tripod, I posed the questions to him. Being Fred, he gave it serious and careful consideration.

"Paul's a large man," he said. "So it would have to be a brave beast to attack from the front. Or one that was trapped and had no way out. I saw a bear maul a man because it could not escape."

"They had bears in Brooklyn?"

"Montana. I stopped on my way west, working on a ranch before I decided that cows were dumber than a kid from Flatbush."

"Your rail-hopping days?"

"Yes. Thought I'd take a peek or two at how the cowboys live. Didn't like it and kept going west."

"So, back to the bear mauling," I said, thinking that might be the size of creature that Eleanor had in mind. "How did the cowboy look after it was done?"

"Like a mess."

"And his clothes?"

"Not good. Not that anybody noticed. You tend to look at the blood and body bits."

I gagged slightly, but persisted. "If the coat is crumpled on the ground, could the camera pick up that it is torn?"

Fred squinted at the coat. "Not really. Maybe we should drape it over a bush?"

"Would a bear leave a man's coat draped over a bush?"

"Sydney's pictures aren't always realistic," Fred pointed out.

"It doesn't seem like a torn coat would scare the audience." I circled round and round the coat, throwing it in different heaps about the ground and then picking it up and shaking it out.

"Maybe that's what they could do?" said Fred. "Perhaps we could shred the coat and tumble it in a heap on the ground in front of the gate. The ladies can pick it up, revealing that it's been cut into pieces."

"A look of horror on their faces," I said, slowly because I was thinking it through. "Then Renee holds out her hand and we see blood dripping off it. Blood from the coat. That works and will be easier to show than stains upon the cloth itself."

Fred nodded. "What will you use for the blood?"

"There's syrup and lard in the pantry. I can mix something together that looks thick and drips slowly. Renee will hate getting it all over her hand."

"We all suffer for art, according to Sydney," said Fred. Rummaging through the tools, he pulled out the head of an old garden rake. "You can use this for claws."

We draped the coat over a couple of crates that we found in the back of the barn. With file and rake, we attacked the coat, mimicking the catching of claws and the chewing of teeth. By the time we were done, the front of the coat hung in long shreds. We agreed that any tramp wearing it would be dead.

"Of course, it doesn't really explain why the coat ended up in one place and the tramp's body disappeared," said Fred.

"Let's hope the audience doesn't think that hard," I said. "Maybe we'll show Paul's body later on."

Humbert came into the barn to collect some clippers for trimming the hedge. He shook his head at my two coats and muttered about the waste of good clothing. "It's art," I said, but Humbert muttered all the more.

Fred made the adjustments that he wanted to the tripod. We hauled all the gear down to the far end of the garden, where a wooded gate opened into a small copse. The path was badly overgrown. When Lulu and Renee arrived, they both eyed the walk with trepidation.

"That will be murder on my stockings," said Lulu, pointing out with one toe and displaying an ankle nicely draped in silk.

"Could we film the scene upon the lawn?" Renee asked. "The tramp could lean over the gate and call to the sisters."

"No," said Sydney. He looked down at the pages clutched in his hand. "Eleanor's scene takes place in the woods. To the woods we go."

Eleanor frowned. "The setting isn't all that important. They could be standing at the gate."

"You wrote that they encounter a mysterious man upon a wooded path," said Sydney. "That is what we are going to do."

"Sydney," said Max. "Is it that important?"

"I think it must be," said Sydney. "Max, things are stirring. But not enough. We need more now. Especially if we are to make the studio happy."

Max nodded. "Very well. Ladies, if you would." He swung open the gate and gestured to the path. "Let's let Sydney direct as he wishes."

"If I snag my dress or Lulu ruins her stockings, the studio pays for them," said Renee, a threat that could often cow Max, with his careful accounting of every penny spent. But this time he just shook his head and gestured at the path. With a sigh she led our small troop into the woods.

It was a little wooded plot, sandwiched between high hedges and fences of the French Hill estates. Back in Arkham's early days, there had been a smaller house on the property, according to Sydney, but it disappeared. An odd word choice, I thought. "How can a house disappear?" I asked Sydney as we walked into the woods.

"Oh it burned, like the big house," he said. "And the trees grew up around it. Trees like fire. Now it is a nice mix of pine, maple, oak, and hemlock. Mostly hemlock, according to my grandfather."

"Isn't hemlock a poison?" said Lulu.

"It's a poisonous wood," echoed Eleanor, pulling a shoe out of a muddy patch of ground. "Ugh, look at my shoe. And listen to those insects. What a noise."

"A poisonous wood," chuckled Sydney. "That's perfect. We'll have to put it on the title card. Nobody could quite agree on who owns this land and the pond in the center. My grandfather said that one summer the nearby houses stocked the pond with fish for the amusement of small boys with poles. It was considered safer than fishing in the Miskatonic River. But the fish died. Now most of the estates keep their woods gates locked."

The crows flew from branch to branch, following us through the hemlock, the muttered cawing rising above the insects' drone like old men grumbling over our heads.

"When I was a boy," Sydney recalled, walking down the path, "I was often the only one playing in these woods. There used to be frogs there too. I'd catch them and put them in a jar. My grandfather said that they cut ice out of the pond in the winter and stored it in an ice house at the bottom of the garden. That's all gone now."

By the time I reached the pond, I felt unbearably hot and sticky. The woods exuded a moist heat that itched under my shirt and damped my collar. No birds sang in these woods but the odd hoot or caw continued as Fred set up the camera. Louder and more persistent was a humming buzz, more like flies around rotting garbage than bees. I kept expecting stinging insects, but none appeared. Just the horrible whining buzz that rose from all around the edge of the murky, weed-choked pond.

Sydney told Paul to emerge from the bushes at the edge of the pond, startling Renee and Lulu on the path. With much muttering, Paul pushed his way into the center of one large and prickly looking bush.

Fred set his beloved Bell and Howell number 242 in the center of the path. The sun filtering through the trees glinted on the camera's black enamel case. The adjustments that he made earlier to the Akeley tripod made him grunt with satisfaction. The Akeley GYRO head proceeded to pan and tilt as Fred cranked the camera. The resulting film, as we'd learned from prior shoots, would give the audience a disorienting view of the sisters as they proceeded to the pond. Despite Fred's usual application of care and grease, the gears whined louder than ever before, nearly drowning out all the other noises in the wood.

Paul crashed onto the path, forcing Renee and Lulu back toward the camera. With a dirty face and ragged coat, he made a fine figure of menace. The pair shrank toward each other as Paul held out a hand covered with a greasy, fingerless glove. My touch to his makeshift character. I remembered a drunk coming up to me one night as I got off the streetcar and headed to my apartment. He'd been a harmless old man, well known in the neighborhood for drinking bathtub gin and then begging a dime for coffee and a little something to eat. But that night, with his fingers bared by a torn glove, he'd startled me. I'd almost run away, but then Renee had come up behind me and spoken to him very gently, digging a quarter out of her purse and pressing it into his dirty hand. I'd been so proud of my sister then. Her kindness was well known throughout the movie community. She never turned down anyone who truly needed help.

I wondered if she remembered that night. Once again, as Lulu shrank away, Renee pressed forward, grasping Paul's dirty hand in her own. This time, and much against her real character, Eleanor's scenario called for Renee to throw Paul's hand aside and threaten to call the dogs if he bothered them again. Paul started forward as if to strike her. Lulu shrank back further, having established that the younger sister feared the world more than the elder. Renee flung out an arm in an imperious gesture, and Paul turned aside, now shrinking away from her.

"That's it," directed Sydney, "go back around the pond as if heading away toward town. The sisters turn back to their house but pause. They hear the sound of real dogs hunting in the distance. A sacrifice in blood about to happen. A way to open. Cut!"

"Now how will they know that?" said Max.

"Know what?" said Sydney, frowning at the bush bent by Paul's struggle to climb back into it.

"Know a blood sacrifice opens the way? Oh and dogs barking," Max said, with more emphasis on the former and the latter – canine howling – sounding like an afterthought.

"Title card," said Sydney. "And instructions on the score for the dog howl. I did tell you that we had to have a score made to send to all the theaters."

"Yes," said Max, a little reluctantly. "But the studio is wondering if that expense is necessary."

"Of course it is necessary," said Sydney. "Everything is necessary. If the studio wants results, if the studio wants *worldwide* results, we need a score to go with the film. That's crucial. It's all in the manuscript. The importance of music as the masked stranger descended into the darkness. How it called forth the shadows."

Eleanor had been standing with Lulu, discussing the scene and possible modifications to her reactions. Upon hearing Sydney's comments, she turned around.

"What are you talking about?" she said.

"The ending. How important it is that everything leading to the ending be as outlined in my grandfather's manuscript."

"About that manuscript…" began Eleanor.

"Your scenarios are marvelous," said Sydney, talking over her. "Just the right touch of foreboding. Paul, get further back into that bush. I want to try your approach to the sisters again. Come onto the path a little faster."

"Sydney, that bush is sticking to my coat," complained Paul as he repositioned himself. "I don't think I can escape any faster."

"Try," said Sydney with no sympathy at all.

Paul did multiple lunges out of the bush as Fred cranked the camera. Then they moved further down the path to show Paul stumbling away from the sisters portrayed by Renee and Lulu. Finally Sydney declared himself satisfied.

We walked up the path to the gate. I pulled the bloodied and ripped jacket out of my basket. I draped it across a bush for the first pass at the scene.

Renee and Lulu walked up to it, hesitated, and then recoiled from the discovery.

"No," said Sydney. "That's too tame. Try again, but with more terror upon seeing this evidence of a terrible accident, a mauling by a wild animal."

Three more attempts left Sydney as dissatisfied as the first try. I couldn't blame him. I had already suffered the same doubts. The unexpected discovery of blood was terrifying. It was just difficult to show. At least in a way that would make some type of horrid sense to the audience.

"Perhaps we should move the jacket?" I said. "Have it across the path so it blocks the gate. Renee or Lulu could pick it up to make it clear that it is ripped."

I explained my idea of dripping blood, but without much hope. Renee, predictably, protested getting her hand smeared with a sticky mixture. "Besides, we've done that before. At least twice," she said to Sydney. "Let's be different this time."

I couldn't disagree. I hadn't liked the idea much and I liked it less the longer we stood in the woods. Splashing blood about, even fake blood, seemed like a very bad idea.

Oddly, Sydney agreed, although not necessarily from the same trepidation that the idea gave me. "Just splattering gore about, that sounds like a Tod Browning film, not a Sydney Fitzmaurice," he said. "Just act as if you see blood. We don't need to show it to the audience."

They tried again, but Sydney waved them back down the path. "That's not right either. Put it on the gate itself."

"Why would it be on the gate?" asked Renee. "What animal would leave it in such a place?"

"Push the back against the gate, as if the man backed up against it. That he was literally ripped apart just steps from safety," Sydney said with satisfaction.

After that, I affixed the jacket to the gate by slinging it over my shoulders, pushing back against the gate as if something was charging up the path at me. Something so terrible that I would rather turn and face it than fumble with the lock. The wood gate scraped against my back. I felt the rough wool coat catch on the boards of the gate. Turning, I shoved the material so it truly caught on the top of the gate. Pulling away, it looked like a sad empty scarecrow dangling in front of us.

Once again Renee and Lulu approached the now filthy coat. They recoiled from it as if the tramp himself stood in front of them.

"That's it," Sydney said. "As if you stand accused of the man's murder, as if your banishment led to his doom," he continued, reciting from Eleanor's scenario.

Renee stood proudly, as if the man's fate failed to move her, while Lulu cringed away from the gate.

"Cut! Perfect. My vision exactly," said Sydney.

Both Renee and Lulu slumped a little. The buzzing in the woods sounded louder and more angry than before. With some relief, I pulled open the gate into the garden. I couldn't wait to leave the woods. For once, I wanted to return to the house. At least there were no insects there.

A large brown dog came charging up the path, with a man following after him shouting: "Duke, Duke, come back here, you mutt."

The man behind the dog was a scruffy sort, dressed in an old worn suit and battered hat. Over one shoulder he had slung a guitar.

We all started to see a real tramp appear in the woods.

"Hello," he said, upon spotting us. "Didn't mean to scare you."

With the rest dumb with surprise, I stepped forward and held out my hand. "Hello, I'm Jeany."

"Pete," said the man. "And this here is Duke. He's a good dog, don't let his looks fool you."

Eleanor followed my lead. She shook Pete's hand and patted Duke on the head. "He looks like a very good dog indeed," she said, with that croon that true dog lovers get in their voices. It did go a long way to explaining why, for all her jibes to the contrary, Eleanor was nearly always the person who walked Pumpkin and made sure that the pug was fed.

Pete looked over our heads at Sydney. "I heard you were back, Mr Fitzmaurice," he said. "Didn't expect to see you in the woods."

"I'm surprised to see you still wandering around Arkham," said Sydney. "How are you doing, Ashcan Pete?"

The man shrugged. "Well enough. Always something to do, something to see in Arkham. Duke was just certain there was something new on this path. Guess he was right."

Duke was sniffing around the gateposts and the ruined coat that still swung from one corner of the wooden gate. The dog let loose a howling bark, which made me start. The dog's deep baying sparked off the cawing and rustling of wings in the trees above us, the ever-present crows of French Hill.

"Oh hush, Duke," said the tramp called Ashcan Pete. "Nothing here at all."

Max stepped forward to shoo the dog away from the coat, trying to drive Duke off with a flapping of his hands that just made the hound wrinkle its brow at him.

"Oh, for goodness sake," muttered Eleanor, stepping around Max. "Duke, go with your master. Go on. Go home!" The last was said with a firm emphasis on home.

Pete chuckled to see the dog retreat from Eleanor's onslaught. "That's right, tell him straight. Can't shillyshally with that dog. Come here, Duke. Come here, now."

With a whine, the big dog backed away from the coat and followed his master down the path. Above them the crows kept up a raucous cawing.

Sydney frowned after the pair as they wandered off. "I wonder how he got in here," he said. "The woods are fenced all the way around. He must have cut across the back of one of the other estates."

"Does it matter?" said Renee. "Are you satisfied yet?"

"No, it needs something else," Sydney said. "Something more."

Eleanor gave the birds in the trees an unhappy look. The cawing was so loud that it drowned out the buzzing in the bushes. "Maybe they could be attacked by crows?"

"No!" cried Lulu. "Eleanor, this is a Paris coat. I'm not getting bird mess all over it."

Sydney nodded. "That's an idea. Fred, how can we stage that? Max?"

"Perhaps one of the guns from the house?" Max said. "You could fire it off. That will scare them out of the trees and Fred could film them flapping around."

Renee frowned. "And we can wait inside while you do it. I agree with Lulu. I do not want to be cleaning bird mess out of my hair."

She rarely spoke so forcefully with Sydney, but I knew that she did not want to see Sydney kill one of the crows with this silly trick. Dead animals always upset her.

"We can scare them into flying about, and do it without any birds getting hurt," said Fred. He too had caught the distress in Renee's voice and knew how much she hated to see animals suffer. Once, back in Hollywood, he had helped me find a good home for a canary given to Renee by an admirer. She loathed caged birds, but we couldn't just set it free as she demanded. The poor thing had had its wings clipped, something that I didn't tell Renee. Instead, Fred found a very nice old lady who lived in a little house across the street from him and had always wanted a canary to brighten up her living room.

Fred adjusted the camera so it was pointing nearly straight up into the trees where the restless crows paced back and forth on low branches, ruffling their wings and croaking at us. "Use the shotgun but fire away from the trees and don't hit any of them. We don't want dead birds raining down in the shot."

Renee winced, and Sydney looked thoughtful. "Well, one or two…" he began and then stopped at a glare from Renee.

"If we tossed some bread or other food on the path…" I said, hoping to hurry the scene along. I wanted out of those woods. "…we can lure the crows down. Then scare them into taking off. Like pigeons in the park. Less dangerous than firing off a gun, anyway." I pushed for a decision. Sydney was capable of standing around all day, and the woods were closing in on me like Lulu being trapped in the coffin.

Fred agreed with me. "You could flap that coat at them."

Max went up to the kitchen and brought back a couple of stale loaves. The crows didn't seem to care for the bread, keeping up their cawing and ignoring our efforts to coax them. So Max trudged back up to the house and returned with aging sausages that somebody had bought for lunches but nobody liked. The smelly, bloody meat brought the crows out of the trees to battle over the bits. Fred cranked the camera, capturing the vicious fighting over the sausages, which Sydney pointed out could be taken for actual human fingers.

"Hays will certainly censure us if we say that," I said, feeling slightly queasy. Sydney was right. It did look like the crows were tearing something living apart.

"We do not have to title it that," Sydney said. "Just drop some hints to a few reporters about the scene where the crows dismember a dead body. Of course if anyone asks directly, we just say we did some wildlife filming of birds eating stale bread and old sausages."

But when I flapped the coat at the quarreling crows, the contrary birds simply hopped or skipped out of my way without taking to the air. Now the birds decided the bread was to their liking and the trees were a boring place to be.

After a couple more unsuccessful tries, I turned to Sydney. "Now what?"

"Rock salt," said Sydney. "We can get some from the kitchen and load the shotgun with it. It will make a bang and a sting, but no dead birds. That should get them back in the air."

"You don't need us to film this," said Renee, who already retreated halfway up the lawn with Eleanor and Lulu. "I'm going back to my room."

"I'll walk up to the house with you," said Max, "and bring back the gun."

Lulu and Eleanor decided to take their car for a drive, since Sydney's efforts to direct crows seemed likely to account for the rest of the day. The pair strolled around the corner of the house, heading to the barn where they stored their car next to the touring automobile that Sydney had leased.

"Well, at least you have not deserted me," said Sydney to Fred and myself. And somehow, I could not leave, much as I hated this little patch of hot, muggy woods. I felt like I was stuck trying to get this right. As if something had to happen now so we could resolve the rest of the film.

Max brought back a shotgun which Sydney loaded with rock salt. "Step away, Max," Sydney said as he took aim at the crows. Max and I sheltered behind the gate. Fred started cranking. Sydney let off the shotgun. There was a tremendous bang and an even greater cry of outrage as the crows took to the air in a black cloud.

Then the cloud turned in midair and began a murderous dive toward Sydney. With a shout, he dropped the shotgun and lit out for the house, running ahead of pecking, clawing birds. Max plunged after him.

Fred swung the camera to follow them, still cranking and muttering a great deal. I ducked behind Fred, but the birds showed no interest in us. We apparently had earned some protection by being the dispensers of bread and sausages, while Sydney had been the god of rock salt and noise. Max should have stayed with us.

Sydney and Max reached the kitchen door and plunged through it. It closed with a great bang. The cloud of crows flew straight up in the air, wheeled a few more times around the chimneys, and then settled down on the roof. We could hear their discontented croaks from across the lawn.

Fred cranked a few more feet of film and then stopped. "That will work," he said with quiet satisfaction. "We can splice that into the beginning, a great ominous cloud of birds flying around the top of the house."

I thought about how it would appear on the screen. "But it could be even better," I said. "if we splice scenes of the crows throughout the film."

"Every time the sisters venture out of doors, we show the crows watching them," said Fred.

"And peering through the windows at them," I said.

"The audience will be terrified of birds by the time they leave the theater," Fred chuckled.

I grinned. It was a great idea, better even than Eleanor's scenario or one of Renee's little edits. One of those touches that made a Fitzmaurice film famous. I suddenly felt a bit more charitable about being stuck in the woods. But not enough to stay any longer.

The crows continued to pace across the rooftop, muttering and watching us.

"They carry the souls of the dead," said a voice behind us.

I gasped and whirled around. Humbert was standing by the gate with a rake over his shoulder.

"Heard Mr Sydney firing at them," said Humbert. "He used to do that as a boy. Take the gun into the woods and pester the crows. Then run back into the house. One time, they caught him. Down there in the woods. Pecked him bloody. Had to call the doctor for stitches and all. Bet he remembers that."

"He didn't seem to worry today," I said, watching the crows finally fly away from the roof and toward town. Off on their own crow business.

"Crows remember," said Humbert. "Crows have long memories. Better than bees, says my aunt. Comes from carrying ghosts around in their beaks."

"Ghosts in their beaks?" I said. I hadn't heard that one. Although I recalled Sydney talking often enough about birds being guides to the realms of the dead. "Psychopomps," I remembered suddenly. "Eagles, cranes, owls, ravens, and crows. Sydney bringing back those weird feather bits and saying they prevent hauntings."

"Yeah, Jeany, all those feathers for *Death is a Woman*," said Fred.

"Plumed hats," I said, remembering how Sydney had wanted us to place different types of feathers in Renee's hats. He bought a stuffed owl for the set, because it was supposed to represent some goddess. Renee had hated that dead bird. "And we couldn't find a crane feather, so we used an egret. So Sydney was furious, although nobody would know the difference."

Humbert watched us with his usual dour expression, but his tone was mild when he added. "Don't know nothing about pomp birds. But crows fetch ghosts out of a house, says my aunt. If you let them. Nobody ever let them into that house. That's why the crows are always so mad at the Fitzmaurices."

With that pronouncement, Humbert ambled away, off to do something with the garden.

I waited for Fred to break apart the camera and tripod, and then took the tripod from him. We started toward the house, discussing Sydney's odder beliefs when it came to beaks and feathers. We were almost at the house when Fred looked over his shoulder and said, "But where's Paul?"

CHAPTER FOURTEEN

We searched for the rest of the evening. It started simply. Walking up to the house, looking casually for Paul, certain that he had slipped by us and returned to his room while we were messing with the crows. But we could not find him.

After dinner, with still no sign of Paul, everyone grew a little more worried. Except Sydney, who said that Paul must have wandered off somewhere for a smoke and would turn up soon. Max kept looking at Sydney in the strangest way, but mumbling that he must be right. After all, what could happen to a man on a warm summer afternoon in a neighborhood like French Hill?

The days were getting longer, and it was still very light in the early evening. Fred and I decided to search back in the woods. "Maybe he fell?" I said as we walked, remembering that movie shoot where we broke the actor's leg and had to ride down the mountain with him. Of course, there we saw him fall. But perhaps it was something like that.

"Or he walked out at a different place. It can't be just the one gate at the Fitzmaurice house," said Fred. "That tramp. The one with the dog. He didn't come through the gate, he was already in the woods when we got there."

"Of course," I said, very relieved. "There's probably another gate or break in the hedges, and Paul went out that way. Only…" Only it wouldn't have been more than a mile in any direction to get back to the Fitzmaurice house. So where had Paul gone?

Fred pushed open the gate at the end of the garden. We walked through it into the hot, sticky woods. The crows were settled on the branches above us now, and the hideous insect buzzing was louder than before.

"Only what, Jeany?" said Fred.

"It's not a very big woods," I said as we walked through the green shadows cast by the trees. "Even if he walked all the way to the far end."

"Maybe he didn't feel like coming back to the house," Fred said, ambling along beside me. His hands were thrust deep in his pockets and his cap was pushed all the way on his head. By the clinking sounds he made, I knew Fred was fidgeting with something in his pockets, probably some bolts and nuts or loose coins. He always did that when he was worried.

"Nothing has gone right on this shoot," I said, which was probably what we were both thinking at that moment.

"No more a disaster than usual," said Fred. "Stuff happens, Jeany. Nothing ever works as smooth as we like."

It was true. And it wasn't. Effects did go wrong all the time. But we didn't all wake from screaming nightmares at the same time. People didn't break legs from props that flew off the wall or get boxed into coffins.

"It feels like we're cursed," I said, and I wasn't joking.

We reached the pond. It looked as dismal as it had before. More so with the shadows creeping around the ends as the sun went down. The water was murky brown with dead leaves floating on top of it. The tangle of weeds on the edge was rimmed with a green slime as the roots trailed into the water.

"Think little Sydney really went fishing here?" said Fred, picking up a pebble and tossing it into the pond. It landed with a deadened plop, and few sullen ripples spread out across the water.

"What would you do with anything you caught in that?" I said.

"Knowing Sydney, he stuffed any fish and mounted them on the wall."

I smiled. "I'm not sure that you can do that with a fish. Besides, he said all the fish died."

Fred poked around the weeds a bit, scuffing at them with his shoe. Neither of us felt like touching any of the plants growing in this dank little wood.

"There's another path here," said Fred as he walked around the bush in which Paul reluctantly hid earlier.

"Where does it go?" I said.

"Not back to the house. Looks like it heads to a different part of the woods. Probably where that guy with the dog went."

"Ashcan Pete," I said. "His name was Pete and the dog was Duke." I circled round the bush to the spot where Fred stood. I saw a thin little path leading through the trees. As we went along it, I started to see paw prints in the damp earth. Pete and his friend had passed this way.

"How can the woods be so wet?" I said to Fred. "It hasn't rained for days."

"Underground springs?" he suggested. "The water for the pond has to come from somewhere."

"But it's at the top of a hill," I said. "Doesn't water run downhill? Why does it collect here?"

"Jeany, I'm from Brooklyn. What do I know about nature?"

"Didn't you spend time with cowboys out west?"

"Only long enough to know that I didn't like cows." Fred stopped. We'd reached a place where the path widened into almost a circle of trees and a bare patch of ground. A few bare stones poked through the tangle of tree roots and weeds.

"Wasn't there supposed to be a house in these woods?" said Fred. "One that burned down."

"They have a lot of fires in Arkham," I said, considering the tales of how the Fitzmaurice house also had burned down and been rebuilt by Sydney's ancestors.

"Like anyone from San Francisco can talk about fires."

"Oakland. It's not the same," I said.

I wandered around the bare outline of walls that no longer existed.

"Looks more like a hut to me," I said as I traced that square. It was tinier than our first apartment in Los Angeles. "Must have been one room only." A large pile of rough-cut stones lay at one end. "Chimney? Fireplace?"

Fred shrugged. "Maybe. There's more paw prints here."

There were. Circles of overlapping prints, huge and splayed broader than my outstretched hand, with deep gouges in the dirt as if the dog had dug around the base of these ruins. Huge gouges really.

"How big was Pete's dog?" I said.

Fred was poking around the other end of the clearing. "Huh? Dog-sized. Not a little thing like that pug of Lulu's."

The paw prints, the claw marks, looked bigger to me than any normal-sized dog. Almost the size of a man's foot or hands. Some of the gouges in the dirt seemed different. Those looked like the mark of a man's hands, a man who had been digging his fingers deep into the muddy earth to try to avoid being dragged by something. I remembered in one of Sydney's movies that we made marks like that in the dirt, to indicate that the hero had been carried off by the ghoul that stalked him.

"Fred," I said, backing away from the edge of the house. My palms felt sweaty and my voice sounded harsher than normal. "Did you come down here today?"

He walked back to where I stood. "No. I don't think anyone went further than the pond."

"Sydney didn't ask Paul to set something else up for filming. Like a man being dragged away by dogs?" Sydney had that habit of asking anyone who was nearby to do a task, whether or not they usually did that. He might have drafted Paul into setting a scene for later shooting. I hoped he had done that.

Fred shook his head. "Eleanor talked about showing the tramp being dragged off by a giant dog. It was in one of her scenarios. Sydney liked it but Max said that it would be too expensive to hire a dog. You'd need a trained animal to do that. Something like Duncan's Rin Tin Tin."

I'd heard Warner Brothers was filming a movie with Lee Duncan's big German Shepherd as the star. Sydney had been very dismissive of it. "Why would people want to watch a dog run around in a film?" he had asked. "It's only interesting if the dog attacks people. That might be worth it. Friendly family dog turns mad wolf and terrorizes town."

"So no faking up some dog paw prints?" I asked Fred. "So Sydney could have his dog bites man to death scene?" I pointed out the prints that I'd spotted. Fred frowned at the marks, also measuring them against his hands. When he straightened up, he looked as green as I felt.

"Sydney liked the whole idea with the sisters just discovering the bloody coat," Fred repeated, but I couldn't tell if he was trying to reassure me or himself. "He thought it worked better."

"Sydney kept talking about a blood sacrifice too," I pointed out, even though I wished I hadn't remembered that.

Stepping gingerly around the pawprints, we found where the path continued to spiral amid the trees. By then we should have reached the far edge of the woods, but the path twisted and turned so much that I could not tell where we were. I knew that the other houses of French Hill were only moments away, just hidden by the heavy growth. Hemlock, Sydney had said, the woods were full of hemlock. Full of poison.

"What's that?" said Fred.

Something was hanging from a tree branch high above our heads. It looked familiar. Getting closer I could see it was a man's coat, shredded and torn and draped across a high branch. A coat very much like its twin, the coat that I had left behind us with Fred's camera equipment. This one, this coat, would be the one that Paul had been wearing when he disappeared. The base of the tree seemed deeply gouged with claw marks.

I clutched Fred's arm. "Do you think?"

He looked wide-eyed at me. "Can't be. It's broad daylight. There's houses all around. A man won't be eaten by a mad dog in the middle of a neighborhood wood. A dog could never drag him into a tree. That's something cats do. Like lions in that film."

I remembered that film. I'd gone with Fred because a woman had shot much of the footage with her husband and, besides, I wanted to see a real lion in Africa. Not some sad old circus cat stuffed and mounted in Sydney's study. Fred had gone because the filmmakers had their camera eaten by bugs and that, according to Fred, had led to the invention of his beloved metal monster.

"No, of course not, there's nothing in New England that would drag a man into the trees," I said. "Except Eleanor said it would be a dog man who would kill the tramp."

A man savaged by a dog-headed man, a beast that could climb a tree like a lion. Except that was just a silly idea of Eleanor's. Just an idea to scare the audiences after we turned it into silver light and shadows on the screens of their movie theaters. It wasn't real. But the mound of black cloth hanging off that tree branch looked exactly like Paul's coat.

"It was probably thrown up there by children. Someone playing pirates," I said, even though I remembered what Sydney said about all the other houses locking their gates into the woods and forbidding their children to play here. I walked forward to check closer. To prove that it was not the coat that I had refitted to Paul's broader frame just a few hours earlier.

That's when I stepped into the pool of blood.

I knew it was blood as soon as it soaked into my shoe. The thick, sticky quality of the liquid, not like water, and how it stained the leather. We went to a slaughterhouse once, Fred and I, just to see how blood spattered and pooled in dirt. We went because Sydney said that the blood we were splashing around on a set didn't look real enough. So we looked at real blood in a variety of places. We went to a morgue and talked to a coroner about how blood looked at a crime scene. We knew a lot about blood, probably too much.

I screamed and backed out of the pool. Fred came running to me.

"Jeany, what is it?" he said.

I scraped my shoe against a stone, again and again, trying to wipe it clean. "It's blood," I whispered, not willing to say it too loudly. I don't know why. Maybe because I was afraid of attracting the attention of whatever spilled that blood in the first place.

"Can't be," said Fred. But he leaned over the pool of liquid and tapped it with one finger. He recoiled. Pulling a handkerchief out of his pocket, he wiped the liquid off his finger. It left the rusty brown stain of congealing blood on the cloth.

Fred looked at me. I stared back at him. Neither of us willing to say what we were thinking.

Finally I said, "It's probably an animal." Although I did not believe that.

Fred said, "Dog, maybe? Dog fight, couple of pets that ran off home afterward."

Neither of us sounded convinced.

Then a bark sounded, the bark of a big dog, and a man's whistle answered. Fred and I stepped closer together and turned to face whatever was coming.

Duke charged into the clearing only to stop at the sight of us. He put his nose down and started sniffing along the ground, imitating a bloodhound that we once filmed. That hound, the one in the movie, had been sent to hunt for a man falsely accused of murder. I couldn't guess what Duke was looking for.

The dog circled around us until he got to the base of the tree with the deep claw marks going up its side. Duke whined a little and backed away. Another sniff took the dog nearer to the pool of blood that I had disturbed. That earned another whine, louder and more distressed.

A man's whistle sounded again. The tramp, Ashcan Pete, strode up the path toward us. "Duke," he called. "Get away from there."

On spotting us, Pete tipped his hat. "Sorry, folks, still working on Sydney's project? Didn't mean to disturb you again. Duke just turned tail on me and came back here again. He gets agitated like that sometimes. Goes looking for trouble. Bad habit for a dog. Or anyone."

"It's all right," I said. "We're looking for a friend, one of the men that we were with earlier. Have you seen him? He's about your size and was dressed like a…" I stopped, not sure how to say bum or tramp to a man who obviously slept rough himself, to judge by the condition of his coat and trousers.

"Dressed like a gentleman of the road?" said Pete with a bit of a smile. "Saw that one of you was playing at that. Dangerous thing to do in these woods."

"What do you mean?"

Pete tapped his leg, and Duke ran over to lean against his master. The man ruffled the dog's ears. I had the impression that he was thinking carefully about his next words.

"There's spots here in New England, odd places," Pete said. "Where you can go off the road and end up where you don't want to be. Works the other way round too. Some things come creeping out that shouldn't be here at all."

Fred shook his head. "It's a small wood in the middle of a grand old neighborhood," he said. "How can something happen here and nobody notice?"

"Didn't say that they don't notice. Don't talk about it. Nobody in Arkham talks about it. But Arkham, Kingsport, and a bunch of other places, there's thin spots. Duke's got a nose for that. Nose for trouble." Pete patted the dog with a loving thump and was answered by an enthusiastic tail wag.

"I don't understand," I said. Blood on the ground, claw marks on the trees, thin spots. None of it made sense. "What do you mean?"

"Just that there are places that you shouldn't go. Not alone, not looking for something, not hunting down paths. People disappear doing that in Arkham. You should ask Florie."

"Florie? At the diner?" I said.

"Yep. Her family has been in Arkham a long time. She hears things. She remembers things. Me, I just took a wrong turn and have been a bit stuck ever since. Of course, I found Duke and that's something." Pete looked around the clearing. "Going to be dark soon. I'll walk you two back up to the gate. Safer that way."

"But we need to find our friend," I said, not wanting to stay but not wanting to abandon the search for Paul. "And we found something. Blood." I pointed at the spot where I never wanted to step again.

Pete looked where I was pointing. He kept a firm grip on the back of Duke's neck. "Could be blood. Could be an animal got loose here and killed something. Not necessarily your friend. Look, I'll walk you back to the gate and then I'll take a little search around town. I know the places that man can go drinking when he's got a thirst. Likely your friend is in one of those joints."

Fred looked as troubled as I felt. "I've known Paul to go on a binge or two, but not when he's working. He's always been reliable."

"We should keep looking," I said. I hated to stop our search even though I felt as if I was being pushed out of the woods. Not by Pete, but by the trees, the buzzing insects, the rotting smell of the place, all crowding in on me like one of the nightmares that kept dragging me out of sleep in the middle of the night. Above us, the black coat swayed like funeral bunting on the branch.

"If Paul is not back by morning," Fred said. "We call the cops."

"Could do that," Pete agreed amiably as he practically shoved us back on the path and walked us toward the Fitzmaurice gate. "Not that the cops have much luck around here. Arkham's a strange town."

"I believe that," I said.

Pete smiled more broadly at me. "Florie said you were one of the clever ones. Well, she'd know."

Florie again! I resolved to go back to the diner as soon as I could. I wanted to talk to Florie now.

The shadows were deeper on the path. Once or twice a bush rustled, which was odd because there was no wind at all. I pretended that I didn't see the odd shapes created by some of the shadows. Shapes like a dog-headed man, hunkering down and loping on all fours like a wolf, only to stop and stretch, and stand like a hunched-over man in the shelter of the hemlock. Duke bared his teeth and growled at the nothing in the bushes, and it remained hidden.

Pete and Fred started talking about airplanes. Pete had no desire to fly in one. Fred wanted to take a camera up in one. "Did you see *The Skywayman*, some of the stunts that they got? But they filmed from the ground," said Fred.

"The pilot died," I said. It had been a horrible wreck a couple of years ago, killing both the star of the film and his co-pilot. Of course, their studio just rushed it into release with plenty of headlines in the press promising a final close-up of the killer crash. Sydney had seen it and reported his disappointment in the whole thing. He said most of it looked false because the studio had used models rather than actual footage for many of the "death defying" parts. "Why would you go up in a plane to be killed?"

"Planes are safe enough," said Fred. "And getting safer all the time. I've talked to some of the barnstormers. They can do tricks without any trouble if they are given time to set up and rehearse. It's like us. They make it look worse than it is, to give the audience a scare."

I had my doubts about that. But luckily Sydney had never liked how airplanes looked in films and never expressed any interest in doing a movie with one.

By the time that we reached the gate, I was almost convinced that Paul had just gone out for a snort on the town. But not quite. The voice in my head that I didn't want to listen to kept insisting that it had been blood on the ground and claw marks on the tree where we'd seen what looked like Paul's coat.

Pete shoved the gate open. Duke, with a happy tail wag, bounded through and across the lawn. We walked more slowly behind the dog. Pete came last. He turned and gave one more long look down the path. Then he shoved the gate shut and lowered the latch to lock it with a decisive snap.

"That's a bad place," Pete said. "The Fitzmaurice men could never resist it. But it's a bad place to get lost."

"Sydney said that he loved those woods. That he liked to go there with his grandfather," I said.

"Florie says he liked to throw stones at hornet's nests," answered Pete. "Lots of men in Arkham are like that. Shove a stick at something to see what will happen. Doesn't make it a good idea."

We bid Pete goodnight and trudged back to the house. "Tomorrow," I said to Fred, "you can take me to the diner again. I need to talk to Florie."

Fred looked up at the flock of crows that seemed to have returned to permanently settle on the roof of the Fitzmaurice house. The birds spread across the eaves like a giant ink blot.

"I think you are right," he said.

The next morning, Max told us that everything was all right with Paul. "He's taking the train back to California," he said.

I was only halfway through my morning coffee. Another horrible night had filled my head with nightmares. I woke with all my bedding, pillows included, in a tangle on the floor. The nightmare left me shivering and sweating with a horrible pain in my neck because I'd been curled up on a nearly bare mattress. There had been no fire in this dream, that I remembered, but something had been chasing me through the woods. My dream featured trees that dripped poison from stone leaves and giant insects, bigger and blacker than crows, that filled the skies with buzzing wings.

Gulping a couple more mouthfuls of coffee, I listened to the others question Max about Paul. Most importantly, how he knew that Paul was going to California and what did that mean.

"He got a job," said Max. "He called from the station and asked me to ship his stuff."

"He just took off in his makeup and tramp clothes?" I asked. That made no sense at all.

"No, of course not," said Max. "He came back here while we were still down at the gate shooting at the crows, and washed up. Found a telegram offering him a part in some project of United Artists and took off. I think he wanted to avoid Sydney. Well, you know how Sydney was about Maggie leaving. Paul just grabbed a couple of shirts and his razor kit. Then he asked if I could send his trunk later as he didn't want to deal with it. It's all locked up and ready to go."

Jim, who was stuffing his face with bacon, just nodded in agreement. Hal, who was eating with more dignified bites, said, "I noticed that his things were missing from the bathroom and closet. His trunk is still in our room."

"I didn't hear the phone," said Eleanor.

Max shrugged and took a bite of toast. "It was a bit later, when Jeany and Fred were out in the woods. I picked up the receiver just before it rang. I was in the hall, about to make a call to the studio, but when I picked it up, there was Paul on the other end instead of the operator."

It made sense. Paul always had been a bit distant with the rest of us. He might take off without telling anyone. Even if he'd promised to work with Hal on his chicken farm.

We heard a clatter on the stairs that meant Sydney was sweeping down to breakfast. Renee was eating up in her room, as was Lulu. Renee stayed upstairs because I'd washed her hair and set it in pins that morning to give her a proper curl for the day's scene. Lulu probably was eating in bed for the same reason. Being half dressed and made up did not do much for glamor over breakfast. Besides, both leading ladies had taken to avoiding Sydney in the mornings. He was either too cheerful to bear before coffee or equally gloomy and insufferable. We never knew which, and it seemed to be triggered by the state of the previous day's filming or whatever discussion that he'd had with Eleanor about the state of her scenarios.

"Hush," said Max. "Don't say anything more about Paul. I'll tell Sydney later. But he's not going to like losing him. You know how he gets when someone poaches one of his actors."

"Well, I know how I get when that happens during a show. How does Sydney react?" said Eleanor.

"Furious and unforgiving, and the rest of us will be questioned for days about our supposed lack of loyalty," said Hal. "He dislikes it most in the middle of a shoot. The last time was the young man who fell down the mountain."

"Selby didn't leave," I said. "He broke his leg and had to stay in the hospital."

"Exactly," said Hal. "Max should keep quiet. Sydney might not even notice for a day or two. Paul doesn't have any specific scenes coming up."

"I won't notice what?" said Sydney as he came in and dropped into his chair with a dramatic wave of the arm at Mrs Mayhew and her coffee pot. "Eggs, bacon, and very well-done toast," he called to her. "With the good marmalade. Not honey. And butter, don't forget the butter."

"Butter and marmalade are already on the table," I said, shoving them toward Sydney. Mrs Mayhew poured Sydney a cup of coffee and filled the rest of our cups to the brim. I sipped mine a little to gain enough room for more cream and sugar.

"You won't notice that Renee and Lulu are breakfasting in bed in preparation for their big scene," said Eleanor with a wink at Hal. "Or resting from yesterday's activities. Lulu was up and down all night. She swears that she was eaten alive by mosquitoes and ticks in your woods yesterday. Not that I could find a mark on her."

"And I'm sure you looked closely," said Sydney.

"Every inch of her pearly white body," said Eleanor. "Honestly, Sydney, you are as bad as those New York reporters. Not that calamine does a thing for my romantic mood, but I stood ready with a jar of the stinking stuff."

"So she can film today?" said Sydney. "No bug bites showing?"

"You have a heart of gold, Sydney," said Eleanor. "Such compassion for your actors."

"I have a film to make," said Sydney, "and a studio to please, don't I, Max?"

Max had buried his head in the financial section of a Boston newspaper as soon as Sydney had entered the room, but he looked up at Sydney's comments. "We are making progress and that pleases the studio," he said.

"I live to please the studio," Sydney replied. Mrs Mayhew returned with his breakfast and placed the china plate carefully in front of him. "Excellent, excellent. Nothing like a hearty breakfast before a hard day's work."

Sydney was definitely in one of his jolly moods, which meant that he liked yesterday's filming. I was a little surprised. I thought he'd still be upset about the crows. After all, the birds had chased Max and him into the house.

"What are we filming today?" asked Betsy.

"Just a couple of simple scenes. A lull before the real terror starts," said Sydney. "You dressing the sisters for a dinner alone in the dining room. The dinner itself. A knock on the door that you answer, only to find no one there. It's all building up to the entrance of the masked stranger."

"No party scene?" said Betsy. She loved the party scenes and being able to do a little extra cameo as a flirtatious maid or guest.

"I thought about it," said Sydney. "I discussed it with Eleanor."

"Endlessly, darling," said Eleanor.

"But we've done those so many times," said Sydney. "I wanted this film to be different. This film *will* be different. The audience will feel as if they are trapped in the house with the sisters and as anxious as they are to escape it."

"But not for a party," muttered Eleanor. "Women cannot be appeased with a simple party, a few drinks, and a pretty gown. They also want power, as our battle for the vote proved. Now we must show that we can use it wisely. We have been kept isolated too long, now we move into a new way of thinking. The sisters step forward into a new world and a new power after being imprisoned by their family's past. That is the current that carries this plot, that is why a party would be all wrong."

Betsy started to say something, then didn't. Obviously there was no winning such a dispute with Eleanor when she framed it like that. Whatever Betsy said, she would either fail to uphold the ideals of those who fought so hard to get women the vote, or label herself as far too easily appeased or too quickly distracted by pretty gowns. I gave Betsy a sympathetic glance. I couldn't figure out the correct answer either.

Eleanor's intellect was formidable. I admired her greatly. She also scared me a little. Which was unfortunate, because she could be the kindest of souls. If I had told her of my fears earlier, the outcome of that summer might have been different.

"We need the isolation of the old house, the anxiety of the sisters to leave their past behind," said Sydney. "They move to a new place and leave behind the shadows of the old. They remake their world as we will remake ours. Besides, it is much easier to frighten an audience with an empty room."

"A completely empty room?" questioned Eleanor. "Cannot be done. There's nothing frightening about that."

"Perhaps not on stage," conceded Sydney. "But it works on film. Didn't it, Jeany?"

I laughed. It had worked. It was a trick that Renee and I came up with to fill a spot in a film where not much happened. Of course, Sydney didn't like it at first. But when he saw how the audience reacted, he claimed it as his own invention.

"We had a scene in the *Witch Woman of the Woods*, where the heroine has to run away from the house into the woods. But why would she do that?" I said, echoing Renee's early arguments against the scene. "Wouldn't a house, even a spooky old house, be safer than running through the forest at night? So we show her enter the house, very afraid, very uncertain. She stands in the hallway looking into an empty parlor room. The audience sees it from the heroine's viewpoint. Just a long, long look through a half-open door at a nearly empty room. Just a chair and the edge of the table."

"No dripping blood, no headless corpses?" said Eleanor.

I shook my head. "Nothing. Everything is completely bare and simple. And we kept the camera on that empty room for a full minute." One minute of staring at nothing can seem like eternity in a crowded theater.

Eleanor caught that and nodded. "Long enough that the audience starts to fidget. Papers rustle. People start whispering."

"People always whisper at the movies," said Betsy. "They are reading the title cards out loud to their friends. But it was a long time with nothing happening."

"That was the beauty of it," Sydney picked up. "A moment of absolute stillness with an audience trained to look for frantic action by those silly Keystone pictures and all the rest."

"A long moment," agreed Eleanor. She looked intrigued by the idea. She was a very intelligent woman. "Then what did you do to make them jump?"

"Slammed the door," I said.

I still remembered the satisfaction of that spectacular hard push after sitting behind the door for a minute. The bang of the door, not that anyone could hear it, and Fred's triumphant call of "Perfect!" as he finished the shot.

"In the theater, the organ supplied the pop of noise, the sound of the slam," I explained. "And Fred had shot so close that it was like the door slammed right in their face."

"Clever. Bet that made them jump," said Eleanor.

I nodded. "It did." The night that Renee and I snuck into the back of a theater to watch, one man yelled so loud in surprise that he nearly frightened us. He certainly caused the rest of the audience to gasp. After that, nobody wondered why Renee as the sweet heroine turned around and ran off into the woods not to meet the terrible witch, but to become her. That was the other twist that kept the audience talking as they streamed out of the theater and into the night. It also marked the end of Renee playing sweet heroines in the movies.

"It's funny," I said. "That scene. The house was very similar. The way that the woods ran in the back." We'd filmed at a mansion that one of the studio heads had built up in the canyons. Sydney had picked it because there was a long lawn in the back that led to a tall iron fence and a gate opening into a wooded ravine. I remember Renee running down the back steps of that house and to the gate to disappear into the place of evil enchantment that changed the heroine forever into the witch in the woods.

"We use bits of our life to inform our stories," said Sydney. "And we are drawn to stories that inform our lives. Like dear Renee, forever transforming herself into something that she is not."

That made me look up. As far as I knew, Renee had never discussed her complicated history with Sydney. Or that I was actually her sister. But given their intimate relationship over the last few years, he probably guessed that she wasn't completely who she said she was. Was this a hint that he knew enough to keep her secret or a threat that he knew so much that could harm her?

"I watched a few of your older films," said Eleanor. "I have friends in the business and they were able to get a hold of the reels for a private screening. I did not see the witch movie but I saw the siren and the vampire. Both were surprisingly good. Renee truly transforms herself. At one moment, you are sure that she is innocent, perhaps the victim, and at the next she's a woman of such power, even of evil. Lulu, as much as I love her, cannot do that. She is always just Lulu. She can hold your eye. She can make you care about her character. She can be unforgettable in scenes. But she can never be anyone other than Lulu."

I knew what she meant. There were two kinds of actors, both equally at the top of their game. One disappeared into their parts so completely that you could not believe it was the same person the next time that you saw them. But each time you saw them, you believed in that role so completely that you couldn't look away. The other also caught your eye but always by playing a variation of the same person. If they strayed too far from that character, you didn't really believe it. Chaplin was like that. Always the Tramp, and you loved him for it, but never truly anyone else.

"But Lulu being Lulu is exactly what I want," said Sydney. "Today we will film them preparing for the dinner, tomorrow the dinner itself, and then we'll record Lulu's scream. The scream that will shatter the mirrors and release the masked stranger."

Fred looked up from his breakfast at that. "You didn't say anything about shattering mirrors. Do you mean the ones in the hall? Aren't they old? Valuable?"

"You cannot break those mirrors," said Sydney. "No, I want to record Lulu's scream. And film her screaming, of course. Then film dozens of mirrors shattering. As if mirrors are breaking around the world. As if doors are opening everywhere. Then we will do the scene with the masked stranger."

Fred sighed. "Dozens of mirrors. Breaking. Cracking and falling apart?"

"No, no," said Sydney. "An explosion of glass. Can't you use dynamite or something?"

Fred swore. "You want to put us all in the hospital? Sydney, we are talking about exploding glass. Is Lulu or Renee going to be anywhere near it? And if we do explosions indoors, we might burn the place down. It's not safe, you lunatic." Fred only called Sydney insane when he was truly worried. They had these fights once or twice before. The one time Fred backed down, Selby broke his leg.

"No, no, Fred," soothed Sydney, obviously recognizing that he had pushed a bit too hard. "You can set it up wherever you want. Buy some cheap mirrors, rig an explosion, film the results. We'll edit it in."

"We can use the back lawn," I said. "Down near the fence."

Fred grumbled a bit but finally agreed. "I can rig it. But everyone must stay in the house. I hate explosions."

"What about you?" I said.

"Somebody has to crank the camera," said Fred. "Humbert and I can rig up some type of barrier, just poke the lens through. Yeah, I can make that work. But, Sydney, between that and setting up the equipment to record Lulu's scream, it's going to be a few days."

"That's fine," said Sydney. "We're nearly to the end. As long as Jeany has our mask done by the solstice, we'll be all right."

"I have a couple of masks," I admitted.

"But I need time," said Fred. "Explosions!"

"You have eight days," said Sydney with a snap of his teeth as he crunched through his marmalade-dripping toast. "You can be ready by then."

Fred muttered more about explosions, screams, and working for lunatics. "We've got just over a week," he said. "That's not nearly enough time."

"Of course it is," said Sydney. "We used to do an entire film in a week. Have you all gone soft? We can do this. Jeany, bring me the masks now."

"The solstice?" said Eleanor, saving me the need to respond. "Is that when we get to see your finale?"

"Ah, yes," said Sydney, finishing up his toast with one last bite. "The longest day of light, the shortest night, the perfect time to finish filming. It will be marvelous. Don't you agree, Max?"

Max mumbled something and folded his paper. He stood up. "I need to phone the studio," he said. "Let them know everything is proceeding on schedule."

As he left the room, Betsy turned to me and said, "Isn't anyone worried about bad luck?"

"What do you mean?"

"You know. Breaking mirrors. Seven years of bad luck."

I shook my head. "I don't think Sydney believes in bad luck. At least not for him."

But it was odd. Sydney was superstitious. Renee once laughed at him for walking out of his way to avoid a black cat. Maybe he did not know that breaking mirrors caused trouble.

Later I learned the truth. That he did not care what luck he brought down on the rest of us. And that he was not the only one with that attitude.

CHAPTER SEVENTEEN

Fred tried different ways of blowing up mirrors in the barn. The constant sounds of shattering glass reverberated through the house, to the point the indoor mirrors seemed to be humming in sympathy. I hated going down that hallway more and more each day. I felt like I had to apologize to the mirrors for the multiple deaths of their brethren. I also wanted to break them all every time I caught a glimpse of a crooked reflection out of the corner of my eye.

Humbert mumbled a lot about the waste of good hay, as Fred used the bales normally reserved for the grass-cutting mule or for mulching the garden as barriers to keep exploding glass from hitting him.

I tried to escape my woes once or twice by watching these tests, but Fred always chased me out with stern warnings about the dangers of flying glass and putting an eye out.

"And what will you do if you lose an eye?" I asked.

"Only need one to peer through the viewfinder," Fred answered far too nonchalantly.

At the house, when Fred did come back from the barn to film the scenes that Eleanor created, things became even messier. Of course, Sydney's assurances that we would only film one or two more scenes before the solstice quickly dissolved into a rush to get several new ideas into the can.

Perhaps it was Lulu or perhaps it was Renee, but neither were thrilled with doing little more than getting dressed for a dinner and then having the dinner alone in the house. They felt it didn't give them much scope to show off their best talents, despite Sydney's reassurances that the finale would be worth it.

"If this is all that the audience has to watch," said Renee on the first night, "they will either fall asleep or walk out." After spending a day watching Sydney direct and then change his directions while Betsy fussed with Renee's curls, the ones that I had already perfectly set, I had to agree.

"Our audiences expect a shock a minute," said Renee. It was a slogan that one of the theaters had used about an earlier film, one where we made the actors jump out of dark corners and rigged props to drop from the ceiling. "This is going to become the snore a minute film if we don't add some terror."

Eleanor became an unexpected ally. "I have to agree," she said. "When we do my horrid little plays in New York, I'm careful to ladle out the blood as thickly and as quickly as possible. You don't want the audience to stop and think. That's the worst thing that can happen to a horrible shocker. Otherwise they'll start wondering why a perfectly healthy young woman doesn't run screaming from the monster luring her to her doom."

"Exactly," said Renee. "Only in this case, it is why don't two bored young ladies leave their lonely house? Sydney, we are not filming Chekhov. Something has to happen."

"Spare me fickle, spineless, drifting people," said Eleanor. "You are right. The sisters should be actively courting their fate, however Sydney wants to arrange the end. Let's make something happen."

But Eleanor's ideas, while exactly the type of frightening and bizarre that Renee wanted, created the next accident.

Eleanor rewrote the dinner scene to include a lightning bolt that struck a guest through the window, slaying or at least maiming the poor man that the sisters have invited into their home.

"How do I do that?" said a much-beleaguered Fred, who was still searching for a mixture to create the proper explosion of mirrors as well as trying to borrow a microphone and other equipment from the University to record Lulu's scream. We all checked the calendar and were aware of time swiftly running out. The solstice was only a couple of days away.

"At our theater, we'd use a prop man," said Eleanor. "One who did a flash of light across the table and a rumble of a thunder sheet. Of course you need sound for that effect."

"We can write noise into the cue sheet for the accompanist. I hope this only shows in large theaters with good musicians," muttered Fred. "We have enough instructions to keep an orchestra busy. But we need something else."

In the end, he decided to use an old-fashioned flash powder. "Lycopodium powder," he said to me, showing me the yellow mixture. "The magician's friend. There was even a French fellow who tried to run an engine with it. Makes quite a flash."

"Where did you get it?"

"That five-and-dime, the one where Lulu wanted to go shopping? I found it. More of a hardware store than some. Even has a bunch of old men hanging in the back around the stove with bad coffee and lots of ideas of how to make and break things," Fred said. It sounded like his description of heaven. "I've been talking to them about different ways to break the mirrors. He had a number of minor explosive mixtures to try."

"Is it safe?" I said.

"Probably not," Fred sighed, "but it's better than some of Sydney's ideas. He wanted me to electrify the candlesticks and actually shock Hal when the bang goes off. Thought it would get more of a reaction."

"Not again," I muttered. Sydney did something like that in a past picture. A mild shock to make the actor jump. Fred had been furious when he'd found out that Paul had rigged that up for Sydney. It was like the balloon without any ropes. It never occurred to Sydney that someone could get hurt. It was one of the many reasons I appreciated Fred watching out for us. And, with Paul gone, I couldn't think of anyone else who could create a stupid trick like that for Sydney.

"Let's just tell Sydney that the bang will be so loud, everyone will jump," I said.

Sydney decided to film the scene at night, to make the flash at the window stand out more with the electric ceiling lights off. We broke out the stage lights that we'd brought from Hollywood to light the characters from the side. The room became a tangle of cords and wires that made Fred snap at everyone.

Then we discovered the real problem. Fred couldn't light the powder and crank the camera. He was too far away. With Paul gone, we lacked anyone that Fred felt was experienced enough to handle such a volatile effect.

"I think we should call it off," he told Sydney.

"No," said Sydney. "I like the scene as Eleanor has written it. We keep it. Can't Jeany or Max light the powder?"

Fred looked horrified at the thought. I hoped it was the idea of Max bumbling with a match and an explosive powder that bothered him. I knew I could do it, but I also had to be across the room to flip the switch on the lights and plunge the room into darkness after the flash. We'd already rehearsed it a couple of times. I knew the cues better than anyone.

As for the rest, Betsy was playing the maid, Pola and Hal were the guests, Jim also was serving, and Renee and Lulu were the hosts.

"Eleanor?" I suggested, because putting fastidious Max in charge of an explosion wasn't workable. And he needed to wave the slate in front of the camera so we could keep track of the takes, anyway.

Eleanor flatly refused. "I hate explosions. Fire. Loud bangs. Reminds me too much of my war days."

"But you wrote it into the scene," I said.

"Of course, you always give the audience something that terrifies you," she said. But she continued to refuse to help with the scene.

"If it is a loud flash and bang," said Lulu, "she won't even watch. She'll be busy writing up a new way to kill my character while we are playing the scene."

"Mister Claude," said Fred. "He could do it."

"Who's Mister Claude?" I asked.

"A stage magician who talked me into buying the powder. He's on the Orpheum circuit but visiting a friend in Arkham. He was picking up things for his act," said Fred, who explained this magician was a fellow fan of small-town five-and-dime stores. "He should know how to handle it." Fred patted his pockets and found a card. "He gave me his card and wrote his hotel phone on the back. Said he'd be interested in seeing how we made movies."

Mister Claude proclaimed himself charmed with Fred's invitation to set off an explosion on a film set. I liked him immensely when we met. If there was ever a man that looked like a stage magician, it was Julius Claude. Even in a simple dark suit, he gave off the aura of wearing a tuxedo with all the trimmings. I almost expected him to produce a dove from his pocket.

"I've often thought that we magicians could use more of the new technology in our shows," he said, looking over Fred's beloved camera with much interest. "There's possibilities in this."

"And we're going to take more and more of your audience every year," said Sydney, sweeping into the room. "Good to see you, Claude, it's been some years."

Apparently, Sydney knew more people in Arkham than we were aware of.

Mister Claude nodded. "A long time. You came to me about an act for your circus."

"Not my circus," said Sydney. "It belonged to Lucinda. Her grandfather had started it and it was a bit run down by the time that I arrived. I tried to build it up. But the time for circuses, vaudeville, and theater is past."

"Indeed," said Mister Claude. "Sally will be heartbroken when I tell her. She's just booked us into six months of playing the Orpheum Circuit."

"Still have that assistant?" said Sydney. "You are a lucky man."

"And the Fitzmaurices remain very unlucky men. I heard about Lucinda's disappearance and the circus fire."

"Tragic accident," said Sydney, moving away from us. "Although nobody knows what happened to Lucinda. They never found a body."

It was a bewildering exchange. Sydney always acted like he'd been away from Arkham for years and didn't know anyone in town any more. Although this sounded like the two men met in Sydney's fabled circus. The circus that left Sydney broke at a nickelodeon in San Francisco, looking for a new art form.

"Mister Claude," I said. "If you come this way, I'll show you where we want to create the flash."

"Please call me, Julius, Mister Claude is my stage name," he said with a courteous shake of my hand. "After all, we are fellow entertainers. And your name is?"

"I'm Jeany, Jeany Lin. I work on the costumes and makeup. Actually, I design the costumes. And the props, and do other things when we need someone."

"A talented young woman," said Julius. "Much like Sally Alexander. My act would not work at all without my assistant."

"Then you are lucky to have her," I said.

"Yes, indeed, although I don't think she always believes me when I tell her that. Is this where you want your flash?" We had gone out the kitchen door and circled back to the window outside the dining room.

We looked into the lit room. "Yes, right here," I said. "They will come in, sit at the table, make some conversation, and then Renee will say that she is waiting for the stranger. That's when you light it. When you hear her say 'I am waiting for the stranger.' Bang goes the flash and I turn out the lights."

"I did not know the actors spoke in the movies. Nobody can hear them."

"They say the lines. At least in scenes like this, where they are supposed to be making conversation. They used to talk all kinds of nonsense, but then lip readers in the audience would report to others what they said. If it was too foul or too silly, it would make the papers."

Julius chuckled. "I can see the embarrassment."

"So they speak the lines or close enough to the lines that will appear on the cards. Sydney insisted on that line: 'I am waiting for the stranger.'" As I said it, I felt a cold touch on the back of my neck. A whisper of a breath sounded in my ear. Once again, I had the feeling of being watched that walking down the hall of mirrors always inspired in me.

The magician noticed my shiver. "You should be careful," he said.

"What is it about this place?" I said.

"Arkham or this house?"

"Both?"

He made a gesture with his hand. A small white card appeared between his first finger and his thumb. He handed it to me. It was a simple pasteboard card with the name Professor Krosnowski on it.

"I know her," I said. "She was at Velma's. She spoke to me. Florie told me her name."

Julius nodded. "I am not surprised. You should talk to both of them again. Those women understand this town. They can help you."

I remembered the tramp, Ashcan Pete, had given the same advice about talking to Florie. I'd meant to go back to the diner, but Sydney had added extra scenes and I gotten caught up in the filming. I mentioned this to the magician.

Julius looked down at me. "Ashcan Pete knows this town and its people. If he thinks you should talk to Florie, you should do so. I also recommend seeking out Professor Krosnowski before the solstice."

"Why?"

"There's something here," he said. "You seem like a sensible young woman. And one who has seen too many stage tricks for me to misdirect you."

"I've only been to magic shows a couple of times. Fred likes them. He says there's a lot of tricks that we could learn, that we could use in the movies."

He chuckled again. "Indeed. I think we could learn from each other. But be careful. There's something about this house, about this family, and, I must admit, about Arkham that is not a stage illusion. I am convinced that there is real magic here. Or at least forces that cannot be easily explained."

His face was half in shadow and his voice, a deep baritone, sounded too serious for me to dismiss him out of hand. But could I believe a stage magician who claimed to know real magic when he saw it?

"Why are you telling me this?" I said again.

"Because little more than five years ago, Sydney Fitzmaurice came to one of my shows. He stayed afterward to ask me about some things that I had said. It was patter, the usual mystic mumbo jumbo that most magicians use in the act. Sydney heard something in my speech that caught his attention."

Sydney liked magicians. I knew that he often went to shows. Renee used to go with him, but magic acts bored her. Also she disliked the stage magician's common practice of hiding birds and rabbits in their clothing. She felt it was unfair to the poor creatures to be stuffed up a sleeve or trapped in a hat.

"Sydney heard me speak some phrases that I learned from a French friend who had died in the War, a man who often spoke of magic as real. So Sydney came backstage with a manuscript that he claimed came from his grandfather. A very odd play, apparently written by the grandfather when he was a young man. But the heroines spoke phrases that were even older than that, phrases very similar to those that I spoke. Sydney thought this was tied to ideas, rituals, that his family had stolen long ago."

I had a suspicion that this was Sydney's manuscript that he kept promising to Eleanor and then hiding from her. It sounded like he'd been doing that particular trick for longer than we'd known.

Julius shifted so the light spilling out of the windows illuminated his face more fully. He looked very serious and much older than he had appeared in the hallway only moments before. "Sydney was very secretive. He wanted my knowledge and he would give nothing in exchange for my advice. But it intrigued me that he claimed Arkham as home. This town intrigues me. I've found the occult library at the University is extensive. A strange thing to discover in a small New England town and enough to bring me back whenever I have engagements nearby. But I understand the dangers. Do you?"

"I can't leave," I said, as troubled as I was by this and the earlier discussion about the Lucinda who had disappeared. Was that the woman who the professor thought Sydney killed? No, she'd spoken of a student. "I have… friends in this company. I cannot leave them." I had to protect Renee. I could not abandon the rest of the company, not friends like Fred and Betsy.

"You may need to make a choice," said Julius. "Lucinda wanted what Sydney offered and failed to take the danger in account."

"You mentioned her before," I said. "Who was Lucinda?"

There were shouts inside the dining room. Sydney barked out instructions for the coming scene. Time was running out. I had to go to my place, or the scene would not work.

"Lucinda was more a creature of the air than the earth. She lived between the two," Julius said. "An aerialist in a small circus. Sydney promised her the moon, stars, and all the rest. He worked as a ringmaster for a season. He tried to create a spectacle with the show. He dressed them all in mirrors. He strung mirrors around the tent, so when Lucinda flew, it seemed a dozen women took flight."

I heard Fred calling me, but I needed the end of this story. "What happened? Please, tell me."

"Sydney came to me, asking for a magic that I did not have," Julius said. "I do not know what he did that night. But there was a fire. It destroyed the circus. And no one ever saw Lucinda again."

"Did he use a mask? Did he put a mask on her?" I said. Then, in response to Fred's shout, I called back, "I am coming. Just a minute."

I asked Julius again. "Did Sydney ask you for a mask?"

"No," said Julius. "He did not ask me for a mask. But I heard that Lucinda had a new costume. One that included a silver mask that reflected the audience, that reflected the flames, when she flew."

Time was up. Sydney was shouting again. "Thank you, thank you," I said as I ran back to the door. Florie, I was thinking, I need to talk to Florie. "You know what to do."

Julius waved in acknowledgment and shouted to me as I ran. "So do you." Then, just as if he was a mind reader as well as a magician, he said, "Go see Florie. She can tell you more."

I reached my spot before Sydney exploded. Fred was already behind the camera. The actors were all in place around the table. Renee looked lovely and, as Sydney exclaimed, otherworldly in a pale shimmer of a dress that I had sewn for another film but we had never used. Lulu appeared young and more pretty than beautiful in a lace dress that I had fitted to her earlier that morning. It was cut from one of the dresses that I had found in the attic and well suited to the character of the younger, shyer sister.

Betsy and Jim whisked around the table, very smart in servant costumes that we had brought from California. Hal and Pola both wore their usual dress-up clothes, a little more formal than they had for earlier scenes, but easy modifications had turned them into a country judge and his wife, out for a dinner with a pair of young ladies.

Eleanor was not watching. I remembered what she had said about her dislike of loud bangs. No doubt she was in her room for rewrites.

"Places," shouted Sydney.

The actors sank into chairs or, in the case of Betsy and Jim, began leaning over the "guests" as if they were serving the nonexistent food in their dishes. A few minutes of meaningless chatter was made to fool the lip readers: "How was the weather? Did it seem too cool tonight? Can I have soup? Thank you for the soup."

After enough of this for Fred to get his establishing shot, Renee spoke the one line that would appear on the title card: "I am waiting for the stranger."

Bang! Julius lit the flash powder. The bright light flooded into the room. I threw the switch that doused all the lights.

As the room plunged into darkness, there was a second arc of blue light, an arc of electricity sparking across the table. A man cried out. There was the terrible thud of a body falling.

I flipped the switch on and flooded the room with light again as everyone began shouting over each other.

Hal was flat on the floor. Pola was on her knees beside him.

"Oh, my God, my God," she said. "Is he dead?"

CHAPTER EIGHTEEN

Hal was alive, but barely. Max calmly called the operator and asked for Doctor Wills to be sent out to the house. Then he sat in a corner, taking notes and talking quietly with Sydney while the rest of us moaned about what a bad luck picture this was turning out to be. When the doctor arrived, she took one look at Hal and called for an ambulance.

"What happened?" I asked Fred after the ambulance came and went.

"I think he was shocked," said Fred, who promptly crawled under the dining room table. I crawled after him as quickly as I could.

"Shocked? How?" This couldn't have happened. We'd checked everything. Fred had checked everything. Hal couldn't be heading to hospital.

Fred pulled up a cable that had run under the table, leading to one of the big lights that we'd brought with us for night scenes. "I don't know how," Fred said, running his hand along the length of cable. "There's nothing wrong here. An arc of electricity like that, it should have fried these cables. And the fuses should be destroyed."

"What do you mean? The lights came on."

"Yes," said Fred. "The lights came on. The fuses worked. After a huge arc of electricity, like a bolt of lightning, strikes Hal. Jeany, that's not normal."

We crawled back out. Fred checked each of the lights in turn. Then he went to the kitchen to look at the fuse box. He found nothing.

We spent the rest of the night going over and over the scene. Nothing made any sense. It should have been as safe as safe could be. It was like the picture that had fallen off the wall or the coffin that closed on Lulu. Simple tricks, the type that we always used, that kept going wrong in this film.

Neither of us dared to speak of Paul. Of blood in the woods or the feeling of something truly wrong.

Well past midnight, we gave up. I dragged myself upstairs, almost too tired to sleep. As I walked past Renee's door, she called out to me. She was sitting by the window, peering out in the darkness. As I came up to her, I could hear the scratch of claws up on the roof.

"Those crows," said Renee. "Still out there."

I pressed my face to the cool glass and let my eyes adjust to the faint moonlight. Dark shapes were visible along the edge of the roof. They bobbed and weaved about, and I could hear the faint mutter of birds waking briefly and then returning to sleep.

"They are not doing anything," I said to Renee.

"No," she said with a shudder, turning away from the window. "They never do anything. They're just there. Like sentinels. Watching us. Waiting for another disaster to happen and somebody to die this time."

I couldn't bring myself to speak of Paul. He was in California. Max told us that Paul was in California. I couldn't bring myself to speak of the pool of blood in the woods or the terror it woke in me.

I'd never heard my sister sound so depressed. Usually I was the one who worried. Who was sure that something we'd done wouldn't work out. Renee just knew she would succeed, that she would become a star, that we would find a place to accept us even though we weren't everything that we said we were.

"It's just crows," I said. "They can't hurt us."

"I hate this house," said Renee. "It wants something from me."

"Renee!" I said, although I had felt the same for days. "It's a house. It doesn't have feelings."

"Are you sure?" said Renee, her voice barely above a whisper, her body slumped in defeat in front of her mirror. "Ever since we went into those woods, I've felt something terrible has happened. Something horrible will happen. Then the house will eat us up. Keep us trapped here forever."

"Renee!" I said again. This was too close to my nightmares. The house engulfed in smoke and flames while I wandered forever through its interminable hallways and was forever caught in the endless reflections of the mirrors downstairs. "We can walk out the door right now. Call a cab and go to the train station like Paul. We don't have to stay."

Renee looked shocked. As shocked as I felt as soon as I said it. But there wasn't any reason to stay. Let Sydney finish the picture without us. We could go back to Los Angeles. There were always more pictures, other directors, and nothing, nothing, was keeping us here.

"I cannot leave Sydney," said Renee. "We have to finish this picture."

"Why?" I said. "We've done enough for Sydney. You've made him famous."

"No," said Renee. "He made me famous."

"No he didn't," I said, suddenly as furious as I'd ever been with my brilliant, beautiful, genius of a sister. "You're the one who thought up the best tricks, the best way to fool the audience into thinking one thing and showing them another. You came up with all the twists, like that empty room. You made Sydney's ideas better and bigger and more amazing than anyone else ever could."

"More than you, with your clever costumes? More than Fred, with all his camera tricks?" said Renee. "More than Pola, Hal, Jim, Paul, and Betsy, with all the characters that they've created? More than Max with his notes and constant calls to keep the studio happy?"

"Yes," I said. "There's dozens like us in Los Angeles. Hundreds more every day, getting off the train and dreaming of work in the movies. But you are the star. You are the one that makes each picture unforgettable."

Renee grabbed my hands and squeezed them, that clasp of an older sister to a younger, the way that she had on the first night in the orphanage, and on the night that we decided to run away.

"Sydney gave me that chance, he let me be the leading lady. Not the treacherous fortune teller screaming curses or the wicked harem girl plotting to knife her master. The only roles that a half-Chinese girl from Oakland would be allowed to play. But Sydney didn't care who I was, what I was, he made me a star."

I shook my head. "You would have been a star without him."

"No," said Renee. "He got us all here, he made us the best at what we do. Scaring the audience, making them dream a nightmare, giving them a memory of something that never was and never could be."

"You sound just like him," I said. "Quoting bits and pieces that don't mean much if you stop and think about it. Renee, there's something wrong here. We should go home."

"No," said my implacable sister. She sat down at the mirror and peered into it, much as she had looked into the night-dark window earlier. What she saw in her reflected eyes seemed to satisfy her. "There is a way forward. We can finish. There's just the final scene with the mask."

I thought of the silver mask and its paper twin lying in my room. There was something about it that continued to bother me. The more that I stared at it, the more I could see the shadow of a face behind it. But not the face of an ordinary woman. The face of a monster, something both organic and metallic, something both hideously of nature and created by an alien science that I didn't want to understand.

But I couldn't tell that to Renee. That was a thought generated by nightmares and not an idea that I wanted to discuss in a house that creaked and groaned around us as dozens of crows slept, muttering crow dreams on the roof.

"I need the mask," said Renee. Her voice sounded peculiar now, an echo of her normal decisive tones.

"Not yet," I said. "We aren't filming that scene yet."

Renee kept staring at her reflection. A shadow stirred in the mirror. I looked over my shoulder at the bed curtains. That impossible canopied bed that she'd claimed from the very first night. No drafts moved the draperies. Renee continued to gaze into the mirror and the shifting reflections, which looked like a creature underwater rising to the surface.

"The mirror is key," she said. "Terror is key."

"Renee," I said, laying my hand on her shoulder and resolutely not looking into the mirror. "What are you talking about?"

She started a little under my hand. Renee blinked like someone waking up. "Finishing the picture. I saw Sydney's manuscript finally. He showed me it tonight."

"Oh, so you know how it will end?" I said. "What happens to the sisters?"

Renee was looking back into the mirror. "What? The sisters? I guess so. It's so much more than that." Her voice drifted off. If her eyes hadn't been wide open and staring so intently at her reflection, I would have thought she'd fallen asleep where she was sitting.

"But what is Sydney trying to do?" I resisted the urge to shake her. Or at least spin her around on her chair so she was no longer looking at those fluctuating shadows in the mirror. It had to be the curtains, or perhaps the crows outside the window, that were causing those agitating shapes. I refused to see a dog-headed man crouching in the corner of the reflected room. When I looked back over my shoulder, it was just Renee's enormous traveling truck occupying that part of the room. When I looked back to the mirror, it looked as if three creatures stared out at us, or a three-headed dog man with snarling mouths.

"What was in Sydney's manuscript?" I asked.

"An ending," said the now sleepy sounding Renee. "An ending of everything normal."

"That sounds horrible," I said as firmly as I could. I liked normal. I liked simple days with friends, chatting over coffee, pinning up hems, sketching ideas in my book, or eating breakfast. I liked Fred being incapable of passing anything mechanized without wanting to tear it apart. Or Betsy counting cards in her head and gleefully pulling in the pot. Or Pola knitting blankets for all the babies of her acquaintance and Hal trying to decide if chickens and eggs would be the best strategy for early retirement. "I like normal," I said out loud. "I don't want it to end."

Renee swung away from her mirror with a yawn. "I'm so tired. I think I'll sleep until noon. Only a few more days until we finish the picture." Her voice shifted again. It was as if she was playing every possible version of my sister, of the persona that she had created for herself when we ran away so long ago. Now she was the daring Renee again. "We should do something amazing, darling. Maybe take the train to New York and shop our way through the city. How would you like that?"

"But, Renee," I said. "What about Sydney's manuscript? What was the end?"

She climbed into the bed, shaking her head. "Don't worry. It is good. Very good. Sydney's right. It will make us famous. Max says the studio is going to be so happy with this picture that we'll be able to do whatever we want."

"And what do you want, Renee?" What do I want, I asked myself. I had no answers.

As I turned off the lamp by Renee's bed, she stirred and said, "Jeany, can you cover the mirror? Please. Just throw a towel over it."

I picked up a shawl from her chair and dropped it over the dressing table mirror so it was covered completely.

Renee gave a sigh of satisfaction and rolled on her side, presenting her back to the mirror. "Thank you," she murmured. "I hate waking up and seeing those reflections. They watch me. I wish they wouldn't."

CHAPTER NINETEEN

The next morning, after checking on Renee who was still heavily asleep with her back to the covered mirror, I found everyone gathered in the parlor. In one corner, Eleanor sat on the sofa with Pumpkin on her lap, looking very wan, leaning against Lulu's shoulder and muttering in her ear.

Lulu finally shook her head and snapped, "Darling, don't be silly. It was an accident. Nobody knew poor Hal would be hurt."

"But it is exactly…" Eleanor started, but Lulu shushed her with far more force than I had ever seen her use.

"It's nothing," she insisted. Then she spotted me and waved me to her. "Jeany, did you see a bolt of lightning come through the window last night?"

"No, of course not," I said. "There was the flash. Mister Claude set that off." I closed my eyes, trying to picture the scene exactly as it happened. "I turned off the lights and then there was a flash across the table. Fred thinks it was one of the cables. That something sparked or there was an electric arc."

"Like the animals, two by two," said Lulu.

"No," said Fred, coming up behind me. "An arc discharge. Or voltaic arc."

Lulu and Eleanor both blinked at how that sounded in Fred's Brooklyn accent.

"He reads science magazines," I said.

"A little lightning bolt. A short-pulse electrical arc. But I can't find what caused it," said Fred. "I thought one of the cables was loose or torn. That might explain it. Why would it ground in Hal's body…"

"Fred!" I said as Eleanor looked sick and Lulu fussed over her with consoling little pats.

"There's no reason a spark should arc like that between the candlestick and Hal," said Fred. "There was nothing touching the candlestick to cause that to happen."

"Exactly as I wrote it," Eleanor said again. "Lightning comes through the window, strikes the candlestick, and then strikes down the old man. All because he is moving the candlestick to see the sisters more clearly."

"But Hal didn't touch the candlestick," I said. "He was supposed to rise from his chair and lift it after the big flash. Just after we switched the lights back on. Then he would have mimed a heart attack and dropped to the floor. That would have been the next scenario to film. But he hadn't touched the candlestick yet. I'm sure that he was just sitting in his chair, waiting, when I flipped the switch."

"I didn't see him move," said Lulu, "although that flash was so bright, I had sparks in my eyes. But it looked like there was just a fizz of electricity going from the candlestick to him. Without him doing a thing."

"A fizz?" said Fred.

"I don't read science magazines," said Lulu. "Sort of a hiss. Like an electrical snake leapt out and bit him."

Eleanor moaned a bit more and dropped her head into her hands.

"Eleanor," Lulu said, very stern. "For all your claims of being descended from witches, you cannot make things happen just because you write them down. Not even little curses. If you could, half the reporters in New York would be lying dead by now."

Eleanor raised her head and looked at Lulu. "I never wrote about the reporters. But I did write that scene with the guillotine."

"That was not your fault," said Lulu very firmly, not like her usual tones. Then, to Fred and me, she said, "It was the very first of our terror plays. Eleanor had a script that she found in France. She adapted it for me."

"Horrific happenings in the French Revolution," said Eleanor, with a resigned sigh. "Murder, mayhem, suggestions of lewd acts, even greater suggestions of diabolism, and a finale with a guillotine. Innocent girl loses her head while the howling mob watches. We called it *Reign of Horror*."

"Sounds like a script that Sydney would love," I said.

"It didn't go over very well with the critics," said Eleanor. "We hired a magician to provide the final scene with the guillotine, but it never worked like I wanted. So we kept making changes in rehearsals. Which just leads to disaster, as you know. Opening night was the worst. The damn thing stuck halfway down. There's Lulu on the chopping block and nothing happens. So we cut the lights, dropped the curtain, and prayed everyone would think that was how it was supposed to go. But we were slaughtered in the papers."

"So Eleanor rewrote the scene that night in absolute fury," said Lulu, "and turned it around so that the magician is suddenly and permanently maimed by the very guillotine that he meant to use to destroy the heroine."

"And what happened?" I asked.

"Exactly what I wrote," said Eleanor again. "The stupid apparatus collapsed. Lulu walked away unscathed. But the stage magician, that poor man, lost his hand."

"But that was an accident?" I said. It had to be an accident. Bad things don't happen just because somebody writes a curse down.

"Gouts of blood and screaming accident. We dropped the curtain even faster. And had fabulous reviews the next day. Everyone wanted to come to our theater. But we never did *Reign of Horror* again," said Lulu. "Eleanor did get her wish. Revenge and fortune, all at the same time."

"That makes it sound like magic," I said, trying very hard to sound skeptical. Except there had been all those hints from Ashcan Pete, Julius, Florie, and even Darrell, that magic existed in Arkham. And if it existed in Arkham, why not New York?

Eleanor looked at me. "I have always been very careful since then to, well, not be angry when I write. My grandmother used to say that it was anger, hate, and other terrible emotions that led the women in our family to black magic. She was always preaching about it. How our wicked witch of an ancestor was burned in Salem for cursing her neighbors and the rest of the family fled south. But that wickedness went with us, even unto the seventh generation, as per my hysterical old granny." Eleanor's sophisticated drawl had dropped into a more blurred cadence, one that I recognized from Southern actors and actresses. Not quite Dixie, but close.

"Eleanor," said Lulu, draping her arms around her. "You are the least wicked woman that I know."

"You didn't mean to hurt Hal," I said.

"No, of course not," said Eleanor, "not at all. I quite adore him and love discussing chickens with him."

"Well, then," said Lulu.

"But I was angry when I wrote that scene," said Eleanor. "I've been angry, just brimful of hateful anger, every time that Sydney teases me about that old manuscript of his. I wanted to show him."

Lulu fussed and petted Eleanor some more. Eventually Eleanor agreed that the whole incident was just an accident. The pair decided to go for a drive, pleading a need to get out of the house.

"Would you like to go to the diner?" I said to Fred, who had sat silent, even slightly stunned through Eleanor's story.

Fred looked at me oddly. "Did Eleanor just confess to being a witch? Do you believe her?" he said, as if I should have reacted more than I had. Except by now, someone telling me that magic might be real seemed like old news.

"I need to talk to Florie again," I said to Fred. "We need to do that if we're ever going to understand what is going on."

Before we left, I hunted down Betsy in her room. I was worried about Renee and her strange behavior the night before. I asked Betsy to check on Renee.

"Of course," said Betsy. "I was going to start writing to other studios. This is the last picture that I'm making with Sydney." She rummaged through her trunk for stationery and envelopes.

"But what about Max?"

"Max is Max," said Betsy with a sigh. "Cannot help loving those three worry lines in his forehead but I don't like how he goes along with everything that Sydney says. He's just a studio flunky."

"Are you sure?" I said. There were times in recent days when I felt Max had more agency that we originally thought. That maybe he told what Sydney to do, and Sydney listened.

"It's always about the studio. Nothing but how the studio trusts him to get things right and the studio knows that he'll do what is necessary. I don't think he even cared that Hal was hurt," said Betsy, and she looked heartbroken at that thought.

Although I hated to agree, I had noticed how cool Max had been through the whole accident. It had been shocking to see Max making notes in his notebook as the ambulance came and took Hal away. And what about Paul? He'd been so unruffled about Paul even before Paul phoned him from the train station. As if he hadn't cared that people were disappearing.

"I'm glad that Pola went with Hal," I said. She'd grabbed her bag of knitting and climbed into the back of the ambulance last night. As far as I knew, she was still at the hospital.

"Yes," said Betsy. "And I'm not sure that they'll be back. Pola said something to me about how as soon as Hal is well, she's taking him back to Anaheim."

"What's in Anaheim?" I said.

"Her brother, and his chicken farm," said Betsy with a slightly hysterical giggle.

It shouldn't have been that funny, but it had been a terrible night. I started to giggle too. "So Hal will find out which comes first, the chicken or the egg?"

Betsy collapsed with a shriek of laughter. A shriek with a razor's edge of hysteria to it. Arkham started to fray even our most determined, hopeful player.

I heard Fred shout up the stairs. "We need to leave," he called.

I met him in the front hall.

"I need to swing by the University to pick up that microphone that they are lending me," Fred said. "We record Lulu screaming and then shoot the final scene as soon as the sun sets during the solstice tomorrow."

"Not another night shoot?" I said. "Not another shoot right after Hal's accident?" What was Sydney thinking? None of us were ready to start filming again.

Fred nodded. "Candles down the hallway, flames flickering in the mirrors, and Lulu screaming at the entrance of the stranger."

"And who is playing the stranger?" I said. It had been vague in all the discussions so far.

"Jim, he's the only actor left," said Fred. "Sydney wants him in the hood."

"The stranger is the hooded man?" I said. That was odd. The hooded man usually showed up earlier in a Fitzmaurice film and never had much to do with the actual plot.

"Yes," said Fred. "Guess the hooded man finally gets something to do. Make Lulu scream."

"Jim wore the hood and cape in the last film, so I won't have to make any changes," I said. As the tallest of our three regular actors, Jim made a fine skinny hooded man with the cape going all the way down to his ankles.

As we passed through the main door out of the house, I glanced down the hallway. The mirrors were playing the same tricks that I'd noticed the first day in Arkham. Showing other rooms in impossible angles. I couldn't see either Fred or myself in the reflections, but I could see through the open doors of the kitchen to Mrs Mayhew arguing with the cook about something. Both of them had hands waving in the air like witches trying an incantation over the cauldron. But I suspected it was just a discussion of the soup for lunch.

The mirrors also showed Sydney and Max entering the library, with the rows of books behind them like dark bricks in a cemetery wall. A wall filled with the dreams of dead men encased in gold-tooled leather bindings.

Betsy had joined Eleanor and Lulu in the sitting room, as if none of them could bear to be alone. Eleanor was still pale, and Lulu was watching her with narrowed eyes. Betsy was writing busily at a desk, planning a future far away from all of us. Max would miss her once she was gone, I thought. But Betsy was also right in thinking that he'd never notice her until she was gone. He was too busy trailing after Sydney, trying to be like Sydney, from his well-tailored suits to his fancy cigarette case.

I looked for Jim, but he was the only one out of sight. Perhaps because he was sitting in the window seat. Knowing Jim, he was probably napping upright.

Fred tugged at my shirt sleeve to get my attention. "Are you coming or going?" he said, while I stood frozen halfway in and halfway out of the door.

"I don't know," I said. "That's the problem. I don't know where we are going next."

"Velma's Diner first," said practical Fred. "It's almost lunch time. You'll feel better after a sandwich."

"That's your answer to everything," I said. "More food."

Fred nodded. "It's a simple answer but it works most of the time."

Velma's was busy, but nobody paid much attention to us. All the booths and tables were full, so we sat at counter stools. After a few minutes, Florie swung by with a coffee pot in one hand and a pair of menus in the other. She slapped the menus down in front of us.

"The movie folk," she said. "But less of you than last time."

"Just us two," agreed Fred. "How's the turkey sandwich?"

"Not bad, but the roast beef is better," said Florie. "Less of you at the Fitzmaurice place too. Hear the woods have been playing tricks."

I must have started, because she put the coffee pot down and patted my hand. "Can't keep secrets in Arkham," she said. "At least not for long. Got one missing, one in the hospital, and one sensible enough to walk herself out of that house, or so I hear."

"Paul went back to California," I said. "Hal's in the hospital and Pola's with him."

"Smart woman. Knitters nearly always are," said Florie, leaning on the counter with her notepad like she was taking our order. "You sure that one of you went back to California?"

"Yes, Paul went back more than a week ago," I counted the days since we had filmed in the woods.

"Guess that's why Mrs Mayhew had Humbert take his trunk up to the attic, then," said Florie.

"No," I said more slowly. "Max shipped it out. Didn't he, Fred?"

Fred nodded, but Florie just shook her head.

"Florie, how do you know about the trunk?" I asked.

"Humbert," said Florie. "He's kin. Besides, he eats here regularly enough. Heavy trunk, he said. Lots of things for a man to leave behind."

"Paul is in California," I said, more firmly. "If not, where would he be?"

"Now that," said Florie, "is a very good question." Somebody further down the counter shouted for more coffee. Florie picked up her pot. "So, turkey or roast beef?"

"Roast beef," Fred said.

"Turkey," I said.

Then, after she walked away, we both looked at each other, remembering the clawmarked tree and the man's coat waving from the branches overhead.

"And that was definitely blood on the ground," I said to Fred as we waited in a noisy, crowded diner for the world to stop spinning out of order.

Fred shook his head. "We don't know it was Paul's blood. Max got a phone call from him."

"Max got a call from somebody saying he was Paul," I said. "Remember, he said that he picked it up and there was Paul. That the phone hadn't rung yet."

"So?" said Fred.

"What if it was Sydney, on his extension upstairs?" There were two phones in the house. The main one was on a little table downstairs just outside the library door but there was another in the little study just off Sydney's bedroom. It had been installed for his grandfather, Sydney told us, after the old man had trouble going up and down the stairs. He used it to talk to Mrs Mayhew downstairs as much to call out, so Sydney said.

Florie slapped our sandwiches in front of us. Fred took a big bite of roast beef and chewed thoughtfully. "Wouldn't Max know it was Sydney?"

"Sydney's good at imitating voices," I said. "Remember last year, at the cast party, when he did everyone, including how you talk about your camera 242 and Betsy's giggle when she slaps down her cards?" It had been a little uncanny, listening to Sydney parrot our pet phrases and vocal expressions back to us. His imitation of Paul asking to borrow a cigarette off Hal was particularly good.

Fred chewed some more but he didn't disagree that Sydney could have pulled off a quick conversation as Paul. "But why?" he said. "Why would he go to the trouble?"

"So we'd stop looking for Paul," I said. "Because if we knew something had happened to Paul, we might stop working."

"We'd never stop filming," said Fred, a little shocked at the idea.

"Why? Why do we keep going? Is a movie so important that we have to finish it, no matter what?" I said. "Even if it kills someone? Because that's what the studio expects us to do."

"Jeany!" Fred said and then stopped. Because I was right. That was what the studios expected. There was money in movies, lots of money and more every day, but only if new movies kept coming out and kept getting bigger, kept getting better, kept bringing people into the theater. Like Eleanor's play where the magician lost his hand. Like the film where the plane crashed. People might have been shocked or even horrified, but as Lulu said, the reviews were smashing.

"Accidents happen," said Fred. "But we don't get paid if the films don't get made and keep getting made. That's all that's happening. Maybe Sydney is cutting a few corners, but not more than usual."

"What if Sydney promised the studio something truly shocking?" I said. "Like that flyer film, where the pilot died."

"Nobody planned on that," said Fred. "It was a night landing and they made an error."

"But their studio still released the film," I said. "Sydney quoted the *LA Times* about it, 'what is gone in the flesh will live forevermore on the screen.'"

Directors cut corners, studios cut corners, everyone wanted something more and the business folks didn't really care what happened to the artists as long as the films were released and tickets sold. Fred was sticking his head in the sand if he thought Sydney and Max were immune to such pressures.

Fred shook his head. His sandwich was nothing but crumbs on this plate. I had barely touched mine as I considered all the ways that Sydney might do something truly horrible to the cast.

"I don't see how these accidents could be anything but accidents," said Fred, more slowly than before. I could almost see the thoughts tumbling through his head. Thoughts too terrible for a nice man who just liked to invent things. "It makes no sense that Sydney would ruin his own work."

"There's something strange about this script that Sydney has," I said. "And this ending with the hooded stranger. I think he promised the studio something terrible."

"Jeany, the studios, all the studios, are getting more and more nervous about moral codes, church protests, and civic investigations," said Fred. "If Sydney did anything dangerous, anything wrong, that might cause the studio to abandon this project. That's why we've got Max. To keep an eye on Sydney. Not just watch the expenses, but to stop Sydney from causing the type of trouble that might land us in the newspapers in the wrong way. They don't want another Fatty Arbuckle."

Florie whipped by us again, and eyed my uneaten sandwich with disfavor. "You should eat that," she said to me. "You are going to need your strength."

"Why?" I said. "What's happening?" I still didn't agree with Fred's assessment and was trying to think of ways to talk him into taking my point of view. Except he was right: nothing had happened that couldn't be labeled an accident, except the possible disappearance of Paul. And that was so vague, so uncertain. I needed more proof that Sydney was planning to create the accidents. That he had deliberately set out to harm the actors to terrify his audience.

And, if that got out, who would work with Sydney again? Would he risk losing his whole company, I asked myself. I shook my head. Of course, he wouldn't lose his actors. Hundreds of would-be stars were getting off the train every day, looking to become rich and famous in the movies. Look at Lulu, look at Renee, intelligent women still following Sydney's directions, even as others were harmed nearby.

Florie slapped down a bill. She looked with greater satisfaction at my plate. I'd managed to eat my entire sandwich while considering how I could prove Sydney such a villain that I could make Renee and all the rest abandon the picture.

"We should talk to Max," I said to Fred.

"Why Max?" he asked as he dug change out of his pocket to pay Florie.

"Because he's nervous about what the studio thinks. He's always nervous about that," I said. "If we can convince him that the studio heads will be angry about Sydney's plans, we might get the picture halted."

Fred tipped up his cap as he scratched the back of his head. "Maybe," he said. "But if the accidents haven't upset them yet, there's not much we can give them."

"There must be something more," I said.

Florie brought back the change and thanked Fred when he told her to keep it as a tip. "Have you talked to Professor Krosnowski yet?" she said to me. "She's a bit worried about you."

"The professor that was here the other night?" I said. "Mister Claude asked me to talk to her too."

"Good advice," said Florie. "You can find her at the University this afternoon. She's teaching today. Try the English department first. If she's not there, then she'll be in the stacks, looking for some dusty old book."

Fred settled his cap more firmly on his head. "I'm heading to the University for a microphone. You could talk to the professor while I'm picking that up," he said.

I nodded and asked Florie, "What classes does she teach?"

"The nasty kind that people like," said Florie. "All about murder, and devils, and curses. Only she calls it poetry and literature. Writes, too. Mostly local history – she just changes the names so nobody recognizes their family in it and calls it fiction to stay out of trouble. If anyone knows what Sydney Fitzmaurice is up to, it's the professor. She's got a powerful dislike of that man and his movies. Rants about him every time a Fitzmaurice picture plays at the movie house."

"But why?" I said, being more than a little tired of vague warnings. "What did Sydney do?"

Florie put down her coffee pot and leaned over the counter to whisper in my ear. "She says that he murdered a girl with magic. On the summer solstice."

CHAPTER TWENTY

During the drive to the University, Fred and I debated the possibility that Sydney might have killed someone. Fred didn't believe it. I almost didn't. Not the way that Florie said. It was Sydney, who I had known for years. He was flamboyant and self-centered and more than a little careless about how his ideas might impact someone else. But murder? Sydney's style was selfish. He put people at risk and probably didn't care if people got hurt. But it was stunts that he could justify as risky but worth it. It was pretty common throughout Hollywood. But deliberately murder someone? That was harder to imagine, but this summer, I was starting to imagine it. And then I thought of Renee and groaned. How was I going to convince her that Sydney was so dangerous?

"And what did Florie mean, a murder with magic? A magic trick that went wrong? Like Eleanor's guillotine?" said Fred.

"I don't think Eleanor likes to think of it as her guillotine," I said, remembering the upset woman that we'd left behind at the Fitzmaurice house. "But I could see Sydney setting up a trick and not being too careful or thinking it through. Like that balloon that he wanted to use. Or directing Selby off the mountain."

Fred nodded. "I cannot see it. Not like shooting or stabbing someone."

"No," I said. "But Mister Claude mentioned something. About a circus performer. One that went missing after Sydney set up a new act for her."

A woman of the air, wearing a mirrored mask, who reflected the flames, as I recalled our conversation. So much like how Sydney described his masked stranger in this movie. Too much like it for my comfort.

"Maybe this professor knew her too," said Fred. "And that's why Mister Claude wanted you to talk to her."

I nodded. That made sense, and apparently both Mister Claude and Professor Christine Krosnowski knew Florie. "I think that all the news in Arkham isn't in the newspapers," I said. "I think it all goes through Velma's Diner."

"Good diner is hard to beat for gossip," agreed Fred.

When we got to the University, Fred was sent in one direction to collect his microphone while I went in search of the English department. We agreed to meet back at the car.

I found Professor Christine Krosnowski in a tiny closet-sized office in the English department. I slid through the partly open door and took the one seat in front of the desk. Behind her was a peeling wall calendar and a bucket with a mop.

"The janitor and I share," said the professor, with a glance at the bucket. "I work days. He works nights. As you can see, I'm highly valued by my colleagues."

"But why do you work here?" I said. It was an odd conversation. It felt like we fell into talking like old friends or at least recent companions. Except we had nothing in common and had only met once, very briefly, at Velma's Diner. "Couldn't you teach elsewhere?" I honestly wanted to know, even though it was the least urgent question that I had to ask her.

"One of the Seven Sisters?" the professor said. "Probably. But Miskatonic has its charms. Especially the library. And teaching leaves me plenty of time for writing. For the pulps." She smiled a particularly wicked smile. "Which does make the old dears on the academic side rather livid. Except they can never prove, never want to prove, that I'm writing about them. So they give me whatever class that they don't want and the worst office on campus. Not that I care. Not as long as I get paid for my teaching and access to the more... shall we say... off-limits areas of the library."

"Florie said that you wanted to see me. So did Mister Claude," I said.

She tapped one finger on the desk. Thinking about what to say next, I guessed. Her face was a little severe but not unfriendly. As a teacher, she must have been one of those with eyes in the back of her head. I met a few nuns like that back in Oakland. The teachers who always gave the impression that they knew exactly what you were thinking and were pondering how best to open your mind to greater possibilities.

"What do you know about magic?" said the professor.

"Stage magic? Like the kind that Mister Claude performs?" I asked.

"No," she said. Tap, tap went the finger. Pay attention was the message, I guessed. "The real stuff. Magic to open doors. Magic to let things out."

"Thin spots," I said, remembering the conversation with Pete in the woods.

The professor tilted her head and pursed her lips. "Deliberate openings, not just natural occurrences. The Macedonians brought it into Egypt with Alexander. Or the Macedonians found it elsewhere and carried it back from further north or further east. It's not like Napoleon's savants understood what they found."

"Napoleon's followers," I said. "Like the first Fitzmaurice."

"Yes, that one," said the professor. "He went to Egypt, following Napoleon's orders, with a whole gaggle of men, called savants, to study history, especially the ruins related to Alexander, another military man dedicated to conquering the world. Some say that the savants went seeking magic to make their general stronger. Almost found it too. But Napoleon abandoned them to go back to Europe, and they started bickering among themselves. Eventually Saturnin Fitzmaurice returned to France, but the wrong way round the Mediterranean, going east, going north, following some map of Alexander's conquests. Picking up items all along the way."

"Sydney's grandfather thought everything was taken from an Egyptian tomb," I said. "At least that's what Humbert says. And Sydney."

The professor shook her head. "There's been a number of people at the University who talked their way into old man Fitzmaurice's parlor to look at his 'treasures.' A hodgepodge of history, one of them called it, a magpie's picking of loot."

It seemed the magpie approach was Sydney's family heritage, I thought, and told the professor about Sydney's own collecting of strange objects from occult shops and bits of stories from everywhere.

"Too many like that. No scholarship. Just collect to collect. But Saturnin Fitzmaurice finally crossed the wrong people in Europe. He fled all the way to Arkham. With a wife who was a priestess by all accounts. Of a religion far older than even the pyramids."

I shook my head. "That's not what Sydney says. He's descended from French nobility." I remembered the stories, the quotes given to Darrell the day he came to the house and had his leg crushed under Saturnin's portrait.

"Descended from a Marseilles wharf rat who deserted the French army and jumped ship for a country as far away as he could get with a stolen bride and artifacts," the professor said. "You shouldn't believe what people say about themselves. Always check your facts." The last sounded like a piece of advice that she gave her students regularly.

"Everyone in the movies invents a new biography," I said, and I wasn't trying to excuse Sydney. But I wasn't sure what she was driving at. What did she really know that wasn't very ancient history?

"It's a very American thing to do, reinventing yourself," said the professor. "But murdering women with magic. That's a Fitzmaurice trick, and one we need to stop."

"This is about the circus performer," I said. "Mister Claude told me about her. But she died in an accident. Or maybe died. Nobody ever found her body." It could not be murder. It was about taking risks, about causing accidents, about… I was terrified and babbling in my head. Because if Sydney was a murderer, he was in a house with my sister. My sister who was not acting anything like herself when I left her last night.

"Lucinda," said the professor, mentioning the same name that Mister Claude had. "She came later. She was his second victim. The woman that I knew, my student, died almost exactly ten years ago, performing that atrocious ritual that

Saturnin brought to Arkham. The solstice ritual of the masked Camilla, to bring forth the hooded Stranger."

"But that's the character that my... that Renee is performing," I said. And inside my head, I was screaming, and Renee was not with me. Renee was in a house with Sydney. And Sydney, if he believed what the professor said that he believed, was beyond dangerous.

"Camilla isn't a name," said the professor, lecturing me as if we were in a classroom instead of a closet and she wasn't discussing murders happening to real people. "The Camilla is, as far as I can tell, a title. The title of the head priestess. The Cassilda is the secondary priestess, the one that opens the ritual with a bird-like scream, according to the notes that I've seen. But that old man, Sydney's grandfather, turned the whole ritual into a play back in the 1850s. A couple of French savants did that in Paris as well. Ended badly there too. Fitzmaurice tried to peddle his version to the Booth brothers before the Civil War, but they never produced it. The brothers fell out. Fitzmaurice moved back to Arkham, where he kept trying to sell various members of the University on performing his ritual."

"The professors here? But didn't they think that was dangerous?"

Christine Krosnowski snorted. "That wouldn't worry my Miskatonic colleagues then or now. They tried at various times to get hold of the manuscript for the University library. Orphaned young, Sydney became his grandfather's pet. A more spoiled brat of a rich man's son..." She sighed. "And handsome too. Still is, I hear."

"Some people think so."

The professor nodded. "I had a student, a young woman who wanted to be a writer and an actress. Violet had so much talent. Sydney talked her into adapting the old play that he found in his grandfather's papers. She brought it to me, in bits and pieces. Asking my advice. And, to my regret, I encouraged her to work on it. It was all about masks and strangers, a woman calling forth a hooded man. Bringing the stranger to our world through a doorway in a mirror. Every time I read what she had written, I'd have terrible nightmares. The dreams lingered for days."

"That's what we've been filming," I said, not that I wanted to confirm her fears. Why hadn't the professor stopped Sydney then? Why was I going to have to do something now? "A movie about two sisters, waiting for a stranger. Only there are mirrors that explode and a silver mask."

Christine Krosnowski sighed. "Then he's still at it. Just like his ancestors. They've tried before. Several times. Always on the summer solstice, always between the thirteenth and twenty-eighth year of a century, in five-year intervals. In Sydney's case, 1913 with my student Violet, 1918 with the circus performer Lucinda, and now 1923."

"With our film," I said.

"If this attempt fails, he might be able to make one attempt in 1928," she replied. "After that, he'll need to wait for another eighty-five years. And a grandson to carry out his wishes."

"Why those dates?"

"Comets. A pair of twin comets, Camilla and Cassilda. Tiny little things, barely visible to the better telescopes. Predicted in 1801 by a French astronomer who had been left behind in Egypt and based on some texts that he discovered in a temple. Texts later stolen by Saturnin Fitzmaurice. It wasn't until 1828 that somebody actually spotted both comets and confirmed their existence. Then they disappeared for eighty-five years, reappearing in 1913. And every five years since."

Rituals, comets, magic. I shook my head. It made horrible sense and it was complete nonsense. "It's all like a fairy tale or a bad Haggard novel."

"Never doubt that there's fact behind fiction," said the professor. "Poets and other writers often use the metaphor of nightmares quite effectively to explain phenomena that scientists cannot. I don't know how or why these comets appear in such a strange pattern. One of my... odder... colleagues here has suggested that they come and go from our universe."

"I'm sorry?"

"Nobody ever said that Neely Chambers made sense, but he's been teaching at Miskatonic since the 1890s. He was a friend of Sydney's grandfather and tried more than once to liberate the Fitzmaurice manuscripts for his own collection. Neely, in his more lucid moments, has suggested that there are comets and other space phenomena that slide between two universes. He also claims that alien entities once colonized the South Pole." She looked a little embarrassed by the last statement. "Some days I think Neely should be writing for the pulps too."

"But what happens?" I said. "What will Sydney do?"

"I don't know," the professor admitted. She shuffled some papers on her desk, not looking directly at me. "I wasn't there when Violet disappeared. I should have been. I had enough doubts about the project. There was a fire. Everyone remembers that. The theater burned down and had to be rebuilt. The audience got out, mostly through sheer luck, as did the cast. But Violet was never found. I tried to push the police to investigate, but they claimed she ran off with Sydney. He took a train out of town that night."

"But that's not what happened?" I wasn't going to panic, I told myself. I was going to leave this closet and this crazy story, and I was going straight back to the house and make everyone leave. Everyone. Nobody was safe if Sydney believed he could open doors between universes with killing rituals.

"Nobody ever heard from Violet again. When Sydney reappeared as the ringmaster of a small Midwestern circus in spring of 1918, I read about it in the *Arkham Advertiser* and asked a friend to investigate."

"Mister Claude." Based on the conversation that I just had with him.

"An intelligent man. We met at an auction, both bidding on occult texts. I won," she smiled. "But we kept up a correspondence after that. He's visited a few times, to explore the stacks. Five years ago, I asked him to look into the circus and see if Sydney and Violet were a couple there."

"And no Violet?"

"No sign of her at all. But Violet had no family in Arkham. She was an orphan and at the University on a scholarship. So nobody cared." The professor straightened the pile of papers to her satisfaction and finally looked directly at me. "Julius made the same mistakes I did. He couldn't believe that Sydney would go so far. And there was so little real proof. Just a woman who disappeared. Strange talk about mirrors and doors. Then Lucinda disappeared, during the summer solstice performance. There was a fire, and confusion, and although nobody saw her get out, no body was found either."

"And no police investigation?"

"Julius tried. But he couldn't get anywhere. Carneys aren't particularly fond of the police. Nor do the police care for vagabonds." The professor tapped her desk. "So Lucinda vanished, and Sydney left the Midwest for the West Coast. That's as much as we knew when the articles started appearing about Fitzmaurice's terror films. His nightmares on the silver screen."

"He started making movies in November 1918," I said, wondering who the "we" was in her story. Florie, certainly, and Mister Claude, but could there be more people investigating the arcane events of Arkham? "At least that's when we met Sydney." However I didn't explain that my "we" meant my orphaned sister and I, either. "He'd married a woman in San Francisco. She gave him the money to start out as director. Then the studio recruited all of us."

"What happened to the wife?"

I shrugged. "Nothing much. A divorce. She wasn't interested in performing and she did have lots of family, wealthy family back in San Francisco."

"So, not the perfect victim," said the professor. "At least not the way that I think he picks his victims."

"No," I said. But Renee did fit that pattern. A woman alone, as far as Sydney knew, with no visible family. A woman who was grateful to him for her artistic career and passionate enough about making that career to overlook Sydney's more obvious flaws. And a sister who was going to save her, I kept telling myself, despite all the mistakes that we had made. "But our leading lady, Renee Love, she's much like the others that you describe."

"Julius said that there were two women playing the sisters."

"Lulu McIntyre. But Lulu has Eleanor, and Eleanor would kill Sydney before she would let anything happen to Lulu," I said. "Possibly with magic."

The professor raised her eyebrows. "Interesting."

"Except," I said, thinking back over our conversations at the house, "Sydney wanted them here. He recruited Lulu, for her scream, and Eleanor, for her witch ancestors. At least, that's the gossip. Eleanor might even know more about Sydney's manuscript. He keeps giving her quotes from it for her scenarios."

"Having a woman of magic translating his work into his current art form," the professor nodded. "That might be the key. Things have never quite aligned for the Fitzmaurice men. Saturnin had the comets and his priestess. But he failed."

"How?" I said, because this was important. I needed to know how to stop Sydney.

"Arkham has its protections. In the first case, Saturnin Fitzmaurice was opposed by a woman of magic, a maid in the house who got the children out. But she kept the terror in."

"That ancestor of Florie and Humbert?" This town, with its secrets and its families, we didn't need to be in such a town, I thought. We needed to be heading home to California, where everyone could reinvent themselves and become what they wanted to be. Not where they were caught up in family stories more than century old.

The professor nodded again. "A useful woman. Also, Saturnin lacked a mask. At least according to what Neely learned from Sydney's grandfather. For that old man, the explanation was the ritual had gone wrong because the priestess was improperly presented. She needed to be masked in silver, according to his notes. But Sydney's grandfather found a mask somewhere."

I didn't tell her that I'd found that mask. That it was sitting on a table in my bedroom, waiting for Sydney to find it and use it.

"But not just the mask, it can't be that simple," I said. I was arguing mystic rituals in a broom closet with a woman who taught poetry and collected occult texts. How had I gotten to this place? And what could I do to save Renee?

"No," said the professor. "We're sure that there is more to it than that. Every time, Sydney has tried this and failed, because he was missing some element. Every time was an experiment in magic, an experiment in opening a door for the Hooded Man. If he fails again, he'll have another chance in 1928, then the comets will be gone. Stop him now, and save your friends."

"But why me?" I said out loud, finally, the cry that was echoing through my head.

"Because you can," said the professor. "You can enter the house. You can pull the others out, like Rebecca Baker."

"But why can't you help me?" I said. "Come to the house. Explain to the others."

She shook her head. "Sydney dislikes me intensely. So the house will keep me out. It barely lets Ashcan Pete and Duke walk across the lawn, and you were with them, an invited guest. Julius made it onto the grounds, again as an invited guest, but he said that he could feel the house pushing him away the entire time. And as for poor Darrell, I understand it bruised his leg. I've tried three times to go up that drive and once through the woods. Neither path would open for me. Turned me right around and left me somewhere that I didn't want to be."

A house that pushed people away. A house that was waiting to devour us. I believed her but I couldn't say why.

I stood up. "I'll go back now," I said. "I still have time to get rid of the mask and get Renee out of the house. All of them." Fred, Betsy, Max, Eleanor, and Lulu. None of them should be hurt because of Sydney's strange obsession. But how was I going to make them believe me? When I barely believed it myself.

As I walked back to the car, I tried different arguments in my head. None of my arguments convinced me. It all sounded like one of Eleanor's scenarios. Only more overwrought and underthought, as Renee had said once about a film that we'd both wanted to like more than we did.

But the mask. The mask was still up in my room. The mask and my paper copy. I could destroy the paper one easily. I could get rid of the other. Bury it, drown it, blow it up with Fred's flash powder. That might make Sydney pause. That could give me time to get the others out of the house.

During the ride back to the Fitzmaurice house, Fred kept talking about the microphone and recording device that he'd borrowed from the University. As well as the size of the Miskatonic laboratory that he'd seen. Apparently the engineering students and their professors had impressed him. Or at least given him ideas.

"Sound as a weapon," he said. "That's one of their ideas. Imagine, a shout that breaks a piece of glass and, if amplified, could crack a battleship."

"I think we don't need any more weapons in the world," I said. "Certainly no more noise."

"Well, just a scream or two," said Fred. "Luckily the professors were interested in what Sydney was trying to do. They want a copy of the recording and the film. One of them has an idea for synching film and sound. And then broadcasting it like radio."

"That sounds…" I was going to say "impossible." But was anything impossible in Arkham?

"It's a big leap," said Fred. "But there's others talking about it. Electric telescopes. But nothing like films. Just a simple image. But somebody will figure it out. There's an invention a minute, big stuff, little stuff."

"Maybe it will be you," I said.

Fred grinned. "Wouldn't it be great? To show films all around the world anywhere you want to watch them? The studio would love that. I can see Max totaling up the dollars."

"Except, how do you sell tickets? Wouldn't you need it to be in a theater?" I said. Because making money, that's all the studio cared about. At least, that's what Max usually said.

"Subscriptions. Like a magazine," Fred said. "Pay so much and get so many movies broadcast to your box. Max would figure something out. He likes money."

Max was smart with money. Max was smart. Fred was right when he suggested earlier that I go to Max. The studio had hired Max to control Sydney. So all I needed to do was to go to Max.

"How did your meeting go?" asked Fred, finally coming down from the clouds of contemplating all the ways that sound and pictures could be broadcast.

"She's an interesting woman," I said. "And Florie was right. The professor is worried about people getting hurt on the set. She said one of Sydney's plays started a fire at a theater here. And there was another at a circus where Sydney worked."

"He's careless," said Fred. "Sydney's always thinking about how something's going to look to the audience. He forgets that there are people on the set. Like his exploding mirrors. But was there really a murder?"

"Nobody knows," I hedged. I wanted to talk to Max before I tried to get Fred to believe in magic. Fred was just too practical for talk of rituals and other worlds. Max probably wouldn't believe it either, but he'd be worried about how such stories would impact the studio. This was much more serious than Sydney's known dabbling with the occult. "They never found any bodies, but two women did disappear."

Fred looked troubled as he turned the wheel and started to drive past the Fitzmaurice gates up to the house. "Maybe you're right, Jeany," he said. "Maybe this is the last film that we should make with Sydney. Hal shouldn't have been hurt like that. Paul had the right idea."

"So you think Paul went to California?"

Fred stopped the car in front of the house. He walked around it to open my door. "Where else could he have gone? But I'll look in the attic. After we record Lulu. If his trunk is there, we can investigate further."

"I'll go look in the attic," I said. After all, I had to pick up the mask in my room. Destroy it, hide it, do something with it. The solstice was almost on us.

As soon as we entered the house, Max and Sydney came popping out of the library. Soon all three men were in a deep discussion about the placement of the camera, the placement of the microphone, the recording equipment, the cords needed, and the sequence of events. Fred thought it best to record Lulu first, that would take the longest to do, then shut off the microphone and film the scene.

Lulu and Eleanor heard the talk and came out of the parlor to investigate. Neither Betsy nor Renee were downstairs. I ran upstairs looking for them, determined to talk to Max later, when I could get him away from the rest. If he listened, we could stop the filming today and all be on the train to California tomorrow.

Renee was in her room, looking much more rested than she had for days. She was looking at a magazine and eating strawberries. When she saw me, she waved me toward the bowl.

"They're delicious. Mrs Mayhew brought them from her garden. Wasn't that kind?"

I nodded, thought about discussing what I learned from the professor, and then remembered all Renee's objections the night before. Better talk to Max first, I decided. I grabbed a strawberry from the bowl, kissed her cheek, and told her that I had things to do.

"Helping Fred record Lulu's screams?" Renee said.

"Something like that," I said. "Looking for Betsy."

"She's out. She's packed a bag for Pola, who is staying near the hospital. Betsy said that she'd take it to her. She called for a taxi an hour or so ago."

"I'm sorry we didn't know," I said. "Fred and I could have taken her."

"Pola rang after you left. Hal's sitting up and talking a little."

"That's a relief."

Renee nodded. She kept looking down at the papers in her lap. What I'd taken for a magazine at first glance was a colored folder containing a few loose sheets of paper, densely written in Sydney's flamboyant handwriting.

"What's that?" I said.

"Camilla's ritual," said Renee. I started, but my sister didn't notice. "It's lovely. All about welcoming the hooded stranger into the world. To make the world anew. It's lovely." She murmured in a lower voice. "To open the way is simple – and the Hooded Man will stride the world in a moment of light."

The mirror behind her was full of shadows, shadows of women lost in smoke and fire, and I almost cried out. I wanted to spin her around on her chair and tell her to look at what Sydney was doing. But she was the elder, and I was the younger, and when had Renee ever done what I had asked? I needed help.

So I ran out of the room and down the hall. In my room, I pulled the mask off my desk and thought about how I could destroy it. But then I stopped. Sydney wanted the mask. He had made that clear. Maybe I could bargain with him. Give Sydney the mask, take Renee and the rest out of Arkham. He could try again in 1928. That's what the professor had said.

It was a terrible, cowardly thought. I was ashamed as soon as that idea came to mind. But I couldn't destroy the mask. The more I looked at it, that simple silver mask, the heavier the air became. It was as if the house was pressing down on me, stopping me from moving, preventing me from doing anything.

"No!" I said and lunged under my bed for my suitcase. I threw it open and tossed the mask into it. I slammed down the lid then I shoved the suitcase back under the bed.

Then the screams began, horrible, terrible shrieks, that rang through the house. Startled, I went out the hallway. What were they doing? We weren't supposed to film Lulu's screaming until tomorrow. Her cries continued. Screams that could break glass, sink a battleship, that could tear your heart from your breast. Lulu was screaming. And she wasn't stopping.

CHAPTER TWENTY-ONE

At the top of the stairs, looking down the long hallway, I saw the mirrors. I saw the mirrors more clearly than I should. They reflected a hallway twice as long as it really was. The mirrors reflected images that shouldn't be there. Not when I could see where people were standing. But, as usual, the mirrors caught and bent and reflected around corners all that was happening in that long hallway.

The reflections showed Eleanor, struggling in Max's arms, as he held her back from Lulu. Fred crouched over a recording machine, a statue of a man, responding to nothing but the whirling gadget before him. Sydney was to one side, watching, just watching.

Then I spotted Jim playing the hooded man. At least it should have been Jim. A tall gaunt figure in a hooded cloak, standing in the doorway, opposite Lulu. But the door was at an impossible, wrong angle to the hallway. The reflected hooded man in the doorway was too tall, too thin, elongated and stretched beyond ordinary human size. Everything was wrong, crooked, and out of true alignment. Everything that I saw was a trick of those mirrors and a deception of the reflections.

In the depths of the mirrors, another house stood, with hallways that opened onto rooms with windows full of alien landscapes. Burning suns and lavender skies, twisted trees and birds with impossible razor beaks, dog men scrambling over the window sills and loping down the hallways, closer and closer, to a hooded man who raised a fist to hammer on the mirror glass.

I froze. Terror held me still. Then I forced myself to take another step down the stairs. The world slid back to a wooden hallway filled with cables and a shiny metal microphone. The tall figure in the hood, the real man standing in the hallway, turned with an uncertain step. It was just Jim, a baffled looking Jim.

"Sydney," said Jim, pushing the hood off his face. "What now? Do we need to keep rehearsing?"

Sydney didn't respond. He seemed fascinated by something outside of our view, something reflected in the mirrors.

Lulu's scream dropped to a whisper as she shredded her voice in terror. Then she crumpled to the ground. Eleanor, with one last vicious kick at Max, broke free and ran to her, sobbing. I hurried down the stairs as Eleanor shook Lulu, trying to wake her.

"What's wrong with her?" Eleanor said. "I never wrote this. I never wanted this."

I turned to Fred, yelling at him, "What are you doing? Help us."

Fred shook himself free of the recording equipment. Blinking like a man who had just woken up, he ran to us. "What is it? Did she shock herself on the mike?"

Eleanor said, "She fainted."

"What happened?" I asked Fred.

"We started recording. Then silence."

"Silence? She screamed forever."

Fred shook his head at me. "I couldn't hear anything."

"What were you doing?" I said. "You weren't filming this scene until tomorrow."

"Max wanted to test the equipment. So no more accidents," said Fred, who still seemed uncertain, almost as if he was sleepwalking through his responses. "This was just a test."

"I could hear Lulu all through the house," I snapped at him. "Eleanor, Eleanor, let go." I pulled at her hands, worried at how tightly she was clutching Lulu. "Let's move her into the parlor and onto the couch."

Lulu's eyelids fluttered and then she opened her eyes. She started to speak, but the only sound that she could produce was a reptilian croaking that clearly frightened her as much as it disturbed the rest of us.

Fred fetched Mrs Mayhew from the kitchen, who listened to our sputtered explanations.

"Hot water, lemon, black pepper, and mustard," she said. "Best cure for a strained voice."

The revolting beverage produced, Lulu sipped it with grimaces. Eleanor watched her with a forced smiled and reassuring comments.

Jim pulled off the hooded robe with a look of near loathing, announcing that he would be smoking in the garden. He pulled a hip flask out of his pocket as he exited through the kitchen.

I dragged Fred back into the hallway. The mirrors, when I glanced at them, were quiet, reflecting only ordinary things. Reflecting us standing there with a silver microphone between us.

"Now," I said again, wanting to understand what had happened. The professor, Julius, everyone seemed certain that we had until the summer solstice to stop Sydney. "What went wrong?"

"Nothing," said Fred. "Lulu started to scream, in fact she kind of played it up, like she does. Showing off. The microphone and recorder worked. But…"

"But what?"

He started moving down the hallway, unplugging cords and winding them neatly over his arm. Deliberate slow moves, like he did when he was worried, and then Fred said, "I couldn't hear anything. Not Lulu, not anyone else. Not you, not until you started shouting my name. It was as if…"

He stopped again and slowly packed the cords back into their box. He dismantled the microphone and put it away.

"As if what?" I said. I'd never known Fred so hesitant to speak, so slow to say what he was thinking. Usually he had a hundred ideas about why, and what, and how something happened, especially when it came to the gadgets in his clever hands.

Fred turned to me, his ordinary pleasant face screwed up into a grimace of remembered pain. "In the War, back when I was driving a truck full of supplies to the boys at the front, I got hit by a bomb."

"Fred!"

"Well, I got missed by a bomb. It exploded right in front of us. And I was deaf for hours. Jeany, it was like that. Like an explosion, and all of a sudden, I couldn't hear."

"But what did you see?" I asked, thinking of the strange reflections in the mirrors, the alien landscape that I thought I glimpsed.

"Nothing," said Fred. "I couldn't hear and… and… no, it's like a dream. When you wake up and you're sure that you remember everything, but nothing is there."

I knew exactly what he was describing. I felt the same. The shadows in the mirrors, already the images were fading. I struggled to hold onto those pictures in my mind. To hold onto other ideas as well. Warnings from the professor, from Julius, from Florie, and Pete. It was if the house knew how much I hated it and was trying to make me forget. Make us all forget how much danger that we were in.

A car honked outside and a door slammed. Quick footsteps tapped across the porch, and Betsy opened the door. "Do you have a dollar for a cab?" she said. "I spent my money on chocolates for Hal and forgot to put extra in my purse."

Eleanor came out of the parlor. "Do you have a cab? Tell him to wait," she said. Turning to us, she added, "I'm taking Lulu to the hospital. Somebody needs to look at her throat. She can't talk."

"Are you coming back tonight?"

Eleanor paused, and seemed to recover a little of the elegant poise that marked her when she first came to the Fitzmaurice house, but then she said, "We may send someone for the car and our things. I want to be out of here now. I never meant this to happen, but I don't dare write another word for Sydney. Here, you take this, I don't want it. I don't want anything to do with movies."

She thrust a piece of paper into my hand and went back into the parlor to fetch Lulu. The pair hurried outside to Betsy's cab. With a crunch of gravel, the taxi left.

"What did she give you?" Betsy asked.

It was a piece of paper covered with Eleanor's neat typing. Two scenes were laid out in two brief, pithy paragraphs. The ending of our film.

The first said, "The Hooded Stranger arrives. The younger sister recognizes that her doom is on her. Cassilda screams, a haunting sound that can never be forgotten, and then she is silenced forever. Her voice is gone."

That was the scene that they had just finished rehearsing. The scene that had destroyed Lulu's voice. But it was the second paragraph that terrified me. It was the second paragraph that described Renee's fate.

The second said, "Camilla dons the silver mask. She becomes a creature of the Hooded Stranger and opens the way, and herself is lost forever in the world of the Hooded Stranger. But the Hooded Stranger advances, stepping straight toward the audience and into our world. The power of the Hooded Stranger cannot be denied by any who watch."

CHAPTER TWENTY-TWO

The rest of the evening was my nightmares made real. Wherever I turned, whoever I talked to, it was if there was a wall of glass between us. As if they could hear nothing that I said. As if I was speaking to reflections in a mirror.

I went to Renee first, with Eleanor's horrible script folded in my pants pocket. My sister barely lifted her eyes from her dressing table mirror to acknowledge my presence. No matter what I said, no matter how I pleaded, Renee only shook her head and said, "Nearly done. Then we go home."

Betsy and Jim were just the same. Mumbling agreement but then retreating to their rooms. Locking their doors against me, even as I knocked, and cried, and in one angry moment, kicked the panels of Betsy's door so hard that it shook.

Fred retreated to the barn to blow up mirrors. Despite all he had seen and heard, he seemed determined to finish the film. Talking to him, shouting at him, I felt as if I was yelling at an imitation Fred, one who kept nodding at what I said but forgot it as soon as he turned away from me.

So I searched the house for Max, hoping to find him and get him to stop everything. To call the studio and tell them. Tell them something, but I found myself forgetting exactly what the professor said and so tired that I couldn't keep searching, so tired that I had to retreat to my room. I forced myself to drag open my sketchbook and began to draw. A young woman consumed by fire; two young women, one flying above the other, a college student and a circus aerialist – two women whose stories had been forgotten except by a few. Two women whose names were slipping away from me as well, the longer I stayed in that horrible house.

By morning, Eleanor and Lulu had not returned. Renee remained in bed, mumbling and rolling away from me when I tried to shake her awake. Everyone else was unnaturally silent at the breakfast table. I could barely hold my eyes open. I certainly felt as if I was being gagged, being smothered, by the atmosphere. We all were like wan ghosts of our normal selves.

Except for Sydney and Max; Max splendidly dressed for the final day of filming, chatting with an unbearably jolly Sydney. The pair spent the entire meal talking about box office expectations and predicting great profits for the studio. It was so horribly ordinary, but I couldn't seem to say anything there, inside the house, even now that I had Max in front of me.

After breakfast I fled to the porch, gulping the fresh air, glad to be out of the house, terrified to go back in, trying to think where to go next. Betsy and Fred followed me, and seemed more alert outside the house. But when I proposed that we pack our bags and leave, they turned shocked stares to me.

"But I'm going to play Cassilda," said Betsy. "Max says with Lulu gone, I can be the younger sister in this scene." Her eyes glittered unnaturally and her voice was brittle. An imitation Betsy, with none of her usual good-humored sparkle. I shook my head at that mad idea. This was one of my best friends, of course I could convince her of the danger.

"I'll wear the white dress and stand in the back, with a veil over my head, the second priestess, Max says. Max will tell the studio what a trouper I was, helping out when Lulu left, and that should help with getting bigger parts." Betsy spoke like a wind-up doll, the words sensible but the tone of her voice flat and almost drugged. How many times had she played the victim of a mesmerist, a vampire, a creature that sapped her will? How had she suddenly become the characters that she played in real life?

"Oh, Max says that," I said with some sarcasm, hoping to provoke a reaction. "And why do you want to stay, Fred? I thought you cared about us. That you wanted to prevent these accidents."

Fred sounded as compliant as Betsy. "I have prevented the accidents. Everyone is safe because of me. You are safe, Jeany." He spoke in a monotone, pointing at a stack of crates on the porch. "It's all in the can. And packed up for shipping back to the studio." He meant the film canisters neatly crated for shipping. "We'll all work together when we get back to California."

"It will all be wonderful, the best picture ever. Max said so," Betsy repeated.

"Max said so." I parroted her intonation from earlier. "But aren't you tired of waiting around for Max? Going to get on with your career?" It was as if she'd forgotten all that had happened in the last twenty-four hours. As if she'd forgotten everything that she'd said to me just yesterday.

"Max says everything will be wonderful," Betsy told me so earnestly.

"Max says the studio is very happy," added Fred. "I need to explode those mirrors. We need that to finish the picture. I have a job to do," He picked up 242. He even patted it on the side as he walked down to the barn.

Betsy grabbed the tripod and hurried after him, obviously not wanting to stay and argue with me.

And, as stunned as I was by their sudden change in attitude, I never thought once about the strangest part of the conversation. Neither mentioned Sydney. Both acted as if Max was in charge.

As the sound of shattering glass and probable bad luck filled the air, I paced the porch. No matter what I said, nobody seemed inclined to leave. We'd been loyal to Sydney for years, putting up with his fits and starts, but this was something different. This was a danger to Renee.

But nothing could happen without the mask, I thought. The mask was well hidden in my room. But was it? The more I thought about it, simply being in a suitcase under my bed wasn't enough.

I entered the house, determined to hide or destroy the mask totally. That would delay the filming. Once past the solstice, the professor had claimed that it would be another five years before Sydney could try again.

Peeking into Renee's room, I saw that she was still a dreaming beauty, lost amid the pile of lace-edged pillows. I closed the door softly and hurried to my room.

Pulling my suitcase out from under the bed, I flipped open the top. It was near bursting with my sketchbooks, each page filled with drawings of strange monstrous women, twisted pale spires rising above a mist-enfolded city, trees that dripped poison, dog-headed men, and the distant figure of the Hooded Stranger. All the records of my dreams during that long strange month in Arkham. And under and over and around the edges of every picture was sketch after sketch of the silver mask.

But as I lifted out the sketchbooks and stacked them on the floor, I realized that the bottom of my suitcase was completely empty. The metal mask and its paper twin were gone.

"Sydney," I gasped. Who else would take the masks? No wonder he had been so pleased at breakfast. He had everything now. Eleanor's scenario, the masks, the recording of Lulu's scream, all the elements that he needed for tonight's ritual, including my beautiful sister as his sacrifice. Suddenly my head was clearer than it had been for hours, anger at Sydney and his manipulations burning away the horrible fog that I had struggled in.

Now I would force Max to listen to me. I would tell him about the women who disappeared. I would make him realize that continuing this film could bring unprecedented scandal to the studio. That he should stop or at least delay Sydney past this year's summer solstice.

I heard the men's voices outside my bedroom window. Looking out, I saw Max and Sydney walking across the back lawn towards the woods. Sydney carried a shotgun in the crook of his arm. Hunting for crows, I thought. As if he hadn't caused enough trouble the last time.

I ran out of the room and down the little hidden stair at the back, exiting through the pantry. The kitchen was eerily empty, all the breakfast dishes neatly washed and stacked beside the sink, but no sign of Mrs Mayhew or the cook. Their hats and coats were missing from their usual hooks beside the door. As if they too had vanished into a mirror.

But it was Friday, I thought, and Mrs Mayhew did her shopping on Friday for the weekend. No doubt Ethel had gone with her.

I crossed the lawn to the gate that led into the woods. I saw nothing of Sydney or Max. From the barn came the sound of more exploding glass. I hoped Fred's barrier of hay bales was protecting Betsy and him from the mayhem. Then I opened the gate and ran down the path toward the pond, determined to catch up with Max and get him away from Sydney long enough to talk. To stop the filming of the final scene.

The woods were worse than I remembered. Sticky hot under the trees and the buzzing of insects more shrill than ever before. As I ran, I heard a horrid panting sound amid the rustling of the bushes. I didn't slow, I didn't look, I just kept running, determined to catch up to the men. Even Sydney, carrying his shotgun, would be preferable to whatever stalked through the trees behind me.

I reached the pond. The murky waters smelled worse than before, a stench of decay, as if a thousand fish had died here. I circled the pond. There was no sign of the men. I kept to the path that we'd followed earlier. My panting shadow kept pace with me but never so close that I could catch a glimpse of it.

But after the pond I could find nothing familiar. Once or twice I thought I heard Sydney's big laugh or a shout from Max. But when I shouted back, nothing answered. Nothing but the buzzing of insects and the huffing bark of my shadow pursuer.

Every turn of the path took me deeper into the trees. The long, pallid trunks stretching above me, the branches bare of all but the most withered leaves, none of it looked like the summer woods that we'd filmed in. Nowhere could I find the foundations of the little burned house or the tree with the black coat swinging from its branches.

Instead I stumbled through my nightmare forest, endless shadowed paths twisting me around and around, until I nearly dropped to the ground, so tired, so hopeless, that I wanted to curl up in the muddy leaves and let whatever pursued me in the shadows finally win our strange race.

Somewhere, somewhere too close, a barking laugh of triumph mocked my despair. I knew I had lost. Renee was lost. I could not save anyone.

Then the crows attacked. With harsh cries they flew in my face, claws tangling in my hair, wings buffeting me. I flung my arms to the side, trying to beat them off, screaming in fear and frustration, as I'd wanted to scream all night. The crows swooped and dived unrelentingly, until I turned in my tracks. Under a rain of black tormentors, I ran through the woods as fast I could.

Every time I stumbled, every time I paused, the crows dived down again and drove me along the path with terrible shrieks and caws. The smell of the pond overwhelmed me. I wanted to stop, to vomit, to give up, but the crows wouldn't let me. I stumbled on.

At last I reached the gate to the lawn. With trembling hands, I wrenched it open and fell forward onto the newly mown grass. With long graceful swoops, the crows flew past me, whirling through the sky to settle on the roof.

As I watched the birds fly away from me, I saw that the sun had moved much further in the sky than I expected. Long evening shadows, the house's shadow the longest and crookedest of them all, stretched across the lawn. I'd lost the entire solstice day in those terrible woods.

I veered toward the barn, determined to find Fred and recruit his help. But the barn was empty except for the shattered remains of a dozen mirrors, the glass winking red reflections in the light of the setting sun.

Tired beyond anything that I had ever known, I turned back to the house. This time, I decided that nothing would stop me. I would find Max. I would keep Sydney from filming on the solstice. I would take Renee out of this cursed house and away from Sydney. Not even those terrible crows would keep hold me back.

I circled round the house to the front door. The crates for the studio were still stacked neatly at the end of the porch, ready to be sent to the train station, ready for the studio to take possession.

The sun was nearly down. Looking through the half-open front door, I could see that Sydney had lined the hallway with candles, the flames flickering brighter than I expected, reflected in every mirror. At one end of the hallway, furthest away from me, Fred was busy cranking old 242. Nearer to the door was Jim, dressed in the robes of the Hooded Stranger. Betsy was arranged beside him in a long veil that covered her hair and face completely. Between them and the camera, Renee stood perfectly still in the long white dress that I had made for her original performance as the murderous siren. But this time, she held in her hand the silver mask. As I watched, she slowly raised the mask to her face. I screamed at her to stop, but nobody moved, nobody looked at me. Once again, just like in my nightmares, I was on the wrong side of the mirror.

Somewhere further down the shadowed hallway, I heard Sydney's voice, not shouting directions, but intoning some sibilant syllables. Nonsense words, but the more he spoke, the greater my feeling of terror grew.

"Stop," I shouted. "Max, you have to stop them."

As I went across the porch, Max stepped into the doorway.

"Max," I sobbed in relief. Finally somebody who looked straight at me. Finally somebody who would listen to me. "You have to stop him. Something terrible is going to happen."

Max looked at me, as mild as ever, pushing his notebook into the breast pocket of his finely tailored suit. "Yes," he said. "That's what the studio is paying for."

"No, no," I cried. "Max, you don't understand. This time the magic is real."

Max laughed. "That's what Sydney promised. Now go away, Jeany." He smiled at me with a broad grin, the bravado of Sydney at his very worst. "We have the mask. We don't need you any more. Nobody needs you any more."

Then Max slammed the door in my face. I heard the lock click into place, even as I rattled on the knob and then bloodied my hands beating on the panels, screaming for my sister, screaming for Fred.

CHAPTER TWENTY-THREE

I quickly realized that bruising my hands upon the door would do nothing to help Fred and Betsy, to save my sister. So I started around the house, determined to enter through the kitchen door. Max had obviously thought of that too. It was locked. No matter how hard I shook it or kicked it, the door would not budge.

All the windows were locked too. Every door barred. All the time, I could feel that horrible, terrible house pushing against me. I remembered what the professor had said. That the house could keep out those that it did not want. That it was part of the terrible Fitzmaurice magic.

I circled back to the porch and then I spotted it. A long heavy hammer sitting on top of one of the boxes on the porch. Humbert must have left it there after nailing the wooden crates shut. It was just what I needed.

I picked up the hammer. It felt solid and so right in my hand. I walked up to the parlor window. Through the glass I could see the smirking smile of that Fitzmaurice portrait, the one that Sydney's ancestor felt was more important than saving his children or his wife. I grinned back at Saturnin Fitzmaurice and swung the hammer hard against the window glass.

It took three strikes, but the windows shattered under my blows. I reached inside, careless of the broken glass, and unlocked the window. I shoved up the sash and crawled in, still clutching the hammer in my hand. Blood dripped from my hands, but I ignored the cuts as I crossed the room. After the crows, after Max's betrayal, nothing stung as much as my anger.

The parlor door, like all the rest, was locked. I used the claw head of the hammer to pry open the lock with a satisfying splintering of wood and screaming metal.

As I stepped into the hallway, I stepped into the hell of my worst nightmares.

Flames lit all the mirrors. But the flames were inside the glass, not outside, an impossibility that belonged to dreams. The smoke flowed out of the mirrors, overwhelming the vague light of the candles as the nebulous figures moved in it, some human, some not.

I did not care. I plunged into the smoke, crying out for Renee, screaming for my sister. I brushed against a long veil and the figure of a woman. It was Betsy. I tore the veil and my second paper mask off her face. She stared blankly at me until I grabbed her and squeezed her hand so hard that my nails dug into her skin and drew her blood to mingle with my own.

With a gasp, Betsy blinked and stared around her. "What is it?" she said.

"Fire," I yelled back, barely able to speak with the smoke choking me. "Hold on to me. We need to get out."

Betsy grabbed my shoulder and we stumbled forward in the smoke. The click, click of the camera turning led me to Fred, bent over the viewfinder, oblivious to the smoke that billowed through a hallway now ten times longer than it ever was before.

I smacked the back of his head and knocked his silly cap forward on his nose. Fred straightened up with a cry. "Jeany?" he said, looking around him with puzzled eyes.

"Fire!" I yelled. "Hold on to Betsy. We need to get out."

Fred fumbled for his camera and hissed. He pulled his hand away from the metal body of 242 with blistered fingers.

"How? What?" he said. "How can that be burning?"

"Get away!" I said, pulling again on his arm.

Fred grabbed Betsy's arm with his unburned hand, and we went forward.

A hooded figure stood before us.

"Jim!" we all shouted, but the figure that turned toward us wasn't Jim. It wasn't like anything that I'd ever seen before. It might have been a man, but a man so impossibly beautiful that he seemed alien, with pallid skin and looking-glass eyes that reflected the flames now springing out of the mirrors. I froze, caught between awe and terror, and then my anger surged up again. This was the figure that had haunted my dreams. This was the creature that was trying to steal my sister.

With a shout, I flung the hammer at him. I swear that the Hooded Man didn't move but a mirror shattered behind him. Then the glass of the mirror ran in liquid drops, melting together until the mirror reformed on the wall.

We stumbled backward, an ungainly trio of three very ordinary humans trying to find their way and not lose their grip on each other.

And we smacked into Sydney. He stood entranced by his own spell, a burning manuscript in his hands. His skin was beginning to smoke, but he showed no sign of pain. He took no notice of the flames at all. But he looked directly at me when I tried to swat the burning paper out of his hands.

"What are you doing?" he cried.

"Leaving," I said. And then, because Renee had loved him, still loved him for all that I knew, "Hold on to us. Help us."

But Sydney turned away into the smoke, walking toward the stranger reflected in the mirrors. "My king, my king, I have found your way into the world. We will capture men's minds and control their simplest thoughts." Sydney's clothes smoked and began to burn, cloaking him in flame.

Horrified, I pushed the others away from Sydney, lost in his delusion, his final scenario, the end of his terror picture.

"Hold on to me," I said to Fred and Betsy. In the mirrors, a masked woman stood behind the Hooded Man. I turned away from the reflection and walked into the center of the smoke.

Renee stood like a glistening pillar of ice, a woman all in white, masked and crowned in silver, not in the costume that I had made but in the one that I had dreamed, the one that I had drawn on page after page of my sketchbook. An extraterrestrial garment summoned by dreams and magic to clothe this goddess, a stranger herself…

Until I reached out and grabbed her hand. I gripped her fingers hard, the way that a little sister will when she wants to lead her big sister to safety.

At first her hand lay cold and lifeless in mine. Then she stirred, and clasped my hand as she always had, a squeeze of comfort, an intertwining of our fingers, that universal language that Sydney sought, the language of love.

I looked into the mask of silver and saw nothing but a reflection of myself. So that I was mirrored and twinned and paired in the smoke and darkness. Dark hair, dark eyes, half Chinese, half Swedish, all American, two sisters lost in a world that called them names and knocked them down. Two women who dared to overcome that. Two sisters who loved each other even when they forgot to say it.

"Renee," I called out, using the name that she gave herself on a train hurtling toward a future that she made happen by sheer force of will, my brave, my beautiful, my wonderful big sister.

"Jeany," she said in so soft a whisper that I could barely hear it over the crackle of flames burning in the mirrors. Then louder, and in the language of our mother, the musical and well-remembered words for "little sister."

I pulled her toward the door, or at least where I thought the door should be. We walked forward through the smoke. My sister holding my hand, my friends with their hands on my shoulders, moving together past the nightmares.

Then, just as we reached the door, there was Max. Still immaculately turned out, still looking more like a bookkeeper than a villain. Not at all what I expected to find in the final reel of a Sydney Fitzmaurice film.

"What are you doing?" he echoed Sydney.

"Getting out," I said, reaching around him for the door.

"You can't," he shouted, pulling at me, trying to shove Renee away from me. "We need this picture. This is for the studio." He cried it as Sydney had cried for his king. "I'll be rich. They've promised me so much money. The Hooded Man filmed for real. Pictures around the world to make his commands into our commands. I will never be poor again."

"Let me go, Max," I said, struggling to get by him. "We have to get out." The house was actually burning now. The smoke was bitter and real and stinging in my throat. The flames hissed, eating through the walls and the floor. This time nobody would try to save the mirrors and a portrait. Because there were more important people to save.

Max grabbed me, shoving me hard against the others, fighting to keep us from leaving.

"Get away from her," said my sister, my defender, who had always knocked down the bullies who challenged us. My Renee, suddenly speaking with all the strength she contained. She lifted her free hand and tore the mask from her face.

Max looked at her and screamed. I looked back over my shoulder and shuddered. For the mask had heated, burning part of her face, creating an unnatural scar of silver dripping from forehead to chin. She looked like a monster. But she also looked like my sister.

"We are done," I said, and pulled past Max. I felt the doorknob under my hand and the metal was still blessedly cool. I turned the knob and pushed with all my remaining strength. The door swung open. We staggered out of the smoke and onto the porch, all of us together.

Except for Max. Betsy tried to grab him as she passed. He reached out for her as if to draw her back into that inferno. Then the Hooded Man appeared directly behind Max, placing a pallid hand on Max's shoulder. Max gave a shout. With one great push he shoved Betsy through the door, sending her flying after us onto the porch.

The door slammed shut. I don't know if it was Max again or the house itself that locked us out.

But we *were* out.

Smoke poured from all the windows. The crackle of flames was louder than our harsh breathing. We ran together down the long drive to the gate, only to be met by a clamor of bells. A firetruck went swinging by, followed by Doctor Wills' rattletrap car and Mrs Mayhew's old farm truck. The professor climbed out of the doctor's car. Then Florie slid from the passenger side of Mrs Mayhew's truck.

I collapsed into my sister's arms, trying to hug her, Betsy, Fred, everyone all at once, unable to breathe for the happiest of reasons as I gathered them to me. We were alive.

Doctor Wills took us to the hospital to be treated for what she called smoke inhalation.

When I tried to explain what truly happened, she shook her head. "Only so much I can note on a chart," she said. "Smoke inhalation works better than saying that you were poisoned by the atmosphere of an alien world. A world that collided briefly with ours through ambition, greed, and magic stolen out of a lost temple."

After looking at the silver scar that ran down my sister's face, Doctor Wills recorded that as the result of burns, burning film to be precise. I stopped protesting to the doctor. Later, Florie, who had followed us to the hospital, leaned over to me and said, "Those who need to know will know. We'll do our best to keep everyone safe."

After the doctor bandaged Renee's face and the nurses gave her something to make her sleep, I sat on the edge of her bed, still holding tight to her hand.

Florie eventually gave way to the professor that night. The two paced outside our room like sentinels, guarding us from who knows what, and rotating in and out of the room to check on us. The professor gripped my shoulder tightly for a moment. "You did well," she said. "You got them out."

"Not everyone," I said. Although I could not mourn Sydney, I saw Betsy's tears when she realized that Max was lost. Nobody could remember seeing Jim at the start of the fire, but he was supposed to have been in the scene. If he was, then I feared that he had joined Paul elsewhere.

"You did your best," said the professor. "Sometimes that is all we can do."

EPILOGUE
Santa Monica, 1926

The wind blows through this little house by the ocean, cleansing it with the smell of salt sea air. The sun shines in every corner. There are no shadows. There are no mirrors to reflect ghosts or strangers. This house is as different as possible from Sydney's strange home in Arkham. It's also as different as possible from Renee's Alhambra apartments. There were, we found, too many reminders of Sydney in those rooms. Gifts that he had given Renee, the flower vases that used to be filled with roses, and even the coffee table Max piled high with newspapers so Sydney could read the reviews out loud. How Sydney would have loved all the press after his death, all the speculation on what had actually happened.

After the fire was put out, the Arkham firemen found Sydney's body. Unlike his ancestor, it was intact. A few months later, the studio claimed to have found a will in their files. It appeared to be signed by Sydney and left everything to Renee, as the muse of his heart. Did he write that? Or did the studio think that if they gave her an inheritance and a love story, she would ask fewer questions and let the verdict stand? I vacillated between the two explanations until Fred said, "What does it matter?"

The studio needn't have worried about Renee. She had no wish to reveal what had happened in those final days before Sydney's death. In fact, she stopped talking about him after we left Arkham. I was more than willing to let Sydney Fitzmaurice fade into a Hollywood legend. But I mourned Max, despite his equal villainy. For at the end, at the very end, I am sure that he pushed Betsy out the door to save her.

"The studio killed Max," I said. "Making him work for Sydney, exposing him to that evil."

"Is he dead?" Betsy asked me again and again. "They never found his body."

We disappeared for a time, so Renee could heal, but her silver scars never faded. Despite my suggestions for makeup and costumes, she shook her head and claimed that she was done. She had no wish to act.

Then Sydney's wife brought the lawsuit. The reporters hunted us down at our apartment, and newspaper stories started about the final, unfinished film and all the accidents surrounding it. The articles confused Renee with her characters, filling their pages with a woman who was more siren, more vampire, than ordinary mortal. Only the *Arkham Advertiser* printed other stories, all illustrated with photos taken by Darrell, about the beautiful Renee Love and her tender relationship with Sydney Fitzmaurice. Darrell's influence, clearly, and Renee sent him a long letter of thanks with an autographed photo from her unscarred days.

Some of the press dealt with the disappearances of those final moments, about the people never found: Max, Jim, and Paul. But Arkham's police refused to investigate, suggesting that Paul had gone back to California for another job, Jim had followed him, and Max had left town with some of the studio's money. I suspect it was someone at the studio that named Max an embezzler because they didn't want to explain why they had given him the money in the first place. Their plan, however outlandish and improbable, to control the world through films created with magic – that might be hard to explain to their shareholders or to a Congress that increasingly liked to hold hearings on the morality of the film industry.

"Movie people," the police and the press finally said, as if this explained the sudden and total disappearances, and left the mysteries at that.

In the end, the court ruled that as Sydney was legally divorced, the first Mrs Fitzmaurice had no more claim on his estate. They gave everything to Renee, including what was left of the Fitzmaurice house in Arkham.

Renee ordered the burnt and ruined house boarded up. A year later, we bought this little house here on the Pacific Ocean, not too far from where Fred lives. It's a short walk to the Pleasure Pier. Some nights Fred and I go dancing at the La Monica Ballroom.

Fred is working more and more on inventions. He has ideas, wonderful ideas, and there's always someone in Hollywood who wants to do the next thing bigger and better than the way it was done before. But Fred cannot run a camera anymore. His beloved 242 was destroyed in the fire and the burns on his right hand made his fingers stiff. Besides, Fred's hands tremble. Not too much, not so most people would notice, but I notice. When his hands start to quiver, I hold them between mine and wait for the shaking to stop. But we both know that he will never crank a camera as smoothly as before. So, being Fred, he is working on a motor and a way to turn the film without using his hands. I draw the plans and help with patent applications. It is one small way that we battle the curse that Sydney brought upon us. It is a battle that we will win.

Eleanor and Lulu write frequently. Ashcan Pete and Duke found Pumpkin wandering by the river the day after the fire. Eleanor wanted to give Pete a reward, but he refused.

After Arkham, Eleanor and Lulu discovered that New York was too much for them. Eleanor found it impossible to write plays. Even with the return of her voice, Lulu disliked the darkness of backstage in their theater. They've gone to Seattle to teach drama at a college there. It's all very Bohemian, says Eleanor in her latest letter, with dancers, musicians, and artists mingling in the classrooms. There's hours of debate about the meaning of art, but nobody thinks they can change the world. At least not the way that Sydney and Max planned to do it. Inspired by Renee, Lulu has bought a cabin on a beach and they motor out to it every weekend. Pumpkin, says Eleanor, would be positively sleek except that the founder of the college, a woman with a pug of her own, insists on feeding pancakes to all small dogs.

I write back as often as possible. I tell Eleanor and Lulu about Hal and Pola and their chicken farm in Anaheim, as well as all our other news.

Betsy is in pictures again and doing very well. Sennett cast her in some comedies. Then she became the "flapper detective" in a popular series. Betsy now leaps from galloping horses or runaway cars. She flashes a silverplated gun in the shadows as she takes down the villain. All her stunts she does herself, seeking out people to train her on more and more difficult tasks.

Fred and I take her dancing and keep introducing her to other young men. Betsy speaks less and less of Max to us, but she keeps up a correspondence with the professor after meeting her at the Arkham hospital. She talks of going back. More and more after last winter, when Jim was found wandering down a road near Kingsport. He's in an asylum now, mostly because he never sleeps, just sits looking in mirrors or other reflective surfaces.

I hear from those we met in Arkham. Mister Claude mails me tickets for when he's playing a theater near Los Angeles. The professor sends me packages of pulp magazines and challenges me to find her stories in their pages. Florie writes the most. Her letters are funny cheerful scribbles, all about the gossip served with pie and coffee at Velma's. She sends clippings from the *Arkham Advertiser*, so I know what Darrell is doing.

Her feet hurt more and more, says Florie, and she's almost ready to give up the tips in return for a long sit someplace warm. Suzie has left Velma's for the brighter lights of Boston, says Florie. There's a new waitress, Agnes, who is a good gal, says Florie again.

If Betsy returns to Arkham, I think she should look up this Agnes. I read between the lines and know Florie means that this Agnes understands that not all doors and paths in Arkham lead to the places that we know. That some ways twist oddly and lead you out of this world. If Betsy does decide to go back, I will tell her to stop at Velma's first, before she tries to open the Fitzmaurice house. To talk to Darrell, whose newspaper stories hint at things unseen except by those who know how to look. To seek out Ashcan Pete and his faithful hound Duke. There are heroes in Arkham, and she will need them.

Renee's typewriter begins its daily clatter. She prefers to write outdoors, sitting at a little table on the deck that overlooks the ocean. Her face healed but the scars will never disappear. Eleanor put her in the way of script work. She'd been doing the work but found it tedious. Renee loves it. She always had a flair for a scene and now is writing whole scenarios, adapting other writers' stories and even creating a few from scratch. She receives requests from many directors who knew her during the early part of her career. All of her work now appears under R. Lin, rather than Renee Love.

I gather up my sketchbook, my pencils, and my fabric swatches. I have costumes to design, meetings to attend later in the day, and Fred will be coming over for dinner.

As I walk through the house, I hear Renee call. "Any letters today?"

There are. Letters from Eleanor, Betsy, and Pola. We will read them together over breakfast on the deck. As I sort through the mail, I find one envelope from the studio. I stuff the others in my sketchbook to share with Renee. This one I slit open and read by myself. The neatly typed letter is the same as all the others. A request for any information that we might have on Sydney's final film, any footage that might have survived the fire, any copies of the script, particularly Sydney's original manuscript. The last part is underlined.

I treat it as I treated all the rest of the studio's correspondence. I rip the letter into tiny shreds and throw the pieces off the edge of the deck. Let the wind take those words. Let the ocean drown them. I will never help the studio that encouraged Sydney and Max in their madness.

I will never tell them about the trunk filled with all those things, including the smoke-stained silver mask that Renee tore from her face. Humbert helped me empty the crates that had been marked for the studio and transfer everything into a sturdy steamer trunk. A trunk now locked and buried under old hay in the barn behind the Fitzmaurice house. Humbert checks on the barn, the house, and the trunk. He has instructions on what to do if somebody comes to Arkham with my key and a letter from me. He will show them the trunk, he will introduce them to the others. Humbert will let the crows know that there is somebody else to protect if they become lost in the woods.

I just hope that it is not Betsy. She wants to find Max. I would want the same if it was Fred. But still I fear for her. Despite her laughter and her courage, Arkham might destroy her. I feel in my pocket for the trunk key. It's there. It is always there. I never go anywhere without it.

The key is a reminder, like the letters, that I led my sister and my friends safely out of the hall of mirrors and flame. I hope that nobody who I love will ever return to Arkham. But if they do, I will help them as much as I can. And I am comforted by the thought that the professor, Pete, Darrell, and the others are still there. The ones who protect those who wander lost in Arkham's shifting ways.

Renee calls again. I answer and stride out into the California sunshine, to begin a new day with my sister.

ACKNOWLEDGMENTS

There is not enough room to list all the people who contribute to the making of a single book. For all of you, especially the many librarians and booksellers who helped me find information about early Hollywood and the lives of Chinese-Americans in 1920s California, please know that your suggestions from idea to finish were greatly appreciated. The mistakes are my own.

I do want to say a special thank you to Dawn, who sent a website link, Lottie, who answered an email with a tweet, and Phoebe, who asked "how many words today?" Without these ladies, there would be no book at all.

While the characters in this novel are fictional, a number of 1920s historical figures are mentioned in passing. I hope you have the time to learn more about Tye Leung Schulze, Anna May Wong, James Wong Howe, and others. Their histories deserve to be better known.

This story would not be possible without the many researchers, preservationists, and historians who documented the vast international silent movie industry, saved what footage they could, and worked hard to present the diversity of the industry. I greatly enjoyed seeing your contributions at film festivals and theaters in Seattle. I look forward to meeting again in the dark to watch the silver shadows.

Best wishes to all the readers who shared this journey and thank you.

ARKHAM HORROR™

The DEADLY GRIMOIRE

An ARKHAM HORROR *Novel*

August 3, 1926
Los Angeles, California

Dear Jeany,

Please don't fuss. I would never ask you to go back to Arkham. But I've had another note from the professor. Jim's started talking. So, hey ho, off I go. It's time I learned what happened to Max.

Mail me the keys. I promise to kiss Humbert for you. And that darling reporter. Do you know I'm probably the only woman in Hollywood with two subscriptions to the Arkham Advertiser? I bought one subscription and then all of a sudden another started arriving! Darrell sent the sweetest note, saying it was a gift to show his appreciation for posting him the publicity photos for The Flapper Detective and the Mysterious Sanctuary. Isn't that a whale of a title? I'm surprised they could fit it all on the poster.

And, if I say so myself, that Sanctuary idea was a bore. We needed some extra press. Far too many episodes of me standing around, waving my silver-plated pistol at the shadows on a wall – that's not an action serial! No leaping off trains or bounding across roofs. I should have had Eleanor rewrite that script. She knows how to put in a good scare or two. The Educational Screen called it "pretty trite stuff." But they say that about everything. The Arkham Advertiser called it "sheer brilliance that will delight any audience." Maybe I should buy a third subscription.

I didn't even drive my new car in the picture. It's a snappy little roadster, and they painted it blue to match my eyes. At least that's what the publicity folks are saying. Actually, it was that blue when I bought it. So much for old Henry Ford and everything being boring black. Wait until you see it.

Still, dull as the movie was, I looked fabulous in your costumes. The beaded dress! I'm keeping it for the next time I go dancing.

This latest script is much better, more like the Waves of Doom. Except it's the Wings of Dread. We will finish up the big aerial scene tomorrow.

Are you going to Don Juan? I know somebody who will want to know how the synchronized sound works! Don't be surprised if he disappears during the screening. Bet you find him sitting up with the projector. Of course, that's if he can tear himself away from you. Honestly, you should put that man out of his misery and marry him. Now don't give me your objections. I know all the difficulties. But other people have found a way.

Not that anyone should take love advice from me. Look what I'm doing. Searching for the one that got away in Arkham. Or did he? And is he the one I love?

Cross your fingers and wish me luck. Here's to not falling off the plane tomorrow.

With all my love,

Betsy

P.S. Did you hear about the rumrunners using a seaplane near Innsmouth? According to the Arkham Advertiser, they were smuggling a thousand cases a month from Canada. Someone squealed to the police. But they jumped bail and flew away. Now wouldn't that make a great story for the Flapper Detective?

CHAPTER ONE

My mother always said that men are like streetcars. If you miss one, just wait fifteen minutes and another comes along. But my granny said to be sure you catch the right streetcar. The wrong one could take you someplace you don't want to go.

I never knew if Max was the right one or not. Three years after he disappeared in Arkham, I still didn't know.

I went to Arkham with Sydney Fitzmaurice to film one of his terror pictures. Max was part of our crew. There were days when I thought he was the sweetie for me. There were days when his love of money drove me nuts. He made decisions that hurt people. I always suspected Max knew more about Paul's disappearance from the film set than he let on. Max wanted to be the next big cheese. Except when everything went horribly wrong, Max ended up toasted.

Or did he? They never found a body after the fire in the Fitzmaurice house. The officials blamed that disaster on us. Our fault for making a movie in an old house as dry as tinder and likely to burn, they said. I escaped, along with a few others, but when the smoke cleared, three men were gone. They found one man dead, but they never found the remains of Max or another actor, my friend Jim. Despite the fact that there was no evidence, everyone from the Arkham police to the Hollywood studio suits were happy to pronounce Max missing, probably dead, and close the book on that story. And while Jim did reappear some time later, his poor health and length of his disappearance meant I had concealed his return from the suits because I knew they wouldn't have believed me. As for Paul, who disappeared before the fire, they just said it proved film people were flighty.

Which drove me nuts. I was a film person, and I was not flighty. I asked questions afterward because I liked happy endings, or at least an ending. I never liked puzzles without solutions. Max was an equation I could not solve, not without more information.

"Anything for the post today, Miss Baxter?"

I glanced up at my butler. I poached him two years ago from Valentino's wife. Farnsworth said he preferred a more tranquil household.

My mansion in Beverly Hills was quiet. Of course, people who knew me from the pictures would have been surprised. They probably thought Betsy Baxter danced all night and slept all day. They weren't trying to run a Hollywood studio and star in one of the most stunt-filled serials ever filmed at the same time. I was lucky if I found my bed before midnight, but it was paperwork that kept me sleepless, not kicking up my heels around the town.

I dropped my letters on the silver tray Farnsworth extended toward me.

"That's all for today."

"Very good. Will you be home for dinner, or do you intend to dine at the hospital in a cast?"

Farnsworth often thought he was a comedian. And, honestly, his deadpan expression was so perfect I was tempted to invite Buster Keaton to the house for a few lessons.

"I'm performing one wing-walking stunt and that wraps the picture. It's as safe as houses," I told my doubting butler.

"Yes, miss. I'll be sure that the crutches are near the door for your return," he intoned without a single twinkle in his melancholy eyes. His voice carried such a plummy undertone of doom that I almost expected to hear the tolling of funeral bells. But there was something about the cock of his head that said he knew that I knew that he was putting one over on me. If they ever perfected talking pictures in Hollywood, Farnsworth would have them rolling in the aisles.

"Farnsworth, one of these days, I will fire you," I said. A cheap shot and not truly worthy of our usual exchanges, but I was in a hurry to finish up the mail and go to the airfield. I couldn't wait to try my wing-walking stunt in the air.

"If you fire me," said Farnsworth, still in his most disapproving tone, "you would have to supervise the cook. And the maids. To say nothing of the gardener, who reports an aphid infestation in one of the rose beds."

Farnsworth had a point. Why I decided to buy a mansion after *The Flapper Detective* became a hit, I don't know. But when a gal checks her brokerage account and finds she has flashed past her first million dollars and is sprinting toward her second and her accountant is touting property investment, then suddenly twenty rooms or more all wrapped up in a Tudor-style estate on Sunset Boulevard seemed like a sensible idea. I admit that I paid little attention to the house when I was purchasing it. I even nodded when the interior designer started nattering about "accommodations for seven master bedrooms and baths with sitting rooms and a guest's gallery." I still have no idea what a guest's gallery is.

That year, I had too many stunts to learn and a business to run because I'd bought the studio lock, stock, and barrel at the same time. When, in June 1925, I moved into the mansion with a couple of trunks, I found myself a bed and went back to work.

Of course, after a few days, it became clear that living alone in a mansion wasn't possible. It needed people to keep the guest's gallery clean, to say nothing of the roses trimmed in the garden. I wanted to walk down the path to the swimming pool without bumping into thorns.

The mansion, at least the running of it, was a disaster before Farnsworth. That's why I offered him a fortune to come and work for me. Even before I had money, I hated housework. After I had money, I found out I hated supervising housework. When I dissolved one cook into tears by spending our time together trying to explain why she should invest in commodities, it was obvious I needed an intermediary. She wanted to talk about fricassee. I wanted to talk about finances and why women would never achieve independence without understanding investing.

Farnsworth made the cook, the maids, and even the gardener happy. He looked like a director's idea of a butler, all straight posture and silver-gray hair on top. The English accent also charmed them. They understood the orders he gave them. The house and the grounds looked gorgeous, and the meals arrived when I wanted to eat. Even my guilt about worker exploitation waned after Farnsworth came up with a savings account system where we quietly banked a legacy for each servant. When they retired or decided to leave for other reasons, such as the cook finally opening up her own bakery, the legacy would be paid out to them. Everyone became fully vested after a year of service and the amount grew the longer they stayed. Nobody could steal my maids or gardeners after that. I already paid the highest wages in Hollywood. The legacy sweetened the deal.

"In England, of course, longtime servants received such a sum after the master or the mistress died," Farnsworth explained.

"Let's not anticipate anything drastic," I said.

"One hopes not," Farnsworth said, "but the wild horses do make one wonder."

"It was not a wild horse," I reminded him. "It was a very well-trained rodeo horse. Yakima Canutt said I made the perfect jump from it to the buckboard. And I did not break my ankle. I just twisted it."

"Yes, miss," he said. Farnsworth had, at my estimation, about seven different ways of expressing disbelief or disapproval with a simple phrase. The "yes, miss" was absolutely devastating.

I tried it on the studio's board once or twice. Not the "yes, miss" because I was the only "miss" in those meetings with the misters. But I had my own tone of absolute disapproval. It's hard to impress a bunch of suits when you're five foot nothing and have a head of red-blonde curls. Men tend to want to pat your head or some other part of your anatomy. I've had to break a few fingers, metaphorically and not so metaphorically, along the way. But I starred in the best-selling movie serial of all time, *The Flapper Detective*, with stunts that made

Pauline's perils look pale, and therefore I was the woman who made them all a lot of money.

Also, the studio suits learned, to their regret, that I owned *The Flapper Detective*, trademark and all, and thus could take their lovely moneymaker anywhere I wanted. Before I even pitched the first script, I tied everything up nice and legal. When the studio agreed to the pitch, I plunged into production, making sure the fact I did my own stunts, from bareback horse riding through to piloting a submarine, was well publicized. The audiences loved it, and the money came rolling in.

When the series became an overnight hit, I used my profits to buy every share of stock I could find. It said BB Pictures on the stationery now and in big iron letters on the studio gates.

So here I was, a millionaire twice over, in a too big house with a swanky English butler and a pool outside that I never had time to swim in. Max thought being rich made you happy. It made me happier than being poor. But it didn't solve the problem of Max and what happened to him in Arkham. "What's the good of being rich if you cannot answer the question that makes you itch?" I once said to the others who survived that fire in Arkham. Except it sounded too much like an advertising jingle when it popped out of my mouth one evening. My friends told me to forget Max and enjoy life. I did enjoy my life. I loved my work. I just wanted to know what happened that day in Arkham. More importantly, I wanted to find Max. Because I was sure they had not died.

Something else had happened that day, something I saw, or thought I saw, out of the corner of my eye. A flicker of a memory that I could never quite catch, except when I woke in that very dead hour between midnight and dawn.

"The car is at the door," Farnsworth said as I wrapped up the last of the morning's instructions to various employees, both at the mansion and at the studio. "Do you want Henry to drive?"

"No, it's a gorgeous day," I said. "I'm going to let it out and make the run to the airfield in record time."

"The wind in your hair?" Farnsworth said in another tone that indicated complete approbation as I hurried out of my office.

"Somebody will fix my hair when I get there! I am a movie star! Besides, I have a hat," I said as I scooted across the hall, grabbing my favorite hat and scarf from the top of the Roman statue of Venus. Why have a marble Venus if she cannot hold your hat?

"Madam will drive herself," Farnsworth said to Henry as I ran down the steps and hopped into my lovely blue roadster. "As usual."

"Figured," said Henry, who started out as a mechanic, worked as a cameraman for a time, and then went back to cars because there was less chatter than what a man heard on a movie set. At least that's what he told me when I hired him. He kept all my cars running like kittens, engines purring, and was modifying a motorcycle for me. I had an idea for a stunt but needed a bit more speed to make it work.

"Thanks, Henry!" I shouted as I let out the clutch of my roadster. "See you for dinner, Farnsworth!"

The car roared down the driveway. I settled into the seat, loving the feel of the wind washing over me. As long as I kept moving fast, nothing could catch me. Not even my memories of Arkham's shadows.

The airfield was full of people. A crowd to watch our stunts always made for good publicity. I pulled my car as close to the planes as I could. Standing up on the car seat so I was above everyone's heads, I waved and greeted the reporters. The wind picked up and sent my scarf sailing over my shoulder. I twirled and smiled and threw my hands high in the air. I may even have kicked up a Charleston step or two. Some of my best performances took place before the press. This one was a doozy.

"Come on, Betsy, we won't have the light forever," said Marian. My director strolled in the direction of the planes. I hopped over the car door and followed her.

"Are you still sure about this?" she said as we walked across the field.

"They won't call us trite," I said.

"How about stupid and reckless?" she answered. Marian always worried before a stunt. In some ways, she was worse than Farnsworth. But she never said that I couldn't do it. Nor was she callous about any of the folks in the cast, right down to the smallest bit player. She was one of those women who asked, "How are you?" and then paused to listen to the answer. I worked with many directors, some crazier than others, and Sydney Fitzmaurice was perhaps the oddest of all. Not just because he liked to frighten people but also how he persuaded all of us to take part in the bizarre production filmed in his hometown of Arkham. Later, I wondered why we never left his strange old house on the day we arrived, except it was bred into the bones of all actors to never question the director. As I learned in the summer of 1923, never asking questions can lead to tragic mistakes. After that terrible final week in Arkham, I resolved never to blindly accept what others told me to do.

Working in Hollywood, I quickly observed that many directors couldn't even be bothered to say hello. And remembering favorite cookies and pet's names and the other small stuff that made up a life? Not a chance.

So I decided if I was going to break my neck on a set, I wanted a director who would at least think to call Farnsworth so he could give the servants a night off.

Marian was much more than that. She was a person who cared about others. After Sydney's callous disregard for our lives, and I must admit Max's loyalty to Sydney didn't help keep us safe either, I wanted a director who saw everyone on the crew as a person. Having Marian directing my pictures was important. At least if I was at risk of losing my life, it was only because of the stunts that I thought up, not the antics somebody else told me to do.

Marian had started out in small parts like many of us, so she understood the challenges we all faced. She happily abandoned acting for being behind the camera early in her career. Lois Weber liked her and recommended her to me. Having a mystery serial about a daredevil female detective directed by another woman helped sell a few newspapers by covering us. A few holy rollers insisted on banning us in their towns, but that never hurt ticket sales.

I couldn't pay Marian near what she was worth when we started. However, I made sure her contracts gave her a share of the proceeds and then stock in the studio. She was a minority shareholder now, and her block and mine made us the majority by far. I voted and ran the business side for her, as she had no interest in it. When she wasn't directing me, she worked on a series of films intended to enlighten others about the pressing social problems of the day. Worthwhile but daunting to watch. I kept paying theaters to show her films.

"What do you think of the flyers?" I asked Marian, who was always a better judge of people than me. I tended to take people at their word, hence the problem of Max, and was wary of making the same mistake again.

"They have a good reputation. You'll like your pilot," she said. "They call her the Woman Without Fear."

"I thought that was my title," I said with a smile.

"No, Betsy," said Marian, absolutely serious, "you're the Fearless Flapper Detective."

We walked up to the biplane where the pilot was talking quietly to her mechanic. I had been practicing on a similar plane for a week, on the ground, along with a professional wing-walker as my partner for this stunt.

The regular wing-walker for the group, Charlie, was already there, all suited up and ready to go. He was a bit taller than the actor playing the villain, but nobody would be able to tell the difference in the long shots. We'd film a close-up with Roger later. Roger was terrified of heights, so we promised we'd do his bit on the studio floor and he didn't even have to watch my flight. Charlie was Mohawk and had worked around planes in the war, including a stint in Ireland. He seemed to regard standing on a wing in midflight the same as standing on the ground. He had been a terrific teacher, too, and his suggestions had helped craft the final scene.

We planned to recreate Gladys Roy's stunt of playing tennis with a partner on the top of the wing. Except instead of waving tennis rackets at each other, we'd brandish guns. Charlie would pretend to get shot and drop to the wing. Then I was set to slither down the wing and back to the front cockpit where my character was supposed to make a heroic landing. All the real flying would be done by the woman in the back cockpit. She made one last check of the landing gear before striding over to us.

"Betsy, this is Winifred Habbamock," said Marian.

"Wini," said the pilot with a calm nod. She was suited up in what I thought of as aviator's gear – leather hat with ear flaps, goggles, and heavy coat over trousers and boots, all to protect her from the wind and colder temperatures above the ground. On a warm sunny day, it must have been uncomfortable standing around in all that. Winifred Habbamock wore it with the panache typical of flyers. Well, the female pilots were the daredevils of the sky and the darlings of the press. That's why I'd wanted this picture to concentrate on a murder at an airfield. With reporters and adoring fans following the flying women around the country, I decided it was time for the Flapper Detective to have more adventures in the sky.

"It's a pleasure to meet you," I said to Winifred and meant it. I heard about this particular troupe of barnstormers from a couple of directors working on adding air stunts to their movies. Everyone said Habbamock was a spectacular pilot and that her crew had an admirable record for safety. Nobody had been killed on their tour, and that wasn't true of all aerial circuses crisscrossing the country. Of course, the possibility of seeing someone killed was what drew the crowds to the flying stunt shows and air derby races. Everyone knew that but just called it "the thrill" of watching planes buzzing above. The same good old bloodlust drew people to the pictures like mine or Sydney Fitzmaurice's horrid horror flicks.

Of course, my pictures had guaranteed happy endings. The Flapper Detective wins over all impossible physical perils… except the day that she doesn't. Underneath the squeals, the cheers, and the applause, there was that indrawn breath as my fans waited for me to fail.

"Charlie says you've been a good pupil," Wini said. "That you know all his signals and are smart about where you step. Are you ready to put on the harness and take to the air?"

"Absolutely! I can't wait. You sure about the tether?" I said. "I could do it without." Most of the wing-walkers didn't bother with ropes or parachutes. The more death-defying the better, but Charlie insisted on having safety lines and a harness with an "amateur" like me. The fact that I parachuted from a zeppelin in one of my earlier pictures hadn't impressed Charlie with my professional credentials as a risk-taker. Or maybe it had impressed him too much, hence the insistence on safety lines. People did call me "reckless", and I usually took such remarks as a compliment.

"Your choice on the tether," said Wini to me with a grin. "Your neck, too."

"Don't tease, Wini, or give me a heart attack," said Charlie. "It's a tether or a parachute."

"And wreck the line of my coat with one of your bulky parachutes? I cannot do that! Besides, we want to scare the audience," I said.

Wini gave me a wink. "Can't cheat the audience of their thrills. I keep telling Charlie the same thing."

He shook his head at the pair of us. "I walk the wing without any harness.

Same as my brothers and cousins walk the steel in Manhattan. But Betsy has never done this in the air. First time, you always go with a tether."

Wini nodded. "I was just teasing. The rules are the rules. We may take risks, but we keep people safe."

Dottie, who acted as my dresser on set, came running up with the fur-lined velvet coat my friend Jeany had designed for the scene. The coat had clever splits in the back and the side, which concealed the harness. We'd already filmed the scene leading up to this where Roger took my supposedly unconscious self out of the trunk of a car, carried me across the airfield, and chucked me in the front cockpit. How we got from there to an aerial gunfight would not be shown. The audience would fill that out in their heads. Nobody ever said my movies made sense. Not even the *Arkham Advertiser*.

"Do you have your gun?" Marian said to me.

I reached into the pocket of the coat and pulled out the silver-plated pistol.

"It's unloaded?" asked Wini.

"Not even blanks," I said, pulling the trigger with the pistol pointed at the ground. It clicked but no bang. While walking out on the wing, which was waxed cloth wrapped around the lightest possible wood frame, the flyers insisted we shouldn't even discharge blanks. Any damage to the plane could be fatal if we were unlucky. Keeping my balance and avoiding a Betsy-sized hole in the wing was important, too, so I wore my lowest, softest slippers. In my head, I kept running through the sequence of steps I needed to make. Put a foot wrong and I might put a foot through the wing. Charlie had made that abundantly clear during our week of practice.

Wini nodded at my demonstration of the unloaded pistol. "Good. The only person allowed to carry a loaded pistol on one of my flights is me," she said.

I climbed up on the lower wing. Charlie mounted beside me and finished clipping the lines to the harness under my coat. One more wave to the press and I was ready to go. Very ready! I truly couldn't wait to get into the air that day. I'd flown before but never been allowed to climb out on the wing. Whenever I left the ground, I wanted to go a little higher, be airborne a little longer. Balloons were nice, and the zeppelin had been thrilling, especially the parachuting part. I kept thinking airship travel would replace trains fairly soon.

"Don't forget to relax," Charlie reminded me as he climbed into the front cockpit. It wasn't really built for two, but luckily I was small enough to slide into the seat. We were squashed, but we fit. "Keep your muscles loose," he added. "No good being tense on the wing."

Wini dropped into her seat. She waved to the red-haired woman mechanic as the prop started whirring, and the woman waved back. I gave one last thumbs-up to Marian, who ran back to the ground camera. Above us another airplane banked in a lazy turn over the field. In the second plane was our other cameraman, who would be filming the fight from above.

Wini's job was to keep the plane steady and low so we could get good shots from both cameras. If she took us too high, Marian wouldn't have much to film from the ground angle. That's why we paid for a barnstormer. They were used to low maneuvers so their audience could see all the action, especially when the wing-walkers did their stunts.

We rose into the air with that bump that said goodbye to the ground. "If you can do it on land, you can do it in the air, Betsy, my girl," I said to myself. The wind hit us full in the face and it felt wonderful. The racket of the plane's engine and the wind made it unlikely Charlie could hear me muttering my usual litany of "up and at them" to steady my nerves. For me, as I explained later to Wini, it was never fear, not exactly, that made me almost quiver at the start of a stunt. It was something headier than that, an anticipation of the excitement to come.

Charlie tapped my shoulder, our prearranged signal, and I stretched my arms over my head to grab one of the struts. He gave me a bit of a boost that got me out of the seat. And then it was step, grab, turn, and step again, and reach for the next handhold. Just like we practiced, only now we were nearly a thousand feet up in the air. Not that I looked at the ground. My focus was all on the plane and the marks that told me where it was safe to place my feet. The wind hit me with a force like I'd never felt before. The plane's vibrations ran into my bones.

But I was in place, and Charlie was in place. I pulled the silver-plated pistol from my pocket. The sun sparkled off it as I mimed shooting at Charlie.

Charlie shot back with his prop gun. I shot again with lots of arm waving to make it evident to the audience that something had happened. Charlie then dropped flat. All went exactly as we rehearsed.

Until the wind turned and buffeted the plane. I felt the shudder as Wini tried to correct, but the plane tilted. All of a sudden, my footing was no longer secure. I bounced a bit on my toes, trying to adjust. It happened so fast I didn't have time to worry, not then. The worry would come just a few moments later.

Charlie's still prone body started to slide toward me. Then Wini adjusted, and the wings went level again, and he slid away. I huffed a little breath of relief. So far, so good. We had the stunt done. I trusted Marian to have captured the footage needed, even if the wind had thrown us off a little. So I started the sequence to return down the wing toward the cockpit.

Only now my lines were entangled with Charlie. His weight was pulling me off my feet. I fought to keep my balance as I slipped nearer to the edge of the wing. Even at that moment, I wasn't nervous. When I was in the middle of a stunt, I always felt this peaceful calm. Maybe that was why I kept challenging myself with harder and harder tricks. To prolong that moment of peace. People always asked me afterward, "Aren't you afraid?" But the fear came later, much later, when I thought about all the others who depended on me and what would happen to them if I fell.

The ground was a blur a long way down. Too far a fall to walk away alive. I remembered Charlie's lectures about not falling completely off the plane. Even if the tether held, I could strangle myself in the ropes before he could haul me back. Best case scenario was that I'd break a few bones.

Farnsworth, I thought, would not be pleased.

Then I fell.

CHAPTER TWO

My stomach hit the edge of the wing hard enough to knock the breath out of me. Charlie struggled with the lines, trying to untangle us and get himself back into the cockpit. He had to go in first for me to be able to slide in after him. Given our difference in sizes, me landing on the bottom would have meant a flattened Betsy for sure.

I kicked with my feet and clawed with my hands to stop my slide off the wing. The lines bit into my ribs. I wondered if they'd break. I had cracked a couple jumping off a speeding train last year. And the doctor had warned me about not breaking my collarbone again after doing a dive off some rocks onto more rocks concealed by the ocean in the first Flapper Detective adventure.

My legs kicked in a grotesque can-can over empty air as I slithered down the wing. I just couldn't reach the bottom wing or propel myself toward the center and the safety of the cockpit. Instead, I slipped closer and closer to the tip of the wing. And after that, well, it was nothing but nothing. If I got out of this, I vowed never to refuse a parachute. Well, maybe I would refuse a parachute if it looked better to the audience to be without one. Then I firmly told myself to stop arguing with myself. Now was not the time for nerves. The time to be afraid was after I managed to save myself, I said very firmly to the inner Betsy who wondered why she hadn't thought up a movie plot with less death and defying in the same scene.

I glanced over my shoulder to gauge the difficulty of dropping down to the lower wing and crawling my way back to the cockpit from there. Or I could just hold onto a strut and ride the wing all the way down to the ground. Some wing-walkers did that. Of course, if the bump of landing knocked me off the wing, there was a chance of being run over by the plane itself. That, and several other warnings sounded by Charlie during our training, echoed through my head.

Far too far away, the people watching us were tiny figures, just little dolls in the distance.

The ropes jerked as Charlie thumped off the wing and back into the seat. He angled forward, extending his arms toward me, trying to catch hold of a leg or other bit that I had waving wildly in the wind.

Unfortunately, I had skidded a bit too far along the wing. I realized I needed to shove myself back toward the center. Then I could descend, or at least fall in a controlled way, into Charlie's arms and back into the cockpit.

I kicked again with my legs. Nothing but the air beneath me and the wind up my skirts. "This is a ridiculous position," I told myself through gritted teeth. I eased the death grip of my right hand on the lines and felt along the edge of the wing. Clawing for something, anything, that I could use to pull myself where I wanted to go, I felt my hand slide along the rough canvas. My lower half also shifted. I was now much more off the wing than on it. I said a word that would have made Farnsworth blush.

Then the plane tilted. I yelled another profanity. One set of wings, the one that I was on, went up toward the sun and the other set waved at the earth. I slid toward the center like a kid going down a banister. Charlie's big hands grabbed my ankles and yanked me toward him. Then he used the lines and my coat to haul me into place like a fisherman reeling in a particularly ungainly trout.

So I completed the most ungraceful return to the cockpit ever done by a wing-walker. Well, Marian could edit that out, I decided. Or film a close-up on the ground. Definitely on the ground, I thought, as I wiggled into place.

If I ever did this again – and why wouldn't I do this again? – I could drop into the cockpit and then pretend to have a battle with another plane. Why hadn't I added that to the script? I wondered. My heart was pounding, my hair was a wind-tossed mess, and I had lost my hat. But it didn't matter. I smiled as we descended.

Looking over Charlie's shoulder, I saw the pilot, Wini, give me a big thumbs-up. I returned the gesture. If she hadn't banked the plane and slid me back to the center, I might have ended my career right there and then.

The plane touched down on the field and rolled without incident to a stop. A crowd of excited reporters waved notebooks and cameras to catch our attention as they swarmed onto the field.

"Give me a boost," I yelled at Charlie.

He lifted me out of the cockpit. I staggered a little but managed a credible little dance along the wing with a neat jump onto the grass. I resisted the urge to sink down and hug the dirt.

"What do you think?" I yelled at the reporters shouting at me. "Is it going to be the most exciting thing ever seen in a theater?"

"Weren't you terrified?" one woman with a notebook asked me. "When you fell?"

"It's all part of the stunt," I claimed. Now was the time when the bumps and bruises started to make themselves felt. Now I knew that cold fear, the one that always ran like a shiver through me at the end of a stunt, when I thought about how I might not come up with anything better ever again. What if the next stunt isn't as terrifying as I think it will be? What if the audience just yawn and turn away? But I quieted those nerves. I had an audience of journalists in front of me, all clamoring for me to be the brave Betsy Baxter, the unflappable Flapper Detective, and I gave the reporters exactly what they wanted.

I said, "I knew my pilot had her plane under control. And my partner here, Charlie, is the best wing-walker in the business. These fine performers wouldn't let anything happen to me. Now, go on, ask them your questions! They have a show tomorrow night. Everyone should come out to see some real tricks."

The reporters turned from me to mob Wini and Charlie as they climbed out of the plane. I walked a few feet away and tried not to collapse. I would be black and blue tomorrow, I knew from the ache along my ribs, but I was sure that I had managed to avoid breaking anything. Being back on the ground in one piece counted as a victory of sorts.

Marian came running down the field to give me a hard hug that made me wince and groan.

"Your own fault," she said over my protests about bruised ribs. "And don't ever, ever do that again. The entire crew nearly died of fright."

"No shoot-outs in midair," I agreed. "But I have an idea about an air battle. Maybe after the Flapper Detective jumps from a motorcycle into an airplane."

"Oh, Betsy," said Marian, shaking her head at me.

Wini walked up to us. "I've seen that done," she said. "Leaping from a cycle to a plane."

"How did it go?" I asked.

"Fool broke both his arms and a leg," she said. "And I tore up my plane crashing through a fence to avoid running over him." She spoke with an accent I couldn't quite place. A bit New England, a bit something else. There was a crackle of humor under her words as Wini pulled her pilot's helmet off her head and shook out her long black hair. "You have courage," she said. "Maybe not much in the way of brains, but definitely courage."

"I thought you were the Woman Without Fear," I said. "Seems like you've done some death-defying stunts, too. And had a few accidents."

"Never said that I was smart," she said. Again, the words were soft spoken, but I could see a smile at the corner of her dark eyes. "I just like to fly. And it takes money to fly. So, we loop the loop or go upside down under a bridge or let somebody jump on our plane from a moving vehicle. That makes the folks come out to see us. But only the first time. Enough pilots do the same trick, the audience loses interest. Then we make the stunts bigger and bigger!"

"It's the same in the movies," I said. "Do the same stunt too often, or too many others copy you, and there goes the box office."

"Well, at least we can put on the posters that we flew with the Fearless Flapper Detective," said Wini. "That should net us some good press in New England. I hear you're popular there."

"You're going to New England? Whereabouts?" I asked.

"A number of smaller towns and cities all the way up the coast, then ending up in Boston for a big show with several different pilots. We are starting with three days in Arkham. Not happy about that, but I want to be back east this fall," she said.

"Why?" I was surprised to hear her mention of Arkham. And I was genuinely curious to know why Arkham made her unhappy.

"On the East Coast? They're talking about launching a transcontinental air derby for women pilots. Taking off in New York and landing in Los Angeles with a prize of ten thousand dollars for the winner. The closer we are to the start, the easier it is to get the plane onto the field in one piece."

"No, I meant why aren't you happy about flying near Arkham?" I asked. I had my own fears about that place, but it was the first time I'd heard somebody outside Sydney Fitzmaurice's small company of actors and crew voice similar thoughts.

Wini stared at me, a long measuring look. The kind of look I'd seen cowboys and sailors who spent time outdoors give to a cloudy sky. The look that said there's a storm on the horizon.

"You've been there," she said. "Arkham." The smile and the humor disappeared from her voice. Instead, she sounded serious and not too sure about continuing the conversation. Talking about Arkham tended to do that to people, at least those I knew who had been there.

No questions, just that statement about knowing Arkham firsthand, but I felt compelled to answer. "Three years ago. I was there. Something happened."

"Something bad," said Wini. It was not a question.

"I think so," I admitted. "Except the memories are vague. I know there was a fire, and some friends were lost. Except one of them turned up unharmed this year. Jim is in a sanitarium. I'm planning to visit him after this picture wraps."

Wini nodded. The crowd around us had moved away to inspect the planes as well as to pepper Charlie and the red-haired mechanic with questions. "Arkham's like that," she said. "The further you get away from it, the more unlikely the memories seem. Once you leave, the more it seems like a dream."

"What happened to you?" I said.

She shrugged. "I flew into an oncoming storm. My instruments were spinning like mad, so I dropped down, trying to find a train track or something to guide me. Except," she said, "nothing looked right. Then something hit my plane."

"A bird?"

"If it was a bird, it was the ugliest one in all creation," Wini said. "No feathers. Never seen anything like it. It had legs like a squid, but it was flapping through the air like a bird."

"A flying squid," I said. It sounded unlikely, but I had once seen another world reflected in a mirror. A world where a flying squid might well be a creature of its skies. A world that had looked so wrong and so terrible.

At least, that's what I think I saw in the mirror on the final day of shooting in Arkham. Like my last memory of Max, it was so frustratingly vague, almost dreamlike when I tried to recall what exactly I had seen and heard.

"Whatever it was, it was big, it was slimy, and it rolled its one eyeball at me like it was considering lunch," Wini remarked.

I shuddered. It sounded like one of Sydney's nightmare movie scenarios or the professor's pulp stories. Come to think of it, both wrote stories inspired by their lives in Arkham. "What did you do?" I said.

"Pointed the plane toward the sun and flew straight through that electrical storm. I don't know if it was the thunder or the lightning that scared it away, but that creature dropped off my wing and disappeared. Still, that wasn't the strangest thing that happened that day."

"What next?"

"When I leveled out above the clouds, everything changed. No storm at all. Just some nice peaceful white puffs rolling by and the ocean below that, very calm and blue, and nothing to be seen but the shadow of my plane dancing across the waves."

"But you were flying over Arkham?" That's how the story had started.

"That's what I thought. Except all of a sudden I wasn't. I was miles off course and cruising above the Atlantic Ocean. Luckily, I had a nearly full fuel tank and all my instruments returned to good working order. I made it to land. At least as far as Innsmouth. They didn't have much of an airfield then, but I found it."

"And now you're going back there. You are the Woman Without Fear," I said, and I meant it as a compliment.

Wini smiled this time, the cautious type of smile you give someone who believed your crazy stories. The type I felt myself giving once or twice discussing my experiences with Jeany and the others who had worked with Sydney Fitzmaurice that summer in Arkham. All of them said they would never go back. I was the only one who wanted to return to Arkham, but then my friend Jeany said I was the only person in our group of friends who was willing to drive a car across a flaming bridge or jump out of a zeppelin wearing a parachute. In many ways, Jeany was one of the bravest people I knew, but she was not and never would be reckless. Wini, on the other hand, might well be an ally that I needed. From everything that she had said, it was clear she understood Arkham. At least the Arkham that haunted my dreams.

"I'm going back and telling myself that nothing strange will happen this time. I don't know if that counts as courage or wishful thinking," Wini said. "I'll earn my money and enter the derby. Why are you going?"

"I lost a man," I said. "And it's driving me wild. But another friend, Jim, is now in Arkham, and I think it's time to return. There's a professor and a reporter who have been sending me stories about a variety of strange happenings in the area. But not enough answers. I plan to investigate."

"Then you really are the Fearless Flapper Detective," said Wini with a laugh.

"Yeah," I said. "Isn't it terrible when you start believing your own press?"

"Can get a woman into trouble," Wini agreed.

"That's exactly what my butler says. You should come to dinner and meet Farnsworth. He'd like you. And you can tell him I was in no danger at all today."

"Well," Wini drawled.

"Or you can say nothing at all and let me lie to him," I said.

Three days later, one gramophone was cranked up in the first-floor ballroom for those who wanted to Charleston or Toddle. A second one was blaring jazz by the pool, my film crew and Wini's flying circus gang having a grand time.

"More drinks, Farnsworth," I said as I moved between the rooms, checking on the overall state of the festivities. "And we are not talking about tea."

Farnsworth sighed at this attempt at a witticism. "Certainly. There are letters for you."

He handed over the post. I scooped the stack off the silver tray and shook out the envelope with a promising bulge. It was the keys to the Fitzmaurice house from my friend Jeany. That's where my mystery had started, and the burned-out house would be one of my stops when I reached Arkham. I dropped the keys into the pocket of my lounging pants and frowned at the note. Jeany wrote her usual warnings. My friend truly suffered in Arkham and I would never force her to return. But I wasn't Jeany. If risking Arkham's horrors meant finding Max, I would go.

"And your two copies of the *Arkham Advertiser* arrived," said Farnsworth. "I placed one in your office and another in the library."

"Oh, good," I said. "Please add another subscription for the staff or some other spot in this house. We need to encourage them."

"Certainly," said Farnsworth. "We could always acquire a parrot. The extra papers could be placed under its pole."

"Farnsworth, you're a genius," I said as I sped off to my office on the second floor. Hanging over the railing, I added, "Buy two parrots and all the newspapers you need. Parrots would be splendid in the greenhouse."

"It is called a conservatory," Farnsworth replied as he moved toward the back of the hall.

"Put them where you want!" I yelled.

In my office, I transferred Jeany's keys to my traveling handbag. I picked up a briefcase and stuffed in the accounts, contracts, and other business papers strewn across the desk. The train trip took nearly a week and with nobody able to reach me, except by telegram, I planned to complete a fair amount of work.

Not as much fun as playing poker with the boys back when I was just an extra traveling with the crew, but I had booked a car all for myself and looked forward to some time away from Hollywood.

Then I spread out the latest *Arkham Advertiser* that was sitting on my desk and read the headlines. "Professor Christine Krosnowski Disappears! Foul Play Suspected!"

I dropped everything else to grab up the newspaper. I corresponded with Christine regularly. She'd helped Jeany in Arkham and answered all my questions as best she could. Which was often in grim detail. Although a professor of poetry, Christine had a definite interest in the strange history of the town. She also possessed a nearly photographic memory when it came to the odder occult volumes stored in the Miskatonic University's library. She used that knowledge to write the most marvelous thriller stories for the pulps, all published under a fictional name so her colleagues in the English Department didn't know and couldn't criticize her more torrid writing. I'd optioned one or two of her humdingers for the studio.

All in all, she was a good egg, and I wanted to know if she was safe. I scanned the article, which was brief and lacking the type of detail that my fan Darrell would have given it. The professor had failed to appear at a dinner where she was expected to present a paper on a new addition to the Miskatonic University's library, some rare volume she'd discovered in a Boston bookseller's catalog. Some more boring bits about how the book was so valuable that it was being transported by hand to the university and the professor was the only one who knew when it was arriving. Then the writer described the crime scene. Or the lack of one. No blood, no body. How had they managed to stick "foul play" in the headline? All the writer said was that friends went to the professor's house, found the door unlocked, and the professor missing. The article concluded with the usual admonishment for the police to take disappearances like this more seriously.

The Arkham police were useless when it came to disappearances. I'd been trying for years to stir them up over three men vanishing from one film set and their response had been, "They probably went back to Hollywood, Miss Baxter." Even when Jim reappeared, unable to speak about what happened, the Irish desk sergeant simply sighed and said on the phone, "Looks like the lad landed himself in a spot of trouble. They'll take good care of him at the hospital."

From all I had learned, it was clear waiting around for the Arkham police to save Christine was a terrible idea. I could add pressure through phone calls or even hiring a private detective, but that might not be enough to help a woman who had become a good friend. I was done waiting for others to find answers to the questions that so plagued me. I wanted to be in Arkham as soon as possible. The idea of sitting for days on a train now made me fidgety. I needed to cross the country more quickly, I decided, and I knew just how to do that.

I ran back down the stairs with my bags clutched in one hand and the *Arkham Advertiser* in the other. Wini was sitting by the pool chatting with Marian. The two had struck up a friendship.

"Wini, Wini," I said, cutting ruthlessly into their conversation, "how fast can you fly to Arkham?"

"Three days if nothing breaks along the way," she answered. "Maybe faster if the wind cooperates."

"Let's go!" I said. "I need to get there as swiftly as possible."

"Wait a minute," said Wini, rising from her seat. She had that look that many of my crew and Marian always adopted when I proposed a stunt, as if they weren't sure whether I quite understood the dangers. I did, of course. And I wanted to succeed much more than I feared to fail.

"Are you serious?" Wini asked. "You want me to fly you to Arkham?"

"Absolutely!"

"Do you know how many airmail pilots and others have gone down on transcontinental flights? Almost twenty percent. I don't mind risking myself, but I don't carry passengers."

"I thought you wanted to win an air derby. You're heading to the East Coast just in case the women's air derby is financed," I said. There had been a great deal of outcry in the press over the past week about encouraging women to participate in the reckless speed flying of the air derbies. Early backers of the race were starting to drop away, and I knew that worried Wini. Like me, she wanted to win. And it was impossible to win if you couldn't even play the game.

Wini nodded slowly, but there was a new look of interest on her face. "I want to fly in that derby. So do many women."

"But if the backers don't come through, the women cannot race." I'd found that out during our chats. Flyers like Wini might be the darlings of the press and a big draw for the air shows. They all wanted to compete but lacked the backing that the male pilots had for the big prize air derbies. For the safety of the women, or so the moneybags said, and for all the talk about organizing a "ladies only" air derby, every attempt to do so had stalled so far. "If this derby falls through again, you won't race this year," I pointed out.

"There's still a chance they will pull it off," Wini said, "and I'll be in a good position to join if we are on the East Coast."

"I know, I know," I said. "Here's the deal. Fly me to Arkham as fast as you can. I'll finance an air derby. One that lets any woman enter. Ten thousand dollar prize, did you say? I'll double that amount. Think about it. Twenty thousand for the winner and serious stakes for those who finish second or third." I stuck out my hand. "Go on. Shake on it."

Wini grinned and grasped my hand to give it a light shake. "You are one crazy lady, Betsy Baxter, but you have got a deal."

"Oh, good," I said, as I raced away to organize this change in plans. Of course, if Wini had said no, I would have still financed the derby. The check was already written and sitting on my desk upstairs. The women deserved to fly as fast as they wanted. So did I.

"Farnsworth," I shouted as we went back into the mansion.

"You bellowed?" Farnsworth said, coming into the entry with my coat over his arm.

I took my coat. "You're a treasure, Farnsworth," I said. "Have my things shipped to Arkham."

"Already done," Farnsworth reminded me. "The large luggage left last Friday. Including the trunk with your hats."

"Excellent! And cancel my train tickets. I'm going to fly," I said.

Farnsworth removed a few of my calling cards from a tray on a nearby table and tucked them into my coat pocket.

"I'm not making social calls," I told him. "I meant that I'm flying to Arkham."

"Yes, Miss Baxter, I heard your discussion by the pool while I was refreshing the beverages," said Farnsworth. "If you have your cards, it will make it much easier for the authorities to identify the body."

"Well, with luck, we'll make it in one piece," I said. "After all, if twenty percent of the planes crash on the way, that means eighty percent make it to their destinations. That's pretty good odds."

CHAPTER THREE

Black smoke trailed us as we made an emergency landing just outside Kansas City. All because a small fire had broken out in the luggage compartment.

I looked at the scorch marks on the single carpet bag that I'd allowed myself. I was thankful my hats were safe on the train. "Farnsworth won't believe me when I tell him we were in no danger. Perhaps I'll lose this bag before I return to Hollywood," I said, brushing some ash off the side of the bag. "At least my stockings didn't go up in flames."

Wini had her head stuck inside the plane. I heard her grunt and then swear.

"Here's the cause," she said, backing out and tossing a still smoldering cigar on the ground.

"Where did we pick that up?" I said.

"Probably that guy who fueled the plane at the last stop," she said.

I remembered him, the man chewing a cigar and muttering, "Dang me if it isn't a couple of dames."

Every stop we made, the ground crews rushed up to us at various airfields, only to gape when two women climbed out of the plane – even though more and more women received their pilots' licenses each year. Wini had said some of the manufacturers hired women pilots to show that anyone could learn to fly a plane. I recalled telling her that I wasn't sure that was a compliment.

"Compliment or not," she said, "it means those women are paid to get their license. And the more of us there are flying, the harder it is for others to say that it isn't a woman's place to be in the air."

"My mother always thought when we won the vote, all the arguments about equality would end," I said.

Wini didn't even bother to comment about such a foolish statement. She just shook her head and told me I had ten minutes to eat and then we needed to be airborne again.

Other than the fire, and that was more smoke than flame, we didn't have another serious mishap until a wing strut wire snapped. But, despite several dire predictions that we were sure to meet our doom, none nearly as awesome as what Farnsworth would have made, we were able to get repairs done very quickly in an airfield outside some town further east of Kansas City. By that time, I'd lost track of what state we were flying over.

Wini grumbled about leaving her favorite mechanic behind, but Lonnie and the rest had needed to wrap up some business in Los Angeles. They were following by a slower route.

Still, Wini flew us safely through every mishap. By the time we landed, without smoke or a wobbly wing, in an airfield near Cleveland, the press had gotten wind that the Woman Without Fear was flying across the country with the Fearless Flapper Detective. The airfield was mobbed by reporters and spectators when we arrived. One intrepid reporter and photographer drove their car after us, trying to catch a picture of us as we taxied down the bumpy runway. Wini barely missed crashing into the car as I shouted at the men to get out of the way.

"Is this a stunt for one of your films, Miss Baxter?" asked one reporter as Wini gulped down sandwiches and coffee, eyeballing the road map that she used to navigate from city to city. She chatted up the airmail pilots as well since they often knew the best routes.

"After my last picture," I said to the reporter, "I'm thinking about more aerial stunts. Or maybe something dangerous like driving a car after a moving airplane." The photographer had the grace to blush. "But this is only a little vacation trip for me. I wanted to see New England again."

"But are you going to keep flying with Miss Habbamock?" he asked.

"If she lets me. I've never had so much fun," I said. I meant it, too. There was something about being up above the ground, the air rushing around you, that made all the everyday worries fall away. I talked to Wini about taking flying lessons, and she said that if I could handle a car and a motorcycle, I could definitely learn to fly.

"I did it backward," Wini told me on one of our stops. "I learned to drive a car long after I could pilot a plane."

"So how did you become a pilot?" I asked.

"Met a man."

"Oh!" I'd landed in a few briars for the same reason.

She shook her head. "Not like that. He was old. Seemed ancient, although he probably wasn't all that much older than me. Nobody in flying is. Ancient means you're turning thirty."

I laughed. "Hollywood is a bit like that. We're getting some gray hairs, but many folks started in the business after the war. I acted in my first picture in 1920."

She looked at me. "How old were you?"

"I told the director I was eighteen," I said. "Really I was sixteen, but I'd been hoofing it on the vaudeville stage in Chicago for nearly a year. Nobody asked too many questions. How old were you when you started flying with your pilot?"

"An ancient seventeen," Wini admitted with a chuckle. "And, like I said, I called my first teacher the old man. He acted like it. All quiet and beat down. He'd flown in the war, and it did something to him. Made him want to stay far away from everyone. So he moved to my corner of nowhere in particular. The only place that he was happy was in the sky. At least that's what he told me. First time I saw his Jenny, I wanted to take it flying. Of course, I had to steal the plane to persuade the old man to give me lessons, but I didn't damage it."

"I like that about you," I said, chewing on my sandwich. You wouldn't think sitting in a plane, watching the clouds racing under you, would stir up an appetite. But I was always ravenous when we landed. "You dare to take what you want."

"I haven't noticed that you're shy about pursuing what you want," said Wini.

"I'm good with math," I said, "and nobody wanted to hire me for those skills, like counting cards or balancing books. And I'm athletic. Love to dance. Love thrills even more. Then I found I could use all my talents in the pictures."

"So you bought a studio?" Wini said.

"Mary Pickford had the right idea. Control your contracts and you make more money," I said. "And I knew the Fearless Flapper Detective was a winner. It's the best of Pearl White's stunts and more but with a woman in charge, not in peril. It's what modern women want to see." Wini blinked and rocked back in her seat as I leaned across the table to make my point. "Sorry, I didn't mean to give you the whole pitch. That's how I sold the studio on taking the serial seriously."

"And your films sell tickets?"

"Of course, same as they come out to see you perform your stunts and buy newspaper accounts of all the fly girls. You ladies receive more press than the men. Same for me and my stunts."

Wini winced. "Fly girls. I hate that nickname the most. I'm fine with aviatrix. But why can't they just call us pilots?"

"Because then they'd have to call us equal," I said.

We both laughed at the truth of that statement.

Wini pulled a silver cigarette case out of her pocket. Balancing it on one corner, she began to spin it on the table. I never saw her smoke or even open the case, but she often fidgeted with it when we were on the ground.

"What is the record?" I said, with a nod to the silver case that she twirled like a top.

"Three," said Wini. She lifted her hand away from it. It spun once, twice, and, on the third spin, it fell over with a clatter.

Wini scooped it up and tucked the case back into her pocket. "Except in Innsmouth," she said. "Whenever I was there, it spun seven times."

"Lucky!" I exclaimed.

Wini blew out a breath that was a bit too gusty to be called a sigh. More a sound of exasperation. "Guess so. Except Innsmouth never felt lucky to me. It's stranger than Arkham, at least according to some of the pilots who fly near there."

"No place is odder than Arkham," I said with the great conviction of sheer ignorance.

"You should visit before you say that. I wasn't the first plane to go off course near Arkham and land outside Innsmouth. Gossip gets around the airfields. Most pilots don't like flying that route. Including the mail pilots, and they will make any run."

I had noticed in our discussions with the airmail aviators that they took the "neither rain, nor snow, nor sleet, nor hail" saying seriously. In part because when the Aerial Mail Service started contracting out bids, it was good steady money for the companies who won those bids, Wini had said. But her biggest praise was for the lighted fields and runways built to help the mail service.

"They've set up hundreds of beacons for night flyers," she said. "And dozens of emergency landing fields for planes." Despite those lighted fields and my desire for all the speed possible, Wini wasn't so reckless as to fly through the night. Sundown always found us safely on the ground, often staying with the family of a local pilot. It made for a few hours of sleep and many hours of stories about flights. One thing I discovered during that trip was that probably the only thing pilots loved as much as flying was talking about flying.

The more I heard, the more I thought Hollywood needed to be making movies about pilots. I must have jotted dozens of notes in those evenings. Everyone agreed the greatest daredevils were the barnstormers, those pilots who made their living entertaining the crowds, and a movie about those men and women would be marvelous indeed.

During those stops, I picked up what newspapers were available, but nothing was written about Arkham or Christine's disappearance. I tried phone calls and telegrams from the airfields. Farnsworth sent what information he could. However, my frustration mounted. Even moving so much faster across the country than a train, travel seemed infuriatingly slow. I wished for a way to walk out the door and simply be where I wanted to be.

Wini watched me paging through a newspaper at one stop. "Anything helpful?" she asked.

I had told her a little about what drove me back to Arkham, but it was hard to explain why Jim's reappearance had spurred such desperation in me to finally solve the riddle of Max. I was never good at examining my own motives. I preferred to act and think about why I acted much later, if ever. My friend Jeany, a much more introspective person, would often shake her head at me and say, "Betsy, one day, you will race right past what you are looking for."

To Wini that day, I said, "Nothing new about Arkham. I guess that's too small a place to make the national news."

"It always seemed too large a place to me," said Wini. "Too big to fit it all in one neat little article. Innsmouth is much the same. Some of the families in that area have been there a long time. There were always odd stories swirling around that section of the coast."

"Odder than fiction," I said, remembering a phrase that Darrell put into one of his newspaper stories.

"Odder indeed," said Wini.

At that point, one of the mechanics came into the canteen to inform us that Wini's plane was ready to take off. I promptly forgot about Innsmouth, except for a niggling memory of some newspaper story about seaplanes and rumrunners. I meant to ask Wini about it but forgot in the rush of getting airborne again. We still had a few hours of daylight left.

The rest of the journey was smooth, with no mishaps at all, and we reached Arkham's airfield in record time. As I was informed by the *Arkham Advertiser* reporter who met our plane.

"Darrell Ethan Simmons!" I squealed as I hopped off the wing. "Look at you!"

It had been three years since I'd seen him, and the reporter had filled out some. I'd slung the most horrible baloney at him, all sorts of fairy tales about the film business, when we'd first met. But he'd been good-natured about it and a regular pen pal since. There wasn't much that happened in Arkham that Darrell didn't hear about. He was a terrific photographer, too, and I kept telling him that he had the talent to come to Hollywood. I'd have hired him in a heartbeat to be the studio's publicity photographer. But he kept writing back that there were things he still needed to document in Arkham.

"Miss Baxter," he said and produced a small bouquet of roses from behind his back. "Welcome back to Arkham."

I smelled the flowers and then grinned at him. "You want some photos," I said.

"If you could stand by the front of the plane and wave," said Darrell, producing his camera. "An *Arkham Advertiser* exclusive! I can sell reprints to the New York papers."

"Hey," Wini said as she climbed out of the plane. "Don't back her into the prop. It's still moving."

"Sorry," said Darrell. "If I could get a picture of both of you. A famous flyer and a glamorous Hollywood star land in Arkham!"

"You're talking in headlines," I said to Darrell as I posed. Wini shook her head at the pair of us joking back and forth, but she also posed with good grace. We made our money off being public figures. Newspaper photographers were just part of it.

When we were done, I begged a ride into town with Darrell. "Are you coming?" I asked Wini as Darrell good-naturedly transferred my carpet bag and documents case from the plane to his car.

Wini shook her head. "I need to stay with my plane until the rest of the crew gets here," she said. "I'm used to sleeping rough." We had heard that morning that the remainder of her aerial circus had nearly caught up with us. Once they reached Arkham, Wini was planning a few days of overhauling the planes before starting up her first round of performances.

"And our advance man quit," she grumbled to me as I handed over the check to cover her expenses for our flight. That had been part of the morning's phone call with her friend Lonnie Ritter, and she was obviously still vexed by the news. "I guess I'll have to figure out the ads and posters and whatever else he did."

"We'll give you an excellent rate for printing whatever you need," said Darrell.

"Thanks," said Wini.

"So now you're the sales rep, too," I said to Darrell.

"Les sells the ads," said Darrell, "but we all need the money to pay our salaries. Even with your new subscriptions, Miss Baxter."

"Oh, good, Farnsworth remembered," I said.

"His telegram said something about the latest being for Polly and Jacks."

"Probably," I said, looking forward to visiting the new parrots in the conservatory when I returned home.

As we started toward town, I waved out the window one last time at Wini, then settled back into my seat for a good gossip with one of the smartest guys I knew. Darrell might look like a regular newspaper joe, but he had a nose for a very special kind of trouble. The sort that Arkham brewed up.

"So, tell me about the professor. What happened? Has anyone found her yet?"

"She reappeared yesterday," said Darrell.

"And what did she say?"

"I couldn't get into the hospital to see her," Darrell said with some frustration. "I tried a couple of friends, but her room was off-limits to everyone except her doctor and the nurses."

I needed to talk to Christine. In her last letter, she'd spoken about understanding more about how Jim might have reappeared in Arkham. But she hadn't said much beyond that. "But is she all right?" I asked. "She can talk?"

Jim couldn't when he reappeared. Not a word for weeks.

Darrell nodded. "I bribed one of the nurses. A nice girl named Hilda. She said the professor was chatting with the doctor when she went into the room. Very animated, Hilda said, but they both clammed up when they saw her."

"I could disguise myself as a nurse and sneak in," I pondered out loud on the feasibility of that plan.

"Or you could wait and see if she's discharged tomorrow. Or go talk to her doctor," said Darrell.

"That seems too easy," I said. "Next you're going to give me solid advice like my butler."

"Oh," said Darrell as he pulled to a stop in front of the grandest hotel in Arkham, "what does your butler say?"

"Life, Miss Baxter, is not an adventure serial."

We both laughed because we knew that wasn't true in Arkham. And that very night, I got caught in a shoot-out with a couple of gangsters over a handsome bookseller with the improbable name of Tom Sweets.

CHAPTER FOUR

The confrontation happened after dinner. I decided the hotel dining room was too fancy for my mood. I needed to walk off my fidgets. With my luggage not due until the next day, I couldn't do much with my appearance but dressed as nicely as possible from the carpet bag. My brown velvet cloche had survived the trip, but I sighed when I put it on. It was the very plainest of my hats. I longed for the others making their way from California, as I was heartily sick of the plain cloche.

Within a short walk of the hotel, I found myself a diner. The food was not nearly as good as Velma's, a place I'd visited before in Arkham, but I needed to think. Nobody recognized me at the restaurant as I chewed my way through a plate of steak and potatoes. And I had to chuckle at my own surprise at not being approached for an autograph. While I might be recognized regularly in Hollywood, they obviously weren't quite as picture mad in Arkham. I blamed my very dull hat. Who would expect the Fearless Flapper Detective, the jazz baby who had "it" appeal, in brown velvet?

The waitress didn't even make any wisecracks to me as she refilled my coffee cup. Everyone was concentrated on their food and no gossip was to be heard. Unusual, really, for Arkham, not at all like my memories of the place or Darrell's articles or Christine's letters, but the anonymity suited my disposition.

Twilight settled over the streets. Shadows pooled in doorways. The whole town felt deserted. Too late for anyone heading home from work, too early for anyone seeking mischief. Just that in between time when the sky turned from blue to violet and the earliest stars began to appear above the streetlights. A quiet hour, so quiet that the sound of a fist smacking into someone's stomach and the soft *oof* of somebody losing their breath sounded exceptionally loud. I paused at the entrance of an alley. It came again, a grunt and a thump, and then the distinctive rattle of a body hitting a garbage can. So of course I had to investigate.

Peering down the alley, I saw two roughs cornering a third man. A big man dressed in a canvas jacket and sailor's cap backed a tall gentleman in a summer tweed suit and Homburg hat against the dirty brick wall of the adjacent building. A smaller guy danced around the pair, jabbing like a fighter warming up in the ring but not actually hitting anything.

"Come on, mister, one last time, Miss Nova wants her package. Give it up," said the larger of the two gents to his captive. The man in the Homburg shook his head and received a punch to the belly that knocked him to the ground.

"Not so smart now, are you?" jeered the little man. He aimed a few kicks at their victim.

The man on the ground groaned and curled his knees up to his chest in that universal move of protection. "I don't have it anymore," he said. "I told you. It disappeared."

"We want the book," grunted the big mucker. The little one aimed another kick at the downed man's head. The man on the ground had good instincts. He rolled away at just the right moment to catch the kick on his shoulder rather than his skull. But it was obvious who was going to lose this fight without a little help.

Never say that a Baxter ran away from trouble.

"Hey," I yelled into the alley. "Leave him alone!"

The larger man turned. Judging by the rough clothes and the broken nose, to say nothing of the meaty fists swinging at the end of his arms, he would have fit right in with the dock workers who fought on the weekends for the entertainment of the swells. The muckers, my grandmother used to call such men. The little guy's shiny suit and flashy tie looked more like the garb worn by some of the Chicago mobsters who used to hang around the stage doors when I was hoofing in the Windy City.

"Leave him alone," I repeated a bit louder. My experience of such mugs taught me you needed to speak loudly and firmly. No matter how afraid you were. And this pair didn't intimidate me. I faced down much worse in Chicago, including one of Torrio's men. Of course, Torrio's takeover of the mob after Colosimo's murder was one of the reasons I hotfooted it to Hollywood. But this was Arkham, and I stood my ground and yelled.

"Stay out of this, ma'am," the big man said. "None of your business."

The "ma'am" suggested I'd overdone the schoolmarm talk. Or maybe it was my hat. No matter. The pair weren't budging.

I planted my feet in the stance suggested by my shooting instructor. Bringing up the pistol that I'd pulled from my purse, I said, "Beat it, boys, before I start shooting. At this range, I can hit both of you with one shot."

The smaller one ducked behind his larger companion, making the probability of me hitting them both with one shot that much greater. Not the brightest criminal, but then this type of brawn was rarely hired for their brains. Little plug ugly pulled out his own pistol and waved it about.

"Hop it," he warned, "or it will be the worse for you!"

"Hey now, don't do something daffy," said the larger one, turning away from the man on the ground to eyeball his partner. "You can't start popping off downtown. Miss Nova won't like that."

The little one growled at the big sailor.

"Well," I said, continuing to talk tough, "you don't want to shoot or to be shot. Myself, I'm not afraid of the first or the second." Well, I didn't want to be shot, but watching how the smaller man handled his gun, I thought I had a fair chance of ducking out of the way.

I shifted a little in the mouth of the alley to line up on the big one. I figured if I could wing him, a little blood would discourage them both. At least that's what I hoped. If the one with a gun took offense, then I'd be diving for cover and saying goodbye to my silk stockings. More than that I refused to contemplate.

"Why, she is only a little doll," said the one with the gun, and he probably didn't top me by an inch. "She will never shoot."

To prove him wrong, I pinged one off the garbage can's lid. All three men yelped. The lanky one on the ground curled up even tighter. The other two goons backed away. The flashy dresser was so startled that he dropped his gun. Luckily, it didn't go off.

"Hey, lady," said the big man, sounding very aggrieved, "that's not nice."

"It will be worse if you don't leave," I said.

His friend dropped down on his hands and knees, trying to retrieve his pistol from where it had skidded under some boxes stacked against the grimy brick wall. He practically had to go flat on his stomach to reach it, which didn't do the suit and tie much good. The boxes teetered above his head, threatening to avalanche down on him.

The little man popped up with a cry. "Got it!" he said in triumph, drawing his hand back with the pistol in it.

The sailor looked at his companion. He shook his head. "Come on, Albie, let's go. If you keep waving that thing around, Miss Nova will do something harmful to our health."

Little Albie ignored his friend and growled at me. "Don't make me get rough… or I will make you sorry." He waved his gun at me. I tightened my grip on my pistol, lining up my shot.

But his companion grabbed his arm and pulled him further down the alley. "Don't talk to the lady like that. Do you want to get us into trouble with Miss Nova?"

As he pushed his companion away from the fight, he looked back at the man on the ground. "Miss Nova will be all churned up if she doesn't get her book. Best you find it for her."

From his position on the ground, their victim moaned and said, "I don't have the grimoire. It disappeared with the professor."

"Scram!" I yelled. Never back down, never let them see you're afraid. That's what another instructor told me. Seemed it worked, as both lugs slunk off. Which was why I kept taking all those lessons. Because if there was one thing I hated more than anything in the world, it was feeling afraid. As long as I was in control, I could not be scared. Not like that day when I lost Max and Jim to the flames and mirrors.

Now all that was left from the confrontation was a groaning knot of humanity lying in the dirt of the alley.

"Miss Baxter?" I heard a voice behind me. "Are you all right?"

I swung around, pushing the pistol into my purse as I turned to confront the hotel's bellboy. Judging from the cigarette stowed behind his ear, he'd been heading to this alley for a quiet break.

"I'm fine," I said, "but my friend needs some help."

Between the two of us, we managed to pull the thugs' victim to his feet. He swayed there, looking like he'd been Jack Dempsey's sparring partner. Although he probably wouldn't have been up to even one round with the heavyweight champion of the world. Tall and gangly, he reminded me a bit of the stunt rider Frank Cooper, who'd been doing bit parts on several Zane Grey pictures.

Under the dirt and bruises, he wasn't a bad looking man. But I had sworn off tall and handsome after Max.

"What should we do with him, Miss Baxter?" asked the bellboy, who introduced himself as Irving.

"Well, if we let him go, he's dropping back onto the dirt," I said. "And that suit cannot take much more."

"I'm fine," said the gentleman, swaying so heavily against my shoulder that he nearly took me down.

"Sure you are, slugger," I said, shoving his weight more firmly onto Irving. "But let's get you cleaned up before we turn you loose on Arkham. What's your name?"

"I thought you said he was a friend," said Irving, looking perplexed as he helped me walk the man into the hotel lobby. The night manager bore down on us, heading across the lobby with a disapproving stare that even Farnsworth would have admired.

"Absolutely he is a friend. I'm a friend to man and beast, especially the ones that I rescue. You should meet my parrots," I said to Irving. To the other one, doing his best to lie down and take a nap on the carpet, I added, "Now, sweet, tell Betsy your name and where she can send you."

He blinked down at me. "That's it. That's my name. Tom Sweets. But who are you?"

"Betsy Baxter," I said, giving the hand draped over my shoulder something between a shake and a pat. I also pulled the brim of his Homburg a little lower to shade his face and hopefully obscure the dirt and bruises. "And this here is Irving. Please straighten up and pretend you are sober."

"I am sober. Sober as a judge," said Tom Sweets. "But, oh, how I wish I wasn't."

He spoke with the tones of a college man, a Harvard type, to judge from the accent and the wide cut of his pant legs. Both matched the style of the Ivy League gentlemen I'd met in Hollywood. We managed to march the staggering Tom halfway across the lobby before the night manager intercepted us.

The night manager's face was stuck between a sneer and frown, which did not improve his looks. I smiled my best winsome young lady smile at him. The smile that Pickford copied from me to play Little Annie Rooney. "Tom had an accident on our way back from dinner. Please send bandages to my room."

"Is this Mr Baxter?" the disagreeable night manager asked. There had already been some unpleasantness about me taking the honeymoon suite without having a bridegroom in tow. But it was the only suite that had a sitting room, a bedroom, and a private bath. I maintained that honeymooners didn't need nearly so much space.

"If he is Mr Baxter, will you let me put him on the elevator without a fuss?" I asked.

"Madam," said the night manager in a disapproving tone. When had I devolved from a miss to a madam? I wondered. It had to be the hat. "Madam," he repeated himself. "Surely you know whether or not this is Mr Baxter."

"You would think that, wouldn't you?" I answered as I maneuvered my tall rescue into the elevator. Irving remained stalwartly glued to the man's side, probably in hopes of a generous tip. I aimed not to disappoint and whispered promises of a reward to the bellboy. Besides, I needed Irving to operate the elevator.

With the grace of long practice, Irving managed to clang the door shut, push the buttons, and keep our rescue from sliding to the floor by propping him in one corner.

"Are we moving?" asked Tom Sweets. His eyes were still closed. At least, one eye was closed. The other was swollen shut as far as I could tell, peering under the brim of his hat.

"Yes," I said. "Next stop, hot water and bandages."

"Oh, good," he said and slumped a bit more.

With a bit of shoving and pulling, Irving managed to drag the man down the hall, retrieve my hotel key from me, open the door, deposit his burden in the nearest chair, and pocket the tip. Buster Keaton couldn't have done it better. I watched the whole sequence with the idea that we might try something similar in my next picture. Or I could sell the idea to Buster.

Sacrificing a couple of towels from the bathroom, we managed to clean the worst of the dirt and blood off the man in the chair, despite his occasional squawk of protest. He muttered the loudest at the removal of his hat and jacket, but I assured him his virtue was safe with me.

"Madam," he said, without opening his eyes, "a Harvard man never fears for his virtue. But he also hangs onto his hat." Then he slid further down in the chair. He looked so beat that I let the "madam" go. Apparently, that was my role tonight, elderly lady detective. Tomorrow, I swore I would go buy myself a new hat in the brightest red possible. Obviously the brown velvet cloche that I wore to dinner was too somber.

"I don't know," I said to Irving. "If he faints again, we should probably call a doctor. Or send him to a hospital."

"No hospital," mumbled the man in the chair. "I did not faint. I am keeping my eyes closed. I simply refuse to accept that I have been beaten in an alley and now am in some stranger's hotel room. Such things do not happen to men like me."

"And what sort of man are you, sport?" I said as I wiped the last of the mud from his face. He certainly looked like Frank Cooper. But he didn't talk like a cowboy.

"I am a bookseller," he said, straightening up and taking the towel away from me. "From Boston. A dealer in rare books and manuscripts. A purveyor of antique volumes. A man who knows an incunable edition when he sees it. In short, a staff member of Sweets and Nephew, provider to gentlemen's libraries since 1778. I am the current nephew, Thomas Alfred Sweets the Fourth."

"That's quite the moniker," I responded.

He nodded gingerly, then opened both eyes with a wince. "My name was the bane of my school days. And the butt of jokes throughout my time at Harvard. But if you call me Tom and ignore the rest, I will be content."

I pulled off my cloche and fluffed out my hair. Tom Sweets narrowed his eyes and gave me a long look from top to bottom. I handed my coat to Irving to hang in the closet, having been spoiled with servants for a few years. Tom's next long look started at my shoes, paused only momentarily at my silk-stocking clad ankles, noted the handkerchief hem of my skirt was barely past my knees, and managed to finish on my face without noticeably stopping anywhere else. I flashed him a smile for being a gentleman.

He straightened even further, and said, "You can definitely call me Tom, Miss Baxter."

I was impressed that he remembered my name from that small altercation in the lobby. "Please, call me Betsy, and how about I call for a Tom Collins? Irving can fetch us the soda water and lemon."

Tom Sweets sat up all the way. "And the gin?"

I sent Irving out of the room with another tip and a few whispered instructions. I held up the flask I'd taken from Tom's pocket while I was brushing mud off his suit jacket. "Homebrew or imported?" I had already sniffed it and discerned the sharp tang of juniper.

"Imported from Canada as far as I know," Tom said. "It was part of the payment my uncle took from Miss Nova Malone."

"The two mugs in the alley mentioned her name more than once."

"Yes, she is not the most patient of customers. We have had a little trouble with her delivery."

"I noticed the trouble. They didn't act like book collectors. Or even the type that reads anything past the betting pages. What's their boss lady like?"

"I have not had the pleasure of meeting her yet. We have only corresponded since my uncle's error came to light." After hearing the rounded tones of this pronouncement, I believed Tom's claim to be a Harvard man.

"And what was your uncle's mistake?" I asked him.

"My dear but scatterbrained uncle sold the same book twice."

I took the bloody towels and chucked them out the door into the hallway. Irving could take them down to the laundry after he returned with the glasses and soda water.

"How can you sell the same book twice?" I said. "And why would that be a problem? Couldn't you just send them a different copy of the same book?"

"Not this one," said Tom. "It's our grimoire." He said it like the book was an unruly pet or undisciplined relative. The emphasis on the "our" as in "our problem" but with that underlying, grudging affection that one gives to a misbehaving child or a dog that tends to snap at the neighbors.

"What's a grimoire when it is at home in the Sweets and Sons bookstore?" I asked. I never could resist a mystery, and this one sounded like a lulu. Besides, now that I had twitted the night manager by bringing Tom up to my room, I might as well hear the full story.

"Sweets and Nephew," corrected Tom. "The owner of the grimoire doesn't have sons. That's part of the curse."

"Curse?" Welcome back to Arkham, I thought. Of course there was a curse.

"The grimoire," said Tom with the exhausted air of someone telling the same story for the umpteenth time, "has been in the possession of a Sweets since 1789. The book was rebound a few times, and the current binding was gorgeously ornamented in 1909 in an attempt to compete with Henry Sotheran's *Rubaiyat*. But after each sale, it always comes back to us. Each time the grimoire returns to our shop, the book brings about a certain amount of calamity. Thus the family leaves the grimoire and the store in the possession of a bachelor uncle. That way the owner has less to lose when it returns. And the grimoire always returns, trailing disaster in its wake."

"But why do you keep selling your grimoire, then?" I said, because the flaw to me in every story like this – and I had been pitched something similar for one of my movies – was the curious reluctance people had to destroy cursed items. "Seriously, why hang onto a book that brings calamity?" Of course, somebody might ask the same of me about returning to Arkham.

"Because we make an enormous profit every time a Sweets sells the grimoire. The antiquarian book trade is an expensive enterprise," said Tom without even a moment's reflection. "Very few of my ancestors could resist a sure sale, even when you must keep it locked in a lead-lined box in the basement."

A knock at the door announced Irving with an ice bag for Tom as well as a pair of glasses, soda water, and the other ingredients needed for cocktails except the gin. I tipped Irving appropriately and shooed him out the door. Tom applied the ice bag to his black eye while keeping the other eye wide open to track my progress on the drinks. After mixing, stirring, and spiking from Tom's flask, I handed him one glass and took the other back to my chair.

"If you have a concussion, a doctor would tell you not to drink," I said.

"Thank all the angels in heaven that there are no doctors here," said Tom. He tipped back the glass and drained it half dry with a couple of swallows. "Nothing like some liquid courage to heal a man."

"Who bought your grimoire this time?" I said, because obviously there was more to his tale, and I never liked to leave a story unfinished.

Tom swallowed again and then set down the glass with a clink on the table-top. "I'm not sure I should tell you. Family business. For all I know, you are a rival bookseller looking to seduce my best clients from me."

"Does that happen often in the antiquarian book trade?" I said with a chuckle. Nobody ever took me for a femme fatale before. I was never cast as the vamp, not even when I worked for Sydney Fitzmaurice, who loved a wicked lady in his films. As the Flapper Detective, my persona was wholesome gamine with the courage to tackle evildoers.

"I haven't been distracted by a Mata Hari so far," admitted Tom. "Most of the dealers and the customers look like my uncle. Short, bald, and so on. Dressed in tobacco-stained tweeds with leather patches at the elbows. But a man can dream."

"Well, I'm not a bookseller. I'm an actress," I said. If he knew who I was, he gave no indication of that. It was rather restful to just be "an actress" again rather than the head of a studio or the star of a popular movie serial. "And I have a friend who disappeared recently in Arkham. Professor Christine Krosnowski."

Tom gave a start. "That's the professor who bought the grimoire."

I nodded. When he'd been attacked in the alley, I had heard Tom say more than once that a professor had the book the goons were seeking. Christine disappeared after acquiring a rare book for the Miskatonic University. It didn't take the Flapper Detective to see those clues scattered about.

"What happened?" I asked Tom.

"The grimoire did what it always does. It made people disappear," said Tom, adjusting the ice bag and settling back into his chair.

"But the professor is back again," I said. "I heard from my friend Darrell that Christine was found."

Tom nodded. "That may be the grimoire, too. It certainly makes people disappear and sometimes lost people appear. Just not where you expect them. Or when."

"But who has the grimoire now?" I asked, thinking about the implications of a book that could make people appear, lost people like Max.

"That's what I need to know," said Tom, "before Nova Malone's goons put some more holes in me. The gin is good, but my uncle should never have sold the grimoire to a bootlegger."

CHAPTER FIVE

The mix-up was partially his fault, Tom had said with a shrug and grimace at how that movement pulled his ribs. "Uncle left the bookstore to attend an estate sale in Providence. While he was gone, I wrote a description of the grimoire for our cabalistic catalog. All the usual about its condition – very good with no markings save one or two faint stains on second signature, foxing on the end leaf, one corner bumped, binding as done in 1909 in ornamented shagreen, and so on. I added a few comments on its provenance, all in my signature style, far livelier than most book catalogs if I say so myself. Then I mailed the catalog to our usual buyers of occult volumes."

"Sell many of those?" I said. The handsome bookseller was definitely perking up as he explained the marketing of grimoires. "Occult books?"

"We send that particular catalog to an exclusive list, mostly academic librarians and a few select collectors," Tom said. "I usually have less than fifty catalogs printed. But it does seem like half the buyers are here in Arkham, including several professors at the university."

"Not surprising." I considered my own correspondence with Christine and her frequent discussions of particular titles that she was hunting to use in her research.

"When the professor called about buying it, I wrapped the grimoire up and brought it to Arkham," he said. "It wasn't until I returned home and Uncle Alfred arrived back from his expedition that we discovered we'd both sold the book. That was an awkward moment. Especially since one of Miss Nova Malone's Boston friends came into the shop to collect the grimoire."

"Do gangsters often buy rare books?" I asked, wanting to get the story straight in my head. This Tom was a bit of a charmer, and that might mean that he was spinning me a whopper. The whole tale seemed unlikely, but I had encountered some strange characters ever since I'd left home. I learned of even more after I started inquiring about disappearances in Arkham.

At my raised eyebrow, Tom chuckled and said, "Most of our buyers are no more gangsters than your average book collector, who will try to wheedle down a price until it is practically highway robbery. But there's a fellow in West Egg who keeps buying volumes to fill the shelves of his mansion's library, and we don't ask how he made his money. Buys books by the yard if the colors of the bindings match the colors of his shirts! Half bound, three quarter bound, quarter bound, he doesn't care what's in between the covers just so long as the book looks expensive. We put all the unsaleable stuff in his boxes. As long as the part showing is bound in dyed leather and trimmed in gilt, he's happy. That's not uncommon for many of our richer clients. They just want a library that amazes the people viewing it," concluded Tom.

"I know what you mean about folks wanting to impress people with objects they don't need," I said. When people suddenly became rich in Hollywood, they tended to throw their money around buying the strangest things. Like a marble Venus for their hallway. So other people then had to act like them just to keep up appearances.

"That kind of competition to have the best of everything could lead a girl to owning a mansion with an English butler and two parrots in the conservatory," I said out loud. "But it sounds like the person who bought the grimoire didn't want just any fancy book. Nova Malone wanted that specific book enough to send a couple of thugs to fetch it for her."

"Both buyers wanted the grimoire for the contents and paid handsomely for it," Tom agreed. "The fact that the book is fully bound in shagreen, ornamented in gold, and inlaid with jewels added to the price, too. Neither buyer would want to lose it so soon after paying so much. Which is why Uncle sent me back to Arkham. He thought I would do a better job of negotiating a settlement. We'll refund whoever gives up the grimoire. Except now neither buyer has it. And both are very cross about it. I assume the professor is vexed, but she disappeared before I could talk to her. I know another party who helped with the university's purchase is angry. I ran into him at the library looking for the professor. You saw Nova Malone's reaction."

"Jewels? Why jewels?" I asked, distracted by his description. I liked my diamonds for movie premieres, but I couldn't see myself pasting any gem on the cover of a book, no matter how occult the interior text. The whole thing sounded a bit ridiculous to me, but the mention of disappearances and reappearances did intrigue me.

"Sangorski and Sutcliffe started it. Jeweled bindings for rich clients. Very rich. And we had to copy them ..." Tom sighed and took another swig. "Nobody ever said anyone in the rare book trade had any financial sense. Commissioning that cover meant my great-uncle used up almost all of his reserves and barely recouped the expense."

"Guess I'm glad that I'm in the movie business and not in the book business," I said. "Most people come to Hollywood to make money and build bigger mansions to astound the neighbors." Which sounded like a joke but was a fair description of Pickfair, Falcon's Lair, and the new "beach house" that Hearst was building for Marion Davies.

Tom chuckled. "At least we don't have those problems in Boston. Uncle and I live in an apartment above the store. The money all goes to the books, their care and proper handling as it were. As well as our constant search for more books to expand the stock and perhaps even sell someday. Although nobody in our family ever seems to be too keen on the selling part. Uncle practically breaks down in tears every time I list a volume in a catalog."

"So when did your bootleggers become bookleggers?" I asked. "You never said how Nova Malone bought the grimoire."

"The usual way." Tom tipped his glass up and drained the last drops from it. "A request through the mail for a certain type of book that matched our grimoire's description exactly. When Uncle called the number in the letter, he talked to Miss Malone, who said she did not wish to haggle nor did she wish for the book to be posted to her. A messenger arrived with a suitcase full of cash and a bottle of gin as a thank you, along with a request to hold the book until another messenger arrived to collect it. Uncle put the gin in the cupboard and the cash in the safe and went off to Providence without telling me about the sale. He was in search of Gould's *A Monograph of the Ramphastidae, or Family of Toucans*. Anyone can see how that would drive thoughts of everything else out of his head."

I leaned forward to pluck the now empty glass from Tom's hand. "I know nothing about toucans and their power of distraction. But what happened next?"

"As I said, I already handed the grimoire to the professor, along with the usual warnings about not reading it aloud and so on. Not that the warning ever works, but we do have a list we give to every buyer. Also a contract saying Sweets and Nephew is not responsible for anything that happens between when we deliver the grimoire and when it may again become available for sale."

I blinked. I doubted bookselling normally involved all that! I glanced at Tom's empty glass and wondered if the booze could be blamed for his story. The whole thing sounded improbable. But still, that summer with Sydney in Arkham there had been warnings from many people, and we had all ignored them. We hadn't believed. Not believing could be as dangerous as believing. As my friends found out.

"And all your buyers are happy to take the grimoire with a warning?" I asked out loud.

"Collectors," said Tom in a grim tone of voice. "They will do almost anything to add a certain book to their collection. Especially the type who purchase the grimoire. The professor seemed savvier than most and she was purchasing it for the university. I told her it was unlikely to stay in their library for more than a decade or so, but she was content with that. After we learned of the mix-up, I returned to take the grimoire to the rightful owner and refund the university's money, as much as the loss of this quarter's profits pained us, Uncle and me. Except the professor was gone along with the book. And Miss Malone's goons found me."

To judge by the two mugs roughing up Tom in the alley, Miss Malone was not a woman to wait patiently for her book delivery.

I set our empty glasses on the tray. At the click of glass on metal, Tom raised his head hopefully, but I shook mine. "That's enough for tonight," I said. "Have you some place to go?"

He looked much better than an hour ago, but his one eye was still puffed nearly shut. From the hesitant way that he straightened in his chair, I wondered if a rib or two were cracked. I knew the feeling.

"If they took your wallet," I said, "I'll pay for the cab to your hotel or to the hospital."

Tom snagged his suit jacket from where I had left it folded across the chair's arm. He groped in one pocket and, with a satisfied grunt, fished out a hotel key from an inner pocket that I had missed.

"That's this hotel," I exclaimed, looking at the oval brass tag.

"I thought I recognized the lobby," said Tom.

"But why didn't the night manager know you?" I said. The small interrogation that we'd received earlier that evening argued that Tom was unknown to the staff.

"I never met him," said Tom. "I checked in during the day and kept to my room last night. Never met Irving either until tonight." He dangled the key's tag in front of his nose and squinted at the number. "What floor are we on?"

"The top one," I said.

"Ah, well," he said, rising to his feet and carefully pulling on his jacket. He even straightened his tie. With the buttons done up, his suit jacket hid his crumpled shirt. "I am considerably further down. I will find the elevator and descend to my more humble bed."

"But what are you going to do about your two buyers for the grimoire?" I said, because now I truly wanted to know how his story would resolve. I hated questions without answers and stories without ends. That was probably my curse. It certainly landed me in trouble more than once.

"Worry about it tomorrow," said Tom, with a second shrug that made him groan.

I never wanted to be responsible for other people. Good time Betsy, that was my plan when I first left home for Chicago, devoting my life to being footloose and fancy-free. Somewhere along the way, I took a great number of people under my wing in the form of a studio and a household. But I definitely wasn't going to add another to the list. Especially another tall and handsome man. All my trouble with Max was enough for a lifetime. I intended to solve the mystery of Max and return to being fancy-free.

"Are you sure you don't want me to call for a doctor?" I asked Tom, ignoring all my resolutions.

Tom limped to the door. "No," he said. "I'll be fine. Tomorrow I'll be at the hospital anyway. I need to talk to Professor Christine Krosnowski."

"So do I. Talk to the professor, I mean. Meet me in the hotel restaurant for lunch, and we can go together."

Tom cocked his head so he could examine me with his uninjured eye. "Why do you need to talk to her? Are you actually after the grimoire? You are the Mata Hari of the book trade!"

"No," I said. "I need to talk to Christine about a man I lost."

Tom grunted at that. "Why wait until after lunch? Why not do it in the morning?"

"Because I never rise before ten, always eat my breakfast in bed, and have other errands in the morning," I said lightly, shoving Tom toward the door. In truth, I usually worked on contracts and other legal rigamarole in the mornings, but who would ever believe that of a gamine ingenue?

"Also, with luck, my luggage will arrive from Hollywood tomorrow," I said to Tom. "I need to see it off the train as well as make some other visits." Jeany's keys were a hard lump buried in my bag. I wanted to check on the Fitzmaurice house and send my reassurances to her before I did anything else.

Tom departed. I locked the door as soon as he was gone. Then I pulled out all my notes about Arkham and added what I had learned: "Jeweled grimoire, makes people disappear and appear." Then I wrote down the question that I wanted to answer the most: "Is this the way to find Max?"

I wondered if I could persuade Tom to sell the book a third time to me. The professor wouldn't mind too much, I knew, not if I bought one or two of her stories for script development and promised a large gift to the university. I thought the gangster, Miss Nova Malone, might be more of a problem.

As I pondered how I could buy off a bootlegger, or at least stay out of shootouts, someone knocked very quietly on the door. Just a couple of quick raps as if they didn't want to be heard by anyone else.

While I respected the discretion, I wasn't in the mood for visitors. Besides, as I glanced at the clock, it was nearly eleven. Far too late for a lady, or even an actress who played a lady, to be entertaining. Then I spotted the Homburg sitting on the side table. Tom had obviously forgotten his hat.

Picking up the hat, I went to the door, unlocked it, and opened it. "Here you go," I started to say. But the person who hurried into the room was not Tom.

Wini dodged inside. She clutched a knife, practically a dagger, in her hand. As soon as she was in the room, she clicked a button on the knife and the blade slid into the handle.

"Thank goodness you are here," she said. "Lock that door." The knife disappeared into a pocket of her leather coat.

Full of questions, I clicked the door shut and turned back to Wini. "What's happened? And what's with the knife?" Over the past few days, I had never seen Wini shaken by anything, even a lit cigar rolling about in her plane, but she definitely looked worried now. "Is everything all right at the airfield?" When I had left her, she'd been planning an evening with a friend, a moment of rest before her crew arrived and they began preparations for their air show.

"Somebody has been hijacking mail runs," Wini said. "And I think they are after my plane, too."

CHAPTER SIX

"I met my friend Stella for dinner," Wini said. "She works for the Post Office. The airmail deliveries for the Innsmouth airfield disappeared twice last month. And there's rumors of more planes disappearing earlier this year."

"Didn't you say a lot of flyers go down on these runs. Especially if it's late at night?" I asked. I'd offered to ring down to the desk for coffee or tea, as the flask had left with Tom, but Wini just asked for a glass of water. I filled a glass from what was left of our jug.

"Yes," said Wini, "but these pilots didn't disappear. Just their planes. The pilots were found but nowhere near the airfield." She'd settled into the chair that Tom had occupied. She picked up the glass of water, started to sip, then put it back down again, clearly distracted. Her hands thrust deep into the pockets of her leather coat, and I heard the distinct sound of jingling as she fidgeted with the objects inside – keys, coins, that silver cigarette case, and presumably her switchblade.

"Where were the pilots found?" I asked, wondering if these incidents were similar to Jim's reappearance a few months ago. He'd simply been found wandering down a road with no indication of how he had gotten there. "Did the pilots all turn up in the same place?"

"Not really," said Wini. "All were found near Innsmouth but in different spots. Down along the shore. Near the old sea caves. Along the cliff road. Always near the ocean. One pilot was found on the beach, sleeping away."

"Odd place to take a nap," I said.

"Very odd!" Wini agreed. "Everyone claimed they had no memory of how they got there or what happened to their planes. Which have not been found yet."

"But why do you think that someone is after your plane?" I asked.

"Stella drove me back to the airfield after dinner," Wini said. "We were sitting in her truck, just gossiping, when we spotted a man coming out of the barn where I stored the Jenny. He didn't notice us, or if he did, he must have assumed we were fetching the mail."

I must have looked puzzled because Wini explained, "We were sitting in Stella's postal truck. The Post Office workers come and go from the airfield at all hours, says Stella, dropping off the sacks and picking up the mail for the area. Farmers want their Sears catalogs and packages!"

I nodded. Sears sold everything from dresses to plows, and everyone needed something that could be found in those catalog pages. I had moved to Chicago to get away from small town life and ordering the Sunday hat from Sears, but I still remembered the thrill of turning the catalog pages and dreaming about all the things shown there.

"So what did the man do?" I asked, watching Wini fidget, sure she wasn't telling me everything. Something about the incident truly rattled her, but I suspected it would take a little coaxing to get the whole story. "Why do you think he was after your plane?"

Wini sprang out of her chair and began pacing back and forth. "There were three planes on the ground at that airfield. The only one that he spent any time around was my Jenny. Then the man got in a Tin Lizzie and drove away. We followed him back to Arkham."

"Where is he now?" I asked.

Wini shrugged and wandered back to the chair. She sat down, dangling her hands between her knees. "I lost him somewhere around this hotel. Stella had to head home. She starts work early. But I wanted to see you."

"Why? What can I do?" I said.

"You're the Flapper Detective," Wini replied, but I had a feeling she wanted to say more.

"I play a detective," I said. "I am an actress. I pretend to be a detective."

"But you're here to investigate a disappearance. You said so."

Now it was my turn to fidget in my chair. "I'm looking for someone as I told you," I admitted, "but I'm not prepared to stop all the crime in Arkham."

"Well, after I left Stella, I kept looking around for the big guy. I finally spotted him heading into the alley behind the hotel," Wini said. I knew she was talking about the alley where I'd saved Tom from Nova Malone's men. "He met with a smaller man and argued with him."

"I know those two," I said. Arkham was hopping these days, it seemed, but what was everyone looking for? Tom? The grimoire? Something else? And why had Wini sought me out?

Wini did not look surprised at my statement. "I hid at the end of the alley, trying to hear what they were saying, but this man in a Homburg came sliding out the back door of the hotel. The big man grabbed him and started yelling about a book."

"The man in the Homburg was Tom," I said. "I'll tell you about him in a minute. But what happened next?"

"Then I heard gunshots and you shouting," said Wini, glancing at the Homburg that I'd put back on a side table. "What are you mixed up in?"

"I truly don't know," I confessed to Wini. "I am here to find out what happened to my friend Jim." I wasn't quite ready to explain all my theories about Max. Because how could I tell Wini I saw a man fall through a mirror and disappear? Even for Arkham, that sounded crazy.

Except Wini understood Arkham, maybe better than I did. All I had to go on was what I had learned over the past three years, from a distance. Darrell's photographs and stories in the newspaper, Christine's letters, and Jeany's reluctant retellings of what she had seen during the final days of filming.

Wini sighed. "I trust you," she said. "But my plane is my livelihood. It's hard enough scrabbling from town to town. If anything goes wrong, we could lose everything. I want the women's air derby to be on the up-and-up. All the pilots deserve that."

"I'm no villain," I told her. "I promise you I'm not mixed up with anything criminal. I want to find out how my friend Max disappeared. Jim was with him. They were both in the Fitzmaurice house on the final day of our filming. A fire broke out and one man died. But nobody ever found any other bodies. Then Jim came back to Arkham. So maybe Max is out there, too."

"So maybe you are a detective," said Wini.

"Stranger things have happened to me," I responded. "And tomorrow looks to be a busy day."

I explained to Wini that I planned to check the Fitzmaurice house where the fire had happened, visit my friend Christine at the hospital, and try to find out more about the grimoire from Tom. Thinking about all that, I giggled. It was late. Perhaps I'd mixed my earlier cocktail a little too strong, I decided, startled by my own laughter.

Wini looked up at me. "Now what?"

"I suppose I will need a vacation to recover from my vacation in Arkham," I said.

Wini grinned. "It will be late tomorrow before my crew needs me," she said. "I'll help you. And you can help me figure out what happened to those pilots who disappeared and then reappeared without their planes. I don't want to suffer the same fate."

"Very well," I said. "Do you want me to arrange a taxi back to the airfield or are you willing to sleep in a real bed? I could call down to the desk and arrange for another room."

Wini shook her head. "I'd better return to my plane. I'd rather stay there tonight."

I nodded. "Can you come back here by lunch tomorrow? I'd like you to meet Tom Sweets, the man with the Homburg hat and a strange story."

"Tom Sweets? Is that a real name?"

"He says it is Thomas Alfred Sweets the Fourth."

She snorted. "That's too horrible to be a false name."

"I thought the same."

With assurances that she would be safe enough at the airfield and that she didn't need any help finding a taxi, Wini left.

I puttered about the room, unpacking my scorched carpet bag and sighing a bit over its condition. That bag had been on many adventures with me, but this might be its last, I thought. An honorable retirement to the attic after this trip, I decided. I was fairly sure my house had an attic. I would have to ask Farnsworth.

The next morning, I was awake and working on some contracts that I'd brought with me when there was a sharp rap on the door. This time I did not fling it open, rather I called through it. "Who is there?"

"Your breakfast, Miss Baxter," said a familiar voice.

"Irving," I said, opening the door with some pleasure. "Shouldn't you be off work by now?"

"Last duty of my shift," he said, wheeling in the cart laden with breakfast elegantly hidden under a silver dome, a pot of coffee smelling delicious, and even a small red rose in a crystal vase.

"Very nice," I said, waving my hand at the chair near the window. "And delightful to see you, too. Can you do me a favor?"

"Certainly, Miss Baxter," said Irving, unrolling the napkin swaddling the silverware and then snapping out the same napkin to lay across my lap. The young man served with a definite panache. "What can I do?"

I nodded at the Homburg hat still sitting on the side table next to me. "Can you return that to Mr Sweets without anyone knowing where you found it?"

"Absolutely," said Irving. "He's on the second floor. I'll stop on my way back to the kitchens."

"Thank you," I said, slipping a tip with the Homburg to the efficient Irving. "Oh, Irving, do you have any copies of the *Arkham Advertiser*?"

"We have all the local newspapers and a selection of the New York and Boston newspapers in the lounge downstairs," said Irving. "Several days' worth."

"Excellent," I said, pouring myself a cup of coffee and thinking about bootleggers and books. "I'll take a look when I come down."

Nearly a month's worth of newspapers were stacked in a room the hotel grandly labeled "The Library" with a small polished brass sign. They had that wilted look of most hotel newspapers. Too many people had idly flipped the pages while waiting for something else. Most of the stories I vaguely remembered from my readings of the newspaper at home. But then I had been mostly focused on unexplained disappearances and the occasional reappearance of someone, like what had happened with Jim. This time I looked more closely for mentions of rumrunning and airplanes. The earlier story that I had seen about a captured seaplane loaded with illicit cargo was there. And it was written by Darrell! But in the days that followed the story vanished from the front pages when no one had been arrested or charged.

The problem with the airmail pilots and their planes disappearing was not mentioned. It seemed nobody wanted to talk about missing planes. Or perhaps only a few people knew. There was a brief mention of the airfield near Innsmouth being expanded as well as night lights being installed by the mail service. In one issue, I found a letter to the editor from a farmer, asking if anyone had seen some lost sheep, blaming this on increased flights over his fields. The noisy contraptions, as he put it, were scaring all his animals and keeping his hardworking family from a decent night's sleep. Then one night a pilot had landed in the middle of his fields, claiming to have lost his way to Innsmouth, and made "an almighty fuss" until the farmer had driven him "a considerable way" to the nearest phone.

I shook my head at this intrusion of modern life. But a nighttime landing of an airplane, the lost pilot struggling across a field of fierce animals (probably not sheep!), and then having her pound on the door of a seemingly abandoned farmhouse was a fetching scenario. It would certainly make a good opening for one of the Flapper Detective's adventures, I thought. I pulled out a small notebook from my handbag and jotted a line or two. The question, of course, was the role of the pilot. Would it be the Detective herself, off to save another lost soul? Or would this be our introduction to the eventual murder victim or even the villain? This was why creating fictional mysteries was so intriguing.

But as to clues for solving my personal mysteries, I found very little of help and left the hotel to complete my other errands before lunch.

The train station was my first stop. With delight, I watched them roll my largest delivery from California down the ramp from the boxcar and onto the ground.

"Oh, baby, how I've missed you," I crooned to my brilliant blue roadster, patting the hood. Farnsworth had arranged the car to be shipped before I had even left California.

"That's a nice machine," said a red-headed woman supervising the unloading of some crates. She looked vaguely familiar.

"Hello," I said. "Do I know you?"

"Lonnie," she said, holding out her hand to shake mine. "We met at your mansion. During that swell party you threw for our crew."

"Of course," I said, pumping her hand with enthusiasm. "You're Wini's mechanic."

"That's me," she said. "The rest of the crew is heading to the airfield. But I needed to pick up these tools and a couple of spare parts."

"Wini's there and waiting for you," I said.

"Oh, I know," replied Lonnie. "I spoke to her this morning on the phone. Sounds like you had some adventures on your trip. Set fire to my darling even."

"Just a little smoke, almost no flames," I assured her. "The Jenny flew like a dream."

Lonnie grinned. "Wini is the best. When we race in your air derby, we're going to take the grand prize."

"You sound certain of that," I said.

"There's many great pilots," said Lonnie. "But Wini can outfly them all!"

"It will be exciting," I said as I hopped into the roadster. Farnsworth had already made arrangements with the railroad for the rest of my luggage to be taken directly to the hotel. "Sure you don't need a ride?"

"No," said Lonnie, pointing at a battered old truck. "I must make some more stops on the way to the airfield for supplies. We have a performance on Saturday. Hope to see you there, Miss Baxter."

"You will," I promised. "I wouldn't miss it for the world. I wish I could try that wing-walking again." I meant it, too. I loved going up in the plane, and the stunt had been grand. I started to ponder how I could persuade Wini to add me to the show. I needed a holiday, and stunt flying would be an amazing vacation.

The next stop was the Fitzmaurice house. The place looked as grim as I remembered, a blackened shell of a place where Sydney's last film had gone so disastrously wrong. The last place where I had seen Max. I drove past the house itself, having no wish to explore its fire-damaged remains. I still recalled the heat of the flames, the searing sting of the smoke in my lungs, and Max pushing me out the door before I collapsed.

I guided the roadster past the house and to the barn where Humbert, the caretaker, was waiting for me. The tallest man in Massachusetts, Jeany once called him. He was a giant, closer to seven feet than six, and rail thin as well. A kind man, he had been tolerant of the ruckus we'd caused during the filming.

"Those trunks are safe," Humbert said to me, pointing to the pile casually stacked behind bales of hay kept for gardening and feeding the mule he still used to pull his old-fashioned lawn-mowing machine.

The pile looked like it had been there forever rather than just three years. A barn cat showed her kitten how to hunt mice over the tops of the trunks, leaving behind a trail of little cat footprints in the dust. Hiding in plain sight, I doubted any of the Hollywood suits still hunting for Sydney's last script would bother to push aside hay bales or pry open locks that were already starting to rust with the exposure to New England's winters.

Humbert pulled a scythe off the wall and began to sharpen it on a whetstone wheel that he kept near the entrance of the barn. Listening to it make that awful screech of steel against stone, I thought that would also discourage any prowler.

"What are you cutting down with that?" I asked.

"Weeds," said Humbert, never one to waste words. "Spreading out back. Coming from the woods. Been a bad summer for weeds."

He stood up and tested the edge of the scythe with a gnarled thumb. "Something has been bothering the crows, too."

Humbert believed the crows were not altogether normal birds. So did my friend Jeany, who claimed I should keep a close eye on any that I saw flying around Arkham. But I saw none in the sky or nearby trees as I walked around the house with Humbert. We went across the lawn, kept trim by Humbert's mowing machine, toward the fence that separated the house from the wooden copse beyond.

The woods were the last remnants of a primeval forest, according to Christine, fenced in and contained by the first families of French Hill. Despite the green canopy shading the path leading past the locked gate, this was a place where people didn't picnic or let their children play amid the shadows of the trees. It was not a nice place.

After we reached the fence, Humbert began to swing his scythe to cut back long olive-green vines growing through the slats. I moved further away, closer to the gate that once allowed the family access to their wood. Turning back toward the house, I could see that the fire had not burned this side as devastatingly as the front. From where I stood, looking back into the sun at the kitchen door and the path leading across the lawn, I almost expected to see the door swing open and a member of our film crew start down the steps. Would it be Jim slouching toward the pair of broken wicker chairs that still sat in the center of the lawn to steal a smoke and a nap while he waited to learn what part he would play? Or Paul packing his pipe as he came out to join Jim? Or even Max, who actually never relaxed enough to slouch in a broken chair and watch the sunset? Not when sitting would have wrinkled the perfect line of his suit. No, if it was Max marching out the back door, he would have been jotting lists in his monogrammed notebook, a place to go, a thing to do, or a person to impress. Max had wanted to be a big man in Hollywood. He saw himself as the next mogul, dwelling in a mansion, and running a studio.

Odd that I ended up living Max's dream.

Something curled around my ankles. Something damp and cold, clutching me with a painful pinch. Like a dead man's hands reaching out of a grave to grasp my legs.

I shrieked and jumped away from the fence. Long tendrils of slimy green vine were wound around my leg, causing me to stumble. The vine pulled me back toward the woods. From the other side of the fence rose an insistent and awful buzzing, a chittering of insects, and suddenly I felt like dinner being dragged into a lion's den.

Humbert loomed in front of me, swinging his scythe in a wide arc behind his shoulder, and then chopping down with the blade.

CHAPTER SEVEN

"Yep," said Humbert. "Those weeds have been awful bad this summer." The one that had entrapped me was now neatly cut in two.

Humbert's expertly swung scythe cut the vine so the protrusion through the slats of the fence was not more than an inch in length. How large it was in the woods, I had no desire to find out.

I reached down and unwound the damp, clinging mess from around my leg. It felt horrible. Sticky and slimy at the same time. I dropped each piece as quickly as possible, relieved to step away from the strange vine. As the last bit squelched through my fingers, a sharp briny scent, overlaid with hints of decomposition, rose from the rapidly disintegrating mess on the lawn.

"That's not a weed," I said, recognizing that peculiar smell. "That's seaweed." The brownish green blades resembled the giant kelp that swept ashore on the beaches of Northern California. The smell also brought to my mind the scent created by rotting piles of seaweed thrown by a high tide so far up the beach that the ocean could not drag it back. But seaweed doesn't grow in backyards, I told myself. We were miles from the coast. Perhaps some bird had flown inland and dropped it, I thought, while knowing that explanation wasn't likely. The woods beyond the fence were more than peculiar. The first of our crew to disappear in 1923, Paul, had vanished in that tiny patch of wild ground. Nobody ever knew what had really happened. Except, later, we were all sure Sydney had lied to us about the dangers and Max had helped him.

"Weeds," Humbert nodded, walking carefully along the fence line, scouting for any other intruders. One or two smaller vines were efficiently severed in two by the scythe. As soon as they were cut, the leaves began to curl up on themselves, drying to an ashy powder in only a few minutes.

"I don't remember anything like that when we were here before," I said to Humbert.

He shook his head. "New this summer, these weeds. Started a few weeks ago. Got worse this week. The mule doesn't like them."

"No, I suppose not." I stirred one small pile of ash with the toe of my shoe and then grimaced at the stain. My stockings were ruined, too. Arkham was proving hard on my clothes. The nearness of the Fitzmaurice house wasn't doing much for my nerves either. I wasn't afraid. Not in daylight, walking along the fence with Humbert, but I didn't like the feeling of those weeds winding around my ankles. Or the prickles going up and down my spine. As if something in the woods was watching me. I thought of Jeany's warnings, but when had I ever turned back from anything? I stared hard at the house. It was just a house. A burned-out old place that deserved to fall into ruin, just as Sydney deserved to become a footnote in some film history. There were better films to be made, ones with happy endings created by smart women who saved themselves. I planned to make those films.

"Thank you for your help, all your help," I said to Humbert. "I wanted to make sure those trunks were still locked."

"I never answer when any of those men come around asking about Mr Fitzmaurice's things," said Humbert.

"About that," I said, pulling a photo out of my purse. "Did any of the men look like this man?"

Humbert stared at the photo of Max and shook his head. "I remember him," he said. "He came with Mr Fitzmaurice that last time. Same as you and the rest."

"But you're sure that you haven't seen him anywhere in Arkham since then?" I asked, although I'd been asking this question through phone calls, telegrams, and letters for nearly three years.

"No, miss," said Humbert. "I would have remembered."

Looking at his long sorrowful face, I believed him. If Max had returned, if Max ever returned, it would not be to the Fitzmaurice house.

I thanked Humbert again and drove away. The answers I was seeking weren't there. If Max was out there, he was somewhere else. How entirely elsewhere I would not learn until later.

At the hotel, I changed my shoes and stockings. Then I realized my trunks were artfully stacked about the room and that I could change even more. Arriving at lunch in a pleated skirt scandalously skimming my knees, a sailor blouse with a red tie, and a bright blue cloche that simply shouted frivolous miss, I was a flapper in all her glory. Unfortunately, Tom and Wini, both arriving in the dining room shortly after I was seated, seemed intent on discussing serious crimes and how we might solve them. So much for renouncing responsibilities with a ritzy hat.

"First, introductions," I said to the pair as they each launched simultaneously into suggestions on what to do next to solve their problems. "Winifred Habbamock, Tom Sweets, bookseller of grim grimoires. Tom Sweets, meet the daredevil of the air, Winifred Habbamock."

"Habbamock," said Tom, after shaking Wini's hand. "That's a New England name, isn't it? I have heard it before, somewhere near here."

"Probably," said Wini.

"My ancestors got off the boat from Scotland in 1772," said Tom, "with a delivery of books for Thomas Jefferson."

"How nice," said Wini. "My ancestors watched the pilgrims splash ashore in the 1600s. And some say we met the Vikings even earlier."

"Ah," said Tom. "My apologies. I remember where I've seen that name before. Habbamock. It's connected to the Praying Indians."

Now Wini frowned. "If there's any name I hate more than fly girl," she said, "it's Praying Indian. Call us by our real names. Call us Wampanoag, Patuxet, Pokanoket, Mashpee, and all the names that your ancestors failed to record but mine never forgot. Don't erase us from history with some fool's map marked with Praying Indians."

Tom had the grace to look abashed. "I am sorry," he said. "I've been cataloging libraries of early American history. I tend to read while I'm cataloging and remember exactly what I read. But I know as well as anyone that history is only one step away from fiction."

"You are not the first to get it wrong, but you're the first to admit it to me," Wini said with a nod at Tom. Seeing my confusion, she added, "Many of the tribes in New England who converted to Christianity were listed on the early maps and histories as Praying Indians. As in, here's a town of Praying Indians."

"Not too flattering," I said.

Wini shrugged. "You could read it as here is a town that's more like us than some of the other ones. Except we weren't. At least not to most of the folks around here. Still aren't. Heck, I didn't officially become an American until 1924 when the Indian Citizenship Act passed. And I'm still not sure if I can vote."

"But I thought we had the vote," I said. "It's why I took off to Chicago. Women are equal now and all the rest." Except I knew that wasn't true for so many people, hence buying my own studio so I could make those rules for myself. As I learned long ago from my older siblings, if you can't win a game by their rules, then make up your own. Betsy Baxter's croquet might not be played the way other people played, but it was a game I could win.

"Maybe yes, maybe no, when it comes to voting," continued Wini. "It's better than it was. Still there are a lot of towns that manage to keep their ballot boxes locked away from the people who live there. Not that I ever stay in one place long enough to figure it out."

The waiter came with our plates. Wini grinned down at her steak and potatoes. She grabbed a roll from the basket in the center of the table and spread butter on it with reckless abandon. She took a big bite, swallowed, and then looked at us. "We can't change the past," Wini said, "but we can change the future. When I win your race, Betsy, there will be no place I can't go. There will be nothing out of my reach. I just need my wings and a good tailwind to lift me there."

I nodded and tucked into my own lunch. The right play of the diamonds and hearts, even if I had to count all the cards in my head, once led to a fat stake and a chance to change my future. I was happy to give Wini a shot at her own big win.

"But before I can even get off the ground for your race," Wini said, "I need to find another wing-walker. The show doesn't pull them in without that stunt. And we need big audiences this trip to make the planes top notch for racing."

"What happened to Charlie?" I said. "He's all right, isn't he?"

"Charlie's fine," said Wini, "but he had to go home. Brooklyn. One of his brothers was injured on a construction project and a cousin died. They work the high steel." She sighed. "Charlie was the best I ever had. But his family needs him. So now I'm down a wing-walker and an advance man."

"That's rough," I said. Charlie leaving would be hard on the act, I knew. I started to consider ways I could help Wini.

Now it was Tom's turn to look confused. "I know what a wing-walker is," he said. "And no thank you. I'm afraid of heights. You'll never see me go up in an airplane. But what's an advance man?"

"It comes from the circus folks, and we're a flying circus. In the old days, the advance man rode into town a few days ahead of the show to put up posters, take out ads, and stir up publicity. Anything to encourage people to buy tickets," Wini explained. "These days it's more a case of working the phones, but we still need someone to take our posters around the route, too."

"Like what I do," said Tom.

We both stared at him.

"What? You think booksellers just sit in the back of their stores and read until some customer arrives to buy a book?" he said. "Essentially, my uncle does think that, but that method doesn't work. As the rising tide of red ink in our account books proved. But a few well-written catalogs and advertisements placed in the proper journals, and sales will come."

"I can see you are a revolutionary in the antiquarian book trade," I said.

"I personally battled through our bookstore filled with the volumes purchased by my dead ancestors far too many times," said Tom. "It became clear that something had to be done before we drowned in literature. Thus I wrote a catalog, mailed it out, and sold some of the books. I wrote an advertisement and sold more books. I unearthed the names and addresses of past customers and sent out personal letters and sold even more books. I then used the money to pay for something other than books, like the water bill."

"Shocking!" I laughed.

"Yes, when my uncle realized his desk was cleared of overdue bills but there was exactly six inches of shelf space empty in the store, he nearly swooned. He feels empty shelf space affronts the booksellers' creed and should be filled as quickly as possible, so he immediately doubled the number of auctions he attended," said Tom. "Hence our need to sell the grimoire this summer.

Although sometimes I fear the reinvention of Sweets and Nephew is coming a little too late in this modern era. They say that the book trade is doomed by the movies. Why would people buy a book when they can spend a dime to see a picture show?"

"The picture people need books," I said. "After all, books and magazine stories account for most of our script ideas. We're even poaching writers from New York to script our shows."

The talk then turned to Wini's performances and how she could make up for the loss of Charlie's stunts.

"I'll call Mabel Cody to see if she knows of anyone to take over the wing-walking. She's the woman I was telling you about," Wini said to me. "The one that jumps from cars to planes. She's working on a stunt with a speedboat."

I liked the sound of that. Such a jump from a boat to a plane would look fantastic on film. I asked Wini for Mabel Cody's phone number, while Tom finished off his ice cream dessert, and began to think about ways I could persuade Wini to let me take Charlie's place.

After listening to us chat about Mabel, Tom said to us, "You know many dangerous women. I think I prefer the bookseller's life."

"You're the one with a gangster named Nova Malone trailing him," I said.

"Ah, true," said Tom. "Apparently our two friends from last night were making inquiries at the front desk this morning. Irving slipped me a warning along with my hat. Thank you for returning the Homburg."

"Two friends?" queried Wini. "The ones I saw in the alley?"

I nodded. "The ones who gave him the shiner."

Tom tapped his black eye and then groaned.

"Don't poke it," I said automatically. Then chided myself internally for fussing. Start fussing over a man and he'll think he has a claim, as I'd found out a time or two.

"Anyway," Tom said, "they wanted both my name and room number. I'm thinking of moving out of the hotel. At least until I can find the grimoire and return it to Miss Malone."

"That might be wise," I said. "Wini, do you have room in your barn at the airfield for an advance man?"

"Sure," she said. "Ours usually sleeps in his car between stops."

"But I don't have a car," said Tom.

"I do," I said, "and I'd be happy to help you with the advance work. You could even sleep in the car. Although, it is a roadster, and the backseat is small." I looked at Tom's lanky frame. "Well, bend your knees and you'll be fine. And I won't have to worry about someone stealing my car if I have a twenty-four-hour-a-day occupant. Just don't scratch the paint."

"The advance work does sound intriguing. I don't want to go back to Boston until we find the grimoire. Besides," Tom said with a smile, "I am beginning to see the appeal of knowing dangerous women. However, I cannot accept the loan of a car. I don't drive."

Wini and I now stared at him. He shrugged. "I live in Boston in an apartment above the store where I work. I am an antiquarian bookseller. I have neither the money nor the inclination to own a car. When I want to go someplace far, I take a train. Close by, I walk."

"Not a problem," I decided. "I will drive us from town to town. You can search for the grimoire as well as promote Wini's show." I decided I could use our trips to investigate mysterious disappearances and reappearances of people. To see if anyone had seen Max. Also, this meant that I would be on hand when the grimoire was found, which might answer all my problems.

"That's a solution!" said Wini, looking relieved. "I hate advance work, so it's kind of you to take it on."

"What do we do first?" said Tom.

"Talk to the professor," I said, checking my watch. "Let's see how our combined charm does at gaining us entrance to that hospital." I waved the waiter over and signed the lunch to my room.

Tom looked a little disturbed. "I know you're a Hollywood actress and all that," he said, "but can you afford this?" He gestured at the meal we had demolished while making our plans.

"It will be fine," I told him as we waited in the lobby for the hotel's garageman to bring my car. "The studio pays my bills." Perhaps I should have said that I owned the studio, but some men acted strangely when they found out I was a boss lady. It was nice being just Betsy Baxter again for this trip. Just Betsy with a larger trunk of hats.

"The studio pays?" said Tom, sounding astonished. "I'd heard that people were getting rich in the movies, but I didn't know it included free lunches."

"Mr Sweets, you would be surprised," I said as we piled into the roadster. Wini took the front seat next to me while Tom folded himself sideways into the backseat.

"I may have to sleep sitting up," he said with a smile.

Wini glanced over her shoulder at him. "We've got cots and bedding at the barn. We'll find you a spot where you can lie flat."

"Now, how do I get to the hospital?" I said.

Tom shouted directions from the backseat. For a man who didn't drive, he had a good, almost perfect memory of the instructions given by the doorman at the hotel. We arrived quickly and without ever having to stop and ask the way.

"I'm handing you the map and letting you navigate on all further journeys," I told Tom.

At the hospital, we were told Professor Christine Krosnowski was well enough for visitors. I nipped across the street to purchase some candy and a few pulps from the five-and-dime.

Wini eyed my offerings as we were conducted down the corridor by a stiffly starched nurse, whose skirts practically crackled with efficiency. "Didn't you say your friend was a poetry professor? Are you really going to offer her some of those magazines?" she said, looking at the pulps in my hand.

"Trust me," I said. "She'll love them."

When we were ushered into the room, we found a doctor standing by the professor's bed.

"Doctor Ezra Hughes," he said, stepping forward to introduce himself to us. He was one of those men whose hair had receded enough to give him a high, domed forehead. I suspected he was younger than the hairline indicated but still guessed him to be in his late thirties. The hand that shook mine was firm. The shoulders beneath his neat suit jacket indicated some athletic tendencies. Further, he had a certain wind-chapped look around the cheekbones and prominent nose to indicate he was an outdoorsman or a sailor.

"Betsy Baxter, Wini Habbamock," I said to him. "And this is Tom…"

"You!" shouted the doctor. "You scoundrel! Where is my grimoire?"

Tom took one wild-eyed look at Ezra Hughes and bolted from the room.

CHAPTER EIGHT

"Now, Ezra," said the professor from her hospital bed. "It is not your grimoire. It belongs to the university."

The doctor turned back to Christine with a frown. "But I need it for my research. Our agreement was that I would have the grimoire in hand as soon as that villainous young man returned it to you," he said.

I thought his description of Tom was a bit harsh. As far as I knew from Tom's story, he was as much a victim of the book thieves as anyone else. On the other hand, perhaps this Ezra Hughes had good reason to be angry at Tom. Out of the corner of my eye, I watched him fuss. There was something odd about the man, but I couldn't say exactly what. Perhaps I preferred booksellers to doctors. Also, I'd never liked hospitals. The way hospitals smelled made me uneasy.

This hospital smelled like hot water and plenty of soap. All hospitals did. But there was always a note under that antiseptic odor. One that reminded me that illness and death lurked around the corner. When I considered all the ways to escape the farm where I had been raised, becoming a nurse had never been an option. The sight of my own blood never scared me, but I hated to see someone else suffer.

However, Christine looked as cheerful as any woman confined to a hospital bed could be. She wore a crown of bandages but still appeared remarkably well. When Tom fled the room, his hasty departure sparked a definite twinkle in her eye. I knew her best from letters and one short visit she made to California the previous year. She'd been on the hunt for some reference book and also gave a few lectures at the University of California's Southern Branch. We had gone to lunch, and I had been charmed by her humor as well as her rather pointed remarks about academic life. She seemed to find my tales of stunts and Hollywood executives equally entertaining.

As I bustled up to the hospital bed to kiss Christine on the cheek and fill her hands with good candy and bad fiction, I calculated the best ways to encourage the doctor to spill more information about the grimoire and his conflict with Tom.

"Dear professor, how are you?" I cooed in as silly a voice as I could manage. Christine raised an eyebrow at my antics, but the doctor looked diverted, much as I intended. Wini stayed by the door of the room, content to watch.

"Miss Baxter," said Christine in a slightly bemused tone, "I did not expect a visit." She leaned into my kiss and whispered in my ear, "How did you get here so soon?" I had written her that I intended to visit Arkham to check on Jim as soon as my current movie finished filming.

"I read of your disappearance in the newspaper," I said loud enough for the doctor to hear, "and simply had to come to make sure that you were well." Then I whispered back to her, "I flew! Tell you all about it later."

"How very kind of you," said Christine, transferring the candy and the magazines to the small table beside her bed. She couldn't resist taking a quick peek at the table of contents in one magazine. Her eyes smiled, but she kept her mouth prim. I winked at her.

Plopping down on the chair next to the bed, I batted my eyelashes in the direction of the doctor and said, "Now tell me all about this grimoire that makes people disappear."

The doctor made a sound like a kettle attempting to boil, but Christine chuckled. "I wonder how you found out about that," she said. "Are you now in the hunt for the book?"

"She found out from the horrible bookseller who just fled the room. As he should," said Ezra Hughes. "And you should not say another word, Christine."

At that point, Christine became very much the professor and gave Hughes a look that would have sent her students scurrying out of her way. Then she turned to me and said very clearly, "Several books in the university's library mention the Deadly Grimoire might open a doorway or path, especially when its spells are invoked in a weaker spot. Of course, like all mystic writings, it's hard to be sure if the authors are talking about a philosophical pathway to enlightenment or something else entirely."

Well, that wasn't what I expected. "Weaker spots?" I said.

"Cold places, shadowed spots, mirrors and windows that do not reflect truth," she said. "Or those that show a truth we don't understand." I gave a start, remembering the fire and my glimpse of Max falling through a mirror, a mirror that didn't break but became a doorway to someplace else.

But I didn't mention Max, not then, although perhaps if I had, I could have saved us all considerable trouble later. Instead, I said, "It's sounds very *Through the Looking-Glass.*" I adored reading about Alice's adventures as a child. One of my earliest acting attempts had been playing out Lewis Carroll's many topsy-turvy scenes for my grandmother in our kitchen. The poems always made her laugh.

By the door, Wini looked troubled. "We had a window like that, one that showed something that wasn't there," she said. "At the schoolhouse. When I was a little girl." There was a tension in her voice and face that suggested it was not a happy memory. I noticed particularly because Wini usually projected such an air of reckless nonchalance, especially around strangers.

Christine gave her a keen look. "You're from this area, then?" she said.

"Further up the coast," said Wini. "When I was very small, before I was sent out west, we went to a one-room schoolhouse. It had been built from parts scrounged from other buildings. The window had this old glass, the kind with bubbles and rings in it."

"Colonial glass, I expect," said Christine.

"I don't know," said Wini. "It was all warped. The other kids said you could see into the past through it. They used to dare each other to look. People said that you'd see terrible things, horrible crimes that had happened long ago, if you looked out that window."

"And did you look?" I asked, but I already guessed the answer. Wini was so like me. She'd march up to such a window as soon as she heard about it.

Wini gave her a fierce smile. "Of course! All it took was one dare and I marched right up to that window," she said.

"And what did you see?" I said, pleased I had guessed her reaction correctly.

"I saw people like me," said Wini. "Mending fishing nets, cooking over open fires, and laughing with their children. I had never seen so many people like me in one place."

"And then what happened?" asked Christine, and there was a sadness in her voice as if she already knew the ending to this story.

"A man walked into their camp," said Wini. She waved a hand at the doctor. "A man who looked like him, except dressed in those funny old pilgrim clothes. All dark and flapping around him. Except it wasn't his coattails waving in the wind. There were dozens of shadows all bunched around him, shadows like snakes, striking out at the people. Then all the people were gone except for the stranger ensnared in shadows."

"That's terrible," I said, remembering fire and smoke and Max disappearing into shadows that stretched like hands or tentacles to engulf him. I noticed Christine did not seem surprised by Wini's tale. Nor did the doctor react to her descriptions with more than a slight bemused shake of his head. Arkham, I thought, makes people believe in ghost stories.

"I was so angry," said Wini. "So angry that the people were gone. I ran out of the schoolhouse and searched all over for them. But, of course, there was nothing there. It was just a reflection in the glass. Such a mad, sad little girl I was that day. Searching for ghosts of a people long gone. I picked up a stone and threw it straight through the schoolhouse window so it wouldn't frighten any more children. Broke it all to bits."

"Good for you!" I exclaimed. "That's the way to handle your ghosts." I meant it, too. It was exactly what I would have done. If I had to break windows or mirrors to find Max, I intended to do just that. After all, I'd never been a patient person. Why start now?

"It's the best way," said Wini, looking straight at me. "Never look back. Keep flying forward."

The doctor's reaction to Wini's story was completely different from mine. "Such a loss," said Ezra Hughes. "There are so few of those items left. Far too many have been broken by ignorant souls afraid of the secrets they reveal."

"So you know of windows like that?" I asked, quite intrigued. Perhaps this doctor could give me a clue or two about what happened to Max.

"Of course," said Hughes. "I used to search for such glass on the beach. Just fragments left from the windows and mirrors thrown into the sea. Ignorant fools would do that to rid a house from a haunting. But if you held those shards to your eye, you would see wonders. As a boy, I had a collection of such sea glass. I still do." He had one hand in his jacket pocket and was fiddling with something, much like Wini tended to jingle the items in her pockets.

"It seems like you had a slightly different childhood than Miss Habbamock," said Christine. Her tone was not complimentary, but the doctor didn't seem to notice.

"I was raised in Innsmouth," he said. "Our house overlooked the town and the sea. It was built by my ancestor, Captain Bulkington Hughes. A great man."

"A whaler," explained Christine to Wini and me. "Call me Ishmael, and all that."

Hughes looked pleased. "Melville may have modeled his Bulkington on my ancestor. After all, Melville is the one writer who realized the genius and glory of the sea and the tribute that must be paid to the waves if men are to prosper."

"Do you know," Christine said to me, "I cannot remember a single female character in that book."

"There was a romance in the movie," I said. "Dolores Costello played the lady. She's why the brothers fight and Ahab loses a leg to the white whale." I'd read the book, too, but why ruin the effect of a spoiled jazz baby? Especially when I could practically see the doctor's face turning purple. In my experience, angry men grew careless with secrets and their cards. Of course, provoking that anger was a dangerous game to play. After a certain poker game went very much my way and very much against a guy named Alphonse Capone, I skipped out of Chicago and headed to Hollywood to try my luck there.

"That travesty of a film," groaned the doctor. "They ripped Melville's meditations apart and made it a melodrama. There is no romance in the novel! There is no place for women in such a story."

"That leaves me wondering where all those men came from," interjected

Christine. "Did Ahab spring from the head of some old sea god like Athena from Zeus, and was that why he was so intent on killing that white whale? Freud would have had a field day with all those references to sleeping partners and cannibalism."

Wini tried to smother a laugh while I refrained from giggling at the doctor's expression.

"You will have your little jokes, Christine," said Hughes. "But there is a spiritual truth to be discovered within Melville's work. As you well know." Then, as if he was a preacher on Sunday, he proclaimed, "Consider the subtleness of the sea; how its most dreaded gods glide under water, unapparent for the most part, and treacherously hidden beneath the loveliest tints of azure. Consider also the devilish brilliance and beauty of many of its most remorseless deities, as the dainty embellished shape of many species of spirits. Consider, once more, the universal cannibalism of the sea; all whose divinities prey upon each other, carrying on eternal war since the world began."

Again, I had to almost physically restrain myself from responding to such pompous nonsense. Hughes had misquoted Melville quite badly, in my estimation, and there was something about his general tone that I didn't like.

"Yes, yes, Melville was a decent writer," said Christine in such a placating tone that I was sure she had simply shut her ears to Hughes or had heard him spout off too often. "But I dread teaching that book. After so many years of freshman literature, I find it so…"

"Fishy?" I said, unable to resist.

Wini gave a muffled shout of laughter and, looking at the doctor's reddening face, ducked out the door, saying she would wait for me outside.

The doctor ignored us both, addressing himself solely to Christine. "I know you do not appreciate the majesty of Melville, but I found the inspiration for my oceanic therapies within the pages of his great work."

"I know you mean well," said Christine. "And there's no doubting the number of people you've helped."

"But I could do so much more with the grimoire," stated Hughes. "If that vile young man hadn't lost it. Or stolen it back. All this talk of selling it twice by mistake. I cannot like it, Christine. I'm sure he is lying."

Now that last statement interested me far more than an argument about the merits of Herman Melville and the movie based on his whale book. I liked Barrymore in *The Sea Beast*, and the scene where his leg was cauterized caused half the audience to shriek and squirm when I went to see it. But the entire movie was far too much men on ships for me. I did remember that one reviewer called the story "quite preposterous". But then again, that reviewer found my films preposterous, too.

"Ezra, we will find the grimoire," Christine said. "Have a little patience. You know its history. It is sure to reappear in Boston if not in Arkham."

If, as Tom said, the grimoire did make people appear, I might find the answers I needed within its pages, especially with Christine's help. And, if Ezra Hughes understood the book as well as his conversation indicated, perhaps he would make a better ally than a butt of fish jokes. If the grimoire ended up being only a load of philosophical nonsense, as Christine suggested earlier, I could give it to the university. Perhaps with a note of apology to Ezra Hughes for teasing him so this day.

The doctor made a dissatisfied noise, more of a snort of disbelief than anything else, and bid Christine a formal goodbye. At the last moment, he recovered his manners enough to thank me for visiting my friend.

"I am sure she will find comfort in a woman's company," he said.

Christine and I refrained from rolling our eyes at each other until he left.

"Does he always quote snatches of old fiction and talk like a character from a hundred years ago?" I asked.

"Only when he's on his high horse," responded Christine. "I have seen him be quite modern at a few faculty parties. His foxtrot is exceptional."

"Hmm," I said, not convinced. "But why does he want to read your grimoire?"

"It's not my grimoire," said Christine again. "It belongs to the university. Ezra teaches on the medical faculty. He was instrumental in procuring the funds to finance its purchase. An anonymous donor, or so he said."

"You don't believe in the unknown benefactor?" I asked, curious to find out why Christine would look such a gift horse in the mouth.

"I think he may have contributed the money himself. Although why he didn't want to take credit for it, I cannot say," the professor replied. "He's the one who brought it to my attention. There's considerable Hughes family history tied to that book."

"I thought it belonged to the Sweets family. In between other owners," I said, remembering the strange tale that Tom had told in my hotel room.

"Yes, but the grimoire appears in Innsmouth more than once in its complicated history. It's said that the sharkskin that forms the cover was from a beast netted out of the waters near the coast. A great green shark."

"I've never heard of a green shark," I said.

"It's possible it is simply arsenic-dyed sharkskin," said Christine. "Which would explain both the color of the shagreen cover and the number of fatalities among the owners. Although the current binding was done in this century, and thus wouldn't account for all the fatalities. I wore gloves when I was examining it to determine if it was the Deadly Grimoire."

"Do you know why it's called the Deadly Grimoire?" I asked, thinking Tom had left a great deal out of his story. He hadn't mentioned arsenic.

"That's one name for the book. Other histories called it the Grimoire of the Sweets, which led to numerous misunderstandings. At least one source listed it as an alchemical cookbook of desserts." Christine chuckled over this error. I wondered exactly what mayhem that had caused. "Then there's the False Grimoire. Which caused considerable trouble for the Hughes family."

"Tell me more," I said. Christine pulled herself even straighter in the hospital bed. I plumped the pillows behind her, then settled back into my chair.

In language as precise and erudite as her letters to me, she explained that a Sweets, back at the start of the last century, had printed up a second grimoire. "The story goes that the Sweets family was unwilling to give up their most valuable book but still needed money to purchase more stock for their store, so they made the False Grimoire to have something safe to sell. Others say that this particular Sweets was paid to create a counterfeit so an unscrupulous sea captain could steal the Deadly Grimoire from a rival."

"Name me names," I said, enthralled. This was better than one of my movies. "I never knew the book trade was so full of crooks."

"You'd be surprised what collectors will do around truly rare volumes," said Christine, in an echo of what Tom had told me earlier. "And the captain who paid for the counterfeit was supposed to be the upright Bulkington Hughes."

"Oh," I said, "this sounds like one of your stories. Why haven't you pitched this to the pulps or to me?"

"Because I'd need an ending and the history of the two books is so murky," said Christine. "All that's actually known is that Sweets did create a nearly perfect forgery, but there was a deliberate error in the final signature."

"Somebody signed the book wrong?" I asked, puzzled by her description.

"No, a signature is the collection of pages within a book, all the pages printed on a single piece of paper, then folded and cut apart to form the pages of the work. Everything printed has signatures, from the oldest books to this magazine," she said, ruffling the pages of the pulp to show me what she meant. "On the final signature of the False Grimoire, the printer inserted his colophon. It may have been from habit, that was a common way to mark a book's end, or perhaps Sweets wanted a way to prove the book false at a later date. According to one bibliography that I found, the colophon is quite small, a fish biting its tail, and printed so close to the interior edge of the page that the fish is almost lost in the spine of the book."

All very interesting for someone who was a student of the book trade, but I focused on the important piece of news in the story. "Then there's a fake grimoire that can be told from the true grimoire by the fish picture on the last page." I jotted that information into the small notebook I kept in my purse. A habit that I acquired from Max. However, I didn't bother to have my notebooks engraved with my name. Rather I used plain brown pads from the five-and-dime. My pencil, however, was chained to the interior of my bag by a sterling silver chain and holder. I so disliked losing pencils that I'd had the silver device crafted for me by Tiffany.

"That's what I said," Christine agreed. "Two grimoires, one Deadly and one now known as the Fake or, to more precise bibliographers like myself, the False Fish Grimoire. That's why Hughes wanted me to purchase the grimoire for the university's collection. So I would examine it and verify it was the true grimoire."

"But if his family has the False Grimoire, wouldn't Hughes know that the other one was the Deadly Grimoire?" I said.

"Both books were lost at sea," said Christine. "At least that's what everyone thought until 1910, when another Sweets revealed he had the Deadly Grimoire. He's the one who ordered the book bound in green shagreen and ornamented."

"Tom told me about that. Jeweled and gold decorations. Quite elaborate and unnecessary," I said. "Although he didn't mention any false grimoire. I wonder why."

Christine shrugged. "It was an embarrassment to the family. They are very proud of their reputation as purveyors of rare books with excellent provenance. After their previous handling of the book, the next generation of Sweets removed the original binding to prove that the Deadly Grimoire being sold was the true grimoire, no fish mark. After being certified as free from the fish colophon, the Sweets replaced the binding with jeweled ornamentation, which was popular with a certain type of collector before the war."

"What happened to that owner?" I asked. "The one who bought the fancy version."

"Drowned when the *Titanic* went down," replied the professor. "It was thought the Deadly Grimoire went into the sea with the ship. But apparently it never left Boston. Sweets sold it again to another owner."

"What happened to him?" I said.

"Killed in the war," the professor said. "His estate went to auction and the Sweets bought the entire library."

Killed in the war was the fate of too many men, and it didn't take a curse to make that happen, I thought, but I still realized owning the grimoire didn't sound terribly lucky.

"What happened to the fake grimoire?" I said.

"No one knows for sure," Christine said. "But I've heard some speculation that it also fell into the hands of the Sweets a few years ago. If that's true, it's almost as valuable as the Deadly Grimoire. I would love to see it."

A nurse rapped on the door. "Almost time for rounds," she said. "You'll need to leave, miss, so the doctor can examine her patient."

"Wasn't that what Hughes was doing here?" I asked the professor.

Christine shook her head. Even the nurse gave me a wintery smile of disbelief. "Now, miss," added the nurse, "no more questions. It's time for visitors to leave."

Christine waved the woman away. "I'd much rather chat with Miss Baxter," she said to the nurse, "than sit in bed staring at the wall. I'm quite tired of the wall's company."

"Very well," said the nurse with a sympathetic smile. "But only ten more minutes." She bustled out the door, obviously intent on sweeping all strays out of the ward before the doctor's rounds.

"Ezra Hughes isn't my doctor. He's wild to see the Deadly Grimoire and wanted to hear about the robbery. He's questioned me almost as many times as the police," Christine said in answer to my earlier question. "But he does treat patients on the mental ward and at his sanitarium. You'll see it soon enough."

"What do you mean?"

"The sanitarium, Bluff Mansion. That's where your friend Jim is staying. Didn't you know?" Christine looked slightly bemused.

As soon as she said the name, I did remember it. I had arranged to have Jim transferred out of the hospital and to private treatment as soon as it was safe to do so. Christine had recommended the place to me.

"I do remember your letter about a doctor who specializes in the treatment of lost memories or amnesia," I told her. "I didn't realize Hughes was the man."

"Yes, he's become quite well known in this area," said Christine. "Rather a local boy made good. He's fascinated by memory loss. Especially among those who claim they have experienced a gap in time."

"A what?"

"I guess you could call it a period of time that can't be accounted for."

"You mean people who have disappeared and then reappeared later some place completely different."

"Well, yes," the professor admitted.

"Isn't that what happened to you?" I finally asked. "Did the grimoire make you disappear?"

CHAPTER NINE

Christine chuckled at my question about the cause of her disappearance and touched the bandage that wrapped around her head. "Oh, no, nothing so unearthly as a cursed book," she said. "Somebody knocked me over the head, dropped me into the back of a car, and drove me a considerable distance out of town before leaving me propped up against a road sign. Considerate of them. They could have rolled me into a ditch instead of leaving me where I was found by the next passing milk truck. However, they also stole the grimoire, so I'm less happy about that. Ezra wanted to question me about my memory loss and offer me treatment at his sanitarium if I felt so inclined. Which I don't. Cold seawater baths and tea made from kelp! Thank you, but I'd rather recover here."

"His treatment sounds horrid," I agreed. I wondered now if sending Jim there had been the right decision. What had poor Jim experienced over the past few months? "Does anyone recover at Hughes's sanitarium?"

"The doctor's treatments have been unusually successful," Christine said with conviction. "It's one of the reasons I was not surprised your friend has recovered some of his memories and begun to talk again. Ezra calls his treatments oceanic therapy. He says he uses the sea to restore memory and well-being."

Her words were reassuring, although I still wasn't certain about cold seawater baths or drinking seaweed tea. I took Christine's view of such treatments – Hughes's ideas sounded unpleasant. I resolved to visit Jim as soon as possible. If he seemed well, then I would allow the treatment to continue. If not, I intended to move him back to California as quickly as possible.

"But who stole the grimoire?" I asked Christine. "Do you have any idea?"

"I do not remember much," she sighed. "I was finishing my examination of the book at home and working on my speaking notes for the evening. It was an honor to present the Deadly Grimoire to the library, and I wanted to make an occasion of it. I was sitting quite comfortably at my desk when somebody struck me on the back of my head."

"I read in the newspaper that your friends found your door open and you gone," I said. "That's why I flew out here."

"Did you really fly?" asked Christine. "I've always wanted to go up in an airplane."

"It's marvelous," I told her. "You have to try it. But how did they get into your house, and who would have stolen the grimoire from you?"

"As for getting in, that was easy. The door was unlocked as I was expecting friends. As for who stole it, Ezra thinks it was your handsome bookseller, Tom Sweets," she said.

"He's not mine," I answered very quickly. I simply did not need another responsibility. "I found him being beaten up by some muckers who work for Nova Malone."

"Ah, the Deadly Grimoire's other claimant," Christine exclaimed. "It was the Malone family who bought the Deadly Grimoire once before and wreaked havoc on the fortunes of the Hughes family and others in Innsmouth. Or at least that's Ezra's story. The other side is the False Grimoire was created to cheat the Malones out of their book. Again, nobody is sure what is true. This all happened in the last century."

"So what a tangled web these sea captains and booksellers did weave?" I said.

"*Marmion*," replied the poetry professor, "Sir Walter Scott, 1808. Betsy, I'm always impressed with your knowledge."

"I run with a smart crowd," I said. I did, too. Folks from all backgrounds landed in Hollywood. "I keep telling you that you'd love teaching out west. They're planning big things for the California universities. I expect Berkeley and Stanford to rival Harvard soon."

Christine just smiled and shook her head. "I am happy enough here," she said. "Arkham can be a strange place, but it is my home."

The nurse popped her head back into the room. "Now, I must insist that you leave," she said to me. "The doctor is almost here."

"They will let me out in a day or so," Christine said. "Let's plan on dinner. Bring your friends. I want to hear about your adventures."

"We will take you flying," I promised.

As I walked out of the hospital lobby, I spotted Dr Hughes talking with two large, roughly dressed men. One of them looked familiar, and I was pretty sure he was Little Albie's friend from the night before. An orderly was doing something with a mop and pail. Despite being hit by a cloud of that horrible hospital soap smell, I ducked behind the orderly to eavesdrop.

The two men seemed to be in something of an argument with each other with quick interjections from the doctor. I wondered if they were patients or friends of patients. Their attitude seemed to indicate the latter. I heard one say to the doctor, "So how long until he can tell us where the boxes are?"

"I cannot rush treatments. As Miss Malone very well understands," said

Hughes. "However, if you would only tell me more about the route that he took and where he was found?"

"We've told you all we can," said the larger man, and I was certain that he was Albie's friend. "But Miss Malone repeats, she doesn't have the book. However, she is not giving up her claim on it either."

Following that intriguing statement, the two men talking to the doctor took off. Restraining my natural impulse to follow and question the roughs directly, I lingered in the lobby for a few moments. Then I ran after the doctor. When I caught up to him, I stuck out my hand. "Thank you so much for taking care of my friend," I said. "And chasing off that lout of a bookseller. That young man pestered me for a ride to the hospital and, I'm sure, will want me to take him back to the hotel again. I had no idea that he was such a goof."

Burbling like the most witless of flappers, I shook the doctor's hand heartily.

Ezra Hughes looked a bit befuddled by my statements – perhaps he didn't know what a goof was – and said with a paternal air, "Now, you must be careful of such men." I glanced out the door at his recent companions and thought he should take his own advice. "A young lady alone can be prey to the most terrible of villains."

Not since the Brontës wrote their gothic novels, I wanted to say but replied, "How kind. I have a friend with me, a regular fire extinguisher, to protect me from Lothario booksellers," I said, although I'm sure describing Wini as a chaperone would have amused her to no end. "Now, you take good care of the professor, and I'll be back to see her quite soon."

"Ah," said the doctor, apparently placing me and my flapper slang in his mental filing cabinet. "You are one of the professor's students."

As if a student could afford such a hat as I wore! But really, one couldn't expect a New England doctor from a small town to recognize Paris fashion. "Ah, I've learned a great deal from the professor," I said, and that was nothing but the truth. "However, I hear from her that you're the true expert on missing men."

Ezra Hughes looked surprised at my statement. "Missing men?"

"People who have been lost and don't remember where they were, even after they've been found," I said, which was Jim's case in a nutshell.

"I am considered one of the foremost experts on the recovery of memory," Hughes said. Obviously, he didn't think modesty was a virtue. Well, I didn't either, so why judge him for that?

"Have you ever treated a man named Max Taelsman?" I said.

"Max Taelsman?" said Hughes. "No, I don't think so." And before he could ask any questions of me, a nurse came to remind the doctor that he was wanted for a consultation on an upper floor.

With another wave of my hands, I dashed out the door. I'd learned a great deal in this visit, but now I had a number of questions for Tom Sweets.

Outside the hospital, I spotted Tom and Wini waiting for me by the roadster.

As soon as I reached them, I said to Tom, "The ancestors of Nova Malone and Ezra Hughes seem to have a history with your family. What's this about a false grimoire?"

"Ah, that," said Tom, rubbing the back of his neck with one hand. He gave me a shy smile, tilting up his head in a way that must have made the hearts flutter among the college girls. "Ancient family history?"

"Not good enough," I said, having a heart of stone and being impervious to the wiles of college boys, no matter how they shyly peered through their absurdly long lashes. Such a waste for a bookworm to have such pretty eyes when he wasn't in the pictures. "Spill the beans, mister," I said, in as stern a tone as I could manage on a sunny day in the summer with a breeze fluttering the hem of my dress and wearing a Paris hat. "The doctor claims you're a no-good character and a danger to the ladies to boot."

"As for being dangerous, I'm not the one who carries a pistol in my purse," said Tom. "Nor am I wearing a skirt that would shock my grandmother and delight my grandfather and a hat that would please them both."

"Thank you for the lovely compliment," I responded, "but tell me about your multiple grimoires."

The pair of men who had been arguing with the doctor had carried on their conversation outside. Having obviously settled something between them, they strolled across the street.

Tom eyeballed the pair. "Let's cover my family's convoluted past in another place," he answered. "I don't like the look of those characters."

Wini, who had been watching the two of us with mild amusement, looked over Tom's shoulder at the men heading toward a parked Model T a little way away from us. "I know the one man," she said. "That's the guy who was snooping around the airfield. The one I followed into town." She pointed at the biggest guy, the one I thought was Albie's friend.

"Those two were jawing with the doctor on my way out. He's definitely the one who roughed you up, Tom," I said. The two men climbed into the Tin Lizzie with a dented fender. Neither glanced at us. Apparently, their discussion was more interesting than idle bystanders.

"I agree, which is why I suggest leaving the vicinity," said Tom. "At least his little friend doesn't appear to be with him. Albie was vicious. But I'd rather not tangle with any of that particular fraternity again."

"At least this time you're close to the hospital," I said.

"But will you be my nurse a second time?" Tom replied with another flutter of those lashes. I frowned at him. Tall, handsome, and trouble was not a combination I needed, I reminded myself, no matter how much he might make me want to laugh.

"That's certainly the car I followed," said Wini as the pair started their vehicle.

"Shall we see where they go?" I asked as I hopped into the driver's seat.

"I'm game," said Wini with a grin. She grabbed the passenger seat beside me. "Let them go down the road before you start after them. That way they might not notice us."

"I know how to trail a car," I said. "I took lessons from a writer who used to work for the Pinkertons." I started the roadster and heard the reassuring roar of its engine. I loved learning a former Pinkerton detective's tricks one winter in San Francisco and was delighted to try a few of the techniques that Dash taught me.

"Are you sure you want to do this?" said Tom as he settled himself sideways in the backseat.

"We can leave you here," I said.

Hughes emerged from the entrance of the hospital. Seeing Tom, he pointed at him and began to shout. There was definitely a shaking of fists, but I couldn't make out the words, except "crook" and "fraud".

"Let's follow that car," said Tom, essaying his own cheerful wave at the doctor as we drove by Ezra Hughes.

I laughed then and shifted into another gear, setting a good pace but not moving too close to the car ahead of us. Of course, in a bright blue roadster, we were not exactly inconspicuous. However, the car in front of us headed down toward the river along one of the main streets. There was enough traffic, including a boy madly ringing his bicycle bell and a cranky horse kicking up the traces in a farm delivery wagon, to keep their eyes on the road in front of them.

"Where do you think they are going?" I said to Wini as we made another turn down a street that looked far more industrial than residential. Small factories and the types of businesses that catered to other businesses rolled by.

"Warehouses?" said Wini. "Look, you can see the river now."

The river glinted green and greasy in this section of the town, and there was a definite odor rising in the warm August afternoon.

"Slow down," said Tom. "Looks like they are turning in there."

The Tin Lizzie pulled through the open double doors of a warehouse and stopped. I drove past without even glancing at them, just as the detective once showed me. "Never let them catch you looking," he'd muttered out of the corner of his mouth when we were trailing a pair of crooks through San Francisco's meaner streets. "If you stop behind them, they'll check you out. Go down the street and park around the corner. Always give them time to go about their business. It also gives you time to find a place to watch them."

Sliding the roadster down an alley, I parked in the shadow of another tarred warehouse. The smell of creosote, hemp, and river waste was strong enough to taste in this Arkham neighborhood. I could hear the hooting of tugs as the barges moved up and down the Miskatonic River in the afternoon heat.

"Now, wait a moment," said Tom as Wini and I began to sidle back toward the warehouse where the two men had parked. "Is this safe?"

"Probably not," said Wini to Tom. "But that's more fun."

"Hush," I said to the pair of them. "Let's see what they're doing." I went first, eager to follow the two men and check what they were up to. Their earlier conversation with the doctor about a lost man had certainly sparked my curiosity about their business.

But when we got to the warehouse, a cautious peep through the windows on the side showed the car parked near some crates and no sign of the men who had ridden in it.

"Let's go inside," I said.

"Let's not," said Tom.

"Where's your sense of adventure?" asked Wini.

"I'm a bookseller," Tom said. "An antiquarian bookseller, which means I don't even have to talk to authors, as all the volumes I sell were written by dead people. The most exciting thing I do is search attics for possibly valuable volumes to auction."

"Ever find any?" I said, still balancing on my tiptoes to see through the window, but I couldn't spy anything unusual.

"Not as many as my uncle would like," Tom said. "Boston attics tend to be stuffed full of old clothes, far too many mothballs, sleds with rusty runners, and portraits of dead husbands. An amazing number of portraits of dead husbands. You'd think their widows would want to keep them downstairs."

"Well," I said, "I suppose that depends on the marriage. No portraits of dead wives?"

"Only if there is a new wife downstairs," said Tom.

"This is fascinating," said Wini in a tone that indicated she wasn't too intrigued. "But are we breaking into this warehouse or not?"

"I don't think it's breaking in," I said, dropping back on my heels. I strolled around the corner to the pair of open doors I'd spotted through the windows. "Not if the doors are wide open. We can always say we are lost and looking for directions back to the hotel."

"But I know where the hotel is…" Tom started to say but then blinked. "Oh, right, we could say that, I suppose."

I hooked my arm through Tom's. "Come on," I said with a chuckle, "this will be more fun than a Boston attic."

Inside the warehouse, we found no one, certainly not our suspicious pair of men, and almost nothing else of interest. The crates stacked around the walls held nothing but the straw lining their insides.

"What do you think they held?" I asked Wini and Tom.

He shrugged, but Wini plunged her hands in and stirred up the straw. I waited for mice or bugs to appear, but the packing was clean. Wini noticed that, too.

"This is pretty fresh," she said. "My guess is that the cargo was something breakable. Like glass. That's odd." From the interior of the box, she pulled a long strand of withered seaweed. The briny smell overwhelmed almost everything else and brought back memories of Humbert's weeds.

"That's ugly," said Tom, pointing at a bony little fish that dropped from the seaweed strand. The specimen had bulging eyes and needlelike teeth that jutted out of its mouth. "Looks like a piranha."

"I wonder how that got in there," I said. I was tempted to poke it with my foot but remembered the demise of my last pair of shoes when I kicked the seaweed at the Fitzmaurice house. Instead, I bent as close as possible without touching the thing. The smell was rank and familiar. Those horrible weeds I'd encountered that morning smelled exactly the same, like seaweed rotting in the sun. Then I noticed something else. "Tom, do piranhas have three eyes?"

"I don't think so," he said.

I looked at the third eye, centered in the creature's forehead, and shuddered a little. It was a singularly ugly fish.

"Do we take it with us?" Wini asked.

"No," said Tom and I in a harmonious chorus.

"It might be a clue," Wini said.

"It's dead, it smells, and I don't want it in my car," I replied. "Let's leave it here and see if there's anything more helpful in their flivver."

The men's car looked exactly like the rest of its Ford's Model T brethren, but one front fender had a slight dent, which would distinguish it if we encountered it again. I did a quick rummage around the driver's seat, finding only a matchbook printed with the insignia of the Strike True Match Company of Ontario.

"Somebody's been in Canada," said Wini, tossing the empty matchbook from hand to hand in the same way she jiggled her silver cigarette case.

I moved around to the passenger side of the car and ran my hands along the seat, then peered under the bench on that side as well. There I found half of a burnt cigarette and a business card with a footprint on it, indicating that someone had dropped it on the floor of the car and other people had stepped on it getting in and out. That much of a detective's explanation I could give to my companions.

"In the detective magazines," said Tom, "that footprint would indicate a short man with a limp who previously worked for a banker in Cleveland."

"I'm not even sure if this is a man's footprint," I said, looking at the dirty mark on the card. "But at least we know it came from a place named the Purple Cat in Innsmouth." The name and address were printed under a very stylish cat. All the art and type were done in purple ink. When I showed it to Wini, she frowned. "I don't know it but we can ask around," she said.

"My guess is that they don't serve just tea," I said, flipping over the card. "This is a membership card." The number five hundred and eighty-seven was written on the back in a distinctive flowing script. Like the front, the number was done in purple ink but definitely in a person's handwriting and not printed. The seven was underlined twice.

"Membership card?" said Tom. "For what?"

Wini shook her head at his ignorance. "Blind pig," she said.

"What?" said Tom.

"Juice joint," I said. "Don't they swill the hooch in Boston? Please don't expect me to believe Harvard men are teetotalers who would never enter a drinking establishment."

"House parties," said Tom with a smile. "And certain places of entertainment, which may have included beverages. There is the Bibliophile Club. But I never had to show a card."

"Probably because you were with people who knew people," I said. With booze being banned, I'd seen all sorts of creative ways to keep the wines flowing but the cops unknowing. As I told Wini and Tom. "Cards like these are common enough. Lets the bouncer at the door know you're legit, not a cellar smeller, out to turn them over to the bull."

"Your butchery of the English language is amazing," said Tom in a complimentary tone. He gave a little bow in my direction.

"If you play a flapper detective, you need to know how the jazz babies talk," I said with a curtsey back at him. I didn't need tall and handsome in my life, but it was fun to flirt.

"But there's no dialogue in the movies. The films are silent," Tom rebutted.

"My lips still move in the scenes where I am supposed to be talking," I said, "so the writers create dialogue for me. Or I give them lines."

"She's right," said Wini, who had kept rummaging around the car and largely ignored us. As was probably wise. "About that being a membership card. I've seen such before. There are probably two levels to the place. The first would look legit, but there's a door in the back or a flight of stairs…"

"To where the drinks and the entertainment are!" I said. "We'll have to find out!"

"Why?" said Tom.

"Why wouldn't we?" I said. "Don't you like to dance? I love to dance. I bet this place has a band." I wasn't altogether kidding. I did love to dance, and such joints usually had wonderful bands. Besides, there was that strange seaweed and other aquatic creatures showing up at the warehouse. Something about the scent of decay and ocean lingering around the boxes made me uneasy. A prickle went down my spine. I thought of fire and smoke, even though it smelled nothing like fire or smoke. But every time I caught a whiff of brine, it made me think of Max. I wasn't sure why.

As we left the warehouse, a roaring sound came from the river. Wini's head snapped up. "That's a plane," she said. "A seaplane."

"More a river plane," said Tom. "Look! There it goes."

Peering between the warehouses, we saw a small plane skimming along the water. Wini practically purred when it skipped up into the air, streams of river water trailing off its floats. Several boats tooted as the plane flew overhead, including a long, grumbling blast from one barge.

"Tricky takeoff with all the boats out there," said Wini, "but a good pilot."

I glanced at the plane, though I was more concerned with the memories stirred by the oddities I'd seen that day. But I was never good at introspection, and I shook off my preoccupation. "Where to next?" I said out loud.

As we walked back toward my car, we argued about where to go. Or rather, Wini and I proposed a visit to the Purple Cat, and Tom wondered out loud if it was a place for ladies and booksellers. We assured him that ladies would be fine in any hooch joint on the coast, even if Boston booksellers needed a little protection.

"I'll take my pistol," I said.

"I have a Mauser stored in my plane," Wini offered. "We could fetch that. Oh, and Lonnie, too, she swings a mean wrench in a bar fight."

"I think going armed makes it more dangerous, not less," objected Tom. "And who said anything about bar fights?"

We rounded the corner of the warehouse to spot a man rummaging in the front seat of my roadster, much as I had searched the Model T just a few minutes earlier. All I could see was his back as he bent over my open car, peering inside.

"Stop, thief!" I shouted.

CHAPTER TEN

The man popped up at my shout.

"Hello, Miss Baxter," said Darrell. "I guess I should have known this swell car would belong to you."

"Darrell," I squealed. "What is my favorite reporter doing here?"

"Following a lead, of course," he said. "And you?"

"Working on some things." I liked Darrell very much, but I was well aware anything I said to him might end up in the newspaper. And I wasn't quite ready to explain about not breaking but definitely entering the warehouse down the road.

"Any particular reason you are here?" said Darrell, who wasn't a fool and also knew to follow up on a question.

"Did you see that plane take off from the river?" I said to stall while I tried to think up a plausible explanation for what we were doing.

"Of course," Darrell said. Then he looked more closely at the three of us, especially Wini, and jumped ahead of me by asking, "Are you planning on a water stunt in the air show? Boat to plane, plane to boat? Will you be performing with Miss Habbamock?"

I knew Wini lacked a wing-walker after our discussion at lunch. Perhaps that could be my excuse for poking around where I shouldn't be. I was famous for learning new tricks for the movies.

Because there's nothing that will convince a reporter faster that he has a story than a denial, I shook my finger in Darrell's face. "Now, I cannot tell you all our secrets. But I will say that anyone who comes to Saturday's show will be in for a surprise!"

Wini rolled her eyes at me, not sure what I'd just promised. But still, I had thought performing as a barnstormer might be the way to shake the blues out of my head. I had an idea already for a trick with a motorcycle, having practiced with one for my last picture.

Darrell spotted Tom, standing close behind us, and waved in a friendly manner. "Are you with Miss Habbamock's circus, too?"

"Oh, yes, he is," I said, since we already discussed Tom's place in the show at lunch. "He's our advance man. Darrell, please give Tom your card so he knows where to call in the stories."

Tom shook hands with Darrell. I kept talking, asking about the possibility of printing posters with the newspaper's press.

"We could probably do the printing," said Darrell, "or I can give you the name of a couple of others in town who do such work."

Both Wini and Tom were whispering behind me, possibly wondering what I was playing at. I tipped my hat to a more rakish angle and settled into turning the questions back on Darrell.

"What are you investigating?" I asked Darrell.

"Disappearances," he said. "Several from this neighborhood."

"Like the professor?" I said.

"No." Darrell shook his head. "That's just a plain kidnapping and robbery." He looked a bit disappointed in the ordinariness of the crime but perked up as he described how he secured an interview with the professor. "I managed to talk to her last night. Dressed as an orderly and delivered her a cup of tea."

"I took candy and magazines this afternoon," I said.

He shrugged at my tame foray into hospital visits. "From everything she said, it's clear they stole that old book for the jewels," Darrell said.

"Well," said Tom, "I'm not so…" But Wini trod on his foot before I could, and he had the sense to shut his mouth before Darrell noticed.

"Guess that's what happens when you dress up an old book with gold and jewels," said Darrell.

"Shagreen cover, gilded not gold," muttered Tom in my ear. "And semiprecious stones."

"I figure that they heard about it and broke into the professor's house to steal it," said Darrell, too busy explaining his theory to listen to Tom's objections. "They probably weren't expecting to see the professor there but were afraid that she'd raise the alarm too soon if they left her. Hence the ride out into the country."

"Perhaps," I said. I thought that it seemed like a lot of trouble for a book, no matter how pretty the cover. "But what about these disappearances you're investigating?"

"Those are very odd," said Darrell. "There's been some planes gone off course. Then the pilots reappeared miles from where they were supposed to be."

"I heard about the airmail planes," said Wini.

Darrell nodded. "And then there were the boats."

"Boats?" I asked.

"A couple of fishing boats out of Innsmouth vanished near Devil Reef."

"Sank?" I asked.

"No sign of that," said Darrell. "Just gone. The crews were found later, asleep in a cave. With stalks of seaweed draped all over them. They are still searching for the boats."

"A storm?" ventured Wini. "Something that blew them off course and off the boat? Perhaps they had to swim for it?"

"If they did, they have no memory of it. None of them could explain what had happened. Then there were the delivery trucks," added Darrell. "At least three have disappeared in the countryside near Innsmouth. Same as all the rest. The drivers are found days later near the shore. No memory of how they got there or where they had been. And the trucks are still missing."

"Hijackings," I speculated, remembering some of the stories I'd read about Chicago and New York. Bootlegging wars weren't unknown, and there'd been some sensational tales in the news recently. I kept a box of clippings, just for script ideas to give to the writers of the Flapper Detective. Still, I'd never heard of bootleggers' victims just turning up with no memory of where they had been. That sounded eerily like what had happened with Jim.

Darrell shook his head. "I don't think it is hijackings. There's something strange happening, and it seems to occur near Innsmouth. It's just a feeling that I have, but my feelings are rarely wrong."

Given some of the stories Darrell had written over the past few years, I also had faith in his feelings. The more I thought about my lost Max, Tom's missing grimoire, and Wini's discovery of vanished airplanes, the more I wondered what was happening in this place called Innsmouth.

As the others climbed into the car, I showed the Purple Cat card to Darrell. "Know the joint?" I asked.

"Oh, sure," he said. "It's on the cliff road near Innsmouth. Just outside the village where the road forks. Follow the left branch to the Purple Cat. It belongs to Miss Nova Malone."

Ah, the bootlegger with the interest in grimoires! I glanced over my shoulder at Tom. He gave a frown and shook his head. Tom also circled around the car, heading for the passenger side, obviously wanting to keep out of the conversation. He climbed into the back, and Wini hopped into the passenger seat. I kept chatting.

"Honest place, this Purple Cat?" I turned back to Darrell.

"What I've seen," replied Darrell. "But there's a purple door inside, just behind the stage, with a big man stationed in front of it. I haven't been able to talk my way past him. Or Miss Malone. You don't want to upset her."

Definitely not on the complete up-and-up, I thought, patting my purse with the membership card inside. That made the Purple Cat even more interesting.

"Ever heard of a sanitarium named Bluff Mansion?" I said.

"Of course," said Darrell. "The sanitarium belongs to Dr Hughes. He's gaining quite the reputation for his work as a specialist and soother of society's nerves. We did a little feature on the sanitarium a few months ago. You can find it on the same cliff road as the Purple Cat. Just take the right-hand lane and drive a little further north. If you go too far and miss it, you'll be at the lighthouse."

Wini leaned over the wheel and lightly tooted the horn. "Are we going now?" asked my impatient friend.

"When does the Purple Cat open?" I asked as I climbed into the driver's seat. I thought it might be easier to go there first. I needed to visit Jim, too, but I didn't want to take Wini and Tom along. That was a conversation best held privately at a later date.

"The Purple Cat never closes. Well, almost never. Maybe for a few hours after midnight." Darrell leaned over the door to answer me. The advantage of the convertible was that I could still hold a conversation and start my car. "It's a nice little place with a small dance floor and a band on Friday and Saturday nights. In the early mornings, Miss Malone serves hash and eggs to the fishing crews. In the afternoon, it's coffee for the ladies coming off the cannery shifts. Everyone in Innsmouth knows Miss Malone's place. Miss Malone even started broadcasting the Purple Cat's dance band on the radio. We did a story about her investment in radio fairly recently."

"Well, I'll be sure to stop there," I said. "And meet the famous Miss Nova Malone."

"Be careful," said Darrell. "Strange things happen to people who upset the Malones." I thought I heard Tom gulp from the backseat, but I didn't want to call attention to his fears of Malone reprisals.

"I'm not rude," I said as I gunned the motor.

"She's not one for sauce," Darrell said firmly. "Of any kind. And Innsmouth can be unfriendly to day-trippers. Folks from Innsmouth stick together, and Miss Nova Malone is one of theirs."

"Point taken," I said. "I'll be on my best behavior."

As we drove away, Wini said to me, "Do we go by the airfield and pick up my Mauser?" Tom choked a bit more in the backseat. Wini grinned over her shoulder at him. "Or maybe just Lonnie and her wrench?"

"No," I said. "Let's make this a friendly visit. If there's coffee and gossip in the afternoon, that's when we should visit the Purple Cat. I'd like to know more about those disappearing trucks, boats, and planes."

As we went down the road, I asked Tom, "Has Miss Malone ever met you?"

"No," he yelled back over the noise of the wind and the engine. "Just her gentlemen friends called on me in that alley."

"Still, they know you are in Arkham," I said. Showing up with Tom at the Purple Cat might lead to more explanations and book discussions than I wanted. "We should drop you at the hotel first."

We left Tom at the hotel to gather his belongings and move out to the airfield. Wini scribbled a note on the hotel stationery to introduce him to her crew. "I mentioned that we had a new advance man coming," she said. "They'll show you where to bunk and what materials we have."

Tom nodded and pulled Darrell's card out of his pocket. "I'll call the local newspapers to set up some publicity," he said. "This should be fun. As long as I don't have to go up in an airplane."

"I promise you can keep your feet on the ground," I said.

Tom rubbed the back of his neck in a gesture I was beginning to anticipate. "I'm not so sure my feet have touched the ground since sometime last night." But he smiled as he climbed out of the car.

"Darrell already has photos of Wini and me when we arrived in town," I told him. "Remind him I'm performing in the show. That will help sell a few papers."

"And tickets," said Wini. "We need a good turnout. And then you and I need to talk about this performance idea, Betsy. One week of training in wing-walking…"

"Is plenty," I said. "Besides, I have an idea. It will be marvelous."

Wini looked slightly skeptical but reminded Tom that she needed advertisements to go out as soon as possible.

Tom scribbled some notes on the back of Darrell's card. "I'll see about some posters," he said.

"We've got a cache that shows the plane with a wing-walker on top," said Wini. "You just need to have the printer overprint with the dates and times of the performances. Lonnie or Bill, my other pilot, will have the list. Bill can run you through the sequence of the show, too. It helps if you know the names of the tricks when calling on the newspapers."

Tom nodded and patted his pockets for more paper to write on when he ran out of room on Darrell's card. I tore a page out of my notebook and handed it to him.

"Be careful at that speakeasy," said Tom as we left him.

"We will," I promised, patting my purse with the silver-plated pistol inside.

The left-hand road was hard-packed dirt and the countryside desolate with trees twisted by the wind blowing steadily off the ocean. The smell of salt was strong in the air, and certain twists of the road brought us close enough to the cliff's edge to spot the white-capped waves. Not a road I'd want to drive in the dark but easy enough on a bright summer afternoon.

Despite Tom's doubts and Darrell's cautions, Wini and I found the Purple Cat as threatening as a grandmother's house with cheerful geraniums in window pots, pale dimity curtains hung café style in the windows, and a purple china cat on the doorstep. A neatly painted sign proclaimed that we had found "The Purple Cat: Open Breakfast, Lunch, and Dinner. Midnight Suppers Our Specialty."

"I wonder what they serve at midnight," muttered Wini as we pushed the door open. A bell merrily tinkled to announce our entrance.

"Probably not just water to drink," I guessed.

We found the interior of the Purple Cat matched the exterior for homey warmth with neat round tables covered in gingham checked cloths, sturdy wooden chairs, and a number of women seated in what were obviously their favorite spots. Most had a cup of coffee clutched in one reddened hand. A buzz of gossip filled the room. A buzz that didn't stop when strangers entered.

"Shuckers," said Wini, looking at the other women there. "And scalers."

I raised an eyebrow in inquiry.

"They work in the processing plants," Wini explained with a nod at the women gossiping at the end of their workday. "Shucking shellfish or scaling fish. I remember helping my grandmother with shucking when I was barely high enough to see over the table. Plunging your hands into buckets of cold saltwater leaves them red and chapped and aching for hours. I could never handle it as a factory job, but there's not that much work available in places like this, especially for women. It's one of the reasons I wanted to be a pilot."

"Corn," I said. "Stripping the leaves. That was the shucking we did as kids. That job motivated me onto a train bound for Chicago. Corn shucking was hot and prickly. The cuts and blisters on your hands stung all night long."

"Chickens," added Wini with emphasis. "There is another chore I don't miss. Pecking and scratching and pooping all over when you're hunting for eggs."

"Chickens, wringing their necks and plucking out feathers, just to fry up a Sunday supper," I agreed with a shudder. "Another reason to leave home."

"My people were good people," said Wini. "Everyone worked hard to make it a little better for everyone else. But the work…"

"Stank, and hurt, and was mind-numbingly dull," I said.

Wini laughed. "Guess neither of us would make good farm wives."

"I can safely say being domestic was never my ambition," I said. Which was true. Even when I was entertaining ideas of marrying Max, I never pictured a country cottage and a picket fence. I'd had to paint too many picket fences growing up as well as wash the stairs every Saturday afternoon and polish the silver before Sunday dinners. Rather, I'd imagined a couple living in a nice city apartment, drinking champagne with breakfast, and dancing at the nightclubs after a day of working in the studio.

"I miss the clambakes, though," said Wini as we found a table and sat ourselves down. "The clambakes at home were the best, especially when all the families would come together. We'd build a big bonfire on the beach. The elders would tell stories until dawn. I always tried to stay awake until the very end, but I'd be so full and warm and curled down into the sand. Then I'd wake up the next day in my bed with my grannie scolding me for sleeping the day away but in a grandmother's cheerful way, which meant she was only teasing and not very mad."

"I went to a clambake in California," I said. "It was at the end of a movie shoot. All the extras and the crew in one spot, and the stars off around their own bonfire, but someone brought a Victrola and a bunch of good jazz records. Then everyone ended up together on the sand, eating, and dancing, and waiting for the dawn."

"Sounds like fun," Wini said.

"It was nice," I said, remembering how cold the wet sand had been on my bare feet with the Pacific lapping little waves over my toes in time to the jazz. It was the first time I had danced with Max. He'd been stiff, and awkward, and so sweet.

"What can I get you ladies?" asked the waitress as she arrived toting a notepad and pencil. She wore a white apron tied around her middle that was embroidered with a small purple cat in one corner.

"How's the pie?" I said.

"Best in the state," the waitress answered. "I've got a tomato tart if you want something to fill you up."

"And for a sweet?"

"Deep dish apple," she replied. "With ice cream, of course. Or cheese if you prefer."

"I'll take mine with cheddar," I said.

"Tomato tart for me," said Wini. "And coffee for both of us."

"Be right up," said the waitress. The food came out as quickly as promised. The summer tomato tart was almost as sweet as the apple pie, I exclaimed upon sampling Wini's dish. She announced herself equally impressed with the apple pie after trying a bite from my plate.

"There's nothing like New England apples," she said. "These taste like Cortlands."

The waitress watched us trade bites with a smile, and she absolutely beamed when Wini named her favorite apple. "Those are Cortlands," the waitress said. "From my grandpa's farm. Miss Nova buys several barrels every fall. That's about the last of the 1925 apples. The new crop will be coming soon." She poured us our coffee and set down a pitcher filled with real cream. "But you gals aren't from Innsmouth. I know all the locals by sight."

"We're with the circus," I said.

"The flying circus," added Wini. "Winifred Habbamock's Flying Circus."

"No!" the waitress exclaimed. "We heard that the show was coming to the airfield. It's exciting watching those airmail boys land and take off. My Willard loves to watch the planes flying overhead. But you do tricks?"

"Oh, yes, ma'am," said Wini. "All the best. Loop the loop, low flying, high flying, barrel rolls, and other feats to astound."

"Wing-walking," I added. "Death-defying stunts. Wini is the pilot, and I'm the wing-walker."

"I never!" exclaimed the waitress. "Wait until I tell Miss Nova that we have celebrities from the flying circus at the Purple Cat."

"Tell me what, Mildred?" said a deep voice behind us. We turned to see the largest woman I have ever beheld. A giantess, well over six feet tall in her stockinged feet and nearly as wide as she was long. This mountain of a woman was dressed all in lavender, very stylishly cut. On her broad bosom she wore a large, jeweled pin, a purple cat made from amethysts and diamonds, that twinkled in the afternoon sunshine.

"Why, Miss Nova," said Mildred the waitress. "These gals are from the flying circus."

"This gal owns the flying circus," said Wini, standing to shake Nova Malone's outstretched hand. Wini's own slender hand disappeared inside the other's mammoth paw, but when I also rose to shake hands, I noticed that Nova Malone didn't squeeze hard like a man. She had no need to demonstrate her obvious strength.

"Flyers, are you?" Nova said. "That's an interesting profession."

"I like it," said Wini.

Nova grabbed a chair at another table with one hand and lifted it easily to a place at our table. She settled herself down with considerable grace, rather like the opera singer I saw portraying Turandot in Buenos Aires.

The chatter at the other tables muted just a little, not exactly silence but more a respectful lowering of voices now that the queen of the establishment had entered.

"Tell me about your show," Nova said. "I have questions about airplanes."

Turandot, I remembered, asked questions, too. And those who gave her the wrong answers lost their heads.

CHAPTER ELEVEN

"It's the most daring air circus you'll ever see," said Wini. "Unless you come twice. Then you'll see just as terrifying a show the second time as the first."

Nova Malone smiled at this. "I have never been afraid," she said. "It might be worth watching to see if I could be terrified."

"Well, they call me the Woman Without Fear," said Wini, "but it doesn't mean that I've never known fear. There's been times in my life when I've been very scared indeed. But I went forward despite feeling afraid. Every flyer must do that."

"People call me fearless," I added. "Fear never stopped me from being in charge of my own life, but I know what it is like to be afraid." Sometimes I ran harder toward trouble just to quiet the fear inside me.

"Oh, I understand the emotion exists," Nova answered, "but I have no such memory of ever feeling fear. There's never been a man nor beast that could knock me down or even set me back. After all my siblings died in infancy, my father took me aboard his ship when I was still a baby. Papa thought a sea-raised baby would thrive. And thrive I did. I grew up with no creed except a healthy respect for the gods of the ocean. But even those I do not fear."

"It seems a lack of fear has done you no harm," I said, noting the jewels on her breast and the diamond rings she wore.

Nova tilted her hands to let the sunlight twinkle on her diamonds. She also wore jeweled bracelets, more likely platinum than silver by the style, that caught the light and reflected it back on us. "I have done well for myself," said Nova Malone, "and every jewel that I wear I bought for myself. I do take some pride in building my own businesses."

"As you should," I said. Nova Malone might be a crook, but I admired her attitude. Also, I had to admit, if BB Pictures failed in its early days, who knows what I might have done to keep my fortune. The lure of easy cash drew many a soul into bootlegging. I knew a few Hollywood women who were now running "clubs" for the elite and anyone else willing to pay well for a stiff drink. I'd even danced at the 300 Club when Wilda Bennett married her Argentinian dancer. Which was how I ended up in Buenos Aires earlier this year at the South American premiere of *Turandot*.

"This is a fine place that you have here," said Wini to Nova, "and a very fine tomato pie."

"My cook is the best in Innsmouth," agreed Nova. "I lured her away from Bluff Mansion, which vexed Hughes no end, but the woman was glad to get away from his seaweed recipes."

"I've heard the doctor has some strange ideas," I said.

Nova narrowed her eyes and looked more closely at me. "Unusual for a woman traveling with a circus to know our local nerves doctor," she said.

I nearly bit my tongue, so annoyed at my slip, but Wini saved me from stammering some excuse. "We met him at the hospital, visiting a friend," she said.

"Yes," I said. "Our friend mentioned that Hughes had a sanitarium near here, but I don't understand about the seaweed." Which was nothing but the truth.

Nova snorted. "The fool thinks that any seaweed has healing properties. Cooks it into a broth or boils it into a tea. Then tips it down his patients' throats. Only Ezra Hughes could be that ridiculous."

"So seaweed has no benefit?" I asked. It sounded awful to me, but people were always touting all sorts of cures. Some even worked, like cod liver oil for rickets. Maybe seaweed was a cure for lost memories.

Nova shrugged. "It's a stretch to see it as a cure-all," she said. "My papa fed me on seaweed mash when I was very young, barely past suckling, and washed me with saltwater every day in an empty codfish keg. My size or health may owe something to Papa's practice."

The talk then turned to flying with the big woman asking several pointed questions about the type of planes in Wini's show, their range, and, without directly saying it, their capacity to carry cargo.

Wini neatly sidestepped certain questions while frankly answering others. It was an interesting tango between the two, but neither admitted defeat.

"It's Byrd's flights that fascinated me the most this summer," said Nova. "Do you think it is true that commercial polar flight will become possible?"

"That's certainly the theory," said Wini. "It would considerably cut the time from the West Coast to Europe."

"Yes, it would," agreed Nova in a speculative tone. "Imagine the possibilities. One of my ancestors spent all his life seeking the Northwest Passage. The ice defeated him every time. But he could not fly."

"Someday," said Wini with conviction, "we'll fly to places we cannot even imagine now. We haven't even begun to hit the limits of what powered flight can do."

"I am convinced science will provide us with many new opportunities," said Nova. "Many trips would be far more successful if the journey was accomplished through the air than by land or sea. Certain recent incidents have persuaded me that air routes could be far superior to other ways."

I wondered what air routes Nova was trying to navigate. Could the missing planes be flying her cargo? Again, I remembered the story of the feds busting up a bootlegging run made by plane. Was Nova trying to fly liquor from Canada to this part of the country? But what use would she have for the grimoire that Christine described, except to use the "routes" in it.

At the end of our discussion, Nova offered us a second slice of pie on the house.

"I would truly like to take a slice," said Wini, "but I fear that I'll explode like a firework if I eat one more bite."

Nova chuckled at Wini's statement and motioned away my purse when I started to pull out the payment for our meal. "You have entertained me very well," she said. "The least I can do is feed you." She waved over the waitress. "Mildred, let's box a few more slices of pie for these ladies." To us, she said, "Please take the pie for a later dessert, when your hunger comes back to you, or to share with others."

"That's very kind," I said.

"Indeed, it is," Wini said. "You must come to see our show. You and all your staff. I'll leave tickets at the gate for you."

"All of them?" Nova challenged her as the cook came out of the kitchen. The Black woman had placed our pies in a neat paper box all tied up with a purple string.

"Everyone," said Wini firmly. "No one is ever barred from one of my shows. I owe too much to Bessie Coleman to do anything else. She taught me the barrel roll and how to parachute."

Looking pleased by this answer, Nova escorted us outside. Glancing at my roadster, she said, "There's a storm coming up. Do you have chains?"

"I do," I said, "in the trunk." I carried chains as a precaution, but I certainly saw no need for them that day. The horizon was clear as far as I could see, and the dirt road was perfectly dry. There was no reason to suspect bad weather was coming.

"You might make it back to the airfield before the storm breaks," said Nova, looking at a few fluffy white clouds racing across the bright summer sky. "But turn off into Innsmouth if it starts to hail."

Once we drove away, Wini let out a whistle. "That's an interesting woman," she said. "I have no patience for rumrunners, but I like her."

"I had much the same impression," I answered. "But never tell me that you marched for temperance."

"Some communities might be better dry. A man or woman who drinks away their money and lets their children go hungry, that's hard on everyone. It is still hard to lose someone that you love to the bottle," Wini said. "But I'm not sure making alcohol illegal solves the problem. The Eighteenth Amendment seems to have made no difference except to jail a few more people for doing what they've always done."

"Smuggling alcohol has made some folks rich, to judge by Miss Nova's diamonds," I said.

"And some end up full of bullet holes," said Wini, "if all the stories that you hear about Chicago and New York are true."

The road turned into a dense wood where the overhanging branches formed a tunnel of dark green shadows. When we drove out the other side, the bright afternoon sunshine was gone. Apparently, Nova Malone was a better weather prognosticator than I gave her credit for.

"That's quite the storm cloud!" said Wini, pointing to the east.

I glanced up to see the sky filling with a great dark cloud. The rising wind buffeted the side of the roadster, yet the road was still smooth and dry. It was a dirt road, though, and if the rains came, I could see it quickly becoming mud soup. Still, the storm clouds building on the horizon were far enough away that I hoped we could outrun the rain.

"Let's avoid that storm," I said to Wini and shifted gears again.

Despite my speed, the storm was faster still. The wind howled and raindrops began to splash on the windshield. The overcast sky made it almost as dark as night. I switched on the headlights, but the beams barely cut through the gloom.

I swore and gunned the motor, trying to outrace the storm. Wini went diving over the seat into the back and wrestled up the roadster's top to protect us from the increasing rain. A flash of lightning lit up the underside of the cloud. A rumble of thunder followed.

The road began weaving in and out of the wooded area. Branches creaked overhead as the wind caught the treetops and sent them swaying. "Keep going!" yelled Wini. "We don't want to stop under these trees." The world turned white as another bolt of lightning forked above us.

I took the curves as fast as I dared. The world narrowed in my vision until it was just the road in front of me, the thunder of the engine in my ears, and the vibration of the wheel clutched in my hands. I felt the addictive sense of being balanced between success and disaster. I forced myself to relax into each swoop of the road.

The final turn brought us back out to the cliff road and the edge was far too close to the wheels. I wrenched the steering wheel around as Wini popped into the front seat again. She dragged the top over us just as the hail hit.

The hailstones pinged like bullets off the hood of the roadster as the road turned into a river of mud under the wheels. Glancing over the cliff's edge, I could see a froth of white waves curling around large rocks far below us.

"Don't slow down," Wini shouted over the storm. "Or we'll be stuck fast."

"Keep an eye out for shelter," I yelled back. The next clap of thunder sounded more out to sea than directly overhead. Slowing slightly, I wondered if I should stop to put on the chains, but I decided Wini was right. Once we stopped, the wheels would sink even further. The road was too far out of town to expect any help to come along. I hadn't seen another car all afternoon. The best we could hope for was a wet hike back to the Purple Cat.

The hail changed back into rain. The sheets of water pouring down on us made the visibility even worse.

Wini practically had her nose on the windshield as she peered ahead. "Take the next turn," she said. "That looks like a gravel road."

With a popping of sticky mud and the squeal of the roadster's engine, I forced the car off the muddy road and onto the better surface. Large drops of rain continued to splash against the windshield, but the wind seemed to be dying down. My relief did not last for long.

"Look out!" Wini yelled.

A rowboat suddenly dropped out of the air and crashed directly in front of us. Shards of wood flew up as the boat exploded on impact. I hit the brakes and fought to hold the wheel steady as I swerved to avoid the unexpected wreck.

CHAPTER TWELVE

"Missed it!" I cried with satisfaction as my lovely roadster ran to a shuddering stop on the grassy edge of the road. Luckily, there was no ditch. But Henry was going to be upset when he saw the state of my poor darling. I decided to find a garage in Arkham and make sure the roadster had a good cleaning before I put it back on the train for Hollywood.

Then, all of a sudden, it hit me. I had just driven around a boat that had dropped from the sky. I had never heard of a storm spitting out rowboats! And where was the storm? Once again, the sky above us was a brilliant blue with no sign of clouds. The whole thing had happened so quickly, I would have thought it an illusion or a dream, except for the scattered wreckage now blocking the road. "Where did the storm go? And where did that boat come from?" I exclaimed.

"I have no idea," said Wini. "Waterspout? They can act like tornadoes, picking things up and dropping them elsewhere." But she sounded as puzzled as I felt.

I got out of the car and walked up to the shattered boat. It looked like a dinghy or small rowboat. A ship's name was painted on the side. *Gulliver*, it said, although that name was now scattered across three pieces of shattered board. I picked up one piece.

"There's too much here to clear away easily," I called back to Wini, who climbed out of the car and scanned the sky for signs of the storm that had overtaken us.

I walked around the wreck. The ground was soft from the hail and rain. I could even see some hailstones still scattered among the grass at the edge of the road. As I squelched around the pile of lumber littering the road, I sighed over another pair of wrecked shoes and stockings. Arkham was turning out to be hard on the wardrobe.

"What do you think?" said Wini when I got back to the car. I tossed the board I had salvaged into the trunk.

"That I need to invest in a good pair of boots like yours," I said as I climbed into my seat.

Wini smirked a little at the mud sticking to my shoes and stockings. "You could have stayed in the car," she said.

"No, I couldn't," I replied. "I'm driving. I need to know what the road is like."

"And?" Wini asked.

"Too much debris to get around or even turn around," I decided as I threw the gears into reverse and backed along the narrow road. I hugged the side furthest from the cliff edge because there was no knowing how that strange storm had softened the ground. Driving in reverse was slow, finnicky work, just the thing to keep me from worrying about vanishing storms and boats appearing from nowhere. "Let's find another road. Ah, I thought I saw a turnoff."

We came even with a smaller track, luckily also graveled and running straight uphill away from the sea.

"What do you think?" I asked Wini.

"I was thinking this is easier when I'm in the air," she replied, squinting at a map we had bought at the hotel earlier. "But if this squiggly line is that road," she gestured up the hill, "then it should loop back around and land us in Innsmouth, I guess. And no telling how long it is going to take. How's your gas?"

"We should have enough," I said, peering over her shoulder at the map. "Especially if we can refill the car in Innsmouth."

"If not, we're sure to pass a farm," said Wini. "Someone will have spare petrol."

"Maybe," I said as I carefully turned the roadster and pointed its nose up the hill. "Let's hope we find something before dark."

"Odd," said Wini as we climbed the hill over the protests of the roadster's engine. Poor thing had taken quite a beating since rolling off the train only this morning, I thought.

"What's odd?" I asked Wini as I worried about the engine lacking Henry's tender care.

"How Nova Malone predicted that storm," said Wini. "I would never have guessed hail or winds like that. I'm pretty good at reading the sky, too."

"I wouldn't have guessed there was a storm coming at all. Or even that one passed through. Nova lives out here," I said. "Guess she knows when storms are expected."

"Maybe," said Wini. "But the way she spoke, she was so certain. Perhaps she's like my grandmother. Granny always said she had a certain feeling when bad weather was coming."

"My grandfather used to say the same thing," I said. "Except with him, it was the first big freeze of the year. He said he could feel it coming in his bones. But it was odd. Maybe Nova's weather predictions come from eating seaweed mash as a baby."

Wini chuckled at my joke. "If that's what it takes to know when a storm is going to blow up, every pilot in the sky would be eating seaweed."

The track continued up and over the hill. As we crested the top, Wini shouted at the sight of a house. "What do you think?" she said. "Do we stop there?"

I glanced at the gauges. The fuel was low, not enough to worry us yet, but we didn't know how far we still needed to go to reach Innsmouth. "Perhaps we should stop and get directions," I said.

Unlike Nova Malone's Purple Cat, this was as unfriendly a house as I'd ever seen. The paint had been peeled off long ago by weather and age, leaving behind a bleak gray house with a sagging roof. The porch that ran around two sides looked ready to collapse into the dirt. Shutters with missing slats were half-closed across the windows. The only door had a conspicuously large and new lock beneath its knob. There was no knocker or doorbell visible.

"Are you sure anyone is living here?" I said as we walked to the door. The place seemed deserted, but I couldn't shake the feeling that someone was watching us. I heard a harsh caw and, glancing up, saw a trio of crows looking down at us.

Wini gestured at the yard and surrounding outbuildings. "Somebody is keeping the place up. At least as much as they can. There's a lot of poor folks in this part of New England," she said. "But there's fresh tire tracks in the yard and not a lot of weeds."

We walked up the creaking steps and across the wobbly porch to knock on the door. There was no answer from inside.

Wini pounded the door a couple more times, but the house remained silent. I cracked open one shutter and glanced through a window. The glass was so dirty that the interior was murky, but it was clear there wasn't much in the way of furnishings. I could make out a bare table and a few plain chairs scattered about. If somebody was keeping the place up, their attention was focused on the outer buildings and the yard, not on the house itself. Despite what Wini had said, I doubted anyone was living there.

"Let's look around the barn," Wini said. "Maybe they're working in the back and cannot hear us."

As we stepped off the porch, the trio of crows took flight. With one long mocking caw, they flew away.

"Think that's an omen?" I said, and I was only half joking. This place was wrong. I could feel it in my bones but, at the same time, I felt that familiar urge to figure out why rather than run. I never could stand to be afraid.

"I don't believe in omens," said Wini. "Crows are just crows." And the way she said it, I caught the echoes of a long-standing argument with somebody. "No matter what they say in Arkham," she concluded.

We walked around the barn. As we got to the far side, we started to hear noises – a steady banging like somebody hammering away at something. Wini walked up to one big shed with a closed wooden shutter. She rapped on it with her knuckles but received no response, so she grabbed the edge and lifted it up to peer inside.

"Oh, damn," Wini said as she looked inside the shed.

"What do you see?" I asked as a man's shout rang out.

Wini grabbed my arm and began to drag me toward the shed's doorway. "We'll have to brazen it out," she said, "but he'll be upset we're sneaking by his workshop. Leave the talking to me."

"What are you jabbering about?" I said. "Who's there?" It wasn't like the woman who'd just told me crows were only crows to suddenly take fright. Except she didn't seem frightened. More resigned and a little wary when a shadow crossed the doorway.

A heavyset man with a thick black beard stepped in front of us. Despite working in a farm shed, he was neatly dressed in a three-piece suit. His maroon tie looked like silk to me. In one meaty hand, he carried a hammer. He smacked the hammer against his other hand when he saw us. It was not a friendly gesture.

"Chuck Fergus," said Wini. "Been a long time."

"Winifred Habbamock," said Chuck, "what are you doing out here? Snooping again?"

"The storm caught us on the road," said Wini, without a blink at the hammer and belligerent tone of Chuck's voice, "and we had to turn off. We're just looking for a way back to Innsmouth."

Chuck looked skeptical at Wini's response but then he spotted me. "Who's your friend?"

"Betsy Baxter," I spoke up. "I'm the driver who succeeded in making us lost. And ruining my shoes in all your lovely New England mud." I waggled one wet foot at him. I figured a man who dressed so nicely on a farm might appreciate the heartbreak of trekking good shoe leather through the muck.

Distracted by my antics, Chuck almost grunted something sympathetic. At least he seemed less inclined to put the hammer to immediate use. "You need galoshes," he said to me, and pulled up his pant leg slightly to show how he protected his good shoes.

"An excellent idea," I said.

As if realizing the hammer didn't send a friendly signal, he turned and tossed it back into the shed. Then he walked us around the shed and back to our car. A better description might have been that he herded us away from whatever he had been working on.

Since Wini made no objection, I followed her lead and went meekly enough. I had questions but sensed this wasn't the time to ask them. Although I couldn't resist a peek through the shed door as we passed it. I spied several crates, much like those we'd seen at the warehouse near the river, only these were all nailed tightly shut.

"Still flying in your circus show?" Chuck said to Wini as we reached the roadster.

"Always and forever," said Wini. "I'm never giving up the sky."

"Lonnie with you these days?" he asked almost shyly.

"She's making the engines purr like kittens every day," said Wini. "She's always up to her elbows with adjustments on my darling or another of our planes."

Chuck huffed at that, almost a chuckle. "Lonnie does love to get her hands dirty," he said. "Give that woman a wrench and she's as happy as some dolls are to get flowers."

When we got back to the roadster, he also looked at the fuel gauge. "You probably have enough gas to make it to Innsmouth," he said to me, "but I've stashed some extra cans in the barn. I'll top you off so you won't have to worry."

As he walked away, I said to Wini, "Who is our gentleman farmer?"

"No farmer and no gentleman," said Wini. "Chuck drives for the O'Bannions. I wonder what he's doing so far out of town."

"Are you going to ask him?" I said, wondering who or what an O'Bannion was.

"Oh, no," said Wini. "You don't ask about O'Bannion business." The way she emphasized "don't ask" told me that an O'Bannion wasn't a local farmer. "But Chuck is a bit sweet on Lonnie, so he's always been friendly with me. As long as he thinks I'm not interfering with the O'Bannions' affairs."

"How does Lonnie feel about him?" I asked as I watched Chuck return with a can of gas.

Wini tugged her ear. "Don't know," she finally admitted. "Lonnie likes the cars he drives."

"Flashy?" I asked.

"Fast," said Wini. "All the better to outrun the law."

"Ah," I said. "That kind of business."

Wini nodded. "Always that kind."

Chuck made quick work of filling up my gas tank, then he gave us some pointers on how to get to Innsmouth, shaking his head over the map Wini showed him and penciling in a lane that wasn't clearly marked.

"These maps," he said. "Out of date as soon as they are printed. It's almost as if the roads move to fool the mapmakers. Better avoid this stretch if you ever come back out here." He ran a thick finger along the cliff road that curved toward the Purple Cat.

"Why that bit?" said Wini, not mentioning that we'd already driven it in a storm.

"The road crosses Malone territory along the cliff," said Chuck. "And funny things happen on Malone's bit of the coast."

"Really?" I exclaimed. "What type of things?" We also hadn't told Chuck about the boat that had dropped out of the sky.

Chuck screwed the cap tight on his gas can. "There's men who have been driving these back roads for years who get lost when they cross Malone land. Same for those who sail along the coast near here," he said. "They say it's the curse of the *Bolide*."

"What's a *Bolide*?" I asked, itching to know more about this particular curse. Curses seemed as common as crows in this part of New England.

Chuck backed away, obviously reluctant to talk, but Wini piped up, "Thanks for your help. Be sure you come to the show later this week. Lonnie will be performing her motorcycle tricks."

His eyes smiled at her invitation, even if the rest of his expression was hidden by his beard. "I'd like to see that," Chuck admitted. To me, he added, "The *Bolide* sailed out of Innsmouth and disappeared when it was returning loaded with enough whale oil and ambergris to make everyone rich. Some folks think Gulliver Malone conjured a devil to destroy that ship and ruin his rival, Captain Bulkington Hughes."

At the mention of Gulliver Malone, I asked, "Any relation to Nova Malone?"

Chuck grimaced at my question but nodded. "An ancestor of Nova's. Gulliver was about the only person in Innsmouth who hadn't invested in the *Bolide*'s shares, so folks suspected him first when the *Bolide* disappeared. Certainly the Hughes family accused him of sabotage."

"Ships go down all the time," I said. "Even the unsinkable *Titanic* sank."

"The *Bolide* disappeared as it was entering the harbor," said Chuck. "It didn't run into an iceberg or a storm. It vanished. Now boats, cars, and even planes have started to disappear when they cross Malone land or sail near their portion of the coast."

"Bad weather," guessed Wini. "Storms blow up suddenly along this coast."

"Or Nova Malone has found Gulliver's book," said Chuck.

"His what?" I said, but I was sure I knew the answer. Chuck was talking about the Deadly Grimoire.

"Everyone knows Gulliver Malone used a book to conjure up some new ways to sail from place to place," said Chuck. "He went searching for a way to corner the trade from east to west and back again. He challenged a number of captains to beat his sailing times, and they never could. Some said Gulliver always won, even when the wind and tide turned against him, because he had other ways of completing his race."

"So he was a good captain or good at cheating," I said. "Winning a race or two doesn't mean magic books were used." Although I had my doubts about the last statement.

"Maybe not," said Chuck, "but then Gulliver Malone turned against the Innsmouth investors when they picked Bulkington Hughes's *Bolide* over Gulliver's ship. That's when they say he spoke the deadly spells in his book and made his rival vanish."

"What happened to Malone?" I asked, but if Chuck's story was anything like Christine's, I knew what had happened to the sea captain. And that his spell book, or whatever it was, ended up back with a Boston bookseller named Sweets.

"His words rebounded against him," said Chuck. The big man looked deadly serious for a man telling ghost stories. With the sun now shining on all of us and no sign of storm clouds on the horizon, Wini unlatched the car top and folded it down behind the backseat. Chuck helped her fasten it back into place.

"They called it the *Bolide*'s revenge," Chuck continued, "as Malone's own ship vanished the next time it sailed out of the harbor."

"There's nothing to fear from dead men. That was all long ago," said Wini to Chuck.

"Except his spells keep working," said Chuck as he opened my car door like a gentleman. Wini shook her head and opened her own door. "At least, that's what they say in Innsmouth. That Gulliver Malone woke the old sea gods, and those gods are still angry about it. Hungry and angry."

I considered the smashed boat tossed onto the cliff road like a child's abandoned toy. How far did those sea gods roam, I wondered.

As we pulled away from the farm, I asked the more obvious and immediate question of my companion.

"So how mixed up are you in the O'Bannions' criminal business?" I said to Wini. "And does that business have anything to do with the fact that you fly with a Mauser in your plane?"

CHAPTER THIRTEEN

Wini grimaced. "I'm not involved in anything criminal," she said. "At least, not now. I run an honest show."

"But?" I said, because I could guess some of the shortcuts Wini might have made.

"Betsy Baxter, you look so sweet that someone might think the rain would melt you away like sugar," said Wini. "Will you refuse to finance the air derby if I tell you that I once worked with the O'Bannions?"

"Heaven knows I've made some interesting choices," I said to Wini, shifting gears as we headed down the road that Chuck had suggested. "You might say playing poker with a bunch of drunken executives when they didn't know you could count cards was… perhaps… slightly dishonest. On the other hand, you might also say telling a gal she could bet her garters if she wanted to was just inviting the lady to cheat those executives blind."

Other than the occasional puddle, there was no sign on the road that a storm had blown through. The further we went from Malone land, the drier the terrain became, and I wondered if the storm had blown out before it reached this section of the coast.

Wini laughed at my last statement and explained her relationship with Chuck as we drove along under the now calm blue skies. "I never played cards with the O'Bannions, but I flew a few messages for them back when I first started my own air business. Messages that the O'Bannions wouldn't trust to the telegraph or the mail. I never asked what was in those envelopes. That's one of the reasons I took the show west as soon as I'd raised enough cash. I didn't want to be anyone's errand girl."

"I thought you didn't like rumrunners," I said.

"I don't," said Wini promptly. Then she turned more thoughtful. "Though I like some of the people fine, like Chuck. Many end up in the business because there's not much opportunity to do anything else."

"Signs might not say 'No Irish Need Apply' anymore," I guessed, "but there's plenty willing to tell you that the Irish or the Swedes or the Mexicans cannot work in their business." I'd run into a fair number of barricades myself and had a great deal of sympathy for anyone who faced similar opposition in trying to do what they wanted to do. That's why I hired Marian and a number of other people on my crew. They deserved a chance.

Out of the corner of my eye, I saw Wini give a thoughtful nod. "Bootlegging is a way to get around that. Although I won't say they don't have their own peculiar prejudices, but I never was an actual member of any gang. I also never saw smugglers as heroes or villains. Most come to a sad end. According to stories that kids used to tell, there was a hanging judge in the area who used to order pirates and smugglers staked out. He said let the high tide drown them and save the expense of a hangman. Only, one time, when the tide went out, the smuggler's body was gone. Only chewed ropes and deep gouges on the stake were left. The story scared me silly as a kid. The idea of being tied down and having something chewing on you while the water filled your lungs."

"Gruesome," I agreed. "But I think the feds just send people to prison these days."

"I have no desire to spend any time behind bars. Not being able to fly, that would be the worst punishment ever," Wini said. "But it's so hard finding honest work. I couldn't get a regular contract with one of the larger flying outfits, not being a woman and with brown skin, too."

"But you're a daredevil," I said. "The Woman Without Fear. I thought you flew those stunts because such flying paid better than contracts." Yet I understood the lack of choices Wini faced. Success came at a price, but some people weren't even allowed to pay that price because of who they were.

"I fly stunts because, like Bessie Coleman, people will buy tickets to see me despite my ancestry," said Wini. "But when Bessie died earlier this year in that stupid accident, it started me thinking. I don't want to end up in a grave, forgotten in a year. I want to make history, make it so nobody can ever forget that a woman dared to fly higher, faster, and better than anyone before her. Eventually I want to beat the men in their own race."

"I'll still back your derby," I said. "And I'll back you against any man in the air. But only if you stay honest with me."

"That's a fair deal," said Wini. "I'd shake your hand, but you're driving."

I chuckled and switched gears so we could go faster. "What do you think your friend Chuck Fergus was doing on an old farm in the middle of nowhere in particular?" I said.

"Not growing potatoes, that's for sure," Wini answered promptly. "My guess is that it's a convenient stop for the distribution of booze."

"You saw the crates in the shed," I said.

"Of course," said Wini. "I'm not blind. Chuck wouldn't hustle us away so fast if there wasn't someone coming to pick those up. My guess is whoever owns the place turns a blind eye once or twice a month when the O'Bannion shipment comes through. Or the O'Bannions own that farm. There's plenty who would sell out for the kind of cash they can flash around."

"Truck, boat, or plane?" I mused on the possible conveyances for smuggled liquor.

"Could be any of the three. Could be all of the three," Wini speculated. "There's a flat enough field out back of the barn for landing. There's plenty of spots along the coast close to the road where a ship could offload. And there's all manner of backroads if you want to run a truck from Canada to here."

"Is it all coming from Canada?" I asked.

"From what I hear, that's true in these parts," said Wini. "The best comes from Europe, of course. Nobody has outlawed whiskey in Scotland."

"Or champagne in France," I said. "Or beer in Germany."

"Which is why we will never be dry in America," said Wini. "Even if we board up all our own breweries."

"Some of the breweries make decent ice cream these days," I said.

"Yes, but those pints will never outsell pints of suds," said Wini. "Hey, there's the sign for Innsmouth."

Chuck's directions had saved us some winding through the back roads and led us straight to the main road running through Innsmouth. As we drove through the outer edges of the town, the impression was of a place far less prosperous than Arkham. I saw many boarded-up houses, some looking as if the building was ready to collapse.

"Is it just me or does the town feel unfriendly?" I asked Wini as we drove down a quiet street leading to a slightly better neighborhood. At least there were storefronts without boarded-up windows or doors. But even those signs of commercial life seemed peculiarly lifeless. "Do you think anyone is out and about?"

"It's not lively," Wini answered as we passed one closed shop after another. No one was on the sidewalks either. "Perhaps it's nearly suppertime for most folks?"

"Seems early for that," I said. "The sun's still high."

"This town is mostly fishing folk," said Wini. "Up before dawn and down before dark."

We took another turn and suddenly overlooked the harbor. Below us, crowds of people were hurrying toward the weathered and dilapidated wharf. I immediately turned the car in their direction, but as the streets narrowed, it became increasingly difficult to navigate around the people suddenly appearing from everywhere. The crowd swelled around and past our car, and I caught shouts about help needed down at the pier. Of course, that made me want to see what was happening. Luckily, my companion was just as curious.

"Guess we found everyone," I said, parking the roadster.

"Follow the crowd?" said Wini as she got out. She looked as eager as I felt.

"Don't you love it when you can hear trouble brewing?" I said as I brushed the dried mud from my stockings and straightened my hat.

"Betsy Baxter, some people head in the opposite direction when they see a crowd forming," laughed Wini. "Will you pass up any opportunity to get into trouble?"

"Absolutely not," I said. "A Baxter is always an opportunist."

"I suspect that I am, too," said Wini. "Let's see what's going on."

We followed the crowd down to the shore. While I could not swear the whole town was there, it seemed likely. On the edge of the crowd, I spotted someone I did not expect.

"Look, there's Ezra Hughes," I said.

Wini turned away from me and pointed in the opposite direction. "And there's Nova Malone, riding in like the Queen of England."

She was quite right about the ride. Nova Malone stepped out of a stately Rolls-Royce Phantom, the 1925 model Henry had kept casually mentioning to me as a possible car. He was dying to look under the hood of the new replacement for the Silver Ghost. Nova Malone's chauffeur looked familiar, too.

"That's one of the men I almost shot in the alley last night," I said to Wini. "The excitable shortie. Albie."

The little man was now dressed in a neat suit and very circumspect dark tie. Albie barely came up to Nova Malone's shoulder, I noticed, but he held the door for her with much more grace than he'd used to wave his gun earlier. After she got out and had a few words with him, he retreated around the Rolls to watch the crowd.

"This is becoming interesting," I said.

Ezra Hughes and Nova Malone exchanged a pair of glares, which should have sizzled everyone in the crowd between them. Then they both turned away from each other.

"All we are missing is your reporter friend Darrell," said Wini.

"Nope, he's here, too," I said, pointing to a motorcycle with a sidecar rolling down the street. The man riding on top of the motorcycle was Darrell. After he parked, a tall figure unfolded himself from the sidecar. I swore when I saw Darrell's passenger. "What's Tom doing here? This will cause trouble." Luckily, neither Ezra nor Nova spotted Tom, and I moved to intercept the men before anyone saw them.

I ran around the edge of the crowd to the pair standing by the motorcycle. "You idiot," I said, smacking Tom on the arm.

"Ow! What did I do?" said Tom.

"Came to a town gathering with at least one person willing to shoot you for your grimoire," I said, tugging him around to point out Nova Malone and her chauffeur. "And one who wants to tar and feather you," I added, pointing out Ezra Hughes. "What are you doing here?"

"I caught a ride into town and took Wini's posters to the printer," said Tom. "Your friend offered to give me a lift back to the airfield after I placed a few ads with his newspaper. But there was a phone call just as we were leaving, and Darrell needed to make a detour for a story. I said I was happy to ride along as we didn't know when you or Wini would return from your riotous outing."

"My perfectly proper trip to the Purple Cat involved apple pie, a muddy road, and a slight detour through the local farmlands," I said, leaving out a few details about local bootlegging that I'd learned along the way. As for the boat that fell out of the sky onto the road, I wasn't going to mention that anywhere near Darrell's sharp ears. Not yet, as it was exactly the type of story he'd insist on investigating immediately, and he would possibly want to take my photo next to the boat. I wanted to answer a few questions of my own before I turned Darrell loose on that particular mystery.

Tom ducked his head and rubbed the back of his neck. "Where's your roadster parked?" he said, shifting his hand to shield his face from any possible watchers.

"Over there," I said, pointing to my car.

He reached into the sidecar and pulled out a leather helmet along with a pair of goggles. "Mind if I borrow these for the ride back with Miss Baxter?" Tom asked Darrell.

Craning his head to see what was happening at the other end of the wharf, Darrell waved a hand in consent as he adjusted the camera strapped around his neck. So intent was he on the possibility of a story, Darrell barely acknowledged me, other than a "Hello, Miss Baxter. Could you please move a bit? I need to get down there."

I stepped smartly aside so the reporter could weave his way through the crowd. Luckily, both Nova Malone and Ezra Hughes also seemed intent on whatever was happening out on the water. Neither glanced toward us.

Tom pulled the leather helmet over his head and adjusted the goggles across his eyes. The gear covered his face as effectively as a mask.

"Slump a bit," I said, worrying his height would make him more visible.

Tom hunched his shoulders forward and practically bent double as we slipped away through the crowd. When we got back to the roadster, he slid into the backseat.

"Better put the top up again," I said to Wini, who gave me an incredulous look. But she obliged and wrestled it back into place for the second time that day. At least we weren't moving while she did the maneuver this time.

"Now, stay put," I ordered Tom. "I want to see what's happening." Wini latched the roof into place, shook her head at both of us, and headed toward the pier.

"I don't suppose you have something to read," sighed the man in the goggles.

I slapped our road map into his hands. "Figure out the fastest way back to the airfield," I said.

Wini was already ahead of me, working her way through the crowd to the edge of the water. When I caught up with her, I saw what had so fascinated the entire town.

A tugboat was coming into the harbor. Rather than towing a ship behind it, the tug pulled a familiar seaplane in its wake. One wing was half gone, and the plane listed terribly to starboard, but the floats still held it above the water.

"More storm damage?" I said to Wini. I didn't know much about airplanes, but there was something not quite right about this one. It wasn't just the damage to the plane. Something about the broken wing made me uneasy. Also, the smell of rotting seaweed as we approached the pier was nearly overwhelming. I wondered how the rest of the crowd could stand it. Perhaps they were used to the briny smell of decay.

"Maybe it was the storm," said Wini, peering intently at the damaged plane, but she sounded unsure. "Look at that wing, though. Does that look like it just snapped off to you?"

"No," I said, taking a closer look as the plane was pulled level with the dock. The curved indentations in the skin of the wing seemed so very familiar, although I'd never seen any such marks so large before. Then I remembered the time a big German Shepherd grabbed a sandwich off an extra. The pair ended up in a tug-of-war over it. The tooth marks the dog left on the disputed lunch looked much like the indentations on the fragile wing of the airplane. "It appears something chewed on that wing."

"And bit it clean off," said Wini with a nod of agreement.

CHAPTER FOURTEEN

"So what would chew on an airplane?" I said as we drove away from Innsmouth.

"And take a bite that large?" said Wini.

"A whale?" speculated Tom.

"Whales are in the ocean. Planes are in the air," I responded. The road from Innsmouth to the airfield was smooth and without any of the challenges of our earlier route along the cliffs. I shifted the gears and picked up speed, enjoying once again the feeling of zooming to a destination. Innsmouth bothered me. Not the accident to the plane, although that was odd enough, but something about the entire place felt wrong. It wasn't that it was poor. I'd grown up poor. Boarded-up windows or unpainted front doors weren't uncommon in the small town where I was from. But Innsmouth felt different. Perhaps it had been the overwhelming smell of ocean debris that blew through the town – there was a depressed air about the place.

"But it was a seaplane," Tom yelled over the engine's roar from his place in the backseat, still arguing for his whale theory, "so presumably it was in the sea at some point."

"I still think it was the wind," Wini finally said after a few more miles of pointless speculation. "Something like a waterspout that tore the wing and hurled the plane off course."

We'd learned earlier that the plane ran a regular route, taking supplies to several isolated island communities before landing each evening in the Innsmouth harbor. A chief investor in the project appeared to be Nova Malone. Several of the townspeople referred to it as Miss Nova's plane.

The plane carried no passengers, but the two-man crew was missing.

"Did you see the name of the plane?" I asked Wini and Tom. When they shook their heads, I said, "It had *Gulliver* painted on the tail." The boat that had fallen from the air to land in front of us was named *Gulliver*, too. I salvaged a board with the letters "Gulliv" and put it in the trunk of my car, I told Tom.

"What? A boat fell out of the air?" he asked.

"Makes more sense now," I said. "The dinghy must have fallen from the plane before they crashed."

Wini shook her head. "I don't think they'd be carrying anything that heavy. If they had any type of lifeboat with them, it was probably canvas or rubber. Besides, didn't people say the seaplane disappeared earlier today? From what I heard, their flight plans went further east."

"Perhaps they were lost nearer to the cliffs," I speculated.

"Well, if that's true, then we should start our search along that stretch." As soon as a call went out for volunteers, Wini asked to join the search parties for the missing pilots. She intended to take up her own plane to see if she could spot the two men. Boats had been launched from the Innsmouth docks before we'd left. Chief among the organizers had been Nova Malone, who promised to set up a round-the-clock meal service for the searchers as well as a reward for any information about the missing men.

"But didn't Chuck Fergus say that area was dangerous to fly over?" I said, remembering his warnings earlier that day.

"Wait!" said Tom from the backseat. "Who is Chuck Fergus?"

"A bootlegger friend of Wini's," I explained.

"Of course! I assume he's one of Nova Malone's men," Tom said.

"No," said Wini. "He's an O'Bannion man. Which makes it interesting that they are operating out here. If this is Malone's territory, I wonder if that's the issue with the missing planes."

"What do you mean?" I asked.

"Sabotage," said Wini. "If there's a battle over who is moving liquor through this area, then they might be sabotaging each other's transportation."

"Cars, ships, and planes?" I asked.

"It's possible," said Wini, with a rare frown. "I wouldn't have thought that the O'Bannions would stoop to such tricks."

"Where there's money," I said, "there's mischief." Look at all the trouble Max caused, running after the riches he decided he deserved, I thought. As I told Darrell earlier, missing vehicles could be as simple as a snatch and grab of each other's cargo. Such tactics in Chicago tended to leave a lot more dead bodies on the ground, rather than just men with missing memories, but perhaps New England bootleggers were politer.

"I hope that's all it is," said Wini. "Mischief and not malice or something more deadly."

"I was just thinking the same thing," I said. "I knew a few of the boys in the trade in Chicago. They wouldn't just hit someone politely over the head and leave them in a ditch somewhere."

"This," said Tom, "is why I much prefer reading about adventure and not living it. Will you go to the police?"

"With what?" I asked. "A boat that fell from the air? I've been calling the

Arkham cops for nearly three years. Even three men disappearing couldn't move them to do much. Darrell might be more helpful if he's not off pursuing some other story."

"I'd rather not involve your reporter friend," said Wini.

I could understand her reluctance. If she had past dealings with one of the bootlegging gangs in the area, the resulting press would do her reputation no good and might impact the circus. Knowing the type of muck the press was often inclined to rake and the harm they had done to friends of mine, I decided Wini was right and it was best to stay quiet for now. If, or when, we needed Darrell, I was certain of his sense of fair play. The trick would be to give the story to Darrell before anyone else started writing about Arkham's latest peculiarities.

"So what next?" asked Tom.

"I will take my plane along the cliff and a few miles out to sea," Wini said. "We might spot more wreckage or even the crew. Although why they would have left the plane when it was still floating, I can't figure out. It would have been safer to stay with the seaplane. They would have been found quickly then." She planned to take her own plane aloft when we reached the airfield to search as long as daylight held. Night searches were nearly impossible, she said, but luckily it was late summer. Sunset was still hours away.

"Perhaps the whale chased them off?" said Tom. He'd pulled off the goggles and helmet as soon as we'd left Innsmouth, but the headgear had left his hair standing up every which way. As he leaned over the seat to join our debate, I couldn't repress a smile at his wildly crumpled hair.

"I still doubt it was a whale," I said. "I've never even heard of them attacking ships. Except in the movies or books."

"Oh, a whale will turn on a whaler," said Wini. "There's more than one story of that happening."

"The *Essex*," said Tom, "was sunk by a giant whale in 1820. That was what inspired Melville to write *Moby Dick* according to some."

"How do you know these things?" I asked him.

"Abandoned in a bookstore as a baby," replied Tom. "I teethed on the *Encyclopedia Britannica*, according to my uncle."

"What did your mother think of that?" I said.

Tom shrugged. "She washed her hands of the family by the time I reached school age. She wanted a career in art and left for Europe. She currently enjoys running a gallery in Lucerne. She once said it was much more serene to deal with cubists than booksellers."

"And your father?" I asked.

"Oh, he's still in Boston," said Tom, "and drops into the bookstore on a regular basis. He's been a book scout for years and prefers that to a settled life."

"A book scout? Anything like a Boy Scout?" I said.

"Not nearly so prepared," said Tom. "He travels around New England, visiting estate sales and auctions and so on. Book scouts sort through the bins of other bookstores looking for treasures."

"So you survive by selling books to each other? Bookseller to book scout to bookseller?" I said.

"Correct," said Tom.

"But how can you make any money doing that?" I said.

"Very astute," replied Tom. "You see the basic flaw."

"You are just passing the money back and forth," I said.

"Exactly, but we always have something to read." Tom sounded very much like a Harvard professor pleased with a bright pupil. "However, that's why the grimoire was so valuable. It helped us acquire cash from new buyers once every decade or so."

"About that peculiar book of yours," I said. "We need to talk. It seems the Deadly Grimoire has quite the reputation all along this coast. And I'm not sure that dealing in curses is the best way to make a living."

"We do not sell curses," said Tom emphatically. "We sell books. What the buyers do with those books is none of our business."

"I am not sure it works that way," I said, but Tom was right. What people did was up to them. Hollywood had been accused of corrupting the morals of the country for years, but I wasn't convinced someone switched from upright virtue to jazz and gin overnight just because they watched Clara Bow. The owners of the Deadly Grimoire could put their purchase on a shelf and admire it as a work of art.

"It is complicated," I reluctantly admitted.

Tom straightened up in his seat. "Oh, look, we're here. There's the airfield."

Wini snorted as I gave him a hard look over my shoulder. Obviously, this wasn't a debate he was prepared to have. And, since I wasn't sure of the answer I wanted, at least not then, I let him off the hook.

Once we parked, Wini jumped out of the car and raced across the field to organize her search flight.

"Won't you go with her?" Tom asked.

I shook my head. "She'll take up one of her crew who is experienced at spotting. I'd be dead weight."

Tom unfolded himself from the backseat. "Well, I have a cot here," he said. "And a few more calls to make. If someone did steal the grimoire to sell it, there's only a few dealers who would take it. I need to let them know the grimoire is on the loose again."

"Would they buy it from a thief?" I said.

"If I ask them to. They will try to grab it back, but if they can't do that, they'll pay for it and call us," said Tom. "It's not the first time we've recovered the grimoire from another bookseller."

"You don't think they'd try to sell it to one of their other customers?" I said.

Tom shook his head. "Most of the dealers who know the grimoire also know about the curse."

"And those who don't?"

"Wake up to the smoking ruins of their store," Tom said nonchalantly. "Sometimes it's not as drastic as that," he added upon seeing my expression. "But whatever happens, it generally persuades the bookseller that it is better to send the grimoire back to Sweets and Nephew. There's a bookplate with instructions on what to do inside the front cover."

"So, you do acknowledge there is some danger in handling the grimoire," I said.

Tom sighed. "We're not completely heartless. Over the generations, we've mollified our doubts with the knowledge that good people are rarely harmed by the grimoire. The types who want it, let's just say they are not the most virtuous of souls."

Which did leave me wondering about Ezra Hughes and his fascination with the book. Nova Malone, I understood. Like her ancestor, she thought it might lead to more riches and, judging by her jewelry, she was a lady who believed in getting rich. But why would the good doctor want it? And was he indeed a good doctor? My worries about Jim being in his care surfaced again. I resolved to go see my friend as soon as possible.

I walked over to the airfield's offices with Tom. We watched Wini's crew push her plane into position. She jumped into the cockpit with her regular co-pilot, Bill, in the second seat. With a wave and a roar, they were airborne and headed to the coast to search for the missing pilots.

After they left, Tom and I followed Lonnie back into the barn to watch her work on Bill's plane. I told her how I wanted to learn how to fly.

"Anyone can learn to fly an airplane in a month or two. It takes real talent to learn how to fix an engine so the plane flies," Lonnie said, grabbing a wrench from the ground. "At least that's what I tell Wini."

"Is it really so hard?" Tom asked.

"Not if you understand the theory of the internal-combustion engine, carburetion, compression, ignition, and explosion," she chuckled at our expressions. "I trot out all the big words when I want to impress someone." Then she shrugged. "Just know absolutely nothing is easier when the engine works and nothing is more of a devil when it breaks," she said. "I've worked on lots of engines. They all have their quirks, but once you get into the guts of one, you'll probably understand the others." She looked a little doubtfully at Tom. "If you understand engines, I mean. It helps if you've worked on automobiles."

He cheerfully acknowledged that he did not even drive.

Lonnie shook her head at that. "Not a career for you," she said.

"Probably not," said Tom, looking at her greasy hands.

"It is more than just keeping the engine tuned," Lonnie said. "There's the rigging checks and truing up the wires and struts. I overhaul every plane after a show to tighten sagging wires as well as looking for any other problems."

She ran her hands along the wing to demonstrate. "A rip in the stitching or any tear in the fabric could be a disaster. Not long ago, a wing's cover ripped off when the pilot went past one hundred and fifty feet. The fall killed him."

She patted the wing with satisfaction. "My planes won't wash out. I keep Wini and the rest of the pilots safe. If you are a mechanic, you need pride in your work. You're responsible for people's lives."

It was fascinating to hear her views, and the more she talked, the more I began to think about a new film, one that featured a woman mechanic who saved the day. Lonnie laughed when I ventured the idea. "People will never believe that mechanics are heroes," she said. "Not the way that the pilots are!"

"Then we will need to show them that," I said. Marian would love to make a movie about female mechanics, and it was time people like Lonnie had their stories told.

"Well, I should make my calls," said Tom.

I left Tom with promises to return the next day to drive him around the countryside and help him place Wini's posters in the nearby towns. I also needed to speak to Wini about the tricks I wanted to do for the show. Despite my earlier fall, I was sure I could climb out on the wing and wave to the crowd without Charlie's harness. I also had ideas about borrowing Lonnie's motorcycle and making a jump to the plane. Or perhaps Lonnie could drive the motorcycle and I could ride behind her. That might work, I thought, as I walked back to the roadster. It was sure to be a crowd pleaser. All I had to do was convince Lonnie and Wini to let me try it. There was nothing like devising a few death-defying stunts to take a gal's mind off her other worries. By the time I started the car to head back to Arkham, I felt much better.

I might not have the answers yet about Max's disappearance, but I had some ideas now on where to look for those answers.

After an unusually quiet night for Arkham, I breakfasted early and requested my car from the hotel's garage. I checked our much folded and refolded map to locate Bluff Mansion.

Once again, I was on the twisting cliff road near Innsmouth, although the turns took me further north than the previous day's journey to the Purple Cat. But like the countryside near Nova Malone's restaurant, the sea winds had twisted the trees and hollowed the hills. Even in the late summer sunshine, the land felt bleak. Or perhaps that was my own emotions as I raced toward a rendezvous I both wanted and dreaded.

Jim had disappeared more than three years ago at the same time Max was lost, and his return was nothing short of a miracle. But why Jim? Why not Max? Those were the questions buzzing in my mind as I followed the road away from the sea and along a high stone wall. The way people kept disappearing around this area and then reappearing in other spots was all part of a larger pattern, I was convinced. I was also certain Hughes and possibly Nova Malone knew more than I'd learned so far. Their entangled family histories suggested that.

Eventually, I came to a pair of handsome wrought iron gates, propped open for the day with a discreet brass plaque that proclaimed I had found Bluff Mansion.

The driveway leading to the sanitarium was smooth and white, made from crushed seashells. With a perfectly centered door flanked by white pillars that stretched past the second-floor windows to the roof, the sanitarium looked like a Hollywood version of a Roman temple. I could see how this place would impress its potential patients with its sense of importance.

I circled a bubbling fountain before drawing up to the grand entrance of the Palladian style house. Opening my handbag, I took a quick check of the contents. My silver-plated pistol was snugly secured in the special pocket designed for it. Unusually nervous, I drew out my compact and checked myself in its tiny mirror. While the prohibitions against ladies painting their faces had faded over the years, this was New England. I didn't want to look too much like a Hollywood actress. Not for this visit. I had represented myself as a close relation of the patient, rather than the studio mogul who was paying for his care.

Satisfied my powder was subtle enough to pass for natural and my dark green hat was somber enough for a visiting relative, I walked up the steps of the mansion and rang the bell.

The door was answered by a neatly dressed woman with dark hair secured in an old-fashioned chignon.

"How can I help you?" she asked.

"My name is Betsy Baxter," I said. "I am here to see my cousin Jim Janson."

"Ah, yes," the woman said, clicking away from me in heels that made a distinct rat-a-tat on the polished marble floor. I followed her inside. "I have you down in the book as visiting today." She settled herself behind a desk set neatly to the side of the door. The whole arrangement, while something like a hotel's desk for checking guests in and out – complete with a wall of cubby holes for mail and keys – was positioned in such a way as to not be clearly visible from the door. Instead, the first impression, most certainly deliberate, was that I had stepped into a mansion of the Gilded Age, complete with grand staircase, impressive paintings in heavy gold frames lining that staircase, and, I glanced up to check, a crystal chandelier that would rival any found in New York or Hollywood. Not exactly a New England saltbox, that was for sure.

At some point, the Hughes family possessed considerable wealth to judge by the marble stairs and mahogany banisters twisting away to higher floors. Looking around the place, it was obvious that an older, more palatial mansion had been converted into a facility that met the needs and aesthetic expectations of a wealthy clientele. I wondered how the family money had been lost and when the need to turn the place from a home to a sanitarium had occurred.

I turned away from the center and followed the woman to the reception desk.

"If you could just sign here," she said, extending a fountain pen toward me and pointing to a leather-bound ledger with cream-colored pages. Like the desk, it bore a resemblance to the type of guestbook you would find in the fancier hotels. I signed my name, the date, and the time as indicated by the signatures above mine.

"Thank you," she said, closing the book on her desk. "I'll call for one of the nurses to escort you to the patient. Would you like to speak to Dr Hughes today? He's available in an hour for a brief consultation."

I pondered the wisdom of another encounter with Dr Hughes so soon after meeting him at the hospital. Oh well, why not, I thought. "In for a penny, in for a pound," I said out loud to the puzzlement of the woman waiting for my answer.

"I'd be delighted to speak to Dr Hughes about poor dear Cousin Jim," I continued. "But can I see Jim now? His mother worries so, and I'd like to give her as complete a description as possible."

"Yes, of course," said the woman at the desk, picking up a phone and speaking a few words into it. In the distance I heard the clank of an elevator door and then the light footsteps of someone wearing rubber-soled shoes. "Ah, Nurse Roberts, can you escort our guest?" said the woman at the desk to the nurse that entered through a side door.

"Certainly," said Nurse Roberts, waving me toward the door she had just come through. "Your cousin is in the conservatory today. We have all the windows open. It's such lovely weather, and our guests so enjoy the view."

"Our guests" seemed to be the name for both visitors and patients, perhaps to give the place a more refined air, I decided as I followed Nurse Roberts down the corridor. Certainly, there was no hospital smell nor the sterile feeling of an institution as we walked along a hallway carpeted in a fine blue wool runner. Other than her uniform, Nurse Roberts might be taken for a superior sort of maid or even a maiden aunt, directing guests to where they could take a light refreshment and a little entertainment before venturing home again.

The size of the sanitarium's bills made much more sense after seeing all this. Hughes obviously catered to the expectations of very rich clientele. I was glad for Jim's sake, for it was as civilized dand comfortable as possible.

"Ah, here he is," said Nurse Roberts, after we had entered a very pretty glass room filled with potted palm trees and delightfully vivid flowers spilling out of porcelain urns. All the windows along one side were cranked open, and a light breeze carrying the scent of recently cut grass played through the room. Glancing out those windows, I realized the gardens were surrounded by high hedges that blocked any view of the sea. Instead, we could have been gazing upon a tranquil garden set anywhere in the world. The flowers outside were a mix of roses with the blowsy open flowers of late summer.

"Wake up, Mr Janson. Your cousin is here," Nurse Roberts said.

Jim was seated in a white wicker chair with his feet up on a stool. In keeping with the rest of the "guests" I saw lounging in similar chairs, he was neatly dressed in what appeared to be casual clothes. No patient's pajamas and robes here. Rather, he wore simple flannel trousers, a blue shirt, and a cotton sweater draped over his shoulders. Only his footwear betrayed him as a patient rather than a visitor, as he wore soft leather slippers on his feet. All of which I'm sure had been billed to the studio, as he'd been found in rags earlier that year.

But I didn't care about the cost. I wanted Jim to recover, and the money was well spent if that was the result. Of all the things that frightened me, and I was no Nova Malone immune to fear, the idea of losing years of memories scared me the most. I wanted to remember every minute of every adventure. I wanted that for Jim, too.

The luxury of the place reassured me. At least Jim looked as if he was being well cared for. Watching Nurse Roberts, I decided she had kind eyes.

Nurse Roberts shook Jim's shoulder very gently. He stirred under her hand and blinked sleepy eyes at me. "Oh," he said, sitting a little straighter in his chair, "is it time for lunch?"

"No, Mr Janson," said Nurse Roberts. "You have a visitor. Your cousin Betsy."

"Hello, Jim," I said to the man I'd last seen being engulfed by smoke in a burning house three years ago. I drew a breath to calm myself. I was finally there. I could finally ask about Max. But first I said, "How are you?"

CHAPTER FIFTEEN

It took Jim a minute or so to come fully awake. Or as awake as he appeared to be capable of. Throughout our conversation that day, I felt that Jim was looking beyond me into some dream that never quite finished for him.

"Hello, Betsy," he said after I repeated my name again for him. "How's tricks?"

"Life's good," I told him. "Living in a big house these days with parrots and an English butler to look after everything. I even have a conservatory but not as pretty as this one."

Jim nodded at me with another fleeting smile, but his eyes slid to the open windows, looking at something I could not see. After disappearing on the day of the fire, he stayed lost for years until someone found him wandering the road near a town called Kingsport. According to the hospital reports I had read over and over again, he'd been completely incapable of speech during his short hospital stay. Also of sleeping without the aid of considerable narcotics. Several doctors expressed worry about the amount of sleeping drugs it took to stop Jim from climbing out of his bed and wandering the hallways, always in search of a mirror or reflective surface. When Jim found a mirror during his nighttime stroll, he would stand in front of it, silently regarding his reflection until fetched back to bed.

Ghost catchers, that's what my mother called mirrors, and she always veiled them when there had been a death in the family. Dangerous was what my friend Jeany believed, and she had banned all mirrors from her home after a stay in Arkham.

But what actress can live without mirrors? I spent far too much of my life looking at myself, first as a dancer and then as an actress in the movies. Mirrors were a necessary part of the trade. A mirror in the studio showed you how your body moved or how your face looked to the audience. I needed mirrors, but I never feared the reflections I saw.

Jim's distraction that day was a frustration. I wanted to pelt him with questions, but at the same time I didn't want to frighten him. From every report I had read, he became most agitated when pressed about the missing years and where he had been. I needed a way to lead the conversation around to the topic without too much fuss.

"How about a stroll?" I asked Jim, glancing at the nearby Nurse Roberts. She nodded encouragingly at me.

"I suppose," replied Jim with no great enthusiasm. He'd been a bit player when we'd first started at the studio. He was also a man without any ambition as far as I could remember. Jim's greatest talent, said one director in my hearing, was his ability to stand or sit perfectly still for hours. Apparently that predilection had not vanished, no matter what had happened to him in the past few years.

With some gentle nudging by Nurse Roberts and myself, Jim stood and wandered toward the door of the conservatory. He even offered me his arm as we walked into the rose garden.

"He's been quite the gentleman during his stay with us," remarked Nurse Roberts as she followed us through the garden.

"His mother will be so glad to hear that," I said over my shoulder. As far as I knew, Jim had no relations. At least, the detective I hired never found any after Jim made his reappearance. Still, it would have been awkward to tell Nurse Roberts that and more awkward still would be to explain why I was murmuring questions to Jim about his friend Max.

Not that Jim had much to say. He'd never been a talker, not like Max, who could talk for hours about his plans and dreams for the future. But I didn't remember Jim as being this silent. Jim responded, although very slowly, to any direct question I asked, but the answers he gave were vague in the extreme.

"So, Jim," I said, deciding at last to force the issue, "where exactly have you been?"

Jim looked down at me with a puzzled frown. "Not here," he said as we paced slowly on the gravel path that wove round and round the rosebushes. The crunching of the stones under our feet was almost louder than Jim's reply.

"No, not here," I agreed. "You only came here a few months ago. But where have you been?"

Jim heaved a great sigh as we passed a fishpond set in the center of the rose garden. He paused to peer down into the murky water, seemingly fascinated by our wavering reflections. Overhung with rose bushes, a few petals and dead leaves floated on top of the water. If there were any fish in this artificial pond, they were in hiding.

"I don't think it is very nice," Jim said to me after several minutes of silent contemplation.

"The pool?" I said, gesturing at it. The brackish water reflected the clouds chasing across the sky. Peering into it, the ornamental pool seemed fathoms deep with twists of seaweed impossibly long and entangled filling its depths. I blinked again and it was only a small fishpond in the center of an overgrown garden, desperately in need of a good gardener with a rake.

Jim sighed again, perhaps at the futility of trying to explain his thoughts, and shook his head. "Where I was," he said. "It always smelled wet. Like the ocean."

We were not far from the sea. In fact, the cliff was on the other side of a tall and neatly trimmed evergreen hedge. Even in this sheltered rose garden, I could smell a faint whiff of brine and seaweed. Very faint but clear, I could hear the boom of the surf as the ocean met the rocks at the base of the cliff hidden by the hedges. But how had Jim gotten himself from a burning house on French Hill to someplace near the ocean?

"Do you remember the fire?" I said. Jim screwed up his face as if he'd bit into something sour but remained silent. "How did you escape the fire?" I pleaded, hoping Jim's answer would give me a clue to Max's own possible route to safety. But that apparently was the wrong question.

Rather than answering me, Jim took off in long strides, startling both Nurse Roberts and myself with his sudden quick action. We followed him as he headed back into the conservatory. Jim continued without pause through the room and up a narrow staircase. This one lacked ornate steps or mahogany banisters, probably once built for the servants needed to keep such a large house running smoothly.

"Where is he going?" I said to the nurse, annoyed with myself for setting Jim off. I knew he didn't like being questioned, and I scolded myself as we loped after him. With his long legs, Jim took a considerable lead.

"I think," the nurse panted a little as we crested another flight of stairs, "he's returning to his room. He will do that sometimes when he's agitated."

Sure enough, Jim turned into a room near the top of the stairs. He walked across the room to yank the curtains closed and then lay down on the bed. Nurse Roberts fussed forward and removed his slippers before he could get any marks on the clean white coverlet. She pulled a light blanket from the cedar chest at the end of the bed and spread it across his legs.

"I'll fetch his tea," she said to me. "He will feel much better after a cup and short nap. Won't you, Mr Janson?" she said to Jim.

Jim nodded into his pillow.

"Can I stay with him?" I asked her. "Until you come back? Then I'll talk to Dr Hughes."

Nurse Roberts looked a little uncertain but apparently came to the conclusion that since we were in the twentieth century, perhaps I could sit with my cousin in what amounted to his bedroom. "But keep the door wide open," she said to me as she bustled out.

"Of course," I said. I pulled a straight-backed wooden chair closer to the bed and repeated the question I had asked earlier in the rose garden. I knew it bothered him, and I pledged silently to make it up to him in the future. But I had to know. "How did you escape the fire, Jim?"

He kept his eyes closed and his face turned into the pillow away from me. But after a few minutes, he whispered an answer.

"Please, Jim," I said as gently as I could. "I cannot hear you."

I hated pestering Jim so. What if my questions undid all the good the doctor had accomplished over the past few months, I worried. But what if Max was lost somewhere "not nice" and needed to be rescued? How else could I find him?

Then Jim raised himself up on one elbow and looked directly at me. "I walked through the mirror," he said with absolute conviction and clarity. I was so astonished by this statement I couldn't form another question.

No sooner had Jim spoken, Nurse Roberts returned. She carried a tray with a steaming cup of tea that appeared distinctly green and smelled quite unlike any tea I had ever encountered. I would have called it a sulfuric odor, not unlike rotten eggs or, more probably, boiled seaweed. It also unpleasantly reminded me of the way Innsmouth had smelled. And the scent rising from the boxes at the warehouse by the river.

With professional efficiency, the nurse swung a small table next to the bed and placed the tray on it. She then helped Jim to sit up in bed and supported his trembling hand as he sipped the tea. Neither of them seemed bothered by the smell, so I held my breath and didn't say anything.

"There now," said Nurse Roberts quite kindly as Jim slid back down in the bed. "Have a nice nap. We'll see you downstairs for supper this evening. Maybe we can even listen to the radio for a bit."

Jim murmured some agreement.

"We have a new radio," Nurse Roberts said to me with a bright smile. She also nearly pushed me from the room. I guessed visiting relations were not supposed to see the patients slide backward on their climb to socially acceptable behavior. "We hear lectures broadcast almost nightly from the university. There's dance music on Saturday nights sponsored by the Purple Cat. Our guests enjoy the entertainment."

I resisted her efforts to remove me from the room. I needed to know Jim was all right. As he drifted off to sleep, I asked Nurse Roberts if he was still being dosed with sleeping drugs.

"Oh, no," she said, sounding a little shocked. "Dr Hughes tries to avoid such medications whenever possible. Mr Janson has been sleeping quite naturally for several weeks."

"Well, that's good," I said. I reached over to touch Jim's hand, giving it a light squeeze in the way that I used to wake my grandmother when she dozed off in the evening.

"I have to go," I said to Jim. "But don't worry. Everything will be fine. I'll take you home to California as soon as I can."

Jim stirred and turned his head toward me. "Oh, Betsy," he said without fully opening his eyes. "Are you going to help Max? Some nights his shouting is so loud in the mirror."

CHAPTER SIXTEEN

Of course, with Nurse Roberts standing over me and Jim snoring quite content-edly into his pillow, I could not do what I most wanted to do upon hearing Jim's extraordinary statement about Max shouting in the mirror. I refrained from shaking Jim awake and peppering him with more questions. Instead, I followed Nurse Roberts out of the room and down the main staircase, this time to the entry hall.

"We do have an elevator," Nurse Roberts informed me. "The doctor made that improvement recently for our frailer guests. It's a blessing when we need to take trays up to the patients, but I thought you might prefer this way." By that pronouncement on my preferences, I took her to mean she wanted to show off the fine paintings and other small luxuries I had glimpsed when I first arrived. Again, I was reminded that a private sanitarium like this relied on the content-ment of the paying relatives, if not the patients, to make ends meet.

As we came to the bottom of the stairs, I saw Dr Hughes standing at the reception desk, chatting with the woman there. He wore a very fine suit and looked quite the dapper doctor in it. He turned toward me with a smile that dimmed as I thrust out my hand.

"Betsy Baxter," I said with no explanation, shaking the doctor's hand with as much enthusiasm as I could manage.

His eyes narrowed. Ezra Hughes said in an almost accusatory tone of voice, "Didn't we meet at the hospital yesterday?"

Oh, bother, I thought, he does remember me. But I flashed my largest smile and pumped his hand up and down like a Fuller Brush salesman, or rather sales-woman, and said, "Why, yes, we did meet yesterday when I was visiting my friend the professor. Today I'm visiting my cousin Jim at your lovely institution."

"You seem to make a great many patient visits," said Hughes with a perplexed look. He gave a definite tug to retrieve his hand. I smiled like a cherub, radiating innocent goodwill with all my acting skills.

"I do try to make the rounds," I said. "At least in terms of spreading a little comfort and cheer to my friends and relations. By the way, I am impressed with the improvement in Cousin Jim." No need to mention that I agitated him into hiding under his pillow not ten minutes past, I decided. "He seems like a new man."

Hughes preened a little at the praise. "I find the patients respond most satisfactorily to rest, well-ordered days, and a diet of my own devising," he said. "We try to rebalance the sentient humors while honoring the connectivity of the human psyche to the primordial substance that grants us all life."

Call me a Scopes monkey, but I couldn't decide if the doctor was advocating for evolution or arguing against it as he lectured me about his theories. But his lecture seemed to contain many references to returning to the ocean that spawned us.

"Of course," he said to me, "not everything is visible to the naked eye. At times we must look beyond what we normally see."

"I am certain you are right," I said, resisting the urge to look about for the nearest exit. Hughes might be a bore, at least when it came to discussing seaweed, but he knew something about disappearances and their peculiar effects on people's minds. I was convinced of that.

The doctor fished a piece of cloudy glass out of his pocket. "The evidence of the transcendent supremacy of the ocean can clearly be seen when examined through such relics," he said. "As a boy, I scoured the shore for these fragments of greater windows and mirrors that revealed the psychic currents. Observe it yourself."

I had no wish to handle the beach glass he thrust into my hand. It felt unnaturally icy to the touch but also slimy as if covered with some mucus. There was something about the feel that reminded me of oysters and how they felt unpleasantly cold as they slid down the throat. Max had adored eating raw oysters. I found them foul.

Still, I raised the piece of glass to my eye as Hughes instructed. Through it, I saw a blurred and distorted version of the room. "I don't see," I started to say, but then the view shifted as I moved away from the window and into the shadows cast by the long drapes. Suddenly the room seemed infused with a purple light, and the shadows became extended tentacles or strands of seaweed, swaying as if observed underwater. It was a repellent view of the world.

I didn't want to look, but like a horrible dream, it seemed to draw me into its distorted realm. I was reminded of the terrible movie we were making that summer in Arkham when Sydney and Max whispered in corners of the house as the rest of us suffered from nightmares. Nightmares like this, of places we should never see.

"Uh, fascinating," I said as I thrust the piece of glass back at Hughes. I stopped myself from pulling a handkerchief from my purse and wiping my hands. But just barely.

Hughes beamed as he took the peculiar piece of glass from me and dropped it into his suit pocket. "Once," he said, "I believe the world was covered in water. This echoes through all the flood myths from Deucalion and Pyrrha in Greek mythology, Bergelmir in Norse mythology, and, of course, the tale of Noah. All of these speak to the power that comes from the ocean to change the world."

As he continued to explain his reasoning to me, despite my obvious backward walk away from him and toward the door, phrases like "divine oceanic currents" and "wisdom of the deeps" threaded through his discussion of his practice. As much as I wanted to learn more about the grimoire, I wanted to be as far away from that piece of glass as possible. My urge to run nearly overwhelmed my manners. However, the doctor seemed used to people edging away from him when in full explanation mode, as he paced along with me.

I smiled and nodded, seemingly the only contribution Hughes wanted, until I reached the door. With the handle firmly grasped in my hand and a quick exit assured, I took advantage of a pause, as Hughes drew breath, to squeeze in a question of my own.

"So, does Jim still sleepwalk looking for mirrors?" I said.

Hughes almost continued his speech over my question, but the word "mirror" caused him to hesitate.

"Mirrors," he began. Then he stopped and frowned at me. "Mirrors have nothing to do with my treatment," he said with an emphasis on the nothing. "Reflections deceive and often mislead the viewer. Windows, certain windows, can increase our understanding of past events and even give us a view into the world under water."

I remembered Hughes discussing this at the hospital in response to a story Wini told. But as I had already received a bucketful of his views, I refrained from inquiring more about windows. Instead, I asked again about mirrors and more specifically: "Do you think Jim hears people in the mirror?"

"My dear young lady," said Hughes, in that amused tone of voice certain men use to deflect the questions of persistent women, "mirrors cannot convey sound."

That, of course, was a scientific fact. But if Hughes thought such a tone or retort could stop me, then he didn't know Betsy Baxter.

"Still, we worry about Jim," I said, leaving vague how many people were inquiring about Jim's health. "Is he talking about Max being trapped in a mirror to anyone?"

Perhaps Hughes inferred that Jim had plenty of protectors, or at least family members, who might stop paying the bills if "Cousin Betsy" didn't have her questions answered. At least this time, he directly responded to the question I was asking about Max.

"The patient spoke once or twice about a nightmare. Perhaps there was some mention of mirrors, and while some counsel removing mirrors to avoid encouraging dysmorphic tendencies, we find that such a practice might create greater harm," said Hughes, now very much the polite and civilized man of medicine responding in ten-dollar words to a worried relative. "Those dreams seem to have faded as his sleep patterns returned to normal. I am certain a few more weeks in our care will find him fully restored."

That didn't answer my question, not completely, but I wasn't exactly sure what I needed to know. As for leaving Jim in care somewhere, I had no disagreement there. I was happy to pay anyone's large bills if it meant Jim was restored to health. And, from everything I had seen, Jim was indeed much better. If he continued to improve, then this was the best place for him, despite my continued uneasiness about the strange shard of glass in the doctor's pocket.

As I dithered, the doorknob was wrenched from my hand and a short man pushed his way inside. I recognized the new guest instantly as Albie, Nova Malone's driver and the gentleman who menaced Tom and me in the alley. Anxious to avoid exclamations and explanations of our past encounter, I twisted away from the door and wished my modest green hat had a veil. Turning my back to the doctor, I pretended a sudden and intense interest in one of the family portraits decorating the entry.

"Could this possibly be a Whistler?" I said, while facing a painting portraying a grim-faced lady dressed all in dismal brown. I found myself talking to the air.

The doctor and his receptionist were intent on the story being gasped out by their most recent visitor.

"Slow down, Albie," said the doctor. "Tell me exactly what happened."

"We found the pilot and his partner," said Albie. "They are just like the others. Sleepwalking down the cliff road. One of them even tried to take a nap right there on the road. Draped in seaweed like all the rest."

I wondered what the seaweed smelled like. Unpleasantly dead like all the other aquatic vegetation encountered in the past two days? Remembering the scene glimpsed through the shard of glass and the cold slimy feel of the piece in my hand, I was beginning to suspect that this seaweed was not entirely natural.

"Have they been taken to the hospital?" Hughes asked.

"Not more than an hour ago," said Albie. "I knew you'd be grateful to hear the news as soon as possible."

"We do have a phone," said Hughes.

Albie had a hand held out, and I realized why he had come in person with his story. Hughes obviously caught the hint, too. With a grumble, the doctor pulled his wallet from his breast pocket and passed a few dollars to Albie.

Albie nodded his thanks as the bucks disappeared into his coat pocket. "I better be going," he said. "Miss Nova will expect me to drive her to the hospital later this evening."

The little man left as quickly as he had come without a single glance in my direction. He did not seem to make the connection with the gal who had waved a pistol at him a few days earlier. There was something to be said for owning multiple ensembles when roaming the countryside investigating mysteries. At least I was wearing a different coat and hat for this encounter.

As soon as Albie's car could be heard speeding away, I made my own good-byes to Hughes and his receptionist, assuring them I would tell the "family" that Jim was well cared for. At the same time, I resolved to cable Farnsworth and set in motion our plans to move Jim to California for his final recovery. The nurses seemed kind and the place well run, but Hughes disturbed me in a way I could not quite fathom.

As I drove toward the airfield to collect Tom, I mulled over all I had learned. Nothing Jim said truly gave me a clue to where Max was. But as Jim improved, perhaps he could tell me more. As for the reappearance of the crew of the missing airplane, I wondered how Nova Malone would react to the knowledge that Ezra Hughes had a spy in her camp. Poorly, I suspected, which argued that the doctor at least had courage. I wouldn't have wanted to make the lady cross, and even Darrell had warned against angering Nova Malone.

But why was Hughes spying on Nova Malone? What was his interest in the missing pilots? Simply more patients for his sanitarium? Or something more? That I couldn't answer. "Arkham," I muttered to myself. "It's as frustrating as always. And Innsmouth is no better."

When I arrived at the airfield, I parked the roadster next to a mail truck. Glancing around, I spotted Wini sitting on a bench outside the small hut that served as the field's office. Seated next to Wini was a good-looking Black woman dressed in a postwoman's uniform.

"Betsy," yelled Wini when she spotted me. "Come meet my friend Stella."

I walked over to the pair. After shaking hands with Stella, I said to Wini, "I heard they found the missing crew of the seaplane."

Wini nodded. "Stella and I were talking about it," she said. "She's the one who found them."

"I was out on the cliff road," said Stella. "The regular postman was sick and the Innsmouth office called us asking for help. Most unusual for them, they generally keep to themselves, but apparently something made several people ill."

"Bad fish for lunch?" I guessed, and Stella gave me a slightly disapproving look for my flippancy.

"The mail has to go out," she said. "So I drove to Innsmouth, picked up the deliveries and started out. I was taking the mail to the Purple Cat and the sani-tarium. I just rounded the corner, right near the cliff edge, when the wind caught the truck."

"I've been on the cliff road," I said. "In a storm. It's frightening."

"I know what you mean," said Stella. "Everyone warns about driving across Malone land. I've never driven to the Purple Cat before, and I wouldn't want to go back unless I absolutely had to. For a moment, I thought the road had disappeared under my wheels. I hit the brakes, and it's a good thing I did because those two men walked right in front of me. I was lucky not to hit them."

"Sounds like luck was with them all right," said Wini. "They might have gone over the cliff if you hadn't found them."

"They definitely acted strange," said Stella. "Like they were sleepwalking. It took some pushing and pulling just to get them into the truck. Then I drove them to Miss Malone's place. Sure wasn't the mail that she was expecting."

"I expect she was grateful to have them found," I said. And I meant just that. Everything I'd seen of Nova Malone indicated that she cared about her employees.

"Oh, yes," said Stella. "She bundled those two men into her Rolls and had her driver take them to the hospital."

"I was visiting a friend who is staying at Bluff Mansion," I said, "when I heard the pilots were found."

"I bet Ezra Hughes was interested," said Stella. "A friend told me that he's been going around the hospital here in Arkham interviewing everyone who disappeared and then reappeared. Then he's been moving them to his sanitarium for treatments."

That answered my earlier speculations about his motives. At least in part.

"You don't say," I said to the pair. "The friend I was visiting had an episode like that. A period of lost memory."

"Then Dr Hughes is the man to cure him," said Stella with considerable conviction. "He started in the war, working with the shell-shocked. Some people consider him quite the hero, according to what I've read in the newspaper."

But there was something about Stella's tone that conveyed a few doubts, too. I wondered if he had ever handed her that peculiar bit of glass he carried with him.

As we chatted, Stella related a story that matched what others had said. That Hughes came from an old Innsmouth family who lost their riches in the last century with the sinking of their ship and had a long feud with the Malones because of it.

"Not that there are many Malones left to carry it on," said Stella. "Nova Malone had a couple of older siblings, but one was lost at sea, and the sister married a man who went out west. There's a niece or two, I've heard."

"And Hughes?" I said. "Any family there?"

"None as far as I know," said Stella, "but he's an Innsmouth man. He may work at the hospital and teach at the university, but he's from there."

Which, her tone implied, meant beyond the reach of the Arkham Post Office. Still, I had learned a great deal from Stella.

"Obviously, every detective story should begin with a trip to the post office," I said, thinking I'd learned more the past few minutes than my entire time racing around the countryside. Of course, there had been other distractions.

Stella nodded. "I'm always surprised folks don't ever wonder more about how their mail appears at their house. Sometimes I think they assume it is magic. And all they have to do to send a package or a letter to a friend is scribble their first name in illegible handwriting on the label, along with a town name… and sometimes not even that! Some of the things that our last postmaster let pile up in the dead letters box. Heavens, you could see why the poor man gave up."

"But you didn't," said Wini. "Stella cleared nearly ten years of lost mail out of the local post office in her first six months."

Stella looked a little embarrassed by Wini's praise. "It's a talent I have," she said to me. "My granny could douse water with a willow stick. Seems like all I need to do is hold a letter to know where it should go. No matter how poorly it is addressed."

"That is a talent," I said. "We could use someone like you at the studio to sort out all the mail that comes in. Half of my mail comes addressed to the Flapper Detective instead of Betsy Baxter."

Stella blinked. "Did you say your last name was Baxter?" she said to me.

"Yes, it is," I replied.

"Oh," said Stella, digging into the satchel sitting beside her on the bench, "then I have a letter for you. It was addressed to a Miss Baxter and the airfield. I meant to ask Wini about it."

I recognized the writing on the outside of the envelope as Farnsworth's neat script. By the postmark date on the letter, he must have sent it just after I left for Arkham with Wini. I tore it open to find another envelope and letter inside the first one. This one had been addressed to me but mailed from Arkham. On a note written on my own stationery, Farnsworth said he was sending it after me to my "last known destination with hopes that madam will still be in one piece to read it." I snorted at this sally, as it clearly brought his voice to me. I did miss Farnsworth's pessimistic attitude toward adventure and thought Tom might enjoy meeting him. They would both withdraw into the library to shake their heads over me.

"How odd," I said to the others. "This letter has been following me around the country. Or at least crisscrossing back and forth."

Once I opened the smaller envelope, I found two more sheets of paper. One looked as if it had been torn from a child's notebook. The other was penned upon a blank recipe card. The writing on the smaller card was odder still. Wini, who openly peered over my shoulder when Stella stepped back to give me some privacy, whistled at the strange little note. "Is it some kind of code?" she said.

"No," I said, after staring at it for a moment longer and then realizing what it was. We'd used a similar device in an early episode of *The Flapper Detective*. "It's mirror writing. Like Da Vinci. You can read it if you hold it up to a mirror." I pulled my compact out of my purse to show her.

The card said, "Help me. Max."

CHAPTER SEVENTEEN

I was so startled by the message that I nearly dropped the letter penned on the second sheet of paper. In a different handwriting, this letter stated:

"Dear Miss Baxter, my wife told me to send this to you as you are the Flapper Detective and certain to know the answer. Ever since my Minerva disappeared and returned, she's been having funny dreams. We talked to Dr Hughes more than once, and he prescribed some mighty peculiar seaweed tea, but it has done nothing to settle my Minerva's nerves. Then we went to the picture show in Arkham and saw you there. You were clever in how you found the villain and helped the poor family who had lost all their money to him. On the way back to our farm, Minerva opined that you would know what to do with these messages that she keeps writing out in her sleep. So please find one enclosed. Should you wish to speak to us, we would be happy to answer your questions. But we don't own a telephone, so please send a letter. Most sincerely yours, Jared Knowles."

I puzzled through the letter, for Knowles's handwriting was almost as hard to read as the note by Minerva, even though it wasn't written backward. Then I read it out loud to Wini and Stella. My voice sounded completely calm, but my mind was in a whirl. First Jim and now this. Where was Max?

"Fancy Farmer Jared writing to a Hollywood actress," said Stella with a laugh. "I wouldn't have thought the old fellow had that much gumption."

"Do you know this couple?" I asked.

"Certainly," said Stella. "They have a farm not far from Bluff Mansion. They don't raise much anymore, the children being gone, but get by with just enough for themselves and what they can sell to the neighbors. I understand both Bluff Mansion and the Purple Cat buy produce from them. I had forgotten about Minerva's disappearance."

"Was she gone for long?" Wini said.

Stella shook her head. "Not more than a day. She went fishing and never came home for supper. It's the first time that had happened in forty years, according to Jared, so he drove into Innsmouth and organized a search. The next day, some kids spotted her in one of the caves near the town. As I recall the story, she couldn't say how she came to be there."

"I would like to talk to her," I said, turning the letters over in my hands. Like to talk to her? I absolutely needed to question her. Here was a clue I couldn't afford to ignore, no matter how strange. "If they don't have a phone, it might be easier to drive out there."

"This time of day, they are bound to be home," Stella said. "I can give you directions. The roads around here are confusing."

"I have a map," I said, running back to the roadster to fetch it. When I returned to the hut, I found Tom had joined the others.

"Are you ready to take some posters around?" Tom asked me, waving the rolled-up paper at me.

"Oh, I did promise to help," I exclaimed. "But I want to talk to Jared and Minerva today."

"Who?" said Tom.

"You can do both," said Wini. "Take Tom and the posters with you and come back through Innsmouth. And maybe decide what we are going to do to replace Chuck's act."

"Oh," I said, suddenly conscience stricken. Wini's livelihood depended on a good show, and I knew she needed a quality act to succeed. "I had some ideas for Saturday's performance. I haven't forgotten."

"Go," said Wini. She obviously took pity on my quivering eagerness to run off. "Go and do what you have to. Later we can decide what stunts are best for the show."

"Here, let me help. I know some of the rural roads outside Arkham," said Stella. She took my map from me and, between us, we puzzled out a route so I could run all our errands from the airfield to the farm to Innsmouth and back again.

Tom listened intently to Stella's suggestions, asking one or two questions, and then nodded. "I can navigate, Betsy," he said.

Remembering how quickly he directed us through Arkham when we visited the hospital, I happily agreed. "I'm sorry to drag you off on my quest," I said as we climbed into the car. "I don't know what we'll find at this farm."

Tom shrugged. "I've made all the calls about the grimoire that I can. Other book dealers know it is possibly back on the market. If the grimoire doesn't show up that way, I'm fresh out of ideas. I might as well enjoy the scenery for now. And we can help Wini with the posters on the way back here."

With a wave at Wini and Stella, we pulled away from the airfield. Tom was an easy passenger full of entertaining stories about the book trade and quick to spot the signs marking turns in the road. If I hadn't been so preoccupied with the strange messages about Max, he might have turned my head. As it was, I sincerely appreciated his calm good humor.

We followed the route laid out by Stella through pleasantly rolling hills and small woods composed mostly of maple and oak. While only a few miles from the sea, at least as a gull flies, the countryside felt vastly different from the area nearer to Innsmouth. The air smelled of late summer flowers and newly cut grass. The wind in my face felt fresh and held no touch of brine in it.

Ever since I had peered through that warped shard of glass, I felt as if I was drowning in a sea of worry and fear. Now the feeling eased, and some of my worries seemed nonsensical. My old confidence bubbled up. I was certain I was on the right road to finding Max, and Tom was the perfect fellow traveler for my journey.

Perhaps it was the late summer sunshine or perhaps it was my handsome companion, but for the first time since coming back to Arkham, I began to sing as we drove along. Tom joined my rendition of "Yes! We Have No Bananas" followed by a spirited version of "California, Here I Come!" that would have put Jolson to shame.

Giggling, I said to Tom, "If you ever visit Hollywood, I can promise you bananas and oranges."

"And how about a sun-kissed miss?" he asked, quoting the lyrics of our last song.

I winked at him. "I may know one or two," I said, thinking that the ladies at the studio would like this man.

"It certainly sounds more fun than sitting in a bookstore waiting for my uncle to uncrate a new shipment of books," said Tom.

"That song has brought many a romantic soul to my state," I said, "and the others are drawn to fame and possible fortune in Hollywood."

"And do all their sunny dreams come true?" Tom asked.

"Mine did," I said. As I said it, I realized it was true. While I worked hard for every penny, I couldn't deny the happiness that I found with my friends. Over the past few years, I had helped many friends achieve their own dreams, and that felt good, too. If only I hadn't let go of Max and lost him in the fire. If I could find him safe and sound, then I could look back at my whole life without any regrets. I could plan my future without any shadows hanging over me. I almost told that to Tom when he looked up from the map and spoke first.

"I think that's the farm," he said, pointing at a neat little house surrounded by a white picket fence. A big old oak spread its branches in the front, shading a porch complete with two rocking chairs and a wicker table.

As we pulled up in front of the house, a gray-haired woman came backing out the screen door. She was carrying a tray laden with a lemonade pitcher, a tall glass, and a plate of cookies.

"Oh my," she said when she turned around and spotted us getting out of the roadster. "I wasn't expecting guests."

"I'm sorry to disturb you," I said, "but I had a letter from Jared Knowles."

"That's my husband," she said. "I'm Minerva Knowles. Wait! I know who you are. You're the Flapper Detective girl, the one who solves all the movie mysteries. Oh my, oh my, you came, and here's me with nothing but a few cookies and lemonade. Come up to the porch and sit down! Sit down. I'll go find a couple more glasses. Jared! Jared! You'll never guess who is out here."

Minerva plunked the tray on the wicker table and rushed back into the house.

"Heavens," I said, blinking a little at the enthusiastic reception, "she seems very well."

"Were you expecting something else?" Tom said.

"Maybe," I said, walking up the porch steps. "Most of the people who disappear seem, well, quieter." I thought of Jim, dreaming away on his bed, and wondered if he might do better with lemonade and cookies than tea made out of seaweed.

The screen door crashed open again as Minerva pushed her pudgy husband out the door in front of her.

"Woman, woman," he moaned, "I'm in my overalls. Oh, dear, I'm sorry. I just finished cleaning out the barn." He looked every inch the farmer from the worn overalls pulled tight over a round belly to his well-worn work shirt open at the collar. A tattered straw hat protected his very pink scalp from the sun. He lifted the hat off his head in greeting and then pulled a red bandanna out of his back pocket to wipe the sweat off the top of his shiny bald head.

"I should apologize for visiting without any warning," I said. "But your letter mentioned you had no phone. I thought it would be easier to drive out here than to go back and forth with letters."

"We're delighted," said Minerva very firmly. Then she poked her husband in the side with an elbow. "Where are your manners? Find these folks some chairs."

"Here," said Tom, bounding up the stairs and fetching a couple of ladderback chairs from the far end of the porch. We settled around the wicker table while Minerva went running off for more glasses and another plate of cookies.

Jared stood awkwardly, shuffling big feet encased in scuffed boots, as Minerva bustled about.

"Please sit," I said, dropping down onto a ladderback chair.

The farmer nodded and gingerly lowered himself into his rocking chair. "You got my letter?" he asked after a long pause.

"Yes, but just a few hours ago. I'm very interested in hearing about what happened," I said.

Minerva was persuaded into the other rocking chair by Tom. She gave it a few brisk rocks, and then said, "I have never been a fanciful woman, so it's been the most peculiar thing."

"Disappearing?" I said.

"No. That happens around here. It's the sleepwalking," Minerva said. "And the spirit writing. My goodness, I haven't been so plagued for a good many years. I think the last time I was this haunted was when I was a little thing of eleven or twelve years old."

CHAPTER EIGHTEEN

Tom leaned forward, obviously intrigued, and asked Minerva, "So you're a medium?"

"Not anymore," the farmer's wife said. "When I was young, my mother was quite the believer in spiritualism. Oh my, that was another century."

"Minerva was famous," said Jared Knowles with shy pride. "We have a scrapbook of articles about her."

"Pshaw," said Minerva. "My mother made that scrapbook more than fifty years ago. She wanted me to have it for my children. Not that I ever wanted to give them any ideas. More recently, I haul it out to shock the grandchildren. None of them ever believe that I was once twelve."

"How about the spirit writing?" asked Tom.

"Oh, I think they find that much easier to believe than their old granny being a child like them," Minerva chuckled.

But I was more interested in her talk of disappearances. It sounded like Minerva had much greater insight than anyone else I had questioned.

"You said that people disappear around here," I said, interrupting their conversation. "Can you explain what you mean?"

Minerva gave a few brisk rocks and then cocked her head at me. She reminded me of the birds around Arkham, the crows with their wise old eyes looking sideways at a person. "You have to be careful where you walk. Don't go into the woods alone."

"Don't cross Malone land," I said, remembering the warnings uttered by Chuck Fergus.

Minerva nodded. "I was foolish when I went fishing. I forgot to watch the tides. Any grandchild of mine would have done better."

"Now, Minerva," said her husband. "The fish were biting. You said so. Not unusual to be distracted by that."

"Fish were biting too well," Minerva retorted. "That should have warned me that I'd drifted into another current. But then that darn old motor wouldn't start, and I needed to use the oars. I was caught contrariwise when the tide came in."

"The fish were biting too well?" said Tom.

"Practically jumping into the boat," said Minerva. "Rising up to the surface and making a feast for the gulls. I had birds diving all around the boat, which is why I wasn't paying as much attention as I should have. When the fish are in a hurry to get out of the ocean, you should ask yourself what's hunting underneath them."

There was a late summer breeze ruffling the edges of our cloth napkins. It carried a bite in it, a chill that was the first warning of autumn. Or maybe it was just Minerva's story with an echo of greedy gulls on the hunt and fish desperate enough to swim into oblivion.

I put a hand to my hat to make sure it was pinned tight in place. I had no time for fancy tales and stray breezes. Ever since I unfolded that note in Minerva's mirror writing, there had been a buzz in my stomach. A feeling that I was finally coming close to the place that I needed to be.

"These notes that you write, the ones that are backward, do you do that while you are asleep?" I said.

"Oh, yes," said Minerva. "My spirit writing only comes out of my dreams."

"I've seen her do it," said Jared. "She just climbs out of bed and marches to the kitchen table. Writes down whatever she's dreaming and then goes back to bed. Most times, it's just reminders to one or the other of us. Things we need to remember."

"Birthdays, shopping lists, chores for the coming season," said Minerva. "I went and talked to that mind doctor Ezra Hughes. Not that he was much help. And the tea he prescribes is simply awful."

"I understand he is quite famous," I said.

"It's hard to take a man seriously when you've known him as a baby and a boy," admitted Minerva. "Ezra used to play with my children back when that big house of his was still a family home. Not that there was much Hughes family left to rattle around in all those rooms. Unlucky, they were."

"And the Malones?" I said, for it seemed that whenever a Hughes entered the tale, a Malone wasn't far behind.

"Unlucky, too. There's only Nova left close by," said Minerva. "She's a bit older than Ezra, but they are much of a generation. She has a sister and a niece or two out west. Ezra has nobody left. Not family, at least. Makes him more than a bit peculiar, I think. Not that he liked me telling him so when I went to see him."

"The analyst was analyzed by the patient?" asked Tom with a smile.

Jared chuckled at the question. "I was waiting for her in the hallway of that fancy sanitarium. Both of them came stomping out of the doctor's office buzzing like angry hornets after her last visit."

"Now, Jared, it wasn't nearly as bad as you tell it," said Minerva, with a swat at her husband.

"Did you tell him to stop poking through other people's dreams and pay attention to his own?" said Jared, ducking out of the way of her friendly swipe with the ease of long practice. "Also, didn't you tell him to try drinking his own tea?"

Minerva winked at her husband and gave a giggle that sounded decades younger than her actual age. In her youth, Minerva must have been a charmer. She obviously still held that charm for her husband. "I may have made some suggestions to Ezra. I'm a mite prone to giving advice, and that's never welcome for some folks."

"She poked him right in the chest," said Jared. "Poked him and told him to stop messing around with seaweed and steer clear of the ocean because he wouldn't like what he dredged up."

"Ezra was always messing down on the beach," said Minerva. "Dragging home all sorts of unhealthy flotsam and jetsam when he was a boy. What the tide brings in should be left for the tide to take out. At least when you're crossing Malone land."

I remembered the greasy bit of beach glass that so fascinated Hughes. I had to agree with Minerva's assessment and told her so. I described the shard Hughes asked me to look through and how unwholesome it had felt.

"There's a reason why people threw those windows in the ocean," said Minerva. "Those bits rolling back on the beach can be dangerous. The things you see through such glass! You never know what's looking back at you while you're spying on it. I told Ezra to be careful. It could be much worse than squinting down a clam hole and having the clam spit saltwater in your eye."

She passed around the plate of sugar cookies and took a large one for herself. After a couple of happy bites, Minerva said, "It was obvious to me that Ezra was going to be no help with the messages I was receiving. But after I saw your movie, I just knew I needed to send the next note to you."

"The next note?" I exclaimed, very surprised at that statement. How many messages had Minerva received?

"I wrote several after I was found down on the beach," said Minerva. "Ezra took them. That's one of the things that made me so mad. He said he wanted to analyze my handwriting for possible personality quirks. As if I don't know all the bumps and tangles of my own self at my age! But after I got home, I went sleepwalking again. It was obvious to me that a message needed to be sent. I rarely write the same thing twice. Not after the right person reads the note. It's only when a delivery goes astray that it happens again. Mother and I figured that out long ago."

"Back then Minerva used to give messages to all sorts of folks," said Jared. "That's why they wrote her up in the newspapers when she was young."

"Who do you think is sending these messages? Is it the dead?" I said. If that were true, how was I to help Max's ghost? "And why did you think that the messages were for me?"

"I told you," said Minerva, shaking her head at my foolishness. "The minute I saw you in the movie, I knew you were the one who needed to hear what that spirit was saying to me. Happens like that. I see someone's picture or hear their name and I immediately know a message is for them."

"And who do you think is sending those messages to me? Do you think it is a ghost?" I said, and I almost dreaded the reply. For what could I do to help the dead?

"Perhaps," said Minerva. "That's what my mother thought. That my messages came from the dead."

Some doubt in her voice caused my next question. "Who do you think is talking to you in your dreams?" I asked.

Minerva heaved a giant sigh. "It's so difficult to explain," she said. She fussed with the plates and the cookies until Jared reached behind her rocking chair and pulled out her bag of knitting. "Show them," he said, placing the bag on her lap. "Like you do for the kiddies."

Minerva clucked. "Oh, my tricks are only for the little ones because it's hard to explain," she said.

"Works a treat for me," said her husband with a twinkle.

She smiled and patted his hand. "That's because you're still a child at heart," she said fondly to her husband. To us, she said, "You should see him at Christmas when he gets to play Santa at the school, handing out presents all around. Spends all autumn growing out his scratchy white beard."

They both chortled at that. Minerva fished her knitting needles out of her bag and began to cast the wool on one. She was fast and had a few rows knitted in a twinkling as she pulled a second yarn into the pattern, making diamonds and stars appear in her work.

"You know why fishermen's wives knit patterns into their men's clothing?" she asked us.

"So they can identify the drowned," said Tom, proving once again that growing up in a bookstore left a person with a head stuffed full of strange knowledge.

Minerva nodded at him. "The women of Innsmouth added something else to their patterns," she told us. "They added maps of stars that we never see. Not when we are awake and wondering. The women knitted the stars and roads needed to guide a man out of the night that never ends." She pulled more yarn out of her bag and added more colors, colors that formed swirls and patterns that did not so much as jar the eye as unsettle it altogether.

"Do you understand tension in knitting?" she said, sweeping both of us with a stern look which suggested she doubted our understanding of the term.

Digging into my memory of knitting lessons from my grandmother, I responded, "Does this have anything to do with purl one, knit two?"

"A bit," said Minerva, shifting to a second pair of needles. It was clear now that what she was knitting would eventually become a mitten. "You have to keep the tension steady or the pattern won't turn out true. If you rush, you end up with a mess you need to unpick and start again. I think," she said as she clicked her way through a few more rows, "too many people rush through the pattern. Innsmouth is a dangerous place to make such an error. To drop a stitch, to create a hole." She deliberately skipped a stitch and a hole appeared in her work. Minerva yanked the yarn, just slightly, and the whole pattern rippled in a way that made Tom and me flinch.

"You feel it, too," Minerva said. "How the world drops away, just for a second, and you land yourself someplace else. Just for a second, just for a breath, just enough to unnerve you."

She gave a vicious twist to her needles and the whole pattern fell apart in a knotted, tangled mess. "Sometimes, though, you can be unraveled into someplace else."

I gave an involuntary cry of dismay at the destruction of her work.

Minerva smiled and picked the yarns out of her lap. "It is nothing," she said soothingly to me, the way that you would comfort a child frightened by a nightmare. "I can always wind it into a ball and start over. Hold your hands up."

I did as I was told, much to my surprise, and Minerva cast her yarn back and forth between my two hands. How many times had I sat just so in the late summer sunlight or close by the kitchen stove in winter while my grandmother did the same, looping me into her skeins and stories.

"If you know where you are, if you know where you are going, if you have a pattern, you can find your way home," Minerva almost whispered. "You can carry it all in your head as easily as you can wear a mitten or a scarf. Remember that. Then you can never be lost. That's what the women know and the men forget."

"Except the ones who learned how to knit," said Jared a little smugly. He'd retrieved another pair of needles from Minerva's bag. In his hands, a sock was growing, covered in the same stars and swirls of Minerva's pattern.

"Ezra's problem," said Minerva, "is the lack of patience in the boy. He thought windows would be a quicker way to where he wanted to go and what he wanted to gain. And Nova Malone is no better, for all that she knows the patterns as well as anyone. She knows her glittering book is just a cheat, a way to shortcut across the old ways."

At this statement, Tom leaned in, obviously planning to ask about his grimoire because what besides a jeweled cover could be described as a glittering book. I shook my head at him just a tiny bit. Tom, bless his heart, leaned back and let Minerva continue at her own pace. I didn't want to distract Minerva, not now, not when I was so close to finding the answer to my own mystery. Later, I told myself, later we can ask about her reference to a glittering book. Except the next few minutes drove it out of my mind.

Minerva unwound the yarn from my hands and into a neat ball on her lap.

Another loop of yarn, and another winding and unwinding, and a second ball joined the first. As she cast her third strand across my hands, my patience broke and I blurted out, "But how do you find somebody who is already lost?"

"By looking, of course," said Minerva as the third ball grew into a neat round shape to match the other two. "Nobody can find anything if they don't look first."

"I'm not sure that is exactly true, ma'am," said Tom. "I've found a great many things I didn't intend to find. Stumbled over them, you might say."

"Are you sure?" said Minerva. "Perhaps you didn't know what you were looking for until you found it."

The last of the yarn slithered away from my fingers. I almost clutched at it if only to tether Minerva to her chair and her story. There was an answer here, I was certain of it, an answer to the questions that had haunted me for three years.

"So how do you bring back someone who is lost, someone who doesn't know your pattern?" I asked.

Minerva nodded briskly at me, the way a schoolteacher might nod at a pupil who finally stumbled upon the point of a lesson. "That's the right question. What do you do if the men won't wear the pattern that you've made? What do you do if they are foolish enough to sail without it? There are words to say, there are songs to sing, but you have to be careful. Drop a stitch, sing the wrong note, make a mistake, and you've opened a hole for a good many things, not just the person who you're looking for. You cannot be reckless."

Minerva and Jared rocked in time with each piece of advice. The creak of the rockers blended with the chittering of the insects stirring at the end of a long hot afternoon. Far away, I heard a crow's harsh cry.

"Who holds your hand and writes words when you are sleeping?" I asked again. "Is it the dead?"

"I think not," said Minerva. "I never believed the dead would try so desperately to speak to us. I think it is the lost souls. The ones still alive who cannot find their way home."

There were shadows under the oak tree. Black shadows, and the shapes made by the branches shifting in the wind looked like tendrils of seaweed floating beneath the water, clutching at a drowning swimmer.

"Ever since I saw you at the picture show," said Minerva, reaching out and patting my knee, "I knew why I dreamed about Max, night after night. The message is for you. Max is trying to reach you."

CHAPTER NINETEEN

When we drove away from the farm, we did not sing. We did not laugh. We did not even talk. For mile after mile, I sat silent. Tom respected that silence. Until we reached the first town where we had promised to display Wini's posters. Even then, I spoke first.

"Where do you want to start?" I asked. It was a tiny town, not more than a few stores clustered on one straight main street called, of course, Main Street. If the town had a name, I forgot it as soon as we left its boundaries. Most of my thoughts were about Max and the terrible weight of the words Minerva had placed upon me.

"General store, dentist's office, and the diner," said Tom. "That's all there is."

"There's the church," I said, pointing to the plain white wooden building.

"Would a church allow a circus poster?" Tom asked.

"They might," I said. I slid out of the roadster and straightened my hat. I unknotted the scarf around my neck and looped it in a more conservative style. "Give me a poster for the church. I'll ask nicely. Where are the free tickets?"

Wini had given us a handful of tickets to spread around with the posters. We were supposed to persuade the most influential people in town to come to the show. Once they came, Wini predicted the rest would follow for the second or third day. In the theater, we called such tactics "papering the house". It was always a good way to open something new and lure in a crowd.

"I'll give a couple to the reverend," I said to Tom. Stepping across the road, I found the church door closed but unlocked. Inside, the pews and pulpit were as plain as possible. Near the door, a woman was dusting a table or perhaps just rearranging something on it. For when she turned to face me, I saw a paper bag in her hand and not a dust rag.

She was dressed in a long skirt and conservative jacket, very much in the style popular before the war, and the whole ensemble looked like it might be ten years old or more.

"Can I help you?" she asked, and her tone suggested she thought I needed more help than I was going to ask for.

"Yes, ma'am," I said, ignoring her pointed stare at my much shorter skirt and darling cloche hat. Apparently my more traditionally tied scarf did not impress her. "I am with the air show and wondered if we could leave a poster on your community board."

I offered the poster to her. She looked as if I had tried to hand her a serpent.

"I am certainly not…" she started to say, but a man's voice interrupted her.

"Now, Mother," said the minister, walking through a door set in the back of the church, "let's see what the lady has to offer."

Like his mother, the minister's suit was old with the black beginning to turn to dark gray along the seams. But his collar and cuffs were shining white and immaculate. Whoever did his laundry did an excellent job. Judging by her red knuckles, I guessed it was his mother, and I smiled at her more sympathetically.

"I am performing with the aerial circus," I told the minister. "A clean and whole-some show, intending to introduce children and their parents to the marvels of flight. It includes a homage to our brave pilots who served so gallantly in the war."

From conversations with Wini, I knew that Saturday's entertainment would include plane rides for a dollar as well as a mock air battle to mimic the dogfights of the last war. Both were popular bits of business to perform between the bigger stunts.

"Of course, we would love to have you attend," I said, turning and handing the free tickets to the minister's mother. "You would enjoy it."

"I don't know," said the woman, turning the tickets over in her hands. It was obvious that very few gifts came her way. Minister's mothers, like minister's wives, were usually expected to do the giving. At least in the small town where I grew up, that was true. "I have never been to a circus. Just a revival tent show once when I was young."

"You will love it," I assured them both.

"A day out, Mother, would be a pleasure," said the minister with a pat to his mother's hand. "I cannot think of a woman who deserves a holiday more." His last statement considerably raised my opinion of the reverend gentleman.

His mother gave us both a tentative smile. "I could wear my new hat," she said, moving away from the table. Rather than covered with church literature or hymnals, I saw that shells were spread across the tabletop. Seashells of all types were arranged in swirls and patterns that reminded me of Minerva's knitting. These unsettling patterns seemed to whirl in front of my eyes.

"That's unusual," I said, turning away from the table before it made me sea-sick. "I would expect flowers for decorations."

The woman looked distressed, but the minister answered smoothly enough. "It's a tradition of the area. Something that the fishermen's families have done for a long time."

"Since the *Gulliver* disappeared," the woman almost whispered.

"The *Gulliver*!" I said. "Do you mean the plane that was lost earlier this week?"

"Oh, no," she said. "Gulliver Malone's ship, the one that vanished from Innsmouth's harbor."

"And not the Hughes's ship, the *Bolide*," I said, recalling the story Chuck Fergus had told.

"The Hughes!" she said with real scorn. "As if they ever cared for the people hereabouts, not the way the Malones did. Not the way Miss Nova does."

"Now, Mother," said the minister with a long-suffering sigh, "we must be charitable toward all."

"Name one basket of food that Hughes has given to a poor family," his mother flashed back. "I can name ten families this week who received help from Nova Malone. The Hughes family only wanted their fancy house and to order around all the rest. The Malones always cared for their neighbors." She was quite the warrior, the minister's mother, when she got started. "What was true in the past is still true today."

"Old feuds, all in the last century," the minister said to me as he walked us to the door. "Ezra Hughes is an educated man, a doctor, and I am sure he has helped many sufferers to heal."

"Good is as good does," sniffed his mother as she waved me goodbye from the church's front door. I did like her attitude. And I couldn't disagree with her assessment of humanity.

Back at the roadster, I found Tom had successfully persuaded the general store, the diner, and the dentist's office to display Wini's poster in their windows. "I even talked the woman at the store into taking a stack of tickets to sell. She'll bring the cash to me on Saturday when she comes to see the show," Tom said.

We drove through several small towns, convincing most of the businesses we found to take a poster, a few to take tickets to sell, and many willing to accept the offer of a free ticket for themselves. Airplanes were still not common in this area, and everyone seemed excited by the chance to see an aerial show.

"Have you decided what trick you will do?" Tom asked as we drove toward Innsmouth. The farther we went from Minerva and her story, the easier it was to bury all she had said underneath light chatter about the possible stunts, the people we met in each town, and the good weather. In short, everything except what Minerva had told us. After all, how do you discuss that the world can fall away as quickly as a knitter can drop a stitch? It didn't fit into a normal day, a day like this, full of sunshine and birdsong.

Rather than trying to wrap my head around the impossible, I proposed a few stunts.

"A jump from a motorcycle or car," I said. "I've done that often enough. I could jump onto the wing if the plane is still moving on the ground. Or onto a ladder. I once did something like that from a little boat to a ship's ladder. Both were moving at the time. It was a tough shot to get, as my cameraman was in a boat, too, bobbing up and down. It took three tries, and I landed in the water twice."

"You're lucky you didn't drown," exclaimed Tom in astonishment.

"I'm a very strong swimmer," I said. "That's why I have a pool. But it is different when you fall into the ocean. Colder. And there are currents, too." I remembered the waves breaking over my head and some screams from Marian that day. Perhaps even a few oaths from Farnsworth when I finally squelched my way home. But it had been an exciting stunt and the pictures of me dangling off the ship's ladder sold tickets galore.

"It sounds like the life of an actress is much more dangerous than I knew," said Tom.

"You have no idea," I said as we turned down a hill. Innsmouth lay below us, the harbor and the town visible in the distance. Driving through Innsmouth revealed another place than the one we had seen the day before. Today the shops were open, and people strolled along like any small town. But there were still sidelong looks at Tom and me after we parked the roadster and started to visit businesses that might display the posters.

"Not exactly friendly," I said to Tom as we exited from a drugstore where the owner had agreed to take both the poster and tickets with as few words as possible. No excited questions about the show like other places.

"Perhaps they are just shy," said Tom, but he also sounded baffled by our reception. "Oh, look, there's a bookstore. Let's see what they have."

"Where?" I said, glancing up and down the street. "I don't see any bookstore."

"Just around that corner." Tom waved a poster at the far end of the street where it curved into another road. The corner of a shop, at least it was probably a shop with a painted name on its door, was barely visible from where we stood.

"How do you know that it is a bookstore?" I said. From the way the sun reflected off the glass, the name painted on the door was mostly obscured.

"I am sure that there is a *B* and a *K* on that sign. And there is enough space for an *OO* between them," said Tom. "See that crate by the door? That's the sort of crate dealers drop five-cent books into. You never know what treasures can be found in such places."

"Serves you right if it is a barber's shop," I said, trying to think of other businesses with a *B* in their names. "Or a baker! Baker's shops have a *B* and a *K*." Then I spotted Nova Malone's driver, Albie, coming toward us. As he was not somebody I wanted to meet again, I pushed Tom into the bookshop. The store apparently specialized in very old and dusty books to judge by the dim interior after we entered. Tom tried not to look smug but failed.

"Go on," I said. "Say that you told me so." Glancing out the window, I saw Albie continue down the street. With any luck, he hadn't noticed us.

"I would never be so rude to a lady as to say I told you so," Tom answered.

"Oh, isn't it wonderful." He took off down the aisle like a hound puppy chasing rabbits.

"It looks like this store hasn't seen a customer since the *Bolide* went down," I said.

"Exactly," said Tom. "It appears many of these books were acquired years ago. It's always a battle to accumulate prime stock."

"I'd say this is a shop where the books won the war, and whoever bought these books is probably barricaded in the back," I said, maneuvering around stacks on the floor. The shelves were stuffed so tight nobody could even pull out a volume without risking an avalanche. "How many shop owners end up crushed under their own inventory?"

"Well, as long as they are not in earthquake territory," started Tom. Then he stopped and dropped back on his heels to paw through one of the piles. "I thought I saw… Yes, indeed! Betsy, look at this. It's Melville's *White-Jacket*. This must be a first." Tom shook the book free from the pile.

"That's a treasure?" I asked, nearly tumbling over another stack of books.

"Oh, definitely," said Tom. "For seafaring readers. Quite famous for its influence, even if Melville didn't much care for the job. He called it a book written for money."

"Oh, aye," said a rumbling voice from behind the shelves. "Melville's story saved many an American sailor's back from a flogging. And I have an affection for the character of Guinea, for I had an ancestor who shipped on a similar voyage, but he successfully used it in his bid for freedom."

Stumping around the shelves came a heavyset old man. Although his tightly curled hair was barely touched with gray, his beard was a white cascade down his chest. He dropped the books he had been carrying onto a pile and shook Tom's hand. "Do I see a fellow bibliophile before me?" he said.

"Tom Sweets," replied my friend. "This is a wonderful store."

The Black man nodded with pride at Tom's praise. "This store has been my great pleasure since I came ashore," he said. "Captain Leonard Pease, at your service. Welcome to Captain Leo's Books." Then he looked at Tom more closely. "Wait, did you say you were a Sweets? Any chance you're from Sweets and Nephew, the Boston booksellers?"

"Yes," said Tom. "I'm the nephew."

"Poor man, it's a hard burden to bear if all the tales are true," said Pease with real feeling. "But I've seen your grimoire quite recently. Being loaded onto a plane."

CHAPTER TWENTY

"The Deadly Grimoire?" exclaimed Tom. "How did you know about that?"

"Who doesn't know about the grimoire in the trade?" said Pease, gesturing to us to follow him down a crowded aisle overflowing with books. "Not the sort of thing I stock, being much more inclined to maritime tales, but I've been keeping an eye out for it since I heard it was stolen. Especially given its history with the *Bolide* and the *Gulliver*."

"Ha!" I said to Tom. "I knew the Deadly Grimoire was to blame for the original disappearances."

The bookseller smiled at me. "Are you a Sweets as well?"

"No, I'm a Baxter," I said. "Betsy Baxter. I'm not in the business of books, cursed or otherwise." Although I was beginning to feel that was slightly untrue. At times, I thought the whole story of the Deadly Grimoire a terrible distraction from my own quest. At others, like now, it seemed the grimoire might be the key to unraveling the whole mystery. After all, it was hard to believe more than one thing could cause people to disappear in this quaint corner of New England. "What was the grimoire's history in Innsmouth, Mr Pease?"

"Call me Captain Leo as the rest of the town does," said the genial bookseller. "What I know is both the Hughes and the Malones once sailed the coast, and further still, into currents and oceans best avoided. Eventually their rivalry grew so fierce that Gulliver Malone went all the way to Boston to acquire the Deadly Grimoire just to outdo Hughes on the trading runs. And it led to bad luck for both families."

"We've heard much the same from several people," I said. "Including Minerva and Jared Knowles today."

"Never argue with Minerva Knowles," said Captain Leo with a twinkle. "The woman knows the whole history of every family in this region. Has it all knotted up in her knitting. She's a terrible force for good, she is, selling her scarves and mittens every winter at the church holiday bazaar."

"Do you own some of her patterns?" I asked.

"I never sailed without one of Minerva's scarves," he replied. "And I never lost my way, no matter how strange the currents ran. Come along, come along, Tom, let me show you what else I have that might interest a Sweets."

As Tom promptly followed Captain Leo further into the store, I glanced back toward the windows and grimaced when I saw Albie's large friend of a few nights ago walking by with a sailor's rolling gait. Best we stay in the shop for a little time, I decided. I didn't feel like another confrontation with either man.

Although my largest problem looked to be liberating Tom from the store, given how he stopped every few feet with a cry of "Now look at this," and Captain Leo would pluck another book from a pile or shelf, saying, "Well, if you are interested in those books, you should see this as well. A second edition but in as good a condition as I've ever found." Soon Tom's arms were full of books. I predicted a crate needing to be strapped onto the back of the roadster in the near future.

The pair finally found "a snug berth" as Captain Leo called his cozy backroom. This den was piled high from floor to ceiling with books, but there was a small fireplace in one corner, and the books gave it just enough space to be safe. A pair of men's boots sat drying on one corner of the hearth. A battered old kettle swung over the flames through a clever arrangement of a hinged iron rod stuck in the side of the chimney.

"One of these days," said Captain Leo, "I will have to electrify back here as well as the front of the store. But I like this old fireplace. The man who sold me the building claimed one of Paul Revere's sons forged the kettle and hook."

"Quite possibly," said Tom. "It always seems to me that you cannot walk ten steps in Boston without seeing some evidence of his industry."

"Did you know the Reveres once held the commission to forge nails for the early navy ships?" asked Captain Leo as he swung the kettle away from the flames with the help of a poker. "Clear off the chairs. Don't let the books stop you from sitting down."

I cleared with a will, wanting to sit down and question Captain Leo about the grimoire. Tom, predictably, became distracted by one stack of books as he lifted it from a straight-backed chair and stood thumbing through a volume.

Using a towel to protect his hands, Captain Leo lifted the kettle off the hook and poured the boiling water into a waiting teapot. "There are some cups," he said. He looked vaguely around the piles of books. "Perhaps by the Conrad?"

I spotted Joseph Conrad's *The Rover* on the table that obviously served as the captain's desk. Beside the novel sat several stout mugs. I plucked three out of the welter of books and papers, holding them aloft. "Here are the cups," I said, handing them to the men.

Tom started to wave off the tea, pleading too much lemonade and cookies only a short time before, but then he saw the hip flask the captain pulled out of his jacket pocket. "Just a drop of rum to sweeten it," said the captain, dropping a generous dollop into each cup. "Better than sugar or cream, I reckon."

Tom finally sat down. He took a sip and sighed with pleasure. "Much better than sugar and cream," he said. "So how did a sea captain become a book-seller?"

"In my early days," said Captain Leo, "I was a poor sailor, but I took the jobs others didn't want, including whaling, although that was a terrible experience. Eventually I worked my way up to owning a boat. At first, I used it for fishing, but as my ambitions grew, so did my ship. I added to it, upgraded the engines, and redid the rigging. It was as ugly a ship as ever sailed the seas, a patchwork of sails and steam, but I loved my *Molly Gee* dearly. I went south to the Caribbean in the winter and north to Nova Scotia in the summer. Wherever the ports were friendliest to me. Carrying a little of this, trading a little of that. But such sailing was a lonely business. Books became my comrades. I found myself haunting whatever stores or market stalls I could find. Being a seafaring man, I tended to purchase books about the sea."

"I'm surprised your ship didn't sink between ports," I said, looking around at the piles. "There's quite a bit of ballast here."

"A bit of ballast," Captain Leo roared. "A bit of ballast! Why, if I'd put all these on the *Molly Gee*, she'd have disappeared beneath the waves. No, no, every time I came home, I left my purchases with my friend Cuffe. When I finally retired, he told me I could live with him only if the books found a new home. Eventually I sold my ship and bought this shop." He pointed at the ceiling above us. "I've added a few more books since then. The attic is practically full now. But don't tell Cuffe. Oh, don't tell Cuffe!"

His shoulders shook with silent laughter. "A bit of ballast." He wiped his eyes with one hand. "What an idea!"

"Still, this doesn't seem like much of a town for a bookstore," I said, remembering the general air of a place past its prime we had seen in Innsmouth.

Captain Leo shrugged. "Property is cheap here, and we need businesses other than shipping and fishing. Devil Reef is a problem for ships, but the world's changing. Miss Malone has some ideas for reclaiming the harbor. She's even been talking about dredging, but that's a good many years away. Sometimes, a little rot can be a help, too. I doubt I'd have bought a building so easily in Boston or even Arkham."

After taking a few fortifying sips of tea, I asked, "When did you see the grimoire?"

"A day or two ago," said Captain Leo. "I was down at the water's edge, fishing off the dock in the early morning, and watching the two young men loading the *Gulliver II*."

"The seaplane?" I asked.

"Yes. Fascinating contraption. Nova Malone named it after her ancestor's lost sailing ship, but her latest vessel sails through the air, right over Devil Reef. If I were younger, I'd be tempted to learn how to fly such a thing. Imagine how quickly and easily you could go up and down the coast," said Captain Leo. "No fear of storms or rough seas. You could fly above the waves and the clouds."

"Well, it can still be pretty rough," I said, thinking about my cross-country trip with Wini. "If you hit a rising or falling column of air, it bumps the plane. Some flights can be very bumpy indeed, just like being tossed around by the waves."

"Oh, have you flown?" said Captain Leo with great interest. "I would dearly like to ride in an airplane."

"Then come to the air show," I said, handing him a pair of Wini's tickets as well as a poster for the show. "Bring your friend, too. There's considerable entertainment, including a daredevil female pilot and an even more daring wing-walker."

"I will," declared Captain Leo. Looking at the line "All are welcome!" printed across the bottom of the poster, he nodded again. "I will indeed."

"But the grimoire?" said Tom, finally looking up from the book he was reading.

"Ah, yes," said Captain Leo. "The cover of the book glittered in the sun so naturally it caught my eye. Albie gave the book to the pilot as they were preparing to take off. I heard him say something about using it for their navigation."

"Albie? Nova Malone's driver?" I exclaimed. That man kept popping up like a bad penny. I wondered why he was wandering the streets of Innsmouth today. I glanced toward the windows, but the bookshelves completely obscured the front of the store. Just as well, I thought. If we cannot see out, Albie cannot see in.

"You know Albie?" Captain Leo asked.

"We have not been formally introduced," I said, "but we've certainly had encounters."

"Yes, when Albie gave the pilot his instructions, I clearly saw the book had a most unusual cover, green shagreen with gilt and jeweled decorations. When you said your name, Tom, that's when I remembered where I'd heard of such a cover. On the Deadly Grimoire."

"It certainly sounds like our grimoire," Tom said.

We thanked Captain Leo for the tea. Tom made a significant purchase of books from the bookseller, and I helped him carry his haul back to the roadster. Quickly checking up and down the street, I saw no sign of Albie or his partner.

"Captain Leo saw the Deadly Grimoire," said Tom. "I'm sure of it. Why, that little... uh..." Glancing at me, he modified whatever he'd meant to say. "That plug-ugly Albie kept saying he didn't have it. He kicked me, too, when I told him I didn't have it."

"Do you think Albie and his partner stole the grimoire from the professor?" I said. "Why would they do that?"

"To retrieve it for Nova Malone," said Tom. "She was furious we had sold the grimoire twice and delivered the book to the professor."

"But you told her you would honor the sale and recover it from Christine," I said, loading Tom's books onto the backseat of the roadster. I was trying to figure out what had happened in the last week. "Why steal the grimoire before you had a chance to make good on your promise?"

"Perhaps she didn't want anyone to know she had the grimoire," speculated Tom.

"Nova Malone arranged to have the grimoire stolen from Christine," I said, "but pretended she was still hunting for it. Perhaps so Hughes wouldn't know she had it. After all, most people would assume if you were looking for something, you didn't know where it was."

Tom nodded. "That makes a devious sort of sense."

"Oh, I suspect Nova Malone is a very devious woman," I said. "And clever, too. Then Albie gives the grimoire to the pilots. The seaplane goes… where?"

"To judge by its condition when it was towed back to the harbor," said Tom, "the flight was somewhere very unsafe."

"And the pilots reappear on the cliff road like others who have flown for Nova Malone," I said. "I bet all the planes that have disappeared recently were flying the same route. Except only the seaplane returned. For the rest, the planes and the pilots are separated, and only the pilots make it back." Perhaps Nova, like Captain Leo, purchased scarves and mittens from the church bazaar designed to lead lost sailors or lost pilots home, I thought.

"But where is the grimoire now?" I said as we climbed back into the roadster. "Still on the seaplane? Then Nova has it. She would have searched the plane for the grimoire as soon as possible."

"Could the book be with the pilots?" said Tom. "If one of them was carrying it in their clothing?"

"Oh, dear," I said, remembering Albie's visit to the doctor. "If it's with one of the pilots, then it's probably at the hospital. Hughes was heading there this afternoon."

I turned the car around as quickly as possible and started out on the road to Arkham.

"Where are we going?" Tom shouted over the engine's roar.

"Back to Arkham," I yelled. "Back to the hospital. To steal the grimoire before Hughes finds it." I told Tom how Albie had visited the doctor and Hughes had been anxious to return to the hospital to see the pilots. "I'm sure Hughes is after the book, too."

"Why?" said Tom, gripping the door handle as tightly as he could. "And do we need to go so fast?"

"Yes," I said. "Hughes is searching for the same thing as Nova Malone."

"And what's that?" yelled Tom as we soared down the road.

"Gulliver Malone's secret way," I said. "His Northwest Passage." Gulliver Malone had found a way to do more than fall through the mirror, I thought.

Gulliver Malone found a way to sail a whole ship to wherever it was that lay behind the windows that so fascinated Hughes. If Nova Malone could navigate a similar route, it gave her a superb way to smuggle liquor from Canada or Europe to the United States and avoid the other gangs. If I could follow the same route, could I finally find Max and bring him home?

We may have hit a bump or two, and the books were rattling around in the backseat, but I was still maintaining a safe speed as we hurtled toward Arkham. Certainly nothing I couldn't handle in the roadster.

But then a battered old delivery van came barreling out of nowhere. It raced alongside the roadster. When I glanced up, I looked into the face of Albie staring down at me with a most terrific frown. His hands were clenched around the wheel as he swerved his vehicle toward my car. Obviously, Albie had seen us in Innsmouth.

"Watch out," I yelled to Tom and sped up my darling car, trying to outrace Albie in his van.

Tom yelled something, but I couldn't hear what as we zoomed along the road.

Albie swung the van at me again. I went up and off the road onto the grass verge, hoping the heavier van would bog itself down in the softer ground.

Albie followed, racing toward us, intent on ramming the back of my roadster. I hit the gas, willing every last ounce of speed out of the engine as I roared back onto the road. Albie's van followed, sounding like some monstrous beast as it labored behind us. But it wasn't built for speed.

"Hold on," I cried to Tom as we came to a turn. I made as sharp a right as I had ever done, yanking the wheel hard and zipping along this new track. Albie tried the same maneuver, but the van was having none of that. It rocked and swayed and tipped over behind us.

Tom looked back and gave a shout of triumph. "You did it!" he yelled.

I geared down and risked a glance over my shoulder. Albie came climbing out of the van with a rifle in his hands.

"No!" I cried as I swerved to avoid being hit.

Albie shot twice. The first shot missed us. The second caught my rear tire. With a tremendous bang, the tire blew and sent us into a long sliding skid.

CHAPTER TWENTY-ONE

"What are you doing?" said Tom as I pulled the car straight and continued on.

"Driving on a flat tire," I said, wincing at the sounds coming from under my car. "At least until we make it behind those trees." I skated around another corner, more on three wheels than four, and brought the roadster to a halt. I reached for my handbag and pulled out my pistol. Enough was enough, and I had had it with that little bully Albie.

"You cannot start a shooting match against a rifle," said Tom, eyeing my gun with some trepidation.

"No," I said. "But I doubt he expects me. This should surprise him." I climbed out of the roadster and stalked back down the road. "Shoot my car! Wait until I catch him."

But Albie was gone. The van was still lying there on its side, but the man was nowhere to be seen. I heard the roar of an engine and spotted the Model T with a dented fender driving down the road. The driver looked like Albie's big friend. Albie was in the passenger seat beside him.

I walked back to my car in an absolute steam. Albie was sure to reach Nova Malone or the doctor long before we could reach the hospital.

"Now what?" asked Tom.

"There's a jack and a spare in the back," I said. "I'm going to teach you how to change a tire. It's something everyone should know."

Tom looked over his pile of jumbled books in the backseat. He straightened them up as I pulled out the tools to change the tire. "I used to have time to read," he mourned, but he accepted the lug wrench from me and began to loosen the wheel as directed. Together we managed to pull off the wheel and roll it out of the way. The spare took just a little tugging and pushing to get it into place. All in all, with Tom's help, it was the fastest I had ever changed a tire.

"You have some amazing talents, Betsy Baxter," Tom said to me after we secured the flat tire on the back.

"Thank you," I said. "Henry insisted I learn how to change a tire. He said

I couldn't go driving all over Hollywood without knowing at least that much about cars."

"Who's Henry?" said Tom as we climbed back into the roadster.

"The man who takes care of my cars," I said. "And how I'm going to face him, given the state of this car, I don't know. Maybe Lonnie can do some repairs at the airfield."

Driving on the spare, I kept our speed down as I wasn't too sure of the tire.

By the time we reached the hospital, no visitors were allowed. Tom and I did our best, but the nurse at the front desk was firm that we had to wait until morning. We could not go into any patient's room, no matter how urgent.

"But what will I tell my mother?" I finally wailed in desperation. "He's quite her favorite son."

"Who, dear?" asked the nurse.

"The pilot…" I burbled on Tom's shoulder as he tried to look concerned and not puzzled by my antics.

"Who is she talking about?" asked the nurse again.

"The pilot, the one found on the cliff road," Tom muttered. Of course, neither of us knew the names of the pilots, which made our inquiries quite suspicious. Even I wasn't sure if this latest attempt at sliding by the nurse's guard would work.

"Oh, why didn't you say so immediately?" said the nurse. "Neither of those men are here. Nova Malone had them checked out hours ago."

"Really?" I said, lifting my head off Tom's shoulder and making as big a play as possible with the white handkerchief Tom stuffed into my hand. "Did she take them home? Mother will be so delighted."

"Oh, no," said the nurse. "They went to Bluff Mansion. The men were sent in an ambulance with all the proper attendants. Miss Malone took Dr Hughes in her fancy car. Everyone knows her car."

I'm sure they did, I thought. The Rolls was hard to miss. Still, I was baffled by this seeming cooperation between Hughes and Malone. Who had the grimoire? Or were they sharing it?

"Was Albie driving?" asked Tom in a casual way.

"Oh, you know Albie," said the nurse, revealing herself to be a local woman. "Yes, he was driving. He'd had an accident earlier, just some bruises and scrapes, but we patched Albie up here while Miss Malone made her arrangements with Dr Hughes. Then they all left together."

Outside the hospital, Tom watched me pace back and forth by the roadster. "Where to next?" he said.

At that point, I was convinced the Deadly Grimoire was exactly what I needed to find Max. Which was foolish, as I had absolutely no idea how to use the thing. Still, I was tired of everyone stealing it and shooting at my car and causing general misery all around. I felt it was time to take the glittering book away from Nova

Malone and the doctor. Eventually, when I cooled off, I might give it to Christine. Then I decided Christine would know exactly what to do with the grimoire.

With everything solved in my head, I still needed a plan of action as I told Tom. "I would go back to Bluff Mansion," I said, "but I've already been to the sanitarium today, and Ezra Hughes might well question my sudden interest in the pilots. Besides, by now, either Nova or Ezra has the grimoire. If it's Nova, she will keep it close. Perhaps a return trip to the Purple Cat would be wise."

"Or perhaps we should find a garage," said Tom. "Is the car supposed to be leaking like that?"

I looked down to see a spattering of oil drops on the ground. Bending further to look right under the car, I could see that my forays over rocks and other debris had done my poor roadster no good at all. "You are right," I said. "I'm not even sure I should drive as far as a garage. Let's find a phone and call for a tow."

We arrived back at the airfield riding in the front seat of a tow truck with my roadster being dragged behind. Lonnie was the first to come running out.

"What have you done to your beautiful machine?" she cried to me.

"A few minor mishaps," I said.

"We ran off the road after being shot," Tom added.

Wini came strolling out onto the field with a grin. "Sounds like fun," she said. "I should have gone with you."

"If you had been driving," Lonnie said as she directed the tow driver where to park my car, "there wouldn't even have been a chassis left!"

"Can you repair it?" I asked Lonnie. "I am sorry to put you to this work so close to the show."

"The planes are fine," said Lonnie as she dived under my car to assess the vehicle's condition. "Betsy Baxter! You cannot drive through fields in a lovely machine like this. Stick to the roads!" Her voice was a bit muffled from being halfway under the car, but her scolding was clear enough.

Tom pulled his stack of books out of the backseat. "I will add these to my luggage," he said. "It will be nice to have something to read on the train trip back to Boston. Although Boston is going to seem very tame after all our adventures."

More clanging and Lonnie's annoyed shout could be heard from under the car. "Honestly, you shouldn't be allowed to drive anywhere, not if you're going to do this to a car!"

"Are you a menace on the roads now?" Wini asked with a grin.

"I'll leave you to explain," said Tom, walking off.

"Coward," I muttered after him. But when I related our adventures to Wini, I gave him full credit for his help. "I'm not sure the nurse at the hospital would have even told us where the pilots were, except he kept batting those eyelashes at her and waving handkerchiefs at me. She asked me if he was married when we went back to call for the tow truck," I said. "And then complimented me on having such a gentleman for a brother."

"He's a nice man," said Wini. "The crew agrees. He's also a whiz on the phones with the press." She pulled a newspaper clipping from her pocket and displayed her smiling photo along with a large paragraph of text on the upcoming show. In bold headlines, it proclaimed "Read All About the Woman Without Fear Who Flirts with Death in Her Airplane." The following story gave Wini's height and weight and mentioned twice she had recently appeared in Hollywood, lending her talents to the movie studios and immortalizing her stunts on film.

Reading the article, I was struck by an idea. "You should show films of your flying along with the show. I can send you reels of our movie."

Wini cocked her head at me. "How could we do that?"

"Set up a projector and a screen," I said. "Lots of small towns just drape a sheet against a wall and set the chairs outside."

"I think people come to see the actual flying," said Wini. "Or to go up in a plane. That's popular and why Bill does the short hops between my stunts. We were going to take people up, circle around Arkham, and then land back down here. On Sunday, we might even fly between Arkham and Innsmouth. There's a little landing strip there used by the mail flyers."

"Movies would be popular while people wait to go up in a plane or for the stunts to start," I said. "We could even cut a special reel from the footage we took in Hollywood. Insert a few cards to explain what is happening."

"Wouldn't we need music?" Wini said. "To accompany it?"

"A wind-up phonograph works," I said. "Or hire a local musician. If you have a talker in your group, have somebody narrate the stunts as they are shown on the screen."

"Who needs a talker?" asked Tom, who returned without any books in his hands.

"Apparently I do," said Wini, outlining my idea to him.

"Five cents for the movie," said Tom, "and sell a pamphlet about your life to the crowd afterward. It's a clever idea, Betsy, and sure to make money for the show."

Wini looked at the pair of us. "I would have to hire somebody to run the projector as well as give the talk. Bill and I need to fly the planes."

"Local crew," I said. "Didn't you tell me you hired a few in every town? This would be only a couple more."

"Sounds interesting," said Lonnie, coming out from under the car. "I wouldn't mind having some cameras to tinker with as well. I had a thought about mounting them in the undercarriage of the plane."

"Aerial footage of your stunts," Tom said. "There'd be a market for that."

Wini nodded. "Perhaps. I'll have to think about it. You and Betsy do have good ideas."

"Fantastic at publicity ideas," said Lonnie, rummaging in her toolbox. "But useless around machines."

"Tom helped me change a tire," I said, feeling the need to defend our mechanical prowess.

"Anyone can change a tire," said Lonnie, unimpressed. She pulled up the hood of the car and sighed. "This is a mess. Betsy, you're a worse menace than Wini to cars."

"Ah, you did make menace status with Lonnie," said Wini with satisfaction. "I'm a bona fide menace to planes and automobiles, according to her. I think it is a compliment."

"It is not!" retorted Lonnie's muffled voice as she practically went upside down under the hood.

"I am not a reckless driver," I muttered to Wini as we left Lonnie to her work. "It's simply been an unusual day."

"Those seem to happen around you," Wini responded. "A car chase and a shoot-out. I'm sorry I missed the action!"

As I told her the story of our day, Wini agreed with me that it was too soon to return to Bluff Mansion. "Hughes may be in love with the sound of his own voice," I finally concluded, "but he's not completely unobservant. I've been a visitor to so many patients in the past few days they should fit me for a nurse's uniform."

Tom then made a sensible suggestion. "Visit the place when Hughes isn't around. He seems to spend a good deal of time at the hospital, and doesn't he teach at the university, too? Go when he's not there."

"I could," I said, "but what if the grimoire isn't at Bluff Mansion? What if Nova already has it at the Purple Cat?"

Wini nodded her head. "I think it is most likely that she has the grimoire now. I cannot see her moving her pilots to Hughes's place and letting the book slip through her fingers. Didn't your reporter friend say something about dance evenings at the Purple Cat? They must have a band on Friday nights. There will be a lot of people there, so we could slip in and look about for the grimoire."

"Oh, I still have the membership card," I said, digging into my purse for the numbered card we had found in the warehouse. "Do we use it to try for the other door that Darrell told us about?"

Wini grinned. "I'm game if you are."

Tom groaned but said, "I have a dinner jacket and some decent shoes."

"Shoes!" Wini said. "I have a pair of dancing shoes. Actually, they belong to Lonnie, but she always lets me borrow them. But I don't have much in the way of party gear."

"When do you think Lonnie will have the roadster repaired?" I asked.

Tilting her head at the clangs and bangs coming from my car, Wini shrugged. "It won't take her long, knowing Lonnie."

"I'll take a taxi back to the hotel. Bring the roadster this evening, say nine or ten? We don't want to get to the Purple Cat too early." Then thinking about how far it was from Arkham. "Maybe you better come by eight."

"It's a full moon night," noted Wini. "Good for flying or driving."

"Or dancing at a bootlegger's club," I said. "You're a bit taller than me, but if you don't mind a scandalously short skirt, I can lend you a sparkly dress and some pearls."

"Trying to turn me into a jazz baby?" laughed Wini.

"You'll be stepping out with one," I said.

"Whatever you can do, I can do better," Wini said. "Bring on your pearls and fancy clothes, Betsy Baxter, and let's go catch some bootleggers in action."

CHAPTER TWENTY-TWO

In my red dress with the crystal beading and a triple loop of pearls around her neck, Wini looked stunning.

"What should we do with my hair?" she asked me as we both peered into my hotel room's mirror to finish our makeup. Since her hair was longer than was fashionable, none of my bandeaus or clips, styled for my bobbed hair, appeared quite right. I looked her over and sighed. "This is so easy when my friend Jeany does it. She always knows the right piece to complete an outfit." Then an idea struck me. "Oh, we could roll it in the back and finish it off with my jeweled comb." I went digging through my jewelry box. The enameled piece I'd purchased in Argentina was probably meant to secure a mantilla, but it looked lovely affixed in Wini's coiled braid. I sprayed some perfume on her hair to help keep everything in place.

"I'm not sure I recognize myself," Wini said with a dubious glance at the mirror. "And I don't know that I could stand to do this much powder and perfume every day."

"Oh, you get used to it," I said, driving a couple more hairpins into Wini's arrangement to be sure it held through a Charleston or similar energetic dance.

"Ow, enough with the hairpins," protested Wini. "I could build an entire fuselage out of the hardware you've stuffed into my hair."

"Never doubt the power of a good hairpin," I said. "You'll be thankful for them by the time the evening is done."

In the lobby, Tom was chatting with Irving, the friendly bellboy, but sprang to attention when we emerged from the elevator. Like us, he was very polished, so much so that I suspected he'd talked Irving into giving his coat a brush and his shoes an extra shine while he waited.

"Don't we all look fine?" I said, looking at my friends.

Tom gallantly offered an arm to Wini and me. We managed to make it out the door without collapsing into giggles at the stunned expression of the night manager when we swept past him.

Between the moonlight and my headlamps, the drive to the Purple Cat was easily accomplished. The place was lit up, with cars parked up and down the road, and the sound of the band very clear as we approached the open door. I always loved a good band, and my toes were tapping on the walk to the door.

Inside, the tables and chairs had been swept to one side. The small dance floor was filled. The quartet on the stage sounded as if they were playing twice the number of instruments as they had. The crowd responded by stepping out with enthusiasm.

"Shall we?" Tom said, offering me an arm as Wini laughingly waved off the advances of the men who had descended on us as soon as we came through the door.

"Don't mind if I do," I said as we took to the floor in a Toddle. As we bounced about the room, I looked for Darrell's mystery door. As the door was painted in purple and had a certain large sailor planted in front of it, it took no great detective skills to spot.

"Isn't that one of our friends from the alley?" I asked Tom.

He maneuvered a turn and even sallied a little cheek-to-cheek to eye the mug by the door. "That's him," he said. "But he seemed a more even-tempered gentleman than our friend Albie."

"I recall that the big man counseled against shooting us," I said with a heel kick and a shimmy.

"Nothing ventured," said Tom.

"Nothing gained," I replied.

We swept in the direction of the door, collecting Wini on the way, much to the dismay of her partner. A little breathless, our trio trotted off the dance floor right in front of the purple door.

The man in charge glared down at me. "Get back to the dance," he muttered.

I pulled the Purple Cat's card from my bag and flashed it in his face. "I have an invitation," I said. "Miss Nova Malone is expecting us."

He blinked at that. "Miss Nova never said..." he began.

Wini turned to me and said, quite clearly, "If Miss Nova isn't interested, we could also discuss our ideas with the O'Bannions."

At this, the big sailor looked astonished. "You'd never give Miss Nova's business to the O'Bannions," he said.

"Why not?" Wini bluffed. "I've flown for them before."

He pulled the door open and motioned us through. "Not the O'Bannions!" he repeated as he slammed the door shut behind us. We were on a rickety landing and a long steep cellar staircase stretched down into the darkness before us. A very feeble light flickered at the bottom of the stairs. While I was pleased we had gotten past the first barrier, I was surprised at what we found.

"Ah," said Tom, "not as welcoming as I expected."

"I was thinking the same thing. It lacks a certain ambience," I agreed as we picked our way cautiously down the stairs. The walls were cold and even slightly damp to the touch, but the railing was far sturdier than one would expect from its decrepit appearance.

"Remind me, who are the O'Bannions?" said Tom.

"Tell you all about them later," I said as we reached the bottom. One small lantern sat in a niche. It cast a pale light in what appeared to be a storeroom. A few dusty cases were stacked against the far wall.

"Uh, shouldn't there be more?" Tom asked, surveying the small space.

"I think there is," Wini said, pointing at the floor.

I looked where she pointed and laughed. "I'd never dare use such an obvious clue in one of my movies."

Three distinct footprints crossed the floor, the owner of the shoes probably having tracked through something wet and sticky. Two were clearly visible, but the third footprint was only half visible, the rest disappearing under the storeroom's east wall.

I examined the wall and guessed that the card was only the first step in accessing Nova's hideaway. Real guests were probably given instructions on what to do at this stage. But I wasn't about to march back up those stairs and ask.

"It cannot be too hard to figure out," I said. "It's set up to discourage the cops and possible gatecrashers, not drive away real customers."

The wall appeared to be ordinary wood, but as the other three walls were brick, I took that to be a sign that this section was more than it appeared to be. "There should be a latch," I said, running my hands along the sides and bottom. Tom joined me and stretched his long arms to the top edge.

"Here it is," he said as something clicked. The wall slid away and revealed another flight of stairs, much better lit than the ones we had just navigated. A faint tick-tick sound drifted up the stairs as well as the clink of glasses and murmur of voices.

"Perhaps I should have brought the Mauser," Wini said.

"It would never have fit under the dress," I replied, pretty pleased with myself for figuring out how to get us this far. I couldn't wait to see what came next. "Besides, if that's not a roulette wheel, I'll eat my best hat."

We descended the second flight of stairs to emerge into a simply gigantic cave. There was indeed a roulette wheel with eager gamblers gathered around it. At the far end of the room, an enormous, polished bar sported two bartenders, mixing, stirring, and shaking cocktails for a thirsty throng. Elsewhere, small café tables and chairs allowed for intimate conversation over the beverages. The rugs underfoot and the silk coverings stretched across the ceiling and the walls gave the entire place the feeling of the sultan's palace straight from Universal's *Thief of Baghdad*.

Beneath my feet, I could feel, rather than hear, the boom of ocean waves crashing against the cliff.

"Welcome to the Smuggler's Cave," said Nova Malone as she advanced upon us. If her sparklers had been splendid in the daytime, her jewelry at night was worthy of a pirate queen. She glanced at the purple-and-white card still clutched in my hand. "I see you've found one of my lost cards. Would you care to explain?"

"It began with a book," I said. "A grimoire. But I expect you know all about it." No doubt about it, the woman was intimidating. Even in my highest heels, she towered over me. But I refused to be intimidated. "I've even heard it called Miss Nova's glittering book."

Nova Malone looked amused. "I expect I do know something. But where are my manners? Please take a seat. Champagne? Brandy? Or something stronger?"

"Champagne is always nice when you've been dancing," I replied. "Excellent band, by the way."

"I think so," said Nova as she lowered herself with regal grace into the nearest chair and waved the rest of us to seats at the table. "Did you know we broadcast our dance music on Saturday evenings? Radio is a remarkable invention. Nearly as remarkable as airplanes. I expect both to change the world, much as the change from sail to steam revolutionized shipping in the last century."

A waiter came to the table. After some whispered instructions from Nova, he left and then returned with a bucket of champagne as well as the necessary glasses. The bottle was popped with a finesse that would have impressed Irving, and the bubbly poured out.

"Now, why are you here?" Nova said as she calmly sipped her champagne. The lights in the room sparkled off the diamonds in her hair, around her neck, and encrusting each finger. Only the purple cat brooch pinned to her breast was not completely covered in the glittering stones.

"Do you have the grimoire?" Tom asked with more bluntness than I had come to expect from him.

"If I have the Deadly Grimoire," replied Nova, "I paid for it."

"I have no argument there," Tom said, "but I would appreciate being allowed to give the university a refund and to return to Boston unmolested by your man Albie."

Nova sighed and shrugged. "Albie is an excitable sort. I've often told him it creates more trouble than it is worth, waving guns around and shooting at people," she said. "I blame the movies."

"Why Hollywood?" I retorted because a bootlegger blaming the movies for moral corruption – well, that was as bad as the congressmen who made such speeches annually. And as hypocritical.

"Those cowboy films. All those shoot-outs, and stickups, and so on," said Nova. "It creates an unreal impression for most people."

"It's entertainment," I said, quite stung by her criticism and, at the same time, aware that we were in far more trouble than I'd anticipated. There was no way out of this fantastical hideaway other than the door by which we entered.

Given the number of large men dressed as waiters and bartenders swarming around the room, it seemed unlikely we could simply walk out without Nova Malone's express permission. I doubted the other patrons would give us a hand, especially since all the entertainment being held here was illegal upstairs.

For once, it seemed I had rushed into a place I could not rush out of. I didn't enjoy the feeling.

"I like your films," said Nova Malone to my surprise. "For all their silliness."

"My movies are not silly," I responded automatically, still trying to figure a way out of our current situation. "Wait, how do you know I'm an actress?"

"My dear," said Nova quite calmly. "I recognized you the first time you visited the Purple Cat. Your movies are quite popular. And your picture is in the *Arkham Advertiser* on a regular basis. I even recommended your films to my nieces. You solve your mysteries with brains, not relying upon some man to rescue you. Or to shoot your way out of trouble. Even if you do brandish your silver pistol in the earlier scenes. You are much too wise to think a gun with only six shots can save the day."

So much for the pistol in my purse, I thought, and shooting our way out. "I never want to disappoint my fans," I said. "They love a clever solution."

"Such an inspiration to other young women," replied Nova with approval. "I fought for many years to secure the vote. And to change the world. To shake it loose from the chains of the past. There are children going hungry in the winter, and farms going fallow in the spring. All because no bank will lend to Innsmouth fishers and farmers. But I will. I'll build this town back up brick by brick myself if I have to. I was born here, I will die here, and I will not let Innsmouth die with me."

I believed her. Her passionate declaration resonated with sincerity. I could see how her vision would appeal to the people of poverty-stricken Innsmouth. I was sure when Nova Malone's shipments came through the Innsmouth docks or down the back roads, people were happy to look away.

"I find all the world's recent changes encouraging," Nova continued. "The technology of today does not rely on strength alone to operate. Electricity, airplanes, and radio. I predict a much brighter future for us all."

"Madam, I hope you are right," said Tom. "If the last war taught us nothing else, technology can be used for good or evil. As can the grimoire."

"I have never feared anything," said Nova. "Not the inventions of this decade or the spells of the past. However, the grimoire has been something of a disappointment."

This last statement obviously surprised Tom. "Our grimoire has never been called disappointing," he said.

"First, I would say that it is my grimoire," Nova declared. "In fact, it could be called my family's grimoire, for we've held it almost as many years as yours. And, of course, Ezra Hughes claims it belongs to him based on his family's history. Although how being a cheat or being cheated gives one a claim, I am not sure."

"There was absolutely no cheating in our transaction," said Tom, sounding as aggrieved and peevish as I had when Nova Malone called my movies silly. She was clever to find all our sore spots. I wondered how she would needle Wini, for it was becoming clear Nova Malone was playing some game with us. I felt increasingly nervous about her ploys.

"Perhaps there was no deception intended this time," Nova said to Tom. "Simply poor bookkeeping by your uncle. But creating the False Grimoire for Bulkington Hughes? A not so innocent ruse by a Sweets."

"Oh, the family truly regrets the creation of the False Fish," said Tom.

"I am sure they did," said Nova Malone. "As much as your friend Betsy regrets what happened to Max, Jim, and, what was his name? Paul?"

At the recital of my lost friends' names, I was startled into an exclamation. "How did you know about Max? About Jim and Paul?" I said. All three had disappeared from the Fitzmaurice house during our filming there, but the newspapers rarely mentioned anyone by name. It was ancient history to most people. And almost nobody remembered Paul anymore. He'd disappeared slightly before Jim and Max, and his exact fate was never known.

"Three years of phone calls to the Arkham police, three years of calls from a studio in Hollywood," said Nova. "It's helpful when there's an Innsmouth woman working on the switchboard. When the same studio pays for the transfer of a man named Jim from the hospital to Bluff Mansion, that's intriguing, too. There are Innsmouth women working there as nurses as well as cleaning the floors and cooking for the patients. It's hard to hide anything from me. If I want to find out, I will."

The battle lines were drawn, and the match had begun in earnest now, I thought. "So you know what I am doing here."

"I might help your Max," said Nova, "if you help me. I'm a far better bet than Hughes for all his fascination with old window glass. He can only show you a glimpse of what is beyond."

"Do you know where Max is?" I said as bluntly as possible. I was tired of games.

"I know more than Minerva," Nova returned. At my look of consternation, she smiled, and it was a very cold smile indeed. "Cortland apples. I buy barrels from Minerva and her husband every year. They have a granddaughter working at the Purple Cat."

I didn't glance at Tom. I didn't look at Wini. I kept my eyes fixed on Nova. When a deadly predator crosses your path, one hunter told me, never look away. "I have no desire to end up in a hospital bed, dreaming my life away," I said. "Wherever Jim has been, it nearly broke him."

"He can be healed," said Nova. "So can my pilots. In fact, as odd as his explanations are, Ezra's ideas are not altogether wrong. I've had good reports of success at Bluff Mansion, good enough to trust my own people there."

Wini, never the most patient of souls, butted into the conversation. "It seems as if you have the book you want. Now, if you promise to stop shooting at my friends, we can all go our ways without any more trouble."

"Oh, no," said Nova Malone. "I need more from you. 1 want to charter a flight, a charting of a route if you will. It seems the Woman Without Fear would be the perfect pilot for me."

CHAPTER TWENTY-THREE

Wini quickly shook her head when Nova Malone asked for her help. "I have more than enough flights booked for the next few months," she said. "After we finish up our tour of New England, I am preparing for a race, an air derby. I cannot take any other business."

It was politely said. Also Wini didn't address Nova Malone's actual business or the legality or illegality of it. As for the lady herself, she gave no appearance of displeasure. But the room felt cold for all its luxurious hangings. Far below my feet, I was too aware of the restless boom of the surf against the cliffs. More acutely, I remembered Darrell's warning to avoid crossing Nova Malone.

"If you fly my route," said Nova, after a long silence where none of us moved, "you will win every race you enter. No one will ever find a faster way to traverse the country or even navigate around the globe. Imagine if you were to become the first woman to fly around the world."

"I have imagined it," said Wini. "I watched those eight men take off from Santa Monica on their flight around the world and wished I was part of that. Last year, I visited the *Chicago* in the Smithsonian just so I could see their plane. But I don't have three hundred or more hours for a flight. Or all the resources of the United States government. The round-the-world flight took more than half a year and plenty of supplies along the way."

"My route might only take a day. Perhaps less," Nova said. "I had a new seaplane delivered today."

Wini didn't quite snort, but she sounded firm when she replied, "There isn't any plane built today that could fly so fast. It cannot be done. That's a fantasy."

"Are you sure?" said Nova. "Even up and over the poles?"

"Circumnavigate via the poles?" said Wini. "Still not possible. I mean, you could fly over…" She paused and fiddled with her champagne glass. If she had had her silver cigarette case, I am sure Wini would have spun it on the tabletop. "Great-circle navigation, that's what you're talking about?"

Tom and I must have looked puzzled because Wini said, "It's about plotting a course around a globe, a circle that allows you to navigate the shortest distance between two points. Except such navigation doesn't allow for weather, air currents, refueling points, and all the rest."

"But what if you didn't need fuel or rest as you flew?" said Nova.

"Air resistance, winds," started Wini.

"What if you were in a space outside of all that?" said Nova. "What about a space that you could travel without gravity dragging you down?"

I finally understood her. "You're talking about Gulliver Malone's route? The one that let him win races," I said. "The one that took him on strange currents outside the world." It was exactly what Minerva warned against when we had talked to her. The cosmos where people could be lost forever without the right pattern to guide them home. The place where Max and Jim tumbled when they fell through a mirror.

Nova Malone smiled at that. "You are a clever woman," she said.

Tom shook his head. "There are no navigational charts in the grimoire. Nothing about great circles either."

"Have you've read it?" said Nova. "I thought the Sweets kept the book locked up and never let the grimoire sully their eyes. Just their bank account."

"It was the only thing I had to read on the train when I came to Arkham," Tom admitted. "I cannot say it made much sense. But I would remember navigation charts or maps. I always remember what I read."

"Do you?" said Nova. "What an interesting thing to know."

All in all, I disliked the whole tone and direction of this conversation. Especially the contemplative look Nova gave Tom after his last statement. Catching her attention was not in his interest. I believed that most strongly. In this subterranean room, with the roulette wheel ticking away like some mad clock, I knew our time was running out. Perhaps it was Nova Malone's almost unnatural calm or the way everyone else in the room ignored our table as if being with Nova Malone set us outside the circle of normal human curiosity.

No matter how thick the rugs beneath my feet, the stone was cold underneath, and the chill was creeping up my legs, the bone-cold freeze of the ocean. I remembered the stunt I'd discussed with Tom, the jump from ship to ship landing me in the Pacific. Even on a sunny day, the cold nearly shocked the breath out of me. The same cold enveloped me now.

I wanted to shake Nova Malone out of her calm, at least enough to create room for us to maneuver a way back up the stairs and out of the Purple Cat.

"You have the charts," I said to her. "The maps and navigation guides. You've been trying for months to use Gulliver's route for your own smuggling. To beat the O'Bannions and stay ahead of the feds."

At the mention of the O'Bannions, Nova's eyes narrowed the slightest bit. "The O'Bannions have their routes. I have mine. We don't interfere in each other's business."

"Not if you want to keep Naomi O'Bannion out of your hair," said Wini. "There's a woman I wouldn't want to upset."

"I am not afraid of the O'Bannions," said Nova.

"But you do have a problem with losing your planes," I said. "Everyone who has flown for you has come home. But what about the planes and cargo? How many have disappeared?"

"That's right," said Wini. "All those missing planes!"

"And ships and trucks, according to Darrell," I said. "All suffered the same fate as what happened to the original *Gulliver*. They all disappeared."

"A truck is easy to replace," said Nova without any concern. "But several thousand dollars' worth of Canadian whiskey. That's more difficult. Buyers grow impatient. Investors begin to ask questions."

The bartenders called for last orders and the customers began slipping away through the door leading upstairs. A glance at my watch showed it was well past midnight. The more the crowd thinned, the larger and more menacing Nova Malone's employees looked. As people left, nobody spared us a glance.

"But your seaplane came through," Wini said to Nova. "They towed it back into the harbor."

"With the wings broken and the pilots wandering the cliff road," I said.

"A better result than our earlier flights without the grimoire," said Nova with a shrug. "Unfortunately, they missed the rendezvous and failed to pick up the cargo. That's still to be done."

"A ship to plane transfer, seaplane smuggling, and you're using Gulliver's routes to avoid the G-men," I said, ticking off my guesses or deductions with my fingers, remembering the newspaper stories over the past few months about bootleggers. "A ship is waiting for you to pick up their cargo, which would be diverted from Canada or Europe."

"You are clever," Nova said again. "A ship is docked at a small island north of here, which can only be reached by a seaplane or boat. We tried boats, but on Gulliver's route, it led to disappearances in the harbor. But, in the air, with the grimoire, I think we could transport our cargo safely. We nearly made it on this last run. Hughes claims his formula will let the pilots fly the entire route, so I'm prepared to make a deal with him. And with you." She stared straight at Wini.

Wini shook her head again. "No," she said firmly. "I'm not flying the grimoire's route or any other for you."

"Unfortunate," said Nova. "Then, for now, I think you should stay here. At least until I've made all my arrangements. Perhaps you'll reconsider your plans."

"We have a show tomorrow," said Wini.

"Yes, you do," said Nova implacably. "I wonder how well your other pilot will perform your tricks and how the newspapers will review the performance when it lacks the death-defying Winifred Habbamock. You may need another source of income sooner than you think. And you," she said, looking directly at me, "you missed the largest clue of all."

"What do you mean?" I said.

"All your running around the countryside," said Nova as she rose from her seat. "Talking to Minerva, visiting Captain Leo, all your snooping, looking for Max. And you could have found all your answers at Bluff Mansion this morning. I spotted it immediately when I signed my pilots into Hughes's care."

"What do you mean?" I cried again as Nova walked away.

She glanced back over her shoulder. "You should look at Ezra's register next time you visit his sanitarium."

The waiters completely surrounded our table. One poked me in the back. I recognized the feel of a pistol against my spine. I had played such a scene in enough movies to know what was what. I hissed at Nova Malone. "I thought you didn't believe in guns."

"I don't believe in shooting indiscriminately," she said to me. "But I'm perfectly happy to let my men use a pistol as an incentive for good behavior. Now, behave and follow their instructions."

The instructions boiled down to "Walk this way, sister" , and a slight shove through yet another storeroom door when we reached our destination. Tom and Winifred settled on packing crates. I tried to pace, but the room was barely wide enough for me to take even a few steps in either direction. Everything had gone very wrong and, worst of all, I'd landed my friends in hot water with me.

"Now what?" asked Tom, who had the temerity or the foresight to snatch the champagne bottle and glasses from the table as we were being hustled away. He sat sipping a glass and looking as if booksellers spent all their evenings locked in storerooms.

"Why are you so calm?" I said to him.

"Would having hysterics help?" he said. "I'd be happy to oblige. I am seriously considering a career change. If gangsters are going to be part of the grimoire trade, I need a new job."

"Bill can handle the basic stuff, and there's always the plane rides," Wini muttered to herself. "But it's still a dirty trick to push us in here."

"And why are you worrying about the show?" I said to her. "We are locked in a room by a woman who thinks she can smuggle goods through … well, I don't know what I would call it, but given the glimpses I've seen, it's not a good idea at all." The world on the other side of the mirrors, the world I saw through the shard of glass Hughes carried should never be allowed to leak into our world. Of that I was certain. Storms and stinking weeds that tried to grab people and three-eyed fish. I was sure those things came from whatever Nova Malone was trying to do.

"I am worrying about my show to prevent myself from being upset," said Wini. "And I know that makes no sense."

"I understand," I said. And I did. I was doing the same thing, focusing on the small things to stop thinking about the larger implications.

"I don't," muttered Tom, but we both ignored him.

"We need to escape. The place should be empty of customers by now," I said, glancing at my watch.

"Nova didn't post a guard," Wini said to me. "At least, I didn't hear her give instructions for one."

"If you're right, now would be the time to escape," I said. "Would they just clean up and leave?"

"Perhaps," said Wini. "If Nova thought we would sit here quietly and wait for her to return."

"Obviously the lady doesn't know you two if she thinks you'll sit quietly anywhere," said Tom.

I stalked to the door and put my ear to the wood. "I don't hear anyone. Do you think they've finally gone home to bed?"

"The only way to find out is to get out," said Wini.

"Are we going to break down the door?" Tom asked.

"Like they do in the movies?" Wini said, looking at me.

"In the movies, those doors are paper," I said. I eyed the packing crates. There wasn't much we could use for tools. Certainly nothing to open the door.

"If I still had my purse, we could shoot the lock out," I said. Of course, my purse and, more importantly, my pistol was the first thing Nova Malone's goons had grabbed from me at the table. Nova had even smirked and said, "I'll have this returned to your hotel. We cannot have the Flapper Detective lose her silver pistol."

"I should have brought the Mauser," Wini grumbled.

"I still don't know where you expected to hide that. In your hair?" I said.

"In my hair? In my hair!" said Wini, springing off her crate.

"What are you doing?" I said as she knelt by the door.

"Picking the lock," she replied as she drew two hairpins out of the arrangement I had made. "It's not as good as my knife or my real lockpicks, but you were right, Betsy Baxter. These hairpins are useful."

CHAPTER TWENTY-FOUR

Wini took less than ten minutes to click the lock open. Once outside our prison, we found only a few flickering electric lights had been left on. The dimly lit corridor was empty of guards and there was no sound of footsteps. I checked my watch. It was nearly three in the morning. Hopefully too early for anyone working in the Purple Cat upstairs. I wondered when they opened for breakfast.

We explored the short corridor. Several unlocked doors revealed other storerooms, many so full of actual stores that all three of us would not have fit inside. The corridor itself ended in a blank wall of stone. If there were any hidden latches or other ways out, we failed to find them.

At the other end of the corridor, there was a door that led back into the Smuggler's Cave. It was the only locked door we had encountered since breaking out, so of course, we decided to pick that lock, too. Wini extracted more hairpins. The first two bent, but the next pair proved effective as she opened the door.

Lit by only one small night lamp, the Smuggler's Cave itself seemed a vast space to cross in the shadowy gloom. We dodged our way around the tables with the chairs stacked for the morning cleaners.

"Doesn't this seem a little too easy?" asked Tom as we approached the door to the stairs.

"Escaping?" I said. "Did you want to stay?"

"Oh, no," he said. "But in the books, there's usually ropes to be cut by bits of broken glass while water rises around the tied-up hero or heroine."

"That's only in the pulps!" I said. "And some pictures. Well, my movies always."

"I cannot believe you're arguing about escaping," Wini said as we left the main room. On the Smuggler's Cave side, a now closed door had a simple and obvious latch to slide it open. With only a feeble light behind us, the stairs were hard to see.

"This is when we could use a match and a candle," I said. "Have you ever noticed how easily those things come to hand in the movies?"

"Or adventure novels?" said Tom. "Well, we know where the stairs are and there is a railing."

We inched our way up the first few steps like intrepid turtles. The long flight seemed even longer this time, ending in the false wall we had unlatched coming down. Once again, we groped along the top of the wall to find the lever. "I have it!" said Tom. The door swung open, and it was pitch black. What light filtered up the stairs from the open door at the bottom did not reach this far.

Walking into total darkness was more than a little intimidating. I knew in my head that there was a floor in front of us and somewhere quite close another flight of stairs that ended in the door to the Purple Cat. But to step into that darkness felt like plunging off a cliff. There was a terrible feeling of the unknown ahead of me.

"All right," I said, grabbing for Tom and Wini, "it's only a room. A small room with a staircase on one side. A staircase going up and not down, so no chance of falling. We are going to find those stairs together."

And my brave, reckless friends stepped into the darkness with me.

"Found it," yelped Tom when he was the first to stumble upon the stairs with his foot. We couldn't see him, and we couldn't see the stairs, but the elation of knowing we had a way out bubbled through my veins.

Wini and I groped our way forward. I felt for the first step and had it under my feet. "Upward," I said.

"I hope the next door isn't locked," said Wini. "I'm not sure I could pick locks in complete darkness."

We went up the stairs, gripping the banister and going slowly, feeling our way. Something about being without any light at all made every sound and smell more intense and even threatening. The clack of our shoes on the stairs was loud, the beating of my heart banged in my ears, and beneath that there was another sound – the booming I had felt more than heard while we were in the Smuggler's Cave. Finally, I said, "What is that? It sounds like waves."

"It probably is waves. The tide coming in," said Tom. "High tide is just before dawn."

"How can you know that?" I said as Wini yelped when she came to a landing and fell against me in the dark.

"High tide?" Tom sounded surprised behind me. "There's a tide chart in the airfield office. I suppose it's common enough around here, being so close to the ocean."

Tom made up the last in our line, the theory being if Wini or I fell, we probably wouldn't knock him off the stairs. If he fell on us, or at least on me, that might well start a chain reaction back to the bottom.

"But how can we hear the ocean inside?" I said.

"Sound carries, and there must be ventilation shafts," said Tom. "The air is fresh."

"And smells like seaweed," said Wini in front of us. "The horrible smell it gives off when it is rotting on the beach."

She was right. There was a strong smell reminiscent of a beach at the end of a hot day. Earlier, I had been too excited to take stock of such things, too eager to search out Nova's hideaway, but now the reek seemed to grow stronger with every stumbling step in the dark.

"I wish they hadn't taken my purse," I said. "I had a perfectly good book of matches in it."

"Oh," said Tom. "I forgot." There was a striking sound, and a match flared up, illuminating two annoyed women looking down at him.

"You forgot you had matches?" I said.

He shrugged and then yelped as the match burned down to his fingertips. The spark of the dropped match fell below us, winking out finally on the stone floor below.

"I don't smoke," said Tom. "I'm not sure why I have matches in this pocket. Oh, right, I wore this jacket to the Bibliophile Club's dinner. Somebody always wants a smoke, and nobody can ever find matches. Cigars, after dinner."

"Keep moving," Wini scolded us both. "We need to get back to the airfield!"

"Yes, yes," I said and proceeded up the rest of the stairs.

The final door, thankfully, was not locked, and we emerged into the Purple Cat. A single ghost light burned on the tiny stage where the band had been playing only a few hours ago. The light seemed almost unbearably bright when we emerged from the stairs. We stopped and blinked, all of us uneasily aware of how vulnerable we were to discovery.

Like the Smuggler's Cave below, the place was full of tables with upended chairs stacked across their tops. It, too, was empty. Everyone had gone home.

The booming sounded louder in the Purple Cat, almost like the giant heartbeat of a primordial beast.

"Are you sure that is the surf?" I whispered to Tom.

"It's night, so you notice it more?" he whispered back.

"Shh," said Wini as she circled her way around the tables toward the outer door.

"There's nobody to hear us," I said with a bravado that was more hope than certainty.

Still, I tiptoed as we crossed the room to leave. Every footstep seemed like a prelude to discovery and another confrontation with Nova. This time, I doubted we would simply be locked in a storeroom.

Reaching the door, Wini snarled to find it locked when she tried to pull it open. "Not again," she muttered, groping in her falling hair for a remaining hairpin.

"It's a bolt," I said, reaching around her to slide the bolt into the open position. The door swung open with a merry little jangle of its bell that caused us all to leap like scalded cats.

"My heart cannot stand much more of this," said Tom.

"Perhaps we should have gone out the kitchen door," I said. But nobody came running.

Outside, the grass was cold and damp as we walked through it, but the sky was still clear, and the moon waxed bright. Oddly, once we were outside, the booming noise disappeared. In fact, the silence seemed utter and oppressive.

Then I heard a long mournful hoot. It was followed by another and another.

"That's a foghorn," said Wini. "Why would anyone be sounding off a fog-horn? It's perfectly clear."

I went around the Purple Cat toward the sound.

"Careful," said Tom, following me. "The cliff is close."

Once I'd gone around the building, the cliff fell away only a few yards behind the back door of the Purple Cat. A sea wind hit my face, carrying a clean salt scent. The wretched stink we'd experienced inside couldn't be detected.

The long mournful wail of the foghorn sounded again. I saw a flash of light.

"I know what that is," said Wini. "That's the Falcon Point Lighthouse. I didn't realize we were so close. A warning for ships and a beacon for night flyers. But I have never heard the foghorn wail like that."

A softer toot sounded, further out to sea. A light flashed three times, twice red and once green.

"There's a ship out there," I said, trying to make out something more. The moonlight gilded the waves and made each rolling breaker appear like the crest-ing back of some gigantic beast swimming beneath the water, but the ship was lost in the blue-black gloom of the horizon.

"Very far out," said Tom. "It's almost like they are signaling back to the light-house."

Wini looked troubled. "I thought the same," she said. "And I don't like it. Let's leave."

The others turned away, but I lingered. The light and the wail of the light-house's horn kept me rooted there. Then I saw a flash of light along the edge of one curling breaker, very faint, perhaps a phosphorescent flash, and suddenly, that feeling washed over me, that feeling of slipping out of one world into the next, the tipping upside down of all our reality I had experienced for a moment on Minerva's porch. Then the lighthouse's beacon turned toward me, and the light stung my eyes. I was simply Betsy again, standing on the edge of a cliff, and my friends were shouting at me to hurry.

"My roadster better be there," I said, concentrating on that worry rather than what had just happened. I didn't want to think about what had happened to me on the cliff's edge. I wanted to get off Nova Malone's troubled property. The wind shifted again and carried the stink of rotting seaweed.

Luckily, the car was still parked on the grass where we had left it.

"What about your key?" said Wini. "Did you lose it with your purse?"

"Of course not," I said. I hiked up my skirt and pulled the key from the pocket sewn onto my garter. Being a pleasant night, we'd left the top down and the doors unlocked.

"Another piece of Henry's advice?" said Tom as we climbed into the car.

"Of course. Never let yourself be stranded. Don't leave your key in your purse. It could be stolen." I started up the engine. The roar sounded far too loud in the predawn stillness, but I drove away from the Purple Cat without any shouts or disturbance.

"I still think it is all too simple," said Tom

"Getting away?" asked Wini.

Tom nodded.

I had to agree with him. "Nova could have locked us up better. Or taken us someplace worse."

"There are all kinds of caves along this coast," Wini agreed. "Many at the base of this cliff. Be glad Nova didn't dump us in any of those. Some flood at high tide."

"I don't think she wanted to hurt us," I said. "I think Nova wanted to delay us or even blackmail us. But I don't think she hurts people unnecessarily."

"She seems to send them off someplace that's not terribly good for their health," Tom said.

"Yes, but she makes sure they find their way home again," I said. I remembered all the people we met that seemed to think Nova Malone was a good woman, or at least a generous one. "But I am worried about Jim being at Bluff Mansion."

"And he is?" asked Tom.

"A friend," I said. "A friend who needs time to heal. But I think he would be better back in California than here." I might want to believe Nova wouldn't be violent, but I couldn't leave Jim unprotected at the sanitarium, I decided. Nova might snatch him to blackmail me and, in turn, Wini. Or Hughes could use Jim as part of his seaweed experiment, which was making me increasingly uneasy. "I think I should get Jim out today," I decided. As for Nova's statement that I should look at the sanitarium's register, I had seen it just the day before. Nothing could be learned there, I almost convinced myself.

"But we're flying today," said Wini as we sped toward the airfield.

"Which might actually be a good time to go," said Tom.

"What do you mean?" I asked.

"Didn't you give free tickets away at the Purple Cat?" he said.

"And we sent some to Bluff Mansion," said Wini. "I posted them yesterday."

"We gave away tickets in the nearby towns," I said. "And more free tickets in Innsmouth," I added, remembering our conversation with Captain Leo.

"Then most folks will be at the show," Tom said.

"And not at the sanitarium," I said. "We could remove Jim while everyone is at the show. To make it truly safe, we could send a special invitation to Hughes. Maybe tell him Wini is interested in his theories. That should draw him out."

"Who is going to remove your friend from Bluff Mansion?" Wini asked. "We're performing."

"We're performing in an airplane," I pointed out. "Couldn't we just fly there, remove Jim, and fly back into the show. You said there was a field in Innsmouth."

"There is," said Wini. "It's not too far from Bluff Mansion."

"But how will you get Jim away? You cannot stash him in the plane, can you?" said Tom. "Wouldn't you need a car and driver?"

"And you don't drive," I said with a sigh. I obviously should have brought Farnsworth to Arkham. He could have organized a rescue or two. But I needed to work with what I had. "Lonnie?"

"No, she needs to stay with the show in case of problems with the planes," said Wini. "But how about a friend with a truck?"

"Who do you know with a truck?" I asked.

"Stella! She can help us," said Wini. "How about removing your friend via the US Mail?"

CHAPTER TWENTY-FIVE

I couldn't hear the crowd over the rumble of the motorcycle's engine and the even louder roar of the plane overhead. Lonnie leaned over the handlebars as if she could push an extra ounce of speed into the bike by sheer will alone. I placed my hands on her leather-clad shoulders and boosted myself off the seat into a standing position like the stance I learned from a bareback rider. The rope ladder trailed back from the plane flying in front of us. Wini had positioned the plane perfectly with the end of the ladder almost hitting the top of Lonnie's head. I went up and off the seat in a single jump, grasping the ladder's rung firmly in both hands.

The crowd roared!

Lonnie shot away. Wini pushed the plane toward the clouds as I pulled myself up the ladder, bringing up one leg and then the other, to anchor myself firmly on the rungs. When I was halfway up the ladder, Wini turned the plane so we would fly back over the field of spectators. The momentum spun me slightly, but it was no worse than dangling from a trapeze. I relaxed into the ladder and let it settle into position.

The great sense of the noise – the airplane's engine and the wind's roar – seemed to fall away. The wind against my face felt splendid. Watching the crowd below thrilled my heart like nothing else. All my earlier fears and worries were gone in the rush of the moment.

Down on the ground, the people of Innsmouth and Arkham raised their faces to look up at us, the daring women of the sky. I unhooked one hand to wave at the crowd. Was Nova Malone below? We'd already spotted Ezra Hughes in the crowd. Tom had pointed him out earlier.

But I forgot all those worries in the thrill of the stunt. I was tired of hunting through the shadows and running after rumors. Let everyone below squint into the sun for once, trying to see us. I was going to rescue Jim. And, I vowed, I would find Max!

We passed the end of the field. Wini held the plane level and steady as I continued to climb the ladder and onto the wing. As we discussed during our drive back from the Purple Cat, I stepped onto the lower wing and hooked my arm around the strut reinforced by Lonnie for a similar trick normally done by Charlie. Wini banked again and flew back over the crowd. I waved one more time from the wing as we passed.

We continued to fly out over the fields. Now the only eyes that turned up to see us were sheep. I popped into the cockpit as we had practiced early that morning. The whole stunt was based on the training I had received earlier in Los Angeles with a few adaptations of my own. Lonnie's clever engineering helped me as the small winch allowed me to draw up the ladder and secure it on the wing. I gave a thumbs-up to Wini in the rear cockpit and saw her signal in return.

If Wini breathed a sigh of relief, I couldn't hear it over the rush of the wind. As for myself, once I had practiced earlier this morning, I'd known that this would work. And it had!

The countryside rolled past us, the late dusty green of summer trees and ripening fields giving way to the silver ribbon of the Miskatonic River. Wini followed the river to the coast, angling away only a few miles from the sea. Soon, we saw the tiny Innsmouth airfield used by the Aerial Mail Service. No other planes were in sight as Wini took us in for a landing.

We hit the ground with the thump and the bounce and the second thump that now felt routine to me. As we rolled to a stop, I spotted Stella's mail truck driving toward us.

As soon as the plane was still, I came out of my seat and onto the wing, dropping to the ground with the ease of an experienced flyer. Wini jumped down after me.

She clapped me on the back. "Well done!" Wini said. "We must teach you how to fly. Next time, I want to try that trick of climbing up the ladder, but I need a pilot I can trust."

I laughed, still so exhilarated by the stunt that I could barely speak. "It was wonderful," I exclaimed. "We'll have to do it again for the film cameras. Can you imagine the audience's reaction?"

Wini's answering grin told me she understood the value of that stunt. "It would be something," she said. "But have you thought of a reason why the Flapper Detective would have to go up in a plane that way? Don't your stunts need to fit into the story?"

With a chuckle, I shook my head. "If it looks good on the poster," I said, "it will work for the audience."

Stella came strolling toward us. We'd called her as soon as we reached the airfield. Once Stella heard our plans, she'd immediately agreed to help.

"Right on time," Stella said. "Even though the Innsmouth Post Office seems to be recovering, they were so happy I volunteered to take the route again today. They wanted to go to the air show."

Climbing up into the back of her mail van, I found a spare uniform neatly folded on one of the shelves next to the packages. A bit bigger than my usual size, the jacket pulled easily over my blouse. I stripped off my pants and pulled on the skirt. A couple of tugs to adjust the hemline, and I was set as a junior postmistress.

Outside, Wini said, "Right, so our next stop is Hughes's sanitarium?"

"Yes," said Stella. "I have some airmail for Bluff Mansion."

"Wealthy patients," I said, climbing out of the back of the van, "if they are getting airmail."

"Hughes only takes those who can pay," said Stella with some disapproval. "No charity cases for him, according to what I've heard. But there's plenty of wealthy folk with bad nerves. And families willing to pay to steady them."

"Are you sure his patients all go home to their families?" said Wini. I had been wondering the same thing. Jim had gone to the sanitarium just a few months ago, but I wondered where he would have ended up if I wasn't fetching him now.

"Where else would they go?" asked Stella as we settled into the front seat of her truck. Stella drove, Wini took the window seat, and I squashed into the middle, trying to keep my legs from interfering with Stella's shifting. From the airfield to Bluff Mansion, it was a short drive.

"They must have to repaint that every spring," said Wini, eyeing the imposing facade from the driveway after we drove through the gates. "New England winters are never kind to exteriors like that." She slid out of her seat and looked at me.

"Jim's room was on the second floor just off the back stair," I said, gesturing toward the rear of the house.

Wini nodded. "Should be easy. I'll bring him down that way if there's no staff around."

Along with the tricks, we'd also discussed who would do what in this little escapade. I decided Wini should fetch Jim. I would look for whatever Nova wanted me to see in the register. "Be quick," I said.

Wini checked her watch. "Bill will be flying loops now," she said. "Then there's the mock battle with Bill and some local flyers. If Tom talks that up enough, we should have at least thirty minutes."

"You saw how excited Tom was to be handed a megaphone," I said. "He'll still be speaking when we get back."

Stella climbed down from the driver's seat and went around to the back of the truck to fetch her mail bag. Wini took off for the rear of the house.

"Let's look at Hughes's register," I said to Stella. We'd talked on the phone about that and how to best go unnoticed into the sanitarium. "Dress as a mailwoman," said Stella, "because they will always look at the uniform and not the face."

"I don't want to run into anyone I met earlier," I told her. "I'm sure the uniform is a great disguise but not if it is Hughes or the same receptionist. She cannot be that blind."

"You'd be surprised, but when were you there?" said Stella.

"A couple of days ago," I said. So much had happened, I was surprised to realize my visit was such a short time before.

Stella shouldered her mail bag and nodded. "Let's hope they have a different person on the front desk on Saturday. It seems likely."

"So, a big staff?" I said, wondering how many were spies for Nova.

"The place employs a fair number from Innsmouth and even Arkham," said Stella. "From maintaining the grounds to supplying the kitchens. I asked around at the Innsmouth Post Office when I was picking up this mail. Lately, they've seen a lot of invoices from the local businesses."

"And are there always as many checks being mailed out as invoices received?" I asked.

"That's a good question," said Stella as we mounted the steps. "I heard the shops need to send their bills twice before payment goes out."

"Interesting," I said as we walked into the lobby. It made more sense that Ezra had approached Nova about treating her pilots with his seaweed cure. It sounded like he needed the bootlegger's money.

As I'd noticed before, the entry would have been a grand entrance hall for a family home. Now, without Hughes talking into my ear and other distractions, I noticed the shabbiness hidden by turning this hall into a receiving area for paying guests. The woman behind the main desk gave us both a slight nod. I didn't recognize her, so Stella had guessed correctly about different staff on Saturday.

"Good morning," said Stella. With a gesture toward me, she said, "This is Betsy. She's traveling the mail route with me today."

Thus Stella neatly sidestepped actual untruths or revealing my true purpose, leaving the slightly disapproving woman with the impression that I was a new recruit to the mail service.

"It's so inconvenient," said the woman at the desk, "when you lot keep changing. And the last postman even lost a few letters."

"Sorry, ma'am, you should see the regular carrier next week," said Stella truthfully.

"It's so interesting," I gushed, taking over the conversation. "Why, this house is wonderful. I'm new to the region, but I've never seen anything finer."

The receptionist puffed up like a pigeon, obviously glad for a little praise. "Isn't it fine?" she said to me.

"Yes, it is," I said. The large visitor's register sat at her elbow. I wanted to see whatever Nova noticed yesterday. I gave a slight nod at Stella. She deliberately turned her back on me and began to unload mail on the desk.

"This one is so blurred," Stella said to the woman. "Can you tell if it is James or John?"

The receptionist leaned forward to check the address. I slid the register book toward me and flipped to the last page. The whole thing really was like a hotel register with patients' names shown as arriving on a certain date and leaving on a later date. Perhaps the families leaving them here pretended this was simply a vacation in the countryside.

There in a bold slash of a signature was Nova Malone's name and next to it were two men's names as arriving patients, probably her two pilots. Then I stared at the name of another patient recorded as arriving the same day. The name was Max Taelsman, the name of my Max. And, more puzzling, he was shown as checked out this morning.

"I think you're right," said Stella. "That's definitely a James."

I barely heard her. I couldn't form a coherent thought. Max's name knocked me for a loop just as if we were going upside down in Wini's plane. Where had Max been? How had he gotten to Bluff Mansion? Why was he gone now?

The receptionist started to turn. Hastily shoving the book away, I smiled brightly at her when she looked at me. The smile was automatic, a cover for the stunned expression that would have been plastered all over my face if I wasn't accustomed to acting one emotion while experiencing another.

"This sure is a swell place," I repeated as a million questions tumbled through my mind. It couldn't be Max? Could it?

Obviously approving of my praise, she returned my smile with her own. "It's one of the finest sanitariums in New England," the receptionist declared. "We're all so proud of the doctor's work."

"Come along," said Stella, "we have a number of stops still to do."

Nodding meekly, I followed her out the front entrance. When we got to the van, Wini was sitting inside, spinning her cigarette case on the dashboard. "Seven," she muttered. "Always seven near Innsmouth."

I decided to keep what I learned to myself. I needed to think it through. I needed to talk to Tom about the Deadly Grimoire. Had Nova's use of the book caused Max to fall back out of a mirror? Or had Hughes seen him through his odd piece of glass? It all seemed too ridiculous and too strange, but I was ready to believe in the power of the grimoire.

When I opened the passenger side door, Wini said to me, "Your friend is in the back."

I nodded and went around to the rear of the van, still thinking hard about what I should do next. What could I do next?

Jim was huddled up against the mail sacks dressed in casual slacks and a shirt similar to the one he'd worn when I visited.

"Betsy," he said with a slow blink. "Am I being mailed somewhere?"

"Yes, Jim," I said as I snagged my clothing. "We're sending you to a hotel tonight. Then home to California." Stella promised to drop Jim off at the hotel after she left us at the plane and delivered the rest of the mail. I owed Stella a lot more than a simple thanks.

As for Jim, I'd arranged for Irving to take him up to a room and for a traveling nurse to pick Jim up from there. The nurse would ride with him on the train back to California. It had taken a very expensive phone call to Farnsworth, but he had everything well in hand with all possible comforts for Jim.

"That's nice," Jim muttered, settling back into the mail sacks. "Oranges would be nice. I miss fresh orange juice." He was almost asleep again, much as he had behaved in the sanitarium. Although he'd always been a champion napper on movie sets as well.

I pulled on my flight pants and folded up Stella's spare uniform jacket and skirt.

Jim stirred in his corner when we bumped over the field back to the airplane. I heard Wini and Stella chatting in the cab. It all seemed so normal, but my world was now officially upside down.

"Betsy," Jim murmured.

"Yes, Jim," I said as I fixed my goggles and helmet for the return flight. What I was going to do about Max, I hadn't decided. I supposed I could return to the Purple Cat to confront Nova. But this time I would keep a pistol in my hand, not in my purse, which meant finding a pistol to carry. I wondered if Wini would lend me her Mauser.

Jim made a distressed sound, the sort of muffled yell that a dreaming man makes.

"Jim?" I said. "Are you all right?"

Jim blinked his eyes open. "Who is Tom?" he said to me in a worried tone. "Why is Tom yelling in the mirror now?"

CHAPTER TWENTY-SIX

We flew back over the crowd with a slow barrel roll. If I had had a parachute, I would have jumped out of the plane. I was that desperate to be back on the ground.

Even when I'd told Wini what Jim had said, she'd reassured me. "We left Tom less than an hour ago," she said. "He was announcing Bill's act and the plane rides to the crowd. What could have happened to him?"

"I don't know, but I don't trust Nova Malone an inch," I said. "And we invited Ezra Hughes to the show, too." I had phoned the doctor earlier in the morning, telling him how much we admired his theories and that we had news of the grimoire. As I hoped, he'd immediately agreed to come to the show.

We circled the crowd with Wini waggling the wings in a salute to the spectators below, then circled again as I nearly wept with frustration. I needed to know what had happened to Tom. But eventually we landed.

Then we were nearly mobbed by the cheering crowd. Wini's crew had to wave them back, mostly to keep them from serious injury from the still spinning propeller.

As soon as I could break away, I searched for Tom. Everyone I asked had seen him earlier, and several people sang his praises. A few more tried to stop me and tell me how much they loved the show, but I waved them off. Nobody, not even Lonnie or Bill, could tell me where Tom was.

I finally went into the hangar where he had been sleeping. Tom's cot was easy to find. There were piles of books around it. I recognized the ones he had purchased from Captain Leo. Nothing indicated Tom had returned to his luggage since we started the show earlier.

Wini came into the barn, stripping off her gloves and her helmet as she spotted me. "Any sign of him?" she said.

"No," I answered. "I've asked everywhere. Everyone remembers him announcing our tricks through the megaphone, but nobody remembers seeing him after Bill finished his performance."

"Yes," said Lonnie, following Wini into the hangar. "I was surprised to see you flying back over the field with no announcement from Tom. I expected him to talk up your return."

"Did anyone see Nova Malone in the crowd?" I asked.

Lonnie, who'd never met Nova, looked puzzled but I explained what she looked like. And described her elegant Rolls.

"I don't remember seeing a Rolls," said Lonnie. "I might not have noticed her, but I definitely would have noticed such a car."

Wini started to look worried. "Even if he wandered off, Tom would be back by now."

"And he wouldn't leave all his books behind," I said. I could have wept with anger and frustration. I was so tangled up. I had found Max, or almost found Max, and I'd definitely lost Tom. If that was my fault because I defied Nova and teased Hughes, I'd never forgive myself.

"Miss Baxter, Miss Habbamock," a voice called outside the hangar.

"Darrell," I said to Wini. I looked through the hangar door to see the *Arkham Advertiser* reporter waving at us.

"A few photos?" he called, holding up his camera.

I went outside to question Darrell. "I'm looking for Tom," I told him. "Have you seen him since the show ended?"

Darrell started to shake his head, then stopped. "I did," he said slowly. "At least I think it was him. He was climbing into a car with Dr Hughes."

"When?" I asked, and I could have shaken Darrell when he paused to reflect.

"Just after you flew away and the other pilot started his aerobatics," Darrell said. "Yes, that's it. Tom announced those. Then a few minutes later, I saw him with Hughes."

"Do you remember what the car looked like?" I said.

"A Model T," said Darrell promptly. "And before you ask me, it was black. But it did have a dent on the front fender. I noticed it was splashed with mud and sand, like someone had been driving near the beach. There was even seaweed hanging off the back bumper."

"You wouldn't pick up seaweed along the cliff road," I said. Although the stuff seemed to be everywhere in Arkham and Innsmouth this summer.

"No," agreed Darrell. "But there's a lower road out of Innsmouth, heading toward Falcon Point, that runs right along the water's edge. It floods out whenever a storm blows in. There's always sand and mud that way. I've driven out there myself to take pictures."

"Anything else?" I said.

Darrell looked worried, never a good sign. "It's a bad area. As I said, it floods frequently. There are several caves, and that road is the only access to the beach. Last time I went, I was experimenting with low light photography in those caves."

"Caves?" I asked. "Like the ones where people were found earlier this summer?"

"Yes, a few of the missing pilots and that one boat crew was found in those caves," Darrell said. "So was Minerva Knowles, a farm wife who got lost on a fishing trip."

"I've met her," I told him.

Darrell looked a little surprised but continued, "That's one of the reasons I went back recently. To take pictures of where people were found. But I wasn't happy with the photos, so we didn't print them. I think I'm going to switch to one of the new Leica cameras. Better control on the shutter speed, better results."

"I don't suppose those caves run under the Purple Cat and Bluff Mansion?" I asked, an idea slowly forming in my head through the haze of worry over Tom.

Darrell nodded. "Yes. But most are only accessible during low tide. The sea goes right into them during high tide."

"Wait here," I said. "I'm going to get a map. Then you show me exactly where those caves are."

By the time Wini finished signing autographs and the crowd had completely dispersed, I knew where I wanted to go. I told Wini what Darrell had seen and what the map showed of the road along the shore.

"Look how it curves here," I said, tracing the route Darrell suggested. "This would put us almost underneath the Purple Cat. What if the Smuggler's Cave had a back entrance and a staircase that led all the way down to the water?"

"You think that's how Nova is bringing in her liquor?" said Wini.

I studied the map. "She could land a seaplane or bring a small boat along the coast here and unload into the caves," I said. "Shipments going elsewhere could be loaded into trucks that take the beach road, then driven wherever needed."

"Makes sense," said Wini. "In which case, calling her speakeasy the Smuggler's Cave seems pretty daring."

"She said she didn't fear anything. I guess that includes investigations by the feds," I said. "Besides, everyone around here seems to avoid that bit of coast due to unusual currents," I finished, remembering Minerva's tale.

"Or Nova Malone's excitable men, like Albie, protecting her stash," Wini said. "Maybe that's why she locked us up. So we weren't out on the cliff road when a ship came in. Remember the noises we heard on our way out of the Purple Cat and the ship flashing its lights?"

"Perhaps," I said. Although those booming sounds seemed stranger than just a seaplane landing or a ship coming close to shore. I remembered the odd flash of light I'd seen, and I was certain that somewhere out at sea, Nova had opened Gulliver Malone's route. "If Hughes took Tom to one of Nova's hideaways, and it does seem like he is working with her men, then that's the most likely place for them to go."

"You're not driving out to those caves alone," Wini said.

Lonnie finished up her inspection of Wini's plane and wanted to know where I was going. When I told her, she moaned. "I just finished putting your car back together. You can't take it down a road covered in sand. You'll probably even try to drive it into one of those caves."

"I'm not sure what's out there," I said, "but it is probably more dangerous than anything we've done so far."

"Then you need me to ride shotgun," Wini declared. "I'll fetch the Mauser."

"There's the Beretta, too," said Lonnie. "I'll get it. There's not much ammo for that, but you can get off a shot or two."

"Did you raid an army depot?" I said when she returned with the rifle.

"Won the rifle off another pilot," said Wini. "He bet the Beretta that I wouldn't copy one of his stunts."

"She flew through an actual barn," said Lonnie, "and only a maniac tries that one."

"I was wonderful," said Wini with a wink.

"You're a reckless daredevil," said Lonnie to Wini. Then she turned to me. "And you better take me with you. Wini is an ace with that Mauser, but I'm better with the Beretta. Also, I'll be there with my tools in case you break something." She heaved her toolbox onto the backseat of the roadster and settled beside it. "Wini, fetch the lanterns and the ropes we use to tie the tarps down. We may need those, too."

"Good idea," said Wini, who ran into the hangar. She came out a minute later and passed those supplies back to Lonnie. "I have extra matches in my pocket, too," she said to me as she climbed into the front seat. "And this." She flashed her switchblade at me. "In case Tom's tied up this time. And if we need to pick a lock–" she held up a case of lockpicks "–these are stronger than your hairpins."

"That's everything but a picnic basket," said Lonnie. "Let's go."

"You're both good friends," I said. "Let's find Tom." I tried to sound cheerful, but the sudden partnership of Ezra Hughes and Nova Malone made me very nervous indeed. If I'd been honest, I would have said, "Let's find Tom before it is too late."

CHAPTER TWENTY-SEVEN

The road ran right onto the beach at the base of the cliff. At times, the road actually disappeared under the sand. We pulled the chains out of my trunk and affixed them to the wheels. It was slow going, and Lonnie winced and muttered about damaging a fine machine every time I went over a bump, but we eventually made it to the very end.

The road stopped at some large boulders, obviously meant to keep idiots like us from driving into the surf during high tides. Getting out, Lonnie eyed the line of dead seaweed marking the tide line. The smell of rotting vegetation was brimstone strong, the worst I'd ever encountered near the ocean. It reminded me of the stench we noticed on the lower stairs of the Purple Cat.

"It looks like the water doesn't come past these rocks," said Lonnie, "but let's back up the car and turn it around."

I was impatient to go along to the sea caves. I could see the dark entrances from where we were parked. "Why waste time?" I said.

"Because if we have to leave in a hurry, we want to be able to leave in a hurry," said Lonnie, pulling two lanterns and the Beretta out of the back. She slung the Beretta over her shoulder. Then she handed one lantern to me and one to Wini.

"Aren't you going to carry one?" asked Wini.

Lonnie shook her head. "You can shoot one-handed with that Mauser, but I need both hands for the rifle." She shouldered a coil of rope and slipped a wrench into her pocket. "Besides, I have a flashlight." She waved the flashlight at us, then shoved it under her jacket.

Rather than stand and argue with Lonnie, who appeared to have a stubborn streak a mile wide, I turned the car around and even drove it up the road a few yards to make sure I parked well above the high tide line. The strong smells and steady moan of the wind playing through the rocks and caves convinced me we were on the right track to finding a secret entrance to the Smuggler's Cave and Purple Cat. I was sure this was what we had been hearing and smelling when we had escaped earlier.

But why had Hughes snatched only Tom? Nova had obviously notified him that we'd escaped her. Why not wait until Wini and I were back on the ground and take all three of us? Fear of the crowd noticing? Or was he using Tom as bait? Why would he want to lure us here?

I rejoined Lonnie and Wini, and we picked our way over the rocks to the closest cave mouth. A glance inside showed it was a shallow cave with seaweed piled against the back wall. By the waterline marked on the cave walls, this was one that filled up at high tide.

"Nobody would store anything here," Wini decided. "It would be carried out to sea too soon."

"It's too close to the road," I said. "If someone was looking for smuggled goods, it would be the first place they'd look."

A couple more caves proved to be similar – shallow and filled only with the detritus brought in by the waves.

We continued down the beach. Right at the base of the cliff, we walked on rocks and shingle, sliding and grinding under our feet. Sometimes it was dry and sometimes wet as the cliff curved away and then back toward the ocean. After clambering over a group of boulders, we found ourselves walking across damp sand.

"Tide comes all the way up to the cliff's base here," said Lonnie.

"Yes, but maybe not into that cave," I said. This cave's mouth was a little above the beach, and there was a clear path leading up to it. As we followed the path upward, we found marks, signs that something heavy had been dragged across the sand.

In the entrance of the cave, some broken boards were piled in a corner and partially burned.

"Ship's pallet," Lonnie pronounced after examining it. She pulled our road map out of her pocket and marked the location of the cave as well as where we had left the car.

I stood by the remains of the fire, looking back out to sea. "At night," I said, "you could see this."

Wini nodded. "You could, but only from the sea. Not from the beach road. Not the way the cliff curves. Nor from above if you were going along the cliff road."

"Yes," I said. "I think you could only see it from out there." I pointed at the waves rolling toward us.

"You might spot it from a plane," said Wini. "Even more likely from a ship."

I nodded and turned away. The floor sloped upward from the entrance. The back of the cave was lost in inky darkness. This looked like a much more promising spot to explore than the earlier caves. I set out without waiting for the others. If Tom was in there, I was going to find him.

Coming behind me, Lonnie pulled her flashlight out of her jacket and directed the beam onto the ceiling and walls. She stopped at one point and used the flashlight to reveal where the cave walls had been chiseled to form shelves and niches. We lit the lanterns as we ventured deeper into the cave.

"Anything stored in these would be above the water, even if a storm surge came into this cave," Lonnie decided.

Wini moved to the front with her Mauser in one hand and lantern in the other. "It goes up here," she called back. "There's some steps carved into the stone, but it's mostly natural passageways, I think."

"Keep going," I said. "Talk later." I hoisted my lantern higher, hoping I would see some sign of Tom. But there was nothing except damp rock, gleaming in our lamplight.

The cave twisted and turned. At points, the stone walls were so close that we had to shift sideways to proceed. At other places, Lonnie, Wini, and I were able to walk three abreast. The further we went, the higher we went, the path ever twisting upward. At various points, Lonnie pulled a compass out of her pocket and compared its readings to our map.

"The way we are heading," she said, "I think we'll be almost under Bluff Mansion soon."

I checked the map and saw how she traced our possible route under the cliff against the road above. I remembered the hedge blocking the view of the ocean from the patients in the garden. But I had heard the surf when I had been at Bluff Mansion.

"I was sure this would lead us under the Purple Cat," I said to Lonnie and Wini.

"No," said Wini, studying the map. "The Purple Cat is here." She tapped a spot on the map at some distance from where Lonnie marked our location. "This passage cannot lead to the Smuggler's Cave."

"What would Ezra need with smugglers' routes?" I wondered out loud.

"Just because the tunnels are here, doesn't mean he built them," said Wini. "My guess is that his ancestors were as crooked as the Malones. Smuggling and piracy were always big on this coast."

"That would explain the mansion," I said.

We continued on. Other than the burned and broken pallet at the entrance of the cave, we saw no evidence of bootlegging or even of anyone using the passage. But the further we went, the more obvious it became that the passageway was no longer natural but rather a carefully carved extension of the existing caves.

"We're almost directly under Bluff Mansion now," Lonnie said as she checked the map. "This is odd."

"What?" I said.

Lonnie had ducked into a niche carved out of the rock, almost a small alcove off the main path. I followed her. As we played our lights around the room, I realized the walls were carved with patterns. Patterns that were eerily reminiscent of those knitted by Minerva and her husband. Similar to the pattern of shells left by the minister's mother on a table in the church's vestibule.

But these patterns were not exactly the same. The strange symbols were carved in sprawling lines across the walls and whirled into spirals that spread across the ceiling and floor of the room. Just looking at them made me feel like I was standing on a ship's deck, a ship tossed by very angry seas.

Lonnie pulled her flashlight away from scribbling across the wall and concentrated the beam at the niche at the end of the room. "Is that glass?" she said.

"I think so," I said, moving closer. The room felt like the interior of an icebox. Goosebumps sprang up across my arms. Somebody had troweled plaster across the back of the niche and carefully placed shard after shard of beach glass into the plaster. It formed the shape of a creature. I would have called it a man for the arms and legs, but the head was wildly misshapen, more reminiscent of a fish than any mammal's head. The jaws were open and pointing toward the sky. The thing had teeth, teeth made of glass, that glittered in the lamplight.

Lonnie took one look and then turned away, following Wini down the passage, but I lingered. This was not Minerva's pattern. This was not what the minister's mother created in the church. This was different, something much colder. I was absolutely convinced without knowing why that this was truly evil.

A jaw big enough to swallow the world, that's what the artist had created. The more I looked at the monstrosity, the more the little pieces of glass forming the horror seemed to melt into one single image, a fish-man shaped window that showed me a view of a world that appeared both familiar and dreadful. When I walked with Jim in the garden and peered into the murky pool, I had seen shapes like this, creatures and plants that swayed as if submerged underwater.

Once before, in a house on fire, I had looked through the smoke and into a mirror that wasn't a mirror, reflecting a world that didn't exist.

At the house, Max pushed me out a door and saved me from the fire. But now I remembered he also saved me from the mirror's fascination. That was the moment in Arkham that I had forgotten, the memory of what had happened that day that had teased my dreams but I had lost until now.

Now I knew why I needed to save Max. Because that day, he had paused, stared into the mirror, and fallen through it to save me.

"Here's a door!" Wini shouted from a little ahead of us in the passageway. I stumbled out of the niche and toward the comforting light of her lantern.

The door that confronted us was sturdy and in good condition, but the hardware of the hinges and handle had the look of the last century. Wini tried it, but the door was locked.

"Now aren't you glad I brought these?" she said, pulling out her lockpicks.

"You have to teach me how to do that," I said as Wini knelt by the lock and fiddled with it.

"It's easy," said Lonnie. "I could teach you."

"Don't forget that you learned from me," said Wini, standing up and twisting the knob. The door clicked open.

"Anything you can do," Lonnie said as we advanced.

"I can still do better," said Wini. "Should I lock this again?"

"Best not," I said. "We may want to exit in a hurry." But I didn't want to go back down the passageway and pass the strange tribute to a mythical creature created in a glass mosaic. I hoped this way out would lead us to daylight and fresh air.

We entered what was clearly Bluff Mansion's cellars. Wine barrels were stacked around all the walls.

"So Hughes is smuggling?" Wini asked, looking at the barrels and crates that filled most of the room. At the edge of our lamplight, I spotted stairs leading up to the mansion.

"I don't think so," I said. A fishy, briny scent filled the room. I went over to one of the barrels. Spotting a crowbar left beside one, I used it to lift off the top.

"Aargh," said Wini. "What is that smell?"

"Not alcohol," I said, peering into the barrel. "Seaweed." Something about the almost gelatinous mass of decaying seaweed caught my eye. "Turn off your lantern," I said as I turned down the flame in mine. Wini looked at me strangely but shuttered her lantern.

"Shine the flashlight away from the barrel," I told Lonnie. She did so. "There, do you see it?"

"See what?" said Wini. "It's dark now."

"No, it's not," I said. "Look at the top of the barrel."

From the opened barrel of seaweed shone a pulsing, purple light.

"That's not normal." Wini sounded surprised, and I was almost as stunned. The purple light created horrendous shadows across the wall, almost as if tentacles reached out of the barrel toward the upper floors of Bluff Mansion.

"Do you think that's what Hughes is feeding his patients?" said Wini.

"If it is," I said, "I'm glad we got Jim out of here." And I needed more urgently than ever to find Tom and keep him away from this horrible seaweed. Whatever experiments Hughes was doing with the stuff were as dangerous as any game Nova played with the Deadly Grimoire.

"Wini, Betsy, come here!" called Lonnie from further into the room. "There's somebody tied up behind these barrels."

"Tom!" I cried, relighting my lantern and rushing toward Lonnie. "Is it Tom?" I felt a rush of relief at finding him.

Lonnie's flashlight revealed a pair of hands tied with rope, just visible by looking between a stack of barrels against the far wall. At our approach, the prisoner's heels drummed against one of the wooden barrels in a staccato signal for help. Muffled shouts also sounded as if the prisoner was gagged.

"Help me move these," I said to Wini, setting down the lantern and pushing the barrels to one side. Wini grabbed another and pulled it out of the way.

"Betsy," said Wini as we rolled away a third barrel. "That's not Tom."

I met the angry eyes of the prisoner as she rolled over to face us. Her hands were tied behind her back. Her ankles were also tied. Somebody had gagged her as well. Her hair was in disarray and one shoulder of her dress was torn as she'd obviously struggled to free herself.

"No, that's not Tom," I said. "Hand me your knife."

And I knelt to cut the ropes imprisoning a furious Nova Malone.

CHAPTER TWENTY-EIGHT

"It was Hughes," said Nova as soon as she had pulled the gag from her mouth. "That no-good skunk of a man stole my grimoire. And my pilots. Who he will use to hijack my plane."

"Why?" I said as I cut through the ropes around her ankles. "Why would Hughes want to fly your secret route?"

"Hughes doesn't want to fly my route," said Nova, shaking the ropes off her ankles. "Hughes never cared about bootlegging, except that I could afford his fees when my drivers and pilots needed his treatments. Hughes wants to be an explorer!"

She spat the last sentence out like a curse.

"What?" I sputtered with surprise. I'd considered several labels for the doctor, but that one didn't fit. "He's a doctor, not Byrd or Amundsen."

"He's going to end up dead if he uses the grimoire," said Nova, climbing to her feet. "That idiot of a doctor believes he can wander along Gulliver's route, harvesting various vegetation and bringing it back here for new medicines and treatments. He's convinced he's found the cure for every phobia. A new and more powerful drug to eliminate fear itself."

"The glowing seaweed?" I said, pointing at the barrels we'd found.

"Every time we sailed Gulliver's route," said Nova, "the seaweed would appear. Not just along the beach but everywhere in Innsmouth."

"And Arkham," I said, remembering Humbert's battles with the weeds on French Hill.

"Probably," said Nova. "I found it around the caves and draped over everything that came back from Gulliver's route, including my pilots. But the more we used Gulliver's route, the more storms happened and the more of the purple seaweed appeared. Ezra started collecting it, telling people he'd pay for any viable pieces if they'd bring it here. It's not easy to preserve. Sunlight or even a dry day will destroy it. It needs to be pickled in brine almost immediately or it will start to rot."

"And what does it do?" I said.

"Apparently, in a tea, it eliminates nightmares," said Nova. "The Innsmouth women who work here let me know. Hughes did find a cure that worked for his patients. It just makes the patients who drink it very calm, very sleepy, and, well, a little bit like Minerva."

"Like Minerva?" I said. The seaweed inspired knitting? I was now completely confused, and my energy flagged. I had been so certain we had found Tom.

"Spirit writing. Receiving messages from beyond," Nova said to me. "The nurses and the orderlies knew. They'd collect up the messages from the rooms and give them to Hughes. He locked everything up in his desk and continued dosing people with his tea. He has plans to manufacture a cure-all and market it over the radio."

"Ambitious," I said with a shudder. The thought of that glowing purple seaweed going down willing people's throats made me queasy. But patent cures were popular. People paid for all sorts of strange concoctions, and this one might very well make Hughes rich. I could understand his motives.

"Don't doubt me," Nova said as she shrugged off the last of the ropes and climbed to her feet. "I would love to find an industry to help Innsmouth prosper. We are going to rot and blow away if we keep waiting for the whaling to return. It's done, and I cannot regret that because it was a hard business. Too many drowned men and too many widows. But there's other fishing, other shipping, other work to be had if people are willing to clear the harbor, repair the seawall, and invest in new technology."

"Like seaplanes," said Wini.

Nova nodded. "This could become a pleasant place for holidays, especially if you could fly up from New York or Boston harbor."

Considering the condition of the town I had visited, I doubted Nova could make Innsmouth into a summer destination.

"Why not manufacture Hughes's medicine if it works?" I said. "Medicines are legal. Booze is not. And you endangered men, too, taking Gulliver's route."

Nova stared at me for a long time in the dim light of that basement with the rotten smell of the purple seaweed rising around us.

"Partner with Hughes and manufacture his cure-all," I urged her. "It's less dangerous than bootlegging."

"Father poured a broth made from the purple seaweed down me when I was a child," said Nova. "It made a sickly babe into a large, strong, healthy girl. But it put the sea in my blood, and I'll never be able to wander far from these shores." She shoved up the sleeve of her dress and angled her arm toward the light. A patch of purple scales ran from elbow to wrist on the back of her forearm. When she shifted her arm in the light, the scales sparkled.

On Nova's arm, the scales had a weird beauty, but such a side effect wasn't desirable. It seemed Hughes's cure-all could prove to be deadly indeed.

Nova rolled down her sleeve. "I stopped drinking Papa's broth when I was a toddler. In those days, the seaweed only appeared in the winter, maybe for a day or two. Many Innsmouth families would harvest it for medicinal tea, but nobody drank it all the time," she said. "I never drank it as an adult. From what I hear, the adults, mostly men, who take it as Hughes's patients don't develop scales, but if they drink too much or too often, they become complacent, sleepy, and unable to think for themselves. They'll do what they're told and little more."

"They become lotus-eaters," I said and quoted, "'Surely, surely, slumber is more sweet than toil…'"

When Wini raised an eyebrow at me, I shrugged. "I had to memorize Tennyson's poem for school," I said. "That line stuck with me."

"Far too many in Innsmouth have become lotus-eaters in various ways," said Nova. "Waiting for something else or somebody else to change things for them but not being willing to do anything more than chant and moan and hope the sea will spit out a solution."

I thought about the niche further down the passageway and the figure made out of beach glass. Had the Hughes family looked for other, darker solutions to their money problems?

"So where is Hughes?" I said. "And Tom? And Max? And the grimoire?"

"Ezra Hughes stole my grimoire," Nova said. "And if you want to see your Tom and Max again, you need to help me get it back."

"What happened?" asked Lonnie, nailing down the lid of the open barrel of glowing seaweed. We all felt a little better with that pulsing purple light and smell once more stifled.

"Ezra had a new patient, a man named Max, when I came to visit my pilots yesterday. Ezra was going on and on about how he saw this man through that shard of glass he carries in his pocket," Nova said.

I remembered the strange world I glimpsed through the same shard and shuddered. If that was where Max had been for the past three years, he must have suffered horribly.

"The man's completely addicted to Ezra's tea," Nova continued. "Yesterday Ezra kept having him demonstrate how he could do simple tasks, like signing his name in the register, while actually in a state like sleepwalking. Ezra seemed to think I wanted men like that working for me. He claimed they'd make the perfect smugglers, never able to remember where they had been or what they had done if questioned by the cops."

Sydney and Max once tried to sell the studio on a script that was supposed to make people who watched the movie susceptible to their suggestions. I'd read the proposal and it had made me shudder. It was also why I helped Jeany hide all the evidence of that last movie at the Fitzmaurice house.

"As if I would poison the men who had lived in Innsmouth all their lives. The husbands, brothers, and sons of women who are my friends!" Nova said. "Ezra tried again today, and I turned him down flat. Then the doctor ordered Max to restrain me. I fought, but he hit me over the head, tied me up, and carried me down here. He stashed me behind those barrels."

"Where did they go?" I asked.

"The seaplane," said Nova. "It's taking off from Falcon Point to complete the rendezvous with my ship. Or at least that's what was supposed to happen. I think Ezra intends it to be a test flight to fetch back more of the seaweed. Or to prove he can control the route to his investors, similar to what his ancestors tried to prove when they set the *Bolide* out on Gulliver's route. If he's poured enough tea down my pilots' throats, they can make the flight safely. They'll also do exactly what Ezra tells them to do."

"But what about Tom?" I asked. Max's fate was horrible, but I could understand why Hughes wanted someone who wouldn't remember any crimes he was told to commit. Did he intend to control Tom the same way? The thought of his funny bright mind ruined by purple seaweed was appalling.

"Your Tom," said Nova, "has memorized the grimoire. He can say the spells without needing the book on the flight. From Ezra's point of view, that's much better than risking the loss of the grimoire."

I remembered Nova's fascination last night upon learning Tom had read the grimoire. Then she had locked him up. "That was your idea!" I accused. "You told Hughes that Tom could help the pilots navigate and you wouldn't have to risk the book. I bet you were even willing to pour that horrible tea down Tom's throat!"

Nova shrugged. "He's not an Innsmouth man. Nor could I risk losing the Deadly Grimoire again. The last time it disappeared on a voyage, with my ancestor, it took nearly thirty years to reappear at the Sweets' bookstore. The spells are vital. Gulliver's charts and maps, which are on the plane, can only take them so far. The spells keep them together, as it were, so everyone can return safely with the cargo."

"We'll have to go back through the passage and around the cliff for your car, Betsy," said Wini. "We might be able to make it to Falcon Point before they take off. Or meet them when they return? Are they coming back to the same spot?"

"They are," said Nova, checking her gold watch. "They won't have left yet. The timing has to be exact on these flights to navigate Gulliver's route. They'll take off right before sunset."

"Then we better start back," I said. "The tide should still be low enough to make it to the car." We needed to get Tom away from the doctor before he swallowed any of that purple seaweed. I eyed Nova, willing to tie her up again for all the trouble she had caused. Nova must have guessed my thoughts because she offered me a bargain I couldn't refuse.

"I know the fastest way there," said Nova, heading toward the steps leading out of the cellar and into the house. "My Rolls is parked in the driveway. Let me make one call upstairs and we'll have a dozen Innsmouth friends at Falcon Point to help us."

"I like how you think," Wini said, "and I'll drive."

"Winifred Habbamock, you are not driving a Rolls," said Lonnie as we surged up the stairs. "If anyone drives the Phantom, it is going to be me."

CHAPTER TWENTY-NINE

The Phantom was a marvelous car, and as we sped toward Falcon Point I decided I would buy one when I returned to Hollywood. The engine had a splendid growl. Lonnie drove at top speed with a steady hand, despite Wini's commentary on how she should have been the driver. Wini rode in the front while Nova and I shared the backseat with the gear we carried through the caves, including the rifle.

Nova seemed amused by the pair but a little distant, too. One of the first things she did upon exiting Bluff Mansion and regaining her car was to hand me back my purse. "I'm no thief. I was going to drop it off at your hotel, but you may need this now," she said. Inside, my pistol was still holstered in its usual pocket.

"Why not partner with Hughes?" I asked her again because the woman was a mass of contradictions, and I couldn't quite figure her out.

"Because a Hughes will never count the costs of what they do. The *Bolide* vanished with all its crew because the captain tried to sail Gulliver's route despite being warned against it. Bulkington Hughes had Sweets create the False Fish to cheat Gulliver by swapping the two books, but he was caught," Nova answered. "I gave Ezra every opportunity, including lending him money to start Bluff Mansion, but then he started using the purple seaweed. I don't sell bathtub gin or wood alcohol colored to look like whiskey. I keep people as safe as I can. Ezra is like all his ancestors, determined to bend Innsmouth's peculiarities to his own advantage."

"But you're the one who opened Gulliver's route," I said as we sped along the road under a stormy sky. Purple clouds were building on the horizon with flashes of thunderbolts, a sure sign Ezra was preparing to open Gulliver's route, according to Nova.

"I never claimed to be without flaws," Nova finally said to me. "Sometimes, lacking fear makes a person... careless, shall we call it? I was careless about Gulliver's route, certain I could outwit the O'Bannions and the feds. But it caused trouble from the day I began to run cargo that way. Then I thought the grimoire was the answer. Now, I wonder…"

But what she was thinking I never knew. We came into sight of the Falcon Point Lighthouse. The sun was very low in the west, and there was another light, a violet hue, that swirled and pulsed along the edge of the water.

"There," Wini shouted, "there they are!"

Lonnie stopped the car as close to the beach as she could. A group of people were there, both men and women, but many wore coats with hoods or cowls pulled up over their heads, so I couldn't clearly see their faces. This cluster of onlookers stood far down the beach, apparently just watching as Ezra Hughes directed Nova's pilots into a boat.

Nova was out of the Rolls as soon as we stopped, grabbing Lonnie's rifle from the backseat. She strode toward Hughes and the crowd. "Clear your people out of here!" I heard her shouting. "That's my plane, Ezra Hughes."

"Look, there's the seaplane," said Wini, pointing across the water. The seaplane was anchored offshore, bobbing up and down in the waves. There was a second boat on the beach, prow up on the sand, the back end floating as the tide came in.

I pointed at it and said to Wini, "Feel like a little piracy or hijacking?"

"I'm in," said Wini. She whipped out her Mauser and ran for the boat. I followed hard on her heels. Behind us I heard Nova shouting and Lonnie yelling something, too.

As we ran for the boat, one of Hughes's cowled watchers made a grab at me with a distinctly animal-like hiss. I had a brief glimpse of a distorted face under the hood, but I pulled my arm free and plunged after Wini.

She leaped into the boat and moved to the motor. Wini tugged on the starter cord, and like all boat motors, it gave an apologetic cough rather than starting. Wini cursed and pulled again. On the second tug, the motor roared to life as I jumped into the boat. Lonnie was right behind us and gave the prow a shove, pushing us out into the water.

There were more shouts from the watchers, and I heard the bang of a gun.

"That's Nova," said Lonnie, who scrambled into the boat and now faced the beach. "She just popped one over their heads. Hughes started running away across the sand."

"I thought she didn't like guns," I said.

"Guess she makes an exception for Hughes," said Lonnie. "Say, who's driving this thing?"

"I am," said Wini, swinging the tiller about so we picked up speed and headed straight for the seaplane. Through the windows of the cabin, I saw two men watching us. Now that we were out on the water and moving toward the plane, my fears fell away. This I could do. I could rescue Tom and Max.

I heard the roar of another engine. Looking around, I spotted a second motorboat speeding toward us, carrying Hughes and the two pilots. On the shore, Nova was holding off the rest of Hughes's followers with the rifle. The blare of a car horn sounded behind us. Twisting around, I saw a couple of trucks careening down the road. They screeched to a halt behind the Rolls, and a dozen people, men and women, jumped out of the trucks. Nova's troops had arrived.

As we approached the seaplane, it began to rock violently. A door in the side popped open. Two men tumbled out, grappling with each other.

"Betsy!" one shouted.

"Tom!" I yelled back, waving wildly and standing up in the boat. Lonnie yanked me down into my seat by the back of my jacket. The boat nearly tipped over.

"Careful," she said. "We are almost there. Then you can leap to the rescue."

Tom struggled to free himself. The seaplane was now rocking dangerously, and both men were almost in the water. Then the other man hooked an arm around Tom's chest and dragged him into the cabin of the plane.

"I can't take a shot," I said, pulling the pistol out of my purse anyway. I might be able to use it when we got to the seaplane if only to threaten them into letting Tom go. "I might hit Tom."

"Or a fuel tank," said Lonnie. "Try not to blow anyone up."

A pop-pop sounded from the boat behind us. Wini ducked and grinned. "Guess those boys have guns, too. Keep low, ladies, and let's outrun them." She banked the boat, taking a long curve that shot up spray and sent a wave of water toward our pursuers. Their boat hit the wave straight on and nearly flew into the air. There were more gunshots, but Wini's wild zigzagging approach to the seaplane made it impossible for them to target us.

I let off a shot at our pursuers with no hope of hitting anything, but the bullet kicked up spray near the prow of the boat following us. The pilot steering the boat jerked away, sending his own vessel crosswise into the next wave and nearly flipping over.

We came up to the seaplane, bumping hard against its pontoon. I scrambled up and over the edge of the boat and into the cabin of the plane. Tom was on the floor, and another man, dressed like one of Hughes's patients, was crouched over him. Tom gasped at seeing me. His attacker grabbed Tom around the throat and began to choke him.

"Stop!" I yelled. He pressed his attack, and Tom's face turned an awful shade of red. I reversed the pistol in my hand and whacked Tom's attacker on the back of his head.

The man rolled off Tom and fell face up in the cabin. It was Max. I had found him, and I had more important things to do. I climbed over Max to get to Tom. "Are you all right?" I said.

Tom sat up, choking and wheezing. "Better," he croaked after a minute.

     Arkham Horror – Visions & Nightmares

I patted Tom's shoulder and turned to Max. "Oh, Max," I said, looking at the gaunt man unconscious on the cabin floor. His hair was wild and streaked with white. His once beautifully manicured hands were scored with tiny scars, and the nails were broken to the quick. He looked so much older and worn. "Oh, poor Max," I said. I could feel nothing but pity for the beautiful young man who was, I had come to realize, much like Ezra Hughes. Max never counted the cost when it came to getting what he wanted. But the punishment seemed far too harsh.

"I don't think he understands English," said Tom. "Or not much. Hughes kept ordering him around, and he did what he was told, but it was odd. Like he barely understood what was happening."

"Or he drank too much of that tea," said Wini, clambering into the cabin with Lonnie. She pointed at a flask lying on the cabin floor. The liquid leaking from it had a familiar scent and was a horrid purple color.

"Yeah," said Tom, "he kept swigging that every few minutes."

"What do we do with him?" said Lonnie.

"Tie him up for now," I said, "so he doesn't attack anyone else." Later, I would deal with the problem of Max. Jim, I reminded myself, was getting better. Surely, with kinder treatment, Max could also recover. Nova never said the effects of the seaweed were permanent.

"Hughes is almost here with his pilots, or Nova's pilots. I'm not sure which they are," Wini reported, glancing out the door of the cabin. "Pistols at sunset?"

The light was almost gone, and the sun was a glowing red ball disappearing rapidly to the west. On the beach, I could see Nova and the other group were still in a standoff.

"Can you fly this thing?" I asked Wini.

"Happy to try," she said with glee, hurtling into the pilot's seat.

Lonnie sighed but closed and locked the cabin door. The rumble of the engines indicated Wini had at least figured out how to start the seaplane.

There was the ping of a bullet off one of the cabin walls, and we all ducked.

"Get us out of here!" Lonnie yelled.

"Going, going," Wini yelled back.

The seaplane began to gather speed, taxiing across the waves. Tom and I were practically flat on the floor, struggling to secure Max with belts and scarves.

"I'm going to start carrying rope with me wherever I go," muttered Tom as he knotted my scarf around Max's hands.

The plane tilted up as we left the water for the air. Tom slung an arm around me and braced himself against the wall of the cabin. "Hey, I don't like heights," he said with a gulp.

"Then don't look out the window," I suggested.

"Good advice," he muttered. "Besides, there's better things to look at." He was staring straight at me.

"What happened to you?" I said.

"Hughes and Albie came up to me at the airshow," he replied. "Hughes sputtered something about the grimoire, and Albie shoved a gun in my ribs. It seemed best to go along with them. They took me to the strange group on the beach. All hoods and no talk."

"I noticed them earlier," I said.

Tom tightened his hold on my shoulders as Wini straightened out the plane. He leaned close and whispered, "One moment on the beach, I felt the world slip. Like Minerva described."

"You felt it, too?" I wrapped one arm around his waist.

Tom nodded. "I may have screamed. But I remembered what Minerva said about holding your place in your head. And, don't laugh, I thought I heard you ask where I was. Then I was in a boat being transferred to this plane."

Bless Jim for telling me about Tom, I thought, certain Tom had heard us talking, although I didn't know how. "I'm glad you're here now," was all I said. Then I exclaimed, "You didn't drink any of Hughes's tea?" I pointed at the thermos now rolling around the floor of the cabin, leaving dribbles of purple behind it.

"Hughes kept handing his friends a sample," Tom said. "And saying the purple stuff would make everyone rich." He pointed at the violet glob now drying on the cabin's floor. "For once, I didn't want a drink. But your man there kept pouring it down his throat."

I looked over at the unconscious Max. "Poor Max," I said. "He always wanted to be in control. The seaweed tea turned him into a puppet for Hughes."

"The doctor ordered him to keep me on the plane," Tom said. "I guess he took those orders literally."

Wini turned the plane toward the shore. "Shall we try a bit of low-level flying?" she called to us.

"What are you doing?" I asked.

"Figure if I buzz the beach, it should scatter the mob around Nova," she said.

I glanced out of the windows. Nova and her companions were backed almost to the Rolls by Hughes's supporters. Further down the beach, a few fistfights seemed to be taking place, but at least there were no bodies on the ground yet.

"Go on," I said, and Wini whooped as she sent the plane into a dive at the crowd.

Lonnie muttered something about "No way to treat a lady," and I think she was talking about the plane.

We passed over the crowd, the pontoons still dripping ocean water and a bit of seaweed. When the plane roared over their heads, the group below scattered and ran. Nova and some of her friends dived into the Rolls. The rest ran for their trucks.

As Wini turned for a second pass at the beach, I saw that Hughes and his boat were heading out to sea, toward the strange purple light glowing near the base of the lighthouse.

"Chase him off," I said to her. "Maybe dump him in the ocean."

"Betsy Baxter, you are a wicked woman," said Wini with a laugh, "and I do like that about you."

She banked the plane and buzzed over the doctor's boat. As we roared overhead, it rocked wildly. Hughes shook his fist at us, but they must have run out of ammunition because no more shots were made. The boat curved away and around Falcon Point. I saw a flash of purple and heard something like the pop of a firework. We circled the lighthouse but the boat was gone.

"Nova's leaving," Lonnie reported as the Rolls roared away from the beach.

"Now where?" Wini said to me.

"Back to Innsmouth," I suggested. "We can land by the wharf and call the police from there."

"Probably best," Wini agreed, "the light's starting to go."

The sun was nearly down. The lighthouse's great beam came on as we flew around it one more time on our way to Innsmouth's harbor.

"But where's the grimoire?" I said to Tom.

"Here," he said, grabbing a knapsack in the cabin. Out of it he pulled a green book ornamented with semiprecious stones in a design that reminded me of Minerva's knitted patterns and the shells on the church's table.

"There are some maps and charts as well," he said. The papers looked old and charred along one edge. "That's another thing Hughes told his buddy to guard until he came back for it."

"Those must be Gulliver's maps," I said. "The ones Nova's pilots were using for navigation."

Tom nodded and stuffed them back into the bag. A second book, also bound in green leather, fell out.

"What's that?" I said.

"Oh," said Tom, looking embarrassed. "That's the False Grimoire."

"Where did it come from?" I exclaimed.

"Ah." Tom ducked his head and rubbed the back of his neck. "My luggage. I've had it with me the whole time. When Hughes grabbed me, I told him I had a grimoire for him, and he made me get it. He said something about both books rightfully belonging to him."

"Tom Sweets," I said. "What were you planning to do with that forgery?"

"Give it to one of the buyers," he said. "I would have told them what it was. Most of the text is exactly the same as the Deadly Grimoire. I thought the professor might like it as a replacement if we had to give the Deadly Grimoire to Nova. I would have refunded the university's money. Well, most of it. A good fake does have value. We've received several offers from various collectors for the False Fish."

"Tom Sweets," I said. "I think your obsession with making a profit is ..."

"Disgraceful for a bookseller?" he said. "I have heard that."

"Admirable," I said, giving him a quick hug. "But you might do better in Hollywood. Set up a store there and sell fabulous books to the stars. They are all building mansions and mansions need libraries. Or work as an advance man for the pictures. My studio could use a charmer like you."

"So you think I'm a charmer," said Tom.

"Hey, there's Devil Reef," yelled Wini from the pilot's seat. "We're going down. Brace yourselves."

"I'll tell you my opinion of you later," I said. "We have a few loose ends to tie up."

Tom groaned and then chuckled. "I'll hold you to that, Betsy Baxter."

Wini brought the plane down in Innsmouth Harbor. We taxied across the water to the sturdiest looking dock. When the plane bumped against the wharf, Lonnie opened the cabin door and jumped out to the dock. "Throw me a line," she said.

We tossed the mooring lines to her and secured the plane to the dock. As we climbed out of the cabin, Tom took the knapsack with the two grimoires and Gulliver's charts.

"Now what?" Wini said as we stood on the dock.

"Find a ride back to the airfield. Send Max to the hospital in Arkham. I can arrange to have him taken to California from there," I said. Glancing into the cabin, I could see Max was still sleeping peacefully. It would take time, but eventually, he and Jim might be cured. I would do what I could. At least I no longer had to worry about what had happened to them.

Of course, I'd have a lot to explain to Jeany and my friends back home. They'd always seen Max as my grand romance. Myself, I hadn't been sure, and Arkham had split us apart before I could make up my mind. But now I knew what I wanted. It was time to catch a new streetcar and head in a different direction. I didn't need a man who schemed to own a studio and, like Hughes, thought being in charge was more important than anything else. I did enjoy dancing with a man who liked to read.

I linked my arm with Tom's. "You'll love California," I promised. "It's much more peaceful than New England, and the weather is better."

"I'm beginning to see the appeal," he admitted.

As we started to walk off the dock, a Rolls came speeding down the street. There was only one Rolls in Innsmouth, so we knew who it was.

"There's Nova," said Wini.

"Good," said Tom, shaking the Deadly Grimoire out of the knapsack. "This is hers. She bought it first."

Nova climbed out of the Phantom and stalked toward us. Her hair was wild around her face, and the light from the setting sun winked off the eyes of the purple cat brooch pinned to her breast.

"I think that's mine," she said, nodding at the Deadly Grimoire.

"It is," said Tom, tucking it under his arm. "As are these." He started to pull Gulliver's charts out of the knapsack.

"No!" shouted a voice from a boat pulling up to the dock. "Those are mine!"

Hughes sprang out of the motorboat as soon as it reached the jetty. In one leap, he was out of the boat and running toward us, waving a pistol in one hand.

"Where did he come from?" Wini asked.

A purple light shone at the end of the dock. Looking directly at it made my stomach lurch as if the world was whirling too fast under my feet. As I watched, it expanded, covering more and more of the dock. Hughes, I realized, had gone from Falcon Point to Innsmouth using Gulliver's fabled route.

"Get away," I shouted at Hughes, pulling my friends toward solid land.

"The book is mine. It was always mine," said Hughes, lunging at Tom and snatching the Deadly Grimoire from his hands. "You cannot have it. It's mine."

"You idiot," cried Nova as she ran past us and grabbed for the grimoire. "What have you done? You cannot open the way and leave it open."

The two of them fought like children playing tug-of-war, lurching back and forth, with the Deadly Grimoire clasped in both their hands. As Hughes pulled and Nova pushed, they moved closer and closer to the purple light consuming the end of the dock.

"Look out!" I cried.

But they never heard my warning. With a horrible scream, Hughes pulled the book completely out of Nova's hands. She leaped upon him like a wild cat with an equally fierce cry. They tumbled backward into the whirling pool of violet and blue light.

It winked out.

We stood there, on the edge of the dock, stunned. Everything looked as it had before. The seaplane bobbed in the water with the other boat moored beside it. Two confused looking men climbed out of the boat onto the dock. But Nova Malone and Ezra Hughes were gone.

"Now what?" Wini said again.

The sun was down. I stood there, staring out into the darkness, listening to the waves breaking over Devil Reef. Far off, I heard the mournful wail of the Falcon Point Lighthouse's horn, warning people away from the dangerous coast.

I regretted Nova's disappearance. I liked the woman for all her criminal ways. However, I thought, if anyone could save herself, it would be Nova Malone. But whether or not she bothered to save Ezra Hughes, I could not predict. I remembered Max's emaciated form and witless stare, and I thought how Hughes wanted to create an army of men like Max for criminal purposes. Nova could save Hughes, or she could leave the doctor to find his own way home. I found I didn't care either way.

I turned around and said in answer to Wini's question, "Now, we go home."

CHAPTER THIRTY

Of course, it wasn't quite as simple as that. It took a few days to arrange for Max's transfer to a pleasant place in upstate New York that came highly recommended by doctors I trusted. It was far from the ocean, something Max requested when he was awake enough to make requests. Like Jim, he tended to nod off in the middle of conversations, and he couldn't stand to have mirrors anywhere in the room.

As to where he had been, Max couldn't say. He claimed he didn't remember. He also claimed not to remember the fire or anything that happened during the making of Sydney's terrifying film three years ago. But when he said he knew nothing about the studio's plans, his eyes shifted away for a moment. I wasn't sure I believed him, but he'd suffered enough, judging by the scars and other signs of trauma the doctors reported to us.

"Are you still acting?" Max asked me during one visit.

"Yes," I said. I didn't discuss the studio or all I had done over the past three years. Max didn't seem to care. I knew it was time for us to go our separate ways. When he looked at me, however much he denied it, he saw smoke, and flames, and a mirror that wasn't a mirror. He flinched whenever I walked into the room.

I only saw a man who had been a friend. A man I hoped healed enough to enjoy the sound of waves and not turn away from mirrors. There were no more regrets or questions to keep me awake at night.

Tom and I spent September touring New England with Wini's air circus. Tom combined being an advance man with book scouting. Eventually, Wini threatened to make him learn to drive so he could ferry all his books from place to place in something other than her van. We compromised. Tom took driving lessons, and I shipped the books back to his uncle in Boston, who inventoried their store with an eye to opening a branch in Hollywood. We gave the False Grimoire to Christine, who pronounced herself enchanted with this addition to the Miskatonic University's collection. As for the real Deadly Grimoire, it fell off the pier with Nova and Ezra. Tom and I both hoped it would stay lost for a generation or two.

My stunts progressed until I was a bona fide wing-walker. But Charlie returned to the show, and the telegrams from Farnsworth about urgent messages from the studio became more and more creative in their polite insults. Apparently, even when you're the boss, you cannot take a holiday forever. And I did like to work.

"Whenever madam deigns to return their calls…" was a telegram which must have cost a fortune but Farnsworth's words made me laugh and decide it truly was time to go home. I was ready to return to Hollywood, but I would miss my friends.

We gathered at the Arkham train station to watch them roll my beautiful blue roadster up the ramp and into the boxcar.

"Take care of that machine," said Lonnie with a hug. "And take care of yourself, Betsy Baxter."

I hugged her back. "Come to Hollywood. I bought a Phantom. You and Henry can give me lessons on how to drive it properly. And I still need a few more hours in the air for my pilot's license."

"We'll see you soon," said Wini, pounding me on the back with her usual enthusiasm. "You have to cheer us at the starting line and the finish!"

"I will, I will," I promised. The air derby Wini had hoped to compete in was canceled. The organizers claimed it was a lack of talent, but several editorials had railed about imperiling women's lives for publicity. It didn't matter. I was going to fund an air derby where both sexes competed equally. Wini was plotting routes with other pilots. We hoped to have more than a dozen women take off from Santa Monica to cross the country. I wouldn't fly in the race, but I planned to fly with them, to be there at the start and the finish.

The train whistle sounded. "Goodbye, goodbye," I called to all my friends as Tom and I boarded the train.

"Someday we'll just fly from coast to coast," I said to Tom. "It will be so much quicker."

"I hope not," Tom answered. "How could you read on a plane?"

As we settled into our seats, Tom pulled several books out of his bag and stacked the volumes beside him with a contented sigh. His visits back to Captain Leo's shop had filled another crate or two.

"What do you think happened to Nova Malone and Ezra Hughes?" Tom said to me.

We chatted about this in idle moments, and there hadn't been much idle time when traveling with Wini, but all we really knew was that neither had been seen since they vanished off the end of the dock in Innsmouth.

"Nova might be lying low," I said, convinced the woman would find her way home if she wasn't there yet. Minerva had implied as much during a second visit to her farm. Besides, I noticed nobody in Innsmouth spoke of Nova Malone in the past tense. Whenever they said anything about "Miss Nova" at the Purple

Cat, it was very much in the present. "The feds were swarming around Innsmouth and Arkham earlier this month."

It turned out that Darrell's stories and some pictures he'd passed to an investigator inspired considerable interest in various government agencies and several raids of Arkham and Innsmouth warehouses. Not as many arrests were made as might have been expected. Both Nova Malone and the O'Bannions apparently had hidden their assets well.

What to do about Bluff Mansion had been more of a head scratcher. Finally, the nurses had organized a cooperative arrangement to run it until Hughes returned, if he ever returned. I helped where I could and made sure all the purple seaweed had been destroyed, and the passage from the beach to the cellar was boarded up. The rest of the treatments were perfectly safe, focused on rest, clean air, and wholesome food. Minerva visited often, teaching knitting to the patients. It seemed to work wonders for many of them.

"I think what happened to Ezra Hughes and Nova Malone is a mystery for someone else to solve," I said to Tom. "It's time for the Flapper Detective to crack a case in Hollywood. I've got a humdinger of a script idea from Christine."

"You've been giggling over her story for the last few days," said Tom. "Let me read it."

I passed the pages to him as the train picked up speed. Arkham disappeared in the distance.

"Betsy Baxter!" exclaimed Tom as he read the opening scene. "You wouldn't dare to do this."

"Oh, yes, I would," I said. "I have it all planned out. Let me tell you how we are going to film that scene."

EPILOGUE

October 30, 1926

My Dear Niece,

It is so kind of you to write, but tell your mother not to worry. Nova Malone is not dead yet. Although it took me a while to find my way home, I am back at the Purple Cat and working on our next radio broadcast. I look forward to experimenting even more with this fascinating invention. The possibilities are truly endless.

While I suffered some setbacks this year, I remain confident that my business will continue to flourish. Certainly, if your sister wishes to attend college, I would be happy to help with her tuition. Your generation shall accomplish such important work, far more than I or your mother could ever have dreamed of.

Do not fret about your own career! There will be forever those who tell us we cannot do what we wish to do because we are women. Ignore them. This summer, I met two amazing young women who offered me great hope for the future.

One was an actress who inspires thousands through her performances and her actions. Some have dismissed her work as silly fictions of the silver screen, but I know the power her films contain. Her stories will cause other women to seek adventures, and they will dare to achieve greatness because of her. I believe the spirit of the Flapper Detective will ripple through the decades to come.

The other young woman races through the skies. Already her flights have carried her far. Her story will lift other women higher than they have ever imagined. Her reckless courage could even take us to the stars someday.

These two women are clever, they are brave, and darkness will never consume them. I believe there are so many more like them, so many more to come. It gives me hope for the future. It gives me hope that we will find a way to restore Innsmouth and remove the trouble from Arkham.

While I know you are discouraged, never give up. Come here, and I will find a place for you.

Your loving aunt,
Nova Malone

ACKNOWLEDGMENTS

The initial inspiration for this novel came from the readers who asked, "Could you go back to Arkham? But don't make Jeany go back. She deserves her happy ending." I agree, for now, and instead had great fun sending Jeany's intrepid friend Betsy to Arkham and Innsmouth. This adventure had many godmothers, including all the ladies of the Monday night card bouts. Thank you to Lynn, Merrily, Susan, Carrie, Sharon, Karyl, Betsy (double thanks since I unwittingly borrowed her first name), and Phoebe for all the kind words about *Mask* and other encouragement. A special thank you also to Aconyte's Lottie and Anjuli for cheering on these adventures, and to Nick and Dan for making both the books and their covers look so good.

Another inspiration for this book came from a pack of cards. The minute I saw the Winifred Habbamock deck, I wanted one. The picture of Wini in her flight gear has been propped up on my computer throughout the writing of this book. I'm very grateful to the designers at Fantasy Flight Games for lending her, and the marvelous Stella, to this particular adventure along with other investigators from the game.

I'm equally grateful to all the aviation historians who documented the many flying women of the 1920s. I like to think Wini's spiritual godmother was Bessie Coleman, of African American and Cherokee descent, who tragically died in 1926. Her early death cut short her efforts to open the skies for other people of color. Coleman's flying career, and her famous refusal to perform before segregated audiences, inspired many people in her time. Her legacy continues to inspire today. Dr Mae Jemison carried Coleman's photo with her when she became the first African American woman in space aboard the space shuttle *Endeavor*.

As Wini notes, women were barred from competing in the popular air derbies of the 1920s. They would finally race in the 1929 Women's Air Derby. The pilots who took off from Santa Monica, California, were Florence Lowe "Pancho" Barnes, Marvel Crosson, Amelia Earhart, Ruth Elder, Claire Mae

Fahy, Edith Foltz, Mary Haizlip, Opal Kunz, Mary von Mach, Jessie Miller, Ruth Nichols, Blanche Noyes, Gladys O'Donnell, Phoebe Omlie, Neva Paris, Margaret Perry, Thea Rasche, Louise Thaden, Evelyn "Bobbi" Trout, and Vera Dawn Walker. Crosson was killed in a crash, others were forced down by a variety of problems, but fifteen finished in Cleveland, Ohio. A crowd of eighteen thousand cheered as the planes came in. Episodes from many of these pilots' adventures made it into this novel but fall far short of the full accomplishments of these women.

The wing-walkers and stunt women who performed in the aerial circuses are less well documented, but there are several archives and collections showing photos of their astounding exploits, including playing tennis midair on the top of a wing. One owner of an aerial circus, Mabel Cody, billed herself as a niece of Buffalo Bill Cody. Her regular stunts involved transferring from a moving car to a plane, including a ladder climb. Many brave performers of both sexes found their way to Hollywood. Such stunts appear in action movies to this day (with a lot more safety precautions!).

As for the female bootleggers of the period, they were just as daring and just as varied as their flying sisters. A favorite of mine was Mary Louise Cecilia "Texas" Guinan, whose career included being an action star of silent Westerns, starting her own motion picture studio, and running a number of speakeasies. Both Betsy and Nova owe a bit to Texas.

While women made incredible strides in the 1920s, not all prejudices or injustices were overcome. Nor was enfranchisement universal. Congress passed the Indian Citizenship Act on June 2, 1924, which granted citizenship to all Native Americans born in the United States. Despite this, as well as the Fifteenth Amendment and the Nineteenth Amendment, access to the polls continued to be regulated by state laws and would vary widely across the country during this period.

Finally, I don't think this story or any of the many female detective stories that thrill us today would have been quite the same without the books written by Mildred Augustine Wirt Benson right at the end of the 1920s and first published in 1930. Her mysteries inspired three women to become Supreme Court justices – what a legacy for any writer! The expectation that young women could achieve as much as the men permeates the adventures of her most famous female detective and her other stories. Follow the clues and you'll figure out who I am talking about.

Thank you, as always, for reading along with this adventure.

ARKHAM HORROR™

The BOOTLEGGER'S DANCE

An ARKHAM HORROR *Novel*

PROLOGUE

A dying man gifted me this blank book so I could write my thoughts, but my thoughts are birds, winging wildly toward the sky, hounds baying below them. My mind is a cemetery full of hideous sounds created by the hungry trees surrounding me. Then I hear your voice and the birds of my thoughts return to my head. I want to ask you, before I forget again, what is your name?

My name changed frequently in my life, almost every time I crossed a border or entered a new city. Many days I forget what I call myself. Then I remember a name and write it in this journal which ties me to a better world.

My name is Paul.

Forgive me. Such a terrible way to introduce myself. My words may frighten you. Do not be afraid. Please do not be afraid. One of us must be without fear. Let me start again.

My name is… but I have written down my name, at least the one that I remember.

So let me begin with a proper beginning, the beginning to the stories we whisper in the dark to comfort children. Let me start again with a sentence to hold back the night terrors. Let me speak it out loud and drown out the baying of the hounds and the whispering of the trees.

"Once upon a time, something happened. If it had not happened, it would not be told."

Let us start there. I remember so little, but I know in my bones how to start a story, even a story as strange as mine. All my life, I have listened to stories. I have taught myself languages by listening to stories.

A creaking graybeard recited "if it had not happened" every night when we were all packed together in a boxcar rolling across a vast steppe, packed as tight as fleas on a well-fed dog. The men on the outer edges of the crowd fell asleep and did not wake. We rolled their frozen bodies out the doors in the morning.

But the rest of us sat shoulder to shoulder so the old man stayed warm in the middle as the train clacked on and winter settled over all of us. His tales quieted the fear. His stories kept us alive.

I have lost so much out of my head, but I remember his tales of the wonderful twins with stars on their foreheads.

I have not seen stars in such a long time. When I first looked up here, I saw only darkness, a night without stars. So I kept my eyes on the ground. Until I heard the howling of the hounds, their terrible baying, and then I ran.

I am still running. I run through cities. I run through time. This something happened to me, but it must be told to you.

CHAPTER ONE

"Isn't it beautiful, Raquel?" my aunt exclaimed as she ushered me out of her Rolls Royce and pointed me to her latest business. The long two-story white building occupied nearly the entire length of the street. The sign high overhead proclaimed in large letters the name of the Diamond Dog. Posters plastered on either side of the double doors promised dances with live entertainment.

Snow swirled through the air while the clouds above looked like a bruise, but the glow of lights outlining the marquee made the whole street seem warmer and welcoming. The rest of the town, from what I'd seen when we'd driven across it, looked like it once modeled for an old-fashioned Currier and Ives print. With snow gilding the rooftops, and even along the edges of the well-shoveled walks, it appeared like a scene from a Christmas card.

My aunt tipped her head back to smile at the lights brightening the gloom of the December afternoon.

"Kingsport," said Aunt Nova with a look of pride that I had come to know in recent weeks, "never had a place like this. It's all the best inside. Wait until you see the ballroom. And–" she pointed to a small door further away, "–we built the radio studio right there. We broadcast one show every day at noon and then live from the dance floor four evenings a week."

"But if they can hear the music at home for free," I said, following my aunt through the double doors and into the Diamond Dog, "why would anyone pay to come to dance here?"

Nova laughed. "It's because they hear our broadcast that they're wild to come to the Diamond Dog. Why, the phone rings off the hook during every broadcast with people asking if they can come the next week to the show." She pointed out the box office inside the lobby, a glass and brass kiosk where couples could buy tickets that allowed them an evening of frolics inside. Prices were posted on a fancy printed card resting on an easel. I noticed tickets for Friday and Saturday nights were slightly higher than Wednesday and

Thursday. All promised tickets included dancing until midnight and a light refreshment during the evening.

Seeing the direction of my gaze, my aunt explained, "We have a buffet supper around 10 PM for the dancers. Just sandwiches and soup, along with coffee, tea, and other beverages."

"No liquor?" I said. Supper clubs in Boston, especially private clubs that required tickets or membership, were notoriously false fronts for the sale of illegal booze.

"No liquor," promised Nova as she walked me through the lobby. "I run a dry house in Kingsport. Not that the police completely believe that. We've had a few raids and they've looked mighty embarrassed to come up with nothing but a kettle of fish chowder and coffee on the stove."

On another easel, a separate printed poster showed pictures of the house band, extolling the keyboard virtuoso Billy Oliver and the chanteuse Harlean Kirk. Across the bottom of this lobby card, printed in red ink with letters as large and flamboyant as those spelling out the performers' names, the poster proudly proclaimed: "As Heard on the Radio."

We crossed the lobby and entered the ballroom itself. The room ran the length of the building, with a gleaming wooden floor, small tables ringing the outer edge, and a stage for the band built along the side closest to the radio studio. I'd been to public ballrooms in Boston as well as many college dances; the dance floor appeared as fine as any of those, with a very pleasant spring underfoot and beautifully polished to a honey glow.

The red velvet curtains swathing the back wall, the crystal chandeliers gleaming overhead, and the white and gold walls decorated in the art deco style showed that Aunt Nova had spared no expense in her creation of the Diamond Dog. The only question was how she could afford so luxurious a place as the owner of a small cafe known for its chowder and its apple pie.

Music swelled through the room, a welcome distraction from the niggling questions raised by even a brief walk through the Diamond Dog. I told my conscience to hush its nagging and turned toward the band.

On the stage the band was practicing, a mix of men and women playing together with exuberant style.

Oh, the music! I could not only hear the notes ricochet off the white plaster walls, but the tune shook the very floor until I felt it throughout my body. Since my illness earlier in the summer, I avoided symphonies, concerts, and even the college's tea dances. In short, I tried to never be in the same space as someone performing on the piano. The Black man on the piano played with brilliant technique as the singer beside him belted out "It's All Your Fault," one of my favorite Eubie Blake songs.

"My poor heart is aching, it's almost breaking. And it's all your fault," the song concluded with a crash of emphasis from the piano.

Aunt Nova walked across the room and said to the pianist, "Billy, I'm not sure about that one. Isn't it a bit old?"

The young man spun around on the piano stool and bounced to his feet. "Hello, Miss Malone. Why, no song ever sounds old, not when Billy Oliver plays it. I make everything sound like it was composed this morning! And everyone can dance to it."

"Oh, leave it in the program," said the singer, a slender woman who topped the dapper Billy by nearly a foot. She was a platinum blonde, with a figure so long and lean that she'd look elegant in anything that she wore. She draped one arm across the shoulders of the piano player. "I love a good heartbreak song. I heard Miss Sophie Tucker sing it once and never forgot the performance. I asked Billy to add it to tonight's list," she added.

"Harlean sings it better than Miss Tucker," declared Billy, "and everyone will love it."

"What does the rest of the band think?" said Aunt Nova with a nod toward the woman playing the saxophone and the man behind the drum set.

"It swings," said the saxophonist. "The people listening to the broadcast will recognize it."

The drummer just gave a crash of cymbals and a nod.

Aunt Nova nodded. "I hired you to play the music so I should trust you to pick the songs."

"It will be a spectacular evening or I'm not Billy Oliver," said the piano player, reaching behind his back to give a glissando of the keys with more of a bop at the end than I'd ever heard in any concert or dance hall. The sound made my fingers itch to try it. "Who is the pretty lady? Is she here to help the radio boys with their broadcast?"

My aunt turned to me with a smile. "Come over here, Raquel, and let me introduce you to the band."

Billy Oliver hopped down from the stage, to be followed more slowly by the two women, while the drummer stayed enthroned behind his drums. From our very first encounter at the Diamond Dog that day through all the years that I sought him out wherever he was playing, I never saw Billy move slowly or even stand still for more than a minute, whether on stage or off it. When he played, all his sizzling energy poured out of him and into the piano until his audience could practically dance on the music streaming through the air. His technique dazzled me. I doubt the world will ever know another virtuoso like Billy at the piano.

"Billy Oliver," he said with a twinkle, "which you may have guessed. This is Harlean Kirk and Ginger Devine. Up there on the drums is my pal Cozy."

"We call him Cozy because he likes to be comfortable and warm. This time of year, he hardly ever ventures out beyond that drum set," said Ginger, shaking my hand. "His real name is Charles Lane, and he comes from Georgia. The New

England winter has been a terrible shock to his system." The drummer gave an impatient double tap on the top of the snare drum. "He's not much of a talker either. So I do the talking for both of us."

"We call her Ginger," said Harlean, "because she is spicy hot on the saxophone."

Ginger laughed at this comment and gave Harlean a little wink. Then she said to me, "Is Billy right? Are you here to help with the broadcast?"

"No," I said. "I'm Nova's niece, Raquel Gutierrez. Why did you think I was with the radio station?"

"Because of the headset, of course," said Ginger with a nod to the gadget sitting on top of my head.

I really had forgotten that I was wearing it. Or rather, I wanted to forget I was wearing it as all eyes turned to the strange contraption. Like a home radio headset, there was a metal disk covering my left ear that amplified conversations picked up by the microphone. The earpiece was held in place with a hair band going right across my head. The round microphone swung like a pendant across my chest.

Another wire snaked into the purse over my arm which held the battery pack.

This latest model was designed for a lady, according to the salesman who looped the wires around my head and neck. He said it looked like jewelry with art deco trim covering the microphone and earpiece. "Please note this battery fits in any handbag," the man bragged as he fought to squeeze it into a new leather purse that my aunt purchased for me. My own handbags were far too small for the battery.

We purchased the listening device in New York after several doctors said it was the only solution. The thing was hideously expensive, but Aunt Nova paid for it without complaint. Everyone told me how lucky I was to have an aunt willing to give me such a marvel.

I hated it.

The hearing aid did amplify sound in my left ear, which was the better of my two ears at this point. I could hear certain people better with the hearing aid turned on than off. But the device also buzzed in my ear and created a jumble of noise which was more distracting than not hearing anything. I often reached into the purse and turned off the battery just to give myself some peace.

But I couldn't tell Aunt Nova how I felt.

Her kindness, her generosity, and her sheer enthusiasm for the hideous device made it impossible to do what I wished to do: tear it off my head and stomp it under my feet.

So I wore it. And tried to forget I was wearing the hearing aid even as the headset rubbed my ear, the microphone pulled on my neck, and the battery banged awkwardly against my hip no matter how carefully I moved.

"No, this isn't for the radio," I said and hoped to avoid further explanations.

I still hadn't come to terms with the fact that a simple bout of fever left me with a significant loss of hearing in both ears, a loss the doctors predicted would only become worse. Because what was more useless than a piano teacher who couldn't hear?

"It's a hearing aid," Aunt Nova boomed. A big woman with a big voice, I could hear her with or without the device. She draped an arm around my shoulders and gave an affectionate squeeze. "The very latest technology."

This was greeted with an awkward silence as everyone stared at me.

"I could hear you even without it," I said to the musicians. "When you were playing. I felt it in my body. I've never seen anyone handle a piano like that."

Billy Oliver's face split into a wide grin while the two women groaned. "Now you're in for it," said Ginger with a shake of her head.

"I was born to play," Billy replied. "From the time I was a little baby, my hands were dancing across the keyboards. I am on this earth to make music."

"I would love to hear more," I said, and I meant it.

"You are a beautiful lady with a rare appreciation for my musical genius," said Billy with a smile so sweet that his boast was obviously meant to make people laugh. "I would be happy to play for you." Billy hopped back on the stage and seated himself at the piano.

I chuckled at his comments as he intended. I loved music in all forms and flavors and was intrigued by how Billy played. However, I knew I wasn't beautiful. The fashion in 1926 was for tall flat-chested women like Harlean or little sprites like the movie star Betsy Baxter. As a tall woman myself, I easily matched Harlean for height, but all similarities ended there. I was broad across the shoulders, and curved in all other places, just like my Aunt Nova and my own mother. What would have looked magnificent when they were young women in the nineties definitely did not suit the current fashions. Instead of trying to look like a flapper, binding my chest and bobbing my hair like one of my college students, I draped myself in sensible sweater sets and tweed skirts. I looked like what I used to be: a piano teacher, although hopefully a young and stylish college-educated teacher, not one of those old ladies in lavender and lace.

Cozy gave a tap of the drums. Billy set off with his hands flying up and down the keys of the piano. For nearly an hour, he played through a medley of songs, the latest jazz pieces and old standards made new by his improvisations. Harlean and Ginger danced on the floor to his music, pulling Nova and me into an impromptu circle. Other employees came out from the kitchen and radio station next door with a whooping shout: "Go, Billy, go!"

He just grinned and waved. The music swelled through the room. The songs shook my worries out of my head. All the anger and frustration, all the sorrow, flowed away as people grabbed my hand and swung me through the dance. They shouted their names at me, welcoming me to the Diamond Dog.

Then Billy started a boogie-woogie version of "Jingle Bells" with everyone hollering the lyrics at him as they swayed across the floor. I dropped panting into a chair beside Aunt Nova, who'd wisely left the dance floor earlier to sit on the side of the room and sip a cup of coffee.

"I never liked that song before," I said to her. As a child, the verses always disturbed me. So jolly but also so sinister, with the line about "Misfortune was his lot." However, the rest of my family adored the song and I could play it in my sleep. I certainly never played "Jingle Bells" like Billy did, and his jazz rendition made my toes tap against the floor.

Nova smiled at the raucous group gathered near the stage. "Billy can make any song into a party," she said. "Some nights he takes challenges from the floor, to see if they stump him with a tune that can't be danced to. Never have, so far. I went all the way to Chicago to recruit him for the Diamond Dog. I'm glad I did."

"He is amazing," I started to say, but the sound of barking distracted me. It sounded like a large hound in considerable distress, so I looked around the room trying to spot it. I couldn't see any dogs. I tapped the earphone of the hearing device with one finger, followed by a similar tap on the microphone. I doubted either gesture did anything for good or ill, but it made me feel better to fiddle with it, as if I controlled the device and it did not control my ability to hear the world around me. A second glance around the room confirmed no dogs, but the howls grew louder. Certain sounds, amplified by the hearing device, could mimic other things as I had found to my confusion while staying in New York. Once I believed that I heard the singing of a canary. It turned out to be a poorly oiled hinge in the hotel dining room. A fact I discovered after questioning the waiter several times and causing looks of amusement or pity throughout the dining room.

Still, this did sound like a hound baying. The deep cry started very low and very far away. When I shifted in my seat, I could swear I heard wind whistling through trees and the call of the hound grew closer. Perhaps the animal was penned up outside and echoes of its barking were sounding in the ballroom.

Just as I turned to Aunt Nova to ask her if she had a pet, the door at the far end of the hall flew open. A tall man dressed in an impeccable suit came striding in, followed by a policeman in uniform.

The music came to a crashing halt. Everyone stared at the intruders.

The newcomer pushed his glasses higher on his nose and then proclaimed with a shaking of his finger, "Do you see? I told you that they were holding illegal dances here." He pointed at Aunt Nova with her coffee cup half raised to her mouth. "And serving alcohol. Do your duty! Arrest that bootlegger."

INTERLUDE

Let me try another beginning. This one I learned from a man in the trenches of a war that I wish I could forget. Why so much of my life is lost while the memories of mud drenched in blood remain, I don't know.

"In olden times, there once was a very poor man who had no coat." My fellow soldier in the trench began his story just so.

Where I am now, I wandered for a long, long time without a coat. Before I became lost in the terrible place, I had a coat, nothing rich or fancy, just a plain black coat like a tramp might wear on a summer day. There was a reason for wearing the coat. Somebody handed it to me and asked me to wear it, but I do not remember why.

But then the hounds pursued me. I barely escaped their sharp teeth and claws. They rent my coat from my shoulders, tearing it with their bloody mouths. I ran away through a forest of trees without leaves, bare branches stretching over my head and a misty starless sky above those hungry trees.

The hounds bayed behind me, horrible mournful cries full of every sorrow in the world and every promise to destroy me. I found a track circling under the trees and ran down it. Eventually the cries grew farther and farther away. I stayed on the muddy path going deeper into the forest despite my terror of the trees.

Have I said yet that the trees here bite? They snatch at you with long twiggy fingers and try to pull you into their open trunks, all lined with teeth and oozing green sap. Twice I narrowly missed being ground up to nothing by their ravenous mouths. I learned to stay on the path and never try to leave it. If you leave the path, the trees will eat you.

Finally, I dropped to the ground in exhaustion and woke up in an alley, surrounded by brick buildings and ashcans. In my ears was the cheerful whistle of a tune, a tune I knew but could not name. A big dog panted in my face.

I screamed, expecting the dog to tear my throat out. Bone-weary with fright, I could not run anymore. I lacked the strength to thrust the beast away. I simply lay upon the cold ground and waited to die.

"Duke, Duke," called a man's voice. "Let the poor man alone. Hey, buddy, don't worry. He's a good dog, my Duke."

The dog sat down in front of me, beating its stubby tail upon the ground. A roughly dressed man held out his hand to me, pulling me into a sitting position.

"You look half frozen," he said as I fumbled through the languages echoing in my head until I realized he was speaking English. An American by his accent, I decided.

My own English came back to me with a stuttering, hesitant "Thank you" to him.

"My name's Pete," he said with the casual friendly handshake that Americans loved so much. I worked for a time in Hollywood and all the men, and many of the women, would grab my hand just so.

I never felt so happy to be touched by another human being. This man could have kicked me or hit me and I would have wept with joy. For his touch meant that this moment was real and not a dream.

"My name is Paul," I told him as words and memories flooded back into my head now I was out of the hungry forest.

"What are you doing sleeping outside with no coat?" Pete asked as he sank down on his heels to look me in the eyes. "This is too cold a night to be sleeping rough like that. The Mission is open, Paul, if you need a bed. Nobody is going to turn you away on Christmas Eve in Arkham."

I struggled to my feet. The kind dog owner held my arm until I was steady.

"Say," he said, "don't I know you? Weren't you in Arkham a while back? Been years, but you look familiar."

I shivered and shook my head. I didn't know him, although I doubt that I would have recognized anyone, no matter how many times we had met. Memories of a forest trying to eat me overwhelmed my mind. I could barely remember my own name, much less the names and faces of others.

The air was cold, far colder than I expected. In my head it was early June and the air, even at night, should have been warm and slightly humid. But as I looked around the alley, I could see signs of snow and frost along the edges. Large icicles dripped from the building gutter overhead. I recognized nothing. I was certain that I'd never seen this dreary place. A trio of ashcans were lined up beside a door opposite us. The dog abandoned us to sniff around these.

Pete laughed. "Duke's treasure hunting tonight. You wouldn't believe what people throw out, and just before Christmas too. You'd think with the stock market crashing they'd want to save stuff. But maybe they figure 1930 will be a better year."

Distracted by the dog, I missed part of his speech, but something sounded wrong. The last year I remembered was 1923 and everyone in Hollywood gossiping about the wealth to be found on the stock market. I rubbed my head wondering if I'd hit it or if Pete was the one confused.

Pete swung a large rucksack and a guitar off his shoulder. Carefully propping the guitar against the wall, he opened the rucksack and stuck a hand inside. "Here, Duke must have found this for you."

To my amazement, he thrust a leather jacket into my hands.

"Go on, take it," he said. "You need a coat."

With trembling hands, I took the jacket from him and pulled it over my dirty shirt. The warmth embraced me.

"Now," said Pete, humming a little under his breath as he pulled the neck of the rucksack closed, "I'll walk you to the Mission. It's not far."

I nodded, willing to follow this man anywhere, as long as it took me away from my nightmares.

"Oh, what sport," sang Pete as he strode ahead of me, whistling to his dog.

The song nagged at me. I started to ask him the name of the tune as I pulled on the coat.

But when I walked out of the alley, I stood again under the terrible trees with their grasping branches. I heard the howling of the hounds, more eerie than the wind. Pete and his dog Duke had vanished. I was alone.

So I ran.

CHAPTER TWO

When the man in the suit began shouting about arresting Aunt Nova, everyone stood completely still, staring at him. Though I could swear my microphone still picked up a faint echo of someone singing "Jingle Bells." It sounded nothing like the raucous way that Billy had been playing the tune, rather a simpler rendition of the melody in a pleasant baritone. I decided the dratted thing had picked up the song from someone out on the street. I put my hand into my purse and switched off the hearing aid.

I truly didn't need it to hear Aunt Nova reply in her booming voice, "Now, Chilton Brewster, you know that there's no liquor here. In fact, if you find one drop in any cup in this establishment, I will pay $10,000 toward your next campaign."

Again, I wondered how my aunt could speak so causally about spending thousands of dollars. Then I stifled my doubts about the legality of Nova's fortune. If she said that there was nothing wrong, I decided to believe her. The alternative was – well, I didn't know the alternative, which was why I persuaded Nova to let me spend Christmas in Kingsport.

"Furthermore, it's not illegal for my employees to rehearse for the dance tonight," Aunt Nova said to the policeman accompanying Brewster.

Brewster strode forward. With his slicked back hair, stiff clean collar, and neatly knotted tie, he appeared a wealthy businessman. His perfectly trimmed goatee and his round glasses gave him something of the look of Dr John Romulus Brinkley, the famed radio doctor.

"Nova Malone," said Brewster. "You may have gotten away with your tricks in Innsmouth, but Kingsport is a different type of town. We don't need you or your sinful dance hall here."

"The only sin is in the eye of the beholder, and this is a ballroom for the enjoyment of anyone who wishes to dance. Don't pretend it's some low-class saloon," said my aunt. She turned again to the policeman. "Well, Mac, are you arresting me for listening to my band rehearse on a Wednesday afternoon?"

"No, Miss Malone," said the man with a baleful stare at his companion. "Mr Brewster and I were just walking down the street when we heard the music. It sounded mighty fine, Billy."

Billy Oliver gave the policeman a wave from the piano stool.

Mac continued, "I told Mr Brewster that there's nothing in the ordinances about people playing music during the day. Figured you were practicing or making a broadcast. Fact is that you could even hold afternoon dances as long as the activity does not interfere with the other businesses on the street."

"Ah," said my aunt with a gleam in her eye. "A Wednesday afternoon dance might be popular in some quarters. We could serve tea and cucumber sandwiches to go with it." The last part she spoke with a fair imitation of a Boston Brahmin drawl, a direct tease, I realized, about Brewster calling her place a low-class dance hall.

"Now, Miss Nova," said the policeman, "you would have to get the agreement of the other shop owners and businesses up and down the street first. They might not like it."

"Or they might consider it a good way to bring business into Kingsport on a slow December day," countered Nova. "It's certainly something to consider."

"When I'm mayor–" interrupted Brewster, apparently realizing that the conversation was running away from him. Certainly, all attention was on Aunt Nova.

"When you're mayor, governor, or senator, you can try to change the law," said Nova. "But until then, you're a citizen like all the rest of us. Even then, you may find the position isn't as powerful as you believe. When you hear the piano playing in the Diamond Dog, you needn't come busting through the door with a policeman in tow. You're welcome to dance whenever you want. I hope you enjoy the broadcasts just as much from the comfort of your home."

"I find your broadcasts disturb the peace of our beautiful city," said Brewster. "When I am in charge, we will clean up, clean out, and keep it clean. Why, just today the Talking Machine and Radio Men's Association sent a proposal to Congress to better regulate the airwaves."

"When they make a law, I'll run my business according to the law. I always do," replied Nova without hesitation. "You need to find a new slogan and a new topic to beat to death in those editorials you read to Kingsport every morning. Radio stations broadcast what the people want to hear. You cannot stop it any more than you can shut down the movie theaters or put folks back into horse-drawn buggies. This is America, Chilton, and Americans do love their contraptions. It's 1926 and nobody is willing to live like it is 1896. Movie theaters, automobiles, radio, and airplanes. It's all here to stay, no matter how strange you find it."

Brewster started to sputter, then he looked around the room. The looks he was getting back weren't hostile – mine was probably slightly bemused as I had no idea who he was then – but the faces weren't friendly either. So his own expression shifted, just smoothed out to a pleasant smile and slight tilt of his head.

"Miss Malone," he said to my aunt in tones which were meant to carry to everyone in the room. Certainly I could hear him almost perfectly. "We welcome new investment in Kingsport. But we cherish the atmosphere of our town as well. If you'd only come to us before you began this venture, we could all have found a way to make it more harmonious."

"I went to the mayor," replied my aunt. "I paid the fees and filled out the paperwork. I did the safety upgrades requested in your letters to the city council. You can inspect the new hose yourself since you are here."

Nova gestured at the red velvet curtain draped across the back wall. One of the men grabbed the edge and pulled it aside to display a coil of hose attached to an oversized spigot. "That's a regulation fire hose," said Nova, "connected to the town's water supply. If any fire breaks out in the hall due to it being electrified for the radio station, we can put it out before the fire station even sounds their bell. You'll note the extra extinguishers hanging on the wall as well. There are additional extinguishers in the station itself and upstairs in my apartment. I had the fire chief himself in the building to oversee the installation of all our safety measures. He told me that this is now the safest building in Kingsport."

The policeman strolled over to the wall to inspect the hose and extinguishers. "Chief was very envious of these," he said, gesturing at the copper extinguishers. "He said you had the very latest, some chemical I can't pronounce."

"Methyl bromide," said Nova. As I'd recently discovered, my aunt loved scientific discoveries and new ways of doing things. She made a habit of searching such stories out in the newspapers and magazines as well as purchasing such items as often as possible. "It's much more effective than the older combinations. I gave a few to the fire station. Even donated extinguishers to the school as well as a considerable sum toward the school's new roof."

"Your donation to the school was most appreciated," Brewster said. He didn't seem like a man inclined to stay silent for long. "The education of the young is one of the most important duties of any civic organization. Our children are our greatest resource to build a better future."

Nova stopped him from launching into a longer speech. "Happy to help the kiddies. As I said just a few minutes ago, everyone is welcome to dance at the Diamond Dog. Further, any good citizen of Kingsport can come to the radio station and contribute to our broadcasts. Mrs Jacob read her favorite ginger snap recipe on the radio just a few days ago. I understand it was popular with our listeners. There's nothing more wholesome than cookies." She chuckled at Brewster's grimace. "Bring your favorite Christmas cookie recipe to the station tomorrow and we'll put you on the air too, Chilton."

He started to frown and then with a strange quirk of his face smoothed all expression away. "I prefer to speak elsewhere," he said, but so blandly that it took all the sting out of the statement.

"Your friend Elmo's station doesn't have half the strength of mine," said

Nova. "Nor half the listeners. Although I do enjoy hearing you read the headlines every morning. You must subscribe to an awful lot of newspapers."

"New York and Boston," Chilton Brewster replied almost automatically. Then he puffed himself up a bit more and his voice was again pitched to reach the back corners of the room so I could hear every word perfectly even with my hearing aid switched off. "A man should be well informed. It's my civic duty to share news of the wider world so Kingsport's good citizens are aware of the dangers outside our town." Then he looked around the room again and spoke directly to the policeman. "Mac, don't you have work to do? Let's be going. I want to talk to you about the new streetlights."

"Yes, Mr Brewster," said Mac with something that was almost but not quite a roll of his eyes.

The two left. The room broke out into such a buzz of conversation that I lost track of all the comments. When one or two people were speaking in a room, I could follow conversations as well as before my fever. Perhaps I missed a word or two, but it was usually easy to fill it in from the rest of the conversation, which is what I've done in writing my story here. I always had a knack for observation too. While not as good at lip reading as I would become, I often guessed correctly what a person was saying even when they weren't speaking directly to me.

This trick served me well as a teacher, interrupting whispered conversations at the back of the room with a telling phrase or two. My college students had called me clairvoyant. As I'd only been a handful of years older than them, it was a reputation that I cultivated to help preserve order in my classroom.

Now I had no students. Once the dean learned of my increasing deafness, my contract was terminated. If Aunt Nova had not answered my letters, I would have been forced to return home to Denver. I hated the thought of having to admit the failure of my grand dreams of becoming a concert pianist. I was sure it would ruin the Christmas celebrations for my entire family. They would be so concentrated on comforting me that there would be no joy in such a reunion. Or so I told myself. The truth was that my family had weathered a greater sorrow, but my own disappointment would sour any homecoming for me. I was barely used to the hearing aid and I dreaded exclamations from strangers. I was certain that it would be much worse to endure the same from people I loved.

I felt a tap on my hand. I looked up at Aunt Nova leaning across the table. "Lost in your thoughts?" she said with a shrewd but kind look. As we made the round of doctors, Nova often broke through my increasing moments of despair with small gestures and pleasant distractions. Shopping was her favorite hobby. She was particularly keen on jewelry and gadgets.

While in New York, we spent considerable time at Tiffany's and almost as much time in tiny walk-up offices where inventors demonstrated everything from electric bread slicers to a strange wristwatch that displayed minuscule maps printed on scrolls. The latter, claimed the inventor, would keep drivers from ever becoming lost. Nova had been intrigued with the invention until it turned out the only maps printed so far showed roads in England.

"Come and meet the rest of the Diamond Dog's crew properly. You can't dance and talk at the same time," my aunt said to me, pulling me out of my chair. "You'll like this lot. They're sure to cheer you up."

I smiled at her. Reaching into my handbag, I switched the hearing aid back on and followed her across the room.

"Let's see," said Nova. "You've met the band. Here's Reggie. He's the genius behind the radio station."

A lanky man in his early forties shook my hand. His hair, despite attempts to grease it into place, stood up in odd spikes around his head, giving him the look of a slightly puzzled porcupine. I recognized the mess created by dragging a headset on and off.

"Nice to meet you," said Reggie, shaking my hand. "Reggie Stubblefield. I'm the station's chief engineer. I keep all the equipment running so people hear sound instead of static."

"And I'm the voice of WKP," said a gentleman with a rich baritone standing next to him. An inch or two shorter and much more solidly built than Reggie, the bearded gentleman introduced himself as Johnny Carlucci. "Giovanni Carlucci, of course," he said. "But we're calling me Johnny Carl on the air."

"My dean insisted I call myself Miss Malone when teaching," I replied, "and not Miss Gutierrez."

"In my father's day they objected to Malone," said Nova, overhearing us. "I'm a bit surprised your Boston college didn't object to the Irish as well. Stuffy place. You're well rid of it."

I knew she meant to be kind, but the loss of my job still stung. The college, while small, held an outsized reputation with Boston's patrons of music. I hoped when I took the position to earn a place in the faculty concerts and, possibly, even be taken to New York to perform. All those dreams were dust and ashes, although only Nova knew that yet. As reluctant as I was to write home and tell the disastrous news to my parents, even worse would be disappointing my younger sister. Clara planned to come back east and take her studies at a similarly prestigious school. I spent many days discussing this with Aunt Nova. I feared my misadventures would end Clara's academic career before it began.

My father reluctantly agreed to my own plans of teaching at a Boston college while making his usual concerned predictions of disaster. There was no man on earth that I trusted or loved more than my father. However, his tendency to wrap all his children in cotton wool, especially after the death of my youngest brother at age eleven, sent us all out into the world aching for adventure.

My older brothers sidestepped banking careers, much to my father's dismay, to join the Navy during the Great War. David seemed intent upon climbing the ladder to admiral. My brother Luis had been bitten by the flying bug and was currently working as a consulting engineer for a company impressed by his passion for propellers.

After far too many family discussions around the dinner table, my father finally agreed that Boston was a reasonably safe city for his eldest daughter to pursue her musical ambitions. "At least she is not interested in Hollywood," he said to my mother.

Clara also scorned the movies, being intent on a career in literature. She wanted to pen intriguing mysteries for the magazines and experiment in theater, being an admirer of the writer Eleanor Nash. Clara talked of the latest trends in modern dance and how those could be incorporated into the type of performance that she longed to see. All of which, she was convinced, could only be truly experienced in New York.

To overcome our father's sure objections, we planned for her to start college in Boston while sharing lodgings with me. Then, with some distance between us and Papa, she could move to New York in pursuit of her literary adventures. However, if I didn't have a position in Boston, her dreams might well be at an end too.

I hadn't had the heart to write Clara. I didn't want to spoil anyone's Christmas with my troubles, even though my aunt kept assuring me that we would find a way to bring about Clara's college career.

Nova clapped her hands, interrupting my gloomy thoughts.

"It's the first of December," she said. "Which means we have twenty-three days until our biggest dance yet. With Christmas Eve falling on a Friday, I plan to make it a true humdinger of a party. Have the special invitations been sent?"

"Yes, Miss Malone," said an older woman in a dark blue dress. She pulled a little notebook and a pencil from one pocket. "I took them to the post office myself yesterday. The box office started selling tickets for the Christmas Eve dance today and we've already had a small rush from the regulars. Now, what shall we do next?"

Nova smiled at the woman. "Lily, you're a treasure. Raquel, come meet Lily McGee. She's the office manager for both the station and the Diamond Dog."

"I was Chilton Brewster's secretary at the bank," said Lily, shaking my hand, "until your aunt hired me away with a fancier title and a better salary."

Nova shrugged. "You deserved it. I could tell that from the first time that I met you. Besides, I need good people to keep this place humming."

"Still, I can't imagine why Mr Brewster came in here making such a fuss," said Lily. "He's been so disapproving of this project from the beginning, but it's a nice high-class business. Just what he said he wanted for Kingsport."

Nova shrugged. "Who knows why one person dislikes another? Myself, I've always thought it was a waste of time to bother about such rivalries. Now, let's decide on the decorations."

As the two fell into conversation, the crackle of my hearing aid increased to an uncomfortable pitch. Besides the two women talking in front of me, I heard a jumble of voices, like the sound of several men speaking all at once. The barking resumed, except this time it sounded more like a hound's baying. I remembered a neighbor's bloodhound sounding off with a similar mournful howl.

I moved away from the others, closer to a pair of roughly dressed men that I hadn't yet been introduced to. I was fiddling with my microphone when I swung it toward one of them. I clearly heard him say to the other, "We'll make the run tonight. It should be safe. There's almost no moon."

"Best ask Miss Malone," said the other. "She'll be hopping mad if we lose this one too." At least that's what I thought he said, although his voice was more muffled and the static of the headset continued to disturb me.

"Nah, the boys will be right where we need them," replied the first man. "Our cookie lady made sure of that."

The other made some answer, but the howling was so loud in my ears that I missed his words entirely. I twiddled the controls of the hearing aid, determined to make the thing behave or shut it off completely. According to the salesman's instructions, I was supposed to shift my body so the microphone hanging across my chest was pointing at a person speaking. I couldn't imagine anything more embarrassing than maneuvering the microphone in such a way. Nor did I want the two men to think I was trying to eavesdrop on them.

My aunt looked around for me. Seeing the men standing close beside me, her eyes narrowed and she called out, "Otis and Tim, don't you need to fetch some supplies?"

"Yes, ma'am," said one. "We're on our way."

They brushed past me without any further conversation and I promptly forgot about them due to my struggles with the hearing aid. Over the following days, I would see both men working around the Diamond Dog frequently. But they rarely interacted with the rest of the staff. Their major responsibilities were carrying in boxes of supplies or working on the truck, a large delivery van, that Nova dispatched frequently to fetch more boxes.

Disturbed by the noise generated by the headset, I left the hall entirely, searching for the dog or dogs that I heard howling. But there were clearly no hounds inside the hall. The salesman had been clear in our discussions that the range of the hearing aid was limited, but I still wondered if I was picking up more noise generated outside than he thought possible.

However, when I looked out the door leading to the street, I saw only the snow falling faster in the waning light. Kingsport still looked like a Currier and Ives picture, like the print decorating the wall of my old music studio. The dusty relic had been left behind by some other teacher with a poor taste in art. I recalled the picture's bare black trees stretching toward a sinister moon masked by wisps of clouds. I always thought it was a singularly unpleasant depiction of winter and quickly replaced it with a sunnier print by Maxfield Parrish.

The wind turned. The icy flakes of snow blew into my face. I shut the door upon the cold and went back into the ballroom to discuss decorations with Aunt Nova.

INTERLUDE

"This happened or maybe it did not." So stories began in the boiler room of the steamer as we crossed the Pacific. The stoker hailed from Cairo, and he told his tales as we shoveled coal and sweated through the voyage.

This encounter happened, maybe, after I met the man with a dog. I was wearing the leather coat, so I think it was after, except it was also before. How can I explain?

The hounds chased me. I stumbled through the woods with teeth until I saw an open space, an ocean of waves which rose and fell but did not reach the shore. All was completely still although it looked as if the water could come crashing onto the shore any second. This ocean of not waves made me giddy to look at it, but I wanted to get away from those terrible trees. So I clambered over the rocks onto the beach filled with gray grit instead of sand.

One step on the rocky shore and I fell, as you fall in a dream, with a jerk and a start. Then I was standing on a wharf. An older Black man was whistling as he loaded boxes onto his boat. I could almost name his sprightly tune. He looked over his shoulder and saw me there.

"Hello, friend," he said in an American accent. "Out late tonight?"

I struggled with the words. It felt as if I had not spoken for days but I had talked with the man who gave me my coat and that had been... well, I did not know how long ago that had been or how far I had run from the hounds.

"Good night," I said and suddenly realized in English those words could also mean goodbye. I did not want to leave. I was speaking only the truth. Now it was a good night for me. I wanted to stay. I desperately wanted to stay.

Luckily, the sailor took the meaning of my words literally and said, "It's not a bad night at all. Clear and cold, but no sign of snow yet. I mean to sail out of the harbor by midnight. Heading south. Soon it will be warm nights and sweet breezes for me and *Molly Gee.*"

"Can I help you?" I said, pointing at the boxes. I meant, "Can I go with you?" but I was afraid to say that. I had tried to follow Pete out of the alley, but the hounds had found me. I had been snatched back to the terrible world of hungry trees and motionless oceans. This time, I thought, perhaps I can sail away. Some tales tell you that you can escape evil spirits by crossing water. I so wanted to escape.

"I'd appreciate your help," the man said. "I'm Leo. Captain and crew of the *Molly Gee*. She might not be the prettiest ship in the harbor but she's all mine. You're not an Innsmouth man, are you?"

I shook my head as I grabbed a box and swung it aboard the boat.

"Didn't think so," said Leo. "Innsmouth is not a friendly town. Look at them, all closed up tight. You'd never know tonight was Christmas Eve."

He pointed toward the end of the dock. I saw the dark outlines of buildings, shadows mostly against the night sky.

"I never like putting in here," he said. "There's not many who do. But it's worth my time to pick up a few commissions from the locals. Miss Malone always deals fairly with outsiders too. What with the war and all, something always needs to be taken somewhere else."

"There's a war?" I said with memories of the trenches bursting in my head. "Another one?"

"I think it's the only one," he replied. "Our boys started shipping over in June and it left even the Innsmouth skippers a bit shorthanded. Of course now that the US is in it, they say the end is coming. Maybe not by Christmas but next year for sure. Did you hear that they even established aero squadrons to beat those Germans?"

"Germany is at war again?" I shook my head. After November 11, I thought Germany was a ruined country. Were they attacked by one of those who hated them?

"Again?" said Leo without ever breaking the rhythm of picking up boxes and loading each carefully on the boat. "Oh, do you mean they've declared war on someone else? This Great War of the Kaiser seems to be stretching all around the world. But I expect it will all be over soon."

"But the war is over," I said, suddenly certain of my facts if not of where I was. "The war ended years ago. Kaiser Wilhelm abdicated."

Leo paused his work and looked doubtfully at me. "Seems to me if Germany's Kaiser left his throne, it would be in the newspapers." He pointed at a stack of paper near the crates. He had obviously had been using them to wrap more fragile items.

I clutched at the papers. Crumpled and well-read but not old. No, every newspaper felt and smelled new. Every newspaper bore a date that was years in my past. "Policies for Allies War Conduct Settled Soon" read one headline. Another proclaimed "10 Killed, 70 Injured in Air Raids on London." I shuffled through other newspapers, reading these in disbelief. The December dates changed but the year remained the same on all of them.

"It says 1917," I said with some indignation to the man watching me with a puzzled look.

"That's because it is 1917," Leo said. "Christmas Eve. December 24."

"But I cannot be here," I said. Because on Christmas Eve in 1917, I knew I was elsewhere, at the edge of a ruined country, deep in a trench where the ground smelled like blood and death. Not on a dock in America.

Once again, I wondered if this was a nightmare. Was I dreaming of this place while in the trench as rockets exploded overhead? I do not remember my dreams from when I slept in the trenches. I remember only the terror and exhaustion as men died all around me. In those days, even this cold dock, with the smell of oil and seawater rising up through the pier, would have been a good dream. During the war, the true nightmares happened when we were awake.

Footsteps sounded on the wooden planks, stopping my contemplation of the newspapers. A man's voice was raised in song.

"There's Cuffe," said Leo. "He'll know what to do. He's a clever chap. He writes for the magazines. Also, he is not an Innsmouth man, which makes all the difference. He comes from Kingsport."

"Hi, Leo, I found a bottle of wine. We can really celebrate Christmas before you ship off," said a rotund man with a bald head gleaming white in the moonlight. His round cheeks were nipped pink by the wind. As he stepped onto the icy dock, he teetered and flung up his arms. Leo gave a shout, hurrying to him as the other slipped and fell. Cuffe rolled as he slid, somehow landing on his back, still waving the bottle of wine above his head.

Leo stopped and chuckled. "Lucky you've had a drink or two already. But you'll feel the fall in the morning, Cuffe," said the sailor.

"Not me! But you're cruel to leave me lying here," cried the other with a mocking grin, pulling the bottle away from Leo's outstretched hand. Then he broke into song: "He laughed as there I sprawling lie."

As Leo and his friend sang the next line of the song together, they vanished. Standing on the edge of the shore with the unmoving waves, I looked at the newspaper still clutched in my hands. The date remained December 24, 1917. "Soldiers Send Xmas Greetings Back Home" said one headline on the front page.

But I lost my home long ago. I drifted around the world. Now I am sending a message to you. I hope you are still reading this.

CHAPTER THREE

During dinner, I asked Aunt Nova about Chilton Brewster and his unforgettable entrance into the ballroom earlier in the afternoon. "An odd man," I said as
I dished out a second bowl of fish chowder for myself. Nova kept a spacious
apartment on the second floor. Dinner had been sent up from the Diamond
Dog's kitchen for my first night in Kingsport, drawn from the supper buffet created nightly for the customers in the ballroom.

"Tomorrow we'll have something more fancy. Thelma comes and cooks for
me most days, but she's off tonight," Nova had said earlier, upon surveying her
neat little kitchen at the back of the apartment. "There's always chowder on the
stove at the Diamond Dog. Good for the dancers when they get tired, and for
the performers too."

I assured Nova that chowder was all that I wanted after being in the car all
day. Sitting in her quiet apartment also made conversation much easier than a
noisy diner or a restaurant. I could, without any apologies, leave the headset in
my bedroom, which was a relief as well.

The soup tasted very good. But my curiosity wouldn't let me enjoy dinner.

"This Chilton Brewster," I asked again. "Who is he?"

"A banker and a busybody," said Nova, pushing her chair back a bit and resting her hands over her stomach with a satisfied sigh. The lamplight winked on
her purple cat brooch. She called it her lucky piece and never went anywhere
without it. Despite dining at home, my aunt wore all her diamond rings and a
pair of gem-studded bracelets around one wrist. Around her other wrist was a
platinum wristwatch studded with diamonds, a beautiful piece that she'd purchased in New York when we had been touring jewelry stores on Fifth Avenue.
Like a magpie, Nova adored anything that sparkled, but she had a particular eye
for diamonds.

"Nothing like a good chowder to set a person up for a day or evening of
work," continued Nova. "We never went a week, your mother and I, without
making chowder when we lived in Innsmouth."

"Brewster shouted so much when he came into the Diamond Dog," I said, refusing to be distracted by family stories. Like her sister, my aunt was very good at sidestepping direct questions. But years of practice with my mother made me persist. I wanted to know more about Brewster and continued to press Nova for answers. Actually, I wanted to ask her directly about the bootlegging allegation, but talking about Brewster seemed easier. "He appeared to be so angry about your business." I emphasized the last word a bit, hoping Nova might be inspired to talk more about what she did when not planning Christmas dances and starting radio stations. "But then Mr Brewster became so very polite and quiet."

"That's Chilton. He's the strangest man. Starts an argument like any fool, shouting and waving his arms as if such actions could persuade anyone to do anything. It's all theater as far as I can tell. The minute he begins to lose his audience, or the debate turns against him, he becomes very quiet and polite. So you're left wondering if he really meant anything that he said before," Nova concluded. "His letters are worse."

"Letters?" I asked.

Nova waved a hand to a neat stack of correspondence on the polished cherrywood desk in the corner of the room. The dining room in the apartment doubled as her office on certain days, according to Nova. On other days, she worked downstairs in the Diamond Dog and still, at least once a week, went to her Purple Cat cafe to oversee its operations.

Her desk, outfitted with a phone and neat black typewriter, was set into an alcove which the builder might have meant for a china hutch or, in pre-Prohibition days, a bar.

"From the moment I moved myself to Kingsport, Chilton Brewster has been writing to me," said Nova. "He wasn't keen on my purchase of the Diamond Dog this fall. The place began as a saloon more than seventy years ago. The owners closed up when Prohibition was passed, determined to wait it out or sell at the best price possible."

"I'm surprised they waited so long," I said. Prohibition had been the law of the land for nearly six years but had been in operation even longer in Colorado. My family had never been much for drinking, other than my parents enjoying a glass of wine with dinner, and nobody at our house cared about the politics of who was "wet" and who was "dry."

My mother frequently and vocally regretted how the debate surrounding the Volstead Act almost overshadowed the granting of the vote to women, an issue that she found far more important. The swirl of discussion around Prohibition in our house largely centered on whether or not to serve wine with dinner when having guests outside of the family. The wine came from Mr Lucianno, who purchased grapes from California. My father often praised Lucianno's red for being as good as anything from France.

"Not many have a use for such a large place," Nova said about her purchase of the Diamond Dog. "I hosted dances at the Purple Cat. I knew how popular it would be if I could find a larger space, a proper ballroom with a bandstand. Also, I wanted to expand the radio station. We have a 50-watt transmitter at the Purple Cat and you could hear it all right a few miles away, especially at night, but we couldn't do much more. I saw at once this building had the ideal setup for a bigger station."

Nova's Purple Cat cafe was located very near Innsmouth, the town where she and my mother had grown up. The sisters once owned one or two buildings in Innsmouth, the legacy of their sea captain father. Nova long ago bought out my mother, who used her share of the inheritance to invest in my father's bank. My mother never spoke about why she left Innsmouth and never expressed any interest in returning to the town. I had never seen the place but understood it to have fallen on hard times. Nova's comments about Innsmouth were almost as vague as my mother's, except she had been living there until her recent move to Kingsport. From one or two comments dropped when we were in New York, I had the feeling that Nova wanted to avoid the place.

Still not answering my questions about Brewster, Nova instead chattered about her plans to expand her radio station in Kingsport. "This building has a nice flat roof for our antenna, and we upgraded the transmitter too. A Western Electric 1,000-watt!" I must have looked properly baffled because Nova laughed and said, "Let's just say I've had my eye on the Diamond Dog for some time. It's perfect for my plans. But I was only able to buy the building in October and Brewster wasn't happy. He wanted to run the one and only radio station in Kingsport, but he broadcasts barely two hours each morning with a 250-watt transmitter run out of his friend Elmo's house. Kingsport might hear him but very few others can. I told Brewster he could have his morning broadcast. I never go on before noon here. Although who wants to listen to a banker read headlines, I don't know. He also gives a little editorial about ways to clean up the town, practicing for his political career, and some rather decent advice related to his savings and loan business – how to calculate the cost of a mortgage and such things. So some of his broadcasts are useful. I'm thinking of adding more like that to our station. Amazing how many folks don't understand business and should."

When we talked, Nova was always happy to share her thoughts about everything from air travel to the robbery of the Bradley home headlined in the newspapers while we were in New York. But when I asked questions about her more immediate past, she was quick to turn our discussion to innocent memories of times shared with my mother when they were children.

As a banker's daughter, I couldn't automatically disapprove of Brewster or easily dismiss his reservations about Nova. Given my family's own attitude toward Nova's wealth as well as the accusations shouted downstairs, I wondered if the allegations of bootlegging might have finally driven Nova from

Innsmouth. She'd been remarkably quiet about where she was and what she was doing earlier in the fall.

We had our suspicions in the family about Nova's nearly inexplicable wealth. It was one of those questions that my mother was so good at avoiding, but nobody who read newspapers could be unaware that bootlegging existed every-where. It could be as innocent as a neighbor making a few bottles of wine for friends every year, or as dire as the stories coming from New York and Chicago about the gangs there. I doubted Nova bothered with brewing "Sugar Moon" or the other hootch generated from homemade stills. But she was definitely a woman of means, and it was hard to imagine how she could have achieved so much through completely legitimate business enterprises.

Still, I liked her enormously. Illness might have forced me to request her assistance, but I was glad to spend time with my aunt. It had been a lucky day when I wrote to her using the address reluctantly supplied by my mother when I moved to Boston.

My mother had given me my aunt's information with many warnings that I was only to contact her sister if I could not wait for help from Denver. Aunt Nova was only hours away from Boston while it could take days for my parents to make the journey from Denver.

"But only if you absolutely must," repeated my mother, pressing the folded piece of paper into my hand. My father pretended that he did not hear our con-versation. While my mother often spoke of her sister fondly, she would quickly follow such statements with a sorrowful shake of the head and a reminder that Aunt Nova was not a good example for us children. This speech drove my brothers and sister wild with curiosity but both parents would then retreat into diplomatic silence when peppered with our questions. My father relied heavily on, "You must ask your mother about her sister." My mother simply said, "Not now, dears, I'm busy."

"You must write," whispered my sister Clara to me the night I received Aunt Nova's address from our mother. "It may be your only chance to meet the fabled Nova Malone."

Aunt Nova was famous in our family for the Christmas gifts which arrived each December, shipped from the most expensive department store in Boston. Other peoples' aunts might send socks or similar sensible items, but our aunt sent the most marvelously impractical gifts.

Christmas packages from Nova brought such things as a wind-up tin train that blew real smoke out of its funnel if you lit a string – although we were only allowed to wind it up and run it through the house without the smoke and sparks. My mother pronounced the train's string a fire hazard after my father lit it and ran the clockwork toy under our Christmas tree. Only one or two branches were scorched, but the train never belched smoke again.

Other gifts included musical instruments such as drums and trumpets (again my mother sighed but allowed us to keep them); porcelain dolls with beautiful brunette curls and long-lashed brown eyes which closed when the doll's head was tipped just so ("Where did Nova find those?" exclaimed my father, who had been dismayed by all the blonde and blue-eyed dolls that we exclaimed over in the toy shop); and for my baby brother when he was seven, the most fierce and terrible pirate costume complete with a plumed hat and a shiny metal cutlass that could actually slice an apple in half ("Oh no!" exclaimed both our parents, but my brother Benny slept with his sword until the day he died).

Our older brothers almost died with envy when they saw the pirate costume. However, that particular Christmas, David and Luis were already enlisted men and recipients of generous checks from Nova, along with a letter from her to use the money for whatever needs that they had as sailors. The pirate costume did much to comfort Benny following the departure of his older brothers in their Navy uniforms.

For my mother, a second letter from Nova similarly consoled her as her two oldest boys, both under the age of twenty, departed for a war which had claimed so many men and ships. "She will always help," she whispered to my father as they sat with hands clasped and made brave smiles at my boasting brothers. "Nova may be a bad woman at times, but she never forgets those that she loves."

Aunt Nova might have had a checkered past, at least according to whispers between my parents and frustratingly vague comments to us children. But her gifts remained magical and highly anticipated. Even as we grew older, Nova's gifts continued to be both thoughtful and delightfully impractical, as well as notably more expensive in the last six years since Prohibition started. I owned a sterling silver desk set, marked as coming from Tiffany's, and Clara received a dresser set, also in silver, from the same store. Upon my graduation from college, Nova sent a string of pearls with a congratulatory note of such warmth and pride that I kept her letter tucked in my jewel box too.

When illness derailed all my plans, I wrote to Nova rather than my parents. It seemed easier to admit to a slightly mythical figure all that had gone wrong in my life rather than deal with the very real fear and grief of my family.

And Nova had come up with a fantastical solution in the form of a very expensive hearing aid. Only it wasn't the solution that I wanted. It wasn't a return to my life as it was before I fell ill.

A now familiar twinge of guilt drove me to smile and ask my aunt, "How can I help with this Christmas Eve dance?"

Nova looked very pleased but asked in a slightly troubled voice, "So you're sure you want to stay through Christmas? What will you tell your parents?"

I reached across the table and squeezed her hand in the same manner she had used to reassure me so many times in the past weeks. "I'll tell the truth. I'm delighted to spend Christmas in Kingsport with my marvelous Aunt Nova and learn a little more about my mother's family. Perhaps we can go see your old home in Innsmouth."

What I would leave out of the letter was all my doubts and fears about my future. There would be time enough in the new year to write about what came next.

Aunt Nova patted my hand and then pushed back from the table. "No trips to Innsmouth," she said. "It's a bad time of year to visit. Besides, we'll be too busy in Kingsport. I'm heading downstairs to check on the crowd."

From the vibrations under my feet, it felt like the band was in full swing. "I think I'll read for a bit," I said, "and then go to bed."

"Whatever you like," said Nova, rinsing off the dishes and piling them in the kitchen sink. "Thelma will cook breakfast and deal with these. I keep threatening her with a dishwasher, but she has taken a strong dislike to every model that we have looked at. She claims they don't clean nearly as well as she does."

"I didn't know about dishwashers for the home," I said. One of our major duties as children was to wash the dishes after the meal. When my brothers complained about the task, my mother told them that it was good to know that for every plate that they dirtied, somebody had to clean it.

"Josephine Cochrane invented a very good model for a hand-powered dishwasher," said Nova, surprising me again with her knowledge of gadgets. "But there's been a number of electrified models installed in large hotels and restaurants. I'm thinking of getting one of those for downstairs at least."

She checked the soup pot. "Maybe enough for lunch," Nova decided, thrusting the pot into a gleaming new Frigidaire Electric Refrigerator. I'd read magazine advertisements for such refrigerators, but never seen one in somebody's home. Back in Denver we still used an actual icebox.

Nova swept by her desk, gathering up Chilton Brewster's letters, and dropped all of them into a drawer that she locked. She pocketed the key. "Goodnight," she said.

"Goodnight," I replied. When she left the apartment, I realized that she'd never answered my questions about why Chilton Brewster was so angry with her.

When I was a boy, I lived for a little time with traveling people. I, who had no home, found a place with folk who forever moved but were always with their family. All the rest of the world treated them as strangers no matter how many times they passed on the roads through their towns. The traveling people, too, treated me as an outsider, but they were kind. "Far, far away, across the great waters," the old women would begin when they told the tales of those they had left behind.

I kept returning to the beach that wasn't a beach. I couldn't find my way back to the dock. I wanted so badly to see the real ocean again. I wandered farther and farther along the shore. Things watched me from the shadows beneath the trees, things with eyes like flames, but if I didn't look directly at them, then they didn't move toward me.

Like before, between one step and the next, I found myself walking down an ordinary street. Snow crunched under my feet. As I passed beneath a slightly open window, I heard a man singing about his longing for a Christmas like the ones he had known before. Transfixed by the sad song, I stood on the street, my heart breaking even though Christmas never meant much to me. But this song was not about the day. This singer yearned for a home.

The song ended. I heard another man's voice saying, "There it is, folks, your most requested song for Christmas Eve, 1944. Just know all around the world our boys are listening to Bing Crosby and thinking of you too."

More music came on and I realized that I was hearing a radio, although the broadcast was clearer and more distinct than any I had heard in Los Angeles. When I lived in California, radios were not common. But that was more than twenty years in the past if this really was 1944. I knew a man who liked new inventions, and he talked me into seeing a demonstration of a radio broadcast. Fred claimed such things would be common in the future. I wondered if I was dreaming about Fred's future or actually living it.

The smell of pipe tobacco drifted out onto the street.

A woman's voice from the room inside said, "Close the window, Michael, and I'll put away the dishes."

"In a minute, old girl," responded a man's voice. "One last puff and a look at the moon tonight."

"Oh, your smelly pipe," she said, but there was great warmth in her voice. "Turn off the light if you're going to open the window. Don't forget the blackout rules!"

The window slid up higher and an old man leaned out. He had a large pipe clenched between his teeth. His head was tilted to the stars. I must have made some noise because he turned his face to me.

"Oh," he said as he spotted me standing there in the shadows of the street. Like all the others that I had met, he spoke with a crisp American accent. "You're not the patrol, are you? I turned off the light."

The minute he said it, I realized no light shone from any window or streetlamp. I could not remember ever seeing any town so dark in America and wondered where I was.

"Strange," he continued, looking up and down the street. "To see our street-lights out. I used to complain all the time about the lights shining in when I was trying to sleep. But now I hate to see Kingsport like this. Still, you can see every constellation tonight."

I looked up. The waning moon shone clear overhead.

"It looks so beautiful," I said, for I had not seen the moon and the stars in such a long time.

"Does, doesn't it?" the man replied. He knocked out the last burning bits of tobacco from his pipe. The shreds fell like small burning stars onto the snow below the window.

"Shh," said the man with a chuckle. "Don't tell the wife! She hates when I leave ash outside. Hopefully it will snow later tonight. Then we'll have a truly white Christmas tomorrow."

He dropped the pipe into a pocket and started to slide the window shut. "Merry Christmas," he called to me.

I stepped toward the window, intent on asking him for help, when a woman spoke behind me.

"You don't belong here," she said.

Startled, I turned to face her in that unlit street. I could only see her outline, a shadow visible due to the pale snow and moonlight. The tilt of the head, the line of her shoulders, and something else, a scent perhaps, told me that the dark shape standing there was a woman. But I couldn't judge her age or see her face clearly. I could hear her voice though, and it was a weary voice. The voice of one who has long ago cried out all her tears and carried her fury at loss under her heart. It was the voice of the orphan, the one without home or family, with strength and protection like broken glass glittering in her speech.

"Agent Adams," a man called from the darkness behind her. "I think we've found it." A flash of red light came from the space between the buildings.

"Coming," she yelled. Looking at me, she raised her hands to her breast and lifted a round object dangling from a chain. Something about it made me uneasy. I had never seen it before, I was certain, but still her amulet reminded me of the forest with teeth.

"It's starting to move!" screamed the man. "Oh, oh, no! That's not possible. Agent Adams!"

"I can't help you," she said to me. "Not here, not now. I am sorry but you must go." She whirled around, racing toward high-pitched screams and squeals of agony.

To my shame, I retreated from the cries. My heart hammered in my chest as terror once again crept over me. The smell of rotting vegetation wafting from the alley covered the street like a damp fog. In the darkness I could not tell where the woman was. Disoriented, I spun around, fumbling for the wall of a building or anything that would give me my bearings.

The window nearest to me opened and the pipe-smoking man leaned out. "What's happening?" he said. "I thought I heard something."

The radio inside his apartment sang out with a merry jingle of bells.

The crunch of snow under my feet became the crunch of sand on an empty beach. When I looked up, there were no stars and no moon.

CHAPTER FOUR

On Friday I watched Reggie set up the microphones for the evening's broadcast. "So many cables," I remarked to Harlean.

"It's a mess," she agreed. Dressed in trousers and a white shirt with a sweater thrown across her shoulders, Harlean waited for Reggie to finish cabling her microphone so she could sing a few test phrases into it. "I'm always having to watch where I put my feet so I don't trip over anything."

"Someday this will be wireless," Reggie told me.

"And all the instruments will be electric," proclaimed Harlean, "if Reggie has his way."

"I'm almost ready to show the world my ideas for electric amplification," Reggie said. As always, his hair stood up in spikes around his head and his own shirt was coming untucked from his exertions. "You could take parts of a phone and use those to amplify the sound. It's just a matter of wires connecting the piano to a speaker."

"I don't know if the world is ready for Billy Oliver to be any louder, Reggie," said Harlean.

Reggie mumbled something that I didn't catch and then crawled under the tiny stage with a trail of cords following him.

"The man's obsessed with microphones and amplifiers and who knows what else," said Harlean to me. "He thinks electricity makes everything better."

"It's a crazy time," I said. "I think there's new inventions every week. But I enjoyed listening to the broadcasts, even the one with Chilton Brewster."

"Mr Brewster lacks poetry," Harlean agreed, "but he does pick some interesting headlines to read."

Nova switched on her radio almost as soon as she got up. For breakfast, we sat at the dining table while Thelma served up fried eggs and hot coffee. Then, to the sounds of Thelma splashing in the kitchen, we listened to Chilton Brewster reading the day's headlines with occasional comments from a man named

Elmo about the expected weather and predictions for the coming year from the Farmer's Almanac.

At noon, just in time to accompany lunch, the deep voice of Johnny filled the room. Perhaps it was family prejudice, but I enjoyed Johnny and Reggie on the radio much more. They also gave a little news, mostly culled from local newspapers rather than the New York headlines that Chilton read, along with comments on the weather and tidbits about people who lived in Kingsport. Quite a few of these stories centered on businesses in the town. Nova revealed over our sandwiches that she'd arranged for local shops to "sponsor" the program in return for being included in the broadcast.

As they talked, the two men often joked with each other and invited the listener into their stories. Then a woman named Mrs Daisy read her favorite sugar cookie recipe with accompanying exclamations and silly asides about ingredients from Johnny. The man made the statement "Two more spoonfuls of sugar would be truly as sweet as you" sound positively flirtatious but in the most endearing manner possible, rather how a younger Johnny might have teased his aunties during the holiday baking. We could almost hear Mrs Daisy blushing with delight as she responded.

After Reggie complimented Mrs Daisy again on how tasty her recipe sounded, Johnny invited everyone listening to tune back in later in the evening to hear a live broadcast of the dance at the Diamond Dog. Altogether I thought it quite a charming way to spend an hour and could see why people enjoyed the noon show.

Nova clicked off the dial and nodded with satisfaction. "We used to broadcast our dances from the Purple Cat," she said to me, "but it was much harder to pick up. Some nights they tell me that you can hear our Diamond Dog broadcasts all the way to Canada. The noon broadcast may not travel as far, but it's popular."

When I went down to the Diamond Dog later to watch them set up the stage, I asked Reggie about how far the broadcast traveled. The answer that I received was confusing.

"During the day you can't expect more than a hundred miles, and that's only in the best of circumstances for your groundwave," he said. "But at night, the skywave can bounce the signal much further."

After that, Reggie tried to explain the differences between groundwave and skywave, and how the earth's atmosphere changed how far radio signals could travel. I understood a little of it, having grown up with a pack of brothers fascinated by all the changes happening in the world. Spending time with Nova, who thought nearly every invention an invitation to a brighter future, also helped.

But Reggie's passion for radio eclipsed even Nova's love of gadgets. It became clear that all advances in listening and hearing devices intrigued Reggie. Every time his gaze drifted below my chin I could tell he was staring at my microphone swinging from its cord. Once or twice he almost reached for it but caught himself before committing any breach of etiquette. In another man, I might have found this attention annoying, but Reggie reminded me strongly of Junior, a high school friend of Luis, who could spend hours talking about airplanes. So caught up in his interest, Junior would often forget all good sense and manners, desperate to impart knowledge to whoever would listen.

Finally, Reggie said to me, gesturing at my hearing aid, "It's like your headset. If we could bounce the signals in the right way, you could be standing here but listening to conversations in Los Angeles. Not just what comes through your microphone."

"But why would I want to listen to people in Los Angeles?" I asked. The thought of voices or sounds coming from far away was vaguely disturbing. I'd caught enough distortions of ordinary noises on the microphone as it was. As much as the salesman had promised clarity from the device and renewed confidence from hearing "every word spoken," I still found the hearing aid more bedeviling than divine.

When I put it on that morning, I could have sworn I heard someone scream. But I'd rushed through the apartment to find only a bewildered Thelma and bemused Nova drinking their first cups of coffee together in companionable silence. The memory of my blunder made me blush hours later.

"I don't think I want to hear someone in California," I added to Reggie.

"Oh, it's fascinating how far sound waves can reach," Reggie replied. "On my own equipment, I've contacted other operators in England some nights. The farthest that I've gotten the signal to work is Nottingham."

"As in Robin Hood?" I asked.

"Exactly." He grinned. "It's quite a thrill when you pick up an international signal."

Johnny walked by. Seeing my confusion at his friend's last statement, he added, "Reggie's talking about his home radio, not this station. He's a ham."

Now I was absolutely baffled. I'd heard bad actors being called hams but didn't think that was what Johnny meant. I wondered if I'd heard the word incorrectly. "A ham?" I repeated with some reluctance. I hated repeating words back at people – I thought it made me sound witless – and preferred to fill in the blanks in my head rather than admit that I hadn't heard what they said. But Reggie's discussion was intriguing and I wanted to know more.

"Home radio operator or amateur radio," said Reggie. "We started a club in college. Got shut down by the war, of course. The Navy didn't want any of us broadcasting and messing up their signals."

"Or giving away their ships' positions to the enemy," Johnny drawled.

That I understood. We'd all worried about the ships and the men sailing on them during the war. Anything which kept them safe was paramount.

"Like a U-boat would have cared about anything we said," Reggie declared. "But Congress finally gave us our radio waves back. Then Miss Nova moved to town and offered to set up this station."

"Did you know my aunt before she came here?" I asked.

"No," said Reggie. "I listened to the broadcasts from the Purple Cat and liked how they handled those. Then I heard she'd bought this place and was looking for an engineer."

"Reggie's dream come true," said Johnny. "A rich lady interested in radio. Most women run farther than the sound of his voice, skywave or no skywave, when he starts on the future of broadcasting."

Reggie just grinned at Johnny, which told me that this was an old tease between the two, much like their banter on the show earlier that morning. "Like you didn't want to be on the radio as soon as Miss Nova offered you a job."

"I wanted the job," Johnny admitted. "I love the sound of my own voice. Even more than Chilton Brewster. Someday I'm going to be a great star."

"Well, you're already famous in Kingsport," said Harlean, joining our conversation. Then she told me, "Half the women who come to the dances want to see Johnny and hear him talk."

"And the other half?" said Johnny.

"They've already been out on a date with you," said Harlean. To me, she said, "If your aunt hasn't warned you, he's known as One-Time Johnny. He only asks a lady out to dinner once. When the evening is over, it's over. He never calls again."

"False claims by jealous rivals! However, I do see all my dates to their door like a perfect gentleman and never even steal a kiss," said Johnny.

"I think that's why they are all so mad at you," Harlean replied. "But it doesn't stop the others from trying to catch his attention."

Johnny just chuckled and strolled out the door. I stayed with Harlean to watch Reggie setting up the microphones and cables until he, too, disappeared back into the studio to check out something to do with the evening's broadcast. I felt a twinge of envy at his industry. He had plenty to do. Simply being an observer was an odd feeling for me. I had spent years in school and then teaching, always with plenty of plans for what would come next. Derailed by my illness, my plans were useless. Less than six months ago, if anyone asked me what I wanted to be, where I wanted to be, in five years' time, I could have answered them in precise terms. Now I simply did not know.

"What do you think about our setup at the Diamond Dog?" asked Harlean, interrupting my melancholy thoughts.

"It's fascinating," I admitted, smiling at her. As glamorous as she was – and even in her daytime clothes, she looked like a star from the silver screen – Harlean seemed genuinely kind and welcoming. I took a renewed interest in the bustle all around me. "When I was younger and played in school concerts, I always liked those moments before the concert began. The anticipation of what came next."

"That's the very best part," said Harlean. "Better even than the applause. Even when I feel like puking out my guts in the bucket behind the curtain."

"I know the feeling," I said. "You too?"

"First time that I went on the stage in *Shuffle Along*, I thought I'd die, but it was the most glorious night of my life. That's how I met Ginger and Billy, they were both on the tour."

"I didn't know there were any white singers in the cast," I said. The musical was famous for its all-Black cast, composer, and director.

Harlean shook her head at me. "I'm not white," she said. "My parents were light enough to pass in the north, but we never lied about who we were." She pointed at her platinum blonde bob. "And this is hair dye, honey."

I felt like a fool, but Harlean stopped my string of apologies.

"It's all right. You're not the first to make that particular mistake," said Harlean. "You're Nova's niece. I never met a woman who tried harder to make everyone welcome. Besides, you told Billy that his playing was magical yesterday."

"It is," I said. "I've never heard anyone as good." I meant it too. My only surprise was Billy played in such an out-of-the-way venue. The Diamond Dog was impressive, but Kingsport was no New York or Chicago. In either city, Billy's band would be in high demand.

Harlean smiled. "I think he's marvelous too. That's why I'm here, that's why I talked Billy into taking this gig with Nova. Someday the world's going to appreciate Billy's talent. I think her idea of broadcasting the dances on the radio is the way to succeed. We'll make everyone listen to what he plays before they can judge Billy on how he looks. Reggie and Nova believe we'll be able to broadcast from coast to coast. And not too far in the future. We could become the dance band of the nation. Even if they ban us in the South. But don't say anything to Billy about my plans and dreams. I'm working on this with Nova. Billy thinks it's success enough just to play for a crowd in a place like this. I like to talk about what will happen in the future, but he wants to talk about what to perform today. Sometimes I think we understand time completely differently. But I know Billy can be a big success!"

Looking at Harlean's determined face, I was sure that she would succeed. Billy was too big a talent to only play ballrooms and nightclubs. If more people could hear him, he would become a sensation. Remembering Harlean's singing during the band's practice session, I felt she also deserved fame and fortune. Nova's radio broadcast seemed to be feeding many people's dreams, including those of Reggie, Johnny, and Harlean. I just wished I had a dream of my own to hitch to that particular star.

"Success at what, darling?" said Billy, bouncing into the room, obviously catching just the end of Harlean's speech. The man walked like he was attached to springs. He hugged Harlean and waved at me.

Harlean bent and kissed him soundly on the mouth. "Why, making everyone dance tonight! I was telling Raquel that this is going to be the best show. We shake out all our early week blues in the Wednesday dance and by Thursday, we're truly sparkling. The crowds just keep getting bigger and bigger as the week goes along."

"Of course they keep coming," said Billy. "I'm playing, and you're singing. Ginger and Cozy have us all hopping. There's nothing but joy as the gentlemen and ladies dance at the Diamond Dog. And they can hear that all the way to Arkham thanks to our radio station."

I tried not to be jealous, but I was. Just a little. Because they would perform, and I could only watch. Harlean was right. Billy would get better and better. All I could hope for was to be able to hear him play. With my hearing slipping away, I would certainly never perform again.

And I would sell my soul for a chance to change that future.

INTERLUDE

Once there was a faithful servant full of good advice and I met him today. If that is not the opening of a story, it should be.

One moment I was beneath the trees, wondering if I should walk into their mouths and end my misery, and the next I was standing outside the door of a tavern. The windows were brightly lit and cast squares of warm yellow light upon the snow. The door swung open. A group of men pushed past me, singing with their arms around each other's shoulders. I stepped inside.

It reminded me of the Bierhallen of my youth. A long bar ran down one end of the room where a giant of a bartender slung mugs upon the counter. Two equally round women gathered these mugs up on trays and moved amid the crowd of men and women seated around the tables. They plunked down the full tankards and plucked up the empties.

"Drink up, drink up," cried the bartender. "Get your whistles wet tonight because next month we're all dry!"

The crowd gave a lusty boo and drained their mugs with shouts for more.

The buzz of conversation convinced me that I was still in America, but where or when I had no idea. In all my time in this country, I had never known it to have such a beer hall. Such things were illegal unless the beer was nonalcoholic. But judging by the red faces of the patrons, and the fumes rising around me, this was beer as the Germans brewed it in the north: light golden in color with a dry hoppy smell.

A fireplace filled one end of the room. Drawn by the warmth, I slid between tables toward it. One table stood a little to the side, half tucked into the corner between the wall and the fireplace. A very soberly dressed man sat there with his feet in well-polished half boots, toes and heels lined straight and tight against each other. What little hair remained on the back of his head was thin and gray. With a high shiny forehead and deep lines under his eyes and nose, I judged him to be a man of mature years. In front of him was not a mug of beer but a small glass containing a red liquid which glimmered in the firelight. Opposite him was the only empty chair in the place.

"May I sit here?" I asked him as one of the waitresses jostled me in passing.

He raised his eyes from contemplation of his glass and nodded. When I sat down quickly to avoid another waitress with a full tray, he spoke. "When one is in service, it comes as a small gift to be served. Every Christmas Eve, I allow myself one hour after the end of dinner and before the final preparations for tomorrow for a glass of sherry in a quiet bar."

"More beer, Hans!" shouted the crowd.

The man across the table sighed. He sat very neatly, elbows tucked into his sides and his hat balanced upon his knee. "I rather underestimated the impact of the Volstead Act. With less than a month to serve his beer, Hans has been encouraging these crowds. I understand that even though he will close tomorrow, the family intends to be open as early as they can on December 26 and stay open every possible day until January 17."

The warmth of the fire, the shouts of the crowd, and the smell of beer, enough of which had sloshed upon the floor to add both odor and stickiness to the bottom of my shoes, all threatened to overwhelm me. I struggled to talk but the old man appeared to take no notice, continuing his conversation more with his glass than with me.

"Carson Sinclair," said the old man with a tap of one finger on his chest. "I have completed so much today including wrapping the master's presents and leaving them under the tree for the children." He looked a little sad. "It seems a great pity to me when a man relies on his servants to purchase his gifts. The master would do better to spend more time with his family." He sighed and shook his head. "I speak out of turn. It must be the season. There was a time when the house was very festive, and the family used to play little jokes with hidden packages and riddles to solve on Christmas Eve to find the prize on Christmas Day. Such games and parties. As a younger man, I remember candles in all the windows and garlands. There was a feeling then, throughout the house, a feeling of joy. That's the trouble with growing old. Along with a certain creaking in the knees, one finds oneself falling into melancholy during the holidays."

"I have no such memories," I said, thinking back to long winter nights alone as a youth and as a man. "This time is simply dark and cold, and I do not think it will change."

The crowd behind me began to sing, the same song that the gentlemen leaving the tavern a little earlier had belted out. This time the singers treated the song as a round, one part of the tavern singing one line and another group picking up the next.

Carson glanced up and the look he gave me was very shrewd. Although I had said so little, I felt as if he perceived my bewilderment and sorrow.

"Take heart," he said to me as the song rose in volume. "You are still a young man. There is time, there is always time even for us who are older, to dream of a world much improved. At least the terrible war is over, and they say that it is the end of all wars if the League of Nations comes to be. If you will allow me to be a touch sentimental in this season, we must hope that even a single act of service can significantly help others. I must believe this is the truth, for the sake of the children."

He picked up his glass of sherry and saluted me with it. "Take my advice," he said. "A single step can place you on a better path, if you are willing to take it."

Once again, I stood in that terrible forest. My shoes were damp and smelled of beer. My coat gave off the tang of woodsmoke. I looked into the mouth of the tree, the gaping red ring of teeth and monstrous tongue, and I stepped away.

CHAPTER FIVE

On Monday, Nova insisted that I walk around the town. I'd stayed as close to the apartment as possible during the weekend, spending most of the time in my room and listening to the Saturday night dance on Nova's radio rather than joining in downstairs. I decided Harlean was right. Billy's performances were just as electric on air as in person.

As far as I was concerned, staying inside avoided any awkward conversations about the contraption on my head. But Nova obviously belonged to the generation who believed walking was essential for good health. Or perhaps she'd had enough of a niece brooding in her living room. "Kingsport is quaint," she said. "And far more friendly than Innsmouth. Take a stroll, enjoy the fresh air, and," in the longstanding habit of mothers and aunts, she added, "here's a list of a few supplies that we need. Nothing too much. Tell the shops to deliver to the Diamond Dog."

The sky was a deceptive blue, looking as innocent as a summer sky, but the cold definitely nipped my cheeks and nose as soon as I ventured outside. I wrapped my fluffy red scarf more tightly around my neck. The heavy wool coat that I'd brought from Colorado was barely enough for wandering the streets in a New England winter. The dratted headset was cold against my left ear, the metal earpiece feeling like ice even though I had covered my head with a knitted cap. I deeply regretted wearing it for my walk around town but lacked the courage to turn back and take it off.

Nova would have noticed if I went out without the hearing aid. She smiled so broadly, practically beaming, when I fidgeted it onto my head earlier. Nova's fascination with gadgets was actually quite endearing. I'd never known another so obsessed with contraptions. The gleaming new electric refrigerator might hold pride of place in her kitchen, but she also possessed an electric toaster, a Hoover vacuum cleaner, and, of course, a very fine radio.

A heavy truck rumbled down the street and turned the corner at the far end of the Diamond Dog. I spotted Otis behind the wheel, which meant yet another delivery to the back door. There'd been a similar, or perhaps the same, truck idling under my bedroom window much earlier that morning. When I'd glanced out the window, I'd caught a glimpse of Otis and Tim unloading heavy wooden crates and carrying the boxes into the Diamond Dog.

I told myself that those boxes contained nothing more than supplies for Nova's upcoming dance. If any crates clinked, I was too far away to hear it, even with the headset turned on.

As Nova claimed, Kingsport was charming, or at least what people expected of a small town in winter. The streets did have an unexpected way of twisting, so I found myself circling the same block twice with no idea how I'd arrived where I started. I thought the town's founders were a bit too fond of clever cul-de-sacs and wondered who designed the labyrinthine tangle of streets. However, given the age of many houses, I suspected that some of the maze was caused by the inevitable building, tearing down, and then rebuilding that cities further west had not yet been obliged to suffer through.

Since hurrying was not a necessity, I lingered on the sunny side of the streets, enjoying the leisure to work my way through Nova's list of needed items. Also, Nova had proved to be right. The more I walked, the better I felt. Many of my worries were forgotten as I allowed myself to be distracted by the holiday displays of the merchants.

Piles of merchandise gleamed in the store windows, designed to tempt the younger members of the community. At the hardware store, a shiny red bicycle and an even more brightly painted toboggan were prominently displayed. A crowd of small boys stood outside the window, chewing on candy cigarettes to impress each other with their swagger, but unable to keep their eyes from straying to the bike and the sled.

I laughed at the sight, so much like my own brothers that I felt a little homesick. Then I hurried into the nearby five-and-dime to find the notions on my aunt's list. The door gave a merry jingle when I opened it. The plump lady in a gingham dress behind the counter put down an angel doll with a porcelain head, fine feathered wings, and fluffy skirts made of silvered lace.

"That's a pretty thing," I said with a nod at the doll.

She smiled at me. "My grandmother ordered dozens of heads years ago for ladies to make up their own dolls. Somehow the box got stored away and the doll heads were never put out. I only found it a year or two ago." Looking closer at the angel, I saw it did have the black painted curls of the last century. The glazed white porcelain face sported very pink cheeks and dots of black glaze for the eyes. "Little girls don't want such dolls," said the shopkeeper. "They want bisque heads and open-and-shut eyes. But my older ladies remember these with affection. I make them up as angels and they buy the dolls as decorations."

"It's very clever," I said. I wondered briefly if my aunt would like such a decoration, but it seemed too sentimental for her. It was hard to imagine Nova playing with such a doll, even as a child. My mother, on the other hand, adored decorating the house at Christmas and rarely left any corner untouched. "I'll buy it," I decided. "Can you wrap it for shipping?"

"Of course," the shopkeeper answered. "I'm Mrs Quick, by the way. I'll put some extra cotton around the angel's head to protect it. Is there anything else you need?"

"I'm looking for hooks," I said, checking the list that I held in one gloved hand. "For putting ornaments on the tree. And tinsel."

"I have both," she said, bustling around the counter to gather up what I had asked for. "How many of each?" The first time she asked the question, I caught the sound of her voice but not the meaning of the words as she was walking away from me. She placed the angel in a box upon the shelf, shifting aside an ornamental string of bells which jangled as she moved them.

A warbling from the headset distracted me from Mrs Quick's chatter. A whining howl sounded in my ear. Then I heard a voice, a man's voice. He said clearly, "I want to ask you, before I forget, what is your name?"

I turned around but there was nobody else in the store. I glanced out the window but saw no one on the street.

"Did you just ask me my name?" I said to Mrs Quick, deciding that the voice must have been hers but was somehow distorted. I shifted my scarf to fully uncover the microphone hanging outside my coat.

"No, dear," she said. "I know who you are. You're Nova Malone's niece, Raquel."

I must have looked rather surprised because Mrs Quick smiled and added, "We've all been keeping an eye on the Diamond Dog since Nova Malone opened the ballroom and started the radio station. Everyone is interested in what's going on there. And I do like the radio program. The gentlemen on it mentioned you on Saturday's noon program."

"They did?" I said. I'd been wandering around the apartment on Saturday, chatting with Nova and Thelma, but not paying much attention to the radio program. There had been a cookie recipe for something with walnuts and raisins, and a particular quip from Johnny about the instructions which caught my attention. Then Johnny switched to mellifluous stories about various people in the town and I'd left the room on some errand or other. My name must have come up in that section of the broadcast.

"Oh yes, quite nice it was, about how you were visiting your aunt for Christmas and enjoying your stay in our town, including dancing at the Diamond Dog. I gather you're a music teacher, an actual college professor."

"I was," I said, not wanting to explain further or admit the only dancing I'd done so far was on Friday night with Johnny. We'd done a whirl around the floor during one of his breaks and then I'd excused myself to return to the apartment, sure that everyone had been staring at my hearing aid. But I did remember chatting with Johnny just before we danced, talking about how I both missed teaching and didn't. Grading people had never been my favorite thing to do. I resolved to have a talk with Johnny and Reggie when I got back to the Diamond Dog. I'd listened to their chatter about various encounters around town with some amusement, but I didn't want to be one of their broadcast anecdotes between reading the headlines and the latest cookie recipe.

I asked Mrs Quick again about the availability of ornament hooks. She eyed my microphone with polite but visible curiosity and then queried how many hooks I wanted. She also informed me that such had been her original question to me.

I didn't know how much was needed. Nova hadn't written anything besides "ornament hooks" and "tinsel" on her list.

"It's for a large tree," I said. "We're decorating it for the Diamond Dog's Christmas Eve dance."

"Ooh," she said, and I heard her excitement with no trouble at all. "I expect the decorations will be something special. And a very big tree. Miss Nova doesn't seem like the type of woman to skimp on such things."

Considering my aunt's larger-than-life personality, I had to agree. "I saw several sets of electric lights to string up on the tree," I told Mrs Quick. Nova also wanted to outline the doors of the Diamond Dog in Christmas lights, but Reggie had protested, saying none of the strings would survive the night if placed outdoors. Looking around Mrs Quick's crowded five-and-dime, I asked her if she'd ever heard of outdoor Christmas lights.

She frowned. "No. I don't think so. But what a good idea. If there were such a thing, you'd probably need to go to one of the larger cities to find it. Or the Sears Roebuck catalog."

Eventually the counter was covered with several boxes of tinsel, hooks for ornaments, a long paper garland I found in a bin, and one very well wrapped angel. I wrote out my mother's name and address. Mrs Quick promised to have the angel shipped as soon as possible. While I paid for the angel and its delivery to my home in Denver, the rest went on Nova's account. "I'll have my son deliver her items," said Mrs Quick. "He won't mind an excuse to stop at the Diamond Dog. He's very curious about the radio station."

I begged Mrs Quick for directions to the grocer, explaining how I had been turned around on the streets more than once. She giggled a little and acknowledged Kingsport was tricky for newcomers.

With her directions, I set off confidently in the direction of the grocer, determined to order the butter and eggs requested on my aunt's list.

As soon as I rounded the corner, I ran smack into a man. We did the awkward little dance of two strangers trying to step out of each other's way. I noticed he was very tall and conservatively dressed in a brown suit. His overcoat wasn't doing much to keep him warm as it was unbuttoned and hung open on his lanky frame, as did his suit jacket.

"Are you all right, miss?" the stranger said. As an afterthought, he also tipped his hat to me, a modest fedora.

"Fine, fine," I replied, embarrassed to cause such a fuss simply trying to walk down a sidewalk. "I wasn't looking where I was going."

"Ah, Tawney, there you are!" Crossing the street was Chilton Brewster, his hand outstretched to catch the other man's hand in a quick shake. The whole move pulled Tawney a bit further off his balance, causing his overcoat and jacket to flap open.

Not wanting to attract Brewster's attention, I ducked around the other man and hurried away.

As I twisted around Tawney, I spotted an odd leather strap and bulge beneath his suit jacket. While I'd never seen such a thing in person, I had seen something similar at the movies. As I hurried to my next destination, I could not shake the feeling that the man was wearing a holstered gun under his coat.

INTERLUDE

"*Es war einmal…*" the grandmothers began the stories. The Grossmutter who whispered into the ears of the Grimm brothers told of nightmares, queens who danced in red-hot shoes and bad sisters rolled down hills in barrels studded with nails.

As a boy, I improved my German by reading a tattered copy of *Kinder- und Hausmärchen,* so old and stained that it practically disintegrated in my hands. I stole it off a junkman's barrow along with a pair of shoes that did not leak.

The shoes pinched my feet and it made my eyes ache to read the fading type under the light of the streetlamps, but eventually the book kept me warm. I burned it one night in a barrel with some other tramps. It was Christmas Eve, I remember, and we passed a bottle of schnapps back and forth which scorched the throat but kept us singing until dawn. I did not freeze to death, although the schnapps on an empty and hungry stomach made me think freezing might have been preferable.

I am never cold here under the trees, but I shiver as I pass beneath their whispering branches. I wish for the warmth of a fire and a friendly hand extending a bottle of schnapps to a starving boy.

Then I see a flame, a blue flame that sputters and then flares in front of my eyes. Between one step on the path and the next, I stood in a laboratory.

I entered, if it can be called entering, near a shelf of dishes and jars, all filled with liquids smelling of brine. I looked into one of the jars and an eyeball peered back at me. In another time and another place, I might have been horrified. But I had stared too often into the hungry mouths of the trees to be frightened of body parts preserved in jars.

I heard voices arguing just past the shelves, so I ignored the eyeball and peeped past the specimens into the room.

At one end of a long table, some type of experiment seemed to be bubbling away in beakers and test tubes suspended over the blue flames of Bunsen burners. I once worked cleaning a laboratory belonging to a chemical factory. It had similar setups which meant nothing more to me than something fragile to be avoided when I mopped the floor, emptied out the trash from bins, and tried, often unsuccessfully, to clean stains from the tables.

At the other end of the table was a set of electrical equipment. At least it was a series of boxes, cables, and switches emitting small sparks and hisses. Standing in front of the equipment was a tired looking man in glasses, twisting a screwdriver on one box to adjust some dial. A red-haired woman, dressed very neatly in a tan jacket and a black blouse, leaned over his shoulder.

I nearly called out to them, but then I saw their audience. A group of men stood around the lab watching. There was something in their gaze. The eyeball in its jar looked upon the world with greater sympathy. All the watchers were dressed alike in brown suits with very white shirts and dark ties underneath. Despite being dressed like clerks, they stood like men in uniforms, very straight and grim. I had never had any luck with such men. I drew back a little in the hopes of hiding from them.

"Dr Maleson," the woman said to the man working on the equipment, "I cannot agree with these changes. The research clearly shows this path cannot be opened using such means. Incantations are indicated. Incantations which are sung. Broadcasting a series of sounds, such as you are attempting to do, may well upset the entire balance of this method."

"Incantations," retorted the other. "Superstitions of the last century. This is 1924! We use science to solve these puzzles. I agree sound frequencies are important, but those created by the human throat are subject to infinite variation. This device—" he patted the thing emitting sparks, then jerked his hand back quickly as if it was stung or hit hot metal. "This device," he continued, "will allow us to duplicate the process precisely every time. When tuned correctly, we will be able to journey to whichever period, whichever moment, we want."

"Dr Maleson," said a tall man in a brown suit. "I have half a dozen federal agents here on Christmas Eve. The paperwork to make this possible, as well as the funding my Bureau has already given your experiment, is staggering. Can you or can you not produce results today?"

"Agent Tawney, of course I can," said Maleson. "This is the start of something big, something undreamed of."

"Not by HG Wells," said the woman with a sour look. "I believed he dreamed of it quite effectively years ago."

"Wells? Miss Thompson, he is a writer!" exclaimed Maleson. "A political radical. Not a scientist. What I have proposed here is something completely different. Not a machine of fiction but a creation that can carry us forward and backward as desired."

"It's my research you're using to create the phenomenon," she said. "I'm telling you that you interpreted it all quite wrong."

"And I'm telling you if this doesn't work today," said the man in the brown suit, "I am shutting off your funding come New Year's."

"Agent Tawney, Miss Thompson," said the scientist. "Prepare to be amazed." He flipped the large lever in front of him and a series of musical notes erupted from the brass metal screen on one end of the box.

A scent rose in the air, not of burning but of something more terrifying than fire. I could smell the forest, the terrible damp fog that breathed from the ground, full of decay and death. I dared not turn around and look. If I did, I was sure I would be engulfed in its horrible depths again. Instead I began to think how I could reach the door. Perhaps if I ran fast enough, hard enough, I could escape this room and whatever was growing behind me. None of my attempts had succeeded so far, but anything was better than standing frozen in fear, every muscle straining as I fought not to look behind me.

"Did you use a music box as the guts of this thing?" yelled the woman over the tinny but loud notes coming from the box.

"Of course," Maleson yelled back over the noise. "The cylinder is larger than normal, my own design in fact, but based on the same principle. As it passes by the comb, the same combination of notes played in the same order resound. Based on the accounts written by Agatha Crane–"

"Yes, yes," Thompson yelled back. "I told you about Crane's research and Sharpe's encounter with a time traveler. But you can't use this method to open the path this way. Didn't you read the account of the grimoire cited by Walters?"

"The grimoire is a family myth of some inbred Innsmouth family, supposedly drowned with the Titanic," replied Maleson. "I refuse to be harnessed by superstition. Or the work of Harvey Walters! He's not a scientist."

"Stop arguing," said Tawney. "Something is happening over there." He pointed to a corner of the room. The shadows shifted, taking on some vague shape. I knew it immediately. It was the shadow of a hound. But only a shadow. The creature was still not in the room. But I swear I could hear a rising whine coming from the corner. A hungry sound shivering through the air. I began to sweat even as I shook from cold terror. So far I had only caught glimpses of those terrible creatures. I never confronted them or stayed long enough to truly look at them. Once they began to howl, I always ran.

Tawney reached under his jacket and withdrew a gun.

"You can't fire that in here," cried Maleson. "There's chemicals."

"There's research! Specimens!" said Thompson. "You could destroy the whole lab."

Something was unsettling about the tune. I knew it vaguely but had never heard it done in such a dirge-like rhythm. The world around me was falling away, the shelves becoming translucent, turning into trees. I finally gave a shout of horror as creatures began emerging from the corners of the room turned into forest.

"The time traveler!" screamed Thompson, pointing at me. I blinked at the woman, as confused as she looked. I was a prisoner of the forest, no traveler, but there was no time to explain.

"Look, Agent Tawney, he just appeared," she said. "By the specimens. It's exactly as Beatrice wrote in her journals."

Tawney swung his gun toward me. "Stop! Halt!" he shouted. "You're under arrest."

I walked toward him, my hands held above my head, knowing that a jail cell would be far safer than this room. But as I stepped forward, a howl sounded through the room and a terrible, scaled creature appeared in the corner filled with shadows.

Tawney screamed as the beast leapt into the middle of the brown-suited men. With one swipe of its long reptilian snout, it bit a man's head off, shaking it briefly like a terrier shakes a rat, and then tossed it across the room. The grisly object sailed through the air and through the trees. I saw a tree whip out an extended tongue and latch onto the head trailing bits of spine and muscle. The tree gulped down its catch.

I sprang away from the shelves, banging into the table. "Run," I shouted. "Run!" Instead, Tawney fired his gun directly at me. Given what was appearing in the room, a bullet would have been a mercy, but I swerved to avoid a hound and the shot missed me. "Run," I screamed at him and then scrambled to save myself.

Even as I ran, the room lengthened, twisted, and turned into a distorted part of the beach beneath the trees. I struggled toward the door.

More shouts and screams erupted as the place became half forest, half laboratory, and complete chaos.

The beasts charged among the men. With horrible wet sounds, they bit bodies in two, even as the men emptied bullet after bullet into the hounds. Tawney kept firing wildly at the creatures, screaming at the others to "Save the box!"

I stumbled back from the carnage, trying to find a way out as the path flickered on and off beneath my feet, as the tune stuttered and stopped and started again from the box now sitting on a flaming laboratory table.

"Get out!" yelled Thompson at the two men next to her. "Get out. It will stop as soon as that stupid box stops. The hounds only appear when time shifts. If we get away from here, they shouldn't be able to follow us."

"My box," cried Maleson, suddenly turning to grab at it. "Mandy, I have to get my box!"

Thompson screamed, "Leave it!"

Tawney shoved Maleson away. "*My* box!" he yelled. "I paid for it. This is mine."

"You traitor," yelled Maleson as the two men wrestled over the wretched music box. One hound lifted its bloody snout from the body of a man that it was efficiently tearing into smaller parts. It fixed its gaze upon the pair fighting over the music box.

"If the music ends, this ends!" yelled Thompson as she picked up a pair of tongs, the type used for handling test tubes, and swiped at the music box. She knocked it to the floor with a resounding crash. The music stopped.

Tawney howled in rage: "That's government property!"

"Look," cried Maleson, "the forest is fading."

Even as I struggled toward it, the door vanished. Maleson, Thompson, and Tawney began to dissolve.

The screaming stopped, leaving a terrifying absence of noise punctuated only by the crackling of the flames. All the beasts, the people, and the music box disappeared.

I was alone under the trees save for a jar containing an eyeball and some parts of men who moments before had been watching an experiment in a laboratory. Beyond that was a hound, still splattered in blood. It raised its head and began to howl.

I walked backward away from it, step by slow step, not daring to breathe, only retreating, forever retreating, under the trees which swiped their tongues along the path and ate the remains of once living men.

CHAPTER SIX

Inevitably, Reggie fiddled with my headset to improve it, which made it both better and worse; he was fascinated by anything that amplified sound. After he worked on it, I could hear some things better. But I also had a much worse time with phantom voices.

However, I'm trying to tell my story in the order that things happened, and I mustn't get ahead of myself.

The voices, or rather one particular voice, became a regular companion on the day after my walk.

As Nova explained over lunch, Tuesday was also a rather slow day as the Diamond Dog didn't offer dances in the evening from Sunday through Tuesday. She once again suggested I take time to see the sights of Kingsport, but I felt I had explored its shops and looping roads enough. Besides, the weather had taken a turn for the gloomy, with overcast skies and a promise of sleeting rain. However, recognizing my aunt might like some time to herself, I went in search of others downstairs.

Reggie and Johnny had finished their noon broadcast and were in the process of locking up the radio station. I'd talked to them the day before about my surprise at being featured in their Saturday broadcast. They'd expressed their remorse for causing any embarrassment. Johnny tried to persuade me into coming on a future broadcast to give "a woman's view" of dance music, but I declined. As fascinating as it all was, I couldn't see myself as a radio personality. I didn't like drawing attention to myself and felt too many people were already staring at me in Kingsport due to my hearing device.

Billy, Harlean, Ginger, and Cozy rehearsed on Tuesday afternoon to prepare for the Wednesday evening dance. As much as their music drew me to the ballroom, the heartbreak of not performing made me want to leave. I knew I was being unreasonable. Billy would have gladly shared the piano with me, or I could have played when he was gone. But I wouldn't be as good as I once was. I tried several times after the infection left my ears, and I could feel in my heart as well as my head the difference in my playing.

As I looked around the Diamond Dog that afternoon, I saw no place where I was needed nor anyone requesting help on a project. Sitting idle in my aunt's apartment for another day definitely did not appeal to me.

When I mentioned that I didn't know what to do next, Johnny told me that they were planning to go to the movies in Arkham, a city not far from Kingsport. "You should come along," he said. "You could see something of Arkham. It's bigger than Kingsport and we could find a good place for dinner too."

This plan sounded much more attractive than anything I could think of, so I said that I would love to go to the movies with them.

"There's a Buster Keaton short," said Reggie.

"And the latest episode of the Flapper Detective's aerial adventures," added Johnny. "That's one of the reasons to go to the Arkham theater. They have the first showing of this adventure."

"My aunt's quite a fan of Betsy Baxter," I said. Nova had written to me about meeting the actress who played the Flapper Detective and her admiration for the woman.

I must admit I liked Baxter's current serial, all about a mystery surrounding a new type of long-distance airplane. I still hadn't figured out who was the villain and who was the hero although I knew the Flapper Detective would save the day. The stunts were spectacular, particularly her shoot-out while walking on the wing of a plane. I certainly wouldn't have the courage to do such a thing.

Reggie pulled a rolled-up newspaper out of his pocket, scattering a few screws and a bundle of wire, and opened the paper to the movie ads. "There's an early screening this afternoon," he said to Johnny and me. "We can just make it if we take the car."

"Let me fetch a coat and hat," I said. I ran up the stairs to the apartment, meeting Nova coming down to check on the stock. As she'd mentioned at lunch, Tuesday was the day that Nova spent in the basement taking inventory and reconciling the books. The basement, which I'd briefly glimpsed on an earlier tour, stretched the entire length of the building. There was a cozy little office tucked next to the basement's boiler where Nova and Lily worked on the accounts together. The office was crammed full, with two desks, two wooden chairs, a very large safe, and a pair of filing cabinets. When both women were in there at the same time, there wasn't room for anyone else.

"Are you coming in or going out?" Nova asked me as I passed her on the stairs.

"Going out," I said. "Reggie and Johnny want to spend the afternoon at the movies."

"Sounds like fun," said my aunt. "If you need cash, there's some in the top drawer of my desk. Look for the red leather wallet. Take the men to dinner if you want. I'll be working until late and Thelma has the afternoon off. It will be leftover chowder and rye bread here for supper."

As much as I liked the fish chowder, I wasn't as addicted to it as Nova. "Johnny mentioned that there were some good places to eat in Arkham," I said as I reached the top of the stairs. Looking over the rail at Nova, who was continuing to descend at a calm pace, I said, "If there's anything you need from Arkham, I'm happy to fetch it for you."

Nova shook her head. Waving one hand at me, she said, "Nothing at all. Enjoy yourself!" Daylight from the windows sparkled off her diamond rings and her favorite purple cat brooch pinned to the front of her dress.

Upstairs I picked up my hat and coat from my room. By Nova's desk, I hesitated. I had quite enough money to pay for my ticket to the movies and my dinner. But I knew my aunt meant it when she told me to offer the men dinner at her expense. She was casually generous with all her employees, which was probably why the rest of Kingsport's business owners complained about the sudden interest in jobs at the Diamond Dog.

I opened the top drawer of the desk, the one drawer that Nova kept unlocked since it held stamps, envelopes, and the grocery money for Thelma. I spotted the red wallet immediately and took out enough to cover everyone's dinner after the movies. As I put the wallet back in the drawer, I saw another letter from Chilton Brewster. It bore today's postmark, so Nova must have dropped it into the drawer when pulling out other supplies. Perhaps fetching a stamp for her reply. Nova did write in response to Brewster's nearly daily letters of complaint, usually a quickly dashed note acknowledging the receipt of the letter and no more.

"It befuddles him to receive a thank you for his unkind words," said my aunt with a chuckle one evening. "I do enjoy keeping him off balance."

I started to take the letter out of the envelope but then thought better of my action. As curious as I was to learn why Brewster wrote to my aunt daily, I couldn't invade her privacy in such a way. If she wanted me to read it, she would share it. Or so I told myself as I shoved the tempting envelope back under the red wallet and slammed the desk drawer shut.

Our drive to Arkham took us through the pleasant, if chilly, New England countryside. Both Reggie and Johnny were talkative companions, pointing out various places of interest including the obligatory spot in the road where the redcoats clashed with the Colonists. I told my own tales of walking through Boston, searching for where Paul Revere and his fellows had met and plotted against the British.

I found Arkham to be a small but interesting city. Like Boston, Arkham felt more like a place of yesteryear than today. It lacked the energetic hustle of New York or the intriguing newness of Denver.

Reggie drove us past a Georgian manse built of mellow brick and fine marble facing which dated from the last century, built well before the Civil War. "That's the Arkham Historical Society," he said with a nod. "There's some very good exhibits inside if you're interested in the history of the Miskatonic River Valley."

As soon as Reggie had pointed out his favorite place, Johnny insisted that we tour what he called "far more interesting spots" including Velma's Diner, the Curiositie Shoppe, and Hibb's Roadhouse. When we slowed past the latter, Johnny made me promise that I wouldn't tell my aunt that he'd directed me there. I assured him that I had no interest in visiting roadhouses with or without him.

We missed the first reel of the Keaton comedy, but it was such silly fare, we soon found our place in the plot, laughing and clapping with the crowd as Buster boxed his way to a romantic conclusion. I truly enjoyed the organist accompanying the film, who took full advantage of the Wurlitzer's more specialized sound effects to add emphasis to Buster's antics. Although I didn't need the hearing aid at the movies, I still wore it. To save the battery, I switched it off during the show. The Wurlitzer was loud enough, I could practically feel every note in my body.

When I mentioned to Reggie how much I liked the organ, he told me that the theater management had added it last year. "Before, they had an upright piano and sometimes a small quartet to accompany the bigger films," he said. "They made quite a show on the first evening that they unveiled the Wurlitzer. Even brought back several big movies, including Fairbanks' *Son of Zorro* movie, to demonstrate all the effects of the organ."

The afternoon was as entertaining as expected. I always liked films as lighthearted as Keaton's *Battling Butler*. Betsy Baxter also didn't disappoint and her appearance as the Flapper Detective was loudly cheered by the audience.

At dinner after the movies, Reggie and Johnny told me about how they'd seen the actress in an aerial circus earlier that summer. "She was performing with Wini Habbamock," said Reggie. "A bunch of real stunts, including jumping off a motorcycle onto a rope ladder dangling from Habbamock's plane."

"I can't imagine such a thing," I said.

"Have you ever been up in an airplane?" Reggie asked as he mopped up a piece of apple pie. Due to the early hour, the restaurant that the men picked was quiet enough for me to clearly hear everything that was said and there were no distracting crowd noises.

"No, I've never flown, and I can't say that I have any desire to," I responded. What I left unsaid was that the physicians all advised against it. Nova had discussed having me fly to California to try a new surgical procedure. With the damage already done to my ears by the fever, the doctors felt a plane flight was too risky. There was even some discussion about whether it was safe for me to return to the higher altitude of Denver.

After so many conflicting doctor visits, I decided to ignore the gloomier predictions and planned to return home eventually. However, those warnings had helped make my case for staying with Nova for a little while longer. To her, I said that it was a chance to make sure that my ears were fully healed and recovered from the infection. Of course the delay in corresponding with my family was not so easily explained. But my reluctance to write bad news at Christmas was between me and my conscience. So far, my conscience had lost that particular battle.

On the drive back to Kingsport, I sat up front with Reggie, chatting about radio technology while Johnny gently snored in the backseat.

Reggie glanced over his shoulder at his friend and smiled. "I told him the turkey and gravy were a mistake if he wanted to stay awake."

"Let him sleep," I said, wedging myself more comfortably in the corner of the front seat. The hills rolling by us were anonymous mounds of white, turning slightly blue in the twilight. The bare hedges and long black branches of the trees overhead once again reminded me of the sinister Currier and Ives print back at the college. The skies were still overcast so there was no friendly moon or stars visible. Such a cold and lonely landscape made me glad that we were headed back to the cheerful warmth of the Diamond Dog.

"Do you like working for Nova?" I asked Reggie. As soon as I said it, I realized how awkward the question was. What could he say to Nova's niece?

"Very much," said Reggie without hesitation, apparently not even aware of the oddness of the question. "There was nothing like the Diamond Dog or the radio station before she came to Kingsport. No matter what they say about people from Innsmouth, she has fantastic ideas. You know she is talking about hooking into the National Broadcasting Company's network. We could be heard from coast to coast. Imagine sitting in California and hearing the band playing in Kingsport."

"It sounds like magic," I said, remembering Harlean's excitement about the idea. Then, thinking more about what Reggie said, I asked, "What do people say about Innsmouth? I've never been, although I know Nova and my mother grew up there. Whenever I ask Nova about it, she changes the subject. My mother does the same."

Reggie shrugged. "I don't know much about Innsmouth, just that they're supposed to be unfriendly."

"That's not Nova's personality," I laughed.

"No, your aunt seems to attract friends," Reggie agreed. "But folks like Chilton Brewster sometimes mutter about bad blood in Innsmouth. I really don't know why."

"Did you grow up near here?" I asked. From earlier comments, I gathered Reggie had moved to Kingsport as an adult.

"I grew up near Boston and moved to Arkham to go to the university there," he replied. "Then I worked for the phone company after I graduated. I modernized the switchboard in Kingsport and made some other improvements, but I was always more interested in radios than phones. Nova's job offer was a dream job for me."

"So you weren't one of the employees that Nova stole from Chilton Brewster?"

"Oh, him!" said Reggie. "There's a man who loves to tell the rest of the world how to think and act."

"I've heard his editorials on the lack of decorum in the modern generation," I told him. "Did you know he also writes letters to Nova? She gets one almost every day."

"Brewster writes notes to everyone," Reggie said with a laugh. "I've helped Elmo out once or twice with his transmitter. He showed me a stack of letters from Brewster, practically one for every broadcast, detailing everything that Elmo could do better or should do better. You think working with Elmo five days a week he could just talk to him after a broadcast if he wanted to change something. But no, Brewster goes home, writes a letter, and then posts it! The odd thing, says Elmo, is that when Brewster is in the same room, he hardly talks to Elmo at all. Just goes in front of the microphone and reads out his bits."

"I wouldn't want to work for a man like that," I said.

Reggie nodded. "Elmo's been hinting that he'd like to come over to our station. If Nova does expand the broadcast, we could use the help. But I hate to think how many letters that Brewster would write to all of us if he lost another employee to Nova!"

When we reached our destination, Johnny roused himself from the backseat and wished us a pleasant evening. He was, he informed us, off home for a quick wash and brush up before venturing out on his date of the night. He'd return for the car, which he shared with Reggie, in an hour or so, he said.

"Two dinners in one night," said Reggie, pretending to be scandalized. "You won't fit into your suits if you keep this up!"

"We plan on dinner and dancing at the Purple Cat," responded Johnny in his velvety voice. "In my case, a light dinner and much quickstepping."

He disappeared into the twilight gloom with a final cheery "Good night!"

When Johnny left, I wondered if I had a book in the apartment to entertain me. My aunt kept no more than one or two shelves of reading material, and she favored nonfiction accounts of polar exploration and sea voyages. My own books were crated up for shipment home. I regretted that my beloved copy of Lang's *Red Fairy Book* was in the boxes stored upstairs in Nova's attic. I'd packed up my boarding house room and shipped everything to the Diamond Dog before departing to New York with Nova, unsure if I'd be returning to Boston or heading to Denver after seeing the doctors. Since then, I'd regretted packing up my childhood favorite. Lang's stories had traveled all the way from Denver with me. I spent many long days stuck in bed with the fever, and the book had been my greatest comfort. The twelve dancing princesses, Jack and his beanstalk, Rapunzel, and Snowdrop were all old friends of mine due to a long-ago birthday gift from Nova. But I supposed reading about Amundsen had educational benefits.

"Are you heading home also?" I asked Reggie. Nova was sure to be in the basement, still working on accounts, or perhaps she had taken the Rolls to the Purple Cat. I hadn't been to the cafe, but I knew Nova held a small dance on Tuesday nights there when the Diamond Dog was closed. Thelma was gone as well. Suddenly the thought of returning to the empty apartment didn't appeal. I had spent enough time there.

"I'm going into the studio to make some adjustments to the transmitter. I have a few ideas for improving the microphones too," said Reggie. "Would you like a tour of the space?"

"Very much so," I said, cheerfully abandoning my resolve to finally figure out the differences between Arctic and Antarctic exploration. Amundsen could wait for another day.

In the studio, Reggie made the technical aspects of broadcasting as understandable as possible. He was a lively and well-informed guide for a novice like me, pointing out many similarities between the equipment in the studio and the device which sat so uncomfortably on my head.

"Do you mind taking it off?" he said, pointing to my headset. "I'd love to take a closer look at it."

"I'd be delighted," I said truthfully. The gadget was beginning to drag uncomfortably on my neck and shoulders. I was happy to surrender it to him.

"Do you mind?" he said, gesturing at the device. "I'd love to see what's under the cover."

"Not at all," I said. If in my heart I hoped he'd break it, it was a very small wish. Nova would not be pleased if the thing was in pieces in the morning. I, however, was relieved to have it gone for even a few moments. A number of sounds might not be as distinguishable without it, but what I heard felt more natural.

"I'll be careful," Reggie promised as he took the hearing aid from me. He produced a screwdriver and began taking the earphone apart.

As he worked, I mentioned to Reggie the recent distortions of sound that I had heard as well as how the device failed to live up to all the promises made by the salesman. "I know it's the best that there is," I said, because Nova had made very sure of that before purchasing the hearing aid. "But nothing ever sounds exactly as it did before the fever. I suppose it's studying music that's made me so fussy. I do know when something doesn't sound quite right."

Engrossed in the device, Reggie mumbled something back about pitch and microphones failing to catch all sounds. Thinking of the opera singers that I'd heard on the gramophone, I thought I understood what he was saying. The full tone of their singing was missing from the recording, while perfectly audible in the theater with no amplification at all.

"It's all to do with the range of what we pick up and translate into broadcast sound," Reggie said. "With the older microphones we could only capture a narrow segment of the audible spectrum. But Western Electric's new microphones and signal amplifiers are making a huge difference. You can definitely hear it in some of the newer recordings. Those systems let us reproduce a much broader frequency range."

"But will it sound the same as going to a concert hall?" I asked skeptically.

"It will sound better," he replied, "and everything that I've seen in the past few years promises broadcasts and recordings will continue to improve. There's even a guy experimenting with broadcasting pictures with sound. Imagine seeing talking movies on your radio!"

I thought of the Wurlitzer resounding through the theater in Arkham. "I prefer the movies the way that they are. With live music in a theater."

"Nobody is going to be broadcasting pictures tomorrow." Reggie tapped the equipment around him. "But even now we can broadcast more of the highs and lows. And softer sounds. I've been telling Harlean with these new microphones she doesn't need to belt out every tune. She could even whisper into the microphone and our radio audience will be able to hear her perfectly, as if she was singing in the room to them."

"A more intimate sound?" I guessed.

"Crooning is what some of the singers are calling it. They're not singing for a theater full of people. They're singing for and to the microphone, and it's a very different technique."

"I'd love to hear it," I said and meant it. I wondered if such microphones and amplifiers could bring back the full range of music to me. Even as radio improved, hearing aids had to improve as well, I told myself. But nothing would ever be the same as it was, I thought a moment later.

Reggie nodded. "Come into the studio during the next dance. I'll put one of our headsets on you. You can listen through it to Harlean and Billy when they're playing for the broadcast. It should be clearer than listening to Nova's radio upstairs. You'll be hearing what I hear when we broadcast."

"Tomorrow night?" I asked, thinking it would be fun to sit with Reggie during the Wednesday broadcast.

"Tomorrow night!" Reggie affirmed. He screwed the plate back on my earpiece and then held it to his own ear, speaking softly into the microphone. "Better," he pronounced, handing the whole contraption back to me. "But not perfect. I'm still hearing something, just at the edge of my range, a slight ringing. Do you hear it?"

"Not quite a ringing," I said, adjusting the headset and hanging the microphone around my neck again. "More like the faintest buzz. Although sometimes it sounds like a dog barking."

"It probably isn't a dog. The animal would have to be in the room for your microphone to pick it up. More likely the microphone is amplifying something that we don't normally hear, like your heartbeat. A piece of jewelry or a button could rub against the microphone while you're walking. It could cause distortions that you wouldn't hear when sitting still."

"No jewelry and I wear the microphone outside my clothes, so the heartbeat is unlikely," I said as I gathered up my hat and coat. "But thank you for looking at it and for the lovely day. I enjoyed the movies, and the dinner, and the lesson about microphones very much!"

"So did I," said Reggie with a smile. "Johnny's right. I'm mad about this stuff." He waved his hand to encompass the whole studio. "Radio is going to be even bigger than movies someday. When we truly understand how to record and broadcast sound so it seems natural, like someone sitting beside you telling a story, we'll change the world."

"I'm sure you will," I said as I left the studio. "Goodnight, Reggie."

"Goodnight," he called back.

I crossed the empty ballroom. The place was nothing but shadows, only a few small lights left on for latecomers like me or Nova working down in the basement. I felt more than heard the clack of my heels as I crossed the wooden dance floor. To amuse myself, I began to hum Billy's rendition of "Jingle Bells" to see how it would echo in the empty room and sound in the microphone slung over my chest. Just as I reached the end of the first verse, I heard a man's voice coming from my earpiece.

He spoke very low and intimately, just as Reggie said people would sound on the new microphones. But he wasn't broadcasting from the stage. There was no one there. He wasn't in the room speaking into the microphone resting over my now wildly beating heart.

With a gasp, I spun around just to be sure that I was completely alone. There was no one there at all.

But still I heard him speak to me. I froze, glancing about me. There was something familiar about this sorrowful voice. I had heard this man before. But I knew the microphone didn't have the strength to pick up anyone outside the room. Reggie had been certain about the range and if anyone knew microphones, it was Reggie.

"Ghosts," I whispered to myself. Clara and I often scared ourselves silly playing with a Ouija board when we were younger (a gift from Aunt Nova, of course). But I never truly believed the dead could speak to us. Because if ghosts existed, it would have been my brother Benny's voice that I heard. This was a man, I decided. Someone my age or older, with a deep soft voice full of sadness and, I was sure of this, an undertone of fear.

"Once upon a time, something happened. If it had not happened, it would not be told," the man said in my left ear as if he was crooning a story just for me. But there truly was nobody there.

I pulled the headset off and slung it around my neck so I could no longer hear any whispers in the earpiece. I switched off the battery as added protection from disembodied voices. Then I ran upstairs as fast as I could, banging into Nova's familiar apartment and hurrying into my bedroom. Luckily, Nova was still out and I didn't have to explain myself to my aunt.

I divested myself of the hearing aid as quickly as I could and retreated to my bed. I sat there for some time just staring at the headset, microphone, and purse containing the battery pack. It was just a collection of wires, I told myself, not a conduit to phantoms.

The longer I looked at it, the more my initial fear faded. I listened to voices coming out of Nova's radio every day. Such sounds couldn't hurt me. To be frightened of a man's voice in my earpiece was ridiculous, I told myself firmly. Just because I didn't understand how I was hearing him, there was no need to be afraid.

My own shillyshallying annoyed me. I used to be a person who made plans and moved forward with those plans. I was never frightened by shadows or odd noises (three brothers cured me of any squeamishness quite young).

"Raquel Malone Gutierrez, don't be a cowardly lion," I said, echoing my brothers' favorite call to bravery when their sisters failed to take a dare. I marched to the dresser. Once again I went through all the bother of placing the hearing aid correctly on my head and then switched on the battery pack. Perhaps Reggie's fiddling had changed so it could broadcast as well as receive.

"Hello?" I said to the night. "Are you still there? How can I help you?"

Because I was sure of the sorrow and the fear that I had heard in the man's voice, I was sure that he needed someone to help him.

I called out again.

Nobody answered me.

"Once there was a princess who was such a dreadful storyteller that the like of her was not to be found far or near," a boy in Norway began his story to me. By which he meant the princess was a liar. I'm worse than the princess. Once I told a man that I was raised on a chicken farm in Iowa, when I didn't even know where Iowa was, much less anything about chickens.

But I'm trying to tell you a story, a story about a dreadful liar that I met, only this one was a prince and not a princess.

I heard him whistling as he walked around a corner. Where I had been a moment before, I couldn't remember. But now I was standing on a street full of fancy houses with evergreen wreaths upon their doors. The sky was as dull as old iron above.

It was all so normal, so calm, that I could hardly believe I had walked into such a place after the nightmares that I had experienced.

"Hey, can you spare a dime? Even a nickel will do," said the man as he walked up to me. Then he shook his head. "Looks like you're as broke as me. Nice jacket! I had one like that, but I threw it out when I got a nick on the sleeve. Those were the days."

I shifted my hand across the cut on my left sleeve. The handsome American facing me was dressed like a wealthy man, with an overcoat lined in fur and a fine suit under that. But the hems of his trousers were frayed and his shoes were unpolished. Even his mustache seemed a bit ragged at the edges and his chin was shadowed by stubble, as if he couldn't afford a good razor or a barber.

"Lovely house, isn't it?" he said to me, but he looked over my shoulder as if seeking a bigger audience. "I once owned the biggest house of all. Of course, the crash took care of all that. Put your money in stocks, Preston, you can't go wrong. You'll always be rich, Preston, just do what your daddy did and you'll never want for anything."

His laughter rang out, a bitter sound. "What does the song say? Traipsing through hell? Walking through it? Slogging, slogging, that's the word," he said to me. "Heard it on the radio and I knew the song was about me. Because that's what I did." He thumped his breast with one hand. "Helped them out, didn't I? Gave them money, didn't I? Slogged through hell, didn't I? And everyone loved me because I was a millionaire."

He waved his bare hands wildly in the air. Each hand was chapped red with cold. The littlest finger on his left hand was crooked, as if he had broken it not long ago. His hands were not the hands of a rich man. His hands were the hands of a poor man, a man who dug ditches or washed plates to eat. His hands looked like mine. So I knew all his talk of wealth was lies.

"Good old Preston," he said, shaking his head. "Good old chump. Thought the money would never run out until it did. Thought I'd spend all my days dancing at the Clover Club and the Diamond Dog. Seems like yesterday, seems like forever ago."

His look turned sly, the glance of a rogue, and he said again to me, "Sure you can't spare a dime? Pay you back twice over. Pay you back with as many silver dimes as your pockets can hold." He tapped the side of his reddened nose. "I have friends, you know, my father's friends. All I have to do is talk to them. Then I'll be me again. I'll be rich again. Just need a small investment in the outer appearance." He gestured at his frayed trousers and shabby shoes. "Get the suit brushed, the shoes shined, and the hair trimmed. If I look like I'm worth something, they'll want me, same as before."

Digging my hands deep into the pockets of my leather coat, I backed away from him, because all his wild talk, all his tall tales, frightened me. Then I felt it, small, and round, and cold as ice in one corner of my pocket. I pulled out the silver coin and tossed it to the desperate man.

He snatched it out of the air and whooped. "A dime! It's my lucky day and yours, too, my friend. 1933 is turning into a good year after all. I wonder what sort of supper they serve for Christmas Eve at the Order. Why don't you come along and find out? I'll tell them you're a friend of the family. What's one more little lie going to hurt?"

I answered his question. I don't know why I did, but it seemed that this man needed to hear what I had to say.

"I have spent all my life lying about who I am," I said. "I did it to eat. I made up stories to stop men from beating me. I lied so I could join an army. I lied again so I could desert my post. I lied every time I crossed a border and became someone new. I have told so many lies about myself that I don't know who I am. I can no longer remember. It would have been best to tell the truth."

He stood completely still, one hand still clutching the dime that I had thrown to him. This poor man in a rich man's tattered suit looked at me with eyes filled with agony, a look I could feel on my own face.

The door of the fancy house opened, and a woman stepped out on the porch. "Preston? Preston Fairmont, is that you?" she said.

He whipped around to face her. "Oh Daisy, darling Daisy, how are you? How is my favorite librarian? Merriest greetings of the season and so on."

"Merry Christmas," she said, coming down the steps with her arms outstretched. "You dear, dear man. It's been too long. When did I see you last? Cairo?"

He sidestepped from her embrace. "Mustn't hug me," he said with a little sadness in his voice. "Not fit for man or beast tonight. I slept rough the last couple of days. Arkham's flophouses lack a certain cleanliness. Not like the Ritz, not like the Ritz at all."

"Oh, Preston," she said with a tender smile. "Come in and get cleaned up. We can find you a bed tonight."

"I don't like to impose, dear lady, I had plans for quite another destination, but–" and he glanced at me, "–perhaps it wouldn't hurt to talk it over. You always were so much wiser than me, darling Daisy." Then he turned and tossed the dime back. "Here, buddy, you need this more than me tonight."

A little boy appeared in the doorway. One hand was wrapped around a candy cane and the sticky evidence of the treat ringed his mouth. The other fat fist clutched a string of bells. "I figured it out," he yelled. "I know when to ring my bells, Auntie Daisy, when the others sing. Come listen to us." He shook the bells at us.

Then they were gone, like a dream, and I was in this place with no stars. For once, despair did not engulf me. My hand was wrapped around the dime that the poor prince tossed to me, and it was warm in my fist. I hoped he would tell the truth to his Daisy.

Unlike the tales that I have told before, the ones I told to deceive and survive, the stories I am writing here are true. But how do I make you believe? When I can barely believe what I see when I raise my eyes from this page.

But I believe you are real. For I heard your name and you spoke to me.

CHAPTER SEVEN

Over the next few days, I heard the unknown man several times more in my earpiece. Sometimes when I was in the apartment, but more often when I was downstairs listening to the band and dancing. Mostly his words sounded like someone broadcasting fairytales.

I'd always enjoyed stories which began "once upon a time." Starting when I was five, Nova had sent me Andrew Lang's fairy books, a few volumes every birthday, until I had all twelve colors, which I loved to read to my baby sister and brother. Nova also shipped us the new Oz book every Christmas.

So when I heard the man's voice saying "Far, far away, across the great waters," I wasn't sure if I was hearing someone outside my head or simply repeating to myself the start of a half-remembered story.

Then, like the miller's daughter in *Rumpelstiltskin*, I discovered the stranger's name. It happened when I was dancing with Johnny at the end of Saturday evening, while Harlean sang "What Can I Say After I Say That I'm Sorry?"

As Harlean gave the final line a nice upbeat twist, Johnny spun me around and the dance ended.

Up on the stage, Billy was joking with Harlean while his fingers rattled out the opening bars of "Jingle Bells." The crowd gave a shout and Billy waved at them. "Next one!" he promised as the band took a break.

In my left ear I heard the stranger say, "My name is Paul."

Without thinking, I responded, "My name is Raquel" just as the music stopped.

Johnny looked at me with a puzzled twinkle in his eyes. "Hello, Raquel," he said to me.

I stepped away from Johnny, scanning the late-night crowd of couples slowly leaving the dance floor. Most were intent on returning to their seats and gathering up their belongings. There would be a call for the last dance in a minute or two, but many would leave now. None seemed interested in me, nor could I spot anyone who might have just declared his name.

I knew it was a man who spoke. That much I was certain of. Every time I heard the stranger, his voice was clear enough for me to judge him a man, not a boy, and – although I was less certain of this – probably not an American. There was something about his accent that reminded me of the Jewish immigrants I had met before, the Yiddish speakers in particular. But, remembering a few visiting musicians who came to play with the college orchestra in Boston, he could have been German or Ukrainian or Polish. I simply wasn't hearing enough to tell, and I was certainly no Sherlock Holmes to instantly know a person's ancestry from their accent.

"Raquel, are you all right?" Johnny said, laying a hand gently on my shoulder to guide me off the dance floor.

"Yes, of course," I replied, sitting down at the small table in the corner that we had taken for our own. "I'm sorry. Just a little distracted. I thought I heard someone I knew."

"See them now?" Johnny asked.

I shook my head, feeling a bit foolish. Could I be suffering from auditory hallucinations? Was such a thing even possible? Joan of Arc, of course, heard voices. Many saints did. But I didn't think this was any angel giving me instructions. This man, this stranger, speaking into my left ear always sounded too ordinary. Just the sort of conversation anyone would overhear by accident. Except it didn't feel accidental or a trick of the microphone dangling from my chest. It felt like someone was trying to talk directly to me.

Sometimes he sounded very far away, but sometimes it was as if he was in the same room with me. As if I could speak to him, if only I knew how.

Still, every time I tried to speak to the stranger – to Paul if the name I just heard was his – I received the same response as I had on Tuesday night. Silence.

"Want me to fetch you a drink before I go do my bit?" asked Johnny.

Johnny announced various songs and spoke a little about the Diamond Dog from the stage during the live broadcast.

"No, I'm still working on this ginger ale," I said, tapping my glass. "I'll wait for the others."

At the end of the evening, Ginger, Harlean, Cozy, and Billy joined me at the table I held for all of us, joking about the evening or speculating about the various couples who circled the floor. They knew most everyone from Kingsport, but the radio broadcast brought many from Arkham and other towns nearby.

Reggie would join us after the broadcast ended. Sitting in the booth and listening through Reggie's headset had been a thrilling experience. On his headsets, I didn't hear the barking of the dog which still disturbed me now and then when wearing my own earpiece. Nor did I ever hear the stranger, I realized, when I was wearing the radio station's headset.

"I'm off then," said Johnny, but he gave a worried glance over his shoulder at me. I resolved to be more discreet in responding to the stranger, to Paul, when next I heard him.

Johnny moved toward the stage to announce the last dance of the evening. Harlean stood at the microphone in a beautiful silk dress with a velvet scarf draped across her shoulders. Her hair was held fast under a sequined bandeau which caught the light and made her sparkle even more.

"She's really good," said a Black man settling into a chair next to mine. He wasn't much older than myself, perhaps he was even a little younger. A good-looking man but one whose face had lines on it that I guessed came from hard times rather than age. He slid an instrument case under his chair. "And Billy Oliver is a genius at the keyboard."

I smiled to hear such praise of my friends. "I couldn't agree more," I told him. "Are you enjoying the dance?"

"Very much," he replied. "Miss Nova holds a swell party. I visited the Purple Cat once or twice. I always thought she had a good ear for performers. These are the best yet."

"I'm her niece, Raquel Gutierrez," I said, holding out my hand to shake his. As soon as I gripped it, I recognized the calluses of a musician. "You're a trumpet player?" I guessed, glancing down at the case now hidden under his chair.

He grinned and admitted it. "Jim Culver," he said. "I do play the horn when I have a chance. Haven't had much work lately, at least not for folks like these."

I raised my eyebrows in inquiry.

Jim shrugged. "I prefer my daddy's horn over any other instrument, but I promised Miss Nova that I wouldn't play it here or any place of hers. Guess she's got a right to say whether it's the living or the dead dancing the night away."

That's what I thought I heard Jim say, although I almost instantly doubted the words meant what they seemed to mean. I told myself that he was speaking as a musician about the quality of the audience. We'd all had performances where the audience seemed dead to the music, unable to respond no matter how hard we tried.

"But I sure do like the way that Billy plays this song. I mean to try that when I get to the graveyard. It will make the old bones hop," Jim said to me.

I wondered if the Graveyard was a club in Kingsport or Arkham, but before I could ask, Billy had swung into his rendition of "Jingle Bells" on the piano. Harlean was shaking a string of bells in her hand while Ginger made her saxophone trip through the notes as Cozy gave the drums the beat of the horses' hooves. As Billy predicted, the couples were dancing with delight, the men swinging their partners about and the ladies kicking up their heels.

Jim mimed the pressing of keys on a horn as he listened, obviously hearing his own horn in his head as he worked his way through this jazz version of the sleighing song. "Yes," he said, "it's downright rambunctious. Should shake a few awake tonight."

He slid a hand under his chair and pulled out his battered old trumpet case. Then, tipping his hat to me, Jim stood up and wandered away through the dancers.

Over the past few days at the Diamond Dog, I'd grown used to folks quite different from those I met in my small Boston college. But there was something about the horn player which bothered me for quite a while after he left. As I sat puzzling through the end of the band's last song, I realized what it was.

The whole time that we were talking, I'd heard very faintly in my earpiece the sound of a horn playing. But Ginger was blowing the sax and Billy was pounding on the keys of a piano. So why had I heard a trumpet playing along with them in that final song? A horn whose notes became more ghostly as Jim Culver danced away from me clutching his closed trumpet case.

Then Paul's voice crackled in my ear again, starting again with "Once upon a time." I forgot all about Jim as I listened to him. The song ended and so did Paul's story. I heard nothing more unusual than the clattering of plates and glasses as the waiters swept around the room, cleaning up the Saturday night dance.

I sat at the table, rapping my fingers against the top, thinking about the stranger who named himself Paul. For the more his voice haunted me, the more I needed to solve this one puzzle. I needed to believe that I could do something for him, even though I hadn't been able to solve anything else in my life.

I saw a strange phrase in a book once. The book was old and tattered and sitting on the very bottom shelf in a public library. When I first came to America, I found cities full of libraries built at the wish of a rich man so even a poor man could sit and read without fear.

One day, in a library with tall, curved windows which let in the foggy sunlight, I opened up a book about knights and ladies. I thought at first it was a child's book so I read it to practice my English.

But it was written in a very strange way and many words made no sense to me. Finally, I went to the librarian and pointed at the chapter heading. "Please," I said, "what does this mean?"

"Divers grisly ghosts," she read out loud, but very softly, as it was a library and people only whispered in its rooms.

"Divers are men who swim underwater?" I asked her, which made no sense in a book about knights and the way she pronounced the word sounded different than what I had heard before.

"It's old English," she said with a shake of her head. "It means diverse or many ghosts."

I remember the Kingdom of Ghosts in the book, where smoke and fumes choke the air and spirits chatter with iron teeth.

Between one step and the next, I walked out of the place where I was and found the kingdom and the musician who rules it. Fog swirled around me as I stepped amid trees dripping with water but thankfully no teeth. As always, it was cold, and the mist made the light so dim that I could not tell if it was morning or evening. I pulled my coat tight around me. If it wasn't Christmas Eve like all the other times, it was certainly the dead of winter. And more than winter was dead in these woods.

In a clearing before me, at the edge of an open grave, a Black man played the trumpet, a song I almost knew.

Staring at the trees, he called, "Mr Ghoul, you should have danced to my tune before. Time to dance, time to shake those bones into the ground."

Something shambled under the trees, something which stank in the darkness there, and groaned with a wet gurgling sound.

"Oh, they ripped out his heart and they ripped out his lungs," said the musician, "but they left the soul for me." He played a more somber tune upon his horn and the moaning creature crawled from beneath the dripping wet bushes. On hands and knees, it crept forward, a gray and ghastly corpse heading for the open grave.

I had never heard such a song before. In Hollywood, I worked for a director who made stories about men being hypnotized and lured to their doom. If he had met this musician, he would have cast the horn player in one of his films. But no movie audience could have heard what I heard or felt what I felt, the terrifying urge to follow the music.

The horn player kept up his tune. I stumbled forward step by involuntary step, seeking only to lay myself down in that muddy grave with the thing that slithered on its belly like a worm into the gaping hole.

But the musician blew one last note and grabbed me by the arm. "You're too late," he said to me with a mournful smile. "Ten years too late and this place isn't for you. Leave the grave for Mr Ghoul."

I stumbled back, too overcome by the silencing of the music to find words.

Shaking my shoulder with his free hand, the musician said, "Go back, go back and try again. Listen for old Jim Culver but listen for a younger Jim. When you hear me playing this, dance to my tune." Lifting his horn to his mouth, he played a jangling tune.

"I know this," I started to say but his music drowned me out.

As the musician played the trumpet, he circled away from the grave. I followed Jim because I had no will to do anything else. He said to me, "You come dancing again on Christmas Eve. But 1926, not 1936. Remember. It's important. You come dancing when Billy Oliver starts playing and Ginger wails on her fine sax. Listen and dance when Cozy beats the drums, or it will be the last dance they'll ever dance. You remember and stay out of Dunwich. This is no place for you!"

Then his music danced me out of his haunted wood with the song I had heard before and names I didn't know. But now I hear your voice. I think you hear mine. I write this warning in hope that you will understand and never see the Kingdom of Ghosts.

CHAPTER EIGHT

We were halfway through the month, and every night brought bigger crowds to dance at the Diamond Dog. All the town was buzzing about how Nova would decorate the place for her Christmas Eve event. Expectations ran high that the decorations would rival the Parker House in Boston. I spotted boxes of crepe paper and festoons being carried into the basement at all hours by Otis and Tim.

Strings of electric lights were draped around the room by Reggie, who constructed the most bizarre switchboard in a corner of the room to control the whole lot. One afternoon he ran me through the switches, showing me how to light up various corners of the room or plunge everything into darkness except the stage. Apparently one of Reggie's past hobbies was amateur theater and he had, in college, run the lights for an amateur theatrical troupe until the theater burned down. The latter piece of information alarmed me until he explained that the fire had broken out on stage during a bizarre play being directed by Sydney Fitzmaurice.

"The film director?" I asked. My older brothers had been huge fans of Fitzmaurice's nightmare movies, although I never liked them much myself.

"This was before he went to Hollywood," said Reggie. "When we both attended the university in Arkham. It was a long time ago, before the war. He was fascinated by the occult and staged this strange show all about a hooded stranger. A fire broke out on opening night. I didn't like Sydney much, so I decided not to work on the production. In fact, I joined the amateur radio society and built my first transformer around that time."

"Didn't a fire destroy Fitzmaurice's final film?" I said, with some vague memories of the headlines around the time that I started teaching in Boston. My students gossiped about the fire for months afterward, as several were fans of Fitzmaurice's leading lady Renee Love.

Reggie nodded. "About three years ago. He came back to Arkham to film in his family home. The fire destroyed the place and his last film."

"Hey, Reggie," said Johnny, walking over to us. "Mrs Orne is here with her recipe for pepper nuts. Do I have the name right?"

"Pfeffernüsse," said Reggie. "It's a great cookie."

"What kind of cookie would use pepper?" I asked.

"Find out along with our listeners. You'd like Mrs Orne," said Johnny. "Come on the air with her?"

"No. I need a walk and to do some shopping." I wanted to buy a gift for Nova, but I couldn't think what she would like. Obviously diamonds, but such jewelry was well outside my budget. Then I remembered the hardware store with the bicycle in the window. I wondered if they carried some small electrical appliances. Nova loved gadgets. I suspected even a clever toy might amuse her.

Outside, it was a simply splendid December day. Not too cold and enough sun to make the snow on the roofs sparkle. Even that slush trodden underfoot didn't look too bad.

I found myself humming Billy's version of "Jingle Bells" as I walked along the streets, smiling and nodding at several friendly faces. In the short time that I had been in Kingsport, the townspeople, especially those who loved to dance, had become familiar to me. And I to them. Nobody stared at my headset anymore or seemed much perturbed if I asked them to repeat their words into the microphone. I began to think that perhaps I could live with the contraption. At least in a place like this, a small town where people could see me as more than a woman with a hearing device. How I would manage in a city like Denver, or how I would tell my family, I still had not decided.

Then, as I stepped from the sunlight into a pool of shadow on a side street, I heard the stranger's voice in my ear. "My words may frighten you. Do not be afraid. Please do not be afraid. One of us must be without fear," he said.

He sounded so sad and so lonely that I spoke without thinking, "I am not afraid. I swear I am not. I wish I could help you."

A sigh, or more accurately, a suddenly indrawn breath sounded in my ear. He said, "How can you hear me?"

"I don't know," I said. "But are you Paul?"

Another ragged breath and with almost a sob, he answered, "I am Paul."

"My name is Raquel," I said.

"I heard you say your name," he said. "Oh, a long time ago, I think. But it gave me such hope."

"It was at the dance a few nights ago," I said. I must have looked so strange. A woman standing on a street corner talking to the shadows at her feet. Luckily this quiet street was deserted so nobody saw me. But I didn't care. I'd finally managed to speak to the stranger, who didn't feel like a stranger at all. I knew Paul, I felt, almost as well as I knew the doubts in my head. During the conversation, I absolutely believed that he was real, a living man, and no ghost of my imagination.

"Time has no meaning where I am," he said. "Tell me what you see."

"I'm on a street," I said, struck by the inadequacy of my words. I tried again. "It's a street in Kingsport, a very pretty town, and it snowed last night. The trees and the bushes are all covered. Oh, and the sun is shining. The sky is perfectly blue."

I stopped, appalled at my lack of ability to accurately describe something right before my eyes, because there were so many details I hadn't mentioned. The small birds hopping in and out of the bushes in search of seeds or bugs. A lopsided snowman decorating the lawn of a house across the street.

"Perfectly blue," Paul repeated. "I look into a sky of nothing. No stars, no moon. Just nothing. Thank you, Raquel, for reminding me of sunlight."

"I wish I could do more," I said. What he said was so strange, so unreal, yet still I believed him.

"You are a voice of hope," he replied. "I have nothing here but despair."

I thought of my own sorrow and anger at losing my hearing through no fault of my own.

"Don't despair," I said as much to myself as to the voice in my ear. "There is a way out of this."

A man rounded the corner of the street, walking toward me. I stepped back to let him pass and Paul was gone. I don't know how I knew that, but I felt his absence keenly.

"Miss Gutierrez," said the tall gentleman as he passed me, tipping his gray fedora.

It took me a moment, but I recognized him as the man who had been meeting with Chilton Brewster the other day.

"Do I know you?" I said.

"We haven't been introduced," he said. "But I was hoping to speak to you. Agent Ralph Tawney, the Bureau of Investigation." He flipped his coat open to show me a badge. Beneath his brown suit jacket, I could clearly see the outline of a gun in a holster.

"I'm sorry," I said, stepping back in surprise. "Why would you want to talk to me?"

His next words shook me even more. "It's about Chilton Brewster. He's made the most peculiar claims about your aunt Nova Malone."

"Snip, snap." I think that is an ending and not a beginning. But the cook made me think of it.

You spoke to me and something stirred in my heart. Not quite hope, it is hard to know hope in this place. But I did not feel its absence so completely. I did not despair as I walked among the trees, not even when I saw the bones of a man lying tumbled at the base of one trunk.

I smelled baking and between one step and the next, I stood at the back door of a restaurant. I had washed dishes in enough places to know this was a good restaurant since the smells coming out of a propped open door were heavy with spice and comfort.

I stepped inside and saw a cook going from tray to tray, icing small ginger cookies in the shapes of stars and crescent moons. From a small box on a shelf, a song crackled through the room. I had to look twice to realize that it was a radio. I had never seen one so small.

"If you're here to help serve today's lunch, you're early" said the cook as she bent over her task, humming a bit to herself; around her neck hung a large silver cross, "And if you're the fool who was supposed to help me with the baking, you're late. It's two hours past dawn already. I need all this done by ten this morning, so I can get started on the entrees. It's not every day we host the Mayor of Kingsport for Christmas Eve."

"A very pretty town," I said to the cook, remembering how you described Kingsport to me.

"What?" said the woman, putting aside her icing to reach for a spatula to transfer the cookies to a rack. "Are you here to work or just hoboing through?"

"I can wash dishes," I said because I knew all good cooks need somebody who is willing to clean.

This cook stopped her work to look at me properly. "Been on the road long?" she said, glancing at my worn leather jacket and stained pants. Even my shoes bore marks of the path's often sudden descent into blood and mud.

"Forever," I replied as honestly as I could.

"Well, the Lord helps those who help themselves," she said. "But there's a lot to be said for charity, especially in this season." She pointed to an alcove behind the kitchen proper where I could see a sink and a large counter with dish racks and draining boards set upon it. "There's a pile of dishes already waiting for a pair of honest hands to clean them. Expect more as the day goes along. Get it all done and I'll pay you."

I set to work. Behind me voices rose and fell as more people streamed into the kitchen.

"Hurry up," said one waitress to the other. "They want the desserts to come out before Mayor Brewster's speech."

The washing continued past lunch as dishes came back to the sink. I had never stayed in one place so long, I thought, since I became lost under the trees. I began to hope that this time I would remain in the pretty town of Kingsport. I was afraid to step away from the sink at all, afraid I would find myself back in the forest.

Eventually the noises behind me died away as people wished each other a "Merry Christmas" and departed. Still I scrubbed, rinsed, and dried, convinced each action would anchor me in one time and place, even though I didn't know what year it was. Whenever it was, there were dishes to be dried and stacked. A job for me. No matter where I wandered, work always made me feel anchored to a place. For a time at least.

Finally, the cook came to tell me that I was finished. "There's not a single dirty dish anywhere," she said. "Just a plate with some leftovers for you. Sit down and eat something before you go."

As I ate, the cook fiddled with the radio dial until eerie music filled the room and a deep voice intoned, "What evil lurks in the hearts of men, the Shadow knows…"

With a sigh, the cook collapsed into a chair and rested her feet on the rungs of the chair opposite me. "I love this show," she said to me. "The first time I heard it I knew Lamont Cranston understood about the monsters lurking out there. Sometimes I'm so tired of fighting, but then I think someone must keep battling. Just like all the people who help the Shadow on this show."

She sighed and shook her head. "I reckon people all over the world are learning the hard way that we must fight evil. Ten years after the crash, I guess we thought life would be getting better by now. But I read the newspapers, all the stuff happening in Europe because of Hitler, and I just don't know."

I ate as slowly as I could as the story of a detective – a detective with the power to cloud men's minds – unfolded on the radio. Children were reunited with their father. At the end, a rich man gave his girlfriend Margo a puppy and the actors wished the audience a "Merry Christmas." I had never heard anything like it before, but it was marvelous. I told the cook how much I enjoyed it.

The cook smiled at me. "It's sentimental," she said. "I know it is. But we need shows like this. Things just keep getting worse, but this gives me hope. Makes me feel like someone will take up the fight."

"But does it have to be us?" I said as I finished the last of the sandwich. It was a question that I had wrestled with all my life. Driven from place to place, I had heard many men and women standing on soapboxes at street corners shouting for change. I'd seen them cut down and I'd seen them rise to power. It seemed to make very little difference. Men slept cold and hungry in doorways. Women still wept at the death of children. If the newspapers of 1939 piled on the table beside me were true, war was once again engulfing the world.

But here I was warm and safe, and for the moment I was content. That much I had learned in a wandering life. The events of the world can change our lives, but we can do little to change the world. All I wanted was a safe and pretty town and to live my life in peace. But the woman across the table from me wanted something very different.

"I don't know about you, son," the cook said as she tapped the cross around her neck, "but I know I have a duty, a calling, to put down monsters. There are days when I am tired, and there are days when I wish the Lord could find another to bear my burdens, but I always know that what I do is good. And I know something more important than the evil in men's hearts."

"What is that?" I asked, touched by her kindness toward me.

She reached out and touched my chest. "I know the good in the most ordinary of people. How much a cook, or a waitress, or a mechanic can do to keep the world a safer place. I have met some extraordinary folks on my travels. I hope you become one of them."

She reached for a handbag and pulled some dollars from it, counting them on the table in front of me. "Use this wisely," the woman said to me. "You're a good worker. I'd have you back, but I'm leaving tonight. There's something in Dunwich that I need to take care of."

As she said the last name, I remembered the grave and the ghoul. "Don't go to Dunwich," I said, thinking about the warning from the trumpet player.

She shook her head. "I don't have a choice. There's a job to be done. Good luck to you."

Even as I gathered up the money, I knew my dream of staying in this Kingsport was impossible. This was not the time, this was not the place, as Jim Culver had predicted. I could feel the world fading as I walked toward the door. The music on the radio became a familiar tune. The kitchen disappeared.

I wish the cook well on her journeys and am sorry that I never learned her name.

CHAPTER NINE

Agent Tawney escorted me to a small diner and insisted on buying me a cup of coffee.

"I'd rather have an Ovaltine," I told the waitress in a small bid for independence. In truth I wished I'd walked away from him when he first invited me to talk to him. Except I was a little overwhelmed. I'd never been stopped by so much as a policeman, let alone a federal agent, and I wasn't sure if I could just walk away. I wished Nova was with me and, at the same time, I was glad that she was safely back at the Diamond Dog, working in her apartment.

"Miss Gutierrez," said Tawney. "Raquel, can I call you Raquel? Please call me Ralph."

"I'd rather not," I muttered, but very quietly and he may not have heard me.

"Mr Brewster has been writing to the Bureau for some time," he said.

"He writes to my aunt daily," I said and then wondered if I should have kept quiet. Perhaps saying that would make Nova look as strange as Brewster.

"I am not surprised," Tawney replied. "He seems to be the very best customer of the US Postal Service. Nevertheless, we must investigate even the most outlandish claims. For the safety of the nation, as I am sure you understand."

"Not at all. What could my aunt possibly do to threaten the safety of the nation? She runs a small cafe called the Purple Cat near Innsmouth and the Diamond Dog in Kingsport. Right now she's home planning a Christmas Eve dance for her ballroom with a live broadcast on her radio station. How could that be of any concern to your Bureau?"

"It's true that investigations of your aunt's activities have fallen to the Prohibition boys until now," he said.

"Oh dear," I said without meaning to speak out loud. Mother would not be pleased if she learned that her suspicions of her sister were shared by the Federal government.

"However," said Tawney, speaking over my interruption, "this is much more serious and well outside the US Treasury's mandate."

"What do you mean?" I asked, while thinking "What could Nova have done?"

"According to Mr Brewster, your aunt – and possibly others employed by her – can travel through time," said Tawney.

I blinked. "I'm sorry, I don't think I heard you correctly," I said. Tawney had one of those rough and slightly low voices that I found hard to understand, even with the help of the hearing aid. But I was looking directly at him and was almost certain he had said "time" as he raised his coffee cup to his mouth and took a sip. Around us the normal clatter of dishes and other people talking also made it harder for me to clearly distinguish his words from others. I shifted the scarf draped across my chest so there was no chance of it muffling or obstructing my microphone. I must have looked like a maiden aunt fussing with her jewelry, except my aunt never fussed and would have demanded answers immediately from Tawney.

"Can you repeat what you said, just a little louder?" I asked, my embarrassment overridden by my curiosity.

"I'd rather not be overheard," he said, leaning across the table toward me. "Read this."

He slid a letter into my hand. Unfolding the heavy cream paper, I immediately recognized the blocky, neat script that covered the entire page. I'd seen Chilton Brewster's distinct handwriting on nearly a dozen envelopes since I had come to stay with Nova.

"To whom it may concern," the letter began. "I have proof that Nova Malone can disrupt the proper progression of time or knows someone who can. She has taken advantage of her knowledge to provide safe passage of illicit goods from one country to the next. Further, her actions have caused an unsettling of previous events to the point of endangering the future of our good town of Kingsport."

I read it twice and then looked at Agent Tawney. "I still don't understand," I said in genuine puzzlement. I could understand an accusation of bootlegging as I had my own suspicions. But time travel? "What does he mean?"

"I asked Mr Brewster that very question. He claims your aunt has traveled through time to accomplish her purchase of the Diamond Dog, an act which may very well impact the history of our nation or at least this corner of it. Since then, he claims she employs time travelers to smuggle liquor into the country for distribution throughout the Eastern seaboard."

"That's ridiculous," I said, pushing the letter back to Tawney. I must have spoken louder than I intended because he made shushing motions with his hands. But I was in no mood to be silenced. "My aunt purchased the Diamond Dog in October after many months of negotiations with the owners. She told me about it herself. She had no need to time travel." I did not bother to comment on the rest of his accusations, which were just as ridiculous. Even if my aunt smuggled liquor, I doubted she had magical employees capable of manipulating time.

Plenty of bootleggers existed throughout the state, and they all seemed to manage just fine with cars, boats, and planes. However, I couldn't say that to Tawney.

At the same time, I wasn't completely naive. There'd been a great bustle of activity around the Diamond Dog these past few weeks. Even if I'd never seen liquor served in the ballroom, I resolved to take a closer look at the boxes and boxes of decorations being carried down to the basement of the Diamond Dog. It was past time that I confronted my suspicions about Nova's other businesses head on. Of course, what I would say to her after I found proof, I had no idea.

Tawney continued, "The records of your aunt's purchase of the Diamond Dog seem clear. But Brewster's letters do suggest something strange happened here. He says he lived through the same day twice. This may be due to somebody's manipulation of time."

"Brewster must be lying," I said, unsure why Tawney would be taking this all so seriously. "Time travel isn't possible!"

Tawney shook his head. "I cannot reveal all our sources but some of Brewster's claims seem to be true. We have evidence something did happen to him on December 24, 1925."

"He says he lived through Christmas Eve twice?" I said. "You can't truly believe him." It seemed a very imaginative claim for a cranky banker who spent most of his time writing editorials about how the "dry" laws enhanced public morality and penning letters of complaint to his neighbors.

"He says he was knocked out of the correct day by a time traveler," said Tawney, as if this was a rational explanation.

All around us the diners continued their conversations. Through the window I could see people hurrying down the street with all the packages associated with Christmas errands. Oddly enough, I found my brief talk with Paul just moments ago felt far more real and urgent than this conversation. My doubt and bemusement at what Tawney apparently felt was a major revelation showed clearly in my face, for the agent reacted very strongly to my disbelief.

"I do have evidence," Tawney said with some ire. He reached into his upper vest pocket and pulled out several small snapshots. "These photos support Brewster's story," he said, thrusting the first picture at me.

Peering at the photograph, I recognized the entrance of the Diamond Dog. Brewster was standing on the doorstep with a portly man that I did not know. When I said as much, Tawney answered with such emphasis that I shushed him, much as he had asked me to drop my voice earlier. "That's one of the former owners, Samuel Morrissen. Who is also a suspected bootlegger," Tawney said with a glare that contradicted all the friendly chatter of "just call him Ralph" only a few minutes earlier.

"Why are you showing this to me?" I asked with some justification and equal brusqueness. "I haven't been in Kingsport before this month. I don't know this person." Which was true, but not completely so. I did remember the name from conversations with Nova about her purchase of the Diamond Dog. The suspected bootlegger part she had not mentioned.

"This was taken during a stakeout of the property by a Prohibition agent. Which is confidential information. I would appreciate your assurances that you won't discuss this conversation with others," Tawney said, completely ignoring my question and increasing my uneasiness.

I murmured something noncommittal. I wasn't about to argue with a man with a badge, but I also wasn't going to gag myself unless I absolutely had to.

"The photo was logged as having been taken on December 24, 1925. As was this one," said the agent.

Tawney slapped down a second photo. Like the first, it showed Morrissen standing on the steps of the Diamond Dog. In this one Morrissen was talking to a man in a leather coat whose face was turned away from the camera. Something about the set of the second man's shoulders and the way he was stretching one hand toward Morrissen seemed desperate. Rather like a man making a plea for help.

"Who is the other man?" I asked.

"Chilton didn't know," Tawney said in such a way that I immediately wondered if the agent recognized the man in the picture. He was certainly scowling at the picture as if the blurred figure was a known criminal. "Brewster claimed that he was an employee of your aunt's, sent to disrupt his business deal by knocking him down. I want to talk to this man and find out what he knows."

"But how is this evidence of time travel?" I said. "Two photos, taken of the same place, showing people on the steps of the Diamond Dog."

"One photo shows Morrissen talking to Brewster on the steps. The other shows Morrissen talking to the stranger in the leather coat, our time traveler," Tawney said as if laying claim to the unnamed man in the leather coat. "Both pictures were taken at exactly the same time." He tapped the ends of the two photos. On each, handwriting noted the date as December 24, 1925, and each did indeed state in the same handwriting that the time was 3:27 PM.

"One of these was labeled wrong," I said with some conviction. The whole thing was too absurd, no matter how convinced Tawney sounded. I wondered again how a federal agent could take such claims seriously.

"The photos were taken with a Vest Pocket Autographic," said Tawney. "The photographer always noted the time and date on the film at the time he snapped the picture."

"He read his watch wrong," I insisted.

"Then this photo appears on the roll and is dated exactly three minutes after the other two," said Tawney, laying down a third picture.

In the third picture, Morrissen was walking away from the entrance of the Diamond Dog, heading toward the photographer. A little further away a figure came down the street. Tawney claimed this was Chilton Brewster, delayed from reaching his destination. Then, in a fourth photo, the man in the leather coat reappeared. Or rather almost appeared. Something must have gone wrong in the exposure, for the man in the leather coat was nearly transparent, a corner of the Diamond Dog improbably visible through his body.

The waitress made another pass by our table, asking if we needed anything. Tawney shook his head at her. I noticed he was careful to shift his hands and cover the photographs, hiding them from her view. But as soon as she walked away, he lifted his hands away and pushed all three closer to me.

"Then there's this photo," said Tawney, setting out a fifth picture like a fortune teller laying out the cards. He shoved it face up across the table to me.

In the picture, again dated December 24 and just a few minutes after the third one, my aunt Nova stood on the street outside the Diamond Dog. She was very oddly dressed for winter, wearing a light summer dress that was torn across the shoulders. Something else about the photo bothered me. I peered closer to be sure. Nova's hair and clothing appeared to be dripping wet. Standing next to her was Chilton Brewster. Once again, a blurry almost translucent figure could be seen further down the street, the man in the leather coat.

"Brewster claims your aunt materialized in front of him and demanded his coat," said Tawney. "She told him that she'd fallen off a pier."

"In the middle of Kingsport?"

"Seems unlikely," Tawney agreed. "Also, at the very time this photograph was taken, the Purple Cat was holding its Christmas Eve dance. According to photos of the event which were published in the *Arkham Advertiser*, your aunt was there. I also have the sworn testimony of two Prohibition agents who attended the dance that your aunt was visible to them for the entire evening."

"She can't have been in two places at the same time," I protested, trying to think of a logical explanation and failing.

"If Nova Malone's accomplice can time travel," Tawney shot back, tapping the figure in the background, "then he could transport her to any number of places at any time that they wish. Imagine, Miss Gutierrez, what damage even one man could do with such knowledge. What malicious attacks could be made by a hostile government agent. As a patriot, Miss Gutierrez, it is your duty to help me apprehend this time traveler." His hand slapped down on the picture of the man in the leather coat.

"But I don't know who he is!" I said.

"Nova Malone does. She was seen with him. Ask your aunt," snapped Tawney.

I nearly retorted, "Ask her yourself." But I held my tongue. I truly couldn't believe a time traveler worked for Nova. Despite Tawney's persistent questioning about the man, I wondered if the agent concocted the photos as an elaborate sham. Did he think to scare me into giving him information? Why would I help him when it was so ridiculous a claim as time travel? No, I decided, he must be looking for evidence of bootlegging.

What I wanted, I thought, truly was time. Time to find my courage. I needed to question my aunt about why she left Innsmouth for Kingsport and where her money came from.

INTERLUDE

"One, two, buckle my shoe," I sing to begin this story.

The hounds are here. I see them emerge from places beside the trees with teeth. Teeth bloodied by their attack in the laboratory. Their howls sound as hideous as their bodies appear. Their faces are so foul that I cannot look them in the eye. They make the ghoul in the Dunwich woods seem clean.

But I found a lady who taught me a way to trick them. This is how it happened.

I don't remember why I left the beach. But I was running under the trees until I burst into an open square. The sun was setting behind large, impressive stone buildings. I stood in a snowy patch of lawn. Around me the walkways had been shoveled to reveal mellow brick. The surrounding buildings were connected by these pathways which all ran in neat lines forming squares and triangles separated by the snowy grass. A group of carolers stood on the steps of one building singing loudly while others gathered around them.

A man pushed past them shouting, "I'll rest you if you don't get out of my way. Classes are over for the year, why can't you students leave us in peace?"

The carolers shouted back, "Merry Christmas, professor!"

In this quadrangle, young people hurried past me, dressed the way that the wealthy Berliners did in my youth. When I was a boy of fifteen or sixteen, years before I was a man lost in the trenches, I'd loiter on the street corners and watch people like these descend from carriages and motorcars, hurrying across the newly shoveled pavement and disappearing into the light and warmth of a theater or restaurant. The women then wore coats of velvet hanging to their ankles and fur collars framing their faces. I once worked for furriers in Berlin, the workshops specializing in trims for the best tailors and dressmakers. I still remember the sable, seal, mink, lynx, and fox furs lying in piles on the back tables to be fashioned into collars and cuffs.

A pair of young women passed me, angling toward a brilliantly lit building at the edge of what would be a great green lawn if it was not covered in snow. These women also were dressed in the slim coats and large fur collars of my youth, but they were not Berliners. They laughed and joked in English, and the coats were cut from more practical cloth, made of tweed or blue wool.

"Hurry, Beatrice," called one woman. "You don't want to miss this party. They promised sherry and cake."

"Without even tasting the sherry or the cake," answered a pretty lady with brown curls springing out from under her hat, "I can predict that with seven members of the Math Club being male, and only two of us being female, the odds of this party being a success are virtually nil."

"That's why Lillian and Gloria are coming," answered the other. "And possibly another girl from the English department, if she hasn't left for home yet."

"That's still seven to four, not quite outnumbered two to one, but far too close for my liking. If Gloria's additional friend does appear, we will be seven to five, Judy," said the one called Beatrice.

"Beatrice Sharpe! You just want to go back to the library," Judy replied. "You've had your nose stuck in that old almanac all semester."

"It's interesting," said Miss Sharpe to her friend. "There's something about it. Every time I read it… well, I can't explain it, not yet, but I will. There's a pattern there. I only need to determine the correct formula."

"Enough studying," cried Judy, linking her arm with Beatrice and pulling her a little faster down the neatly shoveled walkway. "Let's go to this party. Even if it's dismal, it's still better than sitting alone in our rooms tonight."

"Tonight is simply the 24th day of the twelfth month," said Beatrice with a smile as she walked quickly by the other's side. "There's nothing magical about this date. They changed the calendar in 1752 to correct the errors in calculating leap years. But if we want to be mathematically and historically accurate, we should be celebrating in January 1914 and not December 1913."

"Oh look, there's Gloria, and she did bring some friends," said Judy, interrupting her friend's lecture. Three more women joined the group. "Enough talk about numbers and history, Beatrice."

"There will always be math, it is the formula which underpins the universe," said Beatrice, unhooking her arm from her friend so she could gesture with both hands. "And may I point out that we are going to a party of the Miskatonic University Math Club being held in a classroom still reeking of chalk dust due to the equations written on the walls and chaperoned by two members of the faculty. Which makes it unnecessary to even calculate the odds of math being discussed."

I drifted after them, unwilling to approach them but drawn to the comfort of their bright chatter, more warming to my soul than a fire. As a boy, if I had talked to such ladies I would have been chased away with shouts and blows by their gentlemen companions or the police. I would not have dared. But there were no uniformed police here and glancing down at myself, I was no longer the skinny boy who slept in the doorways of furriers, hoping not to freeze overnight or die of starvation. Something about the one called Beatrice made me wonder if I could ask her for help.

As they made their way up the steps of a large and impressive stone building, Beatrice paused at the top of the stairs. She fumbled with the bag hanging off her wrist. "Oh drat," she said. "I left my notebook in the library. I really must fetch it. They'll be locking up soon and the building will be closed for the rest of the week."

"Beatrice!" exclaimed her friend. "You promised to come with me."

"You now have three other women with you who care nothing about mathematics!" said Beatrice. "The odds are in your favor, ladies, especially without me, of having at least a few minutes of casual conversation over the sherry before the talk once again turns to esoteric data. Good luck!" She hurried down the stairs toward me.

"Beatrice, you traitor!" cried Judy, but she swept into the building with the others, still laughing as the door clanged shut behind them.

As Beatrice reached the spot where I stood hesitating about approaching her, she looked directly at me and said, "Do you know that you appeared in this square approximately seven minutes ago in that patch of snow?" She pointed to a white area between the brick walkways. "I observed your footprints begin there and proceed to here. But there's no indication of where you came from."

In the twilight gloom the dark track of my steps was clear, as was the fact that all around them the snow lay white and undisturbed. "Would you mind explaining to me exactly how you did that?" said Beatrice.

I was touched by how she looked at me so directly. Others had spoken to me, but Beatrice saw me. "I don't know what is happening to me," I said. "Do you?"

The carolers behind us launched into a song about a good king.

"I've been calculating and calculating, but I can't find a reasonable explanation for your apparent appearance out of thin air," said Beatrice as if my strange waking nightmare was the most natural thing in the world. "Not unless you want to apply some of the more outlandish but quite interesting theories of that Zurich mathematician Einstein. His papers on Brownian motion, classical mechanics, and electromagnetic fields do suggest time, motion, and energy may be more complicated than Newton imagined." She paused for breath. "Also, the creature following you seems to be untethered to normal patterns of movement. Look how it keeps popping in and out of the corners of the square."

I whirled around and saw one of the nightmares from the forest slinking toward us. Its tongue lolled out of its mouth and it crawled forward on scabrous paws which left no marks upon the icy ground.

"Let's move away," said Beatrice, reaching out to pull my sleeve and tow me after her along the path. "I do want to talk to you, and we can't concentrate with such a thing bothering us."

"Go, go," I said, suddenly afraid I would see her torn apart like the men in the laboratory. But this strange young woman seemed to have no sense of fear. I pushed her away from me, hoping the beast would concentrate on me instead. "Don't let it touch you." The hound behind us had disappeared. Then it popped in front of us, rising out of the corner where one walkway met the other. The stink of the other place, the smell of decay and destruction, drifted through the cold air.

"Very interesting indeed," said Beatrice, cocking her head with curiosity and still no signs of fear. However, she backed up a few steps. "It does like angles, doesn't it? Can't seem to stay away from them." She stepped off the pathway and began to circle the beast. Behind us I could still hear the carolers singing about Wenceslas, but there was nobody else in the square to observe us. The others had gone into the warm and lighted buildings surrounding us on all sides. The hound flickered from spot to spot, increasingly hard to see in the gloom. I could hear its harsh panting and the liquid plop of its tongue swiping in and out of its mouth.

"You must run," I said to her. Running was the only solution. Fighting it would fail. I'd seen these creatures ignore bullets as they tore men apart.

"I was studying the most interesting almanac this morning, and it was all about circles and lines," Beatrice said, not moving at all to my horror. "And nursery rhymes. Most annoying, because I didn't want to be reading children's songs, even one called 'Arithmetick.' But now I wonder."

Because the young lady would not run, I tried to put my body between the hound and her. I had failed those men in the laboratory, thinking only of my escape. This impossibly brave young woman did not deserve their fate.

"Come along, do, you're worse than Judy for lollygagging," she commanded me even as I tried to protect her. "Follow in my footsteps, follow the circle."

She sounded as imperious as the Berlin ladies who once commanded me to sweep the street to keep their hems clean. But kinder too. For still she spoke to me as if I was someone who mattered. As if she wanted to help me as much as I wanted to save her.

So I stepped where she stepped, my larger feet overlaying the prints of hers as we tracked a giant circle around the hound. The beast began to sway back and forth, hunting blindly, always sticking to the straight paths and sharp corners.

"One, two, buckle my shoe; three, four, lay down lower," Beatrice sang as she danced along the curved path we had made in the snow, coming back to where we started. "That rather confused me because I learned it originally as 'knock at the door' but it makes sense here. We don't have a door, do we? I'd duck if I was you."

The hound sprang but Beatrice pulled me aside and down into the snow. The creature sailed over our heads with an odd twisting turn in midair, as if it struck some invisible wall cast up by the outer edge of our circle. It landed back in a sharp corner of the path. It threw up its head and howled, but it seemed as if only we heard it. Behind us the carolers continued to sing loudly, and that may have been the most terrifying moment of all. To know the beast hunted us and only us, and no one could intervene.

Beatrice pulled open her bag and drew out a handful of sharpened pencils, tossing them onto the ground in a pile. The hound whined, a terrifying sound that cut through me, but it was no longer looking at us. Instead it stared at the pile of pencils in front of it.

"Five, six, pick up sticks," said Beatrice, grabbing the pencils on the ground. "Seven, eight, lay them straight." She set the pencils down again in a pattern of triangles. In the sing-song tone that people adopt with pets, she said, "There you go, ugly doggie, look at the nice sticks. Isosceles, equilateral, scalene, obtuse, acute, and right angles. All for you. Good dog, good dog."

She backed away, still walking in a curve, slowly circling us toward the outer edge of the square, closer and closer to where the group of jolly students sang upon the steps of a brick building. The hound dropped its head down, nosing the pattern before it, and, this I swear is true, flickering in and out of existence. With each appearance, it became smaller and smaller until it faded away, no larger than a mouse.

"Fascinating," said Beatrice. "Congruence seems to have confused its ability to hold to this time and place. I wasn't sure so I made a few patterns. Descending patterns would be best if you meet it again, by which I mean a continuation pattern of ever smaller triangles. And, of course, if you go in circles it will have a hard time tracking you."

I tried to stammer out some thanks. All my stunned mind could produce was the broken phrases of my youth, begging on the streets of Berlin. But my gratitude was far truer than when I begged for coins. "Thank you, lady, fine lady, thank you, without your help today we would have died." As soon as I made this speech, I felt foolish. What American would understand me?

Beatrice answered me in far crisper and aristocratic German, "Don't be silly. The book told me exactly what to do. And I was not about to let the creature eat us. I have so many questions to ask you."

As I blinked in surprise to hear the language of my youth, the group of singers on the steps finished up their carol and all pulled strings of bells from their pockets. With much laughter they shook the bells and began to sing again, marching down the stairs toward us.

"Oh, drat that glee club, can't they shut up for a minute?" said Beatrice, switching back to English. "Let's get out of their way. Wait, wait, don't go!"

But I was under the trees again and the hounds were howling in frustration as they tried to find my scent. I began to run back to the beach, and I ran in a wide curve, circling, always circling, to confuse my pursuers.

CHAPTER TEN

Although I would regret my decision later, I did not immediately return to the Diamond Dog and tell my aunt about my encounter with Agent Tawney (I never could bring myself to call him Ralph). Instead I left Tawney and his impossible photographs at the coffee shop while I hastened to the camera store down the street.

When I questioned the clerk about an autographic camera, he immediately knew what I was talking about. He pulled one out of his case and proceeded to tell me about how this particular model was known as "the soldier's camera" as so many had been sold during the war. He demonstrated how to use the autographic feature that allowed the photographer to inscribe the date and time that the photo was taken. "Or you could write the name of a place or the name of the person being photographed," he enthused.

The camera also folded up quite small, perfect to fit into a pocket or purse. "You can always have it with you and never miss a single shot," he assured me.

"That would be quite handy for a detective," I seethed. He looked confused at my bitter statement. Of course he didn't know how a certain Federal agent had thrown down pictures taken by such a camera as the evidence of time travel. Technically, what Tawney said seemed possible. The photos could be dated exactly when taken. But that didn't mean, I told myself, that the two different photos had been snapped at exactly the same time.

Feeling a little sorry for the man – for I shouldn't be snapping at him but rather at the world which continued to complicate my life – I asked about the price. While twelve dollars was not cheap, it was affordable. I purchased the camera and some of the special 127 film to go with it. He wrapped the camera together with the film, adding a beautifully tied bow as a finishing touch. The clerk told me that he would be happy to give instructions about the camera's use to the gift's recipient. I responded that it was for my Aunt Nova, at which he seemed quite delighted.

"Oh, I've been dancing at the Diamond Dog a few times," he said. "I am looking forward to taking my gal to the Christmas Eve dance. We already have our tickets."

"Do you listen to the radio broadcast too?" I asked.

"Always when I'm at home, and I enjoy the noon broadcast while eating my lunch in the store." He pointed to a radio tucked behind the counter, one of the newer table models. "The owner is thinking about offering a few radios for sale along with the cameras. There's a big demand these days."

"It's quite an expense," I said, thinking about the handsome radio sitting in my aunt's apartment and the rest of her new appliances. Only a fool would discount Agent Tawney's claims of bootlegging given the extent of my aunt's mysterious wealth. But bootlegging through time travel? That was a foolish story, a fairytale.

Then I remembered Paul's voice whispering in my ear: "Once upon a time."

The clerk tried to discuss time payments to afford larger items like radios, but I simply thanked him for his help with the gift for my aunt and left the store.

Thinking about Paul, and the fragments of fairytales that I'd heard him speak over the past few days, I set off for the Diamond Dog with my package tucked firmly under my arm. I wished I knew where he was and how I could help him. At that moment, rescuing a phantom man that I'd never seen and only heard through my earpiece seemed so much easier and, frankly, more appealing than sorting out my complicated relationship with Nova. Or deciding what to do with my own future.

Nothing made any real sense. But nothing had made sense to me since the day I realized a simple fever had changed my hearing forever.

To keep up my spirits, I began to whistle the jazzy bouncing rendition of "Jingle Bells" that we now played every night at the Diamond Dog. Billy's version had proved so popular that the dancers demanded it at least once in the evening.

As I turned the corner I heard a howling wail, both like and unlike a dog. Glancing back over my shoulder, I saw nothing behind me. But the sound repeated in my ear and I began to hasten down the street.

Kingsport had played its usual tricks on me and, suddenly, I was walking down a street that I'd never seen before. I paused to get my bearings and figure out the best way back to the Diamond Dog.

Convinced I needed to retrace my steps, I went back to a street that looked vaguely familiar. The buildings in this part of town lacked the overall prosperity of other places, but something about the area reminded me of the streets running behind the Diamond Dog.

The brightness of the afternoon faded away. Clouds gathered overhead, sullen with the threat of snow, and the town which had so charmed me earlier in the day felt unbearably dreary. I noticed an undertaker's storefront, the name and business written in gilt letters on the dark glass. Unlike the shops I'd passed earlier, no warm and welcoming lights brightened these windows or the dark doorways of the other shabby buildings huddled close by. Even the streetlamps cast a sulfurous yellow glow that did nothing to lessen the gloom of this street.

I found myself wondering if this was one of the parts of town that Chilton Brewster wanted to clean up and clean out.

A pair of shabbily dressed women stepped out of a doorway. Both seemed weary, moving with a shuffling gait away from me. One stopped and bent to adjust her shoe while the other leaned against the window of the mortuary. A large white hand appeared in the center of the window. The rest of his body invisible behind the darkened glass, the man rapped sharply against the window. The woman gave a little gasp and sprang away. Tugging at her friend's arm, they hurried down the street and disappeared around a corner.

A completely unreasonable fear settled upon me. While a few people continued to go by, intent on their own business, I suddenly felt unbearably alone and lost. Yet I knew friends and family waited for me back at the Diamond Dog.

My earpiece buzzed and whined enough to set my teeth on edge. I reached my hand into my purse, intent on switching off the battery, convinced the cold or my walk had caused the device to malfunction. But even as I laid my hand upon the battery, I heard Paul's voice more clearly than ever before.

"Five, six, pick up sticks," he chanted.

I passed a wrought iron fence. Laying against the fence were a couple of long sticks. I remembered my brothers grabbing sticks like this and rattling them along a fence for the sheer pleasure of making a racket.

Something about Paul's voice compelled me to act. I snatched up the sticks and spun about, convinced that something stalked me along the street. The fear, the certainty that there was something to fear, nearly overwhelmed me.

Of course I saw nothing. I knew there was nothing there. Yet I also knew my eyes and ears were deceiving me. I could not see it. I could not hear it. But something followed me. It frightened me as much as a hand rapping against the glass of a window had frightened those two women a few moments earlier. Yet the hand couldn't touch them.

But fear is never reasonable, and it was fear that made me believe that something lurked just at the edge of my perception.

"Seven, eight, lay them straight," Paul sang. I tossed the sticks down again so they fell in right angles to the fence. Then I spun about and took to my heels, running all the way back to that afternoon's shops and eventually the Diamond Dog, running as if pursued.

INTERLUDE

When Ivan met his Baba Yaga, she told him to set about his business and his business was all about escaping her with the help of birds, lions, and bees. Made brave by my meetings with the faithful servant and the clever lady, I began to search, as Ivan searched, for a way back to the world that I knew. When I met my Baba Yaga, I tried to follow her home.

Standing on the beach at the edge of the ocean without waves, I heard a tremendous splash. Afraid of what was coming out of the sea, I was retreating under the trees when a woman said, "So much fuss for a book."

Turning around, I saw a large woman wading out of the water. Her dress was torn along the shoulders and her hair was wild about her face. I knew her immediately for the Baba Yaga who walked through the stories of my childhood. On her breast winked a purple brooch shaped like a cat. I could see that she was a woman of great strength and cunning, as a Baba Yaga must be.

When she reached the shore, the woman wrung out her skirt. Then she looked at me and said, "I don't suppose you know the road to Innsmouth?"

I gaped like a fish caught on a hook. It seemed impossible that someone could simply fall into this place like me. I often thought it was my own particular nightmare, and strangers do not join you in nightmares. Besides, I knew bargaining with a Baba Yaga could lead to your head upon a pole in her yard. She frightened me and fascinated me at the same time.

"Perhaps Innsmouth would be a bad choice," she said, and I could not tell if she was talking to me or to herself. She gave me a sideways glance. "I'm not even sure if you're real. Things often aren't here. Try not to turn into anything nasty. I lost my gun in the sea."

Behind me I heard something slither and whine.

"Patterns, I need a pattern for someplace other than Innsmouth," the woman said, walking past me down the beach, still chattering to herself. "Songs make very good maps! But why such a silly tune? Well, it's the one stuck in my head right now. It might fit Kingsport. Here goes."

She began to hum, and it was a tune that I knew. There was a rhythm to it like the ringing of bells. I'd heard this song before in the alley where Pete found me. At the end of the dock when I talked to Captain Leo. I could almost name the song, which had been sung in a beer hall as the faithful servant told me to take heart.

"And soon Miss Fanny Bright was seated by my side," sang the woman, stepping in time to her singing. She began to shimmer around the edges.

With a cry, I sprang after her, more afraid of losing her than losing my head. "Wait, wait!" I wailed like a child chasing after his mother.

Then I was running down a street, an ordinary street lined with shops. People walked slowly along, chattering with each other and clutching parcels in their arms. I dodged around the shoppers. A few glared at me but most simply moved aside as if they barely noticed me. Ahead of me was my glowing Baba Yaga but nobody else seemed to see her. I bumped into a man and he fell into a snowbank. His hat went flying and his round eyeglasses were knocked crooked across his face.

"Watch where you are going!" he yelled at me, but I ran on. I needed to find my Baba Yaga so I could learn her trick of stepping so confidently away from that terrible place. Or I knew it would pull me back under the trees again.

But the street was deserted. Another man, well fed and well dressed, stood on the steps of a long white building. He appeared to be watching for someone.

I ran up to him and held out my hand. "Have you seen her? My Baba Yaga?" I stumbled through the words. I may not have spoken in English. I was so anxious and confused, I may have used the Russian of my childhood.

"What?" he said, turning and looking at me. "What do you want? I don't have anything for you. Get away." He glanced over my shoulder and swore. "G-man. Should have known this was a trick. I'm out of here. Tell Brewster that he can't force me to sell the Diamond Dog by writing letters to the law. They can take all the pictures they want, they have nothing on me."

The man hurried past me to rap on the window of a parked car. "I see you! Hope you captured my good side! Merry Christmas, nosey parker!" Then he laughed and walked away, whistling the same tune that my Baba Yaga sang.

In the distance I heard her voice, still singing. Spinning around, I saw her almost dancing down the street, her feet flying in time to her song. She bumped into the very man that I had knocked into the snowbank only moments before. The two clutched each other, swaying back and forth, but she broke away first. I hurried toward them, determined not to lose Baba Yaga until I learned her tricks.

"This isn't Innsmouth," she said with some certainty. "So the song worked!"

"Madam," said the businessman, resettling his glasses on his nose and glaring at her. "This is Kingsport, and you appear to be drunk."

She laughed at his sour expression. "Liquor never touched my lips today.

But I am indeed one of the wet tonight. Dropped off a pier and into the drink. What's the date, bub?"

"Christmas Eve, of course!" said the man.

"I think I have some time and distance to go tonight before I find myself in the right place," said Baba Yaga. "Be a good sport and lend me your coat. I'm not dressed for this weather."

Apparently wise enough not to argue with such a woman, the man took off his coat and tossed it over her shoulders. "Do not mistake my charity for my approval," he said quite sternly. "Your lack of decorum is appalling. Take yourself home, madam, and be glad that I did not call the police!"

"Bells on bobtail ring," she sang and stepped away from the gentleman with a merry wave of her hands. On every finger sparkled a diamond ring. "Making spirits bright."

Then my Baba Yaga was gone. I was once again on the beach where something slithered underneath the trees near the shore. But I had received a gift from the witch. I knew what I needed: a tune to lead me out of the woods. I know what we must find. Raquel, dare I ask you to go to Baba Yaga and steal her song for us? For if Ivan's friends failed him, their heads would have ended on a pole in Baba Yaga's yard.

CHAPTER ELEVEN

The morning after my encounter with Agent Tawney, Nova asked me to take the previous evening's receipts to the bank. Normally Lily did this, but she'd been feeling poorly. Nova sent her home and told her to stay home for a day or two until she was fully recovered. Knowing my aunt, she probably sent over a pot of fish chowder to aid Lily's recovery. Nova believed in the healing properties of fish chowder the way that other people believed in chicken soup.

Nova kept her money in Chilton Brewster's savings and loan. Whether she did this to annoy him or to placate him, I cannot say, although I suspect it may have been the former. Generally, Nova rarely showed dislike openly, and she often counseled her employees against carrying grudges (despite this, there was a long-standing feud between one waiter and one cook that resulted in a terrible kitchen disaster on a Saturday night).

However, Nova had little patience for those she considered "fools and damn fools too." So it was entirely possible that she wanted Chilton Brewster to be aware of her success at the Diamond Dog by deliberately depositing her increasingly large profits with him.

I had my own reasons for wanting to visit the bank. Following my conversation with Agent Tawney, I decided to question Chilton Brewster about his duplicate Christmas Eve. I still wondered if the whole story was something of a ruse by Agent Tawney – and possibly Brewster – to gain greater knowledge of my aunt's business.

Declining the offer of Nova's car, I set off across Kingsport by foot carrying a remarkably heavy carpetbag. Business at the Diamond Dog apparently had been very good the night before or else Nova had also added the receipts of the Purple Cat to my load. I considered that some of the cash may have come from elsewhere, but I lacked the courage to question my aunt directly. After all, how do you ask over toast and coffee if your host and relative is a bootlegger? It was a question that I had not answered yet in my own head during our breakfast, and one that would continue to plague me on my walk to the bank.

Otis trailed along behind me, which meant my aunt was not completely confident about the safety of Kingsport's streets on a Thursday morning. Although I felt none of the strange chill I experienced the day before, I was glad of Nova's largest employee walking steadily after me.

When I, and the carpetbag full of dollars and coins, reached the bank, Otis watched me climb the steps to the entrance and then left. Presumably he thought the likelihood of me being robbed inside the bank was minimal or simply not his business. I had safely arrived and that was his task completed.

Brewster's bank stood out from neighboring buildings due to its very solidity. Built of stone, it boasted three wide shallow steps leading up to a stout pair of oak doors. Inside, the floor was marble and the counters also oak, with well-polished brass cages to protect the tellers from the patrons. Nevertheless, the customers upon my visit seemed a mild enough lot, waiting in two neat lines for the next available teller. When it was my turn, I heaved the carpetbag onto the counter and said, "Deposit from Miss Nova Malone."

There was a little sighing and fussing, as the bag was too large to pass easily through the teller's window in the brass cage. Instead, I was informed that Miss Malone's deposit was usually handled by the manager and I should take the bag to his desk. Presumably Lily would have done this but why they expected me to know where the bank manager sat, I couldn't guess.

After more fussing, somebody came out from behind a half wall of golden oak to fetch me and the bag to the proper place. My guide turned out to be no less than Chilton Brewster himself.

"Miss Malone?" He bowed me through the open gate that led from the public area to where the officers of the bank sat.

"Miss Gutierrez," I replied. "Raquel Malone Gutierrez," I added in case he thought I was trying to deny my connection to my aunt.

"I don't believe we have seen you here before," he said. I found it hard to reconcile this rather bland man with the one who had shouted accusations of bootlegging at my aunt on my first day in Kingsport or who wrote hundreds of letters to others about their failings.

I wondered if there was a Mrs Brewster and what she thought about his activities. Did the man have any time for her, or did he simply disappear into some office at home to write out all those neatly printed envelopes? Later I would learn there was no Mrs Brewster, which was something of a comfort as things turned out.

"Lily was not feeling well," I explained, "so I offered to bring the deposit for her."

Brewster waved me into his own office and pulled out a chair for me. He circled the large desk (oak again!) in the center of the room and settled into his own chair. An equally impressive bookcase filled the wall behind his desk. It appeared to hold ledgers and a number of smaller leatherbound books, all neatly arranged on the shelf according to the year stamped in gold upon the spine.

Brewster's mouth pursed in an expression of concern at my earlier comment. "I am sorry to hear about Lily. Her work here was always excellent and she was very well liked. I'll instruct my secretary to send some flowers."

That concern, so quickly expressed and apparently genuine for a former employee, encapsulated the problem I had with Brewster the entire time that I was in Kingsport. While I could never like the man, he had his moments of humanity, or at least of good manners, which made it very hard to dislike him as much as I wanted to.

"Oh, Lily is not very ill," I said, heaving the carpetbag onto the desk. I could have sworn the thing had gained a pound or two during my walk and another one while waiting in line at the bank. It landed with a resounding thud.

"Business seems to be doing well," said Brewster, still very pleasant and polite, so much so that I was beginning to regret my resolve to ask about his time travel story. I couldn't think of a way to bring up the topic that wouldn't make me sound unhinged.

"Yes, quite well," I said. "I don't know much about my aunt's business, but she seems to be a success." I paused, hoping Brewster would press me with questions about Nova's business that would allow me to question him in turn.

Instead, he opened the carpetbag and withdrew the bank book and deposit slip resting on top of the cash. He looked it over carefully and just as carefully pulled out the rubber banded stacks of dollar bills and the rolls of coins. He counted the stacks quickly and said, "I'm sure this is all correct. Lily and your aunt are always meticulous and we haven't found an error yet in their deposits." He took the deposit slip from the bank book and placed it with the currency. Then he made a notation in the book, initialed it, and dropped the bank book back into the carpetbag, which he handed to me.

I sat there with the empty carpetbag on my lap, staring foolishly at him over the stacks of bills. In all the mysteries that I read, the detectives came up with clever jokes or sly questions which led their suspects to spill out every possible clue. I couldn't think of a single way to start the conversation. Brewster continued to look at me with the slightly distant but polite expression of a man who must be wondering why I didn't rise and leave his office now that our business was done.

Brewster, probably due to antique notions of propriety, had left his office door slightly ajar. Glancing over my shoulder, I could see other employees walking across the bank's office. A woman typed at a desk just outside the door, the clatter of the keys loud enough for me to hear. A man leaned over her desk, grabbing a stack of paper from a wooden tray while whistling a few bars of Billy's version of "Jingle Bells." It seemed even the employees of Brewster's bank were fans of the Diamond Dog's broadcast.

Then, suddenly in my left ear, the one covered by my earpiece, Paul's voice said, "I believe in you, Raquel."

Feeling momentarily braver, I turned in my seat, looked straight at Brewster, took a deep breath, and said, quite casually, "I met Agent Tawney yesterday."

"Ah," said Brewster, reaching out to rearrange the pens lying on his desk blotter. He set them end to end in a neat line, looking at the desk rather than me.

"He says you wrote him several letters," I went on.

Three almost as straight lines appeared in Brewster's high forehead as he frowned at his desk. "Hmm," he said.

"Did you write to him?" I said, now sounding a little desperate and wishing that somebody, anyone, would tell me exactly what to say. Paul might whisper words of encouragement to me, but how did those smart ladies in Rinehart's mysteries solve the cases? "Did you write to Agent Tawney about my aunt?" I said and hoped that was the right question to ask first.

Brewster raised his eyes from his contemplation of his neat row of pens and looked at me directly. "I wrote to several agencies about your aunt's activities in Kingsport," he said finally. "In my position as a business leader in Kingsport, I am charged with a civic responsibility toward our city. I did not think it would be prudent to keep my observations to myself. Rather, when I saw that significant changes were occurring, and that those changes could be traced to your aunt's acquisition of the Diamond Dog, I felt it was no more than my duty to bring forward the conundrum which I personally experienced on December 24 of last year."

At this I straightened up a little. Tawney claimed that Brewster's letters spoke of a "time travel" incident on Christmas Eve. As I was just about to ask him what happened, he launched into another speech.

"Kingsport can be so much more than it currently is," Brewster said, warming into a cadence that I recognized from his editorializing on his radio show. "I can bring our city to a new level of excellence, a model for all other cities, through programs which harness our resources, both natural and manmade, to serve the greater good."

He spoke very rapidly. I know I lost a word or more, but I've tried to reproduce in this account the general self-important emphasis that he gave to his statements. Although he held no elected office or official position, he truly believed himself to be the center of Kingsport's civic life as his next unsolicited speech would prove.

"To use such a discovery as your aunt has made for the mere satisfaction of a recreational vice can only be abhorred by right-thinking individuals, as I am sure our governmental agencies would agree with me," Brewster continued. "It is my duty to inform them what was happening here in Kingsport. We cannot become another Arkham or Innsmouth."

My own unease grew as I sat there listening to him.

Still he did not shout as he had the first time that I met him. Later I decided he was one of those men who cared greatly about outward appearances. If he had yelled at me in the bank, he would have been heard by his employees through the open office door.

"The Diamond Dog provides innocent entertainment, as do the radio broadcasts from Nova's station. Neither, I think, can hurt Kingsport's reputation," I argued while I tried to figure out how to say, "I'm sure my aunt doesn't use time traveling as a means for bootlegging" without sounding like an idiot.

Brewster frowned at me. "Are you so certain about the innocence of those broadcasts? Have you listened closely to what is said? I have. I advised Agent Tawney to do the same. The cookie recipes threaten us all with a deluge of liquor and vice in our fair city."

I blinked. "The cookie recipes?" I repeated back to him, certain that I heard his words wrong. Weren't we talking about time travel and bootlegging?

"Pepper nuts," said Brewster, "should never contain white pepper according to Mrs Orne. Yet Johnny Carl told the listeners to add two shakes of white pepper. A direction," Brewster emphasized the last word, "which makes no sense in the baking of cookies but contains a great deal of information for others."

He looked triumphantly at me, but I had no idea why. "I don't understand what pepper has to do with anything," I said.

"No?" said Brewster. He pushed back his chair and stood up. He stepped to the bookshelf behind his desk and reached for one of the leatherbound books on it. Like its fellows, the dark brown leather cover was stamped with a year on the spine and, when he opened it, I saw the front cover bore his initials in large gold letters: a prominent CB on the lower right corner.

Brewster flipped a couple of pages and then nodded. "Here it is," he said. "I keep quite meticulous notes for posterity. Someday these will be of great interest to my biographers. Three times in the last two weeks, Johnny Carl has added directions following a recipe. The first time it was 'a pinch of saffron,' a ridiculous spice to use for the cookie in question. Next it was 'improve with an extract of peppermint' and today was the questionable addition of white pepper. About the only flavoring that he's mentioned which makes sense is nutmeg, and even then, he told people to add a dash to a maple cookie recipe which already contained a full teaspoon of nutmeg."

"Johnny jokes around with people when they are on the show," I said. "He would suggest spices to create conversation."

"Do you think so?" said Brewster. "I found the entire pattern of comments suspect, as I informed both your aunt, Agent Tawney, and those laggards in Prohibition who are doing nothing to keep the cities around here dry."

"You told Nova? When? How?" But of course, I should have known the answer.

"I wrote her a letter yesterday after hearing the mention of white pepper. Her code was ridiculously easy for me to decipher," said Brewster. "The idea of sending directions over the air is quite ingenious." Brewster's tone indicated he considered himself quite ingenious too for figuring it out.

"What are you talking about?" I said, completely bewildered on how we had progressed from bootlegging and possibly time travel to cookie recipes in one conversation.

Brewster set his journal upon his desk with a self-important thump. "Directions," he said. "Johnny Carl always says, when he makes those suggestions for the recipes, that he has an extra direction to improve the flavor. Which, obviously, translates to certain listeners as a direction of where to go with their illicit cargo. Extract of peppermint for east, nutmeg for north, saffron for south, and white pepper for west. The last is quite clever, there's very few spices with w in their name."

I remembered how intently Nova listened to the noon broadcast while she generally ignored the evening one. Was she checking each day at noon to see if the directions to her bootlegger friends were being broadcast correctly?

"I suspect the two dashes, one shake, and so on refer to either distance or time, or perhaps a combination of both. Johnny Carl makes other comments during the cookie segment which obviously translate to further instructions on where to go and when to leave a cargo behind," said Brewster.

"So you think my aunt is smuggling liquor into Kingsport," I said with the sinking feeling that his story of radio codes would sound very plausible to law enforcement, however lax Brewster found the local Prohibition agents, and far more plausible than time travel. Still, I had to ask: "Why tell her in a letter that you know how she is doing it?"

"As I said, I am not unaware of the scandal that it would create to have liquor raids in Kingsport," said Brewster. He still stood behind his desk. My neck ached as I craned my head back to watch him. Brewster leaned one hand on his journal and tucked the other in his jacket, obviously striking a practiced pose.

"It is not in our best interests to have our town become as notorious as Arkham. Let Arkham have its Clover Club and its wars among the bootleggers. Let Innsmouth keep its foul secrets. I assumed if Nova Malone realized that her tricks were revealed, then she would cooperate with Agent Tawney, allowing him to gain the information that he seeks. In return, he could grant her certain protections and immunities. In fact, I wrote to her that I would be happy to attend a meeting with both of them and facilitate a dignified exit from Kingsport for her."

"How could Agent Tawney help my aunt?" I asked. "Why would he do so?" Yet Tawney had also hinted during our conversation that he could make "deals" with Nova. Could Tawney be so obsessed with finding a time traveler that he would bend the law or even ignore it? It seemed absurd but Brewster seemed terribly certain a deal could be struck. I wondered how good that deal would be for Nova.

Brewster bent a look at me that I often saw on the faces of certain male professors who could not resist lecturing their fellow faculty members, especially the women, on the most basic of facts. "In return for your aunt's full cooperation, Agent Tawney assures me that she will be removed from Kingsport peacefully. Our town will avoid the shame of harboring such a criminal character as well as, sadly, having lauded her as some type of civic hero. The number of people who have praised her broadcasts and the entertainment at the Diamond Dog is simply appalling. I cannot imagine why they venerate a woman so lacking in decorum." He paused here, perhaps realizing how petty he sounded or perhaps only marshaling his thoughts.

A "peaceful removal" sounded a bit ominous to me. I started to ask for more information, but Brewster continued.

"If Nova Malone cooperates with our government, I will have done my duty and would then be in an even better position to aid my party and my country. I hesitated to run in the recent special election but there will be a Senate seat open again in 1928. I could do a great deal of good for this nation if I were in the Senate," he concluded.

In other men, Brewster's ambitions might have been labeled commendable. But there was something about his tone and his preoccupation with himself which made me uncomfortable. His absurd belief that his private journals held secrets desired by future writers was even rather pathetic.

"Mr Brewster," I said as firmly as I could and not letting him interrupt me again, "my aunt is an honest businesswoman. Not a bootlegger."

Brewster bent a skeptical look at me. "You must hope that is true," he said finally. "But if Nova Malone does not leave Kingsport soon, I will insist the Prohibition agents raid all her places of business. According to the newspapers they've already had considerable success in confiscating liquor bound for Arkham in the last few months. A dry city is a safe city, Miss Gutierrez, and I intend to make Kingsport the safest place in the state."

However odd Brewster was, I realized that he could stir up a great deal of trouble for Nova. My aunt needed to know about his letters to Agent Tawney, I decided. She could no longer wave off this banker's editorials on the radio or write polite notes back to him. Brewster's actions posed a real threat to all my friends at the Diamond Dog.

With all the dignity that the niece of an honest woman should display, I rose from my chair, collected the carpetbag, and left his office. As I hurried out of the bank, my fear was mixed with annoyance. While having a slightly shady aunt was an enchanting tale for children to whisper on Christmas Eve, in reality it was appalling. If the Diamond Dog was raided and I was arrested, the list of things that I could not bear to write to my family about would grow infinitely longer. For people like Harlean, Billy, Ginger, Cozy, Reggie, and Johnny, such an arrest might well end all hopes they had of careers in radio and entertainment. I knew how bitter it was to lose such a dream after giving up my own hopes of being a concert pianist. How could Nova have mixed me up in such a business, I fumed, well aware that my anger was a bit misplaced.

For hadn't I come to Kingsport with Nova willingly and never questioned where all her expensive gifts came from? And didn't I love her, my big, brash, and loud auntie with her generous heart?

"Oh, pepper nuts," I growled as I stomped back to the Diamond Dog.

So the story is told, and here it begins. So the story is told, and here it ends.

Except I can find no endings and the beginnings grow worse. Every time I step out of this place, I lose more of myself. I am no Shadow, adept at fighting evil. I'm not even a cook determined to be brave.

Courage. I tell myself to have courage, but I don't even know what the word truly means anymore. Around me the trees weep blood and all I can remember is the old story of Bluebeard's bride stepping out of the little locked closet. Her shoes are covered in blood. Her heart is cold with terror. The key in her hand cannot come clean but drips blood whenever she picks it up. Courage, her sister tells her, courage for our brothers are coming to save us.

"Down she went, down she went, until she reached the little closet and turned the key," I recite to myself; this story is the only memory that I can keep in my head as the blood pours across the ground and rises around me. "She walked into the little closet and her shoes grew sticky with blood."

No sooner than I thought of the closet full of blood than I stood in the hallway of a house. Light filtered through a dirty window to show a floor gray with dust. I did not know the place, although I had lived in so many houses like this. A remembered smell made me sneeze, a fog of cabbage soups and despairing lives crammed under one roof. I was certain that I stood in the upper hallway of a boarding house. Yet I was equally certain that I was alone, trapped in my nightmare forever.

As I walked down the hallway, I saw my footprints behind me were the only prints on the dusty carpet. All the doors swung into empty rooms, stripped of furniture. A broken window in one room let in the cold wind. An icicle dangled on the windowsill and the walls were blotched with a dark fungus.

Then I heard the bang of a door. I looked back behind me before I realized that the sound came from below me. At the top of the stairs, I found myself overlooking an entryway.

Leaning over the railing, I spotted a woman and a man. All I could see was the top of their heads, and the woman wore the large hat of another era. Their voices sounded neither young nor old. Still, there was an undercurrent of affection and exasperation in their tones that spoke of a couple long used to each other.

"Agatha Crane," said the man. "I don't want to spend our Christmas Eve in a deserted house, not even one with ghosts."

"Wilbur," replied the woman, "there are no ghosts, at least as far as the accounts of this house go. Just a room where the ceiling drips blood, to be precise." She sounded like a woman who always wanted to be precise. When I was very young, I remembered a neighbor who spoke in such a way, a very grand lady in my memory, and one who commanded politeness from small boys. I suspected Agatha was such a woman.

"I don't want blood dripping on my suit either," replied Wilbur. "We're supposed to be at my mother's for dinner tonight."

"We'll be there in plenty of time. Just let me put a new cylinder in the Dictaphone. This will be a very quick experiment. Please rewind the Edison. I have a theory that music causes the vibrations in the ether which trigger the manifestation. You play the song while I dictate what happens for my records."

"We bought the recorder for the office," said the man. "Not as an aid for your research. Why can't you just use your notebook?"

"Wilbur, it's 1908. We must move forward with the century. Why record my thoughts with pen and paper when I can preserve them for posterity on these wax cylinders, which will last for centuries? Imagine, Wilbur, a hundred years from now, two hundred years from now, fellow researchers will hear exactly what I am thinking at the very moment of discovery. These machines are invaluable for research."

"Look, I don't mind you taking the Edison, the thing's nearly ten years old and you can play your old song until the wax melts off. But the Dictaphone is brand new. I don't want blood on it," said the man with a grumble as he cranked on the handle of an old-fashioned phonograph. "It would be the devil to clean, Agatha."

"Don't you 'Agatha' me. If it is blood, it will be spectral blood – ectoplasm, according to all the newspaper articles," Agatha said. "I'm sure any essence produced won't gum up the works or stain your suit."

"I've heard that before," Wilbur said with a sigh. "I love you dearly, Aggie, but you have no respect for machines." He let go of the crank and clicked a switch. The little phonograph began to play a jingling tune.

As the Edison played, the hall where I stood started to melt away. I smelled the scent of blood. Beneath my feet I could see the path through the trees begin to form again. With resignation, I turned away from the landing, knowing nothing I did would prevent me from falling back into the forest. Sometimes I could speak and act with those around me. This time I felt as if I was still half in the other place, dreaming about this couple in the boarding house. Yet beneath my apathy ran a current of fear as I knew that this dream, like so many events before, could turn into a nightmare.

"Hush," Agatha said. "Do you hear dripping? But it's not coming from the closet. Do you suppose it is just a leak in the roof? Blast, I forgot to turn on the Dictaphone. Stop the music. Let's try again."

A click halted the rotations of the wax cylinder player. The hall formed again under my feet, but I still had no power to move or do more than listen to the conversation below. My memories seemed more faded than ever before. If this pair called up to me and asked me my name, I was sure that I could not answer. I stayed silent and watched, like a man in a theater watching a film flickering past him, unable to influence the actors on the screen.

"Aggie," said Wilbur, "we are going to be late for dinner."

"We'll be there on time," she promised. "And I'll play two hands of pinochle with your mother. What I fear is that we will have wasted this time on nothing more than a rumor."

The wind moaned through the broken window in the abandoned house, but Wilbur answered stoutly, "Don't you say there is no wasted research even when it fails? Courage and continue on, that's the motto of my Agatha."

I heard her give a watery sniff. "You old softie," she said with affection coloring her voice. "Now, start the music when I open the closet door. Courage, indeed, Wilbur, and let us continue – the answers are almost within our grasp!"

"Good for you, my dear," he replied.

There was a click of a second machine. Agatha's voice rose from the entryway as she spoke very clearly and slowly into the Dictaphone. "Pursuant to my research, I have determined that in specific circumstances sound waves can manifest certain phenomena which the ignorant might call supernatural. However, I believe these manifestations are natural occurrences created by an intersection of sound and light. The propagation of this wave, passing through the interface between one medium and another, may produce an appearance of matter with varying density."

As the music rose through the empty house, the hallway faded away but the memory of the fond words between Agatha and Wilbur remained with me. Like the others I had seen, they continued with courage. Perhaps it is fear which makes it hard to hear the song, and all I need is the courage to listen for it, the courage to continue the search for a way out of this place.

Then I heard your voice singing. My heart grew a little easier. When I looked down, there was no blood on the ground. I knew my name again and I knew yours.

Courage, Raquel, courage. There is a way through this forest. We will find it together.

CHAPTER TWELVE

I wasted considerable time on my trip back to the Diamond Dog, stopping at the same small cafe where Agent Tawney had bought me a cup of Ovaltine. I may have had a vague idea of questioning Tawney about Brewster. Unfortunately (or fortunately), the man wasn't to be found there so I was spared a very awkward conversation. Instead, I chewed my way through a bacon sandwich and drank the bitter black coffee served from the dregs of the pot. I lacked the will to send back the coffee or request sugar, being so preoccupied with the thoughts buzzing around my head.

The carpetbag sat on the chair next to me at the counter. During my lunch, I avoided the attempts of the waitress to discuss the upcoming Christmas Eve dance. Apparently Johnny chatted up the event on the noon broadcast. I almost asked if he'd given any directions on how to spice Christmas cookies but didn't. I paid for my sandwich, left the coffee to grow cold in the cup, and marched on with the carpetbag now tucked under one arm like a bad puppy.

Finally, I arrived back at the Diamond Dog in the deadest hour of the afternoon, the time when everyone scattered to prepare for the evening. Normally Nova used this break in the day's activities to take a small nap in her apartment, but a quick check proved she was out. With some relief, I left the now hated carpetbag on the kitchen table.

A look outside showed the Rolls parked in the garage. If Nova had left the building, she'd left on foot. This seemed unlikely as Nova liked using her Rolls whenever possible. It was far more probable she was still within the Diamond Dog.

The radio station side of the building was locked up tight as Reggie was scrupulously careful about this whenever he left the building. I knew neither he nor Johnny would return until evening.

After no small debate with myself, I stood at the top of the basement stairs and stared down into the depths of the one area that I hadn't explored thoroughly. Nobody had told me not to go into the basement, or so I reassured myself. But nobody ever went down into the basement except Nova, Lily, Tim, and Otis. If something was needed from there, Tim or Otis fetched it. Lily worked on the receipts in the basement office because the safe was located there. But I gathered from Lily's comments that she never went beyond the small office right at the base of the stairs. Nova worked in the office with Lily, but she also "took stock" on Tuesdays. The latter had something to do with a clipboard, several sheets of paper, and, oddly enough, a small screwdriver that I'd seen her clutching in one hand when she descended.

This was Thursday and not Tuesday, I reminded myself, and it was unlikely Nova was taking stock below. On the other hand, she was nowhere else in the building. I considered climbing the stairs to the roof but knew nothing was there except the antenna for the radio station. The basement remained the most logical place to find Nova.

Switching on the light by pulling the long string that dangled over the top of the stairs, I made my way down to the basement office while humming one of Billy's medleys of holiday songs to keep up my spirits. But the office door was closed.

When I tested the knob, I found it locked. I rapped on the door and called Nova's name. No answer came. Which left only the long hall leading past the boiler and into the storage spaces beyond. The lights were on, indicating that someone else might be in the basement although I heard nothing.

I opened my purse and checked the battery for the hearing aid. Everything seemed fine. When I tapped my microphone with one finger, the tap echoed in my left ear. The silence of the basement was a true silence and not my impaired hearing. Which was not a comfort.

"What fun it is to ride and sing," I sang as I walked down the hall, still intent on making my presence as known as possible.

"Courage," said Paul's voice in my left ear.

"Can you hear me?" I said in surprise, but the reply that came was not in response to my question. Rather it sounded as if he was reciting a story out loud.

"Down she went, down she went, until she reached the little closet and turned the key."

I knew the tale as soon as I heard it. The terrible story of Bluebeard and the closet full of blood had been a favorite of my family, with Clara and I alternating between which was the sister treading in blood and which was the one in the tower watching for their fierce brothers.

By this time, I was so used to Paul's stories that I didn't even consider why he was reciting Bluebeard. Which was altogether foolish of me. For the story was not about a man who liked to murder his wives. It was a warning about how you can never hide from a family secret once you have found it.

"There's nothing in this basement," I said to Paul, even though I was sure that he couldn't hear me. Paul responded directly to me only a few times. Usually hearing him was like listening to the fragments of radio broadcasts from very far away. Reggie demonstrated to me one night how the skywave bounce brought moments of other broadcasts briefly into range. Going up and down the dial, we heard music, news announcements, and call letters fading in and out.

There was something magical about it, as Reggie said, this ability to pluck random voices out of the air. Also, in a cold and seemingly empty basement, something slightly terrifying. Thoughts of phantoms and ghosts intruded. How could we know the voices in the air belonged to here and now, that the people speaking to us were warm and living human beings?

"Courage, Raquel Malone Gutierrez," I said to echo Paul. "There's nothing here to scare you." But I don't know if I believed what I was saying.

No doors were locked in the basement except the door that I just tried. Locked because the ledgers and safe were inside, I told myself, not because seven brides hung on the wall dripping blood upon the floor. Perhaps Nova's gifts of fairytale books were to be deplored for their influence on small children, as the images in my mind were far too vivid.

"Courage," Paul said again, and I took his words for encouragement to explore further.

Walking down the hallway, I opened doors to storerooms full of boxes. When I pried open the lid of a box marked "decorations," ornaments twinkled in the light cast by the bare bulb in the ceiling. I found no sign of illicit booze and began to consider if Nova had been telling the truth about the Diamond Dog being a dry establishment.

Further away from the stairs, the items became more the type of thing stored away in the hope that it would be repaired and useful again someday or else someone would finish discarding it. Tables which rocked sideways on their pedestals, chairs with broken legs, and a pile of chipped dishes. I grew more upset with myself and my suspicions. There was literally nothing of interest here.

The hallway took a sharp turn and suddenly the world wobbled. I can't describe the moment everything changed better than that. One moment I was in a chilly, dimly lit basement and then I wasn't. The smell hit me first, a damp boggy smell, like the areas where water collected in the forest and couldn't drain away. I'd hiked through places like that in the time between winter and spring, when the snowmelt caused flooding and brought down dead trees.

It was an old memory, long before my younger brother and sister were born, when I was the youngest desperately running to keep up with two older brothers who had forgotten the little sister trailing behind them. The trees bordered a graveyard. The boys had dared each other to go through the dark woods and climb over the fence. A fierce winter rain had turned the ground below the trees into stinking mud.

As if I'd tumbled back into my old memory or a dream, I found myself stumbling again over tree roots. Jagged bushes snagged at my clothing. The same queasy fear of my four year-old self returned to me in terrible clarity; I was convinced the forest went on forever and I would never be found. The real woods, the ones I remembered, were a scraggly patch of uncleared land barely wider than a city block.

In this place, I struggled to see in a gloom that still oddly resembled the flickering lights of the basement. There was no beginning or end as I spun around, trying to find the corridor where I had been walking.

I took another hesitant step. Paul's voice sounded in my earpiece. "And her shoes grew sticky with blood."

The mud covering the ground squelched under my feet and splattered over my shoes and stockings. The smell rose with an iron tang, less bog and more like the stink of the sickroom where my youngest brother coughed out his life as I played the piano to distract him.

I fell into a new and worse memory, one which had become a recurring nightmare for many years.

I played, and played, and played, in the hours between midnight and dawn when Benny's coughing always intensified, and my little brother wept with the pain. Overhead, I heard the creaking of the rocking chair as my father held Benny in his arms and sang to him as I played the piano in the parlor below.

The smell increased, the smell of blood and sickness and the shadow of death, all accompanied by the creaking of the tree branches moving overhead, like the rocker I could always hear, no matter how loud I played the piano. The rocker that we could all hear throughout the house as we waited.

I remembered those terrible weeks so clearly, a stronger memory than many things that had happened to me more recently. I played to distract my mother and Clara sitting in the parlor with me, handkerchiefs stuffed in their mouths so my father wouldn't hear their sobs. I played for them and to comfort the pair creaking overhead. I played to console myself.

My father wouldn't allow Clara or me in Benny's room, terrified that we would fall ill even though we'd had lighter bouts of measles as infants. I couldn't hold Benny, my beloved baby brother, but I played all his favorite songs.

After my mother fainted through exhaustion one day, my father also insisted on hiring a day nurse and taking over himself in the evening.

But he couldn't make us sleep through the night while Benny wept from the pain of his fever and rash or coughed up his lungs because of the terrible pneumonia that followed.

I remembered again all too clearly the chilling silence when the rocking chair stopped, when my baby brother no longer cried and moaned. It surrounded me now in this forest place that was not real but felt too real, the silence of my father weeping with his son clasped in his arms. The hideous silence as I closed the lid over the keyboard and sat in the stillness of the dim parlor unable to look at my mother or Clara.

Without thinking, my hands began to move in the pattern of playing those final songs of comfort for Benny, the simple tunes he loved so much, and the music resounded in my head.

Between one step and the next, I was walking through a dimly lit corridor in the basement of the Diamond Dog. Glancing down, I could see my shoes were clean and unstained with mud or blood or any evidence that I had done more than walk through a dream of a best forgotten past.

Shaken, half convinced I had been dreaming but terribly afraid that I had been awake, I continued around the corner. The walls and floor changed again, but for logical reasons. Bare wood rather than painted plaster and a certain roughness of timber indicated a much newer and rather slipshod construction quite different from the basement of the Diamond Dog. Although I wasn't sure of exactly how far I had gone, I wasn't surprised to find a second set of stairs leading out of the basement and into another building altogether.

The narrow wooden stairs ended at a closed door, beyond which I could hear the muffled sound of voices, including the distinctive tones of my aunt. I stood on the top step and eased the door open.

"Seventeen crates of champagne," Nova said quite clearly. "And two more of the port."

A man answered, a voice I didn't recognize. "The boss wants it delivered by Monday. There are big parties planned next week."

"Everyone will have their bubbly by December 20," Nova replied. "Give me your list and we'll take them straight to your customers."

A deep laugh rumbled through the room, but it didn't sound friendly. I crept up one more step and eased the door open. Nova stood in the center of a great bare space, a former garage to judge by the work benches and large barn doors at one end. Near the doors was parked Nova's delivery truck with Otis leaning casually against the hood. As relaxed as his stance was, he never took his eyes off the equally big man confronting Nova.

The stranger was dressed like a businessman in a good suit and heavy overcoat. But his broad shoulders and heavyset features made him look like a boxer. Something about his stance or the way he kept his big meaty hands relaxed at his side also shouted that this was a dangerous man. He ignored Otis, keeping his own gaze fixed on Nova.

"The boss says everything comes to us and we make the deliveries," he said to her.

Nova smiled. "Don't trust me with your list of clients, Chuck Fergus? The Christmas truce holds as far as I'm concerned. We won't overstay our welcome in Arkham."

"Don't forget we helped your people when Innsmouth was raided in September," Chuck replied.

"Poached a few of my men too. How's Albie doing?"

Fergus grimaced.

Nova chuckled. "Can't say I miss Albie. He never was the brightest bulb of a bootlegger."

I held my breath and eased the door open even wider. The stairs were dark at the top so I fervently hoped nobody would notice me. Here was the evidence that I hadn't wanted to find, the family secret confirmed. Like Bluebeard's wife, I had absolutely no idea what to do next with the knowledge. But I knew now that my Aunt Nova was most definitely a bootlegger.

"Still, you did help when I was gone," Nova said to Chuck. "Happy to return the favor and best wishes for the season to Naomi. I'll stay out of Arkham as long as she stays out of Kingsport."

He nodded. "Innsmouth and Kingsport are yours, just as agreed. When and where on Monday?"

"Turn on your radio tomorrow. Johnny will let you know," Nova replied.

Chuck laughed again. This time his amusement sounded genuine. "I didn't believe it when Naomi told me that you were broadcasting to all the rumrunners on the coast, right under the Feds' noses. You've got some gumption, Nova Malone."

"I can't believe you're still relying on telephones and telegrams," said Nova. "Don't you know the Feds are tapping lines all the way to Chicago?"

"We're making some changes at the Arkham telephone company," Chuck said. Then he tipped his hat to Otis and added, "See you on Monday." Turning on his heel, he strode out of the door.

Nova motioned to the truck. "Better go pick up the stash. Make sure Fergus doesn't follow you."

"He wouldn't dare," rumbled Otis as he climbed into the truck.

"It's our luck the Feds found most of their champagne and confiscated it," Nova said to him. "I'll enjoy making money from their misery, but I won't be fool enough to trust the O'Bannions too far. Keep an eye out for trouble."

The rap of her heels crossing the wooden floor toward the door drove me back down the steps. The door opened fully and Nova stared at me. Over her shoulder she said, "Get going." The sound of a truck's engine reverberated through the space. I could smell the exhaust even where I was.

Then Nova said to me, "Are you coming up or shall I come down?"

"Courage," I said to myself and called out, "I'm coming up."

Standing in the garage space, I looked through the wide double doors to the street and realized that we were at the far corner on the opposite side from the Diamond Dog.

Nova wore a fur stole draped across her shoulders with a fox head biting its own tail to keep it closed. I felt rather like the fox under her gaze and waited to find out if she'd shoot me or skin me for discovering her secrets.

Of course, she did neither. Being Nova, she just shrugged and walked to the heavy wooden garage doors. She began to slide one along the tracks to the closed position. "Get the other one," she said, nodding at me.

Shoving the green wooden door along the track with a clatter of wood against the metal runner, I met my aunt in the middle. Once we had pushed the doors into place, Nova dropped a wooden bar across the pair to lock them.

"Used to be a stable," she said, dusting off her hands, "until gentlemen didn't need a place to keep carriages. Then they converted it for automobiles. Morrissen bought the joint a few years ago and added the tunnel from the Diamond Dog's basement to here for his own operation. But after his heart attack this fall, he wanted to retire. Convenient for me."

I circled around the space, not sure what to say, until a closer look surprised an exclamation out of me. "This is smaller inside than it should be," I said, remembering how long the hallway below had run.

"Good eye," said Nova with a nod at me. "False walls were added during the first remodel of this place to cover up part of the horse stalls. Morrissen opened them up again for storage." She walked across the room and leaned one hand on a corner of the wall, causing a hidden door to swing open and reveal a stack of crates behind it.

"We bring the goods through the Diamond Dog and out through here," said Nova with a falsely casual tone. She was watching me very closely.

"And Johnny tells people how to pick it up from Otis when he takes it out again?" I said, trying to act as casual as my aunt.

"Why would you say that?" asked Nova as if we were still discussing nothing more important than what to have for dinner. But this was more important than a fish chowder!

I blurted out, "I met Agent Tawney yesterday and Chilton Brewster today. They know about the cookie recipes." Like Bluebeard's bride, I couldn't keep a secret any longer. I didn't want to pretend I hadn't seen and heard what I just witnessed.

Unlike Bluebeard, Nova's reaction wasn't murderous, although I had never actually believed my aunt would harm me. Not the woman who had done so much to help me in the past few weeks.

Still, her laughter surprised me.

"That's all right," she said, slipping an arm around my shoulders and giving me a hug like she always did. "We're changing codes tonight. From now on, Johnny's going to slip the directions into the weather report. Slightly cloudy, mostly cloudy, almost about to rain, snow expected at ten tonight. There are so many ways to say the same thing in a weather report and still give out more information than the Feds realize."

"Does Reggie know?" I said. "And the rest of them?" I couldn't imagine Billy or Harlean as bootleggers. Or Ginger or Cozy.

Nova shook her head. "Just Otis, Tim, and Johnny. They were running a small operation in Kingsport. This fall, the Feds started raiding around Innsmouth. Most of my old crew left the area. Some people felt it was better that I leave Innsmouth too." She huffed a little, shaking her head almost sadly. "I couldn't believe anyone in Innsmouth wanted me gone but tempers were running hot after a bunch of lawmen poked their noses into certain concerns. I needed to recruit a new crew from a new town. The Kingsport gang were interested. Especially after I suggested the radio station."

I noticed she left out how she came to be in charge of the "Kingsport crew" but then considering the personalities of the three mentioned, I could guess. Nova would have overwhelmed Otis and Tim, as both struck me as more muscle than brain, content to take the money and let somebody else make the plans. As for Johnny, he was definitely the type to take the easiest route. Hadn't he said Nova offered him the chance that he always wanted, to become a star outside of Kingsport?

"One-Time Johnny," I said, remembering Harlean's comment that the handsome radio announcer only went out once with most women.

"That's how they used to pass messages to customers and pick up shipments. Lots of people notice Johnny but they never questioned what the women with him were doing, even when they were the ones driving trucks or boats to pick him up," said Nova. "The radio saves Johnny considerable shoe leather. The Kingsport ladies can still sigh and tell their families that they just like listening to his voice. But the rest of the Diamond Dog employees don't know. It's safer that way."

"But what about you?" My fears remained that a raid could impact everyone at the Diamond Dog. Nova believed she kept them safe by keeping them ignorant. I couldn't be so casual about her smuggling, which apparently involved half the women of Kingsport! What would Brewster say about the decorum of the town if he knew? I felt certain such knowledge would unleash a barrage of letters to every government agency in the country.

"Aren't you scared of being caught?" I asked my aunt.

"No, I'm never afraid. After all, the worst would be time in prison, and I doubt that will happen. I'm not violent, not like some. I even told the boys to stop carrying guns after… well, let's just say after things went a little wrong earlier this year. I decided I would rather lose a load than have someone lose a life."

Suddenly it was all too much. The whispers in my ear, the strange waking nightmare in the basement, and Nova's decidedly casual attitude toward breaking the law and risking imprisonment. My life had already been upended. I couldn't be expected to cope with all of this.

"Why are you telling me this now?" I said.

"Did you really want to know where the money came from?" Nova said with some force. Then she sighed. "No, that's not fair. We never asked my father why he could continue to outfit ships, even purchase buildings, when the rest of

Innsmouth went without. Sometimes it is best not to know. That's the path your mother took. I never pressed her about it. Guess I thought you were the same. Happier not to know."

My aunt wasn't altogether wrong, but I had to ask. "So my mother went west and you took up bootlegging?"

"Continued the family smuggling business, as it were. It's always been done on this coast, but Volstead made it more profitable," Nova said. "Especially after I added a few ideas of my own to the business. Perhaps your mother made the more sensible decision. But I never could resist new science or old ideas. It's fascinating what happens when you mix the two. Even when your neighbors turn you out of town."

Help with the problem in Innsmouth, Chuck Fergus had said just a few minutes earlier. I remembered how my letters to Nova went unanswered in September but received a quick and warm response at the end of October. Nova, I suddenly realized, would never ignore a request for help from family or friends, unless something drastic prevented her.

"What happened in Innsmouth?" I asked more gently than my earlier questions. Because, above all else and against all reason, I wanted Nova to know how much I appreciated all she had done for me, no matter how she paid for it. Because she came when I called for her help, giving me time and space to heal, to sort out what to do next with my life. She invited me into her warm, funny world at the Diamond Dog and I liked them all so much. If I broke with Nova, if I ran away from her, too, then I truly would be alone. That thought frightened me more than any nightmare.

"I may have been a little too bold," Nova confessed, and it would be her last confession of the day. "Two very brave young women nearly died this summer because of me. Then I went on a long journey and had plenty of time to think about what I had done, so much so I came to regret my actions. I was glad that I could help you. It seemed… well, it seemed like the best way to make amends. I've never had much ambition to change the world, not like Chilton Brewster always talks about, but I've always tried to help where I could." She reached out and gave me another of her quick hugs. "But never doubt I would have helped you anyway. You're my niece. We're family. I love you."

Again, my aunt had left me with nothing to say except "I love you too, Aunt Nova. But there's Tawney and Brewster. Are you sure there's no danger?"

"It's nearly Christmas," said Nova. "The Feds may disapprove but they know important people would be furious if they couldn't hold their holiday parties. You watch. There won't be any raids until January. We'll have our dance in every way." With a reassuring pat on my shoulder, she released me.

Her casual attitude toward the Volstead Act was not uncommon. Who hadn't dug out a bottle of wine from a well-preserved stash to give to a friend or even sell surreptitiously to a neighbor in need for a special event? But larceny on this scale was the stuff of big city newspaper stories and movies starring the Flapper Detective. I knew I should disapprove but, being aware of Nova's kindness and generosity toward our family, it was so hard not to love her audacity a little. The more I came to know my aunt, the more I realized that I cared for her a great deal.

"Come on," Nova said, tugging me toward the basement stairs. "Let's go back to the Diamond Dog. I could use a cup of coffee. It's always cold in here and down in the basement."

So I let her lead me back to her warm apartment and an absolutely ordinary afternoon of coffee and cookies. Once again Nova slid away from any hard questions so I hesitated to tell her any more of my secrets too.

Which was foolish. Like the bride's bloody key dripping away no matter how she tried to conceal the evidence, I couldn't hide what I knew. I should have told Nova about Paul's whispers in my ear and the strange nightmare in the basement. But instead, I decided to keep my thoughts to myself, thinking perhaps I could find the answers I needed with just a little more time.

INTERLUDE

I heard you again and suddenly I think there is a way out of this place. Perhaps more than one. I only need to find the right path. But every time I leave the beach, the hounds appear. They do not block me directly. Rather they slink and slither in and out of the trees, and I cannot walk more than ten paces without a howling beginning.

I know how a sheep feels when it is herded by wolves.

I forget things, I know that I do, but I remember the laboratory and the men who died under the teeth of the hounds. The sounds of bodies being shredded by those teeth and claws. The very wet sound of a man's head being torn off his body and gulped by a tree.

And I pause. I cannot lead the hounds to you. I cannot.

The cook trusted me to be a good man. The prince gave me back the silver dime. The good servant told me not to despair. I turn these pages back and forth. In this writing, I begin to see a way out, but I must not let it create new monsters in the world. I must find a way that is safe.

CHAPTER THIRTEEN

With only four days to go until the Christmas Eve dance, a group of us went to find the perfect tree for the Diamond Dog. Which suited me just fine. Nova and I spent our time not speaking to each other about anything important after I discovered her bootlegging operation. I danced as many dances as I could on Friday and Saturday night and accepted an invitation from Lily to spend Sunday dinner with her family. I didn't say a word when every lady in the family gushed about how much they liked the radio broadcasts, especially the cookie recipes and Johnny's banter. Whether they honestly liked to bake, admired the handsome broadcaster, or were part of a smuggling ring of Kingsport matrons, I simply didn't want to know. In those days leading up to the dance, I could have taught ostriches how to bury their heads in sand.

My one regret was that I heard almost nothing of Paul's voice since that time in the basement. Once or twice during the dances I thought he spoke to me, but it was so vague and far away sounding that it left me more confused than ever before. I wanted desperately to talk to somebody about all I had learned. But I couldn't endanger anyone at the Diamond Dog who didn't already know about Nova's operations. Nor would Johnny, Otis, or Tim make good confidantes. Johnny, I suspected, would try to charm his way out of any hard questions and I probably would let him. As I didn't know anything about the other two, I wasn't going to start such a conversation with Otis or Tim. Besides, they would just tell me to go talk to Nova.

So, by the time the others invited me to help them hunt for a Christmas tree, I was desperately glad for an excuse to leave the Diamond Dog and pretend this was an ordinary Christmas with friends and family.

Otis drove us out to the farm owned by a man named Samuel Cuffe. When we arrived at the farm the owner came to greet us, insisting that we all call him "Cuf-fee, just like cuff and coffee combined," he said.

Cuffe was round and pink, with wisps of white hair encircling his bald head. Across his upper lip was a great curling mustache with enough streaks of red in it to suggest as a younger man he had a fiery set of curls. He was, as Clement Moore might have said, a right jolly old elf in green checked woolen trousers and a simply enormous red sweater that was still stretched a little tight across his belly.

Within minutes, this jolly farmer had Harlean and Ginger giggling. Billy, Reggie, and Johnny all joined the ring of laughing discussion about the best place to find a tree of the size that Nova wanted. Once we found the tree, Cuffe promised a couple of hired hands would cut it down and cart it into town for decorating the day before the Christmas Eve dance.

"The best trees are in the back acres," Cuffe said. "It's too far to walk, so I'll take you in the sleigh."

"All of us?" questioned Harlean, looking at our small crowd. We'd fit in Nova's Rolls, but it would have to be an enormous sleigh to take us all.

Cuffe's face fell. "Probably not. There's two benches and I can harness a double team, but five or six at the most."

"Including yourself," said a tall Black gentleman emerging from the farmhouse. "You must count the driver as well as all the passengers." The man was bundled up in a blue peacoat and heavy knit hat like lumberjacks or sailors wore. His beard was full and white, covering most of his lower face. He handed a knit hat, bright red like Cuffe's sweater, to the farmer. "You'll want your hat, too, if you're going driving through the woods."

"You're right as always, Leo," returned Cuffe, popping the hat on his head. It had a great tassel that swung jauntily down the side. "I'll take a few with me to look for the tree. Perhaps the others would like to collect greens and holly nearer the house?"

"And have a cup of something hot with me while we wait for you to return," said the other. "I'm Captain Leonard Pease, at your service. Most call me Captain Leo or just Leo will do."

There was something rather grand about the gentleman. I thought Captain Leo suited him. Obviously the others thought so, too, because there was a chorus of voices then discussing who would stay with Captain Leo and who would go on the sleigh. Otis stated firmly that he would do neither, as he had other errands to run for Nova, but would return with the Rolls later in the afternoon to pick us up.

By the time Cuffe had slid the sleigh out of the barn near the house and harnessed the horses with the help of a burly farmhand, we'd sorted ourselves into two groups. I elected to go on the sleigh with Billy and Reggie. Johnny decided to stay with Harlean and Ginger to pick holly and, if I heard it right, sample Captain Leo's hot buttered rum. Which relieved me mightily, because I wouldn't have to watch my words around Johnny or feel guilty about not pressing him to learn more about Nova's operations. Nova said Reggie and Billy knew nothing about the bootlegging. Which, in my current mood, meant I could pretend I knew nothing about bootlegging while tree hunting with the men.

Cuffe's sleigh was a gleaming beauty, lacquered black with a trim of gold and red stripes along the top edges. Two giant farm horses were harnessed in tandem. The bright silver sleigh bells attached to the straps running across the horses' shoulders rang out as soon as Cuffe led the team and sleigh toward us. He grinned at the sound. "Leo says I put these jingles on the straps as soon as the first snowflake falls. But there's nothing better than the sound of the bells when we're trotting along," he declared. He then whistled and the most beautiful Irish Setter came running around the end of the barn.

"Ready for a sleigh ride, Mab?" Cuffe said to the dog, pulling slightly on her ears while her great feathered tail waved back and forth. "Queen Mab adores riding in the sleigh," he said to me. With a snap of his fingers, the dog bounded into the sleigh. She sat very straight in the front, looking quite as royal as her name.

Reggie and Billy climbed onto the back bench, while I sat in the front next to Cuffe and his dog. He clicked with his tongue to the horses. The sleigh slid smoothly out of the farm's front yard and onto a track winding under the trees. From the tracks of runners visible on the snow and the horses' confident trot, I guessed it was a favorite route. Cuffe soon confirmed that, talking about the woods that we were passing through, the age of a covered bridge that we clattered across, and his enjoyment in being "a hobby farmer." The inherited homestead was apparently too small to bring in much income, but Cuffe had retired from what he called "a city job so boring that its name shall not be stated here." In the winter, he tapped syrup and sold Christmas trees. In summer, he "dabbled" in fresh eggs from the chickens and produce from the garden. Every fall he sold apples from the orchard or pressed his own cider, he told us.

"I write too," he said to me as we swiftly headed to the corner of the farm where he grew Christmas trees. "Over the years I've contributed a few small stories to magazines. Leo is always after me to write something longer and more ambitious, a novel if you will, but I prefer to be the O Henry of Kingsport."

I'd left the hearing contraption at home, not wanting to lug it through a long walk in the woods. Also, I craved a return to what I had known, a world that didn't contain phantom voices, bootlegging aunts, and so much doubt in my own head. The hearing aid was too much of a symbol of everything I had experienced. I needed to leave it behind, I decided, without acknowledging I was once again trying to run away from my problems.

Like the letter that I needed to write to my parents, a letter which was still a blank sheet of paper. Like the questions still unasked and the discussion still not had with Nova about what came next. I even wondered if I was letting Paul's whispers become a way to ignore the other buzzing thoughts in my head. Cuffe's chatter proved an equally good distraction.

With Cuffe sitting on my left side, I could make out what he was saying well enough. The cold air on my face and the friendly ringing of the bells reminded me of Christmases at home, a good memory without any regrets, and that was a blessing too. Mab leaned against my legs and kept my toes quite warm by politely sitting on my feet. I bent to caress her silky ears, very content to be on this winter ride.

Behind me, Billy began to sing in time with the horses' hooves striking on the snow. It was, of course, "Jingle Bells." The rest of us joined in. Cuffe sang with more fervor than perfect pitch. Mab simply thumped her tail a time or two and otherwise ignored our shenanigans.

We crested a small hill and then plunged down into an older, more tangled section of trees with tall bare branches stretching across the narrow road. "The pines are just past this," yelled Cuffe over the singing and ringing of the harness bells.

I peered ahead. A ground mist swirled across the road. In the deeper shadows of the woods, this pale fog appeared almost luminescent above the snowy bushes. From the corner of my eye I saw a strange doglike shadow. When I turned in my seat to catch a better glimpse, I was sure that something was moving in and around the trees, keeping pace with our sleigh. Under my hand, Mab stiffened and then whined.

The air smelt not of snow and pine, but something acrid and almost nauseous, as if a swamp lay beyond the tangle of bare branches or even an open sewer, if such a thing existed in the New England countryside. It reminded me horribly of my waking dream a few days ago.

Billy stopped singing and cried out, "Oh that's a horrible smell. Are you sure there isn't a rotten egg in here?"

Cuffe and Reggie also went quiet. Both sniffed a bit. "Can't smell a thing," Reggie yelled over the ringing of the harness bells, "although I had a terrible cold this week." But even as he spoke, the smell disappeared, as did the doglike shadow that I was watching.

Looking a bit concerned, Cuffe shook the reins and the horses picked up their speed. "This is a bad patch," he said to me. "I forget because most days it's very like the rest of the woods."

The smell evoked the memory of the nightmare in the basement. I stirred uneasily on my seat. Such things couldn't happen here, I told myself. Such things only happened, maybe, in Kingsport. Oh, I was being the perfect ostrich that day!

We left the tall old grove of trees behind and emerged into a patch of cultivated pines where nothing stood more than nine or ten feet tall. The wonderful, fresh and sharp scent of the Christmas trees filled my nose. I quickly, deliberately, forgot the uneasiness of the last few minutes. Cuffe pulled on the reins and brought the sleigh to a gentle halt.

"Go on," he said as we clambered down. He reached down under the seat and pulled out an old scrap of a scarf, as brightly red as his hat and sweater. "Tie that round the branch of the one that you want," he told me. "We'll arrange the cutting and delivery to the Diamond Dog."

One of the many cheerful and completely inconsequential discussions that I carried on with my aunt over the last three days was how she wanted the most impressive tree ever seen in Kingsport. In Nova's words, "One to wow the crowd!" So we stomped through the snow searching for a tree with sufficient wow. Both Reggie and Billy pointed out various candidates, but Reggie championed one with a bald patch and Billy's pick had a distinct bend in the trunk. Mab raced around every tree, a graceful streak of dog giving out a few happy barks before rolling in the snow.

Determined to succeed in finding the right tree for the Diamond Dog, I walked briskly along all the rows. It felt so good to be there with no more bothersome thoughts in my head than the height and width of the perfect pine. When I found it, I summoned Billy and Reggie with a shout. They both agreed the tall Christmas tree with its evenly widespread branches was exactly what Nova would want.

With considerable ceremony, we tied Cuffe's red scarf in a large bow around a branch of what I was already calling "my tree" in my head. I walked a few yards ahead of the others to make sure our marker was visible from the road. Asserting that it was clear and distinct from where I stood, I waved my arms at the others, motioning them to return to Cuffe and the sleigh. Then I turned myself and glanced back at the dark woods bordering this more cultivated area.

The mist was gone but at the juncture where the road angled out of the wood, I glimpsed a doglike shape and two glowing red eyes staring back at me. I squinted, trying to make out what I was seeing. Wolves and coyotes were not unknown in Colorado, although as a city girl I'd mainly seen them in zoos. But though this animal resembled something of that silhouette, there was something strangely wrong about it too.

Mab barreled up to me and barked quite sharply, a warning bark that I felt more than heard. If she'd been a collie, I would have thought Mab was trying to herd me away from the forest. Certainly, she shoved against my legs, pushing me away from where I stood.

"Down," I said, a little more sharply than I meant to. I still strained to see what type of animal lurked beneath the trees. I had a fleeting impression of scales or perhaps even bare skin. When I blinked and looked closer, nothing was there. Wolves and coyotes generally didn't attack humans, I told myself even as I backed away. But if this thing was sick, it might be a danger. The wind shifted and the smell of the mist wafting from the woods was foul, which only heightened my anxiety. The joy of finding the Christmas tree was fading all too quickly.

"Come on, Queen Mab," I said to my companion, "let's go back to the sleigh."

We hurried through the pines. Mab stuck close to me, no longer joyously rolling in the snow or racing her shadow around the trees. As soon as we emerged from the pines, the setter gave a short bark and a wag of her extravagant tail as she rushed to her owner. Cuffe patted her head as he waved us all back onto the sleigh.

The ride back to the farmhouse was quieter. Even the horses' lovely bells seemed muted by the shadow of the older woods. The men said almost nothing, certainly nothing I remembered, and I spent my time peering intently at the shadows under the trees.

But I saw not even a shred of blue mist on our return. For some reason its absence made me all the more uneasy.

At the farmhouse, we found buckets of holly collected by our friends as well as swags of greenery. "There's enough to decorate two dance halls," declared Reggie. "Do you think we can fit it all in the Rolls?"

"Never mind," said the jolly Cuffe. "The men can bring it in our truck along with the tree. Come in, come in." He practically ran up the porch stairs and swung open the door. "You have to try Leo's rum punch."

Inside, everyone was gathered in a long but cozy room. Large, overstuffed chairs were circled around the fireplace while stacks of books covered various patches of the floor nearest the walls.

Cuffe shook his head at the books. "Never mind those. Leo's in the process of moving out of Innsmouth but we haven't enough bookshelves for his entire hoard. We've taken to stacking the books where bookshelves might go."

Captain Leo chuckled as he overheard his friend. "I promise to put it all to rights as soon as Christmas is over," he said.

"You're from Innsmouth?" I asked.

Captain Leo shrugged. "Not really. I lived there for a few years, after I retired from the sea, but the place never took to me nor I to it. I thought it would do for an old sailor who liked to read, but they're odd folk in Innsmouth. I tried opening a bookstore, but nobody ever came into it except a few outsiders, as lost as I was there."

"My mother and aunt were from Innsmouth," I said, "but I've never been to the town. Perhaps after Christmas." Although given Nova's recent revelations, I was beginning to think a trip unlikely.

Captain Leo looked at me. "Are you Nova Malone's niece? The others mentioned you."

"I'm Raquel," I said, holding out my hand to shake his.

Captain Leo started to shake, but then paused. "Raquel," he said in a musing tone. "I have a book for you."

Cuffe overheard him and shook his head with a smile. "Oh, Leo, you try to give a book to everyone that you meet. I don't understand how you can still have so many volumes. Sometimes I think your books multiply when we're not looking."

"Perhaps," said Captain Leo. He walked across the room where he pulled a slim book from a pile in the corner. Bound in leather, it looked very old and battered. "This volume certainly has a strange history, but I think it is meant for you," he said as he held out the book.

"For me?" I said in some surprise, taking it and ruffling the pages. The book appeared to be a journal, the pages filled with a scrawling handwriting that was difficult to make out. I turned back to the first page to see if I could decipher any of it.

"Yes," said Captain Leo, looking very troubled. "I'm sure this one is for you."

I read the first page out loud: "A dying man gifted me this blank book so I could write my thoughts, but my thoughts are birds…" I stopped and stared at Captain Leo, uncertain what the writer meant or why the captain thought this book should be given to me.

The captain must have guessed my doubts because he laid his large hand over mine where it rested on the journal.

"Read it tonight," he said to me, "it's important."

A horn sounded from the yard. Harlean said, "Oh, there's Otis with the Rolls," before I could ask any questions. I slid the book into my purse. We all ran outside, calling our goodbyes to Cuffe and Captain Leo. The pair stepped onto the porch of the farmhouse to wave farewell. Cuffe was beaming and holding on to the collar of Queen Mab to keep the dog from running after us. Captain Leo stood slightly behind him. I thought he looked very sober.

As the Rolls headed back to town, I twisted in my seat and stared back at the strange woods surrounding the farmhouse. As we turned a sharp corner in the road, I thought I saw a flash of something running beneath the trees. The mist rippled along the ground again. I looked again but I could not make it out clearly. It was something like a dog but so strangely twisted and elongated that it was nothing like any dog that I'd ever seen before.

CHAPTER FOURTEEN

Back at the Diamond Dog, Nova wanted to discuss the tree and its decorations. But I wanted to talk about the Wednesday broadcast. During the return from Cuffe's farm, I finally made some decisions, one of which was to persuade my aunt to be more cautious about her radio messages. As much as I believed her repeated assurances that nobody innocent of bootlegging would end up in jail, she clearly wasn't innocent. I had no wish to see Nova behind bars.

"You mustn't have Johnny send any more directions," I said as sternly as I could to my aunt. "Not with Brewster and Tawney listening."

My uneasiness about Nova's operations were justified by the usual warning from Brewster in his distinctive blocky handwriting. Nova shared the letter with me when I arrived back from the farm. I dropped my hat, coat, and handbag on the bed in my room before rejoining her in the sitting area of the apartment. The journal from Captain Leo was forgotten in this new concern. I also dismissed the incident of the strange wolf, if it could be called an incident. We'd been out in the countryside. Strange smells and animals did occur in wooded farmlands.

Instead I concentrated on Brewster's latest letter. I dug through such phrases as "it has come to my attention" and "charged with the ongoing responsibility" while seeing in my mind's eye that impossibly bland man sitting in his journal-lined office penning note after note to the citizens of Kingsport and, apparently, the federal government. When did he find the time to do anything else? I wondered.

The letter exasperated me, full of vague allusions and long words which meant nothing but sounded grandiose and oddly threatening. The word "inadequate" appeared twice for no good reason, although what he found inadequate was unclear. Once he paired it with something about what the larger world should know about Kingsport. Then there was a long paragraph about his ongoing distress that most people outside the town's borders were only aware of Kingsport through the broadcast of music that in no way fit his vision of how the town should be perceived.

"Writes like he swallowed a dictionary," observed my aunt, peering over my shoulder.

"And a thesaurus," I said. "But I think he's saying that if the broadcasts continue to have messages in them, then Prohibition agents will shut down the Diamond Dog and the radio station."

"Since Chilton is not in charge of any branch of law enforcement," said Nova, "his threats don't mean much."

"But what about Agent Tawney? He seems willing to listen to Brewster. I don't think you can count on them staying away until January."

"They haven't done anything yet," Nova pointed out. "Not even come into the Diamond Dog for a bowl of chowder, let alone served us with a search warrant."

"Do they need a search warrant?" I said with some vague memory of a court case in the last year stating the opposite.

"They can search a car, boat, or airplane without a warrant, but not my home or place of business. Or the cars parked in the garage down the street." My aunt grinned at my bemused expression. "I might have left school after the eighth grade, but I make it a point to understand the law. Especially as it pertains to my businesses. Also, I can afford good lawyers and accountants. Accountants are the most important of all. My books are clean. I pay my taxes on time."

"But it's still illegal," I said, trying to sound more disapproving and probably failing miserably. I had never been a heavy drinker, but I didn't objected to others drinking. I'd even thought it was nice how Cuffe and Captain Leo offered rum punch to everyone after hunting for Christmas greenery. If someone as respectable as Captain Leo didn't see the harm, how could I tell others to stay dry? I couldn't. Which, I supposed, was why it was a good thing that I wasn't a politician or a Fed. I suspected men like Brewster or Tawney never doubted themselves. Nova also never seemed to question the rightness of her position, despite the Volstead Act.

Was I the only one, I wondered, who kept seeing the good and bad of both sides and lacked the will to make a decision?

A knock on the apartment door interrupted my gloomy thoughts, somewhat to my relief.

When Nova went to answer it, Lily stepped into the apartment. "There's a man downstairs," she said, handing a card to Nova. "Says he wants to talk to you about some letters."

Nova glanced at the card in her hand and passed it to me. Tawney's name was printed across the top. As she crossed the room to check her makeup and hair in the mirror, Nova said to me, "You should stay up here."

"No," I said, coming to a decision at last. "I want to hear what he says." And, also, I desperately needed to hear my aunt's answers. I went back to my bedroom and rigged the hearing device on my head, settling the microphone around my neck and slinging the handbag with the battery over my arm. As I crossed the room, I noticed my other handbag on the bed with the square bulge of the book gifted to me by Captain Leo. I retrieved the little book and set it on the bedside table. I hung the coat and hat in the closet.

"Are you coming?" said my aunt from the living room.

"Yes!" As much as I wanted to understand what was going on, I'd also been stalling, fiddling with the items in my room. I never liked confrontations and always did my best to avoid them. Perhaps staying with my bootlegger aunt rather than going home for Christmas had been a poor decision. But I reminded myself, it had been my decision, and I needed to live with the consequences. Even help Nova if that was possible. I wanted to pay her back for all she had done for me.

We went downstairs together, with Lily walking a little way behind us, and found Agent Tawney in the lobby area, reading the posters lining the walls.

"Quite the schedule," he said, nodding at the list of upcoming dances. The Christmas Eve dance was printed in red with little holly leaves encircling the line on the poster.

"I do my best," said Nova with a quick shake of Tawney's hand. "How can I help you?"

"Ralph Tawney. Call me Ralph. Do you want to go somewhere more private?" he replied, glancing at Lily and me.

"We'll stay here," said my aunt with a pleasant smile. "I think better on my feet." She raised an eyebrow at the agent.

He raised an eyebrow back at her. Obviously, he'd expected to be escorted to an office or be treated with a bit more trepidation. Nova simply standing there while the rest of us stared at him seemed to disrupt a particular plan.

I admired my aunt's calm and tried to keep my face as polite.

Tawney then shrugged and smiled at my aunt while he fished out some letters from his jacket pocket.

"We've had some complaints from a local gentleman," he began.

"You've been receiving letters from Chilton Brewster," said Nova with a nod at the envelopes. "Same as all of Kingsport. The man is full of complaints and very few facts."

"Do you disagree with his allegations?" said Tawney a little too quickly.

"I don't know what he wrote to you, but I certainly disagree with the letters that he has sent to me. I believe the music played here at the Diamond Dog is of the highest quality and greatly enjoyed by the listeners of our broadcast. Anyone who doesn't like it can simply shut off their radio. Nobody is forcing them to listen."

His bushy eyebrows drew together as if something in Nova's words puzzled him. "What's this about music?"

"Brewster's letters to me are full of complaints about my radio broadcast," said Nova. She quite calmly left out a host of other allegations that I'd seen in

Brewster's latest missive as well as the information that I'd passed to her about my meeting with Tawney. "I strongly object to his characterization of the music played at the Diamond Dog or the musicians playing it as harming the reputation of Kingsport."

Tawney scowled while I bit my lip to prevent a smile. He obviously hadn't expected this turn in the conversation.

"Brewster wrote to you about the music heard during your radio broadcasts?" he asked again, obviously trying to find his way back into the conversation.

"Yes," said Nova. "What else could he complain about?" she added with a bland look almost exactly mirroring Chilton Brewster's most aggravating expression.

I thought Nova was clearly enjoying herself, but also felt some trepidation about how Tawney would react. When I was teaching, my students would occasionally fall into a quarrel with each other. Some mornings simply saying "hello" could set off a storm of tears caused by a greater frustration unvoiced. While I doubted Tawney would break out in sobs, he certainly had the look of someone bottling up too much emotion. A storm seemed to be brewing, but how it would break out I couldn't say.

The federal agent slowly replaced the envelopes in his pocket. "What else, indeed?" he said, looking again at Lily with visible frustration. Since he'd already discussed Brewster's claims of time travel with me, I could only assume that he didn't want to mention it in front of Lily.

Lily, in turn, became very preoccupied with the notebook in her hand as if she expected Nova to begin dictating the day's food orders to her. She barely glanced at the agent.

The silence stretched on. If they ever put up a statue of Nova Malone in Kingsport, and a very unlikely idea that was, then she was ready to be carved in stone. Her hands hung loose at her sides, the light winking off her diamonds. Only the slight rise and fall of the purple cat brooch indicated that she was still breathing.

Nova's serene expression flustered Tawney's attempts to control the conversation. He restarted with, "Now, see here, madam," and then stopped, apparently realizing his tone and words sounded too much like a lawman and not a friendly visitor who asked you to call him Ralph.

"We're a little concerned about some of Mr Brewster's claims, as odd as they might sound," said Tawney in a softer voice, not defining the "we" in his sentence. "Perhaps we could take a look around."

"The Diamond Dog is open to the public every Wednesday through Saturday," said Nova. "Of course, we'll be closed for Christmas this Saturday, but the Christmas Eve dance on Friday will be spectacular. Anyone is welcome if they have a ticket. I'd be happy to leave a pair at the box office for you and a companion," finished my aunt with a smile. "Is that all?"

Tawney seemed stumped for an answer, but his face flushed very red. I stepped back a pace or two, not certain what, if anything, I should or could do.

"I think that's all then," said Nova, walking past him toward the doors of the ballroom. "Raquel, come tell me where you think the tree should go. Center of the floor? In the far corner near the bandstand? Or here in the lobby?" She opened the doors with a last nod at Tawney. "Lily will see you out, Ralph … it is Ralph, isn't it? Thank you for your visit."

She walked into the ballroom. I hurried after her, closing the doors behind me.

"I think the far corner," said Nova, surveying the room. "Then it won't be in the way of the dancers or obscure the view of the band. If we make the tree too visible from the lobby, then there's no surprises when they enter here. I do like wowing my audience."

I blinked at her complete focus on not discussing what had just happened. She certainly surprised Agent Tawney and wowed me. However I quickly gathered that this, like all the rest, was falling into the vast bucket of things Nova would ignore. Unless I forced the issue.

Nova pointed to the left of the bandstand. "Right there. When people come in, they'll be busy chattering and looking at all the holiday finery being worn by their friends and neighbors. Then they'll look up and see our tree glowing with electric lights. Covered with all the silver and gold trimmings."

She had a slightly faraway look in her eyes as if she could see the tree decorated and in place already. "It will be spectacular," Nova said with pride.

Like Tawney, I was baffled as to how to continue the discussion of Brewster's accusations. But I had to try.

"What if Tawney had insisted on talking about Brewster's claims of codes being broadcast in the shows?" I said, because that was the easiest question to ask. "That Johnny was giving directions for bootleggers?"

Nova turned around and shrugged at me. "I would have said that people see patterns everywhere, but such patterns mean nothing at all. Spices as a code for directions? What a charming idea for a Philo Vance novel. I'm hoping for a sequel to *The Benson Murder Case*. A convoluted code cracking would be exactly what Vance would do."

"But that's what you did!" I said with rather more force and then looked around guiltily. Luckily, we were the only ones in the ballroom.

"Well, it probably wouldn't be wise to admit to Tawney that such an idea crossed my mind as soon as I read about new transmitters. Really, it is amazing how clear and how far the signal goes these days. Such an improvement over just a few years ago. As for the rest of Brewster's claims, his letters would sound like so much gibberish to a government man."

"But Tawney believes Brewster!" I protested. "Tawney thinks time travel is possible. Tawney is looking for a time traveler."

Nova spun around to stare at me. A truly worried look crossed her face. "You didn't tell me this before."

"How could I? All you talk about is this dance, and the decorations, and what to add to the Christmas fish chowder. And that's when you weren't discussing cookie recipes with Thelma!"

My anger was perhaps a bit misplaced. I'd been avoiding hard questions as much – if not more – than Nova. But once started, I couldn't seem to stop. "You've said absolutely nothing to me about anything important since last Thursday. Not a word about the bootlegging or what happened to you after you left Innsmouth last fall! I've been waiting days for you to talk to me about your past. About what's happening now! So how could I tell you that Tawney believes in time travel?"

Nova actually deflated a bit before my eyes. I never thought I'd see such a thing from my supremely confident aunt, but she actually appeared sheepish.

"Well," she said after a very long pause. "It's all mixed together. Innsmouth, time travel, and, yes, bootlegging. It started before Prohibition, just a little light smuggling and cutting a few corners to make a better profit in the early days, much like my father did."

I probably looked like one of the fish heads in the chowder with my mouth hanging open.

"There's no reliable way to time travel," said Nova with such calm that I almost believed her. Except what she was saying was impossible. "It's more of a side effect if you like scientific terms. I have a theory that time travel happens when you become lost on certain paths. We used to have a book which helped us avoid such accidental trips."

"We?" I said, rather frustrated with the vague "we" used by both Tawney and my aunt.

She smiled in apology. "The family grimoire. I'm sure your mother never mentioned it. She very much disliked that part of our history."

That I could believe. My mother was a very practical woman who even slightly disapproved of her children receiving volumes of fairytales and Oz books from their aunt. She always gave us novels about plucky orphans.

Nova walked across the room with a brisk click of her heels against the wooden floor that I felt as much as heard. She put a large soft arm across my shoulders and hugged me close for a moment. She dropped her voice low, but I could tell by the way she was pitching her words and speaking directly to my microphone, she wanted me to hear the next bit perfectly. "Our ancestors owned a grimoire once. It let the family smuggle goods along routes difficult to sail without fear. Because of that, they concocted a way to become fearless, a potion of seaweed which left its mark on those who drank it. Your mother always refused her share, which was wise since she moved away."

"And you?" I asked, absolutely enthralled because I loved fairytales and Oz better than Anne Shirley.

Nova gave me another squeeze and stepped back. "Father gave me more than enough when I was a sickly baby." She pushed back the sleeve of her dress and shifted her arm to display a patch of purple scales which glittered like her diamonds in the light. I gaped like a bystander at a carny show and then knew a flush of shame for such a reaction. This was my aunt, no matter how strange the scales, someone who cared a great deal for me.

Nova pulled the sleeve back down. "I never minded the taste. You don't when you've been drinking something since you were a little baby. But the side effects are annoying."

I simply blinked at her, uncertain what to say.

"I become unmoored," Nova said finally. "Oh, how do I explain this? I know a woman who can do this with a tangle of knitting but I'm not a knitter. Sometimes, not by choice, I step out of the world."

I remembered that moment in the basement when the world wobbled as the ground became blood beneath my feet. "But how do you get home?" I said, because it seemed the most important of all the questions racing through my head. Paul, I thought, was lost in the woods, and searching for a way out, according to the stories he whispered in my ear. How does Paul go home?

And, a more treacherous voice whispered in my heart, how do I avoid going home as such a failure? What if Nova's path could lead me to a new future by changing my past?

"If I'm very careful and use the right tune, I avoid being lost on the path and can step back out again," said Nova. "Of course if I'm pushed off course or distracted, or use the wrong song, I can sail right into another time. It's the devil to correct when it happens. That's why it took me nearly a month to begin answering your letters this fall."

I still didn't understand so I picked out the words that I'd heard best and repeated them. "The right tune? The wrong song?"

Nova smiled a little sadly. "It sounds like one of Harlean's blues numbers, doesn't it? But a person can step out of the horrid place if a set pattern is followed. The hardest part is to not be distracted by what's happening there. Some do it by concentrating on a knitted item of clothing and counting the stitches. I find songs with strong repeated melodies work well."

"So you can time travel?" I said, still trying to pick out the sense of what my now chatty aunt was trying to tell me. I might have paid lip service before to accepting only rational explanations, but I wanted the irrational now with all my heart.

"Not intentionally," said Nova. "Because when I do, it causes problems. Like taking Chilton Brewster's coat on December 24, 1925, and not returning it until nearly a year later. I probably should have thrown the coat away. But I try to be honest. Most of the time."

CHAPTER FIFTEEN

According to my aunt, she fell off a pier in Innsmouth at the end of summer and splashed ashore "somewhere else, which means nowhere at all." In leaving somewhere else, she went backward and forward in time, including a stop in Kingsport on Christmas Eve a year ago.

"But why did you fall off the pier?" I asked, because the incident seemed the simplest part of the story and the only part I could visualize.

"A silly battle with a man. I should have known better," said Nova with a shrug and wouldn't say more.

"But why did you take Chilton Brewster's coat?"

"Because I was cold, wet, and angry as a hornet. He looked too warm and too sure of himself as well," replied Nova. She was pacing around the ballroom, checking where she wanted to put decorations and jotting down notes in a small notebook not unlike the one that Lily had held. Although Nova carried hers in her skirt pocket and it had a metal cover set with rhinestones. Like during her conversation with Tawney, she seemed immensely calm, but there was something about the line of her always straight back and the set of her shoulders which made me believe she was gauging my reactions very carefully.

"When did you give the coat back to Brewster?" I asked. Nova's moving about was frustrating me to no end as I had to keep shifting my own position to hear her as perfectly as possible. As usual, her big voice was remarkably clear through the microphone, but I didn't want to miss a single word.

"In October, when I finally arrived back in 1926, close enough to when I fell off the pier to stay here. I popped back into the basement of the Diamond Dog and found the tunnel to the garage across the street. I'd had my eye on the place for some time but that's when I knew it would be perfect for me."

"Perfect for smuggling," I said. "Bootlegging."

"Well, it's been our family business for more than a hundred years. Whatever is wanted at a bit lower price than what is legal. Or whatever is wanted that is completely illegal. Opium was once our trade, and I do think liquor is far less harmful. Your mother never approved of the smuggling or several other things about Innsmouth. She made her choice and a good life too. I stayed and tried to make a difference in the town. I thought the money that fine French wine and good Scotch whiskey brought could make a difference. But Innsmouth hates change even worse than Chilton Brewster."

"And about his coat?" I said, unwilling to be sidetracked in this discussion.

"When I took myself topside, I found it was a warm day for October. I didn't need a coat anymore. I saw Chilton walking by and handed it to him. Unfortunately, he remembered the dress that I was wearing."

"A summer dress with a tear across the shoulder," I said, thinking about the photos that Agent Tawney had laid across the table in the coffee shop.

Nova nodded. "Yes, and more. Brewster remembered not encountering me as well."

"That makes no sense at all," I said. None of the conversation made much sense to me but I kept thinking back to the wobble in the basement and the smell of a decaying forest suddenly surrounding me. Had I been standing in the spot where Nova "popped in" to in October? Was that the place where Paul was? With trees creaking overhead to remind him of old griefs and deep sorrows? A place which felt like stepping into a nightmare for the few moments that I was there.

"Shifting about in time never makes sense," replied Nova with complete conviction. "Some people end up with double memories. What happened when the time traveler interacted with them and what happened when the time traveler didn't. The after and before effect, one theorist called it."

"That's the wrong way round. Shouldn't it be before and after?"

"Only when time is linear. There's a very clever woman named Beatrice who wrote an interesting little paper on an encounter with a time traveler when she was in college. She talks about something similar, that only *after* the encounter can you remember what it was like *before*. Those stuck-up professors at the university simply dropped her work in a cardboard box with some other theories of time travel and forgot all about it."

"How did you read it?" I asked.

"The Miskatonic University professors don't mop their own floors. I pay the cleaning women to bring me information now and then. Earlier this year I was searching for more information about the book I mentioned, the family grimoire. I thought traveling between places by plane would make using those routes outside of our world safer." Nova shrugged. "But it turns out the whole idea is impractical for many reasons. If you're in the space betwixt and between – for I can't call it anything else – you begin losing memories and ending up in the wrong places or the wrong time. Sending codes for normal routes over the radio is much easier."

Nova's revelations left me reeling. But her story also made me wonder if what I had experienced in the basement was possibly real.

Nova closed her notebook with a snap. "Well," she said, looking around the room. "We're almost ready for the dance. Let's go back upstairs."

Which meant, as I'd come to learn, Nova had told me all she wanted to tell me. And I, still trying to understand the information so casually given out, never did mention Paul or what had happened to me in the basement.

Like all relatives who have had an incredibly awkward conversation, or at least as was common in my family, we spoke only of the most mundane things possible over dinner.

With no dance on that night and no evening broadcast on the radio, we then sat in an even more uncomfortable silence in Nova's small living room. At one point, out of sheer desperation, I suggested a game of cards, an activity I usually avoided as my siblings were all much better players than I was. Clara routinely won pennies and nickels from me in various games of chance.

Nova adored cribbage. I knew the minute I saw her lovely board made from a sperm whale's tooth that I was destined to lose badly. But it was worth it for the smile on my aunt's face as she pointed out the features of the board to me. The scrimshaw around the edges depicted a beautifully rigged sailing ship and, rather sadly, the death of the whale.

"It belonged to your great-grandfather," Nova said to me, pulling out the pegs from a cunningly carved little drawer at one end of the tooth.

"David would love this," I said, thinking of my oldest brother. Like Nova, he had his own cribbage board and always insisted on playing at least one game with the rest of us when he came home for Christmas. He preferred three-player cribbage, but gallantly dealt everyone in, even me. My inability to remember the rules correctly often earned me considerable teasing from my siblings.

As I told this story to Nova, she chuckled and admitted that she was another card shark of the family, so much so that my mother rarely played against her as a girl. "I could always persuade our father into a hand or two," she said. "More if he'd had a good run. But by the time I turned thirteen, he could never beat me. Unless the cards were very unlucky. Your mother, on the other hand, is the best at checkers."

"Oh, we know!" I said, remembering many laughing games when my mother trounced even her youngest child with no mercy. As my father once consoled Benny in happier days, no one could come between my mother and an opportunity to king her pieces.

"But what was your best game?" Nova asked me as we picked up our cards.

"I never liked games as much as the others. We had a piano, an old upright, in the parlor so I'd play that when they dragged out the game boards." I still remembered with great clarity those winter evenings, with people shouting out their favorite tunes while I laughed and joked, and played exactly what they didn't ask for. Unless it was Benny. I always played whatever Benny requested because he was my baby brother, and his smile lit up my heart.

After Benny's death, I hadn't played for weeks. I couldn't. Until one evening my father with great solemnity pulled out the checkers board and challenged my mother to a match. With the same gravity, he sat me at the piano bench with Clara beside me to turn the music and sing as she often did.

It had been a strange evening, with Clara and I at the piano, and my parents at the game table. There was a small shadow in the room, the boy who had always sat at the end of the couch, swinging his legs as he gave my father instructions on how to challenge my mother at her favorite game. I know we all felt it, but we knew a great comfort too. And I had played the piano every day since then until my illness stopped me.

Through the cutting of the cards, the creation of the crib, and the little pegs moving relentlessly around the board, I told this story in stops and starts to my quietly listening aunt.

"I am sure they will miss your playing at Christmas," she finally said to me.

"Clara plays well enough," I responded. "She never loved piano lessons like me, but she took them all the same. She's a much better singer too."

"But it won't be you at the piano. Play for them when you go home," she added.

I shook my head. "It won't be as good," I said, remembering my frustration with my playing earlier in the fall.

"For them, it will be," replied my wise aunt.

But I changed the subject and kept our discussion to lighter matters, including what I owed Nova by the end of the evening. She waved away all debts but did suggest I bake cookies with Thelma and her the next day. "We always need so many boxes," she said. "I give them away to everyone who works for me on Christmas Eve. It's something of a tradition for me, to bake on the winter solstice. It's the shortest day of the year, so it feels right to warm up the oven. Besides, Thelma hasn't baked anything since Saturday and the cookie jar is almost empty."

"Are you going to make Pfeffernüsse with white pepper?" I said with a little sarcasm.

"It has a certain bite," said Nova, unrepentant at having me repeat one of her bootlegging directions. Which made me laugh. Then Nova decided that a final glass of cold milk from her electric refrigerator and the last cookies out of the jar would make an excellent nighttime snack.

Far after midnight, I went to bed feeling better about the world and my aunt's shady business. Nova treated the whole affair of Agent Tawney so lightly that I was finally sure that she could indeed escape any serious punishment. As for her claims of a family ability to time travel and former ownership of a mysterious grimoire, I stored that in a corner of my brain reserved for tall tales from relatives. I didn't completely doubt her claims anymore, but I wasn't exactly sure what to do with the knowledge.

As I was turning down the light, I spotted the odd little book that Captain Leo had given me earlier in the day. I adjusted the light next to my bed and began to read the first page.

One sentence leapt out at me. "My name is Paul." I knew immediately I had found the voice who whispered to me and me alone. Next, I read "Do not be afraid. Please do not be afraid. One of us must be without fear."

But I could not follow that advice.

A creeping horror came over me as I read on; the strange mix of fairytales and unworldly descriptions making it impossible to put the book down. One incident seemed to describe both Captain Leo and the jolly Cuffe. Others referred to places that I had at least heard of. All were towns surrounding Kingsport if not Kingsport itself. But the saddest part of all was the man who was telling these tales, a man lost in a terrible place who had never known the family or the friendship that I had taken for granted all my life.

I never believed in love at first sight. I still don't. But I do believe you can read a stranger's words and realize there is a kinship there, a soul that you would like to know better. If nothing else, I wanted to give Paul the courage to find his way out of the terror which held him trapped.

As I turned back the pages and read certain descriptions again, I realized something. As a music teacher, as the girl who always played the piano at family gatherings, I knew the tune that Paul heard, the one sung by his Baba Yaga with the purple cat brooch, the pattern set by Nova Malone. The song which brought Paul back to our world and sent him out of it again.

The tune was Benny's favorite. We played it every night at the Diamond Dog and broadcast it throughout Kingsport. We sang it earlier traveling in Cuffe's sleigh with the horses' harness bells ringing out.

A song I could play from memory, a Christmas song which had nothing to do with Christmas and everything to do with traveling.

I left my bed, wrapping my old blanket robe around me. Then I headed downstairs into the Diamond Dog to experiment on the piano. For I finally knew exactly what I should do next.

I would summon Paul back into the world with "Jingle Bells."

CHAPTER SIXTEEN

Downstairs only a ghost light illuminated the ballroom. The single bulb was left lit in the center of the dance floor all night long in case somebody needed to cross the ballroom or, given Nova's other business activities, wanted to see their way to the basement staircase for a delivery.

I sat on the stool and rested my hands on the keyboard. The cool ivory beneath my fingertips welcomed me home. As much as I hated not hearing the nuance of every note, I loved the music carried from my mind through my fingertips to the piano. While I would never play with the jazz, the fire, of Billy Oliver, I could play, pattering up and down the keyboard mimicking the pounding hooves on the hard-packed snow, the laughter within the sleigh of friends and flirtations, and the ringing, the jingling, of the harness bells. Oh, what fun to know again the life that I had had, to send this tune reverberating through the instrument and the music spilling out into the empty room.

Then I knew it, with the precision that meant I'd always known how my playing should sound, how others should sound, what was perfect for the concert stage, and what was simply acceptable for a family parlor on a winter night: whatever glory, whatever spark, that I had possessed before the fever was still there. I could play – albeit not as perfectly as before, not as beautifully as I had.

So I played the song as ugly as I could.

I hit the keys harder and harder so I could feel it in my hands, my wrists, and all the way up into my shoulders. Harder and harder so I could hear the music shaking through my body, all the anger accumulated and all the sorrow collected. All the love that I had for the music until my body betrayed me. I wasn't even thirty yet. I wasn't supposed to be hampered by illness, weakened by disease. I was supposed to be starting my future, not haunted by the past. I wanted to howl and so I did, screaming through the lyrics until my throat was shredded raw.

I had left the headset behind, forgotten on top of my dresser. In the hours past midnight, I played for my damaged self, hearing only what I could hear without electronic amplification.

As I played, my fury hardened, my intent solidified. I would drag Paul back into the world where he belonged and I would go.

If Nova could fall out of the world, surely I could do it too. I was no longer afraid of the bloody ground, the starless skies, the trees with snapping teeth, and the hounds slithering out of shadowed corners.

I was afraid of the future.

But I did not fear the forest.

I wanted to dive into the ocean with no waves. I wanted to run in circles to conquer the hounds until the music shook me out into the past.

I needed to change my life. I wished for Benny to be alive. I desired (shamefully, oh so shamefully) to have my hearing back just as much as I wanted my little brother.

If my aunt was a Baba Yaga striding into the past, I set my heart on following the same path.

Sweat poured down my face, making my hair cling to my neck. Beneath the blanket robe, my nightgown stuck to my skin. Still I pounded on the piano and sang, the words running together now in one hideous jangling shriek of rage.

Then the world shifted.

Like before, the room wobbled. As Paul had described it, the falling step and drop of a dream overtook me. But the piano keys shook beneath my fingers and the music still reverberated through the wires. My feet banged down on the pedals.

I saw him. In the pause between one note and the next, he was there. Such an ordinary looking man, such an extraordinary person, he was standing under the ghost light in the middle of the room. He was standing on the shore with unmoving water behind him. Both places in the same moment of time were visible to me. In Paul's hands – and I knew he was Paul – was clutched the very journal that lay upstairs upon my bed. After and before, all muddled the wrong way around as time unraveled in the room.

Paul looked straight at me as I stared back at him. His mouth formed a word. I knew it was my name.

But I could not hear Paul.

The hearing aid, the contraption, the hated thing which marked me as different in the world, was lying upstairs. Without it, I couldn't hear him.

I leaped off the piano stool and started toward Paul. I don't truly remember what I meant to do at that moment. Grab him and pull him back into our world? Throw myself into the still waters behind him and hope to surface in a better past?

It didn't matter.

As soon as the music stopped, he disappeared. I fell with a bone-jarring thud off the stage, bruising my already bruised hands as I tried to stop from crashing down. Curling around myself, I lay on the cold dance floor and wept.

I cried like a child, bawling with temper at being denied my heart's desire.

A door banged open. The steady tread of a heavyset woman in sensible house slippers crossed the floor.

"Raquel Malone Gutierrez," said Nova, "what have you done to yourself?"

I saw you. I know it was you. When you looked toward me, I know you saw me too.

You are real. You are Raquel. And I am still here and still trapped and afraid, so afraid now, to hope for more. It was only a moment, but why didn't I act? Why didn't I step forward, grab your hand, and pull myself out of this place?

Even as I write this, the memory of your face is fading. So fierce, so brave, and the moment when I saw you runs out of my mind like sand through my fingers. I must find my way back to you.

If I sit here and tell you a story, then I can keep you in my mind. That's how this works. I think somebody told me that is how this works when they gave me this journal, only now I don't remember. But I wrote it down at the very beginning, that a dying man gave me this pen, this little book, so I could find you.

I turn back the pages to read again the stories that I have told and remember the people who appeared. When I spoke of Bluebeard, it brought me to the house dripping blood and hearts full of courage. When I spoke of faithful servants, I met one.

I know the stories must be told to find you. Somebody told me what to do but I cannot remember who. Was it you?

Can you find me again?

CHAPTER SEVENTEEN

I couldn't confess to Nova what I had done. Not all of it. Not the full extent of my anger or my shameful wish to escape into the past to avoid a future that I didn't want.

Instead I talked about being unable to sleep, playing to distract myself, and then, most improbably, falling off the stage. I let her think the bruises on my hands were from the fall rather than my attack on the piano.

For it had been an attack, an attempt to wrench the world into the pattern that I wanted, and, as I was painfully aware, it was a failed attack.

Nova remained calm and, in the routine that we had established over the last month, didn't ask too many questions. At least not awkward questions like, "Why did you sound like you were murdering the piano?" Hopefully she hadn't actually heard much of my playing.

My big, loud, and often brash aunt demonstrated her own talent for stillness. She sat listening quietly while I clutched a cup of tea and stammered through my story.

Finally, I offered an apology for waking her.

"I never heard the piano," said Nova. "I jolted awake and thought I better investigate. When I was coming downstairs, I heard you fall."

I remembered the whole world wobbling when Paul appeared and wondered if that was what roused Nova. Another thing that I did not confess was that I had been trying for my own "unmooring" from time. Even in my shaken state, I knew Nova would not approve.

After a few more reassurances that I only suffered minor bruising, I retreated to my bedroom. I leafed through the journal again, noting how the writing grew wilder, more sprawling across the page, further into the book, as if Paul was scrambling to put down all the words as quickly as possible. Then an idea struck me. Closing the journal with the final entries still unread, I crossed the room and picked up my headset.

After a moment of thought, I headed back into the dining area to raid Nova's desk for pencils. The lights were out in the kitchen and Nova's bedroom door was shut. I sincerely hoped my aunt had gone back to sleep. I swiped a handful of nice straight pencils out of the top desk drawer and went back to my room.

In every corner of the room, I laid those pencils down in patterns of decreasing triangles as Beatrice had suggested to Paul.

Then I settled myself back in bed and placed the hearing aid on my head. The microphone on my chest, the earpiece in place over my left ear, and the battery placed on the bed next to me. I switched it on, hearing the now familiar electric hum, the faint static just at the edge of my comprehension.

Humming the first few bars of "Jingle Bells," I waited.

"Raquel," said Paul's voice in my ear. As usual, he sounded distracted and worried, even terrified. The howling noise which bothered me before was also audible. I looked at the corners of the room with some trepidation. But nothing appeared.

"Paul," I said as clearly as I could while trying to keep the tune running in my head. Not as simple as it sounds, but I was always good at talking to my pupils while playing examples on the keyboard. Now my fingers drummed silently on the quilt, the same motions as if I played "Jingle Bells" on a keyboard. "Can you hear me? I know how to help you."

"Raquel," he said again, but firmer and more confident. "I saw you."

"You did," I said. My fingers went up and down, playing the melody silently so I could continue the conversation. "I think there's a way to bring you to the Diamond Dog."

"The Diamond Dog?" he said with almost a laugh. "It sounds like something from a fairytale. A little dog who jumps out of a walnut to help poor Ivan."

"I don't know that story." The sounds in my ear were fading, even the howls growing fainter, so I hummed a few bars of "Jingle Bells."

"When I see you again," I heard Paul say, "I will tell you all the stories in my head. That's how I learned to speak other languages, asking for fairytales. I remember them still, all the stories. I heard them everywhere I went. Everyone has a story which begins 'once upon a time.'"

"I always liked the endings better than the beginnings," I said very softly. Because I did not need to shout for this man to hear me. Because I could hear him even as his voice dropped to a whisper. Because we were bound together in this strange bubble of time, memory, and music. "I like the endings where they lived happily."

"Ever after," replied Paul.

A bang and thump distracted me, and the tune dropped completely out of my head.

"Paul? Paul?" I called but nobody answered. I called again and then sorrowfully gave up. It seemed the music could only hold him in our world for a short time. I needed to find a way to make it last. To give him a chance to escape. To give me a chance to escape.

Looking up at the windows, I realized it was dawn already. The thump was probably Thelma coming in the kitchen door with the day's delivery of eggs and milk, I decided. I remembered Nova's grand plans of baking and wondered how quickly I could extract myself from rolling out dough.

For I needed to find Ralph Tawney and I needed help doing that. Help that I couldn't discuss with Nova.

Because I knew the secret of time travel now – and I believed this new secret could buy all of us what we wanted.

I would pay my aunt back by protecting her.

But first I needed to speak with Tawney. He'd given a card to Nova, but I couldn't ask her for it, not without revealing my plans. But I knew somebody else who had Tawney's address. I could go to Chilton Brewster, who would be broadcasting his usual editorials this morning and then proceeding to his office at the bank.

After dressing for baking, I met Thelma and Nova in the kitchen. Nova asked how I was feeling and accepted my assurances that all was well. Which was exactly how I felt. All was well. I knew what to do next.

After that… the future could be changed, I told myself, if I could journey into the past. If I showed our government how to do it, surely they wouldn't interfere with my plans. They would owe me a favor, many favors, favors that I intended to use to help everyone, including myself.

Brewster had hinted at immunity for Nova. Tawney had almost as clearly promised it. To save Paul, I needed the sort of help that our government could give me. I realized that I could tell Tawney what he wanted to know. I could bargain for everyone at the Diamond Dog. I would insist on Tawney helping me in return.

I had forgotten, of course, the first rule of all fairytales. You must never keep anything for yourself. You must sacrifice everything for others. Or disaster will strike, and your happy ending will be overturned.

In the ruins of my memories, I found a story which will link me to you, my Raquel, my Marya Morevna.

Did I tell you about the old lady, the one who was fiercer than Baba Yaga? She lived in my village in a little red house at the very edge of a field of wheat. She grew poppies in her garden. I remember the wheat, taller than my head, golden in the sun. I remember the red poppies lining the path leading to her blue door and the sunflowers planted all around her house. This was years and years ago, when I was very young. I recall her house so perfectly.

Why can I remember this and not remember how I came to this place without sun or poppies or the wind whispering through the wheat?

But my fierce old lady lives in my mind, the hard rap of her silver thimble on the top of my head if I'd done something wrong. But if I did something right, she would tell me about Marya Morevna.

She was brave and led her army into battle, did Marya Morevna, and she was kind, helping her foolish prince even after he let Koschei out of the dungeon.

If I had married Marya Morevna, I told the old lady, I would never have listened to Koschei.

"Koschei the deathless, an interesting character from Russian folklore. The hiding of the heart inside an egg, inside a box, and so on," said the man with a long white beard to a younger man. The two sat together with cups of coffee in a booth. I sat on a stool at the counter, this book between my hands. The waitress hummed a song, a song I have heard before, as she cleaned the counter.

"Be right with you, hon," she said to me. "Just let me get this next order out."

"I used Koschei with my freshman class to illustrate the possibilities of galaxies hidden within other galaxies, stars which can only be detected by their influence on other stars as it were, the heart within the egg within the box," said the older man.

"Afraid that's a bit more complicated than I can understand, professor," said the younger man. "I'm more interested in your thoughts about time travel."

The professor poured a spoonful of sugar into his cup and stirred it three times, clinking the spoon each time against the edge of the cup. "All astronomy is time travel. The stars we see in the sky each night do not exist in the present. At least not as we are seeing them. What we are seeing is what they were, and yet they are brilliant in the sky and very much a part of what we are now. A conundrum for philosophers, this notion of time travel, Ralph. Didn't you ask me to call you Ralph?"

"Please do call me Ralph," said the other. "Are you saying a mechanism for time travel exists, Professor Withers?"

"Not a machine, like HG Wells' story," said the professor. "But as a theory, it already does. We've known as much since Einstein published his work seven years ago. Even as my colleagues debate what relativity means and how his work applies to their own, it's clear we could experience time travel to the future. Going to the past would be the challenge. Yet, as I said, I see the past every night through my telescope. If I could remove myself from where I was standing in the present to the speck of light I am observing, then I would be in the past. I already am in the past in my mind, as it were. It's the matter of moving the body as well." He took another sip of coffee.

"Fascinating to think about. One of my more unusual colleagues at Miskatonic came across some literature which suggested one could dislocate oneself from one's time through use of pharmaceutical concoctions, traveling both forward and back simultaneously while leaving oneself in the present. I think it would be very exciting if it wasn't all theoretical and possibly poisonous."

I turned around and almost yelled at them both that it was not exciting – it was horrible. But then I recognized the face of the man in the brown suit. I knew him. It was the man who had tried to shoot me in the laboratory. He looked almost the same. But when he glanced up, he did not seem to know me.

"But do you have people at Miskatonic University who are experimenting in time travel?" Ralph said, turning back to the professor.

The professor stared at him as the old lady used to look at me before she thumped me on my head with her thimble. "As I explained, such theories can have no practical application. Experiments such as you suggest would be incredibly unwise. If one was to travel to the past or the future, I don't doubt that it would have disastrous results, if only for the time traveler. Such a journey would destroy a man's mind. What government agency did you say you were from?"

A bell jangled as somebody pushed the door open and called out "Merry Christmas, Velma!"

Then I am back in this place without stars, but I know where I am now. I am inside Koschei's egg. I remember the story so clearly as the old woman told it to me: "No matter what Koschei does, he cannot fool Marya. He can kidnap Marya and take her out of our world, or he can cut Ivan up into little pieces and set him afloat in a barrel. It doesn't matter. Marya Morevna always finds the egg where Koschei hides his heart."

Even as I tell this tale, I hear you singing again. I know you will find my heart inside the egg which is this place imprisoning me.

CHAPTER EIGHTEEN

Chilton Brewster was writing a letter when I arrived at his office later that afternoon. He put down his pen without comment. Rising from his chair, he offered me the seat opposite him and then sat again.

"How can I help you, Miss Malone?" he said, as if he was expecting me to open a savings account or ask for a loan.

I didn't bother to correct him about my last name. In this town I would always be better known as Nova Malone's niece. Now I needed to concentrate on how best to help my aunt and the rest of the employees of the Diamond Dog.

"I want to speak with Agent Tawney," I said. Then, because my request came out a little blunt, I added, "Please. You offered to arrange a meeting. You said you wanted to help."

Brewster looked a little puzzled. "Is your aunt willing to talk to Tawney now?"

"This isn't about Nova or bootlegging," I said. The rest came out in a nervous rush of words. "Tawney told me that he wasn't interested in enforcing Prohibition. He wanted to know about time travel. I know how it happens. Well, I know what causes it. Actually, I don't understand why it happens, but I know someone who has traveled through several different times in this area. I can introduce Agent Tawney to Paul."

Then I stopped talking, because I realized I didn't know Paul's last name or anything about him other than what the journal said. My rambling explanation was vague, and probably wouldn't have swayed a skeptic, but Brewster wanted to believe me.

"I knew that woman changed things," Brewster said, and it was obvious "that woman" was my aunt. "I found the two journals from 1925." He pulled down two books from the shelf. The volumes looked identical down to the year printed on the spine and his initials stamped in gold on the cover. "Both books start out exactly the same but change on December 24." He flipped the pages. "In this one, I even copied down the editorial I gave that day." He twisted the book to show me how nearly two pages were filled. "And I noted my disappointment in missing the owner of the Diamond Dog and not being able to finish our transaction."

He had written down everything about his day, including a pithy paragraph about giving away his best winter coat to a woman clearly inebriated and in need of help. I was amused to see he also wrote about how he regretted his action and ran after the woman to retrieve his coat. Apparently, Brewster could even be critical of himself in writing.

"But this journal has a completely different entry on December 24," he said, handing the second one to me.

The entry was much shorter, just a few lines to say he was leaving for an appointment at the Diamond Dog and hoped to take possession of the property shortly. In this book, the pages after December 24 were blank while the pages of the other journal, the one that included the entry about chasing after Nova and his coat, were filled through December 31.

"I always knew there was something wrong," he said, taking back the two journals and setting them side by side. "Every time I walk past the Diamond Dog, I remember things differently than I know how they occurred. It's like remembering a dream, but it feels like a memory."

"Moving through time plays havoc with the memory," I said, thinking of Paul's stories.

"I remember her taking my coat and snatching my journal out of the pocket at the last minute," said Brewster more to himself than me. In fact, the entire time that I was in his office, I felt we both were speaking too much to our own memories and not listening nearly enough to each other.

"After I gave my coat to your aunt, I came back to the office and wrote in it. But later I also remembered writing in the journal and leaving it in the office. When I put away my journal for 1925, I found the other one already on the shelf."

"Writing something down may have caused you to retain the memory of the time before you met my aunt," I guessed. "Although I don't know why there are two journals and only one coat."

"I actually forgot about meeting your aunt until she returned the coat to me," said Brewster. "Then I remembered everything and nothing made sense! I had two journals and the handwriting in both is mine. I remember writing both passages, even though that shouldn't be possible." Strains of anger and even confusion roughened his voice, but again it felt more directed at himself than at me. "She stole my coat. She gave it back. Why do I remember a different day?"

"Something you did after was changed by what happened before but it wasn't the same before, so the after was changed, too," I said, remembering Nova's discussion of time travelers causing before and after to become reversed for some people.

"How do you know this?"

I tried to explain, but it was muddled. I was as confused as Brewster about how time travel worked. Still, I persisted on the one point that I wanted to make. "Paul has been traveling to many places and times. He's the man who knocked you into the snowbank. If the government rescues him, he could explain it all," I said to the banker and hoped the government liked fairytales.

The whole time that I was talking to Brewster, I was thinking Paul needed to be rescued. I didn't know how to rescue him. But Tawney would know who to call, I was certain. When your house was on fire, you called the fire department, you didn't try to pour a bucket of water on it yourself and hope for the best, according to my civics teacher in high school.

There was a reason for agencies like the one that Agent Tawney worked for, and I meant to use every possible resource to help Paul. And protect my aunt. The latter, I was well aware, might be harder. However, I pleaded for her too.

"Nova never meant to be in Kingsport last Christmas Eve," I told Brewster. "It was an accident. She says it is very unsafe, the time traveling, I mean. She never uses it for bootlegging." I cringed a little as I said the last, realizing I probably shouldn't go into details about Nova's philosophies concerning smuggling liquor and what sounded like magic. I did manage not to talk about the grimoire, probably because I was so flustered that I'd forgotten it again.

Twice already in this conversation I called my aunt a bootlegger. But Brewster barely reacted to that.

"I'd forgotten the man who knocked me down," said Brewster. "I was so preoccupied with the coat. I liked my coat and I gave it away! But she was such a demanding woman. I couldn't seem to say no to her. But I regretted it the minute I gave it to her." He shifted uneasily. "I even tried to follow her, but I lost her almost immediately."

"Paul says she's a Baba Yaga," I told him. "And it's probably best if you didn't catch her that day."

"Then, Miss Malone," said Brewster suddenly, focusing again on me and not on the indignation he suffered a year ago, "why are you here? Without your aunt's consent, I think?"

"It's a very good question," a response I'd learned in years of teaching when students asked me a question for which I had no answer. "But to save time," I added without irony, "let me answer it when we meet with Agent Tawney."

I hoped to think out a better explanation for time travel and also a better way to ask for amnesty for everyone at the Diamond Dog by the time we reached our destination. Tawney had promised something like a quiet exit from Kingsport for Nova. How I would convince Nova to accept it, I hadn't decided. But I thought once Paul landed in 1926 and I went to wherever, whenever I could go, it might work out. After all, the future would change. I had great faith that my aunt Nova would survive and flourish in any future.

Brewster finally agreed to help me. He picked up the phone and gave some quiet instructions to someone on the other end of the line. While I was nearly jiggling with impatience in my chair, he put on his hat and overcoat (if it was the one my aunt Nova borrowed, it was a very fine heavy coat with a fur collar).

"I know where Agent Tawney is staying in Kingsport," said Brewster. "I will take you there. You can explain what's happening to both of us."

Tawney was renting a room in a small, neat house on the edge of town. Brewster drove me there in his car, an imposing Chrysler Imperial but not nearly as comfortable as Nova's Rolls. Brewster drove at a slow, steady pace, and stayed silent for the entire drive, which surprised me. I thought he would fire off a dozen questions, but perhaps he wanted to wait to hear what Tawney said to me and what I said to the federal agent.

As usual, after the third turn and twist down Kingsport's picturesque streets, I had no idea of exactly where we were. One or two landmarks looked vaguely familiar, but I hoped Brewster would drive me back to the Diamond Dog after our talk with Tawney.

The neighborhood where we eventually stopped looked prosperous enough: white painted houses with red roofs and large garages behind several places, horse barns converted into shelters for the automobiles now more practical for so many families. We pulled up in front of a house looking as respectable as the rest. Brewster explained the owner was a widow who took in a few long staying guests for the income. "I always recommend her to any business associates who need a place to stay," he said. Which explained how Agent Tawney had found the place.

The weather was incredibly dreary, with heavy clouds and a wind which bit through the best of heavy coats. We hurried from the sidewalk to the front door. I was glad of a small fire going in the front parlor of the house where Tawney's landlady conducted us. The room smelled cheerfully of pine and cinnamon. Rather than a tree, a small swag decorated the mantel. The widow, like my aunt, apparently favored baking cookies three days before Christmas. There was even a smudge of flour on the edge of the neat collar of her conservative brown dress.

Upon hearing who I was, the widow, whose name was something like Mrs Simon or Mrs Smith, asked me about the dances at the Diamond Dog. She admitted that she didn't own a radio but enjoyed listening to the broadcasts at her neighbor's house. "I was thinking of buying a radio after Christmas," she said to me. "One of the smaller ones to set in the kitchen."

"The camera shop is thinking of selling radios on time payments," I told her.

Tawney came briskly into the parlor, fetched by a timid maid or daughter. I never learned which the younger woman was, as the mistress of the house continued to chat with us. Tawney made some efforts to shoo his landlady out of the room.

Undeterred, the widow asked if we would like coffee or tea. Brewster declined both politely. Tawney practically growled something negative. I started to say no as well, but then called her back and asked for the tea. A warm cup to hold in my chilled hands was comforting, a small bit of courage, as I explained all over again to Tawney what I had told Brewster in his office. I was stalling again, but I almost had my explanation and my plea for Nova figured out.

The second time I managed my story better than my confused explanations in Brewster's office. Again I left out the part about the journal given to me by Captain Leo, from some vague idea of keeping Captain Leo and the amiable Cuffe out of my troubles and an even stronger inclination to hold the journal private. Several passages written by Paul felt as if he had been speaking directly to me and I didn't want to share his confidences.

Outside of that, I told the two men as much as I could about Paul. I suggested my knowledge came from our brief conversations, always audible only through my headset and triggered by the tune of "Jingle Bells." I described Paul's visits to Kingsport and Arkham, forgetting entirely the one incident in Dunwich and deliberately skipping the one in Innsmouth to avoid mentioning Captain Leo.

I did tell them that wobbles, as I called them, were created by music played at certain times.

I even told Tawney that it was Billy's version of "Jingle Bells" which seemed to be the most effective in creating those "wobbles" in time.

Several times I reassured them that nobody else knew about time travel, which was almost the truth, and I sounded much more confident of my facts. I thought from my conversations with Nova that she kept the Malones' tendency for "unmooring" fairly quiet, just family as it were.

Again, the men said nothing as I spoke about the most outlandish ideas. Tawney kept making some notes in a small book he carried in his pocket. For some reason that made me even more nervous. Throughout it all – and it felt like hours but was probably only fifteen minutes or so – I made it abundantly clear that I would only help them meet Paul if my aunt received some type of immunity or protection from Tawney's office.

The whole conversation felt like I was walking along a cliff edge, where an unwise comment would plunge me quickly into worse trouble. But I truly didn't know how else to help Paul or Nova. As much as I wanted to escape into the past and change it, I didn't want to leave more problems behind me.

Most of the names that I recited elicited no response from Brewster, except for Preston Fairmont. He mentioned to Tawney that he'd heard of Fairmont, something of a dilettante and a very wealthy man, not the poor prince that Paul described. "I can't think of any reason why a man like Fairmont would lose his fortune in the future," said Brewster, clearly most intrigued by this story. "Unless he made some very unwise investments or withdrew his money completely from the stock market." It was the only time he spoke during my recital.

Tawney seemed more taken by the names of Beatrice Sharpe and Agatha

Crane. Both women, he said to Brewster, had done research of considerable interest to his office.

In fact, all of the discussion after I stopped talking occurred between the two men. Listening to them, it seemed Tawney had met with Brewster a number of times, which surprised me. In the cafe it had sounded like he'd only come out to Kingsport to investigate a few odd letters. I shifted anxiously in my seat, wondering what a close alliance between the two would mean for Nova and for me. As Brewster and Tawney discussed possible implications of Paul's appearances in the area, they ignored me completely. You might have thought they had discovered all this information on their own and I wasn't even in the room. In fact, the pair reminded me of college meetings where two of the more pedantic professors would always conclude with a long-winded discussion of music education theory while the rest of us longed to escape the room. I have sat through more arguments about the ideas of Calvin Brainerd Cady than any woman should be forced to suffer.

Just as I was considering following my nose to the source of the delicious scents wafting from the kitchen at the back of the house, Tawney turned to me and demanded to listen to my headset. I must have looked startled and indeed I was, as I had drifted off into my own thoughts of cookies and future possibilities. Trying to figure out the "after and before" as Nova described the effects of time travel made my head hurt and the discussions of the two men made the headache worse. Tawney modified his bark of a command to a "Please could I" upon Brewster's look of disapproval. Manners mattered to Brewster, even though he did his own version of yapping through his letters – and the occasional bark, I remembered, like the first time I saw him come into the Diamond Dog and accuse Nova of bootlegging.

But today, Brewster played the gentleman, reassuring me that it would be best for Tawney to try to hear what I had been hearing. He asked me to help the agent talk to Paul.

With some reluctance, I disentangled myself from the hearing aid and passed the equipment to Tawney. To my relief, he didn't pull the band across his head. Like most men, Tawney used a strong-smelling pomade to flatten his hair. The idea of cleaning it off the headband or smelling it on my own hair made me wince.

Instead, Tawney held the earpiece up to his own ear. After a moment he shook his head. "Just a hum and you clinking your teacup," he said to me. The microphone was resting on the table next to the tea set.

"Sing a little," I said.

Tawney looked as offended as a seven year-old boy sat down for his first piano lesson. Teaching children helped pay my way through college, but it wasn't easy.

I hummed a few bars of "Jingle Bells" and Tawney dropped the earpiece. When he saw my surprise, he thrust his trembling hands in his pockets and leaned back.

"I heard something howling," he said. "Horrible noise."

I glanced with some trepidation at the corners of the room. The hounds appear at the intersections, at the corners, Beatrice had told Paul. But there was nothing there and the room still smelled of cinnamon, pine, and woodsmoke. There was no reason to be afraid, I told myself.

"But did you hear Paul?" I said to Tawney.

He shook his head, pulled his hands out of his pockets, and picked up the earpiece again. When he nodded at me, I started to sing very softly.

After only a few words, Tawney nodded. "I hear something," he said. "A man talking." He huffed a bit. "It's nonsense words. Maybe another language."

"Paul has an accent," I said.

"Foreign agent?" said Tawney with a hard look at me and Brewster. "Perhaps this is the result of another government's experiments."

My stomach clenched. I didn't want to rescue Paul only to have him imprisoned. "He's an immigrant, a refugee," I said, because I thought that was probably true.

"Perhaps a Russian," Tawney said with a frown. "Well, at least he's not German."

"The war is over," Brewster said.

"For now. But we are keeping our eye on Germany," said Tawney. "He's talking again. He's reciting something. A name. Marya Morevna. Definitely sounds Russian to me."

"It's a fairytale," I said, stopping my singing to explain. "Paul tells himself fairytales to remember things." Paul wrote those stories for me so I would understand. After and before all mixed up. Paul wrote those stories so I could be brave now with Tawney. Paul wrote once upon a time so I could find a happily ever after.

"How do I see him?" asked Tawney, laying the earpiece on the table with a click. "How do I lay my hands on him?"

I didn't like how he phrased it, but I told him, "Come to the Diamond Dog on Christmas Eve. We always play and broadcast 'Jingle Bells' and he should appear then. I think it must be on December 24. I don't know why, but it's easier for him on Christmas Eve." Luckily, they didn't question me about how I would know that, as I still hadn't explained about the journal. Perhaps they thought I picked the knowledge up from Nova.

Thinking about the hounds, I added, "It may be dangerous too. You should be prepared."

"Oh, we will be prepared," said Tawney and his tone did nothing to reassure me.

"You have to keep your promises," I said to Brewster and Tawney as firmly as Nova would. I missed my aunt and almost wished her with me, but I was still convinced that this was the best way to save everyone including myself. "No prosecutions of anyone at the Diamond Dog. Or I won't help you. And Paul won't appear if I'm not there." The last was a complete guess, as I really had no idea if I could repeat my experiment and force Paul to appear in the ballroom through my own fierce wishing. But I had felt something for a moment, as he shimmered into view, as if we were connected. Like Marya Morevna, I had to try to find him, even if he was hidden in a bubble, an egg, of time.

"You can trust me," said Ralph Tawney in a voice that I didn't trust at all.

INTERLUDE

Once upon a time, I despaired, thinking I would be trapped here forever. Now I know hope. All I need to do is find your Diamond Dog. I write this down many times, so I will remember. Every time I write your name as well, so I do not forget you. I remember your name, Raquel. As you remember me.

Now I walk with purpose under the trees and across the beach, to burn away my impatience, as I wait for you. As I walk, I write down another story.

Just moments ago, I found myself striding down a street that I think I know.

As I looked around, I recognized it as the street where Baba Yaga led me on her dance. A movie theater with posters occupied the center of the block. A sleigh being drawn by two bay horses went ringing by me down the street. The signs hung from its sides said, "Buy Your Trees at Cuffe's Farm." Cars tooted their horns in response as a jolly round man waved from the driver's seat.

A couple crossed in front of me to examine the movie posters. "Let's go in," she said to him. "I like Jimmy Stewart."

He turned slightly to her, leaning heavily on a cane. "Looks sentimental to me," he said. "Isn't there an angel in it? And haven't you seen it already?"

"Maybe, and maybe," she said, hugging his arm. "But I haven't seen it with you, and I think it's the best movie of 1946. Let's go in."

I heard the date and looked closer at the street. The cars were wrong, the clothes were wrong. This wasn't my time, not the year I was lost. Not the year that I found you.

"I'd rather go dancing," he said as she pulled him toward the ticket window.

"Baby, they closed down the USO when the war ended. Besides, you just left the hospital," she said.

"Doing a slow waltz with my gal won't put me back in bed. We could go home and turn on the radio, do a few turns around the room," he retorted while still pulling the money out of his pocket to pay for their tickets. "Doctors gave me a clean bill of health at Walter Reed. I'm taking my benefits and heading to college now. How would you like being married to a college graduate, Mrs Parkington?"

"Sounds wonderful to me," she said, hugging his arm a little tighter. "Everything sounds wonderful now you're home again."

As they turned away from the ticket window, the man bumped into me, nearly dropping his cane. "Sorry," he grunted. "I didn't see you there."

"Can you tell me where to find the Diamond Dog?" I asked, being slow and careful with my words, speaking only in English.

"The Diamond Dog?" said the woman. "That's the place where my parents used to go dancing. It's been gone for a long time, twenty years or more." She pointed to the movie theater. "It used to be there." Then, being a kind lady, she paused and asked me, "Did you know it? You look too young to have been there."

"I was there," I said, but so softly that she probably didn't hear me. "I will be there again. I know I will."

The couple brushed past me into the movie theater. Still I did not move, looking at the closed doors and wishing I knew when I would see you next, Raquel. Where are you? How much time separates us now?

A group of boys spilled out of the theater. One of them swung a little silver bell in his hands, small and round like it came off a horse's harness, which he rang and rang. "See! I'm getting my wings," he shouted at the others. One of them swiped up a handful of snow and tossed it in the boy's face. He retaliated by throwing the bell. I reached out and snatched it from the air.

As I shook it for myself, the street disappeared. When I shook it again in the rhythm of the song you sang, the street shimmered into view, but the boys were not there. I almost stepped out again, but I did not know when it was or where you were. If I am to leave this place, I think… I know… I must see you at the Diamond Dog. The more I consider this, the more certain I am.

Jim Culver told me to dance at the Diamond Dog. I will dance with you.

Now I am here again, beneath the trees which no longer frighten me. I have a silver bell in one pocket and a silver dime in the other. With such lucky treasures even the most foolish Simon can find his way out of the woods. I listen for your singing. When I hear you I will start running, ringing my silver bell. This time I will escape.

CHAPTER NINETEEN

On Christmas Eve we could all feel it, the crackle in the air, the anticipation of the Diamond Dog's biggest dance. The tree arrived on Thursday from Cuffe's farm. Nova left it in the yard behind the building to be admired by everyone passing by. A great number of Kingsport residents seemed to find a reason to pass by and speculate on how the tree would look fully decorated in the ball-room.

I was full of nerves, too, but not for the same reasons. I'd made my deal with Tawney and hoped that it would turn out all right for everyone. If I got what I wanted for Christmas, I would disappear into the past and never have to face the future that so frightened me. Paul would be saved. And Nova? Well, I had great faith that Nova would manage no matter what.

On Friday morning, Tim and Otis wrestled the tree through the double doors of the ballroom with the help of two waiters who arrived early to help with the decorations. At one point, as the four men leveraged the tree toward the ceiling, I feared I had misjudged the height and it was too tall for the room. But when the tree stood straight in its cast-iron stand, the very top was still an inch or two short of the ceiling.

"Just enough room for the star," said Nova with considerable satisfaction. Otis and Tim were dispatched to the basement to bring up the multiple boxes of ornaments. As soon as the noon broadcast was done, Reggie and Johnny joined the fun. Reggie doing most of the work and Johnny most of the commentary on what to do next, until the point came when Reggie asked him if he was a con-sulting engineer or an insulting engineer.

"Bit of both," said Johnny without any shame at all and a merry grin at the rest of us.

Reggie unrolled string after string of electric lights upon the floor to make sure there were no tangles. With pliers, cutters, and extra wire, he cobbled them together to make one very long continuous string to loop around the tree.

"Are you sure that's safe?" said Johnny, overlooking the operation.

"Absolutely," mumbled Reggie, talking around the pliers held in his mouth as his hands busily knotted together the strings. "This way it all goes into one socket."

Then came the debate about which should come first: the wrapping of the tree in lights or the placement of the ornaments. Traditionally, it seemed, most people placed the ornaments first, but Reggie claimed that was because they were used to clipping the candles on the tree as the last act of decorating.

"We should wrap these around the tree first," he said, lifting the string off the floor, "and then hang the tinsel."

"Give me one end and I'll start wrapping," I said. At home we always did ornaments first, but Reggie's suggestions seemed sensible to me. Time to try something new, I decided.

Once we looped the electric lights round the tall tree, Reggie placed a silver star enhanced with a small electric bulb on the very top.

I helped Johnny rip open the boxes and hand the ornaments to everyone. Ginger and Harlean took charge of the tinsel. If anyone else tried to add a clump of tinsel to a branch, they quickly removed it, flattened it out, and rehung it so it shimmered straight down like the fringe on a flapper's dress. Only Cozy could hang tinsel to their strict standards. His careful application of each strand earned him a quick kiss on the cheek from Ginger that made him blush and retreat behind his drums.

Billy danced all around the tree, adding glittering glass stars wherever he saw a bare spot. All the while, he sang or hummed his way through "Oh Tannenbaum, oh Tannenbaum" in a manner that suggested it would become a dance hit that night. Cozy caught the rhythm from Billy. Harlean burst into a full throated, "Oh Christmas tree, oh Christmas tree" to accompany them. Soon everyone was singing with her, even me. Billy left the decorating to others as he leaped to the piano stool and turned the traditional song into a syncopated dance that could have come from Tin Pan Alley yesterday.

When it was done, we turned off all the other lights. Cozy did a drum roll of anticipation. Reggie threw a switch and the tree lit up. It glowed in its corner, a pillar of gold and silver reflecting the light in sparkles over the room.

"Oooh," said Harlean, standing by my side. "It's so pretty, I hate to think of it ever coming down."

I just smiled and nodded, because it was too beautiful for words.

"We'll leave it up through New Year's Eve," said Nova. The glow in her eyes demonstrated to the rest of us that the tree matched her inner vision. Tonight's dance would indeed be something to be talked about.

With some regret, I slipped away from the crowd. I was afraid that Kingsport would never forget the bootlegger's dance, but not for the reasons that Nova wanted. I looked once more at the beautiful tree and wished as hard as I had as a child that everything would still be wonderful at Christmas. That this Christmas Eve dance would not lead to disaster.

Outside I went to the street corner to meet Agent Tawney as previously arranged. Out of view of anyone standing at the Diamond Dog's windows, he asked me, "When will your time traveler arrive?"

"Billy is playing 'Jingle Bells' at ten," I said. "I suggested to Harlean that she invite the whole crowd to sing along. We're passing out bells, too, for everyone to shake and ring."

I'd suggested the bells earlier to Nova, who had loved the idea and immediately sent me out to buy up every harness bell or small silver bell that I could find in Kingsport's stores. We'd even driven over to Arkham and raided their stores as well. There were enough bells of all sizes to give one to every dancer. Nova had decided to decorate the handle or loop at the top of each one with a red ribbon and a card that said "Gift of the Diamond Dog" as a souvenir of the ballroom's most memorable night. The whole project made her chortle as Thelma, Lily, and I tied ribbon after ribbon on the bells. For if there was anything Nova loved more than gadgets, I realized, it was giving gifts at Christmas.

Perhaps this shouldn't have surprised me so, considering all the wondrous gifts that she'd shipped to my family over the years or her continuing generosity toward me. Before breakfast was done and we went downstairs to decorate the tree, Nova insisted that I unwrap a long box to reveal a beautiful red sweater with white stars knit into the cabled pattern.

"Nobody should wait until Christmas for all their presents," said Nova, looking me over with some satisfaction when I pulled the sweater on over my pajamas. "Minerva Knowles rarely knits sweaters for folks outside her family, but she was kind enough to do this for me. I knew it would suit you."

"It's gorgeous," I said truthfully, for it was as warm and enveloping as one of Nova's hugs.

As I stood on the corner of the street, dressed in Nova's gift, I felt a terrible traitor as I discussed with Agent Tawney how he and his agents would use the pretense of raiding the Diamond Dog to snatch and hold Paul.

However, I had Tawney's assurances that his men could prevent Paul from being dragged back into his nightmare world. Also, Tawney promised nobody would be arrested during the raid.

"We'll take you and the time traveler with us," said Tawney, "so you can answer some questions in Washington. Then you'll be free to go wherever you want. We may need to hold your aunt for a day or two, just to make it seem like a Prohibition raid, but she'll be free to go before New Year's."

I nodded and made my own promises, although I knew I was lying to Tawney. I simply had to believe he was speaking the truth to me. I had no intention of leaving Kingsport with him. As soon as the world shimmered and wobbled into that other place, I meant to jump into it even as they pulled Paul out. If my aunt could sing her way back to the time she wanted, I was sure I could do the same. I would change my future by retreating into the past.

After I returned to the Diamond Dog, I found it impossible to join in the general teasing and merriment as Nova passed out small gifts to everyone. "For I shan't see you tomorrow," my aunt boomed from the center of the ballroom. "You'll all be home with your families celebrating the best Christmas ever. Just as I know I'll be celebrating with my niece."

I felt horrible as I smiled in response to Nova's speech, because I knew I was about to betray her and ruin her dance.

By nine o'clock, I understood what my mother meant when she said, "My nerves are shattered." My stomach felt as if it had turned into a bowl of acid. Every time somebody wished me a merry Christmas, I wanted to scream or burst into tears. I have never been a hysterical woman, but if one more person asked me how I was feeling, I thought I would indeed shatter.

As the clock ticked too slowly toward ten, Johnny led me out for our usual dance. Even he noticed how tense and stiff I was as we circled the floor to one of Harlean's slower, sadder love songs, all about loss and heartache. The song was far too somber for the night, but the couples loved it as it gave them a chance to lean into each other in a way that the faster dances didn't. More than one couple circled under the giant balls of mistletoe hung in the shadowy corners opposite the tree.

"Relax," Johnny said to me. "You'll be great on the broadcast."

I glanced at the door, looking for Agent Tawney, and so missed his words the first time.

"What are you talking about?" I said as we traversed the floor, keeping to the center and well away from the crowd dancing in place under the mistletoe.

"We're calling you up on the stage during the 'Jingle Bells' introduction," said Johnny, executing a quick two step around a kissing couple who didn't seem to mind the lack of mistletoe above them. "Billy suggested that you play together on the piano, but Harlean wants you at the microphone singing with her. Or you can stand by Cozy and ring the bells."

"That's a terrible idea!" I said, startled out of my worried contemplation of when Tawney would arrive. "I don't play in public anymore. Whose idea was that?" But I should have guessed.

"Nova mentioned how you always played for your family on Christmas Eve. She didn't want you to miss out, so we're being your family tonight," Johnny said. He patted my shoulder as we twirled slowly around the ballroom. "Reggie's got the booth all set up for recording as well so you'll have a record to send to your parents. It's a gift from all of us at the Diamond Dog to you."

"You cannot be nice to me tonight," I said with some emphasis. I probably sounded furious, but it was sorrow rather than anger that roughened my voice.

"Raquel?" Johnny's gaze went from mildly puzzled to completely confused. "What do you mean?"

"Oh, Johnny. I must do something tonight that Nova won't like. It makes it worse because everyone at the Diamond Dog means so much to me."

Johnny danced me to the edge of the floor, back to our regular table, and pulled out a chair for me. "Now, tell me what's wrong," he said, settling into the chair opposite me. "This is more than performance nerves."

But even as he leaned forward, I spotted Agent Tawney entering the room. Right behind him came three more men dressed in plain brown suits. After them came Chilton Brewster. "Oh no," I breathed.

Johnny twisted in his chair and spotted Brewster. "Raquel, don't worry about him," he said, turning back to me. "Your aunt won't let Brewster spoil the fun."

"It isn't Brewster," I confessed. "It's me. I'm going to ruin this dance."

Completely misunderstanding, Johnny patted my hand and said, "Raquel, it's only one song. The whole crowd will be singing along. Everyone will love it."

"They will not," I said, thinking about how the world wobbled and shifted under my feet when I forced an opening with my playing. But I hoped the shift would be as temporary as possible, a few minutes to pull Paul free and for me to escape, and then everything would be normal.

As normal as being raided by federal agents could be, I amended to myself.

The song ended. The excited, chattering crowd drifted back to the tables. With one last pat on my shoulder for reassurance, Johnny made his way back to the stage for announcements. Throughout the evening, a basket with small blank cards had been circulated through the ballroom. The customers were encouraged to write down holiday greetings for people listening on the radio which Johnny then read out loud at every break. As the evening wore on, the messages became sillier and sillier, much to the delight of the clapping crowd who clustered around the stage and bellowed out their own "Merry Christmas!" every time that Johnny paused.

"I see somebody in the audience is a poet," Johnny said, fishing out one card and looking at it. "Or you stole this from somebody else."

"All my own invention," yelled a man in the back.

"Anyway, here we go," Johnny continued. "It takes dough for Christmas presents, all I have is crust, but wish you a Merry Christmas, oh, honey, don't I just!"

"Ain't that like a man," said a woman standing near me. "Any excuse not to go shopping for a Christmas gift."

"I don't know," said her friend, "I think it's sweet."

The group of men in brown suits spread out across the floor, but the crowd was too caught up in Johnny's jokes and their own excitement to take any notice. Brewster remained so close to the door that I could barely spot him, almost hidden behind the rest of the dancers.

Ralph Tawney drew up the chair next to mine and sat down. "Are you ready?" he said, glancing at his watch. "It's almost time."

I wasn't ready at all, but I nodded my head. Near the stage, I could see Nova talking to Harlean and Ginger. In a minute she would turn around. I didn't want her to see me anywhere near Tawney. I stood up and hurried across the room toward them.

Nova turned and caught me in a quick, one-armed hug as I drew near. She seemed so relaxed that I decided she hadn't spotted Tawney, or she truly believed nobody would dare start a raid on Christmas Eve.

"Merry almost Christmas," Nova said to me. "We should have Johnny do messages at every dance. People love knowing their words are being broadcast through the air."

I nodded, unable to say anything. It was almost time for the next song to begin. Johnny kept glancing at me. I waved to him. I had to keep the evening going or Paul would be trapped forever. I would be caught in a future that I didn't want.

"Hey, folks," Johnny said, leaning into the microphone. "We have a special Christmas treat for you. Our own Raquel Malone Gutierrez is joining us tonight for your favorite holiday tune. Give her a big hand and help her send this song out to her family and friends. We may not be with everyone we love tonight, but we can send this greeting out to everyone listening to us!"

The crowd whooped and cheered. Nova gave me a little push toward the stage. Harlean and Ginger hopped up on the bandstand, drawing me after them. Billy slid off his piano stool and offered it to me.

I shook my head. "I can't play in your place," I said as quietly as I could so Harlean's microphone wouldn't pick up my nervous words. Out of the corner of my eye, I saw Tawney and his men spread out through the room. Brewster still remained near the big double doors leading out to the lobby.

"We can play it four-handed," said Billy. "You sit and I'll stand! We'll be fantastic."

"It's your song, Bill. I'll never play as well as you," I said, picking up a string of jingle bells from a pile on the floor near Cozy. Harlean grabbed a string and gave them a shake.

"Come sing with me," she said, looping an arm around my waist and pulling me toward her microphone. Billy hit the keys of the piano with a run of notes that were "Jingle Bells" but also completely his own. Ginger made her saxophone wail in response as Cozy crashed his sticks upon his cymbals.

The dancers yelled as everyone piled back into the center of the floor, men and women stomping and clapping to the music.

Harlean began to sing, "Dashing through the snow."

And the world changed.

In my left ear, I heard Paul's voice through my headset as clear as if he stood next to me. "Raquel," he yelled. "I see you."

Then there he was, an ordinary man in a scratched leather jacket, tumbling through a crowd of dancers. Something was clutched in his left hand, which he held high above his head as he cried out my name.

"Paul!" I cried out, so relieved to see him safe among the dancers. That much I had done right.

Then the edges of the ballroom disappeared. Walls, ceiling, and floor dissolved into a forest and a beach unlike anything existing in our world. It was completely wrong in a way that can't be described, like a nightmare lingering in your head after you wake up.

The dancers were screaming and crying as I leaped off the stage, running as hard as I could toward the nightmare. Beyond Paul's shoulder, I saw the beach and the ocean with frozen waves. My destination was clearly visible if I wanted to change my past and future.

A horrible smell burst through the room and a howl unlike anything I've ever heard, even in my worst dreams. Creatures emerged from the corners of the ballroom, shaped like dogs and scaled like snakes. The monsters snapped their teeth like crocodiles. The crowd shrieked again and rushed toward the doors.

I saw Brewster swept away by the mass stampede, pushed back into the lobby and out of sight. Behind me, Nova was yelling, "Get out, get everyone out, go!"

Whipping around, I saw Nova grabbing at the stunned Harlean and thrusting her toward the doors to the kitchen. Billy, Ginger, and Cozy jumped off the bandstand. Another horrible creature emerged from the wall, launching itself toward them.

Nova picked up Cozy's cymbals, clanging them down on the beast's head. It howled and twisted away.

I put on a burst of speed. Trying to reach Paul, trying to exchange places with him. In the muddle of my thoughts, I persisted in believing that if I could only go there, then the forest would disappear again, taking all the terror away from the Diamond Dog.

Gunshots rang out. Tawney's men pulled out pistols from hidden holsters and fired away at the creatures. One recoiled and crashed back into the Christmas tree. Accompanied by shrieks from the crowd, the great tree swayed back and forth, toppling over with a shattering of ornaments and a shower of sparks from the broken electric lights. Flames sprang up.

"Out, out, out!" yelled Nova at the remaining crowd, those too stunned to run. She dove toward the wall behind the bandstand, tearing at the curtain there. Johnny and Billy ran beside her, helping her wrestle the giant fire hose off its base. Johnny swirled the wheel, releasing the water. Nova turned the hose upon the room.

As the jet of water hit one of the howling monsters, it leapt straight up, clawing at the ball of mistletoe and garlands hanging from the ceiling. The paper streamers broke away, dumping the creature back down into the flames and smoke.

Nova sprayed the water again, blasting the crowd liberally. I was hit by the water, sliding across the floor. But the water cut a straight line between one of the howlers and the crowd rushing toward the door. Snarling, the beast turned aside, charging for a corner of the room, where it popped out of existence only to reappear on the other side of the bandstand, nearer to the radio station door.

As I passed him, Paul clutched at my arm and shouted my name.

"I'm sorry, I'm sorry," I yelled back as I twisted away from him, still intent on trying to reach the path that would take me out of the current time.

"It's you! The time traveler!" Tawney lunged out of the crowd to grapple Paul to the ground.

I screamed at the federal agent, "Don't hurt him! You promised."

With a cry, I shoved Tawney off Paul. Then I heard Johnny yell. Turning around, I saw a frustrated monster galloping toward Nova. She also yelled and swept the hose around to lay a line of water between her and it.

I dragged Paul off the floor, shoving Tawney away. The federal agent skidded in a puddle of water and went down hard.

Before me I saw a path which led under trees with horrible mouths. The beach beyond that of gritty gravel colored purple and blue, like a lingering bruise, and an ocean like glass, murky and frozen forever in one moment between the rising and the falling of a wave.

All around me was chaos. With Nova using the hose to battle the hounds, the fire was springing up unchecked in other places. Johnny and Billy pulled at the velvet drapes, now also alight, trying to wrestle the curtains to the ground and stomp out the flames. Fire licked against Billy's hands. He screamed with pain. Harlean shoved Ginger and Cozy toward the back door as she went back for Billy. Without a moment's hesitation, the other two ran after her, intent on saving their friends.

And I had caused all this, I realized. I had started it. I had to end it. I had to help them. I couldn't do that by relying on Nova to save the day. I couldn't do that by running away.

I turned my back on the path. Grabbing Paul's hand, I pulled him toward my aunt. "We have to help them!" I shouted at him. Tawney was coming up off the floor, starting to wave his gun at the two of us and yelling something that I didn't even try to understand. I elbowed him sharply in the stomach, knocking him down again, as I dragged Paul past him.

Paul never paused. He saw the creatures ahead and ran as hard as I did to help my aunt and friends. But we weren't fast enough.

Smoke rolled through the room, mingled with the horrible stench of that other place. The paper decorations exploded into flames as the fire swept through the room. The world still wobbled, one minute a dreadful forest, the next the ballroom engulfed in fire and smoke. I tripped over a root which became a body upon the floor which then turned into a tar pit of bloody mud.

"Raquel!" Paul yelled as I dropped his arm.

I hit the floor which wasn't a floor, dropping as you drop in a dream with a jolt. I could still see Nova through the smoke, turning the hose upon a snarling beast leaping toward her. The flames swept past me, reaching Reggie's switchboard that he'd set up to control the lights. A dreadful explosion rocked the room.

And then there was nothing as I dropped into a void. The string of bells I still clutched in one hand rang out, one last peal of jingle bells.

INTERLUDE

"This is my best idea ever." I met a man in Hollywood who began all his tales this way. He wove stories out of light and shadows to frighten audiences. We called him the Showman, but we should have named him a wizard for he enchanted us all.

He fascinated me, this Showman, so confident, so certain that the world would want his stories. We were much the same age, but so different. Wherever he went, people saw him. Wherever I went, nobody saw me. I drifted from one place to another, never finding a home. I spoke so many languages, collected so many fairytales, but I talked to no one. Around the Showman there was always a crowd, a laughing crowd, so bright and young. I envied the laughter and the friendship. I never knew what to say.

The Showman knew all the right words, how to draw men and women to him, how to make them carry out his plans. I followed like all the rest, certain it would lead me somewhere. But I still didn't know where I wanted to go.

Now I do.

The Showman was unforgettable, but I forgot him until I saw you again, until I touched your hand.

My life has turned into a story, into a series of stories, that run out of my head as soon as I write them down in this journal. I thought I was done with this, but I'm not. Somehow it is worse now, the trees, the beach, the hounds who crawl amid the shadows. Everywhere I turn, it's different, it's wrong. The trees shift. The beach changes color. Out of the corner of my eye, I thought the ocean moved. Or perhaps something moved under the water, disturbing the shape of the motionless waves.

Whatever swims below I do not want to see it.

I touched you. I felt your hand in mine. I knew hope.

Hope is gone. But is hope gone?

I could not stay with you. I am back here but there is a path and I hold a bell. I ring it and I sing as you sang. I will force the path to take me back to you.

But when I rang the bell, I was somewhere else again, standing at a gate, looking over it at an old house with many windows, a rich man's house. Crows flocked around its chimneys. I knew this house.

I gripped the gate and felt it creak beneath my hands. On the other side, on a lawn covered with snow, was a very young boy and a very old man.

"Grandfather," said the boy, "there's someone in the woods."

"Nonsense," said the man. "Nobody is allowed to go there except the families of French Hill, and we are the only ones left with a proper gate and access to the path. Those woods are your legacy, Sydney."

"No," said the boy, pointing at me, "there's a man at the gate."

"Help me!" I said. More loudly, more forcibly than I had spoken in any encounter before, because I was more afraid than ever before. I saw the smoke and the flames surrounding you. I feared the worst.

"What are you doing there?" yelled the old man, waving a cane at me. "Get out of our woods. You have no right to be there!"

I pushed at the locked gate, determined to enter.

The old man strode up to the fence, leaving a trail of footprints across the snow, and stared at me. "Who are you?" he said. "How did you get here?"

I countered his questions with my own: "Where am I? What year is this?"

"You're on French Hill," he said. "As for the year, it's 1890 as any fool knows." Staring at my scratched leather jacket, he added, "You are not dressed like anyone from Arkham. What path did you take, sir, to come here?"

"The wrong one," I said, turning away from the gate. For I remembered the man who played the horn and told me clearly to dance in 1926. So I rang my bell and sang our song as I followed the path into the woods and out of the world.

CHAPTER TWENTY

A faint knocking on my bedroom door woke me up. Or rather, I was awake, drifting in that limbo between dreaming and being fully conscious, when the muffled rapping made me aware of my surroundings.

I sat up in bed, gasping and sweating. I swore the stink of smoke and that other place filled my nose, but I was in the neat little guest bedroom that I'd occupied all December.

From the other side of the door, Nova called, "Are you ready for breakfast? Thelma has made pancakes." Her words were less clear than usual, as if she was standing very far away from the door or calling me from someplace. She sounded much the way people spoke in my dreams, frustratingly obscure and difficult to hear.

Another thump and Nova called, "Wake up, Raquel."

Scrambling out of bed, I looked wildly around. Nothing appeared damaged or changed. My hearing aid was laid out neatly on the top of the bureau. I was no longer wearing the dress that I danced in the night before. Instead, I wore the silk pajamas gifted to me by Nova when we first went to New York, the very pajamas that I remembered wearing on the morning of Christmas Eve while we ate pancakes and Nova insisted that I open one gift early.

With some trepidation, I opened the door of my bedroom. Nova stood in the hall. A magnificent midnight blue velvet robe decorated with embroidered poppies was swathed around her. In one hand, she held her usual cup of coffee, the smell dispersing the last lingering remnants of my nightmare.

For it had to be a nightmare, I told myself, as we walked into the dining room together. Breakfast was laid out on the table, including a pile of pancakes on each plate. A chafing dish of scrambled eggs was kept warm over a spirit lamp at the center of the table, within reach of both places. The silver-and-crystal syrup pitcher was set close to Nova's plate. Next to my place was a long box wrapped in green paper with a gold ribbon. A box which I knew contained a red sweater with a pattern of white stars down the center.

"An early Christmas present?" I said as I slid into my seat, fighting a sense of dizziness and regret. My actions had literally destroyed the Diamond Dog. But nothing had happened apparently. I couldn't shake the sense that something had happened, that the nightmare continued.

"It's Christmas Eve!" said Nova as she turned to the radio as always to hear the first broadcast of the day. However, just as I remembered it happening before, she took her hand off the dial and exclaimed, "Let's not have Chilton Brewster spoil the morning. I'm sure whatever homily or editorial that he's giving today can be missed. Open your present! I never liked waiting for things as a girl. Still don't. I always think there should be a few presents before the presents. I've got a whole basket of gifts for the employees. I'll give them out later today when we finish decorating the tree." She nodded to the packages sitting by the door, the basket full of gifts that I remembered her distributing.

With trembling fingers, I ripped off the paper of the box by my plate and revealed the sweater.

The last time that I had seen this red cardigan, I had called it beautiful and thanked my aunt. Then I wore it to meet with Agent Tawney and plot the raid on her dance.

The memories of smoke and flame rolled over me again. The horror of seeing Johnny and Billy dragging down the burning curtain. The feeling of Paul's hand slipping away from mine. The awful drop into nothingness. It all washed over me.

I sat in stunned and terrified silence, unable to think what to do or what to say.

Nova set down her coffee. Her eyes narrowed as she looked at me.

"Raquel Malone Gutierrez," she said in much the same manner as my mother. "What's happened to you?"

"What do you mean?" I asked, my hands unconsciously stroking the soft wool sweater and tracing the pattern of stars for comfort.

"Between one breath and the next," said Nova, still staring hard at me, "you faded. Then I saw two of you."

Certain that I had heard her wrong, although I usually understood every word that Nova said in her clear deep voice, I asked her to repeat herself.

"You faded," she said again. "Almost disappeared. I could see the chair right through you when you opened the box. But when you touched the sweater, it was like a double exposure of a photograph. Two women doing the same action in the same place."

She picked up her cup and swallowed almost all the coffee in one gulp. "Time travel can be very dangerous," she said. "And if ever a woman looked unmoored from time, it is you."

"I don't understand," I said. I understood nothing about this day, this conversation, or how I could be holding a gift in my hands that I'd already received.

"Have you seen the forest and the beach?" said Nova.

I thought about those moments in the chaotic ballroom when I almost stumbled on the path, when I'd dropped off it into nothingness. "I ran toward the beach," I admitted, "but then I turned back." Because the Diamond Dog was engulfed in flames, and I wanted to save Nova. But I couldn't find the words to tell my aunt everything that had occurred.

Very calmly, almost too calmly, Nova said, "When did it happen?"

"Today," I reluctantly said. "I think it will be tonight, if this is Christmas Eve."

"It's certainly Christmas Eve for me," said Nova, taking a deep breath as if to calm herself. "I'm not sure where you are, when you are, but I suspect more than one place in time."

I stared down at my hands. If I squinted, I could see two sets of hands, both layered over the white stars, both horrifyingly my hands. In my heart and head, I knew Nova was right. I felt pulled, and pulled apart, as if I was in two places at the same time. Apparently, I was.

I gathered the sweater up, hugging it against my breast. I saw myself do that. I also saw another pair of hands close the lid as I had the first time and place the box politely on the table. The effect was nauseating, making me dizzy. Nova must have had the same reaction, as she set her cup down on the saucer with her usual decisive movement.

But no click. I stared at her and the coffee cup. All month long, I'd sat across the table from my aunt and watched her take a last swallow, replacing the cup in its saucer with a sharp little click. It had always been as clear to me as the ringing of a bell, this click which heralded the start to Nova's day at the Diamond Dog.

But this morning I heard nothing.

Nova said something about correcting what had gone wrong. I looked directly at her and got the sense of the words, both from what I heard and what I saw, but I didn't hear each word as clearly and easily as before. My hearing, my natural hearing, had grown worse since I had stepped on the path and then off it in the burning ballroom.

"You need to do what you didn't do the last time," Nova was saying very slowly to me, like a child who needed instructions, like a woman who needed reassurance. "Turn left instead of right, leave the apartment if you stayed in it, stay here if you went elsewhere."

Even as I stood up from the table, I thought I saw a ghost of myself still sitting there, pouring coffee and discussing decorations. And that version of me had heard every word spoken, every click of the coffee cup, every chink of a fork against her plate as she ate her eggs in stupid, willful ignorance of all the harm she would do in a few short hours.

I was furious with myself, but how could I chastise a ghost from another time who was already fading? As I moved away from the table, the ghostly figure disappeared.

Nova heaved a sigh of relief. "A good start," she said. "We'll keep you moving in opposite directions of where you were before, until we can get you stuck back in this time."

"You make me sound unglued," I said. But I knew what she meant. The apartment didn't seem completely real, as if I was there and not there. It was impossible to describe. Now I knew why Nova talked about being "unmoored in time."

Nova simply nodded. "You said you saw the path and the forest."

"And the beach," I added.

"The beach makes it worse. When did this happen? Do you remember?"

"Ten o'clock, at the start of the 'Jingle Bells' number," I said, retreating across the room to stand near Nova's desk. I hadn't lingered there before, so I thought it was safe.

"Oh," said Nova with a little grimace, "I had such a good idea for the evening."

"You asked Johnny to call me up on stage," I said, looking quickly around the room and relieved to find only one of myself, the one I was, standing there.

"You know about the surprise." Nova looked upset, but then shrugged. "Well of course you do."

I angled back toward my aunt so I could read her lips as well as listen to her words. As I struggled to comprehend her, I prayed the hearing device left in my room would continue to give me some amplification. Apparently, all the hearing in my right ear was completely gone now, and my left was much worse. I'd been warned by several doctors that my hearing would naturally worsen over the years. It seemed time travel accelerated the loss.

"Why did I become unmoored?" I said. "Why here in Kingsport? Why now?" Questions I should have asked days ago, but I'd been so enamored with escaping my unwanted future and rectifying my past.

"Why you?" Nova mused. "Probably because you're a Malone. And you tried to change something, didn't you?"

"I had to do something," I finally admitted. "I don't want my future. I wanted what I had in the past."

"We can't mend the past, but we can always change the future," Nova said, and it was a phrase my mother often repeated to us children. I felt ashamed that I'd forgotten her advice.

"But you went through time," I said to Nova. "You even said you tried to use it for bootlegging."

My aunt grimaced and fiddled with the belt on her robe, an uncharacteristic sign of nervousness or perhaps her own embarrassment. "I made a mistake," she said finally. "I thought we could use the old pathway with new technology, that cars or airplanes could go through it toward the future or escape into the past, just not too far ahead or too far behind. It was a complete disaster for anyone who is not a Malone."

"But why is the path appearing when we sing…" I paused, almost afraid to name the song, "Jingle Bells?"

Nova sighed. "My fault again. After I fell into that place, I needed a pattern to keep my mind from wandering. If you sing, you don't notice other things. Which makes it much easier to direct your steps where you want to go. Even then, it took me several tries to get out again. The tune was the first one I remembered."

Blood under my shoes, the howling of hounds, and the gnashing teeth of the trees, I thought, all summoned or dispelled by a sleighing song. "Everyone sings that silly tune. Why does it cause the world to wobble?"

"Wobble?" said Nova. "That's a good word for it. My father – your grandfather – used to call it rough seas. Those ripples flow into the past, present, and future in unexpected ways. When I started down the path, I fell off into many wrong times before I found the right time. It causes problems."

"So I now exist in two places at the same time? Or do I exist in two times but in the same place?"

"It would take a college professor to explain! But I know it makes you feel like flotsam in a whirlpool," Nova continued. "Best to stay off the path completely and never go there."

"But what or where is the path?" I asked. Paul called it a nightmare in one of his journal entries. I remembered my own brief experiences, the strange dreamlike sensation mixed with best forgotten memories.

Nova shrugged. "Who knows? The grimoire hinted the forest grew in more than one world. Beatrice once told me her equations show it exists both inside and outside of time, whatever that means!"

I checked the clock and it was still early. A look around the room confirmed no ghost of myself had appeared again. Nova's advice of going in the opposite direction of where I'd been before (or was it after?) seemed to be working.

"We'll cancel the 'Jingle Bells' bit," said Nova. "Just to be safe."

I started to agree. But then I thought of Paul. If I failed to open the gate or path or whatever it was which led him in and out of the world, he'd be trapped in a nightmare forever. I couldn't abandon him.

But if I opened the path the same way again, then Agent Tawney would grab Paul. The scaled hounds would leap through. There would be gunfire and mayhem. The Diamond Dog would be destroyed again.

But, I thought, I could sing "Jingle Bells" someplace else. Someplace safe and rescue Paul without ever having to admit to Nova how much I had done wrong in the past few days.

"Cancel the song," I said to her. "Tell the band that I found out about the surprise and decided not to play in public." It was an easy excuse that anyone would believe.

With Nova's agreement to change the evening's entertainment, I went back to my room to dress, thinking all the time about how I could slip away to rescue Paul.

I tried to ignore any worries about more damage to my hearing. What was done was done, as my mother would say. I could only try not to repeat my mistakes in what was now my future.

Once I settled the hearing device on my head with the earpiece over my better left ear, I hummed a few bars of "Jingle Bells."

Almost immediately, I heard Paul's voice, "Il était une fois."

I never heard him speak in anything other than English and a few scattered words that I thought were German or Dutch.

"Paul?" I said. "Paul, can you hear me?"

"I have lost so much," he replied in English. "I can't hold on to the memories. It's all slipping away."

"Paul!" I exclaimed. "It's Raquel! I am coming for you. I promise!"

"It's a terrible way to spend a Christmas Eve," he answered.

"Paul, do you understand me? I am going to save you. Only I can't sing at the Diamond Dog tonight. We'll do it later, when it's safe."

"It's never safe unless Jim plays his horn. Tell them, no matter how often they try, they fail. Tell them that they will die."

"Paul!" I practically wailed, clutching the dresser in front of me, staring into the mirror with wild eyes. "What do you mean?"

"Tell her, tell Raquel, that Jim Culver must play or it goes wrong every time," he said in a fading whisper.

In my desperation, I began to sing full out, the words for "Jingle Bells" tumbling from my lips, trying to force Paul into the room. The mirror in front of me shimmered. I swear I saw the trees, the beach, and the terrible, still water of the ocean which never moved. Then, like a bubble popping, it was gone.

Spinning on my heel, I headed for the door, intent on going down to the ballroom and trying again on the piano. Lying on the table beside my bed, I spotted Paul's journal. Like me, it had changed. Now it was twice as ragged around the edges and dark stains spread across its cover along with something like claw marks. When I picked it up, it smelled like smoke, horrible oily smoke like burned garbage. Or a burned building.

I opened it and rifled through the pages. At the very end of the journal, just filling the final pages, I read an entry that I had never read before. One that I swear just appeared. Yet judging by the stains and blotches on the page, it was as old as all the rest. But it was different too. It was as if Paul was beginning his story again.

"Il était une fois," say the French. Once upon… once on… it was once… all the tales begin the same. With time. With an unknown place in an unknown time. What time am I in? Where is the place I am now? I kneel on the beach with the ocean lacking waves at my back. I scratch dates and places in the grit with my hands as the thoughts run out of my mind. If I can write it down, perhaps I will remember. Already the memory of a snowy world is disappearing. Why snow? Isn't it June? No, it's Christmas Eve, I remember people celebrating, but the kind words and wishes of those I have met are fading, fading too quickly.

How could I have met anyone? There is nothing here. Just me on a beach which makes no sense at all.

I have lost so much. I can't hold on to the memories. It's all slipping away.

The purple sand cuts my fingers and fills in the lines I carve into the ground. When did the sand become purple? I don't remember. I continue to scratch until the scrabbling of my fingers is the only sound in the place.

I dug graves in Paris. The thud of the shovel hitting the dirt reverberates through my body and through my memories. A wet sucking sound when it rained or a bone-jarring dry bang when the sun burned the backs of our shoulders. But rain or burning sun, the stink of a city in despair always rose around us as we dug the graves for the hundreds who died during the fever sweeping the city.

This sand smells of nothing. But I remember the stink of sorrow; it's the stench I carry with me always.

I scratch in the dirt as my hands bleed. Perhaps I am digging my own grave. Perhaps I am already dead. Such thoughts wail in my mind as I see the letters and numbers written in the sand: Arkham 1929, Innsmouth 1917, Kingsport 1925, Kingsport 1946, and all the rest.

My mind is a cemetery full of dead memories, and I do not understand.

Then as the world shifts and wobbles around me, snow fills the names and obscures the dates. I tip my head to the sky and I see clouds. Ordinary clouds, a simple gray blanket of clouds, as the snow falls on my tears. And I begin a new story for you.

I found myself in a graveyard.

The monument before me had an inscription on the top: "They will be remembered in our hearts today and forever." Below was carved: "Victims of the Diamond Dog Fire" and a long list of names, all alphabetical. At the end of the list was a single date: December 24, 1926.

"It's a terrible way to spend Christmas Eve," said a voice behind me. "I hate this place. I come here every year. But I hate it."

I turned around. The man behind me was old, withered, and bent. He leaned upon an ebony cane with a carved silver handle. Watery eyes peered at me though large glasses sliding down to the end of his nose. I had never seen eyeglasses like his. The heavy square frames around the lens covered the entire top of his face, from eyebrow to cheekbone. But the eyeglasses did not hide the tears leaking from his eyes and running down the wrinkled cheeks.

"You're here," he said. "Finally. I'm nearly a hundred. Do you know what I've had to survive to be in this graveyard today? No, of course, you don't. But you will."

I had no words for him. All my languages ran together and the sounds I made with my mouth were like a baby's mewling.

"Take this." He thrust a package into my hands. "Write it down. Write everything you remember, everything you see. If you write it now, after all that has happened, it will change what came before."

I clutched the package to my chest, feeling under the brown paper the outline of a book.

"What?" I finally stammered, the word tumbling out of my mouth like pearls and toads tumbled from the mouths of those bewitched.

"Write your memories on these pages. Pray she reads this in time," the old man whispered to me. "Tell her, tell Raquel, Jim must play, or it goes wrong every time."

When he said Raquel, I heard a voice calling my name. A memory slipped sideways into my head.

"I know who she is," I said to him, joy replacing my sorrow. "I know who Raquel is."

"Change her future and my past." The old man slapped the package in my hand. "Tell Raquel to ask Nova Malone for help or the Diamond Dog burns. It burns every time."

I remembered the fire. I remembered the smoke. I remembered a woman's hand reaching out for mine and then slipping away. "I want to save her," I said. "No, I tried to save her. Didn't I?"

"Stop talking. Just listen. Tell them, no matter how often they try, they fail.

Tell Raquel that they will die," he shouted at me. "It's never safe unless Jim plays his horn."

I tore open the package to see a volume bound in leather and a bundle of pens.

"Blank journal, ballpoint pens, you're supposed to be able to write on the moon with those pens. Damn, they say they'll walk on the moon this summer. I wanted to see that. But I want this more. Write it down and maybe history will change. No, that's not right. It won't be history if you go back. If you go back, you can change the future." He stumbled a few steps away and fell on his side, one hand pressed to his heart. I nearly dropped the book as I moved to help him.

"Don't touch me!" he yelled even louder, arms waving wildly so he created circles in the snow. Great sweeps in the snow like crooked wings sprouting from his shoulders. "Get away from me! Don't lose the journal! Not yet. Later, lose it later so Leo will find it and give it to her. This is all I can do. Please, please let me die in peace. I don't want to dream of their screams one more night. Tell Raquel that I was wrong. Tell all of them that I was sorry." He began to cry even harder as I dropped to my knees to comfort him.

Then the old man sang, a wavering tenor choked with sobs, and the words wrapped around me as he faded away. "Jingle bells, jingle bells, jingle all the way."

Once again, I am on the beach now filled with blue sand. I sit down and I begin to write. I write about how I became lost, and I write about the first time that I heard your voice.

I fill the pages with words untied from time, words which tell about everything that happened, everything that will happen, so it becomes again the story that you are reading.

A long time ago, and yet just moments ago, I began this book. Now the cover changes as I write, the words appear inside, and outside it grows old, older than me, older than us. But I remember again. I scratch down these words. I must try again. I know why the old man cries in such pain. My tears are falling on the page now.

While I write, I pray. I pray like the old man that you will believe.

Because I have seen your name on the monument, Raquel. I have seen so many names that I know because of you. Nova, Harlean, Billy, Ginger, Cozy, and all the rest. Those names are carved into the stone and an old man is weeping next to your grave.

You will all die on Christmas Eve, 1926, unless we can change your story.

CHAPTER TWENTY-ONE

I flew down the hallway looking for my aunt. She wasn't in the apartment, but then I remembered the basket of gifts by the door. I ran down the stairs and into the ballroom. Nova had just handed out the last present and made her little speech. This time, instead of making my way to the door to find Agent Tawney outside, I ran toward Nova.

"You have to help me," I said, thrusting the journal into her hands. "You have to help me save everyone."

The others gawked at me. Nova simply shooed them away, saying we needed to talk. Being Nova, nobody questioned her and everyone did as she asked. Then Nova directed me to a small table at the edge of the room. She propped the book open and read it cover to cover. Whenever I tried to talk or point out a particular passage, she waved me off.

It was agonizing. But this was my aunt who literally could do anything, even travel through time. If anyone understood, if anyone could help, it would be Nova. I finally understood.

After far too long a wait, Nova snapped the book closed.

"I need to see Leo," she said. Raising her voice, she called, "Otis, get the Rolls. We're going out to Cuffe's farm."

"I never went there today," I said. "Not last time."

"Good. Then we're setting a new pattern. Less duplication of you, as it were. Come along."

She swept upstairs for coats and down again, all the time rattling off directions to the others for the setup of the night's dance.

"You can't go forward with the dance," I said as she bundled us both into the backseat of the Rolls. "Didn't you read what Paul said?"

"I read it," snapped Nova. "Now I want to know how Leo found this book. And in the meantime, you can tell me exactly who this Paul is."

So I told her everything that I told Tawney and Brewster, and even more. All the times that I had heard Paul's voice. I even confessed how the world wobbled in the basement last Saturday, and again when I tried to pull Paul out by playing the piano by myself.

Nova just shook her head and muttered a couple of times. I felt very small and miserable by the time we arrived at the farmhouse. Then, as always, my aunt surprised me. "I guess I should have spent less time trying to impress you with fancy gifts and more time talking to you," she said. "I felt those wobbles, but I never thought about how it could be you causing time to shift. I should have looked closer and listened better."

Which made me feel so much worse and so much better at the same time. All I could think to say was. "I do love you, Aunt Nova."

She smiled. "Same, Raquel, same to you. Let's see if we can fix this."

Both Cuffe and Leo greeted us when we arrived at the farmhouse. If they were surprised by Nova's arrival, they gave no sign of it.

She pulled the battered journal out of her bag and waved it at Leo. "How did you get this book?" she said.

Captain Leo looked at her like an old friend. It occurred to me that they probably were. "Come inside and let me explain."

We climbed the porch stairs and entered the living room. "We'll need coffee for this," Cuffe said, bustling toward the back of the house. "I'll put the pot on."

"Don't forget the rum," said Nova. "I smuggled enough of it out here for you to spare me a tot."

Cuffe waved at her as he disappeared into the kitchen.

"I went for a sleigh ride on Christmas Eve with Cuffe," Captain Leo said. "Just after I retired the *Molly Gee* in 1921. It was probably the first time we'd taken the sleigh out. Cuffe had just finished fixing it up and wanted to show it off to me."

Cuffe came bustling into the room with steaming mugs of coffee which smelled more like spiced rum. Nova took a long appreciative drink of hers. I swallowed mine without tasting a thing, so intent I was on listening to Captain Leo's story.

"The sled just flew along, and Cuffe began to sing," Captain Leo said. "It felt like it was all part of the tune, the horses' hooves striking the snow, the ringing of the harness bells, and the whisper of the sleigh's runners. Then the world began to ripple."

"Ripple?" I asked.

"Like looking at a reflection in the water. When you're out at sea and the weather is calm, but then a ship so far out that you can't see it starts the waves and you know something is happening but can't see the cause. Just waves passing on the way to somewhere else, but it changes your perception," he said, his voice very calm in a way that reminded me of Nova. But I could see the tension in his shoulders and his face. Whatever memories were stirred by this description still bothered him. "The woods, the snow, and all the rest. It was the same, but it was changing. A mist came up. Sometimes the mist was in front of us, and sometimes beside us. When I turned my head and looked straight at it, it wasn't mist, or fog, or smoke."

"What was it?" I said, but I thought I knew. I remembered the creature in their woods and Mab's whines when it appeared.

"It looked like a dog. A gaunt, starving dog. I thought we were being chased by a rabid dog. It looked so strange – no fur and the skin seemed almost covered in scales. And a tongue as long as its snout. I gave a shout. Cuffe pulled the reins and stopped the sleigh. The dog was running so fast behind us, and the snow was so icy, it couldn't stop. It crashed right into the sleigh. I'm sure it did. Only then there wasn't anything there. We climbed out to look but couldn't find any tracks. Just that." He pointed at the book.

"It was lying in the snow," Cuffe said. "Anyone could have dropped it."

"I think that dog dropped it. The book had been in its mouth, and it ran into the sleigh and dropped it," responded Captain Leo in a way that made me think this was an old dispute between them. He reached out his hand and traced a semicircle of marks on the back and front that looked something like a dog's bite.

"If a rabid dog dropped the book," said Cuffe, "it certainly didn't stop you from reading it on the way home." He smiled at Captain Leo and tipped his cup to him.

"Of course! A mysterious book appearing on Christmas Eve," said Captain Leo. "I read it from cover to cover. I remembered a man helping me when I put into Innsmouth during the last war. He loaded a few boxes and then disappeared. When I read the journal, I wondered if he was the writer. Perhaps another Jack London, sailing around the world and mixing his stories out of fact and legend. The whole incident was strange, but strange does happen around here. Eventually I stuffed the journal away on a shelf and forgot it. Until you put up the sign for the Diamond Dog. The name rang a bell in my head, so I went looking again for the book. There it was, all the mentions of the Diamond Dog in Kingsport. But I noticed something the next time I read it."

"The stories changed," said Nova, pushing the book across the table to Captain Leo. She looked concerned. "Patterns changed and the thing has changed with them."

Captain Leo flipped open the covers and rifled through the pages just as I had a few hours earlier. Then he paused, reading the final entry in the journal.

"It changed all right," said Captain Leo. "I always remember what I read. Oh, not word for word. I can forget a scene or a chapter and be surprised by it in a new reading. That's half the pleasure of reading old favorites again. But this–" he tapped his finger again on the cover of the book "–was very different the second time I read it. More about the Diamond Dog. More about Raquel." Then he flipped to the final entry. "But there was nothing about the old man dying in the graveyard. I've never read that before. I'll bet my soul on it."

Nova tapped her diamond covered fingers against the tabletop.

"I probably shouldn't have used 'Jingle Bells' for my pattern," she said to us as the clock ticked through my second Christmas Eve of 1926. "But I was in a hurry to make it home and needed something easy to remember. Who can't sing a verse or chorus of that song? But it evokes memories too. Makes you think of Christmas. I was trying for August and kept landing on Christmas Eve. It took a lot of concentration to finally make it to October 1926. I completely lost September this year." She shook her head at the journal. "I did see Paul behind me in Kingsport, but then he disappeared. I should have paid closer attention, but Chilton distracted me."

I wasn't sure if Chilton would call the commandeering of his coat a distraction, but I didn't contradict Nova.

"Paul kept moving around," I said instead, pulling back the book and reading out all the places and people that Paul met. Nova frowned and then smiled through many of the encounters.

"I know them," she said. "I know them all, but not in the times and places he describes. I wonder how the poor man got there in the first place. It's unusual to find anyone on that beach. Although it does happen. There are some mighty thin spots in Innsmouth, even a few in Arkham and Kingsport."

"But why does he keep reappearing on Christmas Eve?" I asked. "That must mean something, mustn't it?"

"It seems I stuck your Paul in the start of my pattern," said Nova, "without taking him all the way out. I went through Arkham, its downtown and the university, too, and Dunwich, which was horrible, the wrong time in Innsmouth, which was worse in some ways, and then back again to Kingsport. By then time would have been unraveling in my wake, so Paul could have been tossed in various directions, even to places and times that I missed."

"Like the wake of a boat?" Captain Leo said. I noticed that neither Captain Leo or Cuffe seemed perturbed by Nova's maritime explanations of time travel and magic.

"I should have guessed you were Baba Yaga. That entry was in there the first time that I read the book," Captain Leo said.

"I've been called much worse," Nova chuckled.

"So how do we save Paul?" I asked her. "How do we save ourselves?"

"We go forward with the dance," Nova declared suddenly.

"But the dance was a disaster," I said, trying to hold on to the memories which were already fading like a nightmare. "We burned down the Diamond Dog. Well, Tawney caused it to burn, bringing out the hounds and trying to hang on to Paul. The whole town wobbled."

"This last entry implies we can change what happens tonight," said Nova, her brow furrowed as she once again read the final passages. "But the suggestion of Jim Culver is troubling. He's bound to stir up something very dangerous."

Captain Leo looked equally troubled. "Jim is a good man, but his daddy's horn has a terrible hold on him."

"Perhaps we just close this book and hide it," I said very slowly, my heart almost breaking as I thought of Paul lost forever in the strange twilight world where the stars never shone. "If Tawney doesn't see Paul tonight, he won't start shooting and the tree won't fall, the hounds won't appear, and everyone will survive."

Nova shook her head. "I never liked the idea of doing nothing as the solution to a problem. Leo is right. Jim is a good man, however wicked his trumpet is." Her eyes narrowed and her fingers continued to tap on the journal's battered, blood soaked, and now charred cover. "Your Paul appears when the music plays, he disappears when the music stops. So how to haul him into this time and place and keep him from slipping away?" She frowned down at the table.

"I almost had him," I said, fighting to recall what happened on the night that hadn't happened yet. Everything had been so clear in my mind only hours before, but now I struggled to remember. "I did hold on to him. I know I did. He didn't disappear immediately, even after the band fled."

"Drag him to the present and hold on? That might work if we reset the pattern. Send a wave to cancel a wave?" Nova sounded as if she was thinking out loud.

Cuffe scratched one ear. "Sounds complicated."

Nova shook her head. "We keep the song playing until it drowns out all the wobbles." Then she gave a very Nova smile. "And we have a town full of the best gadget to do that! I'll send out the word. Every radio in Kingsport tuned to the Diamond Dog's broadcast at ten o'clock. That's when we have Billy and the band play 'Jingle Bells' for all that they are worth."

"But will that be enough?" I asked, thinking of all the times the song snatched Paul away. "Can it anchor Paul to the present?" I added, picking up the maritime analogies from Nova.

"If the old man was right, it will work if we add Jim Culver," said my aunt. "If anyone can make a song behave the way that he wants, it's Jim."

"When Jim is playing, even the dead dance to his tune," said Captain Leo.

"What about the hounds?" I said. While other incidents faded, those terrifying monsters remained clear in my memories.

"We'll start a great circle of dance through the streets of Kingsport, and dance those creatures into corners, into diminishing triangles as Beatrice advised, until everything disappears except Paul," replied Nova as if she planned the confusion of supernatural creatures every day. Given all that I had learned, perhaps she did.

"And Chilton Brewster and Agent Tawney?" I asked.

Nova's smile broadened and it was a dangerous smile. "I can handle a banker and a Fed."

"Dear lady," said Cuffe, "how can we help tonight?"

"We'll need your sleigh to lead the dance through the town," said Nova and Cuffe cheered.

"Oh, he's going to be insufferable about the sleigh," said Captain Leo to me. "He's always claimed it should be the symbol of the farm. By this time next year, he'll have organized sleigh rides for the whole town and probably be advertising Christmas trees on the side."

"Be outside the Diamond Dog at ten and ready to lead the way," Nova told Cuffe. "A great circle of the town, Cuffe, as round as you can make it with every bell ringing on the harness. We'll jingle this town back into time and confound those government agents."

CHAPTER TWENTY-TWO

Avoiding Agent Tawney and Chilton Brewster proved harder than I expected. When I missed our meeting due to our trip to Cuffe's farm, Tawney came to the Diamond Dog and asked for me in the afternoon.

"Bold," said Nova when the message was relayed down to me. We were in the basement office going over the possible permutations of the evening, including re-reading the passages in Paul's journal that outlined the ferocity of the hounds as well as Beatrice Sharpe's calculations to baffle the pursuit of the creatures.

"I wish I could reach Sharpe and speak to her about this," Nova was telling me when the message came that Tawney was upstairs. "But the woman never stays home. She's on one of her expeditions, according to her friend Judy."

"What should I do about Tawney?" I asked my aunt.

"Ignore him," replied Nova. Then to Lily, who had brought the message, "Does Tawney have anyone with him?"

"No," said Lily. "He's alone."

"Tell him Raquel is out," decided Nova. "I don't suppose we can take back the tickets you gave him for the dance."

"Oh, he's sent his thanks for those and bought some more," said Lily. "He said something about bringing friends to see Kingsport's most famous attraction."

"That's more flattering," said Nova, "but will only get him in the door. Well, we know when he planned to arrive last time and must assume it stays the same this time. We'll see him after nine and before ten."

Lily looked a little baffled by this speech, as well she might. So far, Nova had only discussed the repeat of the day with Leo and Cuffe, whom she said she could trust not to spread it around town. "Those men have their own secrets," she said to me and, probably in response to my look of surprise, added, "and it's not up to me to tell their story."

"But I thought they were both retired gentlemen who did a little farming and book collecting," I said.

"You'll find in this town, and several nearby, that there's a number of old men and women who only seem to be retired from their professions. When help is needed, they give it," said Nova.

To distract myself, I flipped through the pages of the journal, noting again the number of new stains and other marks. I worried about what had happened to Paul since I lost hold of his hand. "What about Mandy Thompson and Dr William Maleson?" I said, reading that passage again. "They encountered the hounds very recently."

Like the other entries in the book, it seemed longer and more detailed now, not at all as I remembered. One name popped out at me immediately upon this reading.

"Agent Tawney was with them," I said to Nova. "Look, read this." I thrust the book at her, pointing to Tawney's name scrawled in Paul's account of the attack of the hounds in the laboratory.

"Hmm," said Nova. "I missed that. No wonder he was so quick to respond to Brewster's letter. See if you can find other mentions of him or anyone who sounds like him."

I found one other. At least the man was called Ralph, and I remembered Tawney's frequent insistence that people call him by his first name. "Withers?" said Nova. "I looked at some of his research when I was thinking of using our family grimoire for transportation purposes."

"Smuggling," I said.

Nova shrugged and smiled. "I'm not used to being quite so blunt around you. But yes, for smuggling. Withers, Maleson, and Thompson work at Miskatonic University and the research there can be a bit... well, let's just say esoteric is the polite word for it. Tawney must have tracked down anyone with even the slightest interest in time travel. I wonder if he talked to Harvey Walters. Probably not. Harvey has always been more of an occultist than a scientist."

"Your cleaners seem very well informed," I said, remembering how my aunt said she paid them to keep an eye on the university's activities.

"You never know when they might discover something useful." Nova shrugged. "I'm sure the O'Bannions do the same."

The clicking of Lily's heels on the stairs announced another message delivery. "Chilton Brewster sent a note," she said, handing the envelope to Nova.

"Of course he did," said Nova, slitting it open with a wicked looking knife she kept on her desk. She called it a "gutting knife" and I hoped she was talking about fish. "Full of compliments on our work in civic entertainment and how we've helped to elevate – he always uses such fancy words! – the town's reputation. That's a change of tone! Oh, and he's asking to dance with you, Raquel, tonight. Presumably to tell you what to expect at ten. Quite the Victorian gentleman, asking me for permission to ask you."

"Decorum," I said, "is important to Chilton. But it's 1926 and he should ask me directly if he wants to dance. Frankly, I think Johnny has better manners. And he's a bootlegger!"

"Some of the best gentlemen are," said Nova. "Bootleggers, that is. And even the O'Bannions never burned down my ballroom."

Lily looked completely bewildered at this announcement, but Nova waved her away with the words, "Business analogy. Nothing will burn tonight." To me, she added, "I hope. But I've had the men bring down the extra fire extinguishers from my apartment. They'll be standing by the tree when the time comes."

We spent the rest of the afternoon trying not to do what we'd done before, setting a new pattern as Nova called it.

This new pattern included being honest with each other. I promised my aunt to finally write to my family and make plans to go home. If we survived the night.

By the time the dance started, I felt the same as I had before – a complete bundle of frightened nerves, only even worse. Because everywhere I glanced, it triggered a memory of terrible destruction.

I also faded in and out according to Nova, who kept moving me around the ballroom hoping to counteract the effect. Apparently nobody else noticed, but the tree was capturing a lot of attention.

"Perhaps I should just send you upstairs to my apartment," Nova said at one point when I felt as if there were three of me, all shattering like one of the crystal glasses containing the very innocent fruit punch that Nova was serving to the guests.

"All my strong stuff went to the Clover Club as promised," she said, naming Arkham's most infamous night club as I remarked on the punch. "They're having their own party tonight. Which is best. I hate to think what would happen if Marie Lambeau or Finn Edwards came dancing here tonight."

A waiter dropped a glass. The sound of it breaking ricocheted through the room. I couldn't remember anything breaking the last time and told Nova so. "Good," she said, giving me a close look. "The timeline is changing. You do look more present. I can't see through you at all."

When Johnny came to collect me for our last dance before ten o'clock, I turned away from him and walked straight into the arms of Chilton Brewster, something I definitely had not done before. "You told my aunt that you wanted to dance," I said to the surprised banker. I know he was surprised because he let me lead through the first bars of music.

"I expected her to refuse. Or for you to avoid me," he admitted. Then, coming to his senses, he took over the dance, whirling me in a quick step around a kissing couple. His dance moves surprised me. Who would have thought the staid banker had such a good foxtrot?

"I am not running away from you," I said. Then hearing my own words echo in my head, I said more firmly, "I am not running away from anything. Not now."

Brewster gave me one of his blank-faced looks. The lights above reflected off his glasses but dancing nearly cheek to cheek, I finally got a close look at his face. Great shadows marked the skin under his eyes. He looked as if he hadn't slept in a week.

Or perhaps in a year.

I could feel myself being tugged in all directions, the reverberations of Nova's journey on her path twisting around all of us. What if the same had happened to Brewster? What if he had suffered through more than one day of duplicated time?

"You tried to get the coat back from Nova!" I suddenly remembered how he described the incident in his journal. "You ran after her down the path!"

"I regretted it the moment that I handed my coat to her," Brewster admitted. "So I followed her."

"How far did you go after Nova?" I asked Brewster. "How far forward on the path?"

Two journals in his office for the same year. What else had changed for him? What else did he know? Suddenly Brewster's frustration with the world, the constant letters, and his obsession with driving Nova out of Kingsport made so much more sense. I was surprised I hadn't guessed he was a time traveler too.

Brewster faltered and almost stumbled before he recovered the rhythm of the dance. He swept me off to one side. With a strangely old-fashioned bow, he ushered me into a chair. Then he sat himself in the opposite chair.

"Too far," he said in response to my question. "I knew the minute I stepped on the path what it was. I grew up here in Kingsport, but there were Innsmouth and Arkham relatives on both sides of my family. The Fitzmaurice family, all gone now, but we're related to Saturnin Fitzmaurice's daughter. There's even a Malone back a few generations." He must have noticed my start of surprise because he responded with a small smile, "Something your aunt doesn't know. Innsmouth never liked it when one of theirs married outside of town boundaries. A clannish, almost cultish group, you could say."

"How far did you go?" I asked again, not about to be sidetracked by these claims of kinship.

"Too far," he admitted. "A year ahead, all the way to Christmas Eve, 1926. Then back again to where I started, like an elastic snapping. I lived this year feeling as if I was splitting into two."

I knew the feeling and after less than twelve hours with the same problem, I couldn't imagine days like that. I really would have shattered.

"I haven't slept a full night since it happened," Brewster went on. "Since Nova Malone stole my coat from me. And Kingsport continues to shake. I go forward again and again on the path to this place and this time."

"You feel it too. The world shifting."

"It is getting worse," said Brewster. Then he balled up his hand and banged it down on the table. "I cannot explain. Not in any way that anyone will believe. So I make petty complaints about petty people. But it's not enough! Kingsport could be the perfect place, if only I could correct my mistake."

"But Kingsport is lovely," I said. "Nova opening the Diamond Dog isn't hurting anyone."

Brewster shook his head. "You're wrong. This place will kill everyone here. I know it. We must stop it. I have tried to stop it. I failed." He looked around and then pulled an old-fashioned gold pocket watch out of his vest pocket. He visibly blanched when he saw the time. "I have to leave. If I leave, maybe I can change something next time."

He stood up, obviously meaning to skirt the table and head out the door. I glanced at the doors, seeing Ralph Tawney and his men entering the ballroom. Looking at my own watch, I saw it was ten minutes to ten. Almost time for the band to play "Jingle Bells" and Reggie's broadcast to be heard throughout Kingsport.

Brewster was hurrying across the ballroom, dodging dancers as he made for the exit. I didn't remember him running the last time.

Suddenly I realized what Brewster had said. He had gone forward, more than once! I sprang up out of my chair and chased after him, bumping into a few surprised couples. Closing the gap between us, I grabbed Brewster's arm and swung him around to face me.

"You went forward more than once," I said to him as he blinked down at me. "You saw the fire."

"Every time," he whispered, so low that I couldn't hear what he was saying, but I could read his lips. "Every time they all die in a fire. The building burns to the ground. I hear their screams in my nightmares."

Visibly shaking, he tried to pull away from me.

"Why didn't you write that in your letters?" I said, hanging on to him and being almost pulled over by his eagerness to get to the door. "Why didn't you tell Nova the truth?"

We were now off the dance floor, nearer the lobby doors, almost exactly where I remembered Brewster standing the last time I attended this dance, the time that didn't exist yet but would in just a few minutes. "Why didn't you help instead of just complaining?" I said to Brewster.

He tore his arm free from my grasp and practically yelled, "I tried! I used her song and tried. I failed. I have a great future. I will be a great man. I cannot die tonight." Then Brewster whipped around, straight into the arms of Ralph Tawney, who had come up behind him.

"What are you saying?" said Tawney, with an even harder grip on Brewster than I had managed. "What do you know?"

"There are monsters tonight," said Brewster, trying to shake loose. "The place burns to the ground and releases monsters onto the street. Creatures like hounds. They rip men apart."

Tawney blanched. "You miserable man. You are the time traveler, too, aren't you? You know how to get back to the forest!"

"No, no," protested Brewster as Tawney shoved him into the arms of another agent with curt orders to "hold on to him." Brewster yelped in protest.

"As for you," Tawney said, turning on me, but Johnny was there, having practically sprinted across the ballroom floor.

"Oh, Raquel, here you are," he said in as casual a tone as he could while panting. "Your aunt wants you on the bandstand. We have a surprise for you." The words almost ran together as he tugged me away. However, I guessed immediately what he was saying and followed him as fast as I could.

As we neared the stage, my aunt hugged me and said directly into the microphone of my hearing aid, "What happened?"

"It's Brewster," I told her. "He travels too. Tawney thinks he can find the forest. Does any of that make any sense?"

"More than might be expected," said Nova, still speaking slowly and clearly so I could catch every word. "Four of us traveling the path, all through this point and time. Brewster, Paul, you, and me. No wonder the world wobbles. We need to dance ourselves into midnight and end all this."

Lined up behind the bandstand, I saw Otis and Tim stationed near the fire extinguishers and hose. Other burly men were near the Christmas tree, including Chuck Fergus, trying to look casual with extinguishers propped near their feet. "O'Bannions came through," said Nova with a nod. "All rivalries put aside among bootleggers tonight. I'll owe them in the morning."

All those phone calls by Nova, and everyone answered. I'd never been so proud of my aunt.

Another line of young men and women stood on the other side, directly under the mistletoe. They were armed with what looked like yardsticks and chalk. "The Miskatonic University Math Club," said Nova. "I promised more than sherry for their next party."

"But don't we need…" I started to say as a tall thin Black man carrying a battered trumpet case emerged from the crowd.

"Mr Culver," said Nova, striding forward and shaking his hand. "Delighted you could play tonight."

"Jim," he said with a shy smile. "Just call me Jim. It's an honor to perform here. I cannot wait to play this dance. I do admire Billy Oliver's style."

Billy waved from his piano stool. Jim hopped up on the stage and pulled his horn out of his case.

"Well," Nova said to me. "Are you ready?"

"Yes," I said as firmly as possible. "And Aunt Nova, this time I'm staying for the dance, all the way past midnight. No more trying to run away." This time I would save Paul, I thought, and suddenly there was only one of me there in the hall. All the fractured feeling had disappeared. I knew where I was, when I was. And I knew I was enough.

"That's my niece," said Nova.

I grabbed a string of bells from the basket by Cozy's drums. Ginger gave a little tootle on her saxophone. Harlean pulled me to stand beside her at the microphone. Across the room, I saw Johnny at the broadcast booth's door. He waved at us. Reggie must be ready to broadcast to all the radios in Kingsport. I hoped that all sets were tuned to our station tonight.

"Places, people, places," said Harlean into the microphone. "Grab your bells and get ready to dance!" Waiters circulated among the dancers, handing out the bells for everyone to ring. "Remember, once we start the song, it's out the doors and follow the sleigh. All around the town tonight. This is one dance everyone will remember!"

Harlean turned to me with eyes sparkling with excitement. Behind her, I could almost see my memories of fire, smoke, and creatures dripping with blood. The tree toppling and taking the Diamond Dog with it.

"Not now, not here," I said to myself.

"Ready," I said to Harlean and the world.

"Ladies and gentlemen, grab your partner," Harlean called into the microphone. "And dance!"

Billy's hands crashed down onto the keyboard of the piano. Jim lifted his horn and played right alongside him as Ginger found her own place in the song and Cozy kept the beat.

Harlean began to sing. I sang with her.

The dancers danced in circles, streaming toward the double doors thrown open wide by Nova's employees. Tawney, Brewster, and the other federal agents were shoved off into a corner by the movement of the crowd.

As "Jingle Bells" rang out through the hall, as I rang the bells and sang, the world wobbled and changed. Trees appeared in the center of the ballroom with a path winding under their swaying branches. I saw Paul sprinting toward us, pursued by the scaled hounds.

CHAPTER TWENTY-THREE

I leapt from the stage, grabbing Paul's hands, and they were warm, solid, and so blessedly real. He almost stumbled as he tightened his hands on mine, but his feet found the rhythm. I swung him into the dance. "Circle, circle," I shouted over all the noise, as we waltzed after the last of the dancers streaming out of the double doors.

Behind us the path, the forest, and the hounds wobbled and wavered, one moment there and one moment gone. The band played on, Jim's horn sending notes floating in and above the music, somehow more distinct, as if I was hearing them through my soul rather than my damaged ears. In my earpiece, I heard another world, a howling rising with frustration as the hounds diminished and disappeared before chalked lines and triangles drawn by an enthusiastic group of mathematicians.

Paul and I danced across the lobby. The radio speakers set earlier by Reggie blared the music after us. Out the doors of the Diamond Dog and into the street we followed the dancers.

Ahead of us, the harness bells on Cuffe's horses rang out as the sleigh took its position at the front of the parade. Singers crowded on the back bench of the sleigh caroled with the broadcast floating through the air. Looking up the street, I saw windows open in buildings with radios balanced on the sills. From all rose the song, "Jingle all the way!" as Billy and the band kept the broadcast going from the Diamond Dog.

Then Jim Culver danced down the steps past us, weaving amid the throng. Following close behind him were more slavering scaly hounds, slinking low, crawling on their bellies like snakes, as they flowed into the street. Jim led them all away from the dance, toward the opposite end of the street, and close behind ran the Mathematics Club, chalking straight lines and triangles all around the entrances of buildings and drawing the same symbols in the snow wherever they could.

Every now and then a hound would throw back its head and howl, and I heard it clearly in my earpiece. But on the street, all the music, all the ringing of the bells, drowned the beasts out. The dancers flowed after Cuffe's sleigh, apparently unaware of the beasts being drawn away in the opposite direction.

As we danced, the feeling of being split in two, split in three, split into a multitude of possibilities returned to me. This feeling, I now knew, was time unraveling and then coming back together. It was a wobble but it was more than that; the reality of Kingsport flying away in different directions and nearly overwhelming me. The only thing anchoring me to the here and the now was the feeling of Paul dancing with me and the ringing of the bells.

Settling my grip more firmly on Paul, I followed Jim, remembering Nova saying that Jim could make the music do what was wanted.

I looped my left arm around Paul's waist and rang my string of bells in my right hand. Paul rang a single silver bell clutched in his left hand. Side by side in our strange dance, we followed the wild music of Jim's trumpet.

But the more we danced, the more Paul seemed to be slipping away from me. From the corner of my eye, I could see him fade and reappear and fade away again. The bells grew more and more muffled as if the last of my hearing was also flickering out.

Still we danced. And I held on. Because nothing else mattered but that I hold on.

I gripped Paul tightly and danced, ignoring pains shooting up my legs, ignoring the dizzying sight of two pairs of legs becoming four, eight, or a hundred. Gritting my teeth, I danced. Snow and ice slushed into our shoes. Bright spots of blood marked where we stepped.

And I danced with Paul.

We stumbled through the steps, both of us dragging on the other. Holding tight to Paul, my arm felt like it was on fire. Against my other hand, the string of bells absorbed all the cold of the night, striking like frozen little hammers against my wrist or forearm with every shake. I felt each jarring note, every bruise, as the music blared from every window with a radio.

We danced.

"Here's the spot!" called Nova, who jogged out of the doorway of the garage where she stored her liquor. I realized she must have run through her bootlegging tunnels to beat us there. I was dizzy from dancing, and tired of dancing, and determined never to stop dancing.

"Here's where Chilton, Paul, and I all crossed paths," said Nova. "Hold on to Paul. We're almost done." I heard that. I don't know how, but I heard her when all the world's sound was fading away. Her voice came clear through my earpiece. I heard pride, and love, and fierce determination to never let go of all the future could offer.

"Hold on to me," I said to Paul and though he was shattering into three men, all of them looked at me. All of them saw me. And all kept dancing.

Jim nodded to Nova, never stopping his playing, but his variation on Billy's version of "Jingle Bells" began to change. It became even more compelling, more strident. The hounds twisted and leapt, trying to get away from the music. Paul pulled against my grip as if he felt compelled to dash into the alley's opening. I wound my arm as tightly as possible around him and pulled back, digging my heels into the snow and slush. He nearly pulled me off my feet, and two long drag marks, two straight lines, appeared behind me.

"Stay here!" I yelled at Paul.

With an agonized cry, he started to pull away. "I don't want to go!" he said, the very first words he'd spoken to me that night. "But I must. The dance must continue."

"Not you, not now," I said, toppling against him and clapping my hands over his ears. "Your dance is done."

We fell in a heap in the very same spot where Paul knocked Chilton Brewster off his feet a year ago.

Nova strode to us and without any hesitation sat on Paul's legs. "Hang on!" she said to me. "Almost midnight! We've done enough."

A terrible blue glow shading into horrible purple and green, a sickening light, grew at the end of the alleyway. I shifted my position, so I was kneeling across Paul's shoulders and one of his arms, my hands still muffling his ears. The ice and snow soaked through my skirt and stockings. But all I felt was the fetid warm air which blew from the forest appearing before us, a long path snaking between the grotesque trees.

With a cry, the hounds jumped over us onto the path. They sped away from Jim's playing. They ran away from Kingsport.

"Nearly time," panted Nova.

"It can't be midnight yet," I said. "We only started the dance."

"Time's been playing tricks," said Nova, "but my watch is accurate." She thrust out her hand to display her platinum and diamond watch encircling her sturdy wrist.

"Hold him down until the path closes," Nova instructed me, never budging from where she sat on Paul's legs. "Hold him tight."

I leaned into Paul with a whispered apology for any bruises. His eyes were staring into nothing, and I don't know if he heard me. I wasn't even sure if he was still alive, he lay so still under my hands, but I held on.

Shouts erupted behind us, breaking through the music. One of the hounds twisted its head, looking back over its shoulder at us.

"Stop, stop," yelled Tawney as he raced down the street, his men following him and dragging Brewster with them. "What are you doing?"

"Closing this path for good," Nova yelled back.

Tawney skidded to a halt beside her, looking longingly at the strange road leading through the monstrous forest. "You can't!" he said. "Think what we could do if we could alter the past!"

Brewster was dragged beside him. The once tidy banker twisted in his captor's arms, looking back at the Diamond Dog. "There's no flames," he said in wonder. "It's not burning."

"You can't mend the past," said Nova to both men. "But you can change the future." She checked her watch again. "One minute to midnight. This day will be over. The path closes forever."

"No!" shouted Tawney. "I must return to the night in the laboratory. I need Maleson's machine!" He had his pistol out and waved it wildly at all of us. "Get in there," he said, prodding at Brewster, "show me the way back!"

"I can't!" wailed Brewster. "I can't go there again!"

But Tawney dragged him forward onto the path. Both men appeared to be locked in a strange waltz, a series of steps which I realized matched the haunting rhythm played by Jim. The hound still watching us began to snarl.

"Stop!" I screamed, watching Tawney plunging under those strange trees, taking Brewster with him. But there was nothing and no one to hold them back. I couldn't let go of Paul. I could only watch as they disappeared onto a path that I hoped to never see again.

"Midnight!" declared Nova.

Without a wobble, without any sign at all, the alley was just an alley, cold and empty on a snowy December night.

Nova rose off Paul's legs. I gave him a hand to pull him into a sitting position and then hugged him hard. And, with delight, felt him hug me back.

"Merry Christmas!" Nova yelled at all of us.

"Baba Yaga," said Paul, scrambling to his feet and then shaking Nova's hand. He dropped her hand and threw his arms around her, hugging her hard. "Baba Yaga!" he said again in his husky voice.

Nova patted him on the shoulder once or twice, and then shoved him toward me.

"Go hug Raquel," she told him. "She's the one who saved you."

Paul stood in front of me, his clothing covered with bits of snow and ice where we'd pressed him to the ground. He was such an ordinary looking man. He looked wonderful.

"Oh," I said, not knowing what else to say. "Oh, you're here." I pulled him around, using both hands on the back of his jacket, trying to knock some of the snow away, trying not to cry with relief.

Paul turned impatiently and grabbed my hands. Then he pulled me into a tight embrace. "Raquel, Raquel," he murmured in my ear. I didn't have to hear him to know what he was saying.

Then he pulled back a little, freeing one hand to wipe the tears from his face. "My voice of hope," he said to me.

The sleigh went flashing by us, dancers still whirling in its wake. From all the windows, Billy and the band still played on the radio, loud enough for even me to hear.

"Let's get inside," said Nova, grabbing at us both. "I told the cooks to have pots of chowder ready for everyone."

Pulling me into a one-armed embrace, she whispered in a voice that could have been heard in Arkham, "And if there's sherry in the soup tonight, don't tell the government boys. Not that they seem all that interested in us."

I glanced behind her and saw the remaining brown-suited men searching the empty alleyway, calling for Tawney and Brewster. I linked arms with Paul and turned away.

"Come along," Nova said to us, "it's time to go home."

"But is it over? Truly over?" I said as we all walked up the steps into the Diamond Dog. "Is Paul here to stay?"

He smiled down at us both. "I cannot feel the path any longer."

"It's done," said Nova, not even looking back at the alley where the path had appeared and disappeared. "As I told Tawney, you cannot correct the past. But you can always change someone's future. There were enough people here, enough good intentions, that we shifted time into a new pattern."

The ballroom doors stood wide open. The tree glowed in its corner. Not a single decoration was harmed, not a smidgeon of smoke or ash could be seen.

As we strode through the ballroom doors, Billy gave a shout and brought his hands down on a final crash upon the keys. Poor Harlean, who had been singing straight for apparently two hours, was barely whispering into the microphone, but she saw us and smiled. Cozy banged his sticks upon the cymbals while Ginger played us in on her saxophone.

Back on the street, Jim Culver blew one last note on his horn and tipped his hat to the dancers streaming back into the hall.

"Chowder for everyone!" yelled Nova. "Soup is on!"

I pulled Paul into the line for the buffet table. "Nova says her soup is good for everything that ails you," I told him.

He stared in amazement at the tree and decorations, at the people chatting and laughing all around us, and then, finally, very warmly, he was smiling down at me.

"Then chowder we shall eat," he said.

Such a silly little sentence, and I could barely hear him, but it made me so happy. I adjusted the volume on my hearing aid and held his warm, living hand. I had found the phantom who had whispered in my ear, the lonely writer behind the fairytales in the journal, and he was real. I knew then the future would be worth living, no matter what it held.

Sometime later, we sat at a small table with bellies full of hot soup. Around us the music swelled until it shook the very walls. I could feel it although I would never hear it again as I had in the past. The distortion of the hearing aid gave the tune a hiss and a crackle. But there were no uncanny whispers or howls beneath the electric noise. Although I concentrated, I could hear no shouts from Chilton Brewster or Ralph Tawney. Wherever they were, their voices were silent to me.

I wrestled a battered little book out of my bag, where it had been crammed next to the battery for the hearing aid, and handed it to Paul. "This is yours," I said.

"This is ours," he replied, his hand covering mine on the cover. I turned my hand over and tangled my fingers in his.

"Merry Christmas," I said.

"Happy New Year," Paul said, and his fingers tightened around mine. "Year after year of new years." His voice broke and his hand trembled. "I survived," he said after a pause. "I am here, now, with you. The rest can be forgotten."

I examined the journal with its tattered cover. "I wonder who he was. The old man in the graveyard."

"An angel or a saint. He saved my mind. Without this book, that place would have eaten all my thoughts and left me an empty man."

"I wish we could thank him," I said. "But I think you met him too far in the future to find him now."

Paul nodded. "I don't know how we could thank him. He was dying when I saw him and so sad. I wish I could tell him that we succeeded."

With my free hand, because I was not yet ready to let go of Paul, I ran my fingers over the journal and for the first time noticed a pair of regular indentations different from the other scrapes and scratches. "Look," I said, "there's something here. Initials, I think, stamped on the cover."

Paul looked closer. "There was," he said slowly. "Two letters, in gold, but they wore away."

I traced the outlines of those initials. "CB," I said and then remembered the row of diaries behind the man's desk, all bound in leather and stamped on the corners with his initials in gold. His memoirs in the making, he told me. Every journal carefully preserved, except for this one.

"Chilton Brewster," I told Paul. "This journal belonged to Chilton Brewster. Did he know when he gave you the journal that it would destroy his future even as it saved ours?"

"He was an old man dying full of regret. I do not think he cared what happened as long as the Diamond Dog was saved."

I would never like Chilton Brewster but, in that moment, I found enough mercy in my heart to hope that he would find his own way out of the woods, wherever and whenever that terrible place existed.

Billy ran his hands up and down on the piano keys. He called to the room, "Last dance! Pick your partner! Merry Christmas, everyone!"

I grabbed my headband and took it off, dropping it on top of the journal.

Shrugging off the purse and disentangling the microphone's cord from around my neck, I freed myself from the hearing aid. I left the entire contraption on the table and stepped into Paul's arms.

He pulled me close. We danced to the music that I could no longer hear as clearly as I wished but I would always feel in my heart.

With every movement of Paul's body pressed so close to mine, the music reverberated through my own. Every breath we took, every step, formed its own music. Perhaps I would lose all ability to hear, but I would never lose my ability to feel. It was enough. It was more than enough on this Christmas Day.

Tugging my hand away from his waist, Paul pressed a single silver jingle bell into my palm. I curled my fingers around it and shook it, feeling the vibration against my flesh.

Paul leaned closer and kissed me. Like the bell in my hand, the kiss sounded through me.

When Paul broke off the kiss, he spoke directly into my left ear: "Snip, snap, snout, the tale is out."

I shook the jingle bell one last time and quoted my favorite ending back to him: "With the ring of a bell, they lived happily ever after."

1926 DECEMBER 1926

SUN.	MON.	TUE.	WED.	THU.	FRI.	SAT.
			1 *Chapters One to Three*	2	3 *Chapter Four*	4
5	6 *Chapter Five*	7 *Chapter Six*	8	9	10	11 *Chapter Seven*
12	13	14	15 *Chapters Eight to Ten*	16 *Chapters Eleven & Twelve*	17	18
19	20 *Chapters Thirteen to Fifteen*	21 *Chapter Sixteen*	22 *Chapters Seventeen & Eighteen* WINTER SOLSTICE	23	24* *Chapters Nineteen to Twenty-Three. Interludes. End* CHRISTMAS DAY	25
				30	31	

*Paul's interludes always occur on December 24:
1929 – "Ashcan" Pete and his dog Duke (Arkham)
1917 – Captain Leo (Innsmouth)
1944 – Agent Adams (Kingsport)
1919 – Carson Sinclair (Arkham)
1924 – Mandy Thompson and Dr William T Maleson (Arkham)
1933 – Preston Fairmont (Arkham)
1936 – Jim Culver (Dunwich)
1939 – Zoey Samaras (Kingsport)
1913 – Beatrice Sharpe (Arkham)
1908 – Agatha Crane (Arkham)
1925 – Nova Malone and Chilton Brewster (Kingsport)
1922 – Norman Withers (Arkham)
1946 – Young couple (Kingsport)
1890 – Sydney Fitzmaurice (Arkham)
1968 – Old man (Kingsport graveyard)

ACKNOWLEDGMENTS

Once again, this book could not have happened without my wonderful editor Lottie at Aconyte, who responded to my initial outline about an *Arkham Horror* novel set at Christmas with, "As long as you don't put Cthulhu in a paper hat." Thank you to the equally fabulous folks at Fantasy Flight Games who said, "This sort of thing would happen in Kingsport."

Special homage must be paid to the artist Dan Strange, who has now drawn three covers for my *Arkham Horror* books. He made Jeany, Betsy, and Raquel look exactly as I pictured, and the settings even better than I could describe. Nick continues to be the best art director ever, discovering an old photo which showed what must have been the exterior of the Diamond Dog, and making the insides of each book look as fabulous as the outside.

Finally, this one's dedicated to a lady long gone, a great-aunt who left home to attend music college and returned to become a bookkeeper. According to family legend, she never spoke of why she left college so abruptly and it wasn't until much later that she used a hearing aid in daily life. Her sisters often speculated that her deafness resulted from an illness while away from the family. One of my grandfathers also suffered severe hearing loss after freezing his ears while painting boxcars during the Midwest winters.

Another inspiring ancestor on the family tree was a cabin boy who walked off a ship in nineteenth century New York and kept going until he landed in Chicago. Upon entering a German neighborhood and hearing a language spoken that he understood, he stayed. Where he came from originally remains a mystery and why he left there is also unknown. However, anyone who has studied the history of the thousands who fled poverty, war, and religious persecution in the early twentieth century can find people like Paul.

A source of stories which sparked some ideas was David Armstrong's wonderful podcast *Broadway Nation* and his two-part episode on the writing of "White Christmas" by the Jewish immigrant Israel Beilin, better known as Irving Berlin. Still the bestselling record in history, the song created the notion of the desirability of a snowy Christmas in American culture, to the point that it is rare to hear a weather forecast in December that doesn't speculate about whether or not there will be a white Christmas. The song's most popular recording was done by Bing Crosby, a singer who quickly caught on to the importance of the new microphone technology when he started out in the late 1920s. Although Crosby didn't like being called a crooner, he definitely used the new mikes to make his singing more intimate and immediate for the listener.

David's podcast also reminded me of the incredible contributions of James Hubert "Eubie" Blake to American music. The Black pianist and composer and his collaborator Noble Sissle wrote "Shuffle Along," long credited as the first Broadway musical to not only feature an all-Black cast, but also be created and directed by Black artists. A huge hit in 1921, the musical was performed in New York and toured across the country, launching the careers of such stars as Josephine Baker and Paul Robeson. In 1923, Blake and Sissle performed their popular music in three short films with sound using the Phonofilm process, years before Al Jolson and *The Jazz Singer* heralded the end of the silent movie era.

Radio in the 1920s was as wild and wacky as the early days of the movies. At the beginning of the decade, stations were generally run from homebuilt transmitters and shared the same frequency with each other. Almost anyone with a little technical knowledge or willingness to learn could become a broadcaster.

Competition and the public appetite for content led to bigger live programs and variety entertainment on the radio. The heyday of scripted serials like *The Shadow* would come in the 1930s and 1940s. The 1939 Christmas Eve broadcast of *The Shadow* heard by Paul can be found on YouTube for your listening pleasure.

By the end of the 1920s, stations in larger cities were broadcasting live fourteen hours or more a day and "coast to coast" networks like NBC (National Broadcasting Company) were in place. But American radio still was, and would remain for decades, very flavored by the individuals who ran the stations and the community businesses who paid for the sponsorship of programs.

But what about bootleggers and bankers running radio stations? In 1920s Seattle, a couple ran a popular radio station out of their home. Raided by federal agents, Elise was accused of broadcasting coded information to Roy's rumrunners during her children's story hour. She was not convicted but Roy, who was also the chief of police at the time, did serve five years for his smuggling activity. According to some accounts, he ordered his bootleggers to not carry guns to prevent shootouts and smuggled "good" liquor out of Canada to stop alcohol poisoning from homebrew operations.

Across town a pair of Seattle bankers started a large scale radio operation, bringing in the best musicians from other cities for live programming. In the mess of the stock market crash of 1929, their frequent "borrowing" from their savings and loans to support the station and other business ventures led to fifteen years of incarceration for defrauding their customers and stockholders of $2 million. The station was sold to another banker who also eventually served time for inappropriate use of bank funds to support his radio venture.

The advances in sound technology also led to increasingly smaller and more portable hearing aids. Raquel's device is similar to those that I've been able to find online for the period with some adjustments for plot purposes. All the wonderful gadgets that Nova brought into her home can be found in the magazine advertisements of 1926. Kodak's Vest Pocket Autographic was a real and very popular camera which allowed photographers to jot notes directly on the paper backing of film. According to Kodak histories, 1.75 million were sold between 1915 and 1926.

As mentioned at the end of *The Deadly Grimoire*, female bootleggers operated throughout Prohibition. Many were, at the time, as famous as their male counterparts.

I'm profoundly grateful to my local public library system for access to the newspapers and publications of the era as well as the many enthusiasts who share their love for this history online.

With love and gratitude for all her support, many thanks to my mother for her reminiscences about her family and her own brief career as a teenage radio host (long after the 1920s! she asks me to clarify for you).

Most of all, to everyone who has read this far, thank you for coming on this adventure with me.

OLD TERRORS

A Betsy Baxter Story

Dearest Jeany:

A postcard of the Eiffel Tower telling me that you arrived and are married is not enough! Post immediately reams of paper filled with details and pictures! I look forward to your sketches of all the sights from the Palais-Royal Gardens to Versailles. You must have lunch at Fouquet's, never mind the expense (just send the bill to the studio). Have Fred photograph every dish and you!

Send me information about the fashions. Absolutely everything from what the girl on the street is wearing to the best dressed ladies at the opera. After all, when the Flapper Detective goes to Paris, she needs to be immersed in fashion and return home with loads of new dresses. Never mind what Farnsworth says about the state of my closets. I have to look my very best, don't I? It's all part of the business.

Which means, no matter how often Farnsworth sighs about "vanity, vanity, all is vanity" (please imagine this in my butler's most woebegone tones), I need Parisian gowns for all the Hollywood parties as well as the next serial adventure.

I continue talking to some radio people about adapting my detective stories for them. Sound, they tell me, is the coming thing. Which means I won't have so many excuses to buy dresses if I am simply speaking lines into a microphone. Also, sound effects won't be nearly as much fun as doing my own stunts.

You may now imagine Farnsworth's contribution to my musings on how dull being a radio star might be as "Can madam do anything which does not require her to risk her neck?"

Madam isn't sure. I love the thrill of making the Flapper Detective movies. Although Tom says you can't do the same thing forever, which is an interesting philosophy for a man who is still working in his family business, doing exactly what all those bookselling Sweets did before him.

However, a new film role might make the critics sit up and take notice. You must start thinking very hard about how to make me look like a *femme fatale*.

Which shouldn't be too difficult as you are right in the middle of Paris, where fatal women apparently appear all the time.

There's a new (to me) studio proposing to bring in fresh faces and tell stories in startlingly different ways (which, of course, is what everyone promises when they start a studio). But Lantern Top Pictures is intriguing as they want me as a villainess! Betsy Baxter, a face almost as sickeningly wholesome as Mary Pickford (I wonder if she gets as frustrated being America's sweetheart as I do hearing about how nice my detective is?). The darling flapper, as the *Arkham Advertiser* so kindly calls me, transformed into the latest style of vamp! I hope to persuade Lantern Top to hire you too. You created such a memorable look for Renee and you haven't costumed a proper villainess in ages.

Speaking of Renee, I'm so glad you talked your sister into visiting our friends in Seattle. They will adore showing off their cabin on the beach (I can't imagine Lulu living the rustic life, but I understand they only stay there for the weekends and then retreat back to the city). Just as I promised, I took Renee to the train station myself. She was much more complimentary about my driving than you or Fred.

Renee also asked me to store a trunk for her. Or, rather, the trunk. The one we left behind in Arkham with the reels from Sydney's final film. I remain a little superstitious about that movie. I won't even write down its name. It's like saying Macbeth in a theater. But you know exactly what I'm talking about.

Now don't get excited, but apparently Humbert shipped the trunk to you about the time you and Fred boarded the boat for Paris. It arrived in Los Angeles the same day as Renee was leaving. "Oh darling Betsy," she said to me, looking as appealingly helpless as a small kitten (I used to envy Renee's ability to switch from absolutely chilling to completely vulnerable with just one look. There are still days when I despair of being even half the actress that she was). "What will I do? I can't possibly leave the trunk in storage at the station for a month. I'll cancel the trip and take it home with me." But I saw her shudder and knew she wanted no mementoes of Sydney at your house.

"Absolutely not," I said stoutly as I shoved (in the gentlest way) your sister up the steps onto her train. "Betsy Baxter to the rescue. I'll retain the big strong porter who toted all your luggage here. He can strap the trunk on the back of the roadster and away I'll go with it."

"You mustn't leave the trunk at the studio!" Renee cried as I filled her arms with chocolates, champagne, magazines, and a few small gifts for Eleanor and Lulu. Luckily Farnsworth provided a basket for all these extras. "There are people still searching for those reels."

You had told me that Renee received letters about the film from a few of Sydney's more deranged fans who, sadly, still seem to have connections at the studio even though I've changed the name and the management!

"Don't worry!" I said. "I will take the trunk and its contents home. Farnsworth will lock it up somewhere absolutely safe." Honestly, we probably should have shipped the trunk to Hollywood the last time I was in Arkham, but I was a little distracted then and the trunk seemed perfectly safe with Humbert.

Renee gave me the claim ticket for the trunk as well as a rather odd note from Humbert about how things were soon to be worse in Arkham. According to Humbert, flooding in the near future might endanger the trunk so he felt it would be safer away from the Fitzmaurice house. Which is strange, you must admit. I mean, the house was on the top of a hill so it's hard to imagine the river flooding the barn out back. On the other hand, it's Arkham and, as Tom says, a very unusual place.

"Betsy, you are an absolute angel," said Renee.

"Being an angel is my specialty," I said, because really where would you all be if I didn't organize things properly (with a little help from Farnsworth, who begs me to remember who arranged for the chocolates and so on). I hopped off the train after a few more hugs and waved goodbye.

The porter, a terrifically nice man named Orville, and I immediately went to the portion of the station where one claimed luggage sent from elsewhere. I turned in the ticket. Orville loaded the trunk onto his cart. We were merrily proceeding to my roadster when the most devastatingly handsome man yelled, "Stop!"

Please don't mention the "devastatingly handsome" to Tom, but, seriously, the stranger's cheekbones alone almost made me swoon.

"Have you ever considered being in pictures?" I said to the gentleman as he came up to us.

He seemed a little startled by my question. "Madam," he said, "I am in pictures, as you say. I am Andre Patel. Already I am well known for my roles in movies made outside your Hollywood."

All of which was said in the loveliest baritone voice, exactly like honey dripping over warm croissants, with just enough of an accent to make any American woman sway a bit closer. When the movies switch to sound, this man will outshine us all.

Of course, I recognized his name. There had been some chatter in the gossip columns about Patel being brought to Hollywood to star in Lantern Top's films. A soon as I saw him, I began considering how I could swipe him for a Flapper Detective story or two. Maybe in return for playing their villainess? I would have to talk to the lawyers.

"I'm Betsy Baxter," I said, shaking his hand. "I make pictures in Hollywood but am planning to film in Paris soon."

His eyes widened. "But of course. You are the *Detective à la Flapper!*"

"*Mais oui!*" I responded as I have been practicing that bit of French for our next picture.

"But what are you doing with my trunk?" he said, pointing to the battered old steamer trunk loaded onto Orville's cart.

"I'm afraid it's not your trunk," I said. "I just collected it from the station for a friend."

"No, no," Andre said, but in the kindest of tones. "It's most definitely my trunk. See, here is my name painted on the side."

Which, by golly, was there or at least "A. Patel" in white paint. But, other than that, the trunk was the very make and model of the one that you stashed in the barn on French Hill. However, further investigation of the luggage tag revealed that it was one number off from my claim ticket. When we collected the trunk, the man handing it over was so busy trying to get my autograph, none of us looked at the tag too closely.

"Oh dear," I said, "they've given me the wrong trunk. Orville, let us return to where we began and start again."

"Certainly, ma'am," said the obliging Orville, tipping his cap. We trundled back to the other end of the station with Andre tagging along. He had to. His trunk was on Orville's cart. However, Orville and I offered to take Patel's trunk to the taxi stand before loading mine on my roadster.

But the return to the luggage room proved an even greater disaster awaited us. The correct trunk had vanished! The very apologetic railroad employee explained a large number of trunks had been picked up by an antiques dealer and taken away to his shop just before I had arrived the first time.

"His trunks came from New England too," said the railroad man. "And we assumed yours was part of his shipment."

In short, a bit of a mix up. Actually, more of a catastrophe if anyone knew what was really in the trunk from Arkham.

"But, wait, I know this man," Andre exclaimed when the railroad man gave a description of the antiques dealer. "He is supplying props for our films at Lantern Top."

"Oh dear," I said. This was becoming worse and worse. If the antiques dealer pried open the trunk or anyone at Lantern Top did, they were sure to spot all the costumes and the canisters of film stored under them. What a sensation that would make! Sydney's lost film found again. What a calamity for us all.

"But not to worry, I can take you to his shop so you can retrieve your luggage," said Andre. "Then I can go to Lantern Top with my trunk. It is the problem solved most easily. We simply arrange for a taxi."

"No need!" I exclaimed. "I have my car right outside. Orville can load your trunk onto my roadster, we will fetch my trunk from this antiques shop, and I will happily take you to Lantern Top as my thank you."

"You are too kind," Andre said. "I cannot take you so far out of your way."

"They're filming on Lot C?" I said. "I can get you there much quicker than any taxi, even with stopping at the antiques shop. I know all the shortcuts in Los Angeles."

Which is absolutely true, as you know. If I lost my fortune tomorrow, I could become the City of Angel's very first female cab driver. And very, very good I would be too!

Andre admitted as much as we pulled in front of the antiques store. "Madame Inès Decourcelle could take lessons from you!" he said as he unfolded himself from the passenger seat. "Never have I traveled so swiftly from one place to the next."

"Who is Madame Decourcelle?" I said as we peered into the dusty windows of the shop.

"She claims she was the first *femme chauffeur* in Paris. A cab driver, if you will," said Andre, testing the shop's door. It opened with a tinkle from an overhead bell. "There used to be postcards of her driving her automobile available for all the tourists."

"How wonderful," I said, following him into the shop. "I hope my friend Jeany will send me one. She is in Paris now."

"Oh this was from before the war," Andre admitted. "But you still find pictures of Madame Decourcelle in some of the flea markets."

"I will tell Jeany to look there," I said, and now you have been told. If you find one, send it to me. You know I love such things.

On the other hand, the items in the antiques shop gave me the shivers. I can't say exactly what it was about the place, but everything made me feel unsettled. The taxidermied squirrels lined up on the top of one glass case were particularly gruesome with bulging eyes and teeth much too big for a squirrel. A box of brass and tin ornaments reminded me of those horrible amulets that Sydney used to scatter around the sets. All twisted stars with eyes engraved in the middle.

"They're using this stuff as props at Lantern Top?" I said, inching as far away as possible from the strange collection of dusty globes which showed continents that I did not recognize.

"The producer said such props give the sets more authenticity," Andre said. "Alice Gaither, our director, agreed."

"Oh yes, I heard Alice was directing all the films at Lantern Top," I said. A female director was one of the reasons that I was so interested in the studio's offer.

"Alice picked out a number of items, including a cloak for the film about the countess," Andre said.

I didn't say a word, not one word, against Alice, because I wanted to work with her. But I would never allow a single thing from that creepy shop onto any set at BB. I was more anxious than ever to find the trunk.

"Hello!" I called. "Is anyone here?"

A dusty drape covering a doorway stirred but no one responded.

"Please! I think you have my trunk," I called. "I'll give you fifty dollars if it is here."

Andre looked startled at my sudden offer of cash, but I wanted out of the room as quickly as possible. If waving money at someone would make that happen, I was willing to wave.

Apparently, I had found the magic words, because the drape parted and the most wizened woman ever seen crept into the room. She looked like an animated mummy, one of those horrid ones where the bandages have all been stripped off and the desiccated skin and bones are on display. You remember the photographs in the old Egyptology book that Fred took such delight in showing us when Sydney wanted a scene with a mummy. I was never so glad as when Renee vetoed the idea. Especially since I was the one that you decided to make up as the mummy!

"You are here for the trunks?" the woman said.

"Just one," I replied. "It was mixed up with your delivery."

"I told him thirteen trunks couldn't be right. Nobody would be so foolish to send such an unlucky number," she said to me. "But he went off and left me to unpack everything."

"Have you unpacked them all?" I asked with some trepidation. I glanced around the room, but I didn't see anything that I recognized.

"No, I don't have keys for the thirteenth trunk," she said.

"Oh good!" I said. "That's probably mine. I'll give you fifty dollars for your trouble."

"No trouble at all," said the old woman, holding up the dusty curtain that divided the shop into two rooms. "It's one less thing to unpack." As I passed her going into the depths of the shop, she thrust out her hand. "But I'll take the fifty dollars. Money is money and the owner's always late paying me." I dropped the cash into her hand.

"So this is not your shop, madame?" Andre asked courteously as he followed me into the other room.

The old lady cackled as she tucked away the fifty dollars. "I'm the hired help. The owner's a big man, full of mystic secrets, as he'll tell you himself. He certainly impressed those fools at Lantern Top."

"But I am one of the actors working at Lantern Top," Andre told her with no particular heat. I did like his matter-of-fact manner. A number of actors that we know would make a fuss to hear their studio disparaged.

She shook her head. "That's your bad luck then. Be careful what you touch. There's a reason he sold the stuff so cheap."

I interrupted their discussion with my own exclamations when I spotted the trunk in the corner of the room. "That's mine," I said, pointing at it. A quick check confirmed the trunk was still locked. Our secrets were safe.

Andre and I carried the trunk out of the shop and strapped it onto my car. The roadster valiantly went full throttle to Lantern Top despite being terribly unbalanced by two steamer trunks. Andre was very gracious about the whole trip, not even clutching the door handle when I took a sharper than intended turn onto Lot C.

"Mademoiselle Baxter," he said as he removed his trunk from my car, "you might have a second career as a female racecar driver."

"Oh I have a friend who races airplanes. It's far more exciting," I said. "Although I enjoy a good motorcycle race."

Andre bowed to me. "I look forward to seeing you again," he said. "You are truly the most American daredevil."

"I am considering a role at Lantern Top," I told him. But as I looked around the lot, something about it gave me the heebie jeebies. I cannot tell you why, but it was much like that weird little antiques shop. "You should be careful," I said to Andre, thinking of the warning from the old lady about touching certain things.

"Mademoiselle, it is the movies," he said. "All the dangers are pretend. We understand this, you and I."

But, Jeany, we know differently. Which is why there is a trunk now very securely locked up in my attics.

Oh dear, I started off with such a cheerful letter, but it seems to end with gloomier thoughts. You must not worry. You know me. I'll be on my guard when I visit Lantern Top. And it's probably all nothing, anyway.

Kiss Fred on the Champs Elysees. Remember, this trip is your honeymoon gift from me. Don't pay any attention to my silliness. Have a wonderful time. And do send me sketches of beautiful dresses!

Your friend, always,

Betsy

ARKHAM HORROR™

GATHERING SHADOWS

A Betsy Baxter Story

Darling Tom:

Just a quick note. I nearly sprained my hand writing pages and pages to Jeany. I sent Farnsworth for ice. My brilliant butler brought me back a whiskey and soda (destroy this letter if you see any signs of Prohibition agents interested in your mail or prepare to bake a file in a cake!). But I couldn't wait to write to you. I experienced something so unsettling today and wish you were here instead of Boston so we could have a proper discussion. I've talked it over with Farnsworth, but he simply cautions me not to poke my nose where it could get bitten off. As if that's practical advice.

I can't tell this story to Jeany or Fred, not when they are in Paris enjoying their honeymoon. Because it's so similar to what happened to us in Arkham (the first time, with Jeany and Fred, and the second time when I met you). I don't want to bring up bad memories for Jeany and Fred. You also don't deserve to suffer but I need to share this with someone. Secure your own drink, I'll wait, and then read on.

I went to Lantern Top Pictures today as they wanted me to play a wicked woman. I already encountered one of their leading men, Andre Patel. But I hadn't met the director, and you know how much I care about my directors. So off I went to Lot C to chat about being a villainess. Such a fun idea, maybe I should try a dual role in the Flapper Detective? I could be the detective's evil twin.

When I arrived, they said Alice Gaither was busy directing a scene about monsters on Saturn. "Oh I adore monsters, can I watch?" I asked. Because you learn a lot about a director if you see them at work.

On the set of *A Cosmic Journey*, I found Andre, looking very suave as the hero, and a bunch of costumed extras milling about as you do before shooting begins. I wonder if the public understands how much time we stand and wait, we who labor in Hollywood.

"Mademoiselle Baxter!" Andre said when he saw me. "How is my favorite American daredevil?" I gave Andre a ride in the roadster a few days earlier. He started calling me a daredevil after rolling around Los Angeles with me (I'm sure I can't think why and no comments from you, mister).

"I'm well, and please call me Betsy," I replied. "Is Alice here?"

"No, no, she was called away," Andre told me. "We still lack a few extras, and they needed her help with the Abominable Contessa's next scene."

"Oh yes," I said. "I understand you're filming three movies all at the same time." It reminded me of the stories that Mack Sennett tells about his early days. Apparently Lantern Top embraced such chaotic creativity or lacked the money to hire more than one director.

"Yes, the second is set in the Contessa's castle, and they needed Alice's approval of the tapestries. The third is all about a forbidden jungle island full of secrets," Andre said.

"Oh, that's the one where they asked me to play the seductive priestess of a reptile cult," I said. "I loved the idea."

Andre shot me a strange look. "Perhaps, Betsy, it would not be a good role for you."

"Now wait a minute," I said, pulling myself up to my full five feet and one inch (I was wearing heels). "Are you saying I can't be an evil vamp?"

"No, no." Andre looked a little flustered. "I'm sure you can, how do you say it, vamp as well as anyone. But two women have already been injured on the set."

"I knew I wasn't anyone's first choice to play a villainess," I grumbled as Andre told me about how the original priestess and her understudy were no longer available.

Andre shrugged. "There've been several accidents apparently. I'm not sure what's going on. Everyone keeps telling me it will be fine but…"

"Of course they say all is well," I said. "You are the star. They don't want to lose you. But I hope you'll consider working at BB too. I could use a handsome actor in the Flapper Detective's next serial. We're filming in Paris."

"Mademoiselle Betsy, it would be a delight to show you Paris," Andre said very gallantly.

"Well, it would be me, my friend Tom, and our friends Jeany and Fred," I said. "We've been planning this for some time." See, Tom, I may think Andre would be a fabulous addition to the Flapper Detective series, but I have not forgotten you. Stop muttering at this letter about my flirting and keep reading.

"Don't tell anyone yet," I said to Andre. "I'll ask my lawyers to talk to Lantern Top's lawyers, so nobody's feelings are hurt. Then we can all make lots of money."

Andre laughed. "I love how you Americans approach the movies as a lucrative venture rather than artistic endeavor."

"Oh it can be both," I said. "Perhaps I should peek at this jungle island set. Maybe I can figure out what is causing the accidents. I've done so many stunts, I might be able to spot the flaw."

"Come, I will show you," Andre said. "It looks to be some time before they need me."

The "island" consisted of a sad collection of rubber plants and palm trees with their pots hidden by painted rocks. Just as we started looking about, a flurried looking assistant ran up to us. "Mr Patel, they are ready for you now. Can you come back?"

"Certainly. Betsy, shall I introduce you to Alice?" Andre asked.

"I'll be there in a minute," I said. Something sparkling at the back of the set caught my eye. Andre left as I hunted through the rubber plants. Then, dear Tom, it happened.

As I stretched out my hand to touch a long gilded staff, the world tilted and I was no longer standing amid some drooping potted plants. I plunged into the horrid, fetid, buzzing woods behind the Fitzmaurice house. Or something very like those woods. The air stank and a roar shook the ground. I swear I saw a snake go slithering past me!

I leaped away from the staff and stumbled over a paper mâché rock, plopping right down on my silk-covered behind. After I pulled myself upright, shook out my skirts, and dusted off my pride, I went straight back into the set. But no matter how hard I searched, I couldn't find the staff. It had vanished! As had the jungle.

I probably would be searching still, except Andre returned, leading a nice but rather tired looking woman. "Alice, this is Betsy Baxter," he said. "Betsy, here is our hardworking director."

After shaking hands and muttering a few polite nothings, I made my excuses much to their surprise. But I couldn't stand there, chatting about work, when I could still smell those awful woods.

I keep thinking about how strange Lantern Top seems. Can you rummage through your uncle's books for anything about a staff or a jungle popping up where you don't expect it? You are the absolute whiz at finding such knowledge. Send a telegram as soon as you do.

Obviously, I must return to Lantern Top and discover what is causing the accidents. Andre was right to be concerned. I can't let the poor man handle this on his own. Don't worry about me. I'll take Farnsworth and tell them he's my personal assistant or some such excuse. Did I tell you that Farnsworth joined my judo class? He's surprisingly good.

Now, with my mind made up about what to do at Lantern Top (I knew writing this letter would help me!), I can work on my plans for Paris. I have the most marvelous idea for a stunt at the Eiffel Tower.

Please tell your uncle hello from me. Enjoy your book cataloging. Really, you mustn't lose any sleep over this letter. I promise to be very careful indeed on my next trip to Lantern Top.

With all my love and a few kisses,

Betsy

ABOUT THE AUTHOR

ROSEMARY JONES is the author of the *Arkham Horror* novels *The Nightmare Quest of April May*, *The Arcane Gamble of Harvey Walters*, *Mask of Silver*, *The Deadly Grimoire*, and *The Bootlegger's Dance*. She is an ardent collector of children's books, and a fan of talkies and silent movies. Her other works include *Wrecker of Engines* (Cobalt City 20th Anniversary edition), *Dungeons & Dragons' Forgotten Realms* novels, numerous novellas, short stories, and collaborations.

rosemaryjones.com // x.com/rosemaryjones

Arkham Horror

*A darkness has fallen over Arkham.
Who will stand against the dread
might of the Ancient Ones?*

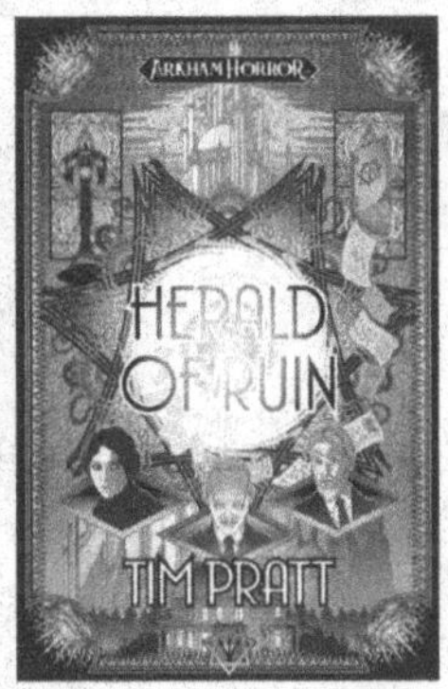

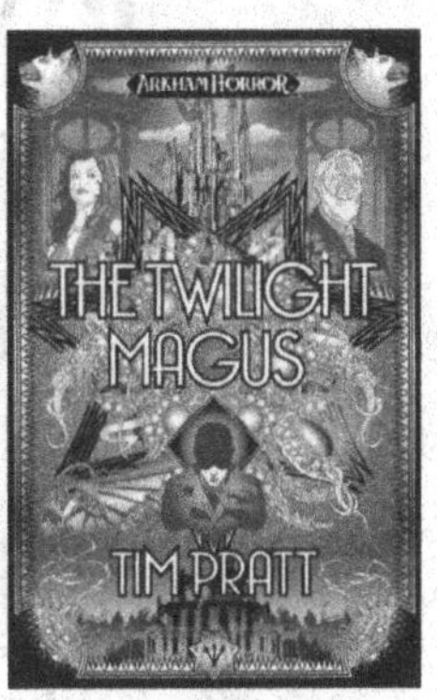

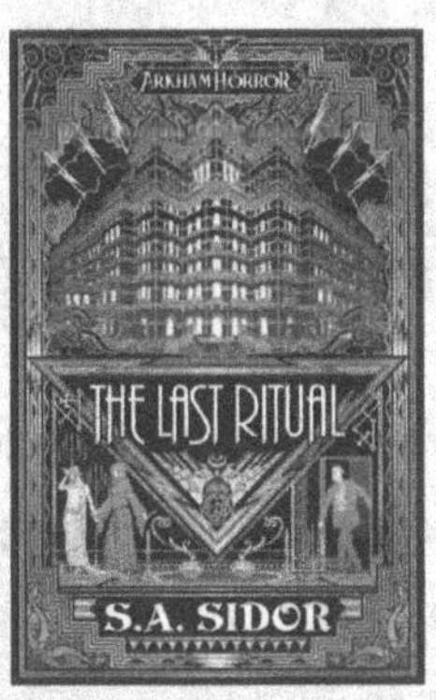

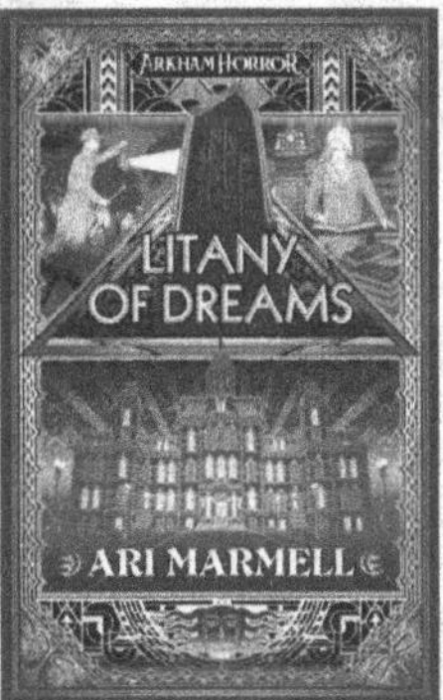

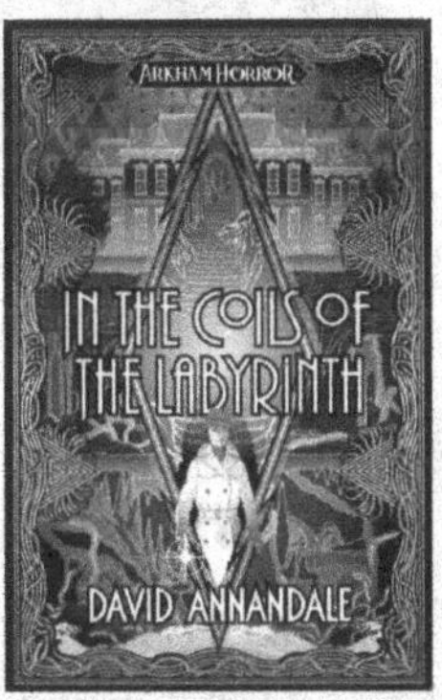

ACONYTEBOOKS.COM
ARKHAMHORROR.COM

CHOOSE YOUR INVESTIGATOR.
CHOOSE YOUR PATH.
DECIDE YOUR FATE.

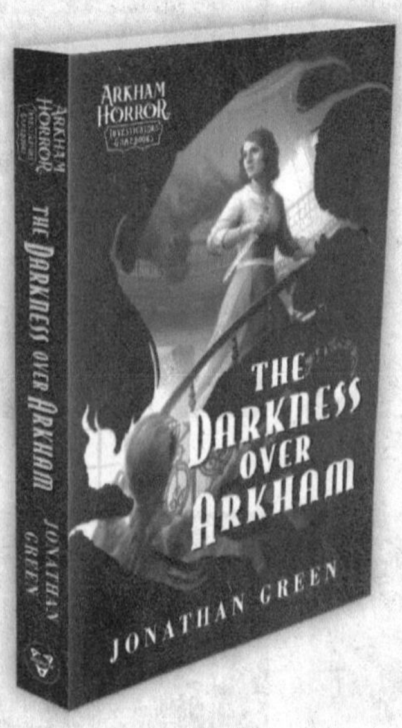

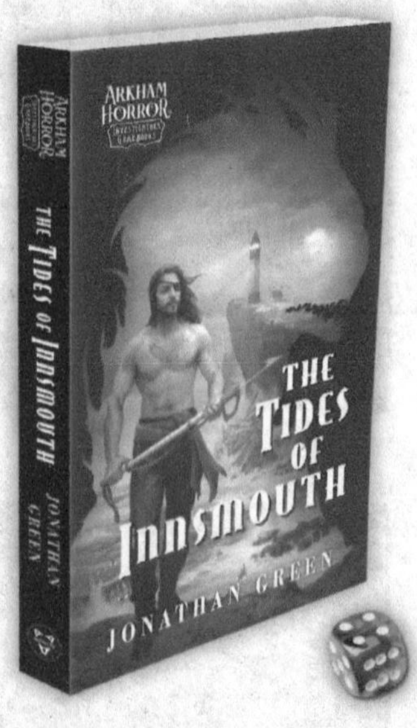

Take on the mantle of Investigator and explore the world of Arkham Horror in a whole new way as your choices change the story.

ACONYTEBOOKS.COM
ARKHAMHORROR.COM